THE
JERUSALEM
PARCHMENT

"*The Jerusalem Parchment* is an exquisitely plotted love story amidst wild adventure that draws the reader deeply into medieval Jewish culture, Christian heresies, and the secrets hidden in the Temple Mount in Jerusalem. Searing apocalyptical obsession forges the three religions of Abraham into a believable synthesis, the Pearl that can bring world peace. This is a page-turner! I held my breath to the very end."

BARBARA HAND CLOW, INTERNATIONALLY
ACCLAIMED CEREMONIAL TEACHER AND AUTHOR OF
REVELATIONS OF THE AQUARIAN AGE AND
REVELATIONS OF THE RUBY CRYSTAL

THE
JERUSALEM
PARCHMENT

A Kabbalist's Search for an Esoteric Map
in the Time of the Crusades

TUVIA FOGEL

Destiny Books
Rochester, Vermont • Toronto, Canada

Destiny Books
One Park Street
Rochester, Vermont 05767
www.DestinyBooks.com

Text stock is SFI certified

Destiny Books is a division of Inner Traditions International

Library of Congress Cataloging-in-Publication Data

Names: Fogel, Tuvia, author.
Title: The Jerusalem parchment : a kabbalist's search for an esoteric map in the
    time of the Crusades / Tuvia Fogel.
Description: Rochester, Vermont ; Toronto, Canada : Destiny books, [2018] |
    Description based on print version record and CIP data provided by publisher;
    resource not viewed.
Identifiers: LCCN 2017013620 (print) | LCCN 2017019411 (e-book) |
    ISBN 9781620556955 (pbk.) | ISBN 9781620556962 (e-book)
Classification: LCC PR9120.9.F64 K33 2018 (print) LCC PR9120.9.F64 (e-book) |
    DDC 823/.92—dc23
LC record available at https://lccn.loc.gov/2017013620

Printed and bound in the United States by Lake Book Manufacturing, Inc.
The text stock is SFI certified. The Sustainable Forestry Initiative® program
promotes sustainable forest management.

10 9 8 7 6 5 4 3 2 1

Text design by Debbie Glogover and layout by Virginia Scott Bowman
This book was typeset in Garamond Premier Pro with Garamond Premier Pro and
Gill Sans used as display typefaces

To send correspondence to the author of this book, mail a first-class letter to the
author c/o Inner Traditions • Bear & Company, One Park Street, Rochester, VT
05767, and we will forward the communication.

THE WORLD OF THE JERUSALEM PARCHMENT
Dramatis personae

Fictional characters are in italics

Christians

Catholics	Heretics	Templars (and a Teuton)
Pope Honorius III	Pierre de Gramazie	Pedro de Montaigue
St. Francesco of Assisi	Pons Roger	Guillem de Montrodon
St. Dominic Guzman	Abbot Boson	*Robert de Bois-Guilbert*
Cardinal Pelagius Galvani	*Arnald Arifat*	*Ansiau de Linniéres*
Jacques de Vitry	*Aillil Arifat*	*Iñigo Sanchez*
Oliver of Padeborn	*Father Makarios*	*André de Rosson*
Ugo de' Borgognoni	*The Old Man*	*Frutolf of Steinfeld*
Galatea degli Ardengheschi	*Mâitre Chalabi*	
Gudrun of Heidelberg		
Rustico of Torcello		
Garietto of Costanziaca		
Bonifacio e Marciana Ottone		

Jews and Muslims

Moshe ben Maimon	*Yehezkel ben Yoseph*
Eleazar of Worms	*Pinhas ben Meshullam*
Yehiel of Paris	*Yaakov of Gerona*
Isaiah of Trani	*Shlomo of Toledo*
Yitzhak of Dampierre	*Yasmine bint Twalia*
Shimshon ben Abraham	
Sultan al-Malik al-Kamil	

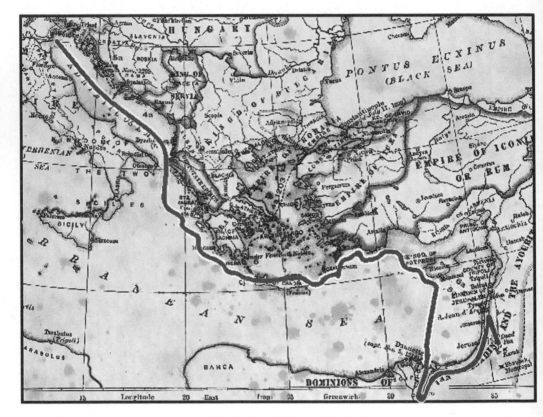

The World of the Parchment

Part One

The

First Day

✡ ✠ ✡ ✠

HEBREW LETTER NUMERIC VALUES

א	Aleph	1	ל	Lamed	30
ב	Bet	2	מ	Mem	40
ג	Gimel	3	נ	Nun	50
ד	Daled	4	ס	Samech	60
ה	Hey	5	ע	Ayin	70
ו	Vav	6	פ	Pey	80
ז	Zayin	7	צ	Tzadiq	90
ח	Chet	8	ק	Kof	100
ט	Tet	9	ר	Reish	200
י	Yod	10	ש	Shin	300
כ	Caf	20	ת	Tav	400

✡ ✠ ✡ ✠

CHAPTER 1

בראשית
ברא אלהים את השמים ואת הארץ

IN THE BEGINNING
GOD CREATED THE HEAVENS AND THE
EARTH

(GENESIS, 1:1)

✡ ✠ ✡ ✠

'εν αρχη
ην ο λογος και ο λογος ην
προς τον θν̄ και θς̄ ην ο λογος

IN THE BEGINNING
WAS THE WORD
AND THE WORD WAS WITH GOD
AND THE WORD WAS GOD

(JOHN, 1:1)

CHAPTER 2

VERUAH ELOHIM MERACHEPHET AL-PNEI HA-MAYIM

And the Spirit of God Moved upon the Face of the Waters

ISLAND OF TORCELLO, 8TH APRIL 1219–14TH NISSAN 4979

With a northeasterly gale whipping waters and flatlands under a full moon, the Venetian lagoon felt like a world in the early stages of its creation.

Someone knocked on the low door of the dyers' cottage.

Avraham, the older brother, got up from the crowded table to open it. A boy, no older than eight, stood on the threshold. A cloak was snapping in the wind, the old pouch and the walking stick were those of a wayfarer, but the upright bearing did not befit a pilgrim.

"Where do you come from, pilgrim?"

"From Egypt!" The wind tore the Hebrew words Mi-Mizraim from the child's lips.

"Have you been freed from your slavery?"

"Yes, I am free!" squealed the figure proudly.

"And where are you headed?"

"To Jerusalem!"

"No, I beseech you, stop awhile and recite the Haggadah (Passover Tale) with us!"

Avraham let Nathan, the youngest, in, hugged him, and complimented him on his interpretation of the prophet Elijah. The small crowd in the dyers' kitchen joyously welcomed father and son back into the warm light of the candles. Rav Eleazar stood up and recited a blessing over the fourth and last glass of wine. Everyone shouted *"Amen!"* and the famous German rabbi sat down with a smile, leaning back on his pillow as prescribed by the ritual of the Passover supper.

There was a pillow for the rabbi because the Ben-Porat brothers would never have neglected a single detail of this ritual, but it was just an old nightshirt filled with straw. Much of the tableware and traditional foods, too, were what poverty and ingenuity had suggested. Avraham and Shmuel Ben-Porat weren't so poor they had to use eggshells for oil lamps, as the saying went, but they could only afford to run a Jewish home on the island thanks to the constant help of the communities close to the lagoon.

In those days—some twelve hundred years after the birth of Jesus—Jews could only reside in Venice for three months, and then only on the island of Spinalunga, a thin strip of marshy land south of the city. For decades they'd been allowed to come and trade with Venetians, on condition that they leave as soon as their trade was done, and since there had to be at least one house where an Israelite could eat and pray according to the customs of his obstinate race, some dyers had arrived to host Jewish merchants.

Dying cloth is exhausting, unhealthy work, done in malodorous vats; an occupation that assures a man he will be spared the anxieties that plague the rich. No community, Christian or Mohammedan, denied a Jew the privilege of adding color to their garments—in exchange, of course, for an appropriate fee, and usually confining him downwind of the town.

The Ben-Porats had been chased out of Spinalunga on a Sunday morning when the Sirocco had blown foul vapors from their vats into a local church for the whole duration of the Mass. They had eventually settled in Torcello, where the kindly abbess of the convent of San Maffìo had rented them a small farmhouse in the borough known as Campanelle, located on the north of the island, close to her community of eighteen Cistercian nuns.

Three months earlier, to their surprise, the brothers had been alerted that their house had been chosen for a secret meeting of six rabbis during Passover week. Hosting traveling Jews was the purpose of their voluntary exile from the mainland, but this time the news had seriously threatened the peace of their home because the dyers' wives were humiliated by the thought of the bleak memories the six luminaries would retain of their sojourn in such a humble dwelling. The two women had become intractable, and their husbands' reasonable objection that the rabbis' choice of Torcello was surely dictated by the need to stay out of the public eye, not by a desire for luxury, had not improved their mood.

A few days before Pessah, the six rabbis arrived—one at a time and with no attendants. One from Trani, in Apulia; one from Gerona, in Spain; another from Lunel, in Provence. Then there were two Frenchmen, one from Dampierre, the other from Paris and finally, from Worms, in the Rhineland, the summoner of the meeting: Eleazar ben Yehuda, spiritual leader of the Hasidei Ashkenaz (German Pietists).

On Rav Eleazar's request, Rav Isaiah of Trani—an olive-skinned, jolly little man whose smile, with a few more teeth, would have been irresistible—had brought with him a scroll of the Torah, protected by ninety-one spells cast by the rabbis of Apulia. For three times a day, despite the pestiferous smell occasionally filtering through from the dying vats, the holy scroll had turned the Ben-Porats' kitchen into a synagogue.

It was, if truth be told, a bizarre meeting. On the night of the Passover meal those reputable rabbis should have been in their homes with their families, after leading prayers in their synagogues. But the invitation each had received from Rav Eleazar had been impossible to refuse.

My wise and honored friend, may God grant you a long life, and peace. I write to you concerning the meeting we have been postponing for two years. A recent dream revealed to me that it must be held, with God's help, on the coming Passover, or we won't hold it at all. A messenger will bring you details of the place, but I can tell you that it will be close to Venice. We shall remember our slavery in Egypt, hear from our brothers about conditions in the Egypt they inhabit today, and discuss the urgent questions of which you are aware. In short, we shall taste the bitter herb of persecution, as our forefathers did, in the hope that the Master of the Universe will hear our cry and send us a new redeemer!

Rav Eleazar, a descendant of the famous Kalonymos family, was a respected Talmudist, but it was as a mystic that his fame had traveled beyond Germany, including claims that he practiced the ancient magical traditions of the Jews of Babylonia. It was rumored that ten years earlier, with the help of some disciples, he had briefly given life to a *golem** on the banks of the Rhine. Be that as it may, Christians generally feared him as a powerful Jewish sorcerer.

But his frequentation of mysteries did not prevent him from being friendly with bishops and counts, and few Jews were better informed than Rav Eleazar of events in the Holy Roman Empire, or in the wider world. This mixture of piousness, politics, and magic was typical of a long line of righteous men (and on a few occasions, women) in

---

*Man-made creature of Jewish esoteric tradition

Jewish history, born in distant lands and epochs—from Babylonia to Andalusia, from Morocco to Bohemia—as if carefully placed there to alleviate the travails of exile.

His fame convinced the rabbis to defy not just Passover custom and the dangers of a long journey, but also the risk of providing Christians with proof of the latest *mamserbilbul,** as Jews referred to the increasingly frequent libels about the Children of Israel. The new one was a rumor, started in Norwich, that spread like wildfire through Christendom, claiming that every year a conference of rabbis in a distant land determined where a Christian child was to be killed as a Passover sacrifice, innocent blood then used by the Jews to bake their ritual unleavened bread.

So when Yehezkel ben Yoseph, the youngest of the six rabbis, arrived at the last minute the day before from Lunel, in Languedoc, in the company of a Christian boy of about ten, the others had been incredulous, the Frenchmen closer to horror than disbelief. They had looked at the blond Christian boy and mumbled a stream of incantations into their beards, stopping short of the formula to be recited before Sanctifying the Name that is being martyred at the hands of pagans. Eventually, after regaining some composure, Rav Yitzhak of Dampierre had blurted out,

"Are our lives not sufficiently at risk as it is, Rav Yehezkel, meeting in secret amid the uncircumcised, without you bringing along a child of the gentiles? What's more, just before their Easter hate-feast! Do you want us all—scholars, dyers, children—to have to Sanctify the Name?"

Yehezkel, a burly thirty-six-year-old, was bigger than all the other rabbis and his was the only beard with no white in it. His deep brown eyes and mild manner belied the strength suggested by a broad frame, a contrast also visible in surprisingly delicate hands at the ends of such muscular arms. He'd worn a simple brown caftan with a wide band of faded yellow silk around the waist and a low, mustard-colored turban

---

*"bastardmurmur"

on his head. A thread of twisted wool hung from his waist to his knees, dyed in a deep, brilliant blue that reminded him of certain wildflowers in the Egyptian desert.

He had wrapped his arms around himself and rocked back and forth, wishing he was back in Egypt as he stumbled over his words.

"Yes, yes, Rav Yitzhak. I'm aware that bringing the boy could be seen as dangerous. But you see, Aillil is the only son of a good friend, a Cathar knight currently in Outremer.* The boy swore he would starve himself to death if he could not join his father, and the passages from Venice start at Easter. I was coming here anyway, so I promised I would try to put him on a ship." He paused. "Also, I heard that in the cities of the Italians the mamserbilbul is not as widespread as in the north." He had looked at the dyers as if hoping for help but then had lowered his eyes and sighed.

"No, there's no denying it, Rav Yitzhak . . . you're right. I acted without forethought, and I ask forgiveness from you and from everyone. The fact is, the boy has grown attached to me over the years. His mother died when he was a baby and . . ."—he'd lowered his voice—"his eyesight and hearing are defective from birth and he is not as . . . quick as other boys, but sometimes I think God endowed him with a strange talent, which. . . ." He realized he was rambling and smiled, throwing up his arms. "What can I say, Rabbi, Aillil is . . . the only family I have!"

Rav Yitzhak—a vivacious scholar known for his love of polemic—gave him a long look, at once severe and wistful, with a trace of what looked like envy.

"You know what Qohelet† said, my friend, 'who can straighten what He has made crooked?'"

The exchange had been in Hebrew, but Aillil knew they were speaking of him. He sat there with a faint smile that could have been thoughtfulness or absence. He was almost thirteen but looked no older

---

*"Overseas." The French word for the lands conquered in Syria was used in most of Europe.

†The author of Ecclesiastes, traditionally assumed to have been King Solomon

than ten, and his beauty imbued anyone who looked at him for more than a moment with a sadness they couldn't explain. He had blond hair and freckled cheeks, and his big gray eyes were covered by a barely visible milky film and converged slightly toward the center. He still had a child's skin and smile, but at times his long lashes, not blinking for long spells, gave him a pensive, strangely adult expression.

Eighteen people sat around the Passover table that night: the dyers' families, the six rabbis, and the young Christian heretic. Two of the Ben-Porat boys were over thirteen, thus ensuring the presence of ten adult males necessary to pray and read from the Torah scroll, something Rav Eleazar had verified before choosing the house for the meeting.

Two copper candelabra stood on the embroidered tablecloth. The big logs in the fireplace spat sparks and bathed the table and celebrants in a flickering reddish light. The commemoration of the Exodus went on late, but after women and children went to bed, a subdued atmosphere settled on the room, much like a wake. A phrase from the Talmud, a sudden word of warning from a prophet, or a loud sigh would break spells of placid silence. Well, near silence: a sizzling candle, a shuffling of slippers, a rabbi humming to himself, a child's moan behind the curtain. Rav Eleazar rocked back and forth, eyes closed, passing his beard through his hands over and over.

An hour before dawn, Yehezkel went outside for a breath of fresh air. He slipped on a *sarbel,** barely managed to get his shoulders through the little door, and stepped outside. Right away, the northeasterly wind wrenched the skullcap from his head, and the rabbi galloped off, chasing it in the near darkness. When he got it, he stood catching his breath and looked at the big moon setting.

"The moon is always full on the night of the seder," he murmured, "as it was when we walked off into the desert toward the Red Sea."

---

*The most common Jewish outer garment in the Middle Ages, a sleeveless mantle with a single opening on the right

The window of the cottage was the only light to be seen. He started walking and soon reached a small pier on the northern shore of the island. He sniffed deeply, searching in vain for the briny flavor that the Bora—as he'd heard the locals call the northeasterly—blowing down from the mountains didn't carry.

Since leaving Egypt, Yehezkel had seized every chance to go to sea. Despite the Jewish theological preference for mountains—and the consequent lack of a seafaring tradition among Jews—he'd fallen in love with boats as a child living near the Nile and still relished sailing with the youngest part of himself. He had become a sailor in the only way there was, by making the right choices on stormy nights when the sea will not forgive the tiniest mistake. Over the years he'd learned to plan for the unlikeliest, unluckiest of circumstances. Then, with time, he'd learned to do so from the first freshening of the breeze. Later, as he delved into the secrets of Kabbalah, he struggled to reconcile a mystic's blind faith in Divine Providence with cold, calculating precaution, but his love of the sea had somehow enabled him to fuse fatalism and prevention in a seamanship all of his own, in which astronomy and maneuvers on deck coexisted with the biblical exegesis of the state of wind and sea.

Ashore, his movements often overshot their intended reach, as if he'd never quite learned to govern his bulk, but the minute he boarded a vessel, be it a Nile *jalabah** or a Catalan *sardinal,* he suddenly acquired an uncanny agility, as everyone who watched him in his element readily admitted.

The wind tore the spray from the crests of the wavelets and slung it in his face.

Yehezkel closed his eyes and imagined himself on a ship's quarterdeck.

He thought he'd heard something, but the wind put back to northeast, so all he could hear now was its erratic whoosh in the nearby reeds.

---

*A boat with a single lateen sail, the medieval ancestor of the felucca, but with no transom.

He concentrated, turning his head slightly from side to side, waiting for another more northerly gust.

There! This time he heard it distinctly. It was a woman's scream.

✡ ✠ ✡ ✠

Galatea degli Ardengheschi was listless.

The Compline bell had rung hours ago, but the candle in the room over the refectory of San Maffìo's convent still burned. Sitting on a wooden stool, the abbess raised her eyes from the Psalter and stretched like a cat, so voluptuously that she found herself standing.

That she was the most fetching nun in the lagoon was the one thing men in Torcello could agree on. Even in the shapeless smock she'd taken to calling her "insomniashirt," her figure was striking: tall and graceful, but with shoulders nearly as broad as a man's. She had violet eyes, and right there, some claimed, one could stop looking for the origin of her undeniable charm. But her white complexion was translucent like alabaster, too, so that her lips, a tiny mole next to them, looked bright in comparison.

Long neck, strikingly slender wrists and ankles—in short, a noblewoman. Even kneeling in prayer, the daughter of Orlando d'Ardenga—who had died a hero's death at the Siege of Acre a month before her birth—knelt differently from other nuns. Not just more composed, but with dignity, like someone who considers it a humiliating but necessary imposition.

She went to the window and gazed at the windswept trees. She watched the Bora shake them fiercely, their silvery foliage twisting and dancing in and out of the moonlight, as if trying to send signals to her. For some time now the stretch of lagoon framed by that window, with its big sky and flat horizon, had weighed on her soul the way a cage stifles the song of a little bird.

That dawn, two doves cooing on the windowsill—an early sign of spring that would normally have put her in a chirpy mood for the whole day—hadn't even scratched this torpor, as nothing seemed capable of doing in the last few weeks. From the taste of food to Sister Erminia's bitchiness, it was all indifferent. At times she felt as if the very salvation of her soul—Madre Santissima!—had become an indifferent issue.

"It is a failure of your will!" she told herself for the hundredth time. "This is not melancholy; it is sloth masquerading as a nobler ailment. That's what Mother Elisabetta would say, and you know it!"

Galatea paced the room like the lioness she had been. "And were you a simple nun, you could accept it as a punishment from Heaven, but you're the abbess of San Maffìo, and if you don't snap out of this *soon*, the whole convent will go to hell in a basket!"

Sitting on the edge of the bed, she wondered gloomily if her detractors, Bishop Ranolfo at their head, were not right to argue that the nuns of San Maffìo should never have chosen a thirty-year-old Tuscan noblewoman—and a widow, to boot!—to be their abbess.

She closed her eyes, letting Mother Elisabetta's familiar smile easily float up before them. A pang of nostalgia, tinged with hopelessness, struck at the thought of her departed teacher. On her deathbed two years before, Elisabetta had advised the nuns to choose Galatea as her successor, because only Galatea could stand up to Bishop Ranolfo to save their community. Ever since the hermit's prophecy on the Island of the Two Vines, ten years earlier, Mother Elisabetta had taken Galatea under her wing and had spent much of the last eight years training the young countess in the fickle politics of the lagoon.

She taught how the ways of the female mind could make running a nunnery more complicated than negotiating with the Saracens. Before long, Galatea found the courage to confide her secret to the Mother Superior. She'd told Elisabetta about the visions, dreams, and premonitions she'd had since childhood. The abbess believed her every word and had commended her on the choice to enter a convent rather than run the risk of such visions being declared as being from the devil. For the first time in her life, Galatea found someone who didn't frown on her dangerous gift and embraced the older woman's friendship like an orphan finding a home.

The bond between them grew deeper than that between teacher and disciple; the two had often talked late into the night about why God tolerated the injustices women suffered everywhere. Popes and clerics said it was Eve's curse, under which every woman would suffer until Christ's return, but both had come to believe that men's words were dictated more by convenience than divine inspiration. No doubt the strength needed to defy priests on the spiritual worth of women came to them from the writings of the Sybil of the Rhine, as people had called Hildegard of Bingen even before she'd died forty years earlier and especially from an idea that Hildegard had called "trust in the soul of woman."

Galatea first heard of the prophetess from a German nun on a pilgrimage to Rome who had actually known her. Then, five years after moving to Torcello, her mother sent a costly copy of Hildegard's *Scivias,* or *Book of the Twenty-Six Visions,* lovingly illustrated by the monks of Monte Amiata. Mother Elisabetta and Sister Galatea had meditated on each vision and on Hildegard's commentaries, coming to trust her spiritual guidance more than that of any male confessor they had ever known. How they had loved Hildegard's answer to why the devil decided to tempt Eve rather than Adam! "He knew that it would be easier to prevail over the sensitivity of woman than over the rigidity of man."

Galatea felt a strong complicity with Hildegard. "She must have been a strange woman, one not many people understood . . . like me," she thought. The Sybil had her visions with eyes wide open and listening with her "inner ear," just like Galatea, who often wondered if her own visions were a prelude to a complete illumination that would come when she was ready. After all, Hildegard had only had hers when she'd been forty-two. "Yes, but she told her sisters everything about those visions. Were I to do the same in the Venetian lagoon, it would cost me what little liberty I still enjoy . . . if not my life!"

She thought back to the winter, when a fisherman's wife on the island of Costanziaca had a vision of the Virgin on a desert shoal in midlagoon. Right away, pilgrimages to the site began, despite the season: sad processions of gondolas and *roscone* bearing the sick. Then the bishop interrogated the woman and determined that the origins of that vision were satanic. The wretch was summoned by the newly established Rialto chapter of the Preaching Friars, and no more was heard of her. The husband, deranged with grief, joined the colonists sailing off to settle the island of Crete.

No, there was no question of telling *anyone* else about these dreams.

Then there was the Sybil's music. Since becoming abbess, Galatea was entitled to commission books and manuscripts for the convent; among the first things she'd sought out were sheets of music by the prophetess, written in that new French notation, with a four-line staff and squares for the notes. Those soaring, celestial melodies changed her life.

More or less since the time her mood had soured, she'd started having a recurrent dream. Six virgins sung a hymn to Hildegard's music. She didn't understand a word the white-clad girls sung, but the music was her favorite of the hymns by Hildegard. She started humming the melody. A month before the dream started, she attempted to replace the music the nuns sung at morning Lauds with that very hymn, causing a scandal on the island. The Cistercian obsession with sobriety is well known: no silver or gold in their churches, only wooden crosses and iron candelabra. Their rule prescribed "the most simple and sombre plainchant," and at San Tomà, the mixed Cistercian house where the nuns lived before San Maffìo, the hooded monks would follow the horizontal line of the melody in a low, dogged bellow so insufferable that Mother Elisabetta had called it a "cilice for the ears."

Naturally, Galatea's idea of singing Hildegard's music at Lauds had met first with Sister Erminia's outrage and then with the bishop's censure. Just as when Mother Elisabetta lost the battle with San Tomà's abbot to keep her nuns in the big house on the canal between Torcello and Boreano, Galatea had to bow to the men on the island on a dozen small but humiliating issues.

She snorted, got up from the bed, and went over to her chest.

No nun would normally be allowed to keep in her cell such a family heirloom, bearing the Ardenga coat of arms and her initials. But the huge trunk of solid oak, with two locks on its iron flaps and endless drawers and secret compartments inside, had been given to the convent by her family for safekeeping in exchange for yet one more donation, thus circumventing the young countess' vow of poverty.

She unlocked it with a key hanging around her neck, looking for the table she'd copied from her latest acquisition for the scriptorium, Hildegard's *Causae et Curae*. She hummed the dream's melody, as if that sudden curiosity were a sign of a recovery, until she found the fragrant, undulated parchment.

AIR	FIRE	EARTH	WATER
Spring	Summer	Autumn	Winter
Morning	Noon	Evening	Midnight
Hot	Dry	Cold	Humid
Childhood	Adolescence	Maturity	Old Age
Lymph	Black Bile	Yellow Bile	Blood
East	South	West	North
Lymphatic	Sanguine	Choleric	Melancholic

That last column ending in the melancholic humor seemed to her a summation of her condition. "But I'm not *old*!" she exclaimed, a little peeved, throwing the parchment back into the chest.

She decided to react; she would take a walk under the moon. She got up, took a woolen cloak from its peg, and slung it over her shoulders. Unlike the cloaks of the nuns, its inside was lined with soft rabbit fur. An owl in the oak on the bank let out a long hoot. She snuffed out the candle on the desk.

"No one will know," she whispered to herself with a flash of the old roguery.

Going down to the small cloister, peering into the kitchen, she heard the regular breathing of the two young scullery girls, curled up by the fireplace. She passed the hospital from which a loud snoring of pilgrims emerged. She took out the key to the door that let out into the kitchen garden and turned it in the hole, trying to make no sound. The moment she stepped out, the Bora filled her cloak. She pulled it to her chest, both fists under her chin. She crossed the garden, raised the pole that barred the wooden palisade, and in an instant was outside the convent.

She was on the northern tip of the island—in her microcosm, the "North" in Hildegard's table. She started walking down to the convent's pier. The moon, still high, splashed whitish light on rocks and puddles on the path. Soon Galatea was calling herself a fool for not wearing proper shoes instead of stupid clogs, more slippery with mud with every step.

The abbess could never say exactly how she slipped into the lagoon. She remembered the low whistle of the wind as she stared at the black water, breaking wavelets slapping the bank. Maybe a gust of wind, maybe a sudden dizziness or a misstep, suddenly she found herself in freezing water up to her neck, the soft slime on the bottom squeezing up between her toes.

She laughed at her own clumsiness and briefly worried that people might find out. But just as in a dream one strives to grasp something as it slips away again and again, so did her efforts to reach the bank only suffice to keep her three feet from it. When her strength started to wane, the shore receded! Only then did Galatea abandon any hope of hiding the incident and begin to fear for her life.

She started shouting under the stars, her white insomniashirt floating around her like an exotic flower. The Bora broke up her screams and slowly dragged her out toward the open lagoon.

✡ ✠ ✡ ✠

The sailor rabbi contemplated the possible scenarios:

If he wasted any time looking for help, the woman would drown.

If he tried to row by himself, standing on the skiff, the wind would capsize him.

The only way to row against that wind was to sit in the stern and use a short paddle.

With God's help, there would be a senseless body in the boat on his way back.

All this went through his mind in a few seconds. Yehezkel started to breathe in the deep, ventral way he learned from his master, a technique kabbalists used to accumulate the energy required to correctly pronounce the secret Names of God.

He stuck his skullcap in his pocket and ran to the pier. He grabbed an oar from inside the dyers' skiff, leaned it against the oak, and jumped on its midpoint with all his weight, snapping it three feet from the blade. He hopped into the skiff with the makeshift paddle, as nimble as a mountain goat.

Crouching on the bottom to dodge the wind, he raised his thumb and lined up the oak with the belltower of the Cathedral behind it, an alignment to help find the landing again. Then he untied the skiff's mooring, sat in the stern and started paddling. With the Bora on a broad reach, the small boat fairly flew on the smooth lagoon, the spray in Yehezkel's face exciting him like a rider's yells spur on his steed.

He saw the round white stain of the woman's gown on the water not two hundred yards from shore. He knew he'd have to grab her on the first attempt, or the wind would carry him beyond her and he would waste precious strength to paddle back upwind to her.

When he got close, Yehezkel realized the woman was no longer shouting. To his surprise, he thought he heard her singing to herself. He had once heard from a survivor of a Greek shipwreck of the calm euphoria that comes over people about to give up and drown. He thanked the Lord she was still alive and wondered how she would react to his appearance.

The moment of the rescue was upon him in no time. As he'd feared, when he slipped his hands under her shoulders she was overtaken by panic and thrashed about with unsuspected strength. Yehezkel took a final deep breath and pronounced four words in Latin in a warm, deep voice:

"Ego sum, nolite timere!"*

On hearing those words, the woman opened her eyes wide, drew a deep breath, and went limp in his arms. In a single, uninterrupted movement, the veins in his forehead pulsating and his beard shining with sweat, the rabbi tore the senseless body from the lagoon's embrace and placed it, belly down, across the low thwart in the center of the skiff.

He sat down and started paddling furiously back in an easterly direction, against the Bora. But every hundred yards or so he gained windward, he lost fifty to turn and gently sit on the woman's back, forcing her to expel great gushes of the water she'd swallowed. Under the brutal pressure of Yehezkel's weight, the woman shook, vomited water, wheezed and coughed horribly. Despite it all, the rabbi could still make out that she was incredibly beautiful.

He used his alignment to find the pier, reached it with his last ounce of strength, tied a line to it almost without looking, and collapsed, exhausted, in the bottom of the skiff. His eyes closed, he wondered if it had all really happened, but the wind and his gasping breaths were not the only sound: he could hear the woman's coughs too, each one turning into uncontrolled retching.

When he had recovered enough, Yehezkel lifted the woman in his arms and managed to carry her, staggering, to the base of the oak. He stretched her out on the grass and tried to revive her, but as he did so some dogs downwind started barking furiously, waking up the fisherman who lived near the convent. Yehezkel saw torches approaching.

Among those running toward him was Gudrun, Galatea's young German protégée. A bearded stranger was manhandling her abbess, and she rushed forward, letting out a fearful scream. Yehezkel stood up,

---

*"Fear not, it is me."

his hands raised in a calming gesture. There were also two men he had never seen.

"It's a Jew!" shouted one of the two. "He was kidnapping the abbess! Let's hang him!"

Yehezkel started his breathing again, but he knew he was too weak and felt the first pang of fear. Whatever he said, these goyim wouldn't believe him. He had always suspected that if his time came to sanctify the Name, instead of doing so with dignified restraint he would likely try to take as many uncircumcised pagans with him as he could. As he watched the savages approach, he felt that the rage mounting inside him was proof that he'd been right.

He tried to keep control. The dyers' cottage was downwind, and he wondered if he should use the power of his voice to call for help rather than try to overcome the rabble.

Suddenly, Galatea came to. She coughed, spluttered, and then gestured to Gudrun to come closer.

The big blonde carefully stepped around the Jew and rushed to Galatea's side, taking her hand.

The abbess whispered hoarsely, "I . . . I was drowning. He . . . he saved me."

Then she passed out.

CHAPTER 3

VAYEHI OR

And There Was Light

ISLAND OF TORCELLO,
TEN YEARS EARLIER—15TH AUGUST 1209

A ripple of sound spread out on the smooth surface of the silence. The big bell had rung Nocturns.

The young nun turned over on a narrow pallet beneath a gauze veil protecting her from insects. It couldn't be—she'd only just drifted off! But the bell chimed again. Galatea opened her eyes. The humid darkness was perfectly still, and the big bed in Castel Romitorio was in another life.

It was five years since she'd joined the Cistercian house of San Tomà; locals called it I Borgognoni. A double monastery in the old style where the church was the only place monks and nuns shared, all other parts of the compound being separated by a high wall, not to be approached at any time. In that summer of 1209, the old cenoby housed thirty-eight monks and fifteen nuns.

Galatea got up quickly; the Rule allowed but a few minutes for bodily needs. She'd grown quite tall for a woman. She gathered her hair

under the cap. It reached to her shoulders again. Sister Erminia had certainly noticed, and soon she would have to cut it again. As she slipped
on a frock, she remembered it was Saturday, and her heart quickened.
Today she would go outside! She felt like singing but didn't. By now
she'd learned to hold back impulses permitted to children that Sister
Erminia called bestial. Laughing out loud, bursting into tears or song,
making faces, screaming . . . all these did not become a nun.

"Oh my dear Jesus, my sweet bridegroom! So many things don't
become a nun." She paused, smiling in the dark, "Or for that matter,
a wife."

The small bell sounded the time for the office. Galatea left her cell
for the oratory, mumbling a psalm. She crossed the tiny cloister and
joined her sisters as they entered the church, their steps on the gravel
the only sound in the night. Hooded monks were walking in from
the opposite nave, the candles on the altar projecting two single files
of sleepy shadows proceeding toward each other along the curved wall
behind the ambulatory, for all the world like ghosts crowding the
dreams of some forsaken pagan lagoon divinity.

Galatea crossed herself before the altar, knelt in her pew, closed her
eyes, and prayed.

She had the vision of the man with the blue shawl again. It happened like the other times, while she was wide awake, eyes open.
Suddenly she was standing on a wooden pier above emerald water sparkling in the sun. Before her, a man stretched out his arms, but over his
head and arms was a shawl of an intense blue, and all she could see were
his hands poking out from under it, dirty fingers strangely splayed out.

What made this vision different from others she'd had all her life
was its capacity to return in powerful yet fleeting shreds. Days after
the vision vanished, the smell of water, or the creaking of planks, or
the blue of the shawl would be there again, sharper than what actually
surrounded her.

Her visions had not frightened her for years, but she still felt the
need to atone for the privilege that she knew to be hers alone. She

would seek out a passing holy man or a cleric returning from a pilgrimage in Outremer and give him a silver *grosso* for his church. Her sin of pride would end up in some windswept monastery in Portugal or Hibernia, and none would ever know of it. Yes, that's what she would do.

After Nocturns, Galatea returned to her cell. Silence would reign until the Lauds bell, just before dawn. She looked around the minute quarters and asked herself once more if two flowers, or even—oh, the nerve!—a caged bird by the small, barred window would really corrupt a nun's devotion to the Lord. She would never be able to go back to sleep. The thought of crossing the crowded island on a market day and entering the cathedral itself; it was so exciting!

Then her eyes fell on the coat of arms emblazoned on her trunk, and she fell on her pallet and pitied herself for her naive enthusiasm. "Galatea degli Ardengheschi, you've been in a convent for just five years, and here you are thinking like an oblate, who never saw the world beyond the walls of the nunnery! A walk to market thrills you like a pilgrimage to Jerusalem. What a sad fate for a countess of Tuscia who used to hunt with men and dreamed of her own fiefdom in Outremer!"

She laid down, feeling a growing shortness of breath. The walls of the cell slowly closed in. Her chest heaved in silent screams. Mother Elisabetta warned her that such nights had not gone away for good, and if they came back, prayer would bring the only possible relief. Sleep finally took pity on her after a while, halfway through an Ave Maria.

Back in her cell after Lauds and Prime, Galatea opened the massive chest and took out an expensive copy of Hildegard of Bingen's *Scivias*, copied by Tuscan monks from a manuscript that had come directly from Disibodenberg. Galatea opened it reverently and tiptoed into the Sybil's visions, the only flight from convent life she did not consider a breach of vows.

Mother Elisabetta shared her enthusiasm for the German mystic, now thirty years dead, and for the past three months the two had been contemplating the first *visio,* the one of the Creator. A week before, they had moved on to the second visio, Hildegard's understanding of evil, temptation, and sin. Since then, the sinister image of the *visio secunda* had drawn Galatea to the book almost every day.

She turned a page, and it appeared, taking her breath away, as it did every time. Above, a blanket of stars; below, Adam asleep with his head reclining on a pool of evil, black water. Fingers from the water became the snake that splashed its black poison on Eve just as she emerged from Adam's rib cage in the form of . . . a piece of the starry sky above!

A few days before, Don Rosalino, the curate of Santa Fosca, had returned into the arms of his Creator. Galatea had been tasked with cleaning up his sacristy. A little after sixth hour, she emerged from the tiny door in the chapter house with two novices.

The three nuns stopped, looking in all directions like anxious birds, at once curious and intimidated, as if venturing into the outside world were something sure to bring its own punishment. Galatea snapped out of it first and led the novices through the throng along the canal between Torcello and Majurbio. Their troubled looks followed beggars, lepers, cripples, and drunks wondering from one *campo* to the next. Under a glaring sun, veiled by the foul vapors rising from the canals, the three nuns crossed the bridge into the borough of Santa Margherita.

Those vapors had been driving Torcello's decline for decades. In the thousandth year from the birth of our Savior the island had hosted forty thousand souls, but now there were barely ten thousand left, the rest driven away by waves of pestilence and foul, unbreathable air. As a kind of consolation, the island was blooming with convents and monasteries as more and more patrician families donated their estates to the church before moving to Rialto.

Traditions in the lagoon told of the flight of the first Christians from the mainland, some six hundred years earlier. The ferocious barbarians on small horses who had raided them constantly possessed no sailing skills—or, in fact, any confidence with water whatsoever—so the inhabitants of Altino found refuge on the islands. It had also been a religious flight of sorts, for those barbarians had also been Christians—*o tempora!**—but of the Arian heresy which at times demanded the persecution of Catholics. The Altinates colonized the islands around Torcello while the Paduans settled Rialto.

Upon emerging on the Square of the Wheel the three froze again, overwhelmed by the grandiosity of churches and palaces, as well as a little shocked by the gaudy dresses of Torcellans. In front of them rose Santa Maria, Torcello's incredibly tall cathedral. To its right was the minute San Niccolò with its wooden gate, and farther right the reddish, round Santa Fosca, surrounded by its graceful octagonal portico. To their left, dozens of boats of all sizes were moored along the quay on the Rio Maggiore. Canals, alleys, and *fondamenta*† stretched in any direction the nuns cared to look, all of them crawling with people. Galatea again wrenched her eyes from a spectacle she could have watched all day. She took her sisters by the hand and resolutely crossed the square to Santa Fosca.

Soon they were ankle deep in dust and cobwebs in the small sacristy behind the church; mice sprinted around them. At first, Galatea was embarrassed to open the doors of Rosalino's closet, decorated with the symbols of the litanies of the Virgin. A wave of sadness overcame her when she did. The priest's whole life was there, on two dusty shelves: notebooks, which he jealously closed when someone approached his desk; the trap to defend these books from mice; a bottle of Chios wine he kept for important guests; a few salamis hanging at the back. And in sacrilegious proximity to those venal possessions, the bronze vessel of the Holy Oil, covered by a cloth cap.

Tears welled as she remembered the little priest, short arms waving excitedly in the air, round eyes as sad as a stray dog's. He would chide

---

*"What terrible times!"

†In Venice, a road alongside water, whether the lagoon or a canal

her for some behavior more befitting a young countess than a nun, but the little smile at the end of the sermon always made her feel forgiven. If only Lupo had smiled at her like that, sometimes.

She noticed two stones on top of the cupboard and took one down. It was covered with strange carvings and brought back Don Rosalino's obsession with ancient Achaeans. For years the curate tried to convince the self-styled erudite clerics of Torcello and Venice that the archipelagos, far from being founded by refugees from Altino, had been settled by the ancient Greeks—whose tongue he studied all his life—and that their island had at one time been the home of Aeneas himself!

The doctors of the lagoon always derided him with the kind of condescension that angered the chubby priest far more than serious, argued condemnations of his theses would have done. One day, after listening to his bitter complaints, Galatea wrote a phrase in the notebook she kept in a secret drawer of her chest. Don Rosalino had said, "There is truth and there is untruth, and if you cling to the truth, even against the whole world, it doesn't mean you're crazy!" On hearing of his death two days before, Galatea read those words again and wept over the vindication of Rosalino that had never come, and over the great injustice that rules in the world.

She gathered the contents of the cupboard in a cloth. Putting the Holy Oil behind the altar would give her an excuse to peer into the cathedral. She told Floridiana and Gualfarda not to leave the sacristy until she came back. On an afterthought she added, in the sternest tone she could muster, that if anyone walked in, they should pretend to have taken a vow of silence. Then, before the novices could question that last instruction, she slipped out, crossed San Niccolò's narthex, and discreetly slid into Santa Maria.

The lion's share of the relics looted from Constantinople in the infamous campaign five years earlier went to Saint Mark's Basilica, still unfinished and more flamboyant with every passing month, but trades and coups de main between Venice and Torcello were not altogether over.

Torcello's Santa Maria, the oldest church in the lagoon, secured no less than a fragment of the True Cross. In five years, the gold-plated reliquary, high above the altar and surmounted by the inscription *HIC EST DE LIGNO CRUCIS*, transformed life on the island. Churches endowed with famous relics soon became fetid, noisy hospitals; the sick laid out on pallets along the naves, their distance from the altar supposedly dictated by the nobility of their birth, but usually determined by the size of their donations.

Galatea's eyes were immediately drawn to the mosaics taking shape at the church's extremities: a Virgin showing her Child in the apse and an immense Last Judgment on the wall opposite. As she admired the triumphant Christ in the Resurrection, taking Adam by the hand and trampling the doors of hell, she suddenly noticed the color of his mantle. It was exactly the same blue as the shawl on the head and arms of the man in her vision!

She gasped. "Oh, Madre Santissima . . . it must be Jesus!"

But two more figures in the mosaic were clad in the same blue. She *had* to find out who they were. She asked a passing monk if anyone in the cathedral could tell her about the contents of the mosaics.

"Abbot Cipriano can tell you anything you need to know, sister. He's here from Ravenna precisely to dictate the contents of the mosaics and knows the meaning of every smallest detail."

She thanked him and walked to the center of the apse. Short, hunchbacked, and with a pointed hood over his head, Father Cipriano looked more like a gnome than a cleric, his head down over the drawings. When he looked up, eyeballs so deepset they looked like they'd been hammered into his skull, Galatea almost jumped back. She curtsied, thinking of monsters and basilisks, and then stammered, "Ego, paupercola et imbecillis forma,* dare to beg for a pearl of the abbot's wisdom. Which Old Testament figures in the Anastasis wear cloaks of the same blue as our Savior?"

---

*"I, poor little ignorant figure"

Cipriano smiled, his upper lip curling just enough to turn the smile into a smirk. "Such questions should not preoccupy a young nun, but you ask with such courtesy and humility that it would be heartless to refuse you."

As he raised his eyes to the mosaic, the hood slipped off. He was totally bald and huge, fleshy lobes hung below pale ears. The similarity with the gargoyles adorning the churches of her Tuscan childhood was complete. Galatea stared at him as if one of those grotesque statues had suddenly addressed her.

"The figures in the blue cloaks are King David and the prophet Ezekiel, sister, but I can assure you that the color of their cloaks bears no significance at all. If it had any, *I* would know. But if you'll forgive a witticism, how come you to seem so interested in the *mosaic* part of the mosaic?"

Cipriano giggled at his own jest. Galatea thought she'd done enough silly things for one day and had better go back to her novices before she caused any more damage. But the abbot started rattling off the sources for the Judgment. ". . . and from Saint Ephrem of Syria and Saint John of Damascus. And, of course, from Saint John's Apocalypse."

At the mention of that book, Galatea became attentive again and turned to the mosaic.

"The Apocalypse? But then, Father, the child sitting in Satan's lap must be the Antichrist, isn't that so?"

The abbot's face darkened. Galatea felt a powerful desire to kick herself.

"You are only supposed to read Psalms and Gospels, sister. . . ." Cipriano looked her in the eyes, and then his expression softened. "But these are dark times; laymen read the Scriptures by themselves, so why should I be surprised that a nun has heard some crazy preacher talk of the Antichrist? That is where you heard that name, is it not?"

Galatea was about to answer, but he raised his hand to silence her, a gesture men often made when speaking with women, which infuriated her. She did not let him cite any other holy texts.

"Forgive me, Father, but I must return to the convent right away."

She left the stunned theologian behind, taking a few steps toward the entrance. When she'd passed the altar, she turned to the east again, bent one knee and crossed herself, her eyes fixed on the enormous ones of the Virgin in the vault.

✡ ✠ ✡ ✠

A little before ninth hour the nuns held chapter in the hall of that name, on the opposite side of the cloister from the church. The prioress introduced a new oblate who had just arrived from Germany. Gudrun, blonde and chubby, was eight years old. Her cheeks were as red as apples and streaked with tears. The poor thing felt much better as soon as her sisters, as befit a new family, smothered her in hugs and caresses that overcame the language difference in no time at all.

After making room for Gudrun on one of the benches, chapter began with the usual litany of complaints: one nun had slapped a sister, one hadn't gone to Mass, another received far too many visitors. Then the sisters sent Gudrun on a child's errand. A commentary on the Song of Songs had been circulating among them, causing sinful fantasies in the minds of those who found their marriage to Christ, so to speak, incomplete, so they started morbidly discussing the weakness of their flesh.

One sister confessed to exploring the recesses of her body; another had been seen by the choir mistress going to a sister's cell in the night. Galatea made a face. Sister Erminia, the choir mistress, had a natural gift for spotting weaknesses and faults in every one of the nuns and had no friends in the Borgognoni because of the pleasure she took in doing so.

After chapter, the prioress asked Galatea to follow her. Mother Elisabetta's bright squirrel eyes shone from minute, tightly gathered features, framed by the linen cap under her hood. To the young nun's surprise, they exited the little door onto the fondamenta, Mother Elisabetta heading straight for the quay.

"Where are we going, Mother?"

"You'll soon find out," said the abbess, refusing the hand an oars-
man offered to help her aboard the *roscona*. Roscone are the size of
gondolas, but twice as beamy and with a short mast, raked aft, in the
middle. In the lagoon they were used for small transport and local fishing. When the women were on board, the men untied the moorings and
took up the long oars. They rowed standing—one forward, the other
aft—as the nuns sat across the boat's middle, the mast between them.
Galatea's eyes begged the Mother, her curiosity unbearable. Finally, as
Majurbio passed on starboard, Elisabetta relented.

"Two weeks ago, a hermit arrived on the Island of the Two Vines. He
doesn't preach and refuses alms. They say he forgives himself nothing
. . . and others very little. He awaits God's imminent judgment and
prays for us all." She paused. "He already cured four sick Torcellans."
Then she lowered her voice. "The abbess of San Zaccaria told me he is
a disciple of Gioacchino!"

Galatea grabbed Elisabetta's hands excitedly. They had heard much
about Gioacchino da Fiore, the Calabrian seer who'd died a few years
earlier. He announced the fall of Jerusalem a month before the news
reached Christendom and wrote a book explaining all the secrets of the
Apocalypse. They had also heard of his prophecy of a third "Age of the
Holy Spirit," after those of the Father and the Son. Mother Elisabetta
and Sister Galatea took great comfort in the similarities between the
visions of Hildegard and Gioacchino of a future world permeated with
love. After his death, some of his monks started wondering apostoli-
cally, preceded by rumors of miraculous deeds. People climbed to the
inaccessible caves the monks chose as hermitages to seek their blessing
or just to watch them meditate.

"I brought you with me, my dove," concluded Mother Elisabetta,
"because I'm going to consult the holy man on the future of our
monastery."

"Here is *real* adventure!" thought Galatea. "Never mind entering
the cathedral! Crossing the lagoon to seek the advice of a holy hermit

is something even a countess in Tuscia would never have done!"

A little later the perfect serenity of the afternoon and the regular rhythm of the oars inspired the nuns to praise the Lord with song. The abbess started humming the Cistercian "Salve Regina," and soon they broke into the soaring arches of Hildegard's hymns, at one point abandoning all musical restraint and singing a B flat, a note expressly forbidden to Cistercians. The harmonies they wove delighted the oarsmen and faded over the water behind the roscona, leaving musical trails that seemed to sparkle in the sun.

Leaving Boreano to starboard, the roscona headed for Sant'Erasmo. The western horizon above Venice filled with black clouds, and soon thunder could be heard in the distance. The air became clear as crystal and filled with the exciting, metallic smell of thunderstorms. When the first big drops began to fall, the oarsmen tied the gaff to the mast along the axis of the boat and threw the sail over it as an awning for the nuns. Then they tied the sail's edges to the gunwales and went back to their rowing stations.

It rained hard, without a breath of wind. The men took turns rowing and bailing, so the roscona wouldn't fill with water. The nuns knelt under the sail, embracing each other and praying softly. Suddenly, the roar of the rain on the canvas brought the vision back to Galatea's senses. The blue of the cloak and that of the lightning over the lagoon were the same. The creaking pier of the vision became confused with the crash of the rain on the water all around.

Galatea sat motionless, eyes wide open and fixed straight ahead.

The Island of the Two Vines lies just north of the bigger one of Sant'Erasmo. The first islanders to land there found a pagan altar whose carved stones would have thrilled Rosalino had they not all ended up in God knows which fondamenta around the lagoon. But the memory of the blasphemous stones remained, giving the island the aura of mystery of a place the ancients considered a residence of the gods.

The boat went ashore where three planks were thrown onto the bank for peasants coming to tend the vineyard. The rain beat down, the smell of weeds was strong, and mud was everywhere, so much that the prioress had to hold on to a man's hand to disembark. The two nuns ran off down the path, habits lifted, as the men settled down under the awning, looking forward to a leisurely wait.

Almost immediately, they came upon a hut built of woven reeds with a little altar inside. A small bell hung from three branches stuck into the thatched roof. The nuns took refuge in the makeshift chapel and squeezed the hems of their habits, still panting from the run.

"You can take off your cap, my dove. I know how long your hair is. I won't make you cut it."

Galatea shot her a look of daughterly love. As she shook her hair, her eyes wandered over the little horizon visible through the hut's door. Suddenly she realized that what had seemed an egg-shaped gray rock was in fact a man. Perfectly still among the reeds, he was hunched up to offer less surface to the rain, just like the birds around him. It could only be Gioacchino's disciple. Galatea tugged on Elisabetta's sleeve and pointed to the shape. The abbess nodded.

"He is supplicating the Virgin on behalf of us sinners," she murmured.

A sudden impulse overcame Galatea, and she dashed out of the chapel bare-headed, wet, and beautiful like the heroine of some Provençal romance running toward her long-lost lover. She squatted down two steps behind the hermit and tried to listen with her inner ear.

His voice startled her. Low and raspy, it seemed to come from far away, as if someone else spoke through the fragile figure hunched in front of her. "What do you see, when you see?"

Her heart missed a beat. He knew of her visions! She felt immense relief, as if some heavenly power had just found her innocent of a mortal sin.

"I see shreds of events. And often they later happen . . . as I saw them." The anchorite didn't answer.

When it was clear he wouldn't speak again, Galatea closed her eyes and tried to commune with his prayers. The rivulets of rain on her face felt like an angel's darting, delicate fingers. Then she made the mistake— as she would think of it later—of letting herself be transported by the sounds of water all around. Suddenly she was staring at the visio secunda, the viscous black liquid looking unbearably malignant.

A finger of the hermit's hand twitched imperceptibly. Galatea shivered. Hildegard's vision took over, and she felt irresistibly drawn to the dark pool as in a dream. She slid into it, unable to scream, and started thrashing in the water, trying to reach a receding bank. In the back of her mind, she noticed it was all happening in total silence. Something grabbed her ankle and pull her to the bottom. She floundered, resurfaced, and then saw that the sky above was full of stars, as in the visio secunda.

"How strange, it's already nighttime," she thought and committed her soul to God, not without a last thought that this was a really stupid way to die.

"Ego sum, nolite timere!" The hermit had laid his hand on her arm, and she felt she was being slowly pulled out of the black pool.

Mother Elisabetta saw the holy man's hand on Galatea's arm and ran out of the hut under the endless rain. When she reached them Galatea embraced her, sobbing, breath short.

The hermit muttered what sounded like a prayer. Then the rain stopped, and in the sudden silence his voice rose clear and strong as a trumpet, the way ancient oracles must have sounded.

The Woman *is* the Jew, and the Jew *is* the Woman!
Only they see, and both are despised because they see!
For this reason they will be redeemed together, in the Last Days!

He turned and pointed a bony finger at Galatea. "Behold the woman who will find the center!"

With the word *centrum*, he fell silent. The nuns exchanged a hesitant glance as the first sunrays lit the thicket of reeds. Elisabetta drew

Galatea's shivering body closer. Was that the answer she'd been hoping for? Was it confirmation that Galatea would be prioress after her and save the nuns of the Borgognoni? Holding her charge tight, she addressed the holy man, who had turned back to the lagoon. "What do you mean by 'she will find the center,' holy father?"

"Oh, the glory of God!" said the old man impatiently, his voice once more hoarse with age as it had been before the prophecy. "That she will solve the enigma in Jerusalem!"

Galatea leaned urgently toward him. "You mean I . . . I will go to Jerusalem? And tread the ground our Lord Jesus walked on. . . . Is it true then that only a woman can solve the enigma?"

"*A woman and a Jew*' is what Gioacchino said. But then, Jesus himself revealed the highest secrets only to Mary Magdalene, the prophetess he took for wife."

The two women were stupefied at the old man's words, but nothing more was said. The birds started singing again, and after a short while the nuns stood up, kissed the hermit's tunic, and made their way back to the Borgognoni.

✡   ✠   ✡   ✠

Just as the hermit in the Venetian lagoon was pronouncing his prophecy, outside the walls of Rome at Ponte Milvio, ten men were leaving the eternal city on the Via Cassia.

They were barefoot and unkempt, their tunics the color of earth, tied at the waist with pieces of rope. Hot dust floated up from their heels and hovered in the air behind them. They couldn't have been monks, for no monks were so destitute, but a well-traveled pilgrim would have found them similar to heretical preachers in Lombardy and Provence and would have been surprised to see such men in the city of the pope. In fact, had you told such a pilgrim that the leader of that ragged band had been received by Pope Innocent III twice in the space of a few days, he would not have believed you.

A leper's bell approached from beyond the next hill on the road.

When they saw the wretched, amputated figure struggling to advance, four of them rushed forward to mitigate his suffering. But the leper was full of bitterness and hatred for the world; he abused and reviled the friars. At first they didn't mind, but when he began to obscenely insult the Blessed Christ and the Holy Mother they backed off, scandalized.

Then the smallest and least handsome of the ten asked his brothers for the traveling pan and water, telling them to continue on their way, saying he would catch up. Once he was alone with the obnoxious leper, the friar addressed him as sweetly as he could. "May God grant you peace, my brother."

"What peace could I have from God, who took peace and everything else from me and made me rotten and stinking?"

"Allow me to serve you; I will bring peace back to you," said the little friar, gentle but firm.

"And what can you do for me that others can't?"

"Whatever you desire, I will do for you."

"I want you to wash every part of me, for I stink so much that even I can no longer bear myself," said the wretch.

And so it was that in the country just north of Rome, on a fiery August afternoon, the small friar lit a fire, warmed water with some herbs, unraveled the bandages, and washed the leper from head to toe, rubbing him with his hands and washing his bandages, too, before wrapping the sores again.

And for the whole time the friar served him in that way, the leper wept without making a sound.

CHAPTER 4

BEIN HA'OR U'VEIN HA-HOSHECH

Between the Light and the Darkness

THE SAME 15TH OF AUGUST 1209, OUTSIDE THE WALLS OF CARCASSONNE

A few hours before the hermit's prophecy to Galatea, the column of survivors leaving the city, their only baggage painful memories and the rags on their backs, stretched down to the river. In the fiery midday sun, they shuffled under a rain of insults and spit from the jeering mob outside the walls. The brief siege of Carcassonne, the mostly heretical city on the banks of the river Aude in Languedoc, had just ended. A short way outside the gate, cross-wearing northerners searched each straggler. The papal legate's orders had been clear: "They are to take nothing, not even an earring. Just their sins!"

A yellow turban caught the eye of a young, armed peasant. The big Jew wore a black sarbel despite the heat and nonchalantly carried a bundled two-year-old in the fold of his elbow in what looked like a very comfortable position for the infant. The youth looked at the olive-skinned face and the black beard, and then shouted, "Hey, you! Hey, Jew!"

Yehezkel had debated with himself for an hour, in the "but on the other hand" style of Talmud sages, on what he should do if he heard those words as he left the city. He turned to look at the barbarian. The lanky, freckled teen was armed with a battered shield and spear. The rabbi stepped out of the stream of refugees.

"Show me the child, Jew! You're crafty enough to have hidden the gold in the wraps!"

Slowly and wordlessly, his eyes fixed on those of the young goy, Yehezkel stripped Aillil naked, shaking the sweaty rags in the air before dropping them to the ground. The toddler squealed with pleasure. The cross wearer looked peeved but unconvinced.

"I know you're trying to fool me *somehow,* Jew! That blond babe can't be your blood, you're from Outremer. . . ." He looked at the ground, rubbing it with one foot. "*I know*! You stole an orphan from the heretics to sell it to your Saracen friends, or . . ." the young man's eyes widened in outrage, "or maybe to raise him as a Jew!"

Visibly impressed by his own acumen, the peasant was already thinking of the prize that awaited him for exposing this perfidious scheme. The kabbalist's voice caught him totally by surprise. "LAMA RAGSHU GOYIM?"*

Lower than a roll of thunder, the first three words of the second Psalm swept the uncircumsized youth with something like supernatural force. It was as if an earthquake had shaken the ground beneath his feet. Like the voice of a dead man from the depths of hell. No, like the voice of all the Cathars who died in Béziers screaming in unison!

The boy swallowed and then pointed toward the river, unable for all his efforts, to detach his tongue from the roof of his mouth. Yehezkel picked up the wraps and turned away.

He'd projected his voice with the secret technique Rav Yitzhak

---

*"Why have the gentiles raged?"

the Blind taught him in Posquiére. From the moment the peasant called out to him, he started breathing the "folded breath." Stripping the child slowly had been an excuse to prolong the preparation and to hold the goy's eyes long enough to reverse the flow of fear between them. Then, his chin pressed on his chest, he had lowered his tone beyond, as Rav Yitzhak put it, "the mere physical size of his sounding chamber" and howled the three Hebrew words in a vibrato of barely repressed wrath.

Yehezkel smiled, imagining the thoughts of the panicked youth. Most likely he was sure to have just survived an encounter with the devil. After all, he must be saying to himself, if Satan needed a heretic infant for his plans, who was *he* to dream of objecting? Yehezkel surveyed the sorry wartime scene to make sure no one had noticed the exchange, and then crossed the sun-baked knoll and rejoined the river of exiles.

Carcassonne and Toulouse are the doors to a corridor connecting the Atlantic and the Mediterranean. At the eastern entrance to the valley known as the Lauragais, the Montagne Noire looms from the north, while sweeping hills overlap southward until they become the Pyrenees. The bulk of the refugees set off on the road that climbs to the doorway to Spain and takes pilgrims to Santiago de Compostela. The Lauragais was like one big forest bewitched with heresy. Lonely watchtowers and menacing fortresses were more frequent on that road than bell towers of churches.

There was no noise of carts—just shuffling feet, moans from the wounded, and the odd woman's sob—all of it blanketed by the shrieking of crickets rising from everywhere like derisory, demonic laughter. Everything spoke of the month-old war: abandoned villages, unkempt vineyards, the desperate bellows of surviving cows—and most of all the whitish, overgrown fields—eerily deserted at the height of harvest time. As the infant slept on his chest and the air shimmered in the heat, Yehezkel mused. "Here I am, the only Jew stupid enough to be caught in a city of Christian heretics under siege!"

He smiled, fingers immediately reaching into his beard to scratch the underside of his chin. "True, I could have left with the other Jews, but what would have become of Aillil in all this?" He raised his gaze to the sky and let out a long sigh.

Yehezkel ben Yoseph, a rabbi and a *medicus,* had arrived in Provence from Egypt five years earlier at the age of twenty-one. He had not just abandoned Fustat and its Nile sunsets but had also given up the shining future that awaited the favorite disciple of Moshe ben Maimon, Salah ad-Din's personal physician and the greatest Jewish scholar of his time, known to Latins as Maimonides. And what was more, given it up for the dubious revelations of a bunch of mystics in the French Midi.

The esoteric schools of the so-called kabbalists had fascinated him for some time, but the truth was he'd chosen exile, and knew it, to escape the gloom that had enveloped him ever since his Naomi drowned herself in the Nile. Naomi—a sweeter name never existed—hadn't given him children, and her smile faded year after year. Jewish law ruled that after ten years of sterile marriage, Yehezkel would have the right—nay, the duty—to repudiate his wife. An unshakable conviction that she somehow deserved that fate caused Naomi's mind to drift into a no-woman's-land where at times he could reach her, while other times she was alone with pure despair.

Yehezkel tried to reassure her. He told her he would never divorce her. He'd explained about the Matriarchs, all three initially barren— Sarah to the age of ninety!—but Naomi was inconsolable. Then one night, in the sixth year of their marriage, she left the house and walked into the Nile. The river that gives life to Egypt took the life of his wife. Custom demanded that he remarry, but Yehezkel escaped to Provence instead, in search of a light in the teachings strong enough to pierce the darkness that had swallowed him.

On his arrival in Posquiére, he'd been accepted on the power of the name of his Egyptian mentor. It would have opened *any* door in the Jewish world, this time into the school of Rav Yitzhak the

Blind, one of the first kabbalists to have received new revelations on the meaning of Scripture directly from the prophet Elijah. The long nights of study with his new teacher had been full of the ways in which the Sephirot, the ten Divine Emanations, manifest themselves in this world. Sometimes, waking up suddenly, his nostrils full of the dry fragrance of veal-skin parchment, Yehezkel would wonder for an instant if he'd fallen asleep in his bed with a book on his face, or if he was still sitting at his teacher's wax-encrusted table, head slowly collapsed onto some holy text.

Yehezkel lived those five years to the hilt, but still they seemed like five months: sea passages, rich cities, markets, sophisticated courts, rabbinical circles. He became the personal medicus of several nobles and learned their *langue d'Occitanie,* a hard, yet musical tongue. As he did with every new language, he had inadvertently learned its singsong before its words or grammar, the result being the total absence of a foreign accent that never failed to amaze the locals. Over five years, Yehezkel turned into one of a growing band of itinerant, rebellious, mostly young thinkers of all three faiths: wandering, polyglot mixtures of hope and disenchantment, mysticism and irony, humility and ambition, who prospered in much of the West to the dismay of the church, even seducing many Christian youths.

In his roaming, Yehezkel witnessed the flowering of a new, voluptuous love for God's creation. The courts of heretical nobles hosted rowdy bands of troubadors—melancholy minstrels—usually afflicted with unreciprocated love and invariably intoxicated by the thick wines of the region. In those courts Cathars, Moors, and Jews competed in poetical, musical, and philosophical contests, courting the attentions of witty, beautiful ladies. And all this while in the Holy Roman Empire the worth of a man was still only determined by birth or by arms, and the virtues of women something yet to be discovered.

The column moved on. Dribbles of refugees left on paths familiar to them until, as the sun melted into the hills, some twenty people climbed the last crest, their legs trembling with fatigue as they sighted the fortress of Montréal. After a little while, they entered the deserted village, its pink Roman roof tiles set alight by the last shafts of sun shining through the tops of the pines. Many dispersed to their homes. The villagers had fled to the mountains, but as in all wars, a strange mixture of cynical old men, young fanatics, and lonely women hadn't left. It didn't take them long to find that these had taken refuge in the kitchen of the Hots, the very family to whom Yehezkel was to entrust the child.

They staggered in one at a time as darkness fell. The big kitchen was divided into three spans by two sturdy pairs of columns joined by arches. At the far end, a huge mantelpiece jutted out over the empty fireplace like a roof, welcoming what was left of the population into its smoky shade. Four men played dice on a low table. A woman sat on a stool suckling an infant. Another followed the game over the head of a man, and a third, old and shriveled, squatted on the floor shelling beans. Five or six more peasants sat on their haunches along the wall. There was a smell of breaths heavy with wine; and a wick sizzled in the bottom of an oil lamp, spreading a foul, sticky smoke.

In an instant the apparent calm shattered. The heretics all talked at once, shouting, embracing, weeping. A ruddy woman dished out broad-bean broth for everyone. Yehezkel declined, pulling out some dark bread and a piece of kosher cheese. Aillil was fed and put to sleep on some straw near the far wall. When he'd eaten, the rabbi went out in the yard to say Ma'ariv, the evening prayer. He used the stars to determine the direction of Jerusalem and then saw some chickens milling around and moved a little farther from the house. Finally, he closed his eyes and prayed, swinging back and forth in the sultry darkness filled with the smell of rotting hay.

Back in the kitchen, Yehezkel pulled the cook to one side. The woman's red cheekbones, nose, and chin were so swollen and shiny they looked like blisters, yet far from making her look clownish, they gave her face a strangely menacing, thuggish expression.

"What is your name, good woman? Are you part of the Hot household?" he asked her.

"I am Germaine, and I have been in this kitchen since I have memory of myself," said the woman.

"The child sleeping over there is Aillil Arifat, the only son of Arnald Arifat. Do you know his father?"

"I held Arnald on my knees. If the infant is with you, am I to understand that his mother . . ."

"Esmeralda didn't survive the siege, may the Lord have mercy on her soul. She died of the fever three days ago, and with her last words begged me to entrust Aillil to the Hot family in Montréal."

Germaine looked war weary but smiled at Yehezkel with all the assurance she could muster. "I'll look after Arnald's son like after my own, sir. I heard he left for Outremer about a month ago."

"Yes, God only knows where he is." Yehezkel fixed his eyes on hers. "Listen, Germaine. Aillil was born with some deficiencies. Sight, hearing, growth. . . . He looks like a babe, but he's over three years old . . ." The rabbi paused, his eyes almost weighing the peasant's heart. "I advise you to find a childless woman to ween him . . . he needs more attention than a normal child, he needs to be . . . *stimulated* all the time."

Germaine was nodding slowly, a knowing smile on her lips.

"I'll come and see him once a year," said Yehezkel, "and I'll try to let Arnald know where he is."

There was a prolonged creak from the door. All heads turned as two perfecti* entered silently, their faces streaked with sweat and dust. They were barefoot, and their patched-up habits were black and hoodless. In the leather satchels across their shoulders was the only nourishment they had need for: a Gospel of John.

The white-haired *bonhomme* was the respected preacher Pierre de Gramazie, but most believers in the room were more devoted to Pons Roger, his young companion with the elephantine ears, whom Yehezkel knew quite well. Despite fasting often, Pons was a handsome youth,

---

*Cathars were divided into believers and consecrated perfecti, also known as *bonhommes*.

whose wide eyes and disarming smile gave him an air of sincerity somehow confirmed by the huge, flapping ears.

The believers stood up and bowed three times to the bonhommes.
Some exchanged the Kiss of Salvation with them; others went down on
their knees and asked for the *melioramentum,* a Cathar blessing.

There were loud requests for the perfecti to give them the Cathar
church's interpretation of the war, but the perfecti knew that the most
reliable source of information on events at Carcassone was the Jew, and
soon everyone was standing around the table at which the rabbi related
the siege to the perfecti. Yehezkel, reluctant to remember the last two
weeks, wasn't very talkative, something unusual for him.

Just five years earlier, a fleet of cross-wearing marauders lead by Enrico
Dandolo, the blind Venetian Doge, sacked Constantinople in a frat-
ricidal massacre for which its leaders had been excommunicated. And
here now was the same pope—as if to prove how far the love of Christ
can go—waging war on other Christians himself. And all this while the
Holy Sepulchre had been in the hands of infidels for over twenty years!
These were indeed dark times.

But the Church had reason to fear these Christians. All through the
previous fifty years, something sweet had been fermenting in Christian
souls. Love of knowledge, of music, of personal illumination, even love
of love. Waves of mystics, new philosophical schools, traveling minstrels,
cathedrals that soared as if to touch the heavens. Rome hadn't liked one
bit of it. An ignorant and corrupt clergy had pushed many Christians to
the brink of spiritual rebellion against Mother Church. Of course, for
the Church the rebels were all heretics: Cathars, Beguines, Waldenses,
Humiliati—in the words of one theologian, "penitents and visionaries
to whose mysticism *nothing* is repugnant."

But there was no denying the spiritual spasm that seized
Christendom in the name of a more apostolic life and of the definitive victory of love on earth. The Cathar heresy spread like a plague,
from Bulgaria to Northern Italy to Provence. News of sacked abbeys

and churches reached Rome with alarming frequency. Innocent III—placed on Saint Peter's throne at the incredibly precocious age of thirty-seven—seemed not to know what he wanted. One minute the Midi was a wasp's nest to be uprooted with fire, the next minute they were a wayward flock of sheep it was his mission to save. Romans joked that their pope was like a blind dog in a meat market.

Then, on a gray January dawn in 1208, hired assassins murdered Pierre de Castelnau, papal legate to Languedoc. The ineptly named Innocent launched a "just war" against the heretics, the cry rising from every pulpit: "Arm yourselves! Go and bring back Christ's peace in Provence!"

It took him a year to rally Christians to war against heresy. Philip II Capetian, the first monarch ever to call himself King of France, dubbed himself "Augustus" to show his appreciation of the choice made by the Grace of God. Yet he declined to lead the ransack of his neighbors to the south, claiming that the constant scheming of the English against his throne left him no time to chase religious lunatics. But greed, much more than outrage at the heretics, sparked the enthusiasm of French nobility, or at least of the families who hadn't been quick enough to grab a place in the sun in Greece or Syria.

The army gathered in Lyon on Saint John's Day at the end of June in 1209. Soon the camp was a riotous city of thirty thousand souls, each one proclaimed a divine executioner by Innocent's bull. By July the only wolf missing was the leader of the pack, the Duke of Burgundy, who kept them all waiting for two turbulent weeks. There were five thousand knights, and for each knight five *ribauds*—feverish peasant-zealots, many with their families in tow—who *knew* that the blood the Cathars would shed for their sins would bring about, as Innocent had said, the mysterious absolution of their own.

The way God chose to deliver Béziers to its executioners was indeed to put many a Cathar's faith to the test. At first light on the 22nd of July, Saint Mary Magdalene's Day, pyres and gallows were being erected outside the walls as monks vied for the privilege of shouting the sermons that would commit the perfecti to the fires of Hell. A mission bearing the offer to spare the city if it would give up the two hundred perfecti it harbored was leaving empty-handed from the Narbonne Gate, when some burghers came out to mock it. A handful of ribauds got in the gate and kept it open until some knights rushed over.

Thus did Béziers fall in one day, and without a siege. The ribauds joyfully drew and quartered men, women, and children They threw them from towers, and burned and boiled them. Not a soul survived, not even the Catholics who had fought the heresy. Arnaud Amaury, abbot of Citeaux and spiritual leader of the campaign, boasted in a letter to Innocent, no doubt inspired by God so later generations should make no mistake about the man, that "twenty thousand corrupted souls" had been exterminated.

Yehezkel's tale began on the 3rd of August, when "Christ's army" had been sighted from Carcassonne's ramparts, singing the "Veni Creator Spiritus" and waving Agnus Dei banners as they marched toward the river.

"It lasted twelve days," said the rabbi glumly.

"The peasants brought their cattle inside the walls out of compassion for the animals and as food in case of a long siege, but this August has been the hottest in living memory, and the water wasn't enough for men and beasts. Not a drop fell from the sky, so they slaughtered the cattle. The carcasses attracted such a plague of flies that Catholic burghers started calling Carcassonne "the city of Beezelbub."* And with the flies came the fevers, killing half the population within days." He turned to Germaine. "Aillil's mother among them. So they decided to accept Amaury's offer to let the survivors leave—except, of course, the perfecti—on condition that they take nothing with them." Yehezkel grimaced as he remembered the previous day's executions.

---

*One of Satan's names, Beezelbub, comes from "Ba'al Zevuv," Hebrew for "Lord of the Flies."

"Your brothers, the perfecti and *perfectae* of Carcassonne, did not try to mingle with the spared believers. Instead they affirmed their faith, mouths wide open on the stakes, with the joy of true martyrs . . ."

"The northern barons want our lands for themselves and will kill us all for it, that's what's happening!" shouted one believer. Pons struggled to achieve a measure of silence and then said, "Yes, the Babylonian prostitute is powerful today; in fact, our Church of Love seems doomed." He hesitated. "This is why I decided to reveal a secret prophecy to you, brothers, one normally reserved to perfecti. I only do this . . . so that you may not lose your faith."

Pierre shot him a glance of undisguised alarm. The pair reminded Yehezkel of kabbalists he'd seen, constantly reproaching each other for excessive revelations made to disciples.

"Have you ever heard of the *Parchment of Circles*?" asked Pons. "No? It's the most precious relic of the Bulgarian church founded by Bogomil! Twenty years ago it almost fell into the hands of the barbarous Serbs, but Nazario of Concorezzo, an Italian *perfectus* who was in Bulgaria to be made bishop, took it to Italy and from there it made its way to Albi, thirty leagues from here. I saw it there six months ago . . ."

Pons lowered his voice, as if Catholics might be hiding somewhere in the kitchen. Heretics and Jew leaned forward, not to lose a word. "It is an ancient, secret prophecy, drawn by Saint John the Evangelist *in his own hand,* in the shape of a circle within a circle with Greek phrases that explain *all* of man's history."

A reverent murmur rose at the mention of Saint John, whose Gospel was the source of most Cathar liturgy. Yehezkel briefly wondered if Pons wasn't making it all up for the sake of the believers' morale but then told himself that Pierre could not have faked his outrage at this young man's revelations.

"The Parchment of Circles foretells the persecution we're suffering today." Pons took a deep breath. "But it says that after it comes the 'Judgment of the Sons of Darkness!' This generation, by its position on the circles, is the last! Saint John's drawing confirms Gioacchino's prediction: the overthrow of the prostitute and the advent of an era of universal love. The same era we have been preaching! This, my brothers, is the Final Tribulation. The Tremendous Expiation is upon us!!"

Many believers fell on their knees and thanked the Lord. Some wept with joy, one or two even danced a few steps across the kitchen. Yehezkel sat motionless, deep in thought.

After Salah ad-Din retook Jerusalem, Jewish expectations of the arrival of the Messiah of David, who would gather Israel again in their promised land, became as thick in the air as the smoke from a town on fire. Excited mystics traveled from one community to the next, spreading tales of miracles performed by the latest pretender to the throne of Judah. Respectable city Jews, as if seized by the Spirit, began prophesizing and explaining mysteries in Scriptures. "And now," thought Yehezkel, "here are these strange Christian prophecies about the overthrow of Rome . . . what a remarkable coincidence!"

"Pons, enlighten me, I beg you," he said finally, "on this Gioacchino's prophecy."

"Oh, it's very simple," said Pons. "Gioacchino divides history into three epochs: of the Father, of the Son, and of the Holy Ghost. The Father is fear, the Son is wisdom, and the Spirit is love. When the Father prevailed, we only knew the rigors of the Law. Then the Truth, which had long lain hidden under a veil, was revealed, and the reign of the Son came. Now man 'fears' and 'knows' but doesn't yet 'love'—the flame of the Spirit doesn't yet warm his heart—which is why the reign of the Spirit must arrive. And just as we were freed from the slavery of mosaic Law when the Son came, so shall we be freed of all dogmas of the New Covenant when the Spirit comes."

Yehezkel listened, all the while calculating if the third era was imminent and the present one dated to the Christian heresy where this Gioacchino placed the starting point of the whole cycle.

"*When?*" he suddenly asked with unintended intensity. "When will this third epoch begin?"

All the believers also stared at Pons, silently awaiting a deadline for the end of their sufferings. "Gioacchino's epochs last forty-two generations of thirty years each, as those in the Apocalypse," said Pons. "The Age of the Spirit will therefore begin in the year of the Lord twelve hundred and sixty!"

"Cursed be the bones of those who calculate the end . . ." mumbled the rabbi to himself.

Both perfecti blanched at a curse by a Jewish initiate. Yehezkel immediately regretted the thoughtless quotation and laid his hand on Pons's forearm. "Don't worry, my friend. It is a curse from the Talmud and only concerns Jews. But why risk disappointment? Surely it is better for everyone to wait and trust God's plan, isn't it? Like Isaiah says: 'Blessed are those who wait for Him.'" The perfecti were silent. Yehezkel tormented his beard as he reflected.

Here I am, trying to dissuade Cathars from believing in the Age of the Messiah, my faith in which is as solid as rock. Why do I do it? Do I fear that if Christian hopes are stronger than Israel's, instead of the legitimate King of the House of David their Galilean magician could present himself again?

Pons changed the subject. "Master Ezekiel, did you hear if the white pig was in Babylon's camp?"

"No," said Yehezkel immediately. "Had he been there, I would no doubt have heard of it."

The "white pig" was Domingo de Caleruega, a Castillan monk who'd been trying to convert heretics for almost ten years. The epithet was a mixture of the older Cathars' hatred for him and the color of his habit, made of the cheapest wool, which turns whitish after two washings. But if truth be told, in the last few weeks fewer and fewer Cathars had been calling Domingo white pig. Since the start of the war he had always been present to help the wounded or stop a burning at the stake.

Pons was one of the souls pulled back from the edge of darkness by Domingo. Two years earlier, in a theological debate held in Fanjeaux, which had been resolved by an ordeal by fire, he had renounced his heresy. But as often happens to the easily converted, he had later repented and slid back into his family's heresy. In fact, to show his zeal, he had become a perfectus at an unusually young age. Cathars were used to accepting the rigors of life as a perfectus only on their deathbeds, and his choice was seen as courageous. In his satchel was the reconciliation with the church that he and Domingo signed that day. Since the start of the war, both afraid of meeting the monk and burning to tear up the document before his eyes, Pons asked every refugee he came across if they had seen the white pig.

An old Cathar, hearing Domingo's nickname, slammed his fist on the table.

"Who, that dry canal? Does *anyone* still believe shitty priests can save their souls? For telling people they could save them when they could do *nothing,* they'll be the first to go to the eternal flames in a procession with the white pig at their head! I'd love to see that monk covered in ulcers and crusts, each one crawling with worms and flies!"

Just then the door creaked open again, and the white pig walked in.

He was accompanied by Guillaume Claret, his partner from the beginning of the mission. They were barefoot and wore whitish, dirty habits, as full of patches as those of the perfecti.

"Ego vos benedico,"* said Domingo, tracing a sign of the cross in the air.

"What sortilege are you attempting with that death sign of yours?" shrieked the old man.

The perfecti stood to face their rival. Yehezkel remained seated. Domingo and Pons looked at each other for a long moment, the tension rising. The monk spoke first. "Pons, Pons," he murmured, almost weeping. Domingo's incredibly blue eyes were full of pain.

Yehezkel noticed their almost frightening intensity. An exaggeratedly ample tonsure contributed to the monk's striking appearance. His partner, in contrast, had sharper yet anonymous features.

---

*I give you my blessing.

"You've become a perfectus, as I'd feared . . ." continued the monk. Pons's outer ears began to redden. Then Domingo turned to Yehezkel. Friar and rabbi surveyed each other wearily, like two beasts in the wild weighing their chances of subduing a challenger.

The old man attacked the monks again. "Away with you, white pig! You're not welcome in this house!"

"Are Jews more welcome than Christians in this house?" asked Domingo with a smile.

"We are all guests in the Hots' kitchen," said Pons, "and should behave as such. Brother Domingo, this is Master Ezekiel, who practices the medicine of the Moors in Lunel."

Domingo bowed his head. "I am Brother Domingo de Caleruega, canon regular and subprior of the diocese of Osma in Castille. And this is my partner, Guillaume Claret."

An elusive smile hovered on his lips. "I've had occasion to speak with your brethren, Master Ezekiel, both in my country and in these gloomy, churchless villages, and they often mentioned your name . . ."

"I hope they were merciful in their judgment," smiled Yehezkel.

"They were flattering, even, but judge you they did, as you expected, because like you they wear a blindfold before the light. We, instead, follow the teaching of Christ: 'Judge not, that you be not judged.'"

Yehezkel parried with ease. "I'm acquainted with the phrase, and it always perplexed me. First, I don't see how Jesus thought to bring justice to the world if everyone ceased to exercise judgment. And second," he added without a trace of irony, "I'm puzzled by the exhortation not to judge others only so as to avoid being judged oneself. I'm ready to be judged for both my words and my actions . . . wasn't Jesus?"

The sight of the blind presuming to lead the sighted was more than Domingo could bear. "You blaspheme, rabbi, a sin your people commit every time you open your mouths. Our church says to the arid virtue of the Law: away, whitewashed sepulchre! I ask for compassion, not judgment!"

Yehezkel confidently landed his thrust. "But my good friar, do you not see that replacing the Law with trust in men's compassion . . . has only brought the ferocious times we live in?"

A murmur of approval for the Jew's unruffled irreverence spread through the heretical kitchen.

Domingo raised a finger at Yehezkel, blue eyes glinting like steel. "Here is the Jewish arrogance the Fathers speak of; I hear it now. Wherever heresy spreads, I find your rabbis have 'debated' the Christians there." Domingo closed his eyes and took a deep breath. This was no time or place to threaten heretics and Jews.

Pons saw where the exchange was heading and had an inspiration. Hoping that the rules of a debate would contain passions, he cried, "I propose a *disputatio* between the three faiths, here and now!"

Domingo and Yehezkel mentioned the late hour and the journeys ahead, but in the end the love of verbal struggle and the urge to convert had the better of both. God was present in the Hots' kitchen and knew who was preaching the Truth. He would make the words of His true messenger triumph, and the souls stumbling off the right path would be saved. The five men exchanged boyish, almost perverse smiles and sat down at the table, surrounded by the heretics, to defend truth against error. Pons suggested that, as in Narbonne the year before, the champion of each faith pose a question to the adversary of his choice that the third party would also have the right to answer. A peasant stepped forward, offering to throw dice to determine who would ask the first question.

With a grim, Spanish look, Domingo said, "I don't mind posing my question last."

Yehezkel had to admire the monk's cunning in passing off as humility what was in fact a clear debating advantage. Pons turned to the rabbi. "Put your question to either of us, Master Ezekiel."

Domingo waited serenely, his eyes now the steady bluish gray of a steel blade.

Yehezkel scratched his chin through his beard, eyes lost in the roof-beams. Finally, he said,

"If you had occasion to speak with other rabbis, Brother Domingo, it was probably because some word in what *you* call the 'Old Testament' made you curious of the Hebrew original. . . Is that not so?"

The monk seemed to weigh the consequences of the admission. "Well . . . yes, I don't deny asking the advice of your sages, but only on issues of translation, as you say. My Hebrew, alas, is shamefully poor when compared with your Latin. I must compliment you on how you speak the Holy Tongue, Master Ezekiel. But I don't see what you're getting at . . ."

"I want you to concede that much in the Old Testament is lost if one doesn't know the meaning of Hebrew words and the rules of the sacred alphabet. God placed secrets in every word and letter of the Torah, so a translation, however much inspired, gives the literal sense only—when *that* is not corrupted, too. We learn the language of a people to trade with them, but how much better should we learn their language if our purpose is to understand God's revelation to them!"

"No, Master Ezekiel, I disagree," said Domingo. "The Septuagint, as you know, is a translation inspired by the Holy Ghost. Not a comma was different in the seventy papyri, so I venture to say that its Greek is probably closer to the message God wanted to reveal than the original Hebrew itself . . ." Domingo started coughing hoarsely.

Yehezkel thought the spirits presiding over the dispute must have choked him for pronouncing such a bestiality. He waited, still quietly shocked at the thought of God speaking Greek, and then pulled out his most polished Latin. "Names, Brother Domingo, define the nature, the very *essence* of people and things. A change of name is a change of destiny. In the Bible, some names change. Abram becomes Abraham, Sarai becomes Sarah, Jacob becomes Israel. The secrets in those changes are not for everyone, and certainly not for those who don't know the language the Torah was written in. I'll give you just one example: if you know Hebrew, you know that the prophet Jonah's name means 'dove,' and new levels of exegesis open up to you, like the parallel between Ark and Whale, and much more. But if you don't know that Jonah means dove, then where are you?"

Domingo hadn't known Jonah meant dove. He thought of the symbol of the Holy Ghost, of the three days in the belly of the whale and those Jesus spent in the sepulchre. His soul was uplifted in the euphoria he always felt when his comprehension of Scripture rose to the next level. He thought:

"Jesus said that Nineveh had repented and been saved, but the Jews, facing a thing greater than Jonah, refused to do so. *Now* I understand the Fathers who learned Hebrew; one grasps aspects of prophecy that this Jew can't even *begin* to understand!" Domingo's thirst for knowledge overcame his Spanish pride. "I'm grateful to you, Master Ezekiel, for the higher comprehension I reached thanks to the meaning of Jonah's name. Can you give me another example, but with some connection to heresy and error?"

Yehezkel was more than ready. "This example is Kabbalah, Brother Domingo, a secret tradition most rabbis would condemn me for divulging, but so be it. The Hebrew letters *beit, yod* and *nun,* if written in that order, spell the word *bein,* which means between. But the same three letters, if written in the order *beit, nun, yod,* spell the word *bnei,* which means sons of. But in Kabbalah, if one changes the order of letters in a word, the total value of the word stays the same, so the alternative meaning was also intended. Are you with me?" He was pleased to see everyone hanging from his lips.

"Now consider the fourth verse in the Bible, 'and God separated light from darkness.' That is all that is left in translation, even in the Septuagint, but it's not everything. The original actually says 'God separated *bein* light and *bein* darkness. It says 'between' twice. Why? My teacher, may his light shine for many years, says that one secret meaning is obtained by shifting the letters and turning the two *beins* into *bneis,* since this does not change their numerical value." Yehezkel paused before the punchline.

"And do you know how the verse reads if we do that, Brother Domingo? 'And God separated *the sons of light from the sons of darkness.*' The secret meaning is that He did so as the second act of creation!"

The believers erupted in a religious battle cry. Almost every page of their theology defined the universe as an eternal struggle between the sons of light and the sons of darkness. Domingo knew it, too, and had to admire the elegance of the rabbi's move. After all, *he* had been the one to ask for an example concerning heresy. He smiled, graciously conceding the round.

"I recognize the power of the tongue the Bible was written in, Master Ezekiel, but the exegesis of the Fathers who studied Hebrew invariably suffered from Jewish influence. I pray God every day to grant that my reason never proceed against His Truth, and that study never corrupts the purity of my faith."

"Ahh, yes . . . study, a dangerous beast!" mocked Yehezkel. "Fear not, good friar, as long as 'study' means only Christian theology to you, I guarantee you'll remain as pure and innocent as a babe. You are known for your erudition, but how could you possibly know that we are in the six hundredth year from the revelation of the Holy Qu'ran to Muhammad, in a cave on Mount Hira? Or that many Jews claim the true Messiah will arrive in three years? What could you know of bar Hiyya's astronomy, or ibn-Sinna's medicine? You're not interested in anyone else's wisdom, since yours is superior by divine decree. But take my word for it, outside Christendom your 'erudition' would make you look downright benighted."

Domingo heard him out in silence. The accusation turned a dagger in an old wound. He'd pleaded with Innocent to let him found a monastic order dedicated to studying and preaching. Now those plans, fed by humiliation, grew into a vow. "It is right that I should swear this before heretics and Jews!" he thought. "Now listen to *me*, rabbi!" His eyes were the bluish lead of stormy clouds. "I shall educate friars to study the sterile wisdom of Aristotle, the Talmud, and the Qu'ran, better to understand the errors of infidels. My preaching knights will lay into the errors of disbelievers with the very 'reason' you brandish today, strong in their faith in Christ, protected by their shining armor of knowledge. And a day will come, as Saint Augustine said, when Jews will recognize the enormity of their sin, swallow their pride, and, redeemed at last, adore their victim!"

Yehezkel was struck by the monk's determination. "Who knows, Brother Domingo, who knows? Maybe a day will come instead when you Christians, comparing your communities to ours, will feel the desire to know what we *believe,* instead of breaking your heads over why we *don't* believe!"

"What *do* you believe? Go ahead, I don't fear any corruption of the Truth you may pronounce!"

"We believe, with complete faith, that Christianity and Islam are but the preparation of the world for the coming of the true Messiah, the fruit of the seed that God planted. So if only we were more enlightened, Brother Domingo, we could shake hands like brothers. That day may come, too."

Domingo jumped from his stool. "Get back, snake! Don't you know what it means for us to touch the hand of one of Christ's executioners, a hand stained with *that* blood?"

Yehezkel also stood up. "With *our* blood! Don't forget it, friar! A *Jewish* womb carried your God, *Jewish* breasts fed him, *Jewish* wisdom spoke through his words!"

"And Jewish perfidy nailed him to the Cross! Murderers!"

"Not true!" A flash of anger lit Yehezkel's dark eyes. "But even if it was, wasn't he, on that Cross, raised above all humanity as a symbol of divine mercy?"

"Well said! The Jew is right!" shouted several Cathars.

Pons rushed to pour water on the fire. "It's your turn to set a trap for us, Domingo. I hope you won't pick on me to avoid the sharp spikes on Master Ezekiel's armor. . . ." Domingo asked for nothing better than to entrap the wily Jew.

"Please help my failing memory, Master Ezekiel. What are the words of the prophet whose name you bear about the warning one should give the wicked?"

Yehezkel thought, "I should have expected this . . ." and then recited,

"When I say to the wicked, 'You will surely die,' and you do not speak out to dissuade him from his ways, that wicked person will die for his sin, but I will hold you accountable for his blood."

"Well, my good rabbi, should we be held accountable for the blood of these heretics for not having warned them, for not speaking out?"

"Mmh . . . you see, we Jews don't punish our heretics with the barbarity I've witnessed in these lands. For us the heretic is still a Jew, whatever weird doctrine he may profess . . . even if he accepts baptism!"

"Come now, I'm sure you don't condemn heresy less harshly than the Church. It would be suicide."

Yehezkel smiled. "Elisha ben Abuya, a heretic from a thousand years ago, was a noted sage before losing the right path. The Talmud calls him a 'destroyer of plantations.' A harsh censure, you'll agree."

"And a wise one, for believers are indeed a plantation that feeds multitudes if well tended but can be ruined completely by tiny insects or birds. But do tell, of what sort was this Ben Abuya's heresy?"

"Er . . . the Talmud is not in the habit of giving details on the nature of heresies . . ."

For an instant, Domingo's hard defenses melted away, and he burst out in a hearty laugh. Yehezkel said, ". . . but it is rumored that he was a Manichean, like these friends of mine, or maybe . . . a Christian!"

"A Christian! Ha! One may as well call adulthood a heretical form of infancy!" jested Domingo.

Yehezkel said, "Listen. A certain sage collaborated with the Romans and justified himself, saying he was only removing the weeds from the Lord's vineyard. But Rabbi Yehoshua told him, 'Let the vineyard's owner clear the weeds himself!' Surely those who elect themselves God's instruments, Brother Domingo, sin with pride. The monks who commit heretics and witches to the fire are falling in a trap laid by Satan. First he blinds justice and then sends his demons to capture the souls *not* of the possessed, but of their executioners!"

"Well said, Jew!" shouted a believer. "This one is too good for you, white pig!" cried another.

Monk and rabbi sat still, avoiding each other's eyes. Pons quoted the Book of Proverbs.

"Starting a quarrel is like breaching a dam, so drop the matter before a dispute breaks out." The combatants nodded, smiling. Pons took advantage of the lowered tension to go outside and relieve himself. Domingo quickly stood up to follow, but Pons stopped him.

"No, Domingo! I don't wish to speak with you alone. Not today."

When he walked back into the kitchen, Pons heard Pierre's voice, all of a sudden apparently fearless. "Why keep pretending one can debate murderers? Were you at Béziers three weeks ago, white pig? Were you one of the monks harassing the dying victims to save their souls? Eh?"

Domingo had indeed been at Béziers, and all his efforts to contain the ribauds had served for nothing. He sat down, weeping at the thought of what he'd witnessed there, but the Cathars didn't relent.

"And at the church of Mary Magdalene, were you there, too? There were seven thousand Christians in that church when it was set on fire, white pig. *Seven thousand!*"

The monk wept silently, Guillaume's arm around his shoulders, as the kitchen slid into chaos. Yehezkel began to breathe the folded breath. Suddenly Domingo seemed to recover, rising with absurd courage. "My mission was to end burnings at the stake! What evil did we ever do to *you*, Pons?"

"Whaat? You dare ask? You only tortured us, burned us alive, drowned us. The walls of every prison in Provence cry revenge to the heavens, friar!"

"I didn't mean that, I meant Guillaume and me. What evil have *the two of us* ever done to you?"

The simple question shattered the young man's last vestige of control. Pons kicked away the stool, fist slamming down on the table, ears fiery red. Domingo's stare was sky-blue serene. Yehezkel thought the monk was imploring Pons to strike him, but Pons held back, his voice filled with contempt. "Now *you* listen to *me*, friar! The Church of Rome is not holy, nor is she the Bride of Christ! She is the devil's church, and her doctrine is satanic!" He was beside himself with rage. "She is the Babylonian whore that John calls 'mother of fornications and abominations!'"

The old man cried, "Here are the words that should have greeted the white pig when he walked in!"

Pons pulled out the reconciliation with the Church as if drawing a sword.

Exploding in the laugh of a man possessed, he tore it again and again. Everyone, as often happens in times of war, understood that violence was an instant away.

A voice rung out from the back, "Get the white pig!"

Pons looked at the two monks and seemed to weigh the consequences of a lynching.

Yehezkel read his thoughts and roared, in the Langue d'Oc, "*Stay where you are!*" The kabbalist's voice bounced off the walls like thunder. Every Cathar felt addressed by the order, and the tension in the kitchen slowly deflated. Only Domingo realized the Jew had empowered his voice in some secret way to scare the Cathars and save his and Guillaume's lives.

Everyone shuffled about in a daze, preparing a corner in which to spend the few hours left until dawn. With straw distributed and candles blown out, an unnatural silence settled on refugees, perfecti, friars, and Jew, broken only by a distant barking of dogs and the calls of an owl.

Domingo prayed for every soul in the kitchen. His heart was heavy for the Jew's blindness, a curse that he knew would last until Christ's return. He thought of the oath he had taken in front of them all, and his heart swelled with a hope that surpassed that for the souls of heretics.

"Sweet Jesus, the learned men of Moors and Jews know the world far better than the ignorant clergy of your Church. If we don't fix that, their missions to the pagans will have more success than ours. My Lord, you know we have to do as I swore to the Jew. And we have to do it soon!"

But even as he prayed, the Parchment of Circles floated up in his mind again. Pope Innocent himself had entrusted him the secret mission of locating the relic, and the Castillan's zeal allowed him to think of little else. Innocent had told him the parchment had come to Lombardy from Bosnia some years before but ended up in Languedoc, and no more had been heard of it.

Domingo had left Toulouse a few days before, headed to Avignon to attend the Council Innocent summoned for September. The desire to check on the health of Pons's conversion made him decide to climb to Montréal, but behind the preacher's scruple lurked the hope that Pons would know of the parchment. When he'd seen him wearing the black habit of a perfectus he'd been pained, yes, but his heart had also jumped for joy: now Pons would be sure to know the relic's whereabouts!

But as the evening wore on, he'd realized that mentioning his search in front of that Jew was out of the question. He'd tried following Pons when he'd gone to relieve himself, but the Cathar had misunderstood his intentions. He would have to question him in the morning, after the Jew was gone.

Meanwhile, Yehezkel lay on the other side of the fireplace, aware of troubling the other man's sleep.

CHAPTER 5

Vayehi Voker

And There Was Morning

TORCELLO, 10TH APRIL 1219

Two days later, the Jew who rescued the abbess of San Maffìo from the lagoon was the talk of the island. The bishop rightly demanded to know what the Mother Superior of a convent—Sant'Eliodoro, protect us!—had been doing on the bank an hour before Lauds, while the fact that a Jew had been out there, too, inevitably fired the imagination of rumormongers.

Galatea was recovering in bed, still wheezing from all the retching she'd done, but reborn in the spirit, her melancholia shed like an old snakeskin. Nothing more than narrowly escaping a premature death illuminates men and women with the intimate joy of saints. Every gesture, every corner of the landscape, every sensation—even unpleasant ones—acquire the taste of a favorite delicacy.

But Galatea knew what dispelled the fog in her life: her rescuer's words.

"Ego sum, nolite timere," she whispered for the hundredth time. "The *exact* words of the hermit! The words of Christ walking on the

66

lake in the mouth of a Jewish savior from the waters . . . and wasn't Jesus a Jew? Not only that, the hermit spoke of 'a Woman and a Jew' . . . Oh, Mother of God, I'm so confused! It seems the good Lord kept a place for me in his plans after all; otherwise, why not take my soul there and then instead of choosing to have me rescued . . . and by a Jew!"

If the descendants of Christ's killers hated humanity, as everyone claimed, then how to explain a Jew risking his life to save a woman he *knew* wasn't one of theirs? Ever since regaining consciousness, Galatea had wrestled with such questions, her lust for answers in itself a confirmation that her listless condition was gone for good. She had reviewed what little she knew about Jews from direct experience and not from the words of priests. She had seen Jews as a child in Tuscia, but from a distance. They had reminded her of crows, all dressed in black with those pointy hats, ample sleeves waving about in eternal arguments. In the lagoon, the only Jews she'd met were the Ben-Porat brothers, who seemed decent people, not afraid of hard work and keepers of their word.

As she considered the timeless question of Christian hatred for Jews, there was a knock on the door, and Gudrun, without waiting for a response, fell into the room clutching a folded note, her breath short from rushing up the stairs—and from the way recent events resembled a Provençal romance.

"One of the dyers' sons just brought this for you, Mother!"

Galatea read the missive as Gudrun shamelessly slid her head on the wall behind the bed, trying to catch a glimpse of the text from above. In good Latin it said that her rescuer was a Passover guest of the Ben-Porats, a medicus from Provence who would be happy to check—in the presence of upright witnesses, of course—the consequences of the incident on her health. It was signed Avraham Ben-Porat.

Of the bulls the church had issued in the last decade prohibiting all sorts of dealings with Jews, by far the most transgressed was the interdiction against using Jewish physicians. Everyone knew that powerful people, from nobles to popes, only entrusted their health to the hands of Jews. But the letter was still an embarrassment to Galatea. There was no question of declining to meet the man who saved her life, of course, but the abbess already knew the bishop would unleash his minions all over the island to make sure he had witnesses to such a reprehensible meeting.

The exchange of notes between convent and cottage during the rest of the morning resulted in the decision to meet in the inn run by Galatea's good friend, Marciana Ottone, and her husband Bonifacio, to whom the abbess had promised to deliver some tablecloths embroidered by her sisters by Easter Sunday.

Meanwhile the rabbis, terrified that the islanders might find out about the meeting, no longer dared go outside, even after dark. Despite their fears, they had discussed with gusto God's intentions in arranging that the only one of the eight men in the house that night with the necessary seafaring skills stepped outside *just* as the woman screamed for help.

"Think of it, Yehezkel," said Rav Eleazar, "how long did the woman scream before resigning herself to her fate? Five, ten minutes? You *had* to arrive on the pier inside those ten minutes to hear her. Who knows how Divine Providence pursues its aims? Maybe our meeting was actually convened because God needed someone to save that nun . . ."

The biggest risk, as they saw it, was Aillil's presence. If it got out that a Christian boy was staying at the dyers', questions were sure to be asked. But keeping Aillil indoors, especially when he could see the Ben-Porat children run and shout in the April garden, would have meant tying him down, so the other children were confined indoors instead. In the end, Rav Eleazar decided they would leave the next day, without waiting for the end of the feast, one at a time as they had arrived. But first, that night, they would discuss the important matters about which he had summoned them.

Rav Eleazar also decided that Yehezkel would row the skiff on the island's canals to his meeting with the abbess, so as to draw less attention. When Aillil heard his tutor would be taking the boat, there was no stopping him from going. The boy simply importuned every adult in the house until they could bear it no more. Yehezkel reassured the others, especially the Frenchmen, that he had credibly justified Aillil's presence several times on his journey from Lunel, but only Rav Eleazar's authority convinced Rav Yitzhak and Rav Yehiel to suffer the boy going along, so sure were they that the appearance in the inn of a Jew with a Christian boy in tow would be followed, as surely as night follows day, by the appearance of a pitchfork-and-torch-bearing mob outside the dyers' house.

Yehezkel picked some herbs in the garden, and Aillil saw him put a strange doll in his satchel. He told the boy to put on his cloak and pull the hood down over his eyes, and as the sun set over Majurbio, the two left the cottage.

The air, after a brief squall, was almost *too* terse. The purple shadows of clouds exaggerated heights and distances, giving things a strangely threatening look. Aillil, sitting astride the skiff's bow, sniffed the air like a hunting dog, now and then laughing out loud, often looking straight into the sun. Yehezkel yelled at him every time he caught him staring at the sun, but it was a losing battle: the boy was irresistibly attracted to lights, almost like a moth.

Aillil grew up with the Hots in Montréal; Yehezkel had often checked on his development, recently taking him on some errands. But only on this last journey from Languedoc to Venice had the rabbi fallen for Aillil's mix of boyish enthusiasms and dreamy absences. From a young age Aillil's left hand was always slightly bent inward, and his left foot dragged a little, but studying him for longer spells had revealed other endearing peculiarities. Aillil could spend hours with his chin on his chest, head slightly turned—like a sleeping bird, thought Yehezkel— fingers running through the soft blond hairs on his leg or forearm. If he was lost in thought and perceived no presences, his hands began to move in a slow, dreamlike dance. Once, seeing him like that, head tilted up at the sky, Yehezkel had asked himself if Aillil was speaking with angels.

Understanding the boy's nasally distorted pronunciation was difficult. "Avyehége," for example, was the sound he made to say "Rav Yehezkel." Yehezkel made a habit of gently prodding adults—there seemed to be no need with children—to involve Aillil in the conversation. He also subjected Aillil to mental exercises of his own devising, to which the boy sometimes reacted angrily. "Leave me alone, Rav Yehezkel! Why do you harass me so?" he would say, retreating into a private world.

He brought his food two inches from his eyes and generally touched everything, passing some things over his cheeks and forehead. He sniffed parchments, at times rubbing them on his face as if better to absorb what was written on them. This last habit reminded Yehezkel of his teacher's idea of the intrinsic power of letters as enchanted amulets made of ink.

In his few days in Torcello, Aillil displayed an uncanny skill with a sling, downing more than one bird that ventured to fly too low over the northern tip of the island. This talent fascinated his tutor, who came out to watch his ward hunt, trying to fathom Aillil's success in hitting fast-moving targets despite impaired sight. He seemed to compensate for blurred vision with a sixth sense, one that the boy could only describe as "letting the stone go at the right moment."

Yehezkel tied up the skiff to a ring on the fondamenta, its stones lit by the last sun. Between Santa Fosca and the Fist Canal—so named for the fistfights held on one of its parapet-less bridges—was the Ottones' famous inn, more crowded on market days than churches on Sundays, often visited by doges and once or twice by foreign kings. The innkeeper was a plump, jovial man called Bonifacio Ottone, married to a Mantuan girl with sharp features and refined manners.

Bonifacio, shining with sweat, welcomed Yehezkel and Aillil with a half bow and led them into the kitchens. Wonderful smells of lagoon specialties filled the vaporous hall. Three nuns and the lady of the inn waited for them in the warm candlelight. Galatea and Marciana faced each other, holding hands and looking straight into one another's eyes with a tender smile, as if consoling each other. Galatea, seeing the rabbi, immediately stepped toward him.

"May God reward your courage, sir! I am Mother Galatea, abbess of the Cistercian convent of San Maffìo," she hesitated for the flicker of a flame, "and Countess of the Ardengheschis of Monte Alcino in Tuscia. And these are two of my nuns, Sister Erminia and Sister Gudrun."

Few people could look Yehezkel in the eyes without raising their gaze, but on seeing the nun standing for the first time, he realized she was as tall as he was, and her bearing somehow made *him* look shorter. He bowed his head. "My reward is to see you up and about, madame, and with a hearty complexion! I am Yehezkel ben Yoseph, of Fustat in Egypt and Lunel in Provence, and this—show yourself, young man!—is my ward, Aillil Arifat of Montréal, in the county of Carcassonne."

Galatea smiled, and Aillil's freckles vanished in a crimson flush. Bonifacio turned away gesticulating, too busy to stop, loudly calling for a tray of *hippocras*.*

Then Galatea lowered her eyes and saw the blue twine hanging from Yehezkel' waistband.

"Madre Santissima!" she thought, "Here I was, already thinking his name says nothing to me, and he's wearing *that* blue! And with such nonchalance, as if it was a ribbon on a fashionable French hat!"

She was shaken but feigned cordiality, "Pardon me, sir, but I fear I'll never be able to pronounce your name correctly. Is there a way I can address you in Latin?"

"Master Ezekiel," said Yehezkel drily, "in the presence of others, but 'rabbi' when we are alone, if you don't mind . . ."

Galatea's eyes widened in violet surprise and then narrowed. "And just what makes you think you and I will ever be alone?"

Yehezkel took a step back. "I ask your forgiveness, madame, I wasn't

---

*Heavily spiced mulled wine

being fresh . . . maybe I said it because . . . because we were alone the only other time we met."

Galatea laughed loud, both hands before her mouth. Sister Erminia's eyes turned heavenward, like someone walking dangerously close to evil. Yehezkel joined the abbess in an embarrassed giggle, and Aillil followed suit, not really knowing what the laughter was about.

When the giggling subsided, Galatea said, smoothing her habit,

"You mean *Je-hes-qél* is the same as saying Ezekiel? You're named after the prophet in the Bible?"

"Yes, madame, my father—may his memory be a blessing—bestowed that honor on me. Can we move on to an examination of your health now, so we can both be on our way?"

Affronted by his hurried manner, she watched him pull out some folded plane tree leaves from his satchel, in which herbs were wrapped, thinking, "He wears *that* blue, bears the name of the prophet clad in that blue in Santa Maria, and pulled me out of the dark pool uttering *those* words! How can I still doubt that it is he? But just what does it *mean* to be *he*? Oh, Mother Elisabetta, what should I do?"

Yehezkel handed her a foot-long straw doll. Gudrun sucked in her breath, thinking the Jew was setting up a black magic ritual. The abbess hesitated for an instant but then understood the doll's function and turned it over in her hands, grinning at the awkwardly drawn smile on the straw-filled face.

"Madame, if you experience pains that began after Sunday night, kindly show me the painful points in your body on the doll."

It was a common solution to the problem of physicians visiting women but an exhilarating novelty to the nuns. Galatea felt like a child again as she tested the doll's consistency amid giggles from Gudrun and Marciana. She pointed out a band of "muscles" in the doll's back, a little above the kidneys.

"Here, Master Ezekiel, at the end of each breath I feel pain along here . . ."

"At the end of breathing in or at the end of breathing out, madame?"

Galatea considered the question and then took a deep breath as the rabbi looked on, smiling. "Both!"

Gudrun was transfixed by the appearance of Mother Galatea's burly rescuer. She'd seen oriental faces before but was discovering that gazing at this one made her feel not unlike drinking a glass of wine. Meanwhile, Aillil exercised his charm on the women in the room, except for frigid Sister Erminia. In fact, had it not been for the presence of a Jew, Marciana would already have smothered him in caresses.

A valet came in with a steaming jar of hippocras, and a strong scent of cinnamon filled the kitchen. Aillil and Marciana were the only ones to sip some in the embarrassed silence that followed.

Galatea took her plunge. "I hope you won't find my question inappropriate, Master Ezekiel, but I am struck by the color of the twine hanging from your waist. Does it hold a religious meaning?"

Yehezkel said, smiling, "Oh, that. It's just a personal amulet to remind me to go to Jerusalem."

"Is *that* what it's there for?" asked Galatea, startled. "Have you ever been to the Holy Land? I've always dreamed of going, but . . . no, no, first I must know, please: how does that color remind you of your vow?"

"To your first question: no, I haven't been, but I trust God to grant me that privilege someday. As for your second question, the answer is complicated, but suffice it to say that for a certain school of Jewish mystics, there is a connection between *this* color and manifestations of the divine . . . in this world."

Galatea's eyes widened in surprise. Yehezkel thought, "Lord of the Universe, this nun is dangerously beautiful. Why did you place her on my path? Are you putting me to the test? Don't you think I could turn around, later, and say: 'if you didn't want me to do it, then why did you pull her out of the water and fling her into my arms?'"

"Manifestations of the divine," Galatea was thinking instead. "What greater authority than a 'school of Jewish mystics' could one turn to for the interpretation of mysteries glimpsed through visions? After all, had I not *known* of the divine nature of that blue?" Embarrassment and hesitation vanished.

"Master Ezekiel, I hope you won't take what I'm about to say as the ravings of a feverish nun . . . but it was no coincidence that *you* were the one to save me! Tell me, do you believe that certain men and women are granted dreams and waking visions of a divine nature?"

"I believe it deeply, madame, more than my reason would like . . ."

"Well, then you must know that I had a premonition of what happened Sunday night, of the name you bear, of the blue you wear, and of an enigma whose solution is in Jerusalem!"

Except for Aillil, lost in his cup of hippocras, everyone was aghast, mouths half open, unable to believe they had just heard the abbess pronounce those words. They were likely witnessing the ruin of the mother superior of a Cistercian house, and in the sort of circumstances that give birth to legends. Then again, the rumormongers would have said, hadn't falling into the lagoon under a full moon already raised doubts about Mother Galatea's mental composure?

Yehezkel was at once flattered by the attention to his person, intrigued by the mention of Jerusalem, and painfully aware of the spell cast by the reckless nun's eyes. He felt the sudden need to avoid the rest of that conversation at all costs and turned to Gudrun. "Sister, here are some wild fennel, wild dill, and horehound. Please prepare a tisane for the abbess by boiling them in wine and straining the decoction through a piece of linen."

Then, to Galatea, with an embarrassed grin, "I am a pilgrim again from tomorrow, madame. Since Divine Providence so strangely brushed us against each other, please accept my blessing."

Galatea bit her lip. "He's leaving tomorrow! I must wrench the secret of my destiny from him *now,* before he leaves the inn. But isn't his departure a denial from above of the role I wish to assign him? No! Only *he* can lead me to the enigma!"

"Forgive my insistence, Master Ezekiel, but I wish to ask you one last question, the answer to which is more important to me than you can imagine. I have a doubt I feel only you can resolve, and if you won't do so . . . well, then it would have been better if you had let me drown!"

Yehezkel remained strangely calm amidst the gasps of shock around him. From the moment he'd seen the senseless, dripping face of the woman he had plucked from the lagoon, he had known in his gut he would not be able to avoid what was happening. He nodded, waiting for her question.

"I would like you to listen to the first two words of a hymn I've been dreaming every night, sung by six virgins. I don't understand a word they sing, but I feel certain you will. It won't take a moment . . ."

With a deep breath, Galatea was about to put the finishing touch to the follies of her Passion Week, breaking into song before everyone like a totally different kind of female guest of that inn, but stopped when she saw Yehezkel gesticulating in horror before he could even get a word out.

"Nooo! Please don't sing, madame! It is expressly forbidden for a Jew to hear a woman's voice singing!" He let out a long sigh, like someone just missed by a galloping horse. "I think . . . I think I've done everything my duties as a medicus required of me, in the circumstances. May God be with you, my good sisters, and . . . Happy Easter!"

He grabbed Aillil's hand, and they left before the abbess could even return the greeting.

As he untied the skiff's mooring, Yehezkel said to himself that the nun seemed to suffer not so much from the travails of a mystic as from the lasciviousness that assails Christians who choose to perversely abstain from what the Torah calls "becoming one flesh" with one's husband or wife.

He stopped. "Now be honest, Yehezkel. You may not be a Christian, but you're one of those, too!"

✡ ✠ ✡ ✠

As soon as they were back in the cottage, Rav Eleazar conducted the evening service of Ma'ariv. Aillil wandered through the dimly lit room, hungry and woozy from the hippocras. After a while, lulled by the drone of ten praying voices, now and then overlaid by a sudden strain of song, the boy drifted off.

The rabbis of course knew of the Christian campaign to retake the Holy Sepulchre, long promoted by Innocent III and finally launched two years earlier by his successor, Honorius III. Damietta, a city at the mouth of the Nile, had been under Christian siege for over a year, and in a corner of the room, Rav Isaiah of Trani was questioning Rav Yehiel of Paris, who had been on board the season's first ship to arrive from Acre and bore fresh news from Outremer. The news Rav Yehiel brought was not good.

"Al Muazzam, Caliph of Damascus and brother of the new Sultan of Egypt al-Malik al-Kamil, may God grant him long life, has ordered Jerusalem's walls demolished. Work was to begin last month."

"Whaat? It can't be!" cried Rav Isaiah, throwing his short arms in the air. "That means al-Kamil intends to return the city to the Christians!"

Yehezkel and another rabbi moved closer, intrigued. Rav Yehiel explained. "I'm afraid you're right, Isaiah. Two months ago, al-Kamil had to abandon his camp in the Delta and rush back to al-Kahira* to deal with the plot of a Kurdish son of a dog from the Hakkarite tribe."

Everyone except Rav Eleazar had now gathered around the Parisian rabbi and hung on his every word.

"The troops woke up without their leader and ran after the Sultan, leaving everything in the camp: arms, horses, tents, supplies. The cursed Franks took everything. And that's not all: the Franks—may God confound them!—crossed the Nile branch west of the island and reached the foot of Damietta's walls. The city has been completely encircled for two months!"

Yehezkel tried to insert a sarcastic comment on the behavior of the Sultan's army, but the others shushed him, urging the Parisian to continue.

---

*Cairo

"Mercifully, God came to al-Kamil's assistance. His brother arrived from Damascus in the nick of time, and together they dealt with the plot—many Kurdish heads rolled on the sand! Nevertheless, al-Muazzam's orders, as Isaiah rightly says, imply that the sultan feels he may have to make a deal on Jerusalem with the Franks to save Egypt."

Rav Eleazar prefaced their last talk with the by-now-customary prayer for martyrs. It was particularly moving pronounced by the German mystic, since everyone present knew that on a winter night in 1196, in Mainz, cross-wearing knights had forced their way into his home and killed his wife Dulcina, his daughters Belat and Hannah, and his son Yaakov. Though badly wounded, he had escaped alive.

After the prayer, he began, "My friends, sages of Israel, I asked you to come here because Satan has found out about our Talmud! That Christian attitudes toward us have changed for the worse is not news, but now I fear they're turning their deadly attentions to the work of our blessed sages . . ."

Rav Eleazar chose his words with care to describe the dangers hanging over the Talmud. "The bishop of Heidelberg is a friend of the Jews. On coming back from a trip to Rome, he told me what is happening in the church. Behind most accusations against the Talmud are Jewish apostates."

"May they be cursed for eternity!" cried Rav Yitzhak. "They hate Israel more than Satan does!"

"But they must not be underestimated," said Rav Eleazar. "As you know, once they accept baptism, the fools goad the monks against the Talmud, the very thing that kept us alive in exile these thousand years. They whisper in their ears that it is not from Sinai but is a recent work that contradicts the Torah . . ."

He lowered his voice. "The bishop told me that a certain Domingo of Guzman, as sharp and fanatical as only Spanish monks can be, seeks out Jewish converts. He has convinced the pope to recognize his preaching order and wants the church to declare the Talmud a Jewish heresy!"

Rav Isaiah said, "Yes, I heard talk of him in Italy. They say his mother dreamt of giving birth to a dog that set the world on fire. They call it a divine omen, but now her *dog* wants to burn the Talmud!"

Yehezkel saw himself in another kitchen, the Spanish monk weeping on a stool in front of him. "I met him, ten years ago," he murmured. "He claimed no connection to Guzman nobility then, and only called himself Domingo de Caleruega. We both spent the night in the house of the Cathar family who took in Aillil on the day Carcassonne fell . . ."

Rav Yitzhak gave him an incredulous look. "*You* were at the siege of Carcassonne?"

Yehezkel nodded silently and then said, "There were two perfecti there that night, too. I remember having the better of Domingo in a sort of disputatio, but a child could have done so in those days. The monk was so distraught he wept for the dead in Béziers as if he were a Cathar himself . . ."

"So *that's* why," said Rav Yitzhak. "Carcassonne fell in August, didn't it?"

"Yes, on the fifteenth, to be precise. Why?" asked Yehezkel.

"Because that was a month before the council at Avignon, in September. I read *all* the bulls issued at Avignon, Yehezkel. Your disputatio with Domingo was enough for the pope to forbid not just trading with Jews, but talking with them about 'any topic whatsoever!' *Now* I understand that phrase. The Spaniard must have insisted on including it after meeting *you*. You must have really provoked the cursed monk . . ."

Rav Eleazar took back the reins of the conversation with unusual force. "Enough, Yitzhak. We're here to defend the Talmud against that dog, not to discover why he hates it." He hesitated. "There are things I cannot speak of, but it's becoming clear that the church has decided to eliminate all threats to her continued control over the minds of goyim. The weakest threat, the Cathars, was the first to fall, and now they're coming after us . . . when they have isolated, expelled, or massacred the

Jews they will turn to their strongest enemy, the one they could never defeat today."

"And who might that be, Rav Eleazar?" asked Rav Isaiah, perplexed.

"The Order of the Temple! Listen: Jews in Paris and Lisbon have heard rumors of a group ensconced in the heart of the order, who are enemies of both the Church and Christian doctrine."

The Hasid* was touching on confidential matters and didn't want to say more than his audience needed to know. Not one of them, not even Yehezkel, would have dreamed of interrupting him.

"The head of the group is a well-known cleric everyone thinks dead, but apparently he staged his own funeral, and now that he's dead, he fights the pope from *inside* an order that only answers to the pope!"

Rav Eleazar smiled, enjoying the looks of utter disbelief on the rabbis' faces. "Also, there's an ancient parchment involved, but I don't know much about that, only that they call it the Parchment of Circles and that the church wants it badly." The Hasid paused. "It seems the head of the secret cabal inside the Temple is also after it . . . this is only a hunch, but I suspect the secret cabal and the parchment are connected in some way . . ."

Yehezkel had a fleeting vision of Pons Roger's big red ears. "The night I met Domingo, one of the perfecti spoke of that parchment before the monk arrived. He called it a Cathar relic, 'a circle within a circle' drawn by Saint John the Evangelist, with writings in Greek that he called prophecies."

"Mmh . . . very interesting," murmured Rav Eleazar. "What do you think, Yehezkel, would their Saint John write in Greek? I rather think he used Hebrew, or Aramaic. . . No, no, we haven't the time to discuss things we know so little about."

The Hasid stood up slowly, as if to give weight to his next pronouncement. "Although some elders disagree with me, I feel the time

---

*From the root *hesed,* loving kindness, a Hasid is a pious, righteous man. Also the root of "Hasidism."

has come to seek allies and prepare defenses. With God's help, I intend to have copies of the complete Talmud buried in secret locations in France and the Rhineland. If you agree to be part of this enterprise, you will all travel to the places I will tell you, and report to me—by trusted messengers only, *no* letters—on the missions I am about to assign you."

As Rav Eleazar hoped, an unseemingly warlike spirit imbued the five scholars. Each one waited excitedly to know his role in the plans of that holy league for the defense of the Talmud. The Hasid pointed a finger at the Spanish rabbi first.

"You, Yaakov, will go home and from there to Portugal to speak with astronomers and navigators at the Court, especially Templars. I want to know all about the unknown continent some of them claim lies three thousand leagues west of their coast. The day will come when Jews have to leave Christian lands for good; so we should look for somewhere else to go until God relents and takes us back to Jerusalem."

He turned to Rav Yehiel. "You, my friend, will go home and seek out trusted allies among the more enlightened knights of the Paris temple. I've heard there are quite a few."

Rav Yehiel nodded. Next was the little Italian. "Rav Isaiah, you'll go to Rome and speak with Jews close to cardinals to find out who supports what regarding legislation on Jews. Also, start spreading the notion we intend to demonstrate: that the Talmud already existed in the time of Jesus!"

The next mission was Rav Yitzhak's. "You'll go to Provence and seek out the perfecti who survived the first ten years of this war between Christians. Yehezkel knows many of them already, but I can't send him because he might run into the Spanish monk again. Oh, and try to find out, as discreetly as you can, what the Parchment of Circles might be, and who the mysterious long-dead cleric really is . . ."

Yehezkel was asking himself if being left for last was a good or bad sign when the Hasid turned to him.

"I hope I didn't bore you with all these politics, Yehezkel. After all, you're a kabbalist, a mystic . . ."

"No, no, don't worry, Rabbi. I'm a bit of a strange Jew, a mystic who loves politics and sailing."

"When you're older, Yehezkel," said the Hasid with a smile, "you'll find that *all* Jews are a bit strange. . . . As for sailing, you prophesied well. You'll be going to Eretz Israel on a Templar cog taking pilgrims to Acre that sails in two weeks. If all goes according to plan, on board the cog will be Don Sancio de la Palmela, known as Doctus, the learned one. He was secretary and scribe to Guillaume of Chartres, the master of the temple who died at the siege last year, and has been summoned to the Christian camp at Damietta."

Yehezkel breathed deeply, a wide grin on his face. Erez Israel! The prophecy hidden in his name would be fulfilled! His heart on fire, he struggled to focus on Rav Eleazar's words.

"The Templar cog is waiting for Don Sancio before it sails. This is why I chose Venice as the venue for our meeting. You, Yehezkel, will find out from the scribe whether any document was found when the order dug under the Temple Mount a hundred years ago that can be used to prove the antiquity of the Talmud."

Rav Eleazar looked into Yehezkel's eyes. "But that's not all. Rumor has it that the head of the secret cabal is in Eretz Israel, so the second half of your mission, should the scribe be unable or unwilling to help, will be to find the long-dead cleric and convince him to help you find the right parchments. Fighting Domingo seems to be his priority, too."

The strategy convinced everyone except Rav Yitzhak, who made a face at the idea that some ancient-looking parchment would dissuade the Castilian monk from his plan to outlaw the Talmud.

Rav Eleazar saw a shadow cross Yehezkel's eyes as the huge responsibility settled on his shoulders. "Your mission is the most important one, Yehezkel, and since I also consider it the most dangerous, I chose you for it, because I know you are a widower with no children. I might have wished for a quieter emissary, one with no ambition to become a *maskil*,* but

---

*Pronouncer of God's Names

everything comes from above. That you survived the siege at Carcassonne speaks well of your sangfroid, though it seems you're also not afraid of beautiful Christian nuns. Sshh! No, no, Yehezkel, I know what you want to say, there's no need to explain; God knows what he's doing! If I sent a Talmudist, I would just get a list of the transgressions committed by every Jewish community between here and Jerusalem!"

A good part of the night was gone. The rabbis recited some psalms, and then the Hasid blessed them all and concluded, raising his eyes heavenward, "Master of the Universe, I implore you, redeem Israel! But if you really don't want to redeem your people yet, then at least redeem the goyim!"

✡   ✠   ✡   ✠

Two days later, on the Square of the Wheel, she saw him again.

Galatea and Gudrun emerged from the bishop's palace. The abbess immediately recognized Yehezkel's ample shoulders and Aillil's blond hair as they stood outside the Ottones' inn. She almost broke into a run and then remembered how she constantly rebuked her novices for such impulsive behavior, and set off at a quick march, followed by her German pupil, to whom that brisk pace seemed to come naturally. As she crossed the square in long strides, her mantle flapping, she thought, "He only said he was leaving so he wouldn't have to see me again . . . the arrogance of these people is truly unbelievable! Did he really think I wouldn't find out he was still on the island?"

Yehezkel's face, on seeing her, lit up in a smile that undermined the basis of her resentment. "Good day to you, madame! It's a pleasure to see you again."

"Good day, Master Ezekiel." Gudrun, with an embarrassed giggle, also stuttered a "Good day," the first words she had ever spoken to a Jew.

Galatea's eyes demanded an explanation. Yehezkel remembered what he'd told her and blurted out, "Oh . . . you're right, of course; I said I would leave yesterday! But you see . . . that night at the Ben-Porats' a renowned German rabbi who was passing through entrusted me with some letters for two sages in the Holy Land." He stood straighter, almost proud. "I'm happy to tell you, madame, that in two weeks I shall embark in Venice for Acre and from there, with God's help, go up to Jerusalem!"

Galatea was silent, but in her thoughts she screamed, "*Take me with you! Please take me with you!*"

She noticed two or three passersby already pointing to the unusual assembly and felt trapped. "I haven't a single good reason to restrain the Jew of the hermit's prophecy from going to Jerusalem without me, to solve an enigma to which only *I* have the key!"

As if throwing a load off her back, she spat out, "*Bereshit!** That's the word!"

Yehezkel froze. He had just resolved to ignore the pleasant tingle the nun's attention gave him, and there she was, throwing the first of ALL words in his face!

"Wha . . . what did you just say, madame?"

"I said Be - re - shit ! It's the first word sung by the chorus of virgins in my dream. Does it mean something to you, Master Ezekiel?"

"No . . . it doesn't mean something, madame," said the kabbalist, visibly paler. "It means *everything*!"

The abbess let out a long sigh, like someone accused of being crazy for her whole life and suddenly disproving it with one word. From one moment to the next, she was no longer the one asking questions, the rabbi was, and so earnestly it almost made up for their first meeting.

"Madame, please tell me more about this dream . . . do you remember any other words, beside Bereshit?"

Galatea smoothed her habit. "Well, let me see . . . they are six white-clad girls with gold bands on their foreheads, but I know they're virgins . . . the way one knows things in dreams. As for the other words . . . the second one is short, just two syllables, both in 'aahh.' Right now I can't remember exactly . . ."

---

*Hebrew for "In the Beginning," the first word of the Bible.

"Is it Barah?" prompted Yehezkel.

Galatea intoned without thinking, "*Baa..ràààà.*" She stopped, remembering the Jewish interdiction. "The second word is Barah, as you say. I have no doubt. You know the whole phrase, don't you?"

He didn't answer. "And what do they sing next, madame? What is the third word?"

Yehezkel's slightly choked voice made her anxious about something she had always found sublime. "I don't remember, Master Ezekiel! You forget I don't recognize the words. You do, don't you?"

Yehezkel nodded but didn't say anything. Galatea had an idea. "When you said Barah, I knew it was the second word. Why don't you pronounce the third word; I'll recognize it!"

"Heaven protect us, madame, don't you understand? The third word is God's name, which I can only pronounce while praying! Try to remember, and I'll wait in silence."

Galatea lowered her eyes, smiling. She hadn't known her rescuer for long but already found it unlikely that he could live up to that simple promise. She concentrated. "In the last weeks I dreamt them every night; no other dream has ever been so persistent. But only until the night of . . . the incident. I've not dreamt the choir again since that night."

"Not good news," said Yehezkel. "Soon you'll forget the little you still remember." He noticed the growing number of goyim who had stopped to ogle.

"But it's a dream, Master Ezekiel! If I'd heard that marvelous hymn while awake, I assure you I would remember all seven words!"

"Seven? Did you say *seven* words?"

"Yes, I thought I'd told you that already. Wait, wait, here it is, it's coming back to me . . . the third word, it's sung with great power, by five voices . . . three low ones and two high . . ."

Yehezkel's eyes widened in a mixture of fascination and horror, as if he expected lightning to incinerate her before his eyes should the nun sing God's sternest name.

At first Galatea hummed it, as if to herself. The musical phrase was low and solemn for two syllables and suddenly high-pitched in the third. When she was sure, she sang it. "*Eeehh . . . looohh . . . hhiiiiiiim*!!"

Yehezkel was sweating despite the breeze. The onlookers' curiosity turned to apprehension at the muffled scream from the abbess. Galatea perceived the frightening speed of the Jew's thoughts, and for a moment it made her head spin. Yehezkel went after a detail that puzzled him. "You said that God's name is sung by five girls, madame, but there are six of them. What does the sixth one do, is she silent? And how many voices sing Bereshit?"

"Holy Mother of God, let me catch my breath, Master Ezekiel! Bereshit is the only word sung by all six virgins, while Barah is sung by . . . wait, by just three of them. Yes, three!"

That was when Yehezkel abandoned all scepticism about the nun's dream. Each of the three words was sung by the same number of voices as the letters that make up the word. The numerological harmony convinced the kabbalist that Divine Providence was intervening in his mission, and that he would be a fool to ignore what the Spirit was doing.

"But why a Christian?" he thought. "And a *nun,* at that? As for dreaming *that* verse, of all verses . . . , well, there was no better honey to catch *this* bear, was there?"

Behind the diffidence, something in the way Yehezkel and Galatea were looking at each other made Gudrun uneasy. The group of onlookers was now less than twenty feet away. The two knew they had to talk more about her dream but that it wasn't the time or place to do so. Yehezkel wasn't a Talmudist, but he suddenly remembered a detail of the sages discussing the issue of a woman's voice. "One may not hear a woman sing," he suggested, "but several women, such as a choir in a synagogue, that is not forbidden . . ."

Galatea reflected and then said, "There's a path along the edge of Sant'Antonio's marsh, near the southern tip of the island. Be there at dawn tomorrow, Master Ezekiel, and please come alone. God be with you!"

The next instant, the two nuns had turned away and were marching into the Ottones' inn.

That night Galatea paced her room like the lioness she was again. During the months of despondency, she had often wondered if her dreams and visions were just the restless yearnings of a warrior's daughter. Now she knew that her purpose in life was greater than praising God and weaving wool: she had to solve the enigma in Jerusalem!

"I must go on a pilgrimage to the Holy Sepulchre! I'll make the necessary arrangements for a long absence of the mother superior . . . No! What am I saying? I can't just leave; that would be running from my responsibilities. If I left for two years the convent would collapse . . ."

Her hands went to her mouth. "But *this* is what I was born for! What kind of life would I have in the lagoon, soaking in the damp regret of not having seen Jerusalem? And what of the hermit's prophecy? No, this is my call, like Hildegard's, I must not let it pass me by. Madre Santissima, give me strength!"

She stood at the window, looking at the distant, flat edge of the lagoon that had been the boundary of half her life, and suddenly knew it was one of the last times she would stand there. "I'll give the bishop his victory. Let *him* choose the new abbess, even Sister Erminia, if he wants!"

When the Compline bell sounded, her decision was made. She had thought of everything. Gudrun couldn't stay behind, for she would suffer the rejection of a fallen favorite, so she would take her with, as Elisabetta had taken her to the hermit's island. She also decided to hire two armigers for protection on the dangerous roads of Outremer. The idea reassured her, as well as being an image of herself on a journey she found pleasing. After all, was she or wasn't she a countess?

She considered how many golden Bézants she'd have to ask from Uncle Rénard—Blanche's brother who lived in Rialto and fifteen years earlier had secured a place for her at the Borgognoni—and where to hide them. She even tackled the question of how to take her chest along, since the thought of leaving without it had not even occurred to her.

Just then, Gudrun knocked and came in without waiting for an answer.

"One day, Gudrun, I'll prescribe you penance for *every time* you entered a room without waiting for permission. Can you imagine the discipline I'll have to impose on you?"

Educating Gudrun put Galatea's virtues to the test, but the harsher the Tuscan abbess disciplined her, the more the young German worshipped her. Over the years, she had attached herself to the abbess like a mongrel and was only happy if she could follow one step behind Galatea, whatever she was doing.

The day Galatea met her rescuer, Gudrun had silently mouthed a formula against the Jew on the way back from the inn. "Crafty Jewish wizard ensnaring the soul of my abbess! May she be protected from your evil filters and dolls, in the name of God the Father, God the Son, and God the Holy Ghost, Amen!"

Then, seeing her fall for his animal sensuality in the square, she had determined to prevent six nuns being alone with a Jewish wizard in a lonely marsh the next dawn.

Galatea caught her totally by surprise. "You must prepare yourself spiritually with meditations on the Holy Sepulchre, my dove, because very soon you and I . . . are going on a pilgrimage to the Holy Land!"

Gudrun forgot everything and fell to her knees, kissing Galatea's hands. She pushed an unruly blonde tress back under her cap, weeping with childish joy. "Oh Mother, will we see the wood of the True Cross with our own eyes, and the signs of the nails?"

That night Galatea couldn't sleep, her only thought: the Holy Sepulchre.

The next morning, before dawn, Yehezkel tied the skiff to the roots of a willow along the path Galatea described. Night vapors lingered over the putrid water and the marsh was dimly lit by a bluish glow. Frogs croaked everywhere, perhaps to exploit the stage before leaving it to the choir he was there to hear.

The fog made the corner of the marshes feel suspended in the middle of fluffy nothingness. Though he expected them, the six nuns startled him. Their voices singing a psalm preceded them, silencing the frogs, and they appeared among the low swirls of fog like a vision before the eyes of a feverish anchorite.

Yehezkel greeted them with a nod of his head. Galatea appreciated his choice not to break the preternatural silence. The nuns wordlessly lined up elbow to elbow on the grass in front of some reeds. At a gesture from Galatea, they sang the first verse of the Bible in Hebrew.

"Bereshit Baràh Elohim Et Ha-Shamayim Ve'et Ha-Aretz."

Storks and herons took off as they began, the fluttering of wings adding a background drumroll that sent a shiver down Yehezkel's spine. When the last of the four voices singing "Ha-Aretz" stopped, he made a slow rotating gesture with his hand. Galatea understood at once and signaled to the nuns to sing it again. After the second performance they all stood silently as the colors of the lagoon emerged in the first light.

Yehezkel was lost in the first morning of the universe, still without a dawn.

Galatea was close to tears. "A melody worthy of angels," she said, "especially 'Ha-Shamayim'! You know, Master Ezekiel, this music was composed by Hildegard of Bingen, a German prophetess. I already knew it before hearing it with these words. When I heard it in my dream I thought I was hearing . . . the beginning of life! And now tell me, I beg you, what did we sing, and . . . did we sing it in Hebrew?"

Considering she doesn't know its meaning, her grasp of the verse is miraculous, thought Yehezkel. "You sang the first verse of the Bible, madame, 'In the Beginning God Created the Heavens and the Earth,' and yes, you sang it in Hebrew, the tongue in which God *created* the world." He paused. "As for the music, you're right . . . it's like spring blossoming in your heart!"

There was another silence. They wanted to speak of Jerusalem, but didn't dare. Yehezkel murmured, "Do you . . . do you often have dreams of this kind, madame?"

Galatea had been waiting for those words. "Oh, Master Ezekiel, if only you knew! I suffer from a veritable *plague* of dreams! From the age of ten, I've dreamed shreds of events which then happened every time. As I grew older, I learned to keep my dreams to myself, lest I be accused of having dealings with the devil!"

The words of the abbess troubled the nuns but didn't surprise Yehezkel, who suspected the nun to be touched by grace from the night he'd set eyes on her. He was moved by the obvious relief she felt in confiding her secret to someone, even to a Jew! Galatea felt his empathy and emptied out the rest of her supernatural baggage.

"The last premonition to be fulfilled was being saved from drowning while hearing Christ's words on the lake. . . . Did you know, Master Ezekiel, that 'Ego sum, nolite timere' are the words Jesus spoke when he reached the apostles in the middle of the Sea of Gennesaret, walking on the waters?"

"No, by my beard! I knew Jesus had walked on water, but not the words he spoke to his disciples!"

Galatea blurted out, "I want you to know that I've decided to go on a pilgrimage to Jerusalem!"

Yehezkel's heart skipped a beat. He was overjoyed but didn't let it show. "In the inn you spoke of 'an enigma whose solution is in Jerusalem.' Is that your purpose?"

"Yes, but not only. I've wanted to make that journey for years, and now you turn up and boast that you're sailing in ten days! I can't just rot in these marshes while you, Master Ezekiel, embrace a destiny that should have been . . . *ours!*"

The reddish top of the sun appeared above the haze, stained with flying birds. Yehezkel reflected on the truly transcendent power of the word "ours." After a while, he asked Galatea to step aside with him, out of the nuns' hearing. "Let me handle it, madame," he said. "We will board a Templar cog, which sails ten days after Easter. Don't tell anyone we're . . . traveling together. There must be no connection between your pilgrimage and the journey of a Jew. We will just *happen* to be on the same ship."

The precaution seemed wise to her, and she nodded approval but was also irked by the male way in which he reserved to himself responsibility for arranging the passage.

"I'm not a child, Master Ezekiel; I can assure you I shall not be a burden to this . . . expedition."

He said, "There are other questions I'd like to ask you about your dreams and visions, madame, but there will be time enough for that when we're at sea."

She felt excited by the imminent adventure but vaguely apprehensive, as for a premonition about being "at sea." She swept the thought away, telling herself that four days after being saved from drowning, anyone had a right to look with suspicion on the idea of being "at sea."

The white-clad chorus took leave of its bizarre audience—made of a single listener, and that one an unbeliever—and walked off down the path. Far away, across the fields, the tolling of the iron bell called the faithful to their knees, to hear the softly spoken magic spells.

CHAPTER 6

BEIN MAYIM LA-MAYIM

Between Waters and Waters

TORCELLO, 20TH APRIL 1219

The nine days before they met again were a trying time for the abbess, who announced her pilgrimage to her sisters on Holy Friday and spent her thirtieth Easter torn between euphoria over the endeavor—a true Paschal resurrection from her previous condition—and teary separations from her heartbroken nuns.

Aillil, instead, was beside himself with happiness. The news that Rav Yehezkel would sail to Syria and help him find his father had injected a feverish enthusiasm into the boy, not unlike—Yehezkel told him—the effect of the bite of some scorpions. He ran from one person to the other, showering each with chivalrous vows and resolutions that didn't excite in that humble Jewish dyers' home the kind of admiration the boy seemed to expect.

That Sunday churches were so full birds didn't dare enter them. Torcellans praised God with jarring but sincere songs, their booming voices rising heavenward from the whole archipelagos. Sequestered in the dyers' cottage, the other rabbis gone, Yehezkel could hear the bellow of their prayers. Fifteen years earlier, when he'd left Muslim lands, he'd been horrified to discover that the role Christians assigned to the Children of Israel in the story they commemorated at Easter was that of Satan's emissaries.

Two days after Easter, having learned of the two guards who would accompany the abbess—raising San Maffìo's contingent to four— Yehezkel went to Venice to ensure the ship's consul would allow the group to board. He was looking for a cog named *Falcus,* belonging to the Templar commanderie of Acre. The Templars had a base near the Church of Ascension, but the order's ships—the waters of the Canal Grande and the souls of Venetians both being narrow—had to stay at anchor at Spinalunga.

Once there, it didn't take the rabbi long to find the northern-type round cog, almost two hundred feet long, weighing, he guessed, some 250 *millaria* (about 125 tons) and with two masts rigged for square sails. He wondered how to obtain an audience with its consul. Within an hour, he'd bought a Greek sailor a drink and been taken on board, his nonchalance on the tallowed gangplank raising seamen's eyebrows. He was introduced to the Cypriot scribe, a shabby little creature with a spark of something human in his eyes. The scribe knew of a Jew among the passengers, but his reaction to the news that Yehezkel intended to bring *five* more people with him—two of them women!—was undisguised mirth.

Yehezkel discovered that the presence of women on pilgrim ships was forbidden but also learned—after a first taste of money by the scribe—that the prohibition didn't apply to princesses. He cautiously inquired about the kind of sum that might suffice to bend that rule to include countesses, and after a lively and enjoyable negotiation, the two men made a deal.

On the 22nd of April, three days before sailing, they met again in the Ottones' inn. When Yehezkel and Aillil walked in, Marciana was again being consoled by the abbess. Not only was she about to lose her only friend in the lair of weasels she considered the communities in the lagoon to be—she had just discovered Bonifacio was having an affair with a trollop from Equilio and was planning to leave her for the younger woman. If she had the courage, she'd just told Galatea, she would join her and make a new life in Outremer.

A little later, Yehezkel was explaining the harsh rules that governed a pilgrim's passage. "It's important—I don't say it to boast, God forbid—that I secured passenger status for all six of us. You see, crew, merchants, and passengers, but *not* pilgrims, have a right to a chest, a mattress, and a supply of water, wine, and flour. You'll be grateful, you'll see, not to be part of the rush to the tables when the meal bell rings."

The abbess listened, a little embarrassed by a nun's ignorance of things every Venetian knew.

Marciana said, "If that's the case, we must rush to the pantry and start loading enough provisions to feed you all until you reach the Holy Land!"

By a twist of fate, on reaching the pantry, Marciana realized she had the wrong key. With a suspicious glance at Ychezkel, she went back to the kitchen. Embarrassed to be alone with a nun, Yehezkel leaned against a pile of chopped wood in a corner, a good ten feet from Galatea. He had forgotten their first conversation and was startled when she suddenly addressed him differently.

"I'm a good cellar keeper, Rabbi, but you probably know better what to take on a sea passage . . ."

Her voice calling him "Rabbi" felt like he'd been kicked by a mule. He sucked in his breath, remembered he had asked her to address him that way when they were alone, and for the first time thought he might be underestimating this nun.

But what was for Yehezkel the poignant memory of his Naomi mockingly calling him "rabbi" when he hadn't yet been one was instead, for Galatea, a kind of spiritual epiphany. Addressing him as the apostles had addressed Jesus lowered her into the Gospels with the sudden sharpness, so familiar to her, of a vision pushing out reality. She listened to Yehezkel pontificate on the maritime virtues of eggs and salted fish with a dreamy expression, only coming back to her senses when Marciana returned to the small courtyard.

Back in the kitchen, Galatea asked Yehezkel gingerly, running her hand through Aillil's hair, already almost a habit, "Don't get me wrong, Master Ezekiel, I don't mean to judge the way you treat the boy, but your apprentice is baptized, and . . . " She looked at Aillil, making an effort to speak the words clearly. "Tell me, Aillil, did you go to church on Easter Sunday?"

Aillil shook his head violently. Yehezkel told himself this had to happen sooner or later. "Ehm . . . Aillil is a Christian, madame, but . . . how can I put it? He's not a Catholic! He professes the faith of the Cathars of Provence, whom the church has declared heretics and massacred in the thousands. I'm sure you know what I speak of . . ."

Galatea was startled. "He is an orphan of *that* war? I hadn't imagined . . ." She kissed the top of Aillil's head and gestured to Yehezkel to step aside with her. "Is it true the Cathars worship *Satan*?" she asked in a whisper, horror and concern in her voice.

"No, they abhor him. But they don't consider him weaker than God," answered Yehezkel.

"Yes, that's right . . . they believe in an eternal war between a good God and a bad God."

"It's more complicated than that, madame. They think it was Satan, not God, who created this world. When we're at sea, if you wish, I can tell you more about the beliefs of Manicheans."

Galatea looked at Aillil again. In her eyes, Yehezkel saw the anguish for the tragedy of war exceed the outrage for the sin of heresy. He quietly thanked God for choosing a Christian, yes, but one with a soul.

Presently the group left the inn and stood by the bridge, by now impervious to the islanders' curiosity. After arranging the rendezvous at dawn on Wednesday, they went their respective ways.

Before casting off, Yehezkel stood on the stern of the skiff, arms across his chest, watching Galatea walk toward Santa Fosca in short, determined steps, like those of an aggrieved little girl.

"Even if Satan tried to ensnare this woman, he would fail," he thought. "She's as stubborn as Job."

✡ ✠ ✡ ✠

At dawn on the 25th of April, Saint Mark's Day, the six pilgrims sailed on a roscona to Santi Pietro e Paolo, on the eastern edge of Venice. They walked along fondamenta reeking of tar and rotten fish lined with chandlers, boatbuilders' yards and sailmakers' lofts, huge warehouses looming behind them.

The abbess and Gudrun marched along the Riva degli Schiavoni feeling like children on Christmas Eve. Galatea wore a new habit, white as snow with light-blue borders. Three steps behind them, muttering under short breaths, the armigers carried the chest, while twenty steps farther back, with no apparent link to the other party, came Yehezkel and Aillil. The rabbi couldn't get the boy to walk next to him; Aillil hopped and skipped back and forth between his tutor and the nuns, wondering about that curious game.

Finally they came out on the Canal Grande. Their departure day was consecrated to Saint Mark, evangelist and patron saint of Venice, and the city was celebrating unprecedented power and wealth. Never in the previous ten years had lighthouses, columns, and standards in the Mediterranean seen such a proliferation of winged lions. With the possible exception of the Golden Horn in Constantinople, Saint Mark's Square, with its basilica nearing completion, was the most breathtaking sight in the world.

Shafts of sunlight shone down between the clouds, turning portions of canal to bright silver, the ships inside them screaming out their identities in the colored standards flapping on their masts. There was no end to them: ships of the Doge, of Venetian Constantinople, of Cyprus, of Acre, of the Hospitallers, of the Templars. What with the flags ashore, Venice on Saint Mark's Day looked like the venue of a gigantic jousting tournament.

They stood on the edge of the bedlam, by the Doge's palace, not far from the quay where pilgrims embarked. Before them stretched a vociferous sea of faces from all corners of the world: Franks, English, Germans, Normans, Spaniards, Magyars; but also darker complexions and higher cheekbones: Saracens, Turks, Slavs, Tartars. Even Yehezkel, who knew the markets of al-Kahira, had never seen such a variety of features, or for that matter of dresses and headgear. Venetians in floppy woolen hats, oriental merchants in silk turbans, monks in habits, beggars in rags, whores with painted eyes, penitents both barefoot and bareheaded. The crowd heaved, shouted, laughed, sang hymns.

Suddenly four Templar knights, preceded by their squires, crossed the square like the prow of a ship cleaving the waves. Yehezkel, realizing it must be their companions on the passage, gestured to Galatea and slipped in right behind them. At the sight of the white cloaks with the blood-red *croix pattées,** the crowd opened up like the Red Sea before the Israelites. The warrior monks, members of an order founded to protect pilgrims, looked down on them as nobles look on plebs, with ill-disguised contempt.

Galatea noticed a whore coming toward them, so scantily dressed that a nipple had escaped the edge of her dress. Used to men twisting their necks to follow such sights, she was surprised to see that not only the rabbi but all four knights paid no attention to her. Sobered by the sight, she reflected that it would be a mistake to underestimate these brothers of the Temple.

Within moments they were at the *Falcus*. She no longer resembled the ship Yehezkel boarded a few days earlier, every flag hoisted and a platform as wide as a street where the greasy plank had been. The queue of pilgrims stretched down the quay as far as they could see. The knights ignored the clerks at the foot of the gangplank and marched

---

*A type of cross whose arms are narrow at the center and broader at the perimeter

straight on board, Yehezkel one step behind them. The official register-
ing pilgrims' names chased him up the gangplank, but when he caught
up, Yehezkel had already reached the Cypriot scribe at the base of the
quarterdeck, who waved the clerk away, "These are passengers, not pilgrims. They're none of your business!"

The abbess mentally congratulated the rabbi on his presence of
mind. She'd heard that Jews never seemed in awe of anyone, as if they
were all of noble birth. She looked around. The deck was huge, yet she
wondered how the hundreds of pilgrims waiting ashore could possibly fit. Then she saw a few vanish down the hatchway just forward of
the mast and understood there would be room for all because most of
them would spend almost a month belowdecks where goods were normally stowed, lying on planking laid on the gravel ballast in the hold.
Yehezkel whispered to her, "Now you see why it's important to be a passenger and not a pilgrim, madame. We've been assigned a small portion
of the deck where we can sleep under the stars."

Galatea noticed that almost all the men had let their beards grow
and asked Yehezkel the reason. He said they'd almost certainly been
told that being clean-shaven among Saracens, especially for blond men,
was rife with unmentionable dangers. Embarrassment froze the abbess.

Some three hundred pilgrims boarded the *Falcus* that day. Galatea
noticed that some men were women in disguise, the dress-up so superfi-
cial it was obvious money had changed hands so the scribe would close
an eye as some pilgrims took their wives along. She had to laugh at
those who, seeing the sailors climb the rigging, thought they had just
sighted the famous "monkeys" of pilgrim lore.

The group installed themselves by the port gunwale, a little aft of
the small forward castle. With the help of the armigers, Yehezkel secured
Galatea's chest with nails and lines so it wouldn't budge in rough seas
and then set up a curtain falling from lines stretched between the gunwale, the chest, and the nearest shroud of the foremast. He placed a
mattress behind the curtain and stood back to survey the result. The
abbess naively imagined pleasantly watching the sea from the privacy

of that lair as they waited for the Holy Land to appear and shot him a grateful smile. Then her eye fell on Rustico, and she smiled, remembering his expression when he'd first set eyes on the chest he and Garietto would drag all the way to Jerusalem.

On the roscona taking them to Venice, Galatea had introduced her bodyguards to the rabbi. The older one, Rustico Bobizo, was a lanky Torcellan named after one of the islanders who'd stolen Saint Mark's body, and proud of it. His ear bore the unmistakable sign of a convict who had survived the rowing benches of Venetian galleys. That he'd grown up without the benefit of an education was clear from the austere simplicity with which he stuck to the male gender.

The younger one was Garietto Zanin from the island of Costanziaco, almost as big as Yehezkel and with hair as wild as Samson's. A rich mane of chestnut curls fell to the middle of his back, and he wore big, soft moustaches like people in the far north. His Viking appearance and a winning smile made women's eyes follow Garietto, so much that on the *roscona* Yehezkel glimpsed the stern look with which the abbess had fulminated Gudrun when she'd caught the younger nun staring dreamily at Garietto's curls.

At last, to the sound of trumpets and drumrolls, the great adventure began. All the pilgrims came out on deck. Relatives and friends on the quay waved banners and shouted blessings that mingled with the boatswain's orders directing the maneuvers. Some sailors hauled in the mooring lines as others hoisted a small foresail, the *Falcus* lacking oars for maneuvers in a harbor. Yet other men weighed anchor, all of them shouting as they pulled, so that hearing the people ashore above the din was impossible.

Then the boatswain cried toward the bow, "Is your work done?" When he heard that the anchor was on board and the ship free, he turned to the pilgrims, "Let the clerics come forward!"

A few priests and monks advanced through a gap in the crowd, bearing big crosses of dark wood.

"In the name of God, sing!"

Every pilgrim knew the ritual by heart and three hundred voices—at first hesitantly and then growing to a roar—joined in the hymn it had become customary to sing at the start of a pilgrimage to Jerusalem by sea.

> *We sail in the name of God, To obtain His grace.*
> *May He be our strength and the Holy Sepulchre our*
> > *shield.*
> *Kyrie Eleison!**

When he saw enough free water in all directions, the boatswain gave the final command, "In the name of God, make sail!"

As the red-crossed mainsail was hoisted, flapping lazily in the breeze, only the hardened sailors weren't weeping openly at the spectacle of sunshine and standards, crosses and spray.

✡ ✠ ✡ ✠

The third day of the *Falcus Templi's* passage began with the kind of gray dawn that the sleeping watch claims is still nighttime, while for the waking one the day has clearly started. The boatswain, whose voice would ring in the pilgrims' ears for years to come, climbed the mast to the crow's nest and shouted the verdict of the hourglass to the four winds.

> *Blessed be the light, and the Holy Cross,*
> *The one God of Truth and the Holy Trinity!*
> *Blessed be our soul and the Lord who gave it to us,*
> *Blessed be this day and the Lord who sends it to us!*

A sleepy murmur rose from the deck, quickly turning into the pilgrims' ritual response, their voices groggy but still full of enthusiasm.

---

*Lord have mercy

Pater Noster, Ave Maria, Amen!
May God grant us a good day and a good passage!

The abbess spent most of the night gazing at the stars. That morning, for the first time, she feared that her illness of spirit might be raising its ugly head again. "Maybe the velvety black of these two nights," she thought, "or the water all around . . . something stirred up the humid melancholic humor that plagued me. I am again indifferent to everything around me, and all I want to do is lie where I am . . ."

She chewed listlessly on a biscuit, only because Master Ezekiel told her to put something dry in her stomach. She decided to react, drank a swig of water, tidied her hair, and got up. She bent a knee in the general direction of the sun and crossed herself. Then, pushing aside the curtain, she left Gudrun sound asleep and ventured on the deck alone for the first time.

She headed forward, mindful of Master Ezekiel's injunction, "One hand for yourself and one for the boat, madame. *Always*!" She had to bend to go through the passage under the forecastle and emerged at the bow of the ship, where a short bowsprit stuck out a few feet. Raising her eyes, she suddenly saw a man standing on the base of the bowsprit, his back to her, tied to the forestay like a human figurehead. She gasped in horror, thinking it must be a pillory for pilgrims who'd broken ship's rules. Then she leaned out, first from one gunwale and then from the other, and noticed a thin black leather strap wrapped around a bare left arm. Finally, she saw the blue twine and recognized the rabbi.

In order to pray undisturbed on a ship full of pilgrims, Yehezkel had started putting on his phylacteries and tying himself to the forestay. Galatea stared at him, mouth open. She instinctively stretched out a hand to touch the fringed edge of his prayer shawl but couldn't quite reach it.

From amidships, pilgrims' voices intoned the first responses to Mass. She hurried, with due caution, to the foot of the mast for the rite. Afterward, she found Yehezkel leaning on the gunwale next to her chest, and he confirmed he had been praying on the bowsprit.

The ship's bell rang, announcing the first shift of the morning meal, and the bedlam of the first two mornings was unleashed again. The nuns pulled the curtain against the beastly spectacle, but not before Yehezkel had time to notice that the abbess hadn't touched the previous day's food. He deduced the ship's motion must be starting to affect her. Gudrun, meanwhile, was wolfing down the equivalent of both armigers' rations. After the meal the watch changed, and the boatswain once more climbed to the crow's nest to deliver his shouts, which reminded Yehezkel of the muezzin's calls.

> *The hours that just passed were good ones,*
> *Let the coming ones be even better!*
> *As they go by, may our passage be a good one!*
> *Eyes open ahead, and a good watch to all!*

Yehezkel was delighted to be at sea again. The sailors soon noted that unlike pilgrims and other landlubbers, the Jew's gaze was constantly in the air checking sails, sheets, and rigging in a way that is second nature to seafaring folk. For the second day, clouds made it impossible to measure the sun's height. Yehezkel wondered if the ship's pilot possessed a loadstone like the one he had. In any case, it was time to attempt to speak with the Doctus, so after asking the nuns to keep an eye on Aillil, he walked aft.

The quarterdeck, atop the castle at the extreme stern of the cog, was a square balcony surrounded by a parapet of elegantly turned wooden columns. Yehezkel climbed the ladder and found five men, all slightly bothered by the Jew's arrogance, going where he wanted without asking for anyone's permission. When he bowed and introduced himself, Don Sancio de la Palmela, a sharp-looking white-haired old man, dressed in a black overcoat not unlike Yehezkel's sarbel, crossed the quarterdeck toward him with a welcoming smile.

"So you're the rabbi I was told would be on board. Glad to make your acquaintance, Rav Yehezkel."

"Thank you, Your Excellency. I bring you the greetings of Rav Yehiel the Parisian, whom I met in Torcello. He was coming from Outremer, and I was headed there!"

Don Sancio often consulted Rav Yehiel in Paris, both on matters of scriptural exegesis and on relations between the temple and King Philip Augustus.

"Please don't call me 'Your Excellency'; plain Don Sancio will suffice. I hope you found Rav Yehiel in good health! 'Youth and vigor are meaningless,' says Qoheleth. And tell me, what news was he bringing from Outremer?"

"Oh, nothing you wouldn't already know, unless you're not aware of why al-Kamil had to abandon his camp in al-Addillyiah two months ago . . ."

"No, by the Blessed Virgin! I was traveling and didn't receive a full report." He took Yehezkel's arm and walked him across the balcony. "You'll have to tell me everything, but first let me introduce everyone. This is the master of the *Falcus,* the renowned Templar skipper Friar Vassayl of Marseille."

Yehezkel bowed and proffered his hand to each man.

"This is his pilot, Arnulf." Yehezkel guessed from the ginger hair that he was a Norman.

"And these are two of the four knights on board—Iñigo Sanchez of Sporreto and a Frankish novice, André de Rosson of Aullefol, in the Aube." The young Frenchman wouldn't shake the Jew's hand, let alone grasp his wrist, and retired to one of the parapets.

Moments later, Don Sancio heard from Yehezkel the kind of information on the siege of Damietta that could only have come from the Saracen side of the war. In the next corner of the balcony, in a rite as old as war itself, the veteran knight mimed skulls shattered and guts trailed on the ground for the novice, his gestures making his white mantle pirouette through the air. Finally, in the corner to which a chart table was bolted, Friar Vassayl and his pilot acrimoniously debated something they clearly wished to hide from the Jew, the result of their efforts being a comical whispered row.

Don Sancio quoted Ecclesiastes twice more in the next five minutes, and Yehezkel, amused, informed him that if Ecclesiastes and the Song of Songs had made it into the Jewish Canon, it was thanks to Eleazar ben Azaryiah—a sage of the Talmud—but also a lover of poetry.

"May his name be blessed for all centuries!" said the scribe, amused and a little moved. Then, with a smile of theological malice, "Did you ever read the Gospels, Rav Yehezkel?"

"Yes, I did," said Yehezkel. "I even came to the conclusion that Saint John was an embittered Jew . . ."

The two men started talking Scriptures, and Yehezkel soon discovered that the scribe was a secret admirer of Averroes,* and as such anathemized by the church as theologically indifferent. They were wallowing in that intellectual complicity when Yehezkel noticed Friar Vassayl angrily whisper something to Arnulf and pour the water from an iron bowl overboard.

What explains the embarrassment on the quarterdeck of the *Falcus* is that in those years the use of loadstones—small pieces of rock that, when free to orient themselves, always point to the north—was not yet widespread. Those who knew of them, like the possessors of a good map, kept it to themselves. Yehezkel immediately grasped the meaning of the bowl of water and suspected that their problems were caused by the stone being floated in an iron container.

He casually mentioned to Don Sancio that he had a loadstone. The old man, pretending not to know what the rabbi was speaking of, peered at the horizon as he weighed the implications of those words. A few moments later, he gestured for Yehezkel to follow him and walked over to Friar Vassayl.

---

*Moroccan philosopher (d. 1198) whose real name was Abu al-Walid Muhammad ibn-Rushd.

"Qoheleth says 'The toil of fools wearies them; they do not know the way to town.' You two would argue over how much gulf is left before the straits until we were on the rocks!"

He gathered his robe about himself and crossed his spindly arms on his chest.

"I represent the master of the temple, who is the owner of this ship, and I hereby take responsibility for involving Rav Yehezkel in its navigation. Many Jews are excellent astronomers and pilots, and this rabbi could be another one. Come on, Arnulf, pull out the loadstone!" The last words were addressed to the pilot, who disapproved of such confidence with a Jew but knew the limits of his authority and pulled out a small, dark piece of rock about the size and shape of a pine nut shell. Friar Vassayl was already pouring fresh water in the bowl, but Yehezkel stopped him.

"If you had bad results so far, Master Vassayl, it's because you floated the cork on which your stone rests in that container. You must use a clay one, or your stone will always behave as if it has lost its mind. . . ."

Friar Vassayl turned to Don Sancio, outraged. "By all the bulls in the Camargue! The stone points north out of love for the Holy Virgin, not for Moses! Why should I listen to a Jew's advice on how to second the stone's love for God's Mother, whom Christ killers call an adulteress?"

Yehezkel's anger welled up at the goy's superstition. "I suppose now you'll tell me the stone hates what spills blood, so armors and swords 'upset' it, or that it hates garlic because it causes lascivious thoughts, which are anathema to the Virgin. I've heard these wives' tales, Friar Vassayl. . . ."

Young de Rosson heard him and grabbed Iñigo by the arm, pulling him to the chart table. "In the name of God, Master Vassayl, can you not see that *iron* is what all enemies of the stone have in common? If garlic wasn't eaten in iron bowls, loadstones would react to it like all stones react to garlic!"

Iñigo's tales filled André with chivalrous furor, and the Jew's tone was more than he could bear. "Oh happy day, on which I am chosen to defend the honor of Our Lady against an emissary of the Synagogue of Satan!" he cried, throwing himself at Yehezkel.

In the middle of the balcony he collided with Don Sancio, who jumped in front of him with the agility of a habitual faster. The scribe was smiling, but his voice was ice. "'Wisdom is better than weapons of war,' says Qoheleth. Brother André, repress your anger, which is a sin, and have someone bring a clay bowl, before I lose *my* patience. . . .'"

A little later, five men crowded round the chart table, watching Arnulf deftly compensate for the ship's roll as he gently lowered the stone onto a cross-shaped cork *calamus* floating in a clay bowl. They quickly determined where north and south were and, knowing how long past midday it was, proceeded to work out their latitude, which told them how far southward they had sailed from Venice.

Friar Vassayl, seeking another confirmation, asked Arnulf for the average speed of the *Falcus* over the three days. Arnulf answered, "We never covered more than eight, at most ten leagues, in a watch, maître. The stone tells the truth; we're past Zara; and soon Spalato will be on our port beam!"

Just then, the voice of the man in the crow's nest rung out, "Galleys on starboard!"

The next instant, all six men were leaning out the starboard parapet, eyes narrowed to glimpse details of the warships. The flotilla of fast Venetian galleys, their decks hidden behind long rows of leather shields against Greek fire, were rowing north at great speed in nearly becalmed seas. The oars raised no spray as they sunk in the lead-like water and emerged perfectly aligned, leaving just a trail of drops on the surface. The regular shouts of the overseers, muffled by the distance, reached to the balcony on the *Falcus*.

"The Captain of the Gulf goes to see the Provveditore da Mar!"* decreed Friar Vassayl darkly.

---

*The civilian official charged with overseeing the actions, in this case maritime, of captains hired by the Venetian Republic.

The Captain of the Gulf ruled waters from Venice to the straits of Otranto, beyond which the Captain of the Levant, based in Corfu, took over. They had found something they could all agree on—captain and pilot, scribe and warriors, Jew and Christians: the arrogance of Venetians.

"Loutish, ill-disposed people with gold buckles on their cloaks, who board your ship without asking permission and move the freight around to count it better, as if it was their goods!" hissed the captain to everyone's approving grunts.

As the galleys shrunk behind them, Yehezkel decided to take his leave of the quarterdeck and check on the nuns. An impatient Aillil waited for him at the foot of the ladder, a head full of nautical questions.

There was not a breath of wind for the rest of that afternoon. The oarless *Falcus* drifted aimlessly, its flaccid mainsail snapping with each roll of the ship, fooling landlubbers into thinking that some wind had finally filled it. Soon the gunwales were dotted with pilgrims leaning out, more dead than alive, passing on their last meal to the fish as some compassionate soul held onto them to stop them from falling overboard.

Galatea was white as a sheet and covered in sweat. She no longer cared about anything or anyone: not the pilgrimage, not the Holy Sepulchre, not the enigma in Jerusalem. She just wanted to be left in peace, possibly with her head perfectly still.

A little before the change of watch at Vespers, the bell rang for the second and last meal of the day, provoking a mere shadow of the enthusiasm it sparked earlier. Yehezkel didn't even try to convince the abbess to swallow anything yet wasn't surprised to see that Gudrun's appetite had not suffered in the least, not to speak of young Aillil and the voracious two men raised in the lagoon.

As he studied the abbess, he was reminded of the Greek philosopher who once declared, having been caught by bad weather sailing home from the Black Sea, that there were three categories of humans: the living, the dead, and those who go to sea.

Galatea's chest didn't even rise in the barest of breaths. The only thing that told Gudrun her abbess was still alive were slight tremors of her nostrils whenever the blandest smell of food reached them. In reality, every tremor felt to Galatea like her stomach tying itself in knots. Gudrun thought that stretched out on the mattress, hands clasped on her chest, covered to her chin by a dark shawl, Galatea didn't just look dead, she looked like the relic of a saint!

Just before dark, the boatswain shouted, "The watch is in place, the hourglass turned!

We wish everyone a good passage, God willing!"

In those becalmed conditions, Yehezkel found the addition of an Insh'Allah particularly appropriate.

The pilgrims, nauseous and depleted of all fervor by the third sunset, answered weakly,

> *"Blessed be the hour in which the Lord was born,*
> *Pater Noster, Ave Maria, Amen!*
> *May God grant us a good night, and a good*
>   *passage!"*

Silence fell on the *Falcus,* broken by creaking wood and pitiful moans. Even Yehezkel was groggy from the erratic swinging in the dark. Suddenly, he saw a candle advance toward him, making its way cautiously around the many sleeping bodies. Flames were strictly forbidden on board, so Yehezkel guessed the bearer of the candle must be someone not subject to the rules. Don Sancio brought a pillow and sat down, Saracen style, in front of the rabbi. He let some tallow drip on the deck on which to steady the candle.

"Qoheleth says: 'Even in the night, man's heart knows no rest.'"

In the flickering light, Yehezkel saw what it was that had belied the scribe's tolerant wisdom since the morning: he insisted on shaving, but without much success, and the short, whitish stubble on his cheeks robbed him of the gentleness of wizened faces, giving him instead the air of an aging outlaw.

Nighttime conversations at sea have something at once languid and adventurous that makes them feel somehow important. Relishing the feeling, Don Sancio plunged back into their theological banter. "Pope Gregory the Great already recognized that our faiths were incompatible, Rabbi. 'If Christianity is Truth, then the Jew is in error, *and vice-versa*,' he wrote. So you see, each is convinced he possesses the Truth. . . Sometimes I think we could *all* be wrong! After all, doesn't Qoheleth say, 'He set eternity in their heart, but so that man cannot find out the work that God has done from the beginning to the end'?"

"I'm not being provocative, Don Sancio," replied Yehezkel, "but I rather agree with Pope Gregory. There is right and there is wrong, and each one of us is free to choose where to stand."

Galatea couldn't sleep and heard every word. But just as she emerged unsteadily from behind the curtain, the vicious cog's starboard side rose, and the abbess slipped, falling straight into Don Sancio's arms. The old man fell backward, entrusting himself to Saint Martin, and rolled away into the darkness.

Galatea stood up when the scribe reappeared, apologizing profusely and introducing herself. Don Sancio insisted the abbess take his place on the cushion. What had started off so clumsily was Galatea's most heroic effort to ignore her nausea since the rolling motion had begun. In simple, elegant Latin, she intervened in their dialogue. "But what if we were all not wrong but *right*? Tell me, my learned doctors, if salvation of the soul were a garden on the far side of a river, and religions were bridges across it, what difference would it make, once in the garden, which bridge we had taken?"

"No, madame, I beg to differ," said Yehezkel gently. "Like most Christians, your heart and mind are set on the garden, but I dare you to deny that we spend our whole life on the bridge we chose!" After a pause, he added, "It's a very narrow bridge, and the river roars below, but the thing is not to be afraid. . . ."

Don Sancio mumbled, "Ahh, bridges, gardens . . . Qoheleth says 'The living know they will die, but the dead know nothing.'"

Those words moved the abbess to ask Yehezkel, "According to Jewish doctrine, what becomes of souls when they're separated from the body? Do they have feelings and memories, or is the time between death and Judgment Day just a big void, like a spiritual . . . sleep?"

"Mmh . . . all I can say, madame, is that Jews don't believe in what you Platonics call 'immortal soul.'"

"We . . . Platonics?" asked Galatea.

"You haven't read Plato? Oh, of course, you are a woman . . ."

"*Yes,* I am a woman and *no,* I haven't read Plato!" she said angrily. "But I know he was a philosopher of the pagans. So for Jews, we Christians are all . . . pagans?"

Yehezkel grimaced, but by now he knew that this nun had no time for mealy-mouthed hypocrisy. "Well, in all honesty . . . yes. I understand that such a view displeases you, but did you ever stop to think of the quantity of statues you're used to bowing to, or of the necromantic ritual in which you claim bread and wine magically turn to flesh and blood, or of the several 'persons' your divinity is made of, one of whom is even the offspring of another. . . Come now, madame, if *you* are not pagans, who will *ever* deserve that epithet?"

Don Sancio laughed. The abbess, not finding words strong enough to express her outrage, emitted a low hiss, her tongue behind her teeth. "Sssss. . . . You have the right to your opinions, Master Ezekiel, but if this joint pilgrimage is to have an end as well as a beginning, this is one opinion I would ask you not to express in my presence *ever* again!"

To Don Sancio, Yehezkel seemed to grow physically smaller. The scribe, like many before and after him, said to himself that there was far more countess than abbess in this stunning lady.

Yehezkel decided he couldn't waste the opportunity that such intimacy with the Doctus represented for his mission and gathered his wits. "The time may not seem well chosen, Don Sancio, but I'd like to pose a question that is very important to me—in fact, that is important to Jews everywhere. . . ."

Scribe and abbess immediately felt how serious the rabbi was.

"Brother Domingo of Guzman wants the Talmud declared heretical with respect to *real* Judaism, which the Church protects. The Spanish monk says that the Talmud is much more recent than the Torah and that it . . . corrupts Jews. The work of our sages is in danger. I have been tasked to look for parchments that will demonstrate the antiquity of the Talmud . . . now if the Templars found any ancient parchments when they dug under the Holy Mount in Jerusalem, *you,* Don Sancio, are the man who would know. . . ."

Galatea hadn't seen such determination in Master Ezekiel's eyes before. Her gaze fell on the blue twine on his thigh. It seemed almost black in the dark, but she could have sworn it shone with an iridescent, cavernous light. Don Sancio was nodding slowly.

"Yes, Rabbi, there *is* a page of Talmud in Paris . . . and it's strange you should ask now, because I dug it out again recently after forty years and once more had to give up on trying to understand it!"

Yehezkel leaned forward. "But if you don't understand what it says, with all due respect, how can you say it *is* a page of Talmud?"

The scribe smiled. "My Aramaic is not Rav Yehiel's, but I've often studied with him, and I recognize the style of a debate between your sages. The parchment is old, of that there is no doubt. It was found while digging the foundations of the Tiberias castle. In my opinion, it is a page of Talmud."

"Can you remember some words of it?" asked Yehezkel.

"My memory made me secretary to the master of the temple, Rabbi. I remember the page as if it was before my eyes, not least because its sense escaped me for so long I must have read it a hundred times!"

"What *did* you understand of it?" asked the rabbi.

"A sage accuses another one of hiding a page from the book of a prophet, 'with the oil, so it would not be hidden,'" recited Don Sancio, still bitterly amused by the strange text. "And claims he hid it because of a prophecy about the Messiah in it, which had already been fulfilled in the life of someone else. . . ."

"Why do you mention no names?" asked Yehezkel. "Who are the sages and the prophet involved?"

"That's the mystery!" said Don Sancio. "The accuser is Acher, 'another one,' the accused is Satmetaz and the prophecy was fulfilled in the life of Mevipaz Zithagam! Do *you* know who these people are? They sound almost Babylonian. . . . Is that an enigma?"

"It looks like one, indeed, though I can easily tell you who Acher was."

"Please do! I've waited forty years for someone to tell me!"

Yehezkel sat up. "Then listen. There was a sage called Elisha ben Abuya who abandoned Judaism and probably became a Christian. In normal circumstances, nobody would ever have mentioned his name again in a debate, let alone written it down if someone else had inadvertently done so. But circumstances were that Elisha, until his apostasy, had been one of the most brilliant minds in extracting Law from the Torah, so a compromise was reached to record his opinions as those of Acher, 'another.'"

"Extraordinary, my friend, simply extraordinary," said the scribe. "Before the monks I am a doctus, but before a rabbi of the Jews I am like an infant learning his aleph-bet!"

"But those strange names, Satmetaz, Mevipaz . . . there seems to be a code involved here; the scribe recording the accusation didn't want a casual reader to grasp *who* this was about."

"Yes, it's what I thought, too," murmured the scribe, disappointed even a rabbi couldn't fathom them.

The hours without breeze finally calmed the waves, and the ship's motion subsided. Without her being aware of it, color returned to Galatea's face. Yehezkel swung slowly back and forth on his hips. Galatea stared at him with curiosity, fascinated by the singsong that was taking over both his body and his speech. The rabbi's dark eyes shone with excitement like when he'd first heard her pronounce the word

"Bereshit." He asked, "Does not the page say from the book of *which* prophet the prophecy was removed?"

"From the book of Missad'techà," answered Don Sancio.

"Lord of the Universe!" cried Yehezkel, waking up the armigers and Gudrun, who peeked sleepily from behind the curtain. "Did you just say *Missad'techà*? How was it spelled?"

"Mmhh . . . let me see. *Mem, yod, samech . . . daled, tav . . . caf*!"

"It is as I hoped . . . we're in luck, Don Sancio! Several codes were in use in the time of the Talmud sages, and I don't know many, but I know the one called At'Bash! All you do is take the twenty-two letters and reverse their order. Instead of the first you write the last, instead of the second the one-before-last and so on, until the last one is actually the first. An *aleph* is a *tav* and a *bet* is a *shin,* so the code is called ATBASH. Simple! As a boy, I tried to encode my own name with it. Can you guess what came out?"

"Missad'techà?" ventured Don Sancio.

"Exactly! So according to Acher, the prophecy came from the book of Ezekiel! Come on, don Sancio, let's apply the Atbash code to Satmetaz and that other weird name!"

They started counting letters, Don Sancio on his fingers, Yehezkel swinging back and forth, eyes closed. Galatea watched him wrap and unwrap the blue twine around his finger. The solution of the mystery, almost certainly the name of some other rabbi from a thousand years before, didn't excite her as it did the two men. To her they looked rather like two hunters discussing the habits of their prey, two overgrown boys playing their favorite game. She felt a fleeting motherly tenderness for the big, bearded unbeliever with the delicate fingers, always chasing a word, a number, a correspondence.

"Satmetaz is Rav Hanina!" cried Yehezkel, beating Don Sancio to it, but not by much. "So according to Elisha, Hanina hid one of Ezekiel's prophecies. As you would say, Don Sancio, extraordinary! But *which* Hanina is he talking about? There was a Hanina ben Dosa, a Hanina bar Hezekiah . . ."

He slapped his thigh. "But of course, donkey that I am! Hanina bar Hezekiah was the man who saved the book of Ezekiel from being excluded from the canon!"

Don Sancio smiled as he removed some tallow from the edge of the candle. "I didn't know Ezekiel risked being left out, but it doesn't surprise me. . . . How did Hanina save it?"

"The Talmud says he locked himself in an upstairs room with I don't know how many barrels of oil for light and didn't come out until he'd reconciled *all* the contradictions between Ezekiel's pronouncements and the Torah. And it seems there were quite a few . . ."

"If that's so, Hanina may have had good reason to hide a prophecy he'd found no way of reconciling. That's it! That's what Elisha means by 'he hid it so it would not be hidden.' It was a prophecy that would have made the entire book apocryphal!"

Yehezkel was ecstatic. "What could the sublime, reckless seer whose name I bear have prophesied?"

"Come on, Rav Yehezkel!" said Don Sancio. "Let's decipher the name of the man in whose life the prophecy was fulfilled. Let's see who this Mevipaz Zithagam was . . ."

It took a little longer than before, and again the rabbi was quicker than the scribe. Galatea saw him grow pale and then abruptly get up and wander off down the deck, mumbling to himself.

A few moments later, Don Sancio's mouth fell open. She heard his incredulous words just as Yehezkel reappeared next to her. "Yeshu ha-Nozri! I can't believe it . . . Acher says the prophecy was fulfilled in the life of . . . Jesus the Nazarene!"

All three fell silent. The boatswain chose the moment to shout, "Midnight, and all is calm!"

CHAPTER 7

HAMAYIM ASHER MI-TAHAT

The Waters Below

ON THE SAME 28TH APRIL 1219, OUTSIDE AUBAIS, NEAR MONTPELLIER

The same day, a rider climbed a dusty white road as the Provence countryside dozed in the afternoon sun. The winding path led to Aubais, a wealthy little feud of the lords of nearby Lunel, built on top of a spur of rock that rose from the vineyards as abruptly as an island from the sea.

Arnald Arifat trotted lazily, swinging in the saddle like someone who knows how to gallop with no reins. Handsome enough to make the saintliest of women recoil from her own thoughts, Aillil's father had long curly hair and a short, curly beard, both as blond as summer. His gray eyes were speckled with golden shards like the plumage of certain buzzards, and a diagonal scar crossed his brow, as if pointing at the gold ring that hung from his left ear.

A distant relative of the count of Foix, Arnald was a free spirit, the kind who is outraged by stupidity and can wrench a laugh from the somberest of men. A man of action—in fact, as his friend Yehezkel ben Yoseph put it, a man incapable of sitting still—he'd been a champion

of the Cathar church for as long as he could remember, from brawl-
ing with Catholic children to defending Cathar bishops in trials by
combat as a teenage knight. On inheriting his father's tiny château in a
round clearing at the center of a forest, Arnald had hosted and become
friends with many troubadours, the traveling minstrels who spread the
teachings of the Cathar church by dressing them up in the language of
"courtly love."

Later, he had become a messenger and spy of the Cathar church and
sailed to Outremer several times on missions for the bishops of Albi
and Carcassonne. Ten years earlier, with war looming, he'd been sent
to carry the Parchment of Circles to safety in the Holy Land. Aillil had
been just three, and stricken in his senses, but he'd not been able to
refuse. Then, from some pilgrims in the autumn that year, he'd heard
of Esmeralda's death in the siege and of his own excommunication. The
news convinced him to stay in Syria, and he'd allayed his misgivings
about the fate of little Aillil by telling himself that Yehezkel, unable to
save Esmeralda's life, had surely brought his only son safely out of the
besieged city.

He spent the following ten years in Outremer, fighting under various lords. But despite many battles against Saracens—which had twice
left him hanging between the living and the dead—he came to appreciate his enemy's noble spirit, disenchanted wisdom, and sensible customs.
After ten years among infidels, he believed that self-righteous clerics
and the drunken fervor of English and German knights had destroyed
what could have been an enlightened and fruitful coexistence. As he
climbed to Aubais, he mused that he'd been away from Outremer for
two months and was already homesick. He couldn't wait to get back to
that land of sand and sky.

In Acre, he sipped Cyprus wine with nobles from all Christendom
and with knights of all fighting orders, seldom hiding his heretical
beliefs *or* his excommunicated status in the discussions on the loss
of Jerusalem and the kingdom's prospects. He'd met heretics of all
three faiths. Once or twice, he had been tempted to ask a bearded old

Jerusalem sage about the Greek words on the Parchment of Circles, but something always held him back.

Then a year earlier the Cathar bishops in Albi heard rumors of a group hidden inside the Order of the Temple who recognized the satanic nature of the Roman church. It was whispered in Acre that this cabal pulled the strings of the Hashasheen, an elusive sect of Shiite fanatics who assassinated clerics and nobility without ever being caught alive.

In those years the loss of Jerusalem made it so difficult for the order to recruit new knights that even excommunicated heretics—mostly Cathars—had been allowed, after confessing their sins to a bishop or an abbot, to become Templars. There were by now tens of *seigneurs faidits* who wore the mantle with the red cross. Aware of this development, the Cathar bishops decided that their trusted agent, Arnald Arifat, would become a warrior monk and try to contact the secret cabal.

The small Templar house in Aubais had the exotic name of Commanderie de Tipheret. Tipheret is the Hebrew name of the sixth of the ten divine emanations in the tree of life of the kabbalists. It can be rendered with "beauty," in the way Plato meant it. The unusual name was the result of liaisons between certain Templar knights and certain kabbalists in Lunel, a town where most Christians were heretics and most Jews were kabbalists. Their ties concerned alchemical questions, but recently Templars, kabbalists, and Cathar perfecti were meeting secretly in the chapel under the fort's tower to discuss opposition to Rome, in just the sort of meetings that kept Friar Domingo of Guzman awake at night.

Through the Templar Master of Provence, it was arranged for Arnald to take his vows there, but before that he galloped home to Montréal to find out what had become of Aillil. When the Hots told him that his son, after vowing to find his father if it cost him his life, had left with the rabbi to find a passage from Venice to Syria, Arnald had first stared incredulously and then burst out laughing.

"My boy has balls, after all! But he missed his last chance to speak with his father before he becomes a monk!" he spluttered, laughing some more.

Then, three days earlier in Narbonne's Church of the Magdalene, he confessed his sins to Abbot Boson, a courageous Cathar bishop under high-placed Catholic disguise, who knew all about Arnald's piratesque missions against the church of Peter—a few of which he had conceived himself.

As it passed under the stone arch, revived by the sound of its own hooves on the cobbles, the horse picked up its pace without asking its rider.

"Me, a Cathar heretic, become a monk?" Arnald was still asking himself. No more sweet old age in the countryside with a loving woman looking after him. No more Jerusalem sunsets talking about God before some wine. Instead, after three days of prayers and fasting, he was about to become a Poor Fellow-Soldier of Christ and of the Temple of Solomon, destined to lose his head, sooner or later, under a short, curved Saracen scimitar. What's more, it was a vow from which one could only be released by the pope himself. Pure folly, that's what it was!

The small Templar fort consisted of a single round tower a hundred paces across and the buildings around the courtyard behind it, protected by a wall that encompassed an austere little church. The tower's barely inclined conical roof was covered with tiles of the color that only the sun of Provence is able to produce. In the square in front of the fortress, the village elders sat on a bench built around a huge lime tree. From inside the flowering lime came the angry buzz of battling bees.

Arnald entered the courtyard, rode to the stables on the far side, and dismounted. After tying up his horse he hesitated, unsure if he should enter the commanderie carrying his sword. Then with a shrug he strode toward the entrance of the tower. As he walked, the horizon swayed to the rhythm of his horse's haunches, as it did after long rides. He reached the base of the stairs and was told to wait while his arrival was announced to the commander of the house.

The knight commanding the Aubais fort was napping in his room on the tower's top floor. Ansiau de Linniéres, a corpulent Burgundian, was a "Western" Templar, one of those for whom it was still Syria, not France, that was "Outremer." He had only been to the Holy Land twice and didn't care much for it. He muttered a few words of circumstance, not even trying to hide that his siesta had been disturbed.

"Ah, so you're the gallant noble who asks to enter the order. . . ."

This was the hundredth anniversary of the order's foundation, so Ansiau knew there were by now several versions of the Templar Rule. Arnald wasn't the first knight to come to Aubais from Syria, take his vows in the chapel, and sail right back to Acre. Ansiau guessed they must be excommunicated knights. For him, it was nothing if not one more example of Christendom's decline after the loss of Jerusalem.

Arnald introduced the zealous persona he had agreed with Boson to present to Templar officials. "Yes, Monsieur, I've been in Syria for ten years and have seen the infidels pile manure on the altars of the Holy Sepulchre. I've had enough and decided to get away from the feckless nobles and join the only knights still fighting the infidels for our Lord Jesus Christ."

Ansiau listened like someone following a beloved melody, then chimed in. "Everyone knows the kingdom is debauched! They dress like infidels, speak their tongue, walk around with little black boys fanning them and rubbing smelly ointments on their feet. They even smoke that evil stuff. I tell you, those 'Christians' in Syria—God is my witness!—get on better with the heathens than with pilgrims from their own lands! How can military defeats surprise us when decadence is everywhere?"

A young page knocked, came in, and announced the *praeceptor* had arrived. The news wiped any residual sleep from Ansiau's eyes. Every Templar province had "visitors," fearsome inspectors nominated by the master of the province. One of them had just arrived at the fort.

Ansiau feigned nonchalance, but Arnald felt the burly Frenchman grow tense. "I would gladly have spoken some more with you, Arifat, but I've official business to attend to. Have someone show you your cell, and when you've settled in, go and see the chaplain. He'll explain everything about the initiation rite."

Arnald quickly deposed his few belongings in the cell he was shown and hurried back to the tower to catch a glimpse of the *praeceptor*. The door to the commander's room was ajar. He'd been right! No wonder the commander was worried: this time the visitor was no less than Guillem de Montrodon in person, the master of Aragon and Provence! Arnald had only met him once, in Acre, but was aware of his reputation. While the masters of the orders spent their time fighting in Outremer (all three were outside Damietta), Guillem was the temple's mediator between the pope and young Emperor Fredrick, much like an abbot between two quarrelsome monks. What on earth was such an important man doing in this godforsaken tower, halfway between a fortress and a farm?

"If I'm going to be a Templar with a secret mission," thought Arnald, "knowing this man will be an asset." He decided to inadvertently bump into Montrodon as he emerged from Ansiau's room. The master of Provence strode toward him instead, catching him completely by surprise, and grabbed his forearm in the shake that knights in Outremer had learned from Saracens.

"Arnald Arifat! Happy to see you, and overjoyed that you've chosen to become a brother," boomed Guillem. "When I saw your name in the list of novices, I decided to initiate you myself!"

"I . . . I am humbled that you even remember who I am, Master, and will be honored to take my vows before you," replied Arnald, nonplussed.

"I also have some questions for you about your time in Syria, *mon brave seigneur,* but that can wait until after the ceremony," added de Montrodon.

"No, no, tell me what you want to know, and I'll answer you right away," said Arnald.

The master smiled. "Come now, man, don't be naive. I'll question you *after* your vows because then, hiding something from your superior will be a mortal sin."

The master of Aragon and Provence turned on his heel and left Arnald standing on the top landing.

Arnald found the next three days a greater torment than the first week after a wound in battle. Like all fighting men around thirty, he'd looked forward to the opportunity to meditate, perhaps even try to pray, but by the first night, he recalled why he preferred action to contemplation: because the latter invariably drove his thoughts to dark, melancholy considerations. From that moment, he became restless.

At long last, before sunset on the third day, a handful of brothers met for the ceremony in the chapel below the tower. The crypt was known as the Chamber of the Bronze Serpent since the time, thirty years earlier, when Salah ad-Din had gifted to Master Roncelin the famous biblical relic that cured the Israelites in the desert, and it had spent a night there on its way to the Paris temple.

The round little hall, lit by dozens of candles, was brighter than the dying Provence day outside. The neophyte was welcomed by a small crowd of knights in white and the chaplain, the only black habit. The buzz quieted as Arnald knelt before the commander, his hands joined on his chest.

"I, Arnald Arifat de Montréal, humbly implore you in the name of God and our Holy Lady to accept me into your company, and let me partake of the benefits of the house!"

"Beloved brother, perhaps you ask because you only see the outer trappings of the order: beautiful horses, armor, cloaks, so you think you will be happy with us. But you don't know that harsh rules prevail on the inside. Those of noble birth, like you, have no idea how hard servitude can be . . ."

The commander coughed and then droned on. "You will never again do as you please: if you wish to be on one side of the sea, you'll be dispatched to the other. If you go to sleep you'll be woken up, and if by chance you would like to be on watch, you'll be told to go rest."

It was clear from Ansiau's tone that it was years since he'd felt those sacrifices would suffice to reconquer Christ's sepulchre, but he wouldn't have dreamed of changing even an "atque" in the ritual.

"*And* you'll have to accept the harshest reprimands with humility. Consider well, sweet brother, if you'll be able to bear all these hardships. . . ."

"Yes, my lord," answered Arnald. "I will bear them all, God willing."

There were more ritual questions, but thanks to his confession to the abbot he was not asked if he was excommunicated, and he answered them all truthfully. The commander made him swear to God and to the Virgin Mary that he would never leave the order, neither for a softer one nor for a stricter one, and that for the remaining days of his life he would strive to reconquer the Holy City of Jerusalem.

Then Arnald waited outside the chapel door as prescribed by the ritual. His life was about to change. "How will I care for a thirteen-year-old unable to fend for himself?" he thought. Then, anguished, "And how will I survive without *women*?"

He felt like a teenager again, his thoughts strangely jumbled and his breath a bit short. A hand on his shoulder told him the time had come. Arnald walked to the altar and knelt down again, but this time it was de Montrodon who solemnly threw a Templar mantle on his shoulders, gestured for him to stand, and kissed him the kiss of vassalage on the mouth. He was a knight of the temple!

As was the custom in Western commanderies, the brothers sang the 133rd Psalm in French. Arnald joined them, finding it even more moving than in Latin.

> *Oh, qu'il est bon, qu'il est doux*
> *Pour des frères de se trouver réunis ensemble!*
> *C'est comme l'huile précieuse, repandue sur la tête*

Qui coule sur la barbe, sur la barbe d'Aaron,
Qui coule jusqu'au bord de ses vêtements.

Despite the white cloak with the red cross, he wasn't quite like the other monks yet, his blond mane contrasting with his new brothers' shaved heads. But Arnald, as he sang, wasn't aware of it.

The next morning, de Montrodon summoned him to the tower. Skipping all monkish rhetoric, the master of Provence came right to the point.

"What made you stay and fight for ten years? You don't look like a knight in search of martyrdom. If you were, you would have joined an order much sooner. Why become a Templar *now*, Arnald?"

Arnald expected this question from his superiors and had prepared a sentimental response. "It's Jerusalem, Master. The Holy City cast a spell on me. Christian knights can only visit as unarmed pilgrims, but I managed to stay with some Saracens for months at a time."

De Montrodon was listening with a puzzled look on his face.

"You see, Master," went on Arnald, "After a while, it's no longer the holy places or even the promise of salvation that matter. It's the city herself, her light, her alleys. . . ."

"And how does that answer my question, Brother Arnald?"

"I want Jerusalem to be Christian again! I want thirty years of humiliations of Christians there to end! Only the Templars really want that to happen, so if I'm going to fight anyway I decided to do it in the only way that will make a difference."

"Mmph!" snorted de Montrodon, a cloud of cynicism casting a shadow on the smile in his eyes. "Nice try, Arifat. With your trouba-dour background, it could have worked, but I've no time for games. The temple knows all about your past role as an agent of the Cathar church. More to the point, we know that before Innocent's war started, you took the Parchment of Circles to the Holy Land!"

Arnald was caught off balance. *This* was why de Montrodon was here, not because he knew him from Syria! But the old man to whom he'd given the parchment was a chaplain of the temple! The safety of the order was what the Cathar bishops sought for the parchment, so why did they not have it? What had the chaplain done with it? Or had the Templars lost it?

"Lost your tongue, Arnald? You know Cathars have nothing to fear from the temple."

Arnald was thinking as fast as he could. This was more than he or Boson had anticipated. The best he could do at this point was try to find out what the Templars knew. "What do you want to know about the parchment?" he asked, feigning coolness and failing miserably.

"First, what was on it, and second, whom you gave it to," said de Montrodon drily.

"Well, I saw it ten years ago, as you know, and my Greek is nothing special. I remember nine phrases or single words, symmetrically placed on two circles so that they formed a cross: four on the outer circle, four on the inner circle, and one in the center. . . ."

"But surely your bishops, your superiors, knew enough Greek to read the text. Don't tell me you were forbidden to know what it said."

"No, no! That would be the Catholic way!" exclaimed Arnald, piqued. "They did tell me; I just don't remember that much. You know, theological formulac don't have that strong an appeal for me. . . ."

De Montrodon threw off his mask of cordiality. "You're a monk now, Brother Arnald. I could order you to stay in this Godforsaken post for the rest of your days."

Arnald shook his head glibly, appalled at the prospect. "All right, all right. I don't remember everything, but the five Greek phrases across, from left to right, were 'Heart of the Messiah' on the outer circle, 'Soul' on the inner one, 'The Heavens' in the center, 'the Oil' on the right side of the inner circle, and 'Sacrifice of the Heart' on the right side of the outer one. The words on the vertical arm of the cross included 'My Spirit' and at the bottom, on the outer circle, were the words 'In Jerusalem.' There, that's really all I remember!"

De Montrodon was nodding slowly. Then he asked, "And who has it now?"

"That's what I don't understand! We thought *you* had it!"

De Montrodon smiled an "I knew it" smile. "I see. Well, Brother Arnald, the man to whom you gave the Parchment is a crafty old bastard indeed. The trouble is he had the last Grand Master's ear for a long time. But Guillaune de Chartres, as you know, died at Damietta last August and the new master, Pedro de Montaigu, is unlikely to fall for the old man's fables."

The master got up tiredly. "I assume your real reason for entering the order is that your Cathar bishops want a spy in our ranks. We can handle that, Brother Arnald; we'll keep an eye on you. Don't worry your head about it. Start training to fight by the Rule, and when the commander says you're ready, go back to Acre and present yourself to the new Grand Master . . . if you can find him."

De Montrodon walked away, leaving Arnald wondering if in those "old man's fables," he had just come across the first trace of the secret cabal his bishops were looking for.

✠   ✠   ✠   ✠

Hidden behind the scaffolding for the construction of the bishop's new palace, the Church of the Magdalene in Narbonne was a modest affair, all that was left of the monastery behind the cathedral of which Boson would be the last abbot, since the bishop's plans envisioned new buildings all the way to the end of the Rue Droite.

For ten years, Narbonne's bishops had once more been elected by the pope and not by the Count of Toulouse. There was no more tolerance for perfecti, and Cathars were chased out of shops like bandits. Abbot Boson led a dangerous life and knew it. He gave refuge to perfecti on the run from Domingo's friars and passed messages between his harried hosts, supporting what troubador Raymond Jordan had named la Resistance.

The sacristy was in an old Merovingian tower behind the church.

In his study on the third and last floor, the abbot was poring over a manuscript on his scriptorium, a carved wooden pulpit on top of which, instead of standing and preaching, one sits and writes. He heard noises in the yard, followed by heavy steps on the stairs. His heart froze in sudden premonition, and he entrusted his soul to God.

The Templar entered without knocking and went to stand in front of the window, his back to the scriptorium. His right hand swept his cloak back over the left shoulder, exposing the hilt of his sword.

Robert de Bois-Guilbert, thickset and not very tall, was in his late forties. His face, even from thirty paces, was that of an English noble of Norman descent, with the smile of a man who cannot be surprised by anything, be it even the trumpets of Judgment Day. In this he was like his father, afraid of nothing on earth or in Heaven. In the glory days of Coeur-de-Lion, Brian de Bois-Guilbert had been the bravest Templar fighting for the king. As well as fighting skills and a kind of atheist bravado, Robert had inherited all four vices sadly associated with Templars: conceit, arrogance, cruelty, and lewdness.

Just as Boson was feeling relief at the white cloak—after all, a Templar knight would never be doing the bidding of Domingo's friars—the contempt in Bois-Guilbert's voice struck him like a whip. "Come down from there, Boson! I don't like having to look up when I talk to Cathar scum!"

Robert, a hugely vain *tombeur de femmes,* was nearly bald and hid the fact by wearing a leather cap, but with no chainmail coff under it. He pulled it off as he waited for Boson to descend the spiral staircase and then suddenly struck him a backhanded slap so strong it sent the old cleric flying across the floorboards. "I know everything about you, you heretical worm!" he said, calmly slipping off the only glove he was wearing as he watched the black habit struggling to get up. "I know you host Cathar bishops, and you hide forbidden marriages from the church. I even know of your Jewish friends! What I don't know is what that serpent Arifat was doing here yesterday. But you're going to tell me that, aren't you, Boson?"

The Templar lifted the abbot with his right arm, keeping him at a distance, as if disgusted by the bad smell. He curled his nose, as if suffering from an attack of bad digestion.

"But . . . but you're a Templar," murmured Boson weakly.

"Yes, but not one of those *you*'re used to speaking with! My loyalty is to the pope and to the Holy Trinity, not to the masters of a corrupted order!"

"Good God, a zealous Templar," thought Boson. "My hour has come . . ."

"There is . . . there is nothing to tell about Arifat," he stammered. "He came to confess himself because he has decided to join your order . . ."

"Pfui! Another rotten apple. Soon there will be more heretics than Christians in the temple!"

Robert smiled and then grabbed the collar of Boson's habit with both hands and lifted him a foot off the floor. His face was distorted into a mask of hate. The mouth in it hissed, "He confessed to *you,* scum, because he couldn't tell a *real* bishop the things he told you, which you will now repeat to me, including any details your hobbled mind may find irrelevant."

He dropped the black habit. He had known that torturing the old man wouldn't be of any use, so he'd told his partner—the Teutonic knight with whom he carried out Father Domingo's wishes—to grab two urchins in the street below before he came into the sacristy. At Robert's low whistle, the German dragged them up the stairs. When Boson saw Frutolf enter the study, he blanched.

The Teuton was huge, nearly seven feet tall, his head so incredibly square it seemed drawn with a ruler. Fleshy lips made his expression one of petulance on the verge of violence. In a single hand he clutched, just below the shoulders, the skinny arms of two children, no more than six or seven years old. He dragged them into the room as Robert unnecessarily revealed his intentions to the abbot.

"Listen, scum. If you don't repeat Arifat's confession word for word to me, these innocents will die before your eyes, their throats slit like lambs, and their blood will stain your soul in eternity"—he paused—"together with all your other sins, of course."

Frutolf pulled a dagger from his waist with his free hand and placed the point against the neck of a child, so terrified it wasn't even whimpering.

"Then we'll put the bodies in a sack and throw them in a Jew's house—eh, Frutolf? What do you say?" joked the Templar. The German laughed, but without enthusiasm.

Boson gathered his wits and addressed Robert in a low voice. "Do I have your word of honor that if I tell you everything you will let the children go?"

"Oohh, look at the heretic's beautiful soul! Did you hear, Frutolf? He doesn't want the innocent to suffer in his place. So be it! You have my word."

The murmur of the abbot relating Arnald's confession was only broken by the occasional sob of a child. He hesitated before mentioning the Parchment of Circles but went on as soon as Frutolf's blade had drawn a trickle of blood from the smaller child's neck. Frutolf had to put the dagger back in its sheath to stifle the child's cries with his free hand.

As soon as he'd mentioned the Parchment, Boson knew they'd have to kill him, so that none would find out a Templar knew where the Holy Texts were taken. As he related the many occasions in which Arnald had sinned in Outremer, the abbot prayed ceaselessly, asking God to save not his soul, but the lives of the children and Arnald's.

When Robert was convinced—at the price of some more innocent blood—that the old man really didn't know in which commanderie Arnald's initiation was to take place, he went back to the window and gazed out over the roofs of Narbonne.

"I decided not to have Frutolf follow the *seigneur faidit,* despite knowing that I risked losing his tracks, and now it turns out I did the right thing, as always! Instead of shaking us off, the stupid Cathar has gone and joined the temple! Now finding him again will be child's play! And what I learned from this heretic abbot is sure to please my mentor. . . ." He turned around with a sticky smile and gestured for the abbot to join him. When Boson stood next to him, he whispered, "And now, *mon brave Boson,* you'll save the lives of the infants once again by jumping from this window. I've heard that taking one's life is a very respected religious sacrament, among perfecti. . . ."

"But you gave me your word that if I told you everything . . ."

"I gave you my word I would let the children go, and I will! I never said what I would do with *you.* . . . Jump from this window *now,* or you'll see the little ones die first and then be dealt with yourself!"

The old man mumbled a prayer, climbed awkwardly over the sill and stepped into the void.

The Templar's silence made him seem moved, but the German knight's guttural laugh behind him ruined the effect he had sought.

✡ ✠ ✡ ✠

Twelve years earlier, Domingo had founded a convent for converted ex-Cathar women near the village of Prouilhe, down the hill from Fanjeaux on the way to Montréal. Endless demands on his time pushed the founder of the Order of Preachers from one realm to the next, but his advancing sickness convinced him not to travel during Lent, and he only left Guadalajara after Easter. Robert knew he could find his mentor in Prouilhe from the middle of April until early May, when Domingo would press on to Paris.

Prouilhe was a day's ride from Narbonne, a distance Bois-Guilbert hadn't ridden in years. He forced Frutolf's horse to a pace that was too slow for both beasts, making the Teuton seethe in silence. Robert thought back to the night hunts with his father in Berkshire, galloping through the forest, torches suddenly splashing the onrushing trees with red and yellow. His father, Brian de Bois-Guilbert, a minor member of the royal household, left his mother when Robert was a child to join the temple and spent years in Outremer trying to climb the order's hierarchy, chasing a dream of becoming master. When Robert was fifteen, he died in a stupid joust in England, fighting to prove the guilt of a Jewish sorceress. Robert never forgave his father *or* the order, and later joined the temple himself to bring about its ruin from within, the only revenge for his mother he found fitting.

His dark spleen made him rule out the existence of any salvation for the scum of humanity, which to him meant all of it except perhaps a man in a thousand. Then he'd met Domingo, and the monk's spiritual guidance miraculously undermined his cynicism. Though he would have denied it, Robert loved his Spanish mentor like a father and would have done anything he asked. Following Domingo's cunning instructions, he befriended the powerful in the order, intimidated the weak, and gathered information on everyone, none excepted.

The two riders sighted Fanjeaux two hours before sunset. They were worn out, and a cold breeze slipped through their clothes. They slowed the horses and took the path to the convent of the Predicatores. The place was deserted, as if abandoned.

Open doors slammed in the wind, animals wandered around the buildings, and a wheelbarrow full of hay sat in the middle of the yard. The knights dismounted and split up to reconnoiter. In a clear sign that their experience came from Outremer, not from jousting tournaments, they moved around the convent as if expecting an ambush behind every well-trimmed hedge.

The first nun they nearly frightened to death solved the riddle. Father Domingo had not been well on the trip from Castille and started work again too hard and too soon. An hour earlier, while hearing a sister's confession, he suddenly fainted. The nuns, every one a soul rescued from heresy, dropped everything and rushed to the founder's bedside.

For the hundredth time—the Teuton was no longer counting—Robert left Frutolf outside as he met someone important. Frutolf knew Domingo had the pope's ear, and that since word spread of his illness he was sure to be sainted the minute he left this vale of tears. Not meeting him was the latest humiliation Frutolf suffered since he'd been assigned to do the Templar's bidding.

Robert entered the founder's room. Floor and shelves were full of codices, and there were parchments everywhere. Domingo lay on a cot in the corner, and two women, one a nun, the other a local peasant, both young and pretty, hovered over him. Domingo saw the knowing smile on Robert's lips and pushed the girls away and then greeted him in a voice so weak the Templar almost didn't recognize it.

"Christ's peace be with you, Brother Roberto. Yes, despite my best efforts, I cannot help preferring to spend my time with young women than with old ones. . . ." The monk smiled as he pulled himself up on his pillows. "But these are things for my confessor, not for you, Roberto. And the time for adding up my vices and virtues has not come yet. I still have too many things to do."

Honorius, the new pope who had replaced Innocent three years earlier, had been showering donations on his Predicatores, and everything he'd planned for ten years started happening at a frightening pace. Ironically, in the same three years, his illness became more severe.

He sat up in bed as a nun rushed to rearrange the pillows behind his back. He was recovering from the lastest bout of fever, and the visit by his protégé inside the temple helped revive him. Robert bent over his teacher. Domingo kissed him on the cheeks and drew a sign of the cross on his forehead.

"Reverend Father," said Robert, "do you remember that seigneur faidit in Outremer you asked me to not lose sight of, some years ago?"

"Certainly. Arnald Arifat. The memory of the time I learned his name still plagues me."

Domingo thought of the morning after the disputatio with the rabbi, when he convinced Pons to tell him what the Jew had been doing in the Hots' kitchen. If that Master Ezekiel was looking after the child of a heretic, the man couldn't be any old Cathar. Now Roberto was bringing him the fruit of the seed he'd planted. Robert eagerly announced that Abbot Boson made some interesting revelations.

Domingo nodded. "Abbot Boson," he murmured, "there's a heretic of moral stature. I admire him more than most of *our* bishops. I've talked philosophy with Boson; he is an adversary worthy of respect."

Robert looked embarrassed, but it lasted a mere instant, and he went on to relate of Arifat's confession. Domingo couldn't help wondering how Roberto obtained the information, but then, eager to know the movements of a major Cathar spy, he told himself it was all for the best of causes. He remained calm until Robert pronounced the words "Parchment of Circles" and then threw off his covers, jumped out of bed, and paced the room excitedly with a nun in chase, entreating him to lie down again.

"At last . . . at long last! I knew God wanted us to find it!" he kept repeating as the sister grabbed his arm and dragged him back to bed.

"Please leave us now, Sister. We have vital matters to discuss."

Suddenly, his teacher's voice was as Robert remembered it, at once suave and authoritative. When the nun exited, Domingo sat him down by the window and pulled up a small stool for himself.

"You must know that rumors about that parchment have circulated for three centuries. Some in Rome say it is truly ancient. According to one monk in Bologna, the circles on it were drawn by none other than Saint John the Evangelist! ¿Entiendes, Roberto?"

The Castillan was smiling the famous smile that female heretics couldn't resist, blue eyes sparkling. He was in his element now, the quest for the parchment combining faith, politics, and books in a mix that was more irresistible to him than the smile of a pretty girl.

"Really, Roberto—*verdad!*—I couldn't be happier with your work. That relic is a precious possession of the Synagogue of Satan. Even if it isn't Saint John's work, the church considers it a genuine ancient text. Every pope has wanted to see it for centuries, and now you, Brother Bois-Guilbert, have discovered where it is!"

"Your words are more than adequate reward for my efforts. But tell me, is it known what the parchment actually *says?*"

Domingo hesitated. "There are two circles, it seems, one inside the other, and writing in Greek on them, though some say it is in Hebrew." The founder allowed himself a confidence. "You know, the vision of the Christian faith propagating itself in ever-growing circles has always intimately exalted me. . . And then of course there is the matter of the circular maps of Jerusalem."

"What do you mean, Father?"

"Circular maps of the Holy City started appearing a hundred years ago, just when the Templar knights started digging in Solomon's Stables. Many thought the monks found a copy of the Parchment of Circles. Why would the Parchment spawn dozens of circular maps of Jerusalem?"

"Because it was itself a map?" smiled Robert.

"Exactly! And why does one draw a map, if not to find something hidden? Do you understand now why everybody is looking for that parchment? *It leads to something that was hidden in the time of our Lord Jesus Christ!*"

Friar Domingo's eyes gave out blue flashes that could have been the light of the Holy Spirit or the sign of a secret madness. He looked like his collapse of an hour earlier had never happened.

Robert sat silently by the window, considering the enormity of the quest's prize as Domingo went to open the door and summon one of the sisters. Then he turned to his disciple.

"Go to Syria, Roberto. Whatever the excuse, have them send you to Outremer, and start looking for that parchment! Send your reports only by trusted messengers, no letters! Find that parchment; I don't care how, just find it! Use whatever means you have to, but wrench it from Satan's grasp. ¡Todo modo es bueno para buscar la voluntad divina!" They embraced. "May the Lord protect you and grant you success and a happy return among us!"

After the Templar left, Domingo stood at the window watching the sun set behind the crest of Fanjeaux's hill and reflecting on what the map led to, something he could *never* tell Roberto, even if he should find it and deliver it.

Three years earlier Cencio Savelli emerged pope from the conclave in Viterbo with the name Honorius III and had been shown all the church's secrets. At once, he summoned Domingo to share the disastrous news of the Confession. Honorius learned that the Templars had used the Parchment of Circles as a map and found a document with which they had been blackmailing the church since the Council of Troyes in 1128.

"What 'document' could *possibly* give them such unearthly power?" Domingo had asked, incredulous.

"The confession by the thieves who stole the body from the tomb," the pope had answered grimly.

CHAPTER 8

SHAMAYIM

The Heavens

ABOARD THE *FALCUS*, SOUTH OF THE PELOPONNESUS, 4TH MAY 1219

The *Falcus* glided over small, orderly waves. After a brief stop in Corfu she sailed in sight of the coast past Modone and was now south of the Peloponnesus. Friar Vassayl set an eastern course to Rhodes that would take them past the small island of Antikythera, leaving on starboard the big island of Crete, renamed Candia by the Venetians. On her port beam could just be seen the arid, bony middle one of the three fingers that Greece stretches lustily toward Africa since time began.

Four days earlier they had docked in Corfu, where the cook loaded water and victuals while Don Sancio met the Captain of the Levant to review the temple's commercial rights and exemptions in Candia and Rhodes. The stopover was for one night only, and pilgrims were not allowed off the cog.

That noon was the first chance Aillil had to accompany his mentor on the quarterdeck. His senses were heightened by ten days of sun, wind, and spray. Normally people grew bored trying to follow his speech, but that morning the boy's enthusiasm charmed sailors and knights; no one minded the effort needed to understand his happy grunts. Iñigo Sanchez was engaging him in some mock fighting moves across the balcony. When he stopped, Aillil stared at him, mouth agape.

"Is it . . . is it dangerous to be a Templar?"

"Yes, young man, it is. We're always the first into battle, and we are *never* taken prisoner. The infidels chop our heads off!"

Aillil swallowed. "Why . . . why did you become a Templar, then?"

"You mean why didn't I join the Hospitalliers? Puah!" Iñigo spat on the deck and burst out laughing.

Aillil faced him, suddenly serious. "Have you killed many infidels, sir?"

Sanchez returned the serious gaze, nodding. "You know, my boy, sometimes I think they'll all come back one day and ask me to return the limbs I chopped off, or the brains I spilled . . ."

A shiver ran down Aillil's back as the breeze played with his blond hair. His eyes searched out the rabbi's black sarbel. He saw Yehezkel standing at the chart table, beard ruffled by the wind.

Aillil sniffed the air like some male forest animal and let out a long, high-pitched howl of joy. The rabbi, used to his ward's lunar expressions, went on surveying mast, sail, shrouds, and halyards. After checking the rigging for the tenth time, his gaze fell on the nuns' niche again.

During the day, for half a watch and in groups of thirty at a time, the pilgrims in the hold were allowed on deck, where they wandered aimlessly, inebriated by the sunlight and fresh air. Few pilgrims knew Latin, and almost none could read, so most fought the tedium of the high seas by conversing with those who spoke their tongue. Others passed the time playing dice, which sparked brawls, especially between pilgrims of different lands. Galatea and Yehezkel occasionally commented on some amusing sights, like a woman putting her hands over her child's ears when the sailors substituted scurrilous verses for the prayers they were supposed to chant with every maneuver.

For an hour Galatea and Gudrun had been subjected to the stentorian voice of an English pilgrim just outside their tent, relating unbelievable stories in a Latin that made the abbess cringe. The man's eyes had crossed Galatea's for an instant earlier in the day, and he was searching his memory for marvels, miracles, and wonders he'd heard of, anything that might draw the stunning nun out from behind that curtain.

Four or five pilgrims sat at his feet listening to his tales with a mixture of delight and horror, when the Englishman saw Yehezkel coming toward them. The presence on board of a Jew was often the preferred topic of such gatherings—nothing new, for Yehezkel—with most pilgrims finding it a bad omen. But the Englishman had watched the Jew speaking at length, and intimately, with the Italian nun, and before Yehezkel could ask Rustico to tell the abbess he was there, he interrupted his vane prattling to introduce himself to the rabbi. Yehezkel heard the nuns fidget behind the curtain, looked around for escape routes, and then resigned himself to the fact that the pilgrim—who insulted the Latin tongue more than the Jews who refused to speak it—had cornered him, at least for a time.

Minutes later the nuns emerged from their lair, and for the bored men on deck it was as if the sun just broke through after a week of clouds. To Yehezkel's dismay, they stopped by the English pilgrim, who now had a dozen listeners and was in seventh heaven, booming like a monk preaching holy war. They heard how the bishop of Saint Alban in person pinned the red cross to his shoulder, and how he'd sworn to complete his pilgrimage on the sacred relic of Saint Peter. What, they hadn't heard of the most potent relic in all of England? Well, it was a small silver crucifix, and inside it were iron filings from the chains that shackled the Apostle Peter!

When she stood close to them, Galatea's nose curled at the sharp odor wafting from the pilgrims. Yehezkel smiled. The familiarity of Christians with dirt—and its companion, stink—was no longer a source of wonder and disgust for him as it had been when he'd first arrived from Egypt. He was happy to see the abbess as bothered as a civilized person should be by the smell on deck, which was growing more intense. Pilgrims were starting to feel hot under their cloaks as the sun's brightness grew behind thinning clouds; there was no escaping the reek that came from three hundred unwashed, sweating bodies confined on a floating wooden prison in the middle of the sea.

Yehezkel had already reached the same conclusion as the crew: the pleasant westerly breeze that had blown for two days was dying. After a while Galatea, bored by the pilgrim's tales, retired to her open-air cabin on her own, since talking philosophy with a Jew behind a curtain all day was out of the question. Gudrun instead stayed in the Englishman's ample rhetorical embrace. Yehezkel smiled, relieved, and made off aft with Aillil hopping and skipping in circles around him.

The *Falcus* entered the Aegean on a sweet night, fragrant with perfumes floating on the residual breath of breeze, as befitted the waters from which Aphrodite emerged. That evening, during the pater noster, the black silhouette of Kythera—the island Venetians call Cerigo—stood out against the sunset like the tip of a sword on the coals of Vulcan's forge. The spectacular end to the tenth day of the passage raised the pilgrims' spirits, and the calm seas favored sleep for the mass of landlubbers, who had by now more or less adapted to life at sea.

The steadiness of the cog put the abbess in the best mood she'd been in since they left Venice, so that her smile was the most sought-after commodity on board. Yehezkel took advantage of it, convincing her to climb to the quarterdeck to enjoy the starry night away from the effluvium on deck.

"I must confess that I have a problem with heights!"

"Oh, don't worry! Should you fall as you climb the ladder to the castle, I'll be right below you!"

The abbess didn't show the relief he expected. If Galatea finally found the courage to climb on the quarterdeck with the ship's leaders, it was only because the near-total darkness prevented her from seeing the deck below.

Despite the late hour, six people were on the balcony: Friar Vassayl and his pilot, Don Sancio, Galatea, Yehezkel, and Piero Vidoso, the cog's Venetian consul.* For an hour, stars and conversation sparkled as they only do on certain nights, blessedly free from mists and bad thoughts. The abbess's presence made the men solicitous and verbose. But the balcony's height above the deck added a greenish tinge to her pallor, and she always seemed on the point of losing interest. She was listening to Yehezkel speaking with Arnulf in a low voice about the stars.

"Of course, the constellation rising above the prow is the one you call Orion." Yehezkel moved to the middle of the balcony and gestured for some attention from his audience. "My honorable friends, my revered Lady. Listen, if you will, to what our Talmud has to say about the constellation of Orion. Shemhazai and Aza'el are the only two names our sages give us of the rebel angels who disobeyed the Creator. They came down to earth, took wives, and generated the giants of Scripture. Aza'el was also the inventor of ornaments and perfumes women use to seduce men. After a time Shemhazai repented and hung himself upside down in the southern sky. For Jews, *he* is the constellation the Greeks named Orion." Yehezkel paused before his punchline. "Aza'el, instead, never repented, and to this day, he pushes women to be the ruin of men!"

Everyone laughed heartily. Yehezkel obtained silence and went on. "Only one virgin resisted the wicked angels' wiles and remained chaste. Her name was Istahar." He smiled. "When they made their lewd propositions, she said, 'All right, but first lend me your wings.' As soon as she had them, she flew to Heaven"—Yehezkel, amid loud laughter, flapped his elbows across the balcony in an impression of a flying virgin—"and hid behind the divine Throne. God transformed her into the constellation you call the Virgin." Yehezkel paused for effect again. "The angels, deprived of their wings, had to wait for our father Jacob to dream his ladder, so they could go home!"

The abbess loved the explanation of the traffic of angels up and

---

*A consul was appointed to keep order among the pilgrims and enforce ship rules.

down Jacob's ladder. Her crystalline laugh rung out in the night, to everyone's delight.

A little later, Yehezkel and the pilot were discussing a reddish star low on the horizon which Arnulf called *Arcturus*. The rabbi sunk his hand inside his sarbel, excited as a boy, and brought out a small, heavy-looking pouch. At long last he would use the *astrolabium** forged for him in his Narbonne laboratory by the nephew of the ibn-Tibbons!

Yehezkel ben Yoseph had always loved maps—of cities, of desert trails, or of the sky at night—and could travel inside them with the excitement that others only experienced in the real places they represented. Winding rivers, jagged coastlines, the haphazard stretch of constellations held an irresistible fascination for him. And what he always found most intriguing about maps were place names. Kabbalah taught him that when playing with names, men stumble on mysterious truths. Yehezkel knew there were no coincidences in that game.

As a child, he liked giving things his own secret names. Instead of asking an adult what a thing was called, he would rename it in his mind with a secret name. He'd often asked himself as an adult if playing that game into adolescence would have resulted in his inventing a grammar for his private vocabulary and developing a whole secret language in which he would only have spoken to himself.

A visceral attachment to words over images—in memories, in abstractions, even in emotions—was the salient characteristic of Yehezkel's mind. He was, in effect, a natural kabbalist. His memory was exceptional but almost never relied on images. He remembered numbers and names effortlessly but confused faces in sometimes embarrassing ways. He talked to himself, even debated himself, and invented new words if he couldn't find one, in any of the six languages he spoke, that expressed what he meant.

---

*Now called astrolabe, an inclinometer used to determine the latitude at sea by measuring the sun's noon altitude

When he'd started learning Torah, he'd been struck by how living creatures received their names. The Creator brought them before Adam one by one, "to see what he would call them," and whatever name Adam chose for them, that would be their name. The Hebrew words *hu shemò* do mean "that is its name," but because of the lack of a present tense in the Hebrew verb "to be," they also mean "the animal *is* its name," in the sense that the name Adam chose contained the essence, the secret nature, of that animal. The similarity with his childhood game flattered him. After all those years, he still felt a boyish complicity with Adam, as if they were old nursery mates.

The predictability of the paths that stars followed through the heavens was another thing he found divine. His love of the night sky was born on the roof of his teacher's house in Fustat. Moshe ben Maimon, the greatest Jewish thinker in generations, treated Yehezkel, the orphan of a friend from his childhood in Cordoba, like a grandson. When Yehezkel declared his love of astronomy, Maimonides—as his mentor was known to Latins—taught him the rules of the heavens, the names of stars, and the celestial alignments he should use to find them. After a year of those lessons, Yehezkel became so expert that one night his teacher—not a man generous with compliments—told him that not even a Persian Gulf pilot could recognize more stars. That night, the boy felt as if he were the only possessor of the keys to the heavens.

Yehezkel extracted the astrolabium from its soft pouch and handed it to Arnulf. The pilot couldn't read the Hebrew names or numbers on the instrument but appreciated the superb workmanship, the precision of the 360 graduations, the soft movement of bronze on bronze, and the simplicity of the curled pointers indicating the positions of major stars. He expressed admiration for the man who forged the precious object.

Don Sancio stretched his hand out impatiently. "Qoheleth says, 'What do people gain from all their labors at which they toil under the sun?' You, rabbi, toil under the stars, but the result is the same. I have little time for strange contraptions that measure God's universe as if it were ours, and not his . . ."

Galatea intervened with mock seriousness. "I am just a poor lagoon abbess, Don Sancio, but if that instrument helps sailors find their way home again, I feel sure God himself inspired its conception."

"Well said, madame!" exclaimed Friar Vassayl.

Arnulf began explaining to Yehezkel the way Christian astronomers and mariners order constellations. Three great crosses are drawn by the twelve constellations, four of them at the extremities of each cross. "The cross we call 'fixed' is formed by Taurus, Leo, Aquarius, and Aquila," said the pilot. "I guess you know that those are the symbols of the four Evangelists: Luke, Mark, Matthew, and John."

"Wait a minute," interrupted Yehezkel. "Those four constellations would be the ones presiding over the four seasons—if you hadn't substituted Aquila for Scorpio . . ."

The moment he pronounced the name of the poisonous creature, the rabbi understood why Saint John was instead represented by the Eagle—the king of birds—which flies highest and looks straight into the sun. He changed course radically. "And have you noticed that Aquarius is the only one of the four with a human form, like the angel you use to represent Matthew?"

"Of course; why do you ask?"

"Because my teacher, Yitzhak the Blind—may his candle burn for many years—says that the sun will be in the house of Pisces for eight hundred more years, but when it then moves into the house of Aquarius . . . the Children of Israel's exile will end, and the Messiah of David will finally arrive!"

Piero Vidoso had been trying for half an hour to get a word in in that learned sequel of stars, angels, and philosophers. But this time he was sure of the level of his contribution and made his plunge. "Those beasts are found in the heavens and on statues of the Evangelists for the same reason: because Saint John, in his Apocalypse, saw those four 'beasts' around the divine throne!"

Don Sancio shared a smile with Yehezkel and then turned to Vidoso in an indulgent tone. "Your knowledge of the New Testament does you proud, my man, but if you were as familiar with the Old one, you would also know where Saint John took both throne and beasts in his vision: from the book of the prophet Ezekiel!"

Galatea felt a pang of sympathy for the poor consul, caught stammering of Scriptures in the presence of two bottomless pits filled with knowledge of them. Don Sancio said, "I must go and have a rest now, my friends, and you, Rav Yehezkel, can go on talking about the stars with Arnulf here, who seems as dazzled by them as you are."

Yehezkel scolded himself for not cornering the scribe earlier to ask him if he'd heard of the Parchment of Circles, preferring instead to prance about like a jester. "Oh, Don Sancio, may we come down with you? There's something I'd like to ask you."

The stunning discovery they made in a Talmud passage, that a page from the Book of Ezekiel had been hidden because it contained a prophecy fulfilled by Jesus, had shaken all three. Galatea still couldn't believe the thousand-year-old parchment in the Paris temple really spoke—in Hebrew!—of Jesus Christ. Two nights later, she sat on deck in the dark once more, arms around her knees, listening to the two formidable exegetes compare Ezekiel's prophecies with events in the Gospels, searching for the episode in Jesus's life that the eccentric prophet foretold by the rivers of Babylon.

A silent bond formed between the three, for no one had ever deciphered that page of Talmud before, so they were the only people in the world to know of the as yet unidentified prophecy. The rabbi confessed he was disturbed by Elisha ben Abuya's accusation, for Ezekiel's book was a part of the Bible, which all Jews were intimately sure had never been tampered with. In any case, rabbi and scribe agreed that the hiding place of the page from the prophet was almost certainly in Jerusalem. Don Sancio said that the Templars, in their digs under the Temple Mount a hundred years earlier, never found anything that looked remotely like a piece of Ezekiel's book—"Or I would know of it!"

A verse from Qoheleth brought Galatea back from her musings to the corner of the deck where they whispered in the dark and breathed in Greek air as sweet as the ambrosia of the gods must have been.

"Aah, Don Sancio! Of all people I've met, you're the one who makes the most discouraging, pessimistic use of Scripture!" laughed Yehezkel. "But I like you. I know people of unassailable faith to whom I would never offer my friendship, but yours would honor me!"

"But you already have it," said the scribe, "as does our most gracious abbess!"

"Forgive my frankness, Don Sancio," said Yehezkel, "but by now you know how important it is for me to prove the antiquity of the Talmud. Well . . . did you ever hear talk of a Parchment of Circles?"

Don Sancio was silent for a while and then whispered, "Yes, I saw it, just once. The Old Man has it."

Yehezkel asked with sudden urgency, "And who is the Old Man?"

"Mmh . . ." Don Sancio smiled, a little disappointed. "I thought *you* might enlighten *me* about that. The fact is none knows who he *really* is. Everyone calls him the Old Man. He must be over ninety, and today he is the chaplain of the new fortress of Château Pélerin. But rumors have it that he was once a famous man, a theologian, an adviser of kings."

Yehezkel thought, "The head of the secret cabal in the Temple! The man who Rav Eleazar said staged his own funeral!"

Don Sancio went on. "He certainly advised Guillaume of Chartres, my master who died last year." He hesitated. His companions thought he was going to quote Qoheleth, but he didn't. "I might as well tell you the reason I've been summoned to Damietta is to find out if the new master, Pedro de Montaigue, will keep me as his secretary or give the position to someone else. . . ."

Ignoring Sancio's personal drama, Yehezkel leaned forward, pressing. "But what about the parchment? If you did see it once, what did it *say*?"

"Oh, I just saw it for an instant, in the Old Man's hands. I remember two concentric circles with Greek writing at certain points on both circles."

Yehezkel leaned back, excited and disappointed at the same time. "And I suppose you don't know who drew those circles, do you?"

Don Sancio smiled wistfully. "Qoheleth says, 'That which is far off and exceeding deep, who can find it out?' Who drew them? Who knows? The Old Man says it was Saint John the Evangelist. . . ."

✡ ✠ ✡ ✠

At dawn on the 5th of May, the boatswain shouted his repetitive auspices. It started blowing a little after dawn. For two hours it blew from the northwest, and the *Falcus* took on an exhilarating pace. Friar Vassayl set a course a little north of Rhodes so they wouldn't drift too close to Candia. But in the second watch the wind turned from the north and freshened. The north seas were not yet formed, so Friar Vassayl decided to keep his course, lowering the mainsail a little and sailing eastward as close to the wind as the fat-bellied *Falcus* was capable.

From the quarterdeck, Yehezkel's gaze fell on the nuns' niche just as Gudrun emerged. As she raised the curtain, he glimpsed the sweat-soaked face of the abbess and, even from that distance, knew she must be going through hell.

Galatea, by now, was only afraid that she might *not* die. Her first thought when the wind picked up had been that it would blow away the fetid smell, but as the waves grew, the cog's movements confined her to the mattress, her will crushed. Now and then, she thought to end her suffering through sheer willpower: simply get up, splash some water on her face, brush her hair. But the thought dissolved almost immediately, and she fell back helplessly.

The first time she had to vomit she realized she didn't have the strength to call for help. "I'll wave a hand," she thought, but it wouldn't move. Her arm across the bucket supporting her forehead, she felt her gut contract and opened her eyes wide, shocked by the loudness of the retch. She stared at the remains of her last meal, unable to even move her head to escape the spectacle. The acrid smell brought on another retch. Her last thought was that she should chew her food longer, as

Sister Marianna had always told her as a child. The lumps of bread in the bucket were surprisingly big.

Everyone who walked past her bucket glanced into it, to see if it needed emptying overboard. She thought, "Do they think I wouldn't do it myself? I'm not an animal!" But when she tried, Rustico took it from her hand. "Leave it, Madre, I'll take care of it!" She tried to insist but fell back in her corner, drained, on the point of crying from humiliation.

"I've become like a baby again, I can't even look after my physical needs . . . God must be punishing me for pride. Maybe Mother Elisabetta was right that pilgrimages are just vanity!"

She turned on her side. "For which sin, I wonder, is the punishment to be seasick in eternity?" The very thought made her shiver, imagining herself wandering around hell with a bucket, like a Christ with his Cross. The image gave her some relief, though, for she thought, "After all, what is all this when compared with our Lord's suffering on the Cross?"

During her passion on the high seas, passersby gave Galatea well-meaning advice. She appreciated their concern, but her attempts to smile were distorted grimaces. "May you be cursed for the humiliations you inflict on me!" she thought every time. "Leave me alone; do you not understand that the worst of this ordeal is the loss of my dignity?"

Gudrun by now didn't feel much better and had spent time draped over the gunwale with Garietto hanging onto her. When she asked Galatea if she needed anything, her abbess answered in a whisper: "No, my child . . . no one ever died of seasickness. Master Ezekiel said so . . . just leave me here with my bucket and forget about me."

But Yehezkel's attentions touched her. Twice the rabbi had come down from the balcony, felt her pulse, and offered some bitter leaves to suck on. Having a "real seaman"—as she heard Arnulf call him—by her side, gave a sense of safety and raised her morale a little. If

Master Ezekiel said she would survive, Galatea refused—despite all evidence to the contrary—to doubt it.

The northerly went on freshening until it whistled in the shrouds with the unmistakable voice of a storm. Yehezkel climbed down again and asked the almost senseless abbess for the key to her chest. He stowed some bags and satchels inside, keeping the astrolabium in his pocket, then used some rags to caulk the edge of the lid. As he worked, it occurred to him that if the *Falcus*—God forbid!—should capsize, the trunk would have to be untied, lest it sink with the cog. Perhaps he could put Aillil and the women in it, if they survived. Suddenly, he had a vision of survivors struggling in the water for possession of the chest.

Yehezkel felt a sudden sensation of danger and turned. A crowd of pilgrims, their faces warped by panic for the gathering storm, were advancing on him from both the bow and the mast. Yehezkel guessed that they had convinced themselves that the Jew was the cause of the storm, and that only throwing him overboard would save them from certain death.

Galatea, who had somehow reached the gunwale with her hands and dragged herself up, was watching, outraged and powerless, the menacing gestures of the approaching cloaks. The pilgrims, soaked by spray and always on the point of slipping on the wave-splashed deck, threw curses at the rabbi, and some of them clutched short belay pins in their hands.

One of the Bible books Yehezkel loved best, for the unabashed irony of the story, was Jona's. He said to himself grimly, "This is the *opposite* of Jonah's story, where the prophet asked to be thrown in the sea! This is where Don Sancio would quote Qoheleth: 'What advantage have the wise over fools?'"

He started breathing the folded breath. What was he going to shout to stop the terror-stricken pagans? He let his rib cage fall, expelling every last pocket of air in his lungs and holding them empty, eyes closed. A few moments before the pilgrims reached the shroud closest to where he stood, Don Sancio appeared beside him out of nowhere and bellowed over the wind, "The Jew is under the protection of the master of the temple! Whoever pulls a hair of his beard will answer for it to Pedro de Montaigue in person!"

The four Templars formed a wall around Yehezkel, swords drawn, and the pilgrims retreated right away. But one of them, eyes on fire, lunged between two knights, belay pin raised in the air. André de Rosson would have pierced him like a pig, if Yehezkel hadn't grabbed his wrist first and dragged him in a long slide down the foamy deck.

A few minutes later, twenty pilgrims were in irons and the rabbi was safely back on the balcony.

When the *Meltem* declared itself in the late morning, the *Falcus* had been forced to run before the wind, which had now turned slightly to the northeast and formed seas the *Falcus* could no longer defy.

Friar Vassayl ordered the mainsail lowered to a strip of canvas along the boom and the *Falcus* took the wind from port side, almost full in the stern. In its gallop south, the cog threw its prow first to port and then to starboard, like a horse trying to throw its mount. In the gallery below the stern castle, where two helmsman normally handled the tillers connected to the cog's two rudders, three men now did their best to contrast each tiller, the strain on them showing. For all that, conditions on board with the *Falcus* running before the sea improved; the storm's howl lessened and a strange calm prevailed, even among the pilgrims.

The balcony swung obscenely with the cog's every roll, the wind turned every mantle into a whip, but despite that it was crowded, for it was where the fate of the *Falcus* would be decided. Only three men up there had full comprehension of charts and winds, of loadstones and hull weaknesses. Friar Vassayl, Arnulf, and Yehezkel knew that if they made the right choices, perhaps the *Falcus* could be saved, but if they made one wrong decision, even an apparently irrelevant one, more than three hundred lives would be lost.

"On this tack, with the wind from port, the stone says we're heading exactly south," said Arnulf, who in such circumstances acquired almost more authority than the *patron* himself. "In other words, if when sailing due east, before the north wind started, we had already passed the beginning of Candia, we now run the risk of sailing into it, and with this gale behind us." The pilot, red mane in the wind, looked each man around the table in the eyes in turn and concluded, "Which would be a disaster."

Don Sancio unnecessarily jutted out his chin. "Arnulf, we all understand the danger of Candia being downwind. Even *I* know that most cogs are lost because they can't sail upwind and are thrown on the rocks. What we want to know is if you think we should seek the other tack, the more westward one, *now,* lest the *Falcus* plunge onto Candia's rocks like . . . like an angel falling after thinking the unthinkable!"

Friar Vassayl answered in Arnulf's place, announcing what everyone already knew, "But if Candia was not downwind for long, and we drifted further west than we think, then if we tack now we'll be blown south right past it . . ."

"Which would mean reaching Cirenaica* within a day," Arnulf finished for him.

It was Don Sancio's turn to comment, the pessimism in his voice more appropriate than usual. "Indeed, Cirenaica. Where those who survive the fury of the infidels will spend the rest of their days on earth as mamluk† slaves."

Iñigo knew that slavery might be in store for pilgrims but that a different fate awaited the Templars should the *Falcus* make landfall in Africa: martyrdom. But not before sending a hundred infidels to hell! He murmured the first words of the Templar battle cry under his breath. "Non nobis, Domine, non nobis."

---

*The eastern half of present Libya
†Infidels captured by Muslims, forcibly converted and sold into slavery or trained as soldiers for the caliphate

✡ ✠ ✡ ✠

At dawn on the same 5th of May, before the storm that struck the *Falcus* began to blow, a noble knight rode into the Christian camp that stretched over leagues of desert, just south of the city of Damietta.

The huge red sun was just above the sandy horizon, the metal fittings topping tents and pennants shone like mirrors. Thin threads of smoke rose from scores of bivouac fires smoldering outside the tents. The camp was slowly waking, and already the knight heard a chorus somewhere intoning a sad funeral litany. Funerals, like everything else in the delta, had to be held early before the blanket of heat came down. Bells called crosswearers to morning Mass. Pages ran to fetch water to cook breakfast. Soldiers led horses to the water troughs, the poor animals rearing and whinnying when they crossed each other, unsure if this was already battle.

The breeze brought a sickly stench of death from inside the city walls, together with the muezzins' voices. After a fruitless year-long siege, the whiny sound angered and discouraged the Christians. There was the fortress, leading its usual, infidel life. Some thought it would never fall. Those mighty walls and square towers burned their eyes; they could no longer bear the sight.

The rider approached the two biggest tents, in the east of the encampment, surmounted by the fiery-colored standards of John of Brienne, king of Jerusalem, and Cardinal Pelagius Galvani, papal legate a latere. He asked to be announced to the legate and a minute later crossed the purple-bordered entrance of the tent. Cardinal Pelagius received him while consuming a frugal breakfast. He was a short, intense cleric, rigid and snooty as only certain military and monastic types can be, accustomed as they are to passing judgment with the wave of a sword or a cross.

"Leopold has left!" announced the count.

Pelagius stood up with a start, toppling the wine jug. "The Duke of Austria ran off in the night, like a common *thief*?" he cried, slamming a fist on the table.

"He'd been secretly embarking his personal guard on two Frisian cogs for a day, it seems," reported the nobleman. "They sailed an hour ago . . ."

"Just when the sultan lost a thousand men in fifteen days!" cried Pelagius, crushing something in his hand. "I hope his cog is pulverized on the rocks!" He was struck by a fit of coughing, and his valet patted him timidly on the back.

"I'll write to Honorius!" spluttered the legate. "His soul won't get away with this, you'll see!"

CHAPTER 9

VA-TERA'E HA-YABASHA

And the Dry Land Appeared

ABOARD THE *FALCUS*, SAILING WEST OF CANDIA, 5TH MAY 1219

With every small increase in the wind's strength, the cog seemed smaller to Yehezkel's eyes compared to the seas around it. The things he looked at assumed an unnatural clarity, as if he could see their secret internal pulsing, that quid of life present even in canvas, wood, or iron. But his other senses seemed to have also sharpened as the gusts grew more violent. Despite the wind's howl, he could hear the creaking of the tillers.

Every time a wave lifted the stern, the rabbi feared the prow would not climb out of the trough and rise in its turn but would instead be submerged and the *Falcus* would plunge, in one elegant movement, straight *into* the Aegean Sea. But every time, after an endless moment of hesitation, the prow came up again, and Yehezkel grabbed the parapet before him, leaving his stomach behind.

Arnulf, excited as a teenager at his first tournament, shouted, "I swear we are not covering less than thirty-five leagues in a watch, perhaps even forty! If they were leagues toward Syria, we could best the time of the Duke of Austria's passage, a year and a half ago!"

"So how long did Leopold take?" asked Don Sancio.

"His fleet was caught by a long, furious September westerly and flew from Spalato to Acre in sixteen days. An arrow!" cried Arnulf.

Just then, the maître shouted, "Look! Over there, twenty degrees starboard of the bow!"

All eyes on the quarterdeck followed his finger and saw two shafts of rock rising through the haze on the horizon, no more than two leagues from the *Falcus*. Yehezkel passed a hand over his beard, trying to recall all the maps he'd ever seen of these waters, and then said, "I know that none willingly speak of the maps they know, but I would really give something to know where those two strange rocks are . . . wouldn't you, Friar Vassayl?"

Don Sancio said menacingly, "This is no time to guard secrets or hide maps! If anyone here knows where those rocks are located, let him speak now! Arnulf?"

"No, sir. I never saw those rocks, either sailing or on a map. But experience tells me Candia cannot be far. They wouldn't stand there like that, far from any coast, or I would have heard of them!"

This time the consul had no doubt he was about to become the hero of the passage. "I know what those rocks are! They're the Strofades! They . . . they opened up for Saint Mark!"

He ran to the table, grabbing a chart. "The two Venetians who stole Saint Mark's sacred body from Alexandria were sailing home through here and were about to be thrown on to a lonely rock just west of Candia. But the rock, aware of the sanctity of the boat's load, split in two just before the impact, and the boat sailed safely through the hundred-foot gap that had been created. So from the one island it had been, it became the Strofades, two fingers jutting out of the sea just off the westernmost tip of Candia!"

"Mmh . . . if that is the case," murmured the scribe, "this cog sailed out of *his* city on the day of *his* feast . . . perhaps the saint is taking us close to these rocks so we will know where we are."

Don Vidoso's face lit up. "But of course, that's it! Saint Mark is saving us from certain death, like he did that day for Buono of Rialto and Rustico of Torcello! It's a miracle! Saint Mark be praised! Hallelujah!"

The knights complimented him on the intervention of his patron saint as if his champion had just won a joust. The consul danced for both joy and barely repressed terror, but the cog's leaders, not yet sure how the identification of the rocks was going to save the *Falcus,* looked at him with sympathetic smiles. Vidoso went down on his knees, but in that position the *Falcus* surprised him—and him a lagoon man—making him roll indecorously into one of the parapets with a Te Deum on his lips.

The maître expressed his opinion. "If the consul is right, and we're about to leave Candia on port, we could try to sail a little closer to the wind and head more eastward, which should bring us into sheltered waters south of the island."

"I thought of that right away," said the pilot. "But the western coast of Candia is some twenty leagues long and without a map with those rocks *on it,* we don't know how far down it they are. If we head east too soon, we could crash into it . . ."

Don Sancio intervened in a grim tone, "But if Vidoso is right and we continue galloping south . . . it's Africa for us!"

Every thought flew to the African coast, where they would all be subdued and sold as slaves, down to the last man, not to speak of the fate of the mercifully few women. The thought of the abbess imprisoned in the harem of some local sheik precipitated the rabbi's choice. "We must find Candia! We can't risk everyone on this cog falling into the hands of a band of Tuaregs!"

"You're right, Rabbi," said Don Sancio tiredly. "And if the coast appears in front of us, we can always bear away again and try to follow it south until the end of the island. But if Vidoso is right, and we don't take a more eastward course now, the pilgrims' fate is sealed. Give the order, Brother Vassayl!"

"No, wait!" It was Iñigo. André de Rosson, standing next to him, urged him on with his eyes. "It's true, there are no arms or horses on this cog," said Iñigo, "and you can't make a company of these three hundred wretches. But there are still four Templar knights on board, with their sergeants and squires! It's unheard of for a group of knights of *our* order to run from a fight with infidels, even if imposed on them by the raging seas! You can't oblige us to suffer such dishonor!"

Don Sancio needed no time to reflect on the issue. "Nice words, Brother Iñigo, but the lives of three hundred Christians are more important to me than your honor . . . Go on, Vassayl, do as I told you."

The maître gestured to Arnulf, who leaned over the parapet and shouted instructions to the sailors below. The stern wind caught his words and carried them through the *Falcus*.

"Hoist a quarter of the main, and take her an eighth to the east!!"

The moment the *Falcus* came closer to the wind by some forty-five degrees, all hell broke loose on board. The seas were just aft of the beam and cross-waves struck the hull from all directions. Every object, big or small, not properly tied down was thrown across the deck, once more awash with waves. The prow rose and fell; every crash made the cog tremble to its most hidden timbers.

Arnulf gave more orders, and soon the boatswain shouted, "All pilgrims below! All sailors on deck! Come on, you ruffians! On deck, all of you! No more watches till the end of the storm!"

The deck looked like a herd of sheep scattered by a wolf. Pilgrims ran in all directions, falling all by themselves or over each other. Some tried to climb out of the hold, but the sailors brutally pushed them back down. The hatch would stay locked for the duration of the storm, and pilgrims could shout all they wanted. They would be thrown against the hull by every wave, and the noise of raging seas, echoing in the hold as in the sounding chamber of a huge musical instrument, would drive them out of their minds, just as the Greeks claimed the gods like doing to those they decided to destroy.

Yehezkel detected a change of pitch in the wind's howl. The northerly was still growing stronger, and the gusts were longer. They pushed
streaks of white foam down the backs of the waves and tore the crests
off the higher ones, slapping the sailors' faces with them, as if provoking the exhausted, growling men. The rabbi suggested that Don Sancio
tell the knights to remove the hauberks they had donned when the cog
came out of the Adriatic, in the secret hope of seeing a pirate dhow
appear on the horizon.

"That chain mail is useless!" shouted Yehezkel. "It will hinder you if
you try to help the sailors, and in the accursed eventuality of the *Falcus*
going down it will drag you straight to the bottom! Take it off and stay
calm. Above all, stay calm . . ."

"I could never be calm aboard this cog!" burst out young de Rosson.

In midafternoon, an hour after luffing by an eighth, the fingers of rock
could still just be seen aft of the starboard beam, and the *Falcus* labored
over the waves roughly toward the southeast. The rabbi's eyes scoured
the horizon, as well as every part of the rigging and every flexing of
the mast. His surveys always included the group he'd started calling his
"little flock." They were hunkered down in the lee of the hatch, pushed
up against three feet of wood, none with the courage to push their head
above them to see what was happening to the cog. Aillil was curled up
in Galatea's arms, in turn embraced from behind by Gudrun, firmly
gripped by Garietto, who was back to back with Rustico.

All were visibly ill—one more, another less—but Galatea's face
was a true mask of suffering. Yehezkel was momentarily gripped by the
expression of surrender he thought he saw on her face, but soon he was
scanning the horizon again, checking that the presumed Strofades were
receding in the correct direction, anxious as everyone on the quarterdeck to see on which side of the cog, with respect to the direction of the
wind, the mountains of Candia would appear.

Suddenly, the elected representative of the pilgrims on board, a
man named Ayrald of Troyes, climbed onto the balcony and presented

himself. Friar Vassayl, who almost lost his love of the sea when the ship's load was a human one, spat, "What do those wretches want now?"

Ayrald hesitated, then said, "The pilgrims are more afraid than I've ever seen them, your excellencies. In the certainty of imminent death, they want to be confessed en masse."

Friar Vassayl, taking the request as a declaration of distrust in his seamanship, retorted, "And why are they so certain of perishing? Maybe it's the weight of their sins that makes them think that way. I've seen worse storms than this one, and I don't share their pessimism!"

"Ah, but you haven't seen the situation belowdeck, *monsieur le maître*. There are two dead, broken arms and legs, water is coming in everywhere . . . your cog will not last long, believe me."

Friar Vassayl barked, "What the hell do *you* know of this cog, or any other? What do you know of the resilient spruce of her mast, of her canvas as tough as chain mail, of her shrouds that weigh two tons? You know *nothing,* so shut that ignorant gob of yours!! Go back to the pilgrims and tell them to look after themselves, and I will look after the cog!"

When Ayrald climbed down, the maître turned to the scribe. "And of these dregs of humanity, what does Qoheleth say, Don Sancio? Eh?"

The scribe didn't answer, but no one doubted for an instant that he had chosen an appropriate verse.

The maître's estimation that the pilgrims should look after themselves profoundly disturbed the rabbi. He would never have left the balcony when the mountains of Candia could appear two or three leagues from the *Falcus* at any moment, but hearing Ayrald's description of the situation below gave him pause.

"Broken arms and legs . . . but I am a medicus, by my beard! I took a vow fifteen years ago—I swore that I am first a rabbi, second a medicus, and third a sailor! I cannot stay up here. . . ."

His decision taken, Yehezkel followed Ayrald of Troyes down the ladder. Bracing his feet against the cog's pitching, he patiently reopened Galatea's chest and took out some herbs, some vinegar to revive the senseless, and ointments against the pain of the fractures. Then he asked a sailor to open the hatch.

The reek of stale urine and the chorus of moans swept over him two steps down the ladder into the dark. When he'd adapted eyes and nose as well as he could, he immediately saw the amount of water splashing out of the bilges and on the planks that were the hold's floor. Waves struck the hull on both sides and almost every seam leaked, some literally spraying water into the hold. Pilgrims filled every available space, including the recesses between the cog's sturdy frames. Every time the *Falcus* fell from a crest, dozens of them couldn't hold onto anything and ended up in a jumble of limbs on the floorboards, semi submerged in the filthy seawater like shattered dolls.

He turned around at once, climbed out, and called the boatswain with the considerable voice he could summon even with no preparatory breathing. Ten minutes later, as Yehezkel set broken ulnas and femurs amid cries of pain and wrapped them in torn shirts as tight as he could, five sailors were busy bailing the bilge. Pilgrims sang as the sailors passed buckets up and down the ladder. Their livid, angry curses rose to a livid, angry sky entwined with the terrorized prayers of the pilgrims, in a Babel-like mixture that well represented, thought the rabbi, the confusion in those gentile minds about God's role in the storm.

He tried to ensure the pilgrims were all wedged in or tied down, but there wasn't enough rope for all. After a big wave that felt like it could have broken the cog's back, Yehezkel took advantage of the pause and dashed to the ladder. In three leaps he was on deck, where he told the first sailor he saw to cut fifty lengths of line, about six feet long, for pilgrims to tie themselves down. The sailor hesitated. He'd seen the Jew on the quarterdeck for most of the passage, but that didn't mean he should take orders from him. The rabbi repeated his request, and this time something in his voice had the sailor's legs moving before the man had even decided to obey. Yehezkel went back below.

Friar Pacifico, a Benedictine monk from Capalbio, had been praying for hours, beseeching the Holy Trinity to let him carry at least a part of the pilgrims' sins so that maybe, if he paid for them with his own life, the cog could be saved. At one point Yehezkel, kneeling down not far away, heard him proposing the barter in a murmur and couldn't help himself. "Friar Pacifico, this is no time for a *disputatio*, but believe me, offering up your life for the sins of others is a meaningless gesture in God's eyes. In your Bible *or* ours, he only asked for a human sacrifice *once,* and stopped Abraham from offering it up . . ." Not wanting to provoke the monk, Yehezkel finished the phrase in his mind. "And he certainly didn't ask for the sacrifice of the man you call his 'Son.'"

Then the rabbi stood up in the middle of the hold and raised his voice, addressing the pilgrims. "I suggest you remind the Lord of his neglected powers! Pray the verse in the ninety-third Psalm, 'The seas have lifted up, Lord, the seas have lifted up their voice, the seas have lifted up their pounding waves. But the Lord on high is mightier than the thunder of great waters, mightier than the breakers of the sea!'"

The words of the psalm spoke to the pilgrims, and soon the Latin verse was being chanted across the hold. "Elevabunt flumina fluctus suos . . ."

When all fractures were seen to, feeling himself choke in the foul darkness, Yehezkel went back to the quarterdeck. Despite the dire circumstances, he couldn't deny the euphoria he felt standing up there. He was more alive, his senses perceiving more of the world, a feeling he attributed to the heady mixture of the danger they were running and the beauty of the sheer power of the sea.

Suddenly, the cry that condemned the *Falcus* went up. *"There, look! Above that black cloud! It's a mountaintop!"*

Candia's mountains were to the south, and they were *downwind*! The consul had been wrong, and now the storm would inexorably throw them on the rocks. Friar Vassayl didn't lose a moment. "Arnulf! A quarter to the west! Jibe the mainsail, and hoist six more feet of it! Now!! We must keep away from the island until we reach its end!"

It was the one thing to be done, and they did it right away, but the men on the balcony soon divided into two camps. Of the first were those who knew little of the sea and believed the *Falcus* had a decent chance, with God's help, of keeping her distance from the coast to the end of the island. Of the other were those who went to sea and knew how little a round-hull cog could resist a gale blowing on her beam, and how quickly she drifted downwind. The members of the second camp understood that in less than two hours the wind and seas would wreck the *Falcus* on the shore.

Despite his preference for words, Yehezkel couldn't chase away a vision of multiple, savage impacts of planks on rocks. "When it becomes inevitable," he thought out loud, "we'll have to let the pilgrims come out and jump in the water. They'll have a better chance of surviving than if they stay in the hold . . ."

"And so it was revealed to all that the *Falcus Templi* was in effect a great White Hawk," said Arnulf dejectedly, finally resigned to his fate.

"What do you mean?" asked Don Sancio, up to that point the coolest of the men on the balcony.

"He's comparing our fate to that of the *Blanche Nef*, Don Sancio," said Friar Vassayl.

Yehezkel thought of the famous wreck, still talked about among mariners though it had happened exactly a hundred years earlier. King Henry I of England launched the *Blanche Nef*—a brand new cog, faster than any other—in November of 1120 and watched her leave for her first cruise with a hundred feasting nobles on board, including his seventeen-year-old son, William Adelin. Yehezkel had heard that every single soul on board was drunk when she hit rocks off Normandy and sunk, that very night. Nobody survived, and King Henry never smiled again. No other ship, it was said, ever brought so much misery to England.

Friar Vassayl leaned out of the balcony on both sides and shouted:

"Hoist another foot of that main! Pull in that gaff, by the blood of the Virgin!!"

They heard thunder, and soon dark, low clouds hid the peaks again. But everyone knew the shore was there, where the wind was relentlessly driving them, wave after wave. Yehezkel knew the book of Ezekiel almost by heart and recited the right verse for the situation to himself, between folded breaths:

"But the east wind will break you to pieces far out at sea... You and everyone else on board will sink into the heart of the sea, on the day of your shipwreck!"

He pictured the hull crushed by the rocks so many times that the idea of trying to beach the cog came to him almost naturally. The image of splintered timbers was replaced by the far less anguishing one of a keel slowing to a halt after digging a channel in the sand of a beach. Suddenly, he remembered hearing a merchant in the synagogue in al-Kahira, as a child, telling just such a story. The master of a cog, caught in a deadly storm, found a beach among the rocks and threw her onto it. The vessel ploughed up the beach and slowly keeled over on one side, with little damage and few victims. The witness quoted the prophet Jeremiah, and Yehezkel heard the verse again in his mind. He turned to Don Sancio. "Do you remember the verse in Jeremiah that says, 'I made the sand a boundary for the sea, an eternal barrier it cannot cross. Waves may roll, but they cannot prevail; they may roar, but they cannot cross it'?"

"I know what you're thinking, Rabbi, but we would need far better visibility than this to locate a beach, if one exists. I fear this thunderstorm has made that impossible . . . is that not so, Brother Vassayl?"

"You both know very well," answered the patron gruffly, "that even if we found a cove with a beach at its end, with such seas we would hit rocks in its entrance, off one of the tongues of land enclosing it."

Yehezkel thought grimly, "Maybe Rav Moshe was right . . . maybe sailing is for goyim. If God decides to leave me among the living at the end of this, I shall only sail again when there is no alternative!"

Don Sancio was at once sobered and exhilarated by the thought that the lines they were reciting were probably the last ones the actors on the quarterdeck would ever deliver. "I want to express my admiration, Master Ezekiel, while I still can, for your precision in quoting Scripture. You have a truly exceptional memory . . ."

"Thank you for the kind words, Don Sancio; your own memory is no less remarkable. Oh, by the way, since the storm started I heard no quotes from Ecclesiastes. Did Qoheleth never go to sea?"

His words made everyone smile, Friar Vassayl laughing openly. The scribe seconded the rabbi's attempt to relieve the tension. "No, Master Ezekiel, I don't believe King Solomon ever went to sea, but I feel sure that if he had, he would have found it futile!"

They all laughed, and then the maître brought their minds back to the fate of the *Falcus*. "At this point, it is probably true that the way to save most lives would be to beach the cog, but it would take a seer to know behind which promontory lies a beach."

The word hit Yehezkel like a slap in the face. "But we *have* a seer! The nun is going to save us all!" he screamed in his thoughts.

He feverishly planned how to bring her up there and then, without explaining, charged down the ladder. He reached his little flock and tried to convince the abbess to drag herself to the foot of the ladder but realized she would never find the strength. With a deep sigh, under Gudrun's shocked stare, he picked her up and carried her aft. The gesture seemed to bring some life back into Galatea's eyes. When she realized she was in the rabbi's arms, her face went through three expression: first the outraged nun, then the cornered animal, and finally total abandon.

Yehezkel thought of the night, a month before, when he'd carried her senseless body from the skiff to the oak outside the monastery. The *Falcus* was doing her best to send them both sprawling down the deck, and as he tried to keep his balance, his hand ended up on the edge of her pelvis. He felt the softness just inside it, as he had that night, and something moved in his loins, like the distant rumble of thunder. As he deposited her at the foot of the ladder, Yehezkel thought, "If we survive, sooner or later this nun will cause me to sin. But not trying to save the cog would be like fishing her out of the Venetian lagoon only to throw her into the Aegean Sea!"

Now he had to get her on the quarterdeck. He thought of

everything. He shouted to a sailor to bring the bosun's chair,* and while the pulley that would hoist her was being set up on the balcony, he tied her down and stepped into the galley. The sheltered clay furnace hadn't been used that day. Contrasting the cog's rocking—he twice called the *Falcus* an evil whirligig!—he managed to light a small fire and warm some vinegar with strong herbs.

A few minutes later, Galatea was sitting on a short plank for all the world like a child's swing, tied for safety and rising in brief tugs as the men on the balcony hoisted her up. Yehezkel climbed the ladder next to her, holding on to her habit to contrast the swinging with the cog's motion. Her eyes regained some awareness of what was happening, but she didn't find the strength to comment.

Finally, she stood with the men on quarterdeck. Yehezkel gave her the infusion. She gulped it down and grimaced as she listened to him explain their predicament and the decision to try to find a beach.

As he spoke, perhaps two leagues away, the rocky cliffs of Candia's shore appeared for the first time, through a thick mist of rain and sea spray.

"We should let the pilgrims out on deck," said Yehezkel, "to take their fate into their own hands."

"The heavens are most unkind to the intentions of these penitents," commented Don Sancio drily.

As Vidoso went off to let the pilgrims in the hold know the full extent of the tragedy, Yehezkel made his first attempt to stimulate the visionary talents of the abbess. "Close your eyes and think of a beach, madame. Think fine, white sand. When you have that picture in your mind, please try to guess where, along the shore in front of us, there may be sand. Can you *see* sand anywhere?" Yehezkel was in control, yet his voice came out a little squeaky.

Galatea concentrated, grasping the parapet, eyes closed and chest heaving. "I don't know . . . I see no sand, only different colors, depending on where I look."

---

*A device used to suspend a person from a rope to perform work aloft

Yehezkel shouted, "Depending on where you look? Then where is the blue, madame? The blue of your visions, the blue of my wool thread, where *is* it?"

"It's not there . . ." sobbed Galatea. "Every one is an earth color, browns, yellows, greens . . ."

In the end, thought Yehezkel, he insisted on taking them to certain death when most, even as mamluk slaves, could have survived. The darkest of Ezekiel's words came out of his mouth by themselves. "Hear what the Lord says, 'Disaster! Unheard of disaster! See, the end has come! The end is here!'"

Young de Rosson, abandoning all chivalric fervor, moaned, "Ooh . . . Saint Pierre, Sainte Tecla, Saint Martin! Oh . . . Maman!!"

Friar Vassayl thought the sky was a dark place, and God was malicious.

"There it is! There's the blue! It's there!" cried Galatea all of a sudden.

She pointed a finger toward a point of the shore where the waves crashed on rocks that had fallen from the promontory above. Friar Vassayl didn't hesitate. "An eighth to the east! Ease out the main!"

A few moments later a cove appeared, hidden between a small island and a round promontory. It was bigger than they expected, with a long white beach at the end, which to their eyes looked like the gates of paradise. For the second time, Yehezkel told himself he *must* stop underestimating this woman.

Friar Vassayl and Arnulf's superior seamanship brought the *Falcus* into the cove without getting close to either side of its rocky entrance. The cog, sheltered from the gale and in nearly still water, was suddenly steady and calm, but it was still fast. They had five minutes at most before it reached the beach to hurriedly organize the collective jump into the sea. The boatswain shouted:

"Everyone jump overboard as late as they have the courage to! Those who can't swim, jump with someone who can! Leave everything here or you'll drown, you'll get your things when the cog is beached!"

Yehezkel entrusted Aillil to Rustico and Gudrun to Garietto, then climbed on the chest and pulled Galatea up with him. He shot a last glance at the end of the cove, now some three hundred feet away. He couldn't help thinking of the apocalyptic vision appearing to people ashore: a huge ship, sails aloft, angrily leaving the sea, as if it had had enough of it, and venturing onto dry land.

Then he turned around, put an arm around Galatea's waist, and jumped.

The dive seemed to last forever. For the rest of his days, Yehezkel would never forget the feeling of Galatea's body clinging to his, or her scream in his beard.

CHAPTER 10

VAYIKRAH ELOHIM
And God Called

FOUR LEAGUES NORTH OF KALIVIANI, IN THE EXTREME NORTHWEST OF CANDIA, 5TH MAY 1219

"Con . . . fi . . . teor,"* whispered the pilgrim. The young Greek monk bending over him saw the word form on his lips and tightened his grip on the dying man's hand.

"All rancor must remain here, brother. Are you at peace with everyone?"

The pilgrim raised his head with a grimace of pain that resembled a smile, exhaled, "I've no more loads," and fell back on the sand. The monk made small signs of the cross on his forehead, his chest, and the soles of his feet, murmuring the words of the ritual. When he was sure the man's soul had left this world, he stood up and gestured to the sailors assigned to the burials.

An hour after the beaching, the sea was still bringing pilgrims ashore, both dead and dying. Thirty-two of them had not answered Vidoso's roll call, and twenty-two bodies had been buried so far.

---

*I confess

The *Falcus,* her underbelly indecently exposed, lay on her side in the sand like a stranded leviathan. The small cove crawled with men recovering their belongings. The cog had majestically sailed up the beach, hesitated as if trying to remain heroically upright, then settled down onto her starboard flank, slightly crushing a central section of the hull, as if to make herself more comfortable.

The rabbi's flock was intact, but Don Sancio had been grabbed by the current, and before André could reach him and drag him ashore, the waves flung him twice onto the low rocks at one end of the beach. Now the scribe lay under a rosemary bush, senseless but breathing, and the rabbi thought that with God's help, he might survive.

The bulk of survivors, some two hundred people led by Vidoso and the Templars, just set off to the nearest village, Kaliviani, four leagues from the cove. Yehezkel climbed to the shrubs behind the beach and was sitting there, drained, surveying the scene. In a corner of the beach the drowned were being buried, one or two relatives mourning them and a row of corpses awaiting their turn. The sun was about to sink into the choppy sea, still full of whitecaps. In the distance behind him, storm clouds crowned the mountaintop in a purplish, crepuscular light.

For the past hour, people from nearby hamlets had flocked to the cove—which he'd learned was called Gramvoussa—and now either helped the survivors or stood around the edge of the beach, chatting. More were arriving despite darkness falling, for everyone wanted to witness an event that all western Crete—the Greeks never accepted the Venetians' name for their island—would weave into tales for generations.

The rabbi snapped out of his reverie and helped Rustico and Garietto build a stretcher for the scribe. Friar Vassayl ordered two sailors to take the stretcher so that Galatea's armigers could carry her chest, which they'd unloaded from the cog under Yehezkel's direction using pulleys, suffering small injuries, and cursing in their lagoon dialect all through the process. Just as they were ready to head for the village, Don Sancio came to with a moan, which Yehezkel thought was a good sign.

Galatea's mood as they set off was so good it embarrassed her. She was probably the happiest of all the survivors, and not because her gift had saved so many people from drowning, nor because everyone in their little group was safe and sound. No, the abbess was secretly happy because for the first time in eleven days, she wasn't seasick. Was it right to praise God and be relieved, she asked herself, when a storm had just taken thirty-two lives?

Then she raised her eyes—and thought she was back on the *Falcus*. The hill ahead of them leaned to one side and the ground gave way beneath her feet just as that cursed deck had done. She felt light-headed and instinctively grabbed the rabbi's arm not to fall. Yehezkel almost jumped back to avoid contact with a woman, saw the nun's expression, and put his arm around her waist just in time to stop her falling headlong on the rocky path. When she was over her fainting spell, Galatea turned to him with a frail little smile, the back of her hand on her forehead. "It was certainly God's will, Master Ezekiel, but you saved my life twice in the space of a month, once by pulling me out of the water and once by throwing me into it! For the rest of my days, I won't be able to look at water without thinking of you."

Yehezkel laughed for the first time since the peaks had appeared downwind of the *Falcus*.

After walking for over an hour they saw white square patches in the moonlight: the roofs of Kaliviani. The first house was crumbling, with the roof beams half exposed and its walls rising to different heights, here above the door, there just to the window sill. Yehezkel guessed it must have been set on fire in one of the innumerable raids on the island by Normans, Saracens, or pirates.

Standing in front of the house was a woman with a folded kerchief on her head. A little stout, neither fair nor ugly, she wasn't old but had wilted early and seemed to have been placed there to complete the picture of desolation. Yehezkel thought no woman in the world could have been more clearly a widow.

When she saw that the man on the stretcher was an aged cleric, the woman stepped into the path and said in a mixture of Greek and gestures, "Someone said 'Show *hospitality* to strangers, for thereby some have entertained *angels* unawares.' Come in for a drink of water."

Galatea recognized the apostle's words but didn't catch Yehezkel's response in Greek, which lit a smile on the woman's face that wiped ten years off it. Galatea asked him what he'd said, and he answered, "That comparing you to an angel is a slight exaggeration, but comparing me to an angel is blasphemy."

The abbess stepped into the house, giggling at the compliment, but with her back to the rabbi.

The woman said the big group of survivors had gone on to Chania, the biggest town in the west of the island, some twenty-five leagues to the east. Yehezkel asked if there were any Jews in the village and when she answered negatively, he gratefully accepted her Christian hospitality.

Friar Vassayl and the four *Falcus* men with him chose to follow the main group and took their leave. The maître entrusted Don Sancio to them and then gripped Yehezkel's forearm, sincere friendship in his eyes. Twenty minutes later, only Yehezkel's flock, still white with sea salt and quietly stunned by the storm and the beaching, was left in the derelict house.

"I am Albacara Mudaciol, widow of Vidal Cordier, a settler from Rialto," said the woman with a curt bow to Galatea. Her features reminded the abbess of Bonarina, her nanny at Castel Romitorio.

"And I am Galatea degli Ardengheschi, abbess of San Maffìo, in Torcello," answered Galatea.

"Oh, you're from Torcello! I have a cousin there! Do you know a man called Raniero Zanin?"

Soon the two women were deep in lagoon gossip. A little later, after Galatea introduced the others to the widow, they hung sheets to divide the big kitchen, men and women improvising pallets to sleep on in the two halves of the room, which, like all Greek homes, smelled strongly of myrrh. Now and then the rabbi checked Don Sancio's pulse and raised one of his eyelids with a finger. The scribe reacted well and as the evening turned to night was increasingly aware of his surroundings.

When the chorus of regular breaths indicated everyone was asleep, Yehezkel went outside to pray Ma'ariv. After thanking the Lord with all his heart for the presence of the Christian prophetess on the *Falcus,* he reflected on the situation. The Templars said they would rest in Chania and then purchase mounts and ride on to the capital of the island, Heraklion, also unsuccessfully renamed Candia by the Venetians. Yehezkel's hope, both to save Don Sancio's life and to get his flock off the island, had been the presence of Jews, if not in Kaliviani, then at least in Chania. What to do?

The night was so dark that though the only light in the house was a candle, the derelict structure was incapable of containing it. Light seeped from the gaps between the roof beams, from every fissure in the walls, and from the small kitchen window, splashing onto the rocks and shrubs outside. Yehezkel thought it looked like a bonfire was raging in the kitchen, yet it was just a candle.

Sun, sea, and silence filled the next days. The widow's guests did little and said even less. Don Sancio improved and began to speak but felt weak and complained of pains in his abdomen. Yehezkel laid him on his side, palpated gently to see where he felt the greatest pain, and concluded that one of the scribe's organs had probably broken its envelope. Galatea suggested that they carry him to Chania.

"Has ve-Halilah!"* cried Yehezkel in Hebrew. "A Greek medicus would kill him! I can do more for him in this village than half the physicians in the Polis, madame, even if you don't seem to think so. . . ."

Galatea felt the haughtiness that occasionally escaped Master Ezekiel's

---

*God forbid!

control, but since Don Sancio was visibly better—he had even taken some warm milk with honey without vomiting—chose not to insist.

In the days before the scribe's condition took a turn for the worse, a strange friendship, of the kind that sometimes blooms between old people and adolescents, developed between Don Sancio and Aillil. When asked, "Do you like it?" the boy would often answer, "I don't quite know what to think of it," an attitude that soon endeared him to the old philosopher.

Don Sancio began to instruct Aillil in those subjects that most intrigued the boy, trusting Aillil's nose to lead him to the best all-round education one could hope to impart in a few days of conversations. Aillil was enthusiastic. Released from the cage of the rabbi's verbose ethical sermons, he was fascinated by the theory and notation of music, and found that even the conjugation of Latin verbs had a strangely satisfying logic. On the second day, Don Sancio asked him, "Did your father ever tell you about Outremer?"

Aillil smiled disarmingly. "I never met my father, sir, but knights who were there told me of white towns and palm trees, of castles watching over desert trails, and strange animals unknown in the West. I've thought of nothing else for years. It's why I'm going there. *And* to find my father."

When Yehezkel thanked him for his efforts with Aillil, Don Sancio mumbled, "Qoheleth says, 'Better a poor but wise youth than an old but foolish king who no longer knows how to heed a warning.'"

That afternoon Galatea, Yehezkel, and Don Sancio were sitting in the shade of a fig tree behind the house, discussing how the presence of sand behind the rocks had been revealed by the blue. The rabbi explained the importance kabbalists attribute to the color Scripture calls *saphir,* the celestial blue beneath the divine throne when Moses ascended Mount Sinai.

"I always knew it," sighed Galatea. "Did I not tell you how many times that heavenly blue appeared in my visions?"

"Interesting," murmured Don Sancio. He spoke with difficulty, pausing often.

"Forgive my bluntness, Don Sancio," butted in Yehezkel, "but do you really not know any more about the Parchment of Circles than what you told us that night on the *Falcus*?"

The scribe's eyes were closed, his breaths shallow. He reflected for a while and then murmured, "This is one secret I would like to let go of before I leave this vale of tears . . ."

Rabbi and abbess both leaned forward, hanging on every word.

"The Order of the Temple has become the power it is . . . by blackmailing the popes for ninety years. The Parchment of Circles is in reality a map that leads to the hiding place of the most dangerous document the church of Peter has ever had to deal with."

Don Sancio hesitated, but he'd known from the moment of the impact on the rocks that he would not survive for long and hadn't said enough to break the balance of powers, so he grimaced and went on. "It is allegedly the confession by the thieves who stole Jesus's body from the tomb . . . the Templars claimed to have found it, but *I* know they didn't. Saint Bernard, ninety years ago, convinced Honorius II that they had, and they have reaped the benefits ever since." Don Sancio let out a long sigh from both effort and relief.

Galatea's mouth hung open, the foundations of her world teetering. "You mean . . . you mean they blackmail the church because if the body was stolen, then . . . then there was *no Resurrection?* But that's . . . *impossible!*"

Yehezkel said nothing, a sly smile on his face. Then, "I always wondered how the temple managed to keep those hundreds of donations . . . and they answer only to the pope, eh? *Now* it all makes sense! But tell me, Don Sancio, who else knows of this 'confession'?"

"The pope and the Old Man for sure, but maybe Domingo of . . ." Don Sancio was stuttering and seemed on the point of passing out.

"That's enough, Master Ezekiel!" cried Galatea, pulling Yehezkel off the scribe by the sleeve of his sarbel. "Can't you see he's in no shape to answer more questions? We must let him rest!"

Yehezkel had been too excited to notice that Don Sancio's face was the color of ash. Feeling guilty, he helped the old man into the house and onto a bed. Don Sancio felt the chill of the approaching end. He heard people shouting on the path and murmured, to no one in particular:

"Says . . . says Qoheleth, 'People go to their eternal home, and whiners go about the streets.'"

Four days after the beaching, Don Sancio was so weak he could no longer stand. Blood had drained out of his face, and his pulse was barely perceptible. Now and then, feeling someone bustle around his pallet, Don Sancio murmured, "Why are you fidgeting so much? Just let me die in peace . . ."

That day Don Sancio wrote his testament in his own hand.

His last wishes were concerned with the division of his books among his students in Paris. Then, too weak to write more, he dictated to Yehezkel a letter to Pedro de Montaigue, his new master, who was in the Christian camp outside Damietta. In it, he heaped praise on the rabbi and the noble abbess for saving hundreds of Christian pilgrims by successfully beaching the *Falcus* in the middle of a storm.

His last letter was to the temple commander in Heraklion, asking him to arrange for the recovery of the *Falcus* by sending boat builders and carpenters to set up a yard on the beach at Gramvoussa. Yehezkel explained to him that after hauling the cog upright and propping her up, they would have to repair the planking where it was crushed and then, to put her back in her element, dig a ditch around her and let the sea into it.

Then Don Sancio prepared himself, with great decorum, for his last journey. "I've been preparing to die all my life, Rav Yehezkel, but now I've been dying for three days, and I'm already tired of it."

There was no pain or fear in the scribe's eyes. He hadn't asked for a priest, not because the Greek rites of the monks in the nearby monastery didn't agree with his Christianity, but because he'd always known that if Heaven and hell existed, one was not assigned on the basis of hurried, last-minute rituals. He knew all the tales about hell and expected that in the end *it*, too, would be a disappointment.

•••

Yehezkel and Galatea had not spoken again of Don Sancio's words on the confession. That evening, unable to vent her outrage near the dying scribe, she dragged the rabbi out of the house and said, sternly, "It's calumny, Rabbi, and you *know* it! People spread denials of the Resurrection in the same way they spread rumors about Jews killing Christian children at Easter for their blood! And anyway, if *that's* what the map leads to, how would it help you to prove the antiquity of your Talmud?"

Yehezkel secretly had no doubt that Jesus's body had been stolen by his followers, or by someone paid by them, but after witnessing Galatea's rage when he'd implied she was a pagan, there was no way he was going to let his own opinion on the matter air.

"Madame, in truth I'm as surprised as you that five or six popes have given credence to a rumor—for without seeing the document it *is* just a rumor—to the point of making the temple what it is today. But I beg you, let us suspend judgment—at least between ourselves—on the existence of this confession until we see the famous Parchment of Circles: if God helps us find it, that is."

"The church giving it credence is what makes it so frightening," murmured the abbess to herself.

At nightfall, Don Sancio became convinced that his Averroism would cost him salvation of his soul and panicked. Garietto ran off to fetch a monk, and the old man confessed himself, but his fear did not abate. Only Yehezkel, sitting at his deathbed the whole night, somehow managed to calm him down a little. At one point, a half-asleep Galatea heard the rabbi whisper in the dark:

"You really believe the Almighty is *that* mean?"

At dawn the scribe asked to be laid on the ground, as is the custom for dying Christians. First light was seeping into the house when Don Sancio, with a last sigh, passed away.

His body lay in the widow's house for the whole day as the monks arranged funeral rites worthy of a temple official. There was no wake for Don Sancio, and that night the curtain didn't spare the women from the sickly smell wafting from the one among the five men on the other side who had been dead for twenty-four hours. Everyone was oppressed in the spirit by the presence of the corpse and dazed by the fragrance of the big candles around it.

Iñigo Sanchez, before going on to Chania, had told Yehezkel that if Don Sancio should succumb to his injuries, he was to be buried in the monastery two leagues from Kaliviani. Yehezkel fished out six silver *grossi* to ensure the monks would erect, in the tiny wildflower garden that was their cemetery, a stone cross with the name and dates of Sancio de la Palmela. Galatea was moved by the gesture, considering it was made by a Jew. "It's true, as they say," she thought, "that nobility is in one's actions, not in one's blood."

With the exception of Aillil's sobs, the six pilgrims stood silently in the sun as the monks lowered Don Sancio into the hard Cretan earth. During the brief ceremony, Yehezkel and Galatea felt the hand of fate pushing them toward the Holy City. They hadn't talked about the confession any more, but it was clear to both that Don Sancio had been the bearer of clues to the enigma their journey was all about. There was no denying it: some kind of Holy Grail lay at the end of their Quest. They were looking for something that no one, monk, pope, or emperor, had so far been able to find.

The nun and the kabbalist, without having to say it, shared the certainty that if "Deus vult" meant God wills it to all pilgrims, in their case God in his unfathomable wisdom had more elaborate plans.

✡ ✠ ✡ ✠

KALIVIANI, 13TH MAY 1219

Yehezkel wanted to go alone, but Galatea wouldn't hear of it. They had to find a passage to Acre, and she was responsible for Gudrun. Not that she didn't trust the rabbi—she would have been an ingrate—but she wasn't in the habit of letting others make traveling arrangements for her, so she would accompany him to Heraklion. She asked the widow where they could find horses. Yehezkel rolled his eyes.

"This island is all steep, rocky hills, madame, and a horse is a shy, moody animal, frightened by narrow paths. Its health is fragile and its value such that one is chained to it as to a galley mate. Believe me, what you and I need are two small, sturdy beasts; tranquil, tenacious, and *cheap*. In a word, two donkeys!"

"I shall *never* be seen astride a donkey, sir! At least, not while I'm alive," huffed Galatea.

She was instead seen sitting composedly across the saddle of one for a good quarter of the island's perimeter. As a girl, she'd learned to kick a horse in the belly so it would draw in its breath and allow her to tighten the saddle one last notch. When she tried it on a Cretan female donkey, she discovered why the reputation of those animals, despite their humble appearance, is so rotten.

For the whole way to Heraklion—a one-hundred-league, three-day ride—wherever the odd couple was sighted, villagers rushed out of their homes, pointing out the donkeys with a nun and a Jew, as if that very scene was a prophesied sign of the imminent end of the world.

On the afternoon of the third day, less than two weeks after the beaching, they entered the walls of Candia, as the Venetians had been calling Heraklion for seven years to no effect. They rode fifty feet from each other to avoid giving scandal in a city. It was Thursday, which Albacara had said was market day, but their plan to arrive in the morning was sabotaged by Galatea's donkey, a specimen worthy of being called stubborn even by other donkeys.

As long as it was on a path, it proceeded in a straight line, but the moment it entered a meadow or a field, it was gripped by a kind of dementia and started to walk in circles with uncanny single-mindedness. All of Galatea's strength barely sufficed to force it back onto the path each time.

They had missed the recruiting of sailors for local boats, a market-day event Yehezkel counted on to find out about vessels due to sail east. They left the donkeys in a stable by the gate and headed to the port to make inquiries. As they descended a narrow alleyway—which, judging by the donkey traffic, must have been one of Heraklion's main thruways—Yehezkel saw a Jewish boy running head down, dodging everything and everyone. He stopped the boy with his belly and asked in Hebrew, "Where are you running like that, to study?"

"There's a rabbi among the slaves they disembarked half an hour ago!" the boy gasped.

Galatea saw Yehezkel's eyes narrow. He said, "Follow me, madame!" and dashed down the alley as the boy ran off to alert the Jewish authorities. Galatea lifted the hem of her habit and ran after him. In a few moments they were in the opening where the harbor's quays converged. Yehezkel grabbed her hand and dragged her through the crowd toward the cries of the slave auction.

In those years, slaves were sold right on the quay where the boat that captured them—usually pirates pretending to be merchants—was moored. The readiness of Jewish communities in the Mediterranean to ransom Jewish prisoners made Jews the favorite prey of pirate ships.

Galatea surveyed a scene similar to Rialto: fish stalls, mutilated veterans, obscenely painted prostitutes. But the abbess, who had grown up in the quarrelsome city-states of Tuscia, also recognized the palpable tension of a city occupied by strangers.

She heard the salesman shout that all the girl slaves—Circassian, Bosnian, Georgian, Bulgarian, Tatar—most between twelve and fourteen, were "healthy and without blemish, in their hidden parts as well as in the visible ones!" She felt impotent anger at the poor girls' fate.

The Jewish slave on sale was about Yehezkel's age, but scrawnier; in fact, almost skeletal. His haunted, expressive face stood out among the other prisoners. The owner of the lot was in the ample tent behind the auction stage. Yehezkel and Galatea watched him without leaving the anonymity of the crowd.

It was a sun-baked, stout Greek around fifty. He had a fleshy, olive-skinned face with few yet deep wrinkles and a thin moustache on the top lip, giving him a classic Levantine look. When he laughed he squeezed his eyes in a porcine way and turned a bright, strawberry red. He was dressed in local fashion, but with a black waistcoat covered in medals and crosses. Yehezkel whispered in Galatea's ear, "He looks like something halfway between a court jester and a fake relic."

Galatea watched the Greek drink wine and tell dirty jokes, slapping a client's shoulder or a slave's buttock with the same gusto. His gestures made his dialect comprehensible to anyone, but now and then he switched to an atrocious Latin, blaspheming in an oriental cadence. She heard him shout, "Saracens may get seventy-two virgins, Iannis, but when Venetians and Templars go to Heaven, they get to bugger the saints!"

She whispered to Yehezkel, "The man combines the most depraved aspects of two races and two civilizations in one person."

Yehezkel laughed loud, always amused by how the abbess left no stone standing of what she criticized. Hearing him laugh, the merchant saw his black sarbel and decided this must be the emissary of the Jewish community, come to ransom the prisoner. Waving his short arms, he invited Yehezkel under the tent. The abbess followed as the Jew made his way around the platform, causing a murmur in the crowd.

The merchant introduced himself with an ironic half bow. "Spiridione Masarakis, *servo vostro.** Ha, ha! Get it? Servo vostro, ha, ha, ha!"

"How much do you want to free the prisoner?" Yehezkel had no intention of spending more time than strictly necessary in the company of this individual.

"A while ago, a Jewish shopkeeper offered me a measly two hundred dinars for him. Parasite! But it was strange; usually the physical condition of a Jewish slave doesn't influence your offers."

The prisoner's lips curled in an ironic smile. Yehezkel reflected, breathing deeply, and then plunged his hand in his pocket and brought out a leather pouch, smaller and softer than the one with the astrolabium. He turned his back to the Greek and poured out the contents into the palm of his hand. When he turned to face Spiridione, he held between his thumb and forefinger a ruby the size of a pigeon's egg, and the exact color of the two drops of blood that roll out of that bird's nostrils when it exhales its last breath.

---

*"At your service," but literally, in Italian and Venetian, "I am your slave"

Spiridione's eyes shone almost brighter than the stone. He looked at the Jew, wondering how many more stones were in that pouch, and then glanced around to check how many people had seen the ruby, every thought crossing his mind as legible as the statues on a cathedral.

Galatea glanced at the prisoner to take her eyes off the slave trader. The man's smile now said he thought the Lord was the best of storytellers.

The ruby was clearly worth more than what Heraklion's Jews could have collected for the ransom, so Spiridione waited to hear what further pretences the big Jew would have. Yehezkel kept turning the stone in his fingers before the Greek's eyes, smiling, until Galatea thought he was overdoing it. Then, suddenly, in a deep voice that silenced everyone around them, he boomed, "I want a passage to Acre for six people!"

The abbess bent down and pretended to straighten the hem of her habit to recover from the fright the rabbi's voice just gave her. Her bones—nay, her very soul—reverberated with those everyday words as if she'd just heard a divine revelation. Suddenly, she remembered his voice when he had spoken Jesus's words that night in Torcello. At first she'd thought it was God himself, come to take her soul to Heaven. Now she understood that he had just used the same, unearthly skill.

Spiridione was also struck by the surge of power unleashed by the Jew. He swallowed slowly, already thinking which boat he would use for the pilgrims. He *had* to be the one to carry the Jew, the beautiful nun, and above all the precious stones eastward, at least for a portion of the way.

They struck a deal. The rabbi declined to tell Spiridione where they resided, saying only they would be back on the first Sunday in June. The salesman removed the prisoner's irons as the Greek lifted the ruby to the light, happy as a child. The prisoner embraced Yehezkel, a broken blessing on his lips, "May God bless you, my brother . . . I would not have lived much longer."

Yehezkel realized the other Jew was worse off for the ordeal than had seemed at first. He'd thought of entrusting him to the local community, but something in the man's dark eyes, he couldn't have said what, made him decide to take him back to the widow's house and look after him himself. They had to find another donkey for the ride back and were slowed by the condition of the ransomed prisoner, who was so weak he was often close to falling off his animal.

He was a Spanish itinerant rabbi called Shlomo del Medigo. Talking with Yehezkel in Hebrew during the journey, he expressed surprise that a rabbi should be traveling with a nun, but when he heard of the circumstances of their meeting and her role in the beaching of the *Falcus,* he agreed Divine Providence was undoubtedly at work.

The slave market had shaken the abbess; she was silent for most of the first day of the ride back to Kaliviani. Then, thinking back to the unearthly roar into which Master Ezekiel transformed his voice, she began interrogating him.

"It was really nothing special, madame," said Yehezkel.

"I'm not a child, Master Ezekiel. You must explain *exactly* how you draw that thunder from your chest, or I won't give you a moment's rest about it from here to the Holy Sepulchre!"

"Oh, dear me! God protect me . . ." laughed Yehezkel.

The Spanish thirty-year-old's resilience and Yehezkel's herbs ensured a quick recovery, and soon the two were studying together in the middle of the night—the best time for kabbalists for attempts to "raise the heavens"—whispering as they commented on one of the codices Yehezkel stowed in Galatea's chest.

Galatea could watch Aillil snoozing for hours, motherly love in her eyes. The widow noticed the way the abbess looked at the boy. At one point, seeing her moved to tears, she came close and took her hand. "He is so beautiful, like a young angel," said Galatea, as if to justify her emotion.

"Yes, he is graceful and pure, but fragile. Born from too young a mother," said the widow.

Galatea changed the subject. Albacara, to survive after the death of her Vidal, had to sell her skill as a weaver, so for a while they talked about fabrics. Then Galatea tried to tell her about Hildegard but soon realized that the widow's faith was as simple as the centurion's. She listened as the other woman quoted Saint Bruno, fear making her voice tremble, "'Careful! Satan is in the air, in the dust that hangs in every sunbeam. He is in the sudden breeze, in the gust that topples men in the field and ruins the crop. All these things are the devil whistling.' Do you see what I'm trying to say, Mother Galatea?"

The village of Kaliviani was a little paradise on earth: two dozen houses surrounded by a green belt of oranges and lemons that stood out against a gray, olive-covered hillside. The sea was an intense cobalt blue teeming with white and red sails. The morning light was sharp as crystal, and the fresh air was touched with lemons.

The pilgrims were guests at weddings with singing, dancing, and great roasting of goats. They witnessed disputes that turned into brawls and at times showed the promise of becoming feuds. This was, Yehezkel explained smiling, because despite being small, the village hosted three of the four Mediterranean faiths: Latin Christians, Greek Christians, and Saracens, but lacked the soothing presence of Jews, whom all three could otherwise have blamed for their troubles.

One day, Galatea was talking with Yehezkel about the Holy City and what would be revealed there. The widow, who'd been waiting for the opportunity, fell on her knees embracing Galatea's thighs.

"I beg you, signora, take me with you! My life on this island without my Vidal has lost all meaning! He was a saintly man, an evil word never passed his lips. I am . . . I feel so *useless* without him!"

Albacara burst into tears. Galatea raised her up and put her arms around her. The widow went on, "I know what I must do: go on a pilgrimage to Jerusalem! My poor Vidal built this house with his own hands, but I shall gift it to the monks and go from one tomb to the other in Jerusalem on my knees!"

Yehezkel turned away, moved by that sudden baring of a whole life in a few moments. He realized the abbess wouldn't consent to the widow's request without his approval. He was the shepherd of their mangy flock. "The important thing, after all," he said to himself, "is that we will be seven souls instead of six."

He turned around. Galatea's violet eyes were fixed on him, as he'd expected. He smiled a consent. Albacara followed the wordless dialogue, astonished that the Jew had the last word over the abbess of a Venetian convent. Still, she thanked the rabbi profusely for "accepting her in the company" and then slipped into the sublime transformation that pilgrims go through once their decision is made.

The noble word "company" the widow used struck Yehezkel as a far better term to describe the little group than the flock he had considered them so far. What turned them from sheep to humans wasn't the presence of the widow, but the power of the number seven.

Despite declared gratitude for having been accepted into the company, Albacara showed an ill-disguised mistrust of the Jew. Once, when she was alone with Galatea, she confided her worry about the influence the rabbi seemed to have on her. "You can't imagine, dear mother, how much the men of that sensual race are experts at winning the confidence of Christian women. . . ."

Galatea reassured her. She'd known this Jew for a month and owed her life to him twice over. She'd felt the same misgivings at first but now understood they were unfounded fears based on calumnies. The widow seemed convinced and smiled broadly. For an instant, Galatea saw the young girl who, years earlier, had embarked for the great adventure with the settler she'd just married, cheeks scarlet with sun and love, full of dreams and trust in the doge's promises.

A strange thing happened in the days before their second trip to Heraklion, connected to the blue of Galatea's visions. One morning, Yehezkel, transgressing his vow to no longer sail for pleasure, joined a local fishing boat. A crewman promised to show him some secret magic. From the animal in a brown-streaked shell as big as a child's fist, he squeezed a yellowish juice and soiled his shirt with it. Then he pompously announced that an ancient magical formula from the desert of

Cappadocia would turn the yellow stain into the blue of the sky.

At the words "blue of the sky," Yehezkel started paying attention to the fisherman's ravings. When the boat was a mile from shore, before they lowered their nets—either through magic or, as Yehezkel rather thought, from the effect of the sun on the juice—the stains on the man's shirt turned a brilliant blue, the very blue of Yehezkel's talisman: saphir. The rabbi couldn't contain his excitement: he had just rediscovered *t'chelet*.*

Back at the house, he feverishly told Galatea and Rav Shlomo of his discovery, citing the verse in Numbers in which the Lord commands Israel, "Make tassels on the corners of your garments, with a blue cord on each tassel." Then he explained to Galatea that tassels had been white since the Saracens' takeover of the Holy Land, because in the confusion of those decades the source of the blue dye had been lost.

"Today," he shouted, jumping up and down on the spot to Rav Shlomo's amusement, "I discovered that what had been lost was the knowledge that dyed materials have to be left *in the sun* for the yellow to turn into blue! Do you understand, madame? Jews now have t'chelet again!"

Galatea, literally under the spell of that color since childhood, was nodding slowly.

The rabbis were as excited as two knights who had just found the Holy Grail. They couldn't wait to find a synagogue to announce the discovery to the Jewish world, so sure were they that finding the source of t'chelet was a sign of Israel's imminent redemption.

To celebrate the historic occasion Galatea wove a linen scarf for Yehezkel on the sturdy little loom Vidal Cordier constructed for his wife. Then she bought fifty shells from the fishermen and used the juice from the disgusting animals to dye the scarf as she had seen the Ben-Porats do in Torcello. When it had lain in the sun for an hour, the scarf filled the abbess with perfect joy by becoming the exact same blue as the mantle of Christ Triumphant in the Last Judgment of the cathedral in Torcello.

●●●

*The term the Bible uses for the color of the blue cord in the tzitzith.

The company spent days of near-perfect serenity in Kaliviani, the kind that later shine in memory. Yehezkel and Galatea took to sitting outside the house at sunset, watching the fiery display in the western sky. The song of crickets bounced off every rock, endlessly repeating the same phrase, like a liturgy stuck on the first two notes of a hymn. One evening Yehezkel said dryly, "Healthy children shout together like these Cretan crickets, a habit adults find bothersome. I wonder what makes them so happy . . . or maybe something prevents grown-ups from letting themselves go to such noisy celebrations. Maybe bigger animals are just more solemn."

Galatea smiled and then stood up and went inside. She set the table, served supper, and sat there, watching him eat. Meanwhile, the widow was lighting candles all through the house, as she always did when she heard the unburied dead scream in the wind.

✡   ☩   ✡   ☩

IN THE PREACHER'S HOUSE ON THE UNIVERSITY'S PREMISES IN PARIS, 25TH MAY 1219

The same evening in late May, Domingo of Guzman was dining with a friend, Bertrand of Garrigue. "Dining" is perhaps too strong a word, since before the friars were only some black rye bread, a hard piece of cheese from the Pyrenees, and a big radish. Domingo said a blessing, and they dug into their banquet.

The Spaniard was exhausted but, as usual, didn't show it. He looked older even than when he'd met Bois-Guilbert in Prouilhe just a month earlier, the frantic pace taking its toll ever more visibly. He now wore a reddish beard, which, together with his blue eyes, was ample evidence of his Visigoth ancestry.

After despatching thirty friars to establish new houses in Orléans, Reims, Metz, Poitiers, and Limoges, he was preparing to return to Bologna. He knew he didn't have long to live and was in a race against time to ensure that the work of a lifetime became irreversible. But through it all, the danger the confession posed to the church was foremost in his mind. He often told himself he must build houses of preachers as if there were no confession and look for the confession as if there was no Order of Preachers.

"Only two days to the Pentecost," remarked Bertrand. "As usual, you did the right thing when you wrote to Francesco of Assisi, saying you would not be back in Italy in time for the chapter of his order."

Domingo smiled. "I have a confession to make, Bertrand," he said. "I only met Francesco once, at the council, four years ago, and don't doubt his good faith for an instant, but I found him strongly influenced by the Cathars' misguided talk of love . . . most of all, I think he doesn't believe in studying and educating priests. He quoted Jesus's words on the lilies in the field and kept saying that where there is love there is no ignorance. But I had the feeling that holy, mystical ignorance is what he is actually about."

Bertrand smiled. "So you're not sorry you'll miss the Pentecost chapter of his 'mendicants'?"

"No, I'm not. It would only have resulted in misunderstandings and a spirit of competition between our friars, if not between him and me." Domingo stood up and started pacing the room. Bertrand knew better than to interrupt the founder's reflections.

Domingo had recently begun to ask himself if the confession really existed, if it wasn't just a plot by the Jews of Jesus's time, a false document redacted to counter the claim of Resurrection. After all, no pope, from the Honorius at Troyes ninety years before to this one, had ever actually *seen* it.

"Could Saint Bernard have been taken in by the Templars and sold the pope a fictitious end-of-times danger? And what if it's all just a Templar ploy? No, no, I must proceed as if the thing exists," he smiled bitterly. "They say Innocent dreamed that Francesco was saving the soul of the church. That may be so, but if *I* don't find and destroy the confession, there will be no church for Francesco to save!"

Part Two

Second
and Third Day

CHAPTER 11

OSE PRI LE-MINO

Bearing fruit after their kind

KALIVIANI, 27TH MAY 1219

Pilgrims set off with a devotional purpose. Absolving a vow, expiating a sin, saving their souls are the focus of their thoughts. All this for a hundred or two hundred leagues, maybe three hundred in the more pious ones. Then something in their heads shifts, like the light on a landscape, and the important thing for them becomes walking. One foot in front of the other, one step after another. A leaf, a lizard, a forest, a river ford, a hostel, a walled city, a desert, a mountain range. Walking forever, beyond the end of the world and down *another* path, no longer remembering the destination and with no more need of a purpose.

Rav Shlomo of Toledo had become such a pilgrim and was trying to explain it to Galatea. "A pilgrim's *real* journey, señora, is inside himself. Man's mind is a landscape, and walking is a way of crossing it. Pilgrims know it . . . oh, do they know it! When they cross each other, there's a certain smile in their greeting; they are secret adepts of the *religio* of never stopping again."

"Yes, I always suspected something of the sort," smiled Galatea. "I could see it in their eyes."

"Of course," said Yehezkel, "should a luckless pilgrim set off on a donkey like the one you rode, madame, he could go in circles in a field near his home until the end of time."

Galatea threw her head back and laughed, the sight of her long white neck making both rabbis fear for their integrity.

"Oh, since we are talking of circles, Shlomo . . . did you ever, in your wanderings, hear talk of an ancient 'Parchment of Circles,' apparently a relic of the Cathar heretics?"

"Parchment of Circles? Yes, let me think, where have I heard that name before? Of course! It was Makarios who mentioned it! Two years ago, in Famagusta, I was discussing Coptic traditions with a very erudite priest of theirs. His name is Father Makarios, and both Latins and Greeks call him a heretic. He said that a big trove of parchments was found near Jericho some four hundred years ago, and the one that caused the greatest sensation was the Parchment of Circles you speak of."

"That's all? Your Father Makarios didn't know what the parchment *was*?"

"No, but then he was only repeating what he'd heard from other Copts in Egypt . . . but why do you want to know about that parchment?"

"Don't laugh, Shlomo, but do you remember Mother Galatea's dream I told you of, the choir singing the first verse of Bereshit in Hebrew? And do you remember the page of Ezekiel that the other said Rav Hanina had hidden? Well, I suspect—nay, I have the strange certainty—that both things are connected to this Parchment of Circles, and that all three are somehow part of a single, arcane scheme."

Galatea smiled. "Perhaps the role kabbalists attribute to *names* that Master Ezekiel told me of is justified. After all, *you*, sir, are called Shlomo and possess the wise moderation of King Solomon, while your friend here rants and raves just like the prophet whose name he bears."

Rav Shlomo laughed, charmed by her wit, and asked, "Has

Rav Yehezkel tried writing your name in Hebrew letters, señora, to tell you what can be glimpsed in it?"

"Wait, wait, what did you just say? Write my name in Hebrew letters?"

"Of course, señora. It is the sacred language of Scripture! No mystical secrets are accessible to anyone using a different language," answered Rav Shlomo, as if stating the obvious.

Yehezkel snorted. "I'll do it, sooner or later. I'm beginning to think that this won't be a short journey. We left Venice a month ago, and we're still riding donkeys back and forth on a Greek island."

Galatea blurted out, "You're an ingrate, Master Ezekiel! Thirty-two people . . . no, thirty-three with Don Sancio, died in the beaching of the *Falcus,* and all you can think of is the time you lost!"

"Sorry, I won't speak another word," mumbled Yehezkel.

"If that were to happen, I would think there was a saint among us," said Galatea drily, "because only *they* perform miracles!"

The next day she asked about the things he promised to teach her when they would be at sea.

"The Hebrew alphabet, for a start. But Manichean theology, too, and your—what is it called—Kabbalah?"

Yehezkel shilly-shallied, without explaining. To overcome his reluctance, she said, "I promise, Master Ezekiel, I'll never reveal to *anyone* who taught me to read and write Hebrew!"

"Madame, I've never been jealous of my knowledge . . . but Jewish tradition frowns on the excessive instruction of women."

"Aah, is that so?" said Galatea. "I should have imagined it; Jews don't consider women capable of leaving ignorance behind them. You're no different from Christian men, after all."

Yehezkel's face reddened under his beard. He found the accusation intolerable. "No, no, it's not the way you think! The Talmud says women are less likely than men to surrender to base instincts, the opposite of what your Saint Augustine held!" He floundered, bringing ten arguments at a time. Galatea noticed his breathless good faith and smiled.

In the late afternoon of the next day, Yehezkel abandoned all scruples and scratched the twenty-two letters of the aleph-bet on a wax tablet. Then, under a fig tree in a remote corner of a Mediterranean island, far from the prying eyes of priests or rabbis, he taught his Christian pupil the appearance, pronunciation, and numerical value of the first five letters.

Galatea was a fast learner. Something in the sound and shape of Hebrew letters resonated inside her like a memory. At times, after dawn, Yehezkel heard her practicing pronunciation by singing the first verse of the Bible in Hebrew to herself as she walked around the house, like that dawn in the lagoon.

One day, the rabbi overheard the women commenting on the saltiness of the meat the widow just cooked. He rushed to the fireplace where the stewpot was hanging.

"Don't eat it!" he exclaimed. "Listen to a medicus. The excess salt was rubbed into it to hide the taste of rotten meat. It is probably poisonous!"

They all followed his advice except Garietto, who thought that throwing out fine Greek goat stew was an offense to God and men. In the evening, the young Venetian looked like a man possessed by demons, writhing with spasms terrifying to watch, froth drooling from his mouth. Yehezkel immediately dragged him out in the garden to make him throw up and picked some chamomile flowers—luckily in bloom.

In the following days Garietto recovered, lovingly cared for by Gudrun. The feeling between the two eighteen-year-olds had been evident on board the *Falcus,* but the abbess had been in no condition to notice temptation sneaking up on her ward. But the German girl being a Cistercian nun, in Kaliviani the story took on the characteristics of the impossible romances sung in every court of Provence.

They were a fetching couple. She hovered over him, blonde tresses swaying, sunburned freckles, and worried blue eyes. Garietto, all muscles and hair, was normally a picture of vigor, and watching the pangs of pain on his sweat-soaked face moved something in Gudrun's deepest spiritual recesses. Garietto, on the other hand, when she bent over him, which was all the time, had before his eyes her irrepressible breasts, which had already caused one villager to have a jug smashed over his head by the virago.

In those lazy Cretan days, as he watched Garietto unabashedly flirting with the girl, Yehezkel mused that the two nuns in the company couldn't have been more different. Gudrun, like all chubby girls, was always rushing somewhere, flushed and panting, in stark contrast to Galatea's poise, as well as her figure. He admitted he couldn't begin to fathom the strange way in which the abbess and her younger sister alternated tender gestures with bouts of sulking.

The abbess continued Aillil's musical education. Yehezkel would hear them singing Hildegard's hymns as they wandered in the low shrubs outside the house. Aillil smiled every time Galatea approached, and for some reason, the boy's weakness for the abbess bothered Yehezkel more than it should have.

Some days before they left the village to see Spiridione again, a meeting neither looked forward to, Galatea mentioned she'd not forgotten the voice he used in the slave market, nor her threat to give him no rest until he taught her how to summon it.

The idea of teaching the techniques for pronouncing God's Names to a Christian woman would have made Lunel's kabbalists recoil in horror, but Yehezkel had reflected on her prophetic gift and her role in his mission and concluded that he sort of . . . owed it to her. In any case, nobody would ever find out. But there had to be method and logic to his instruction. He couldn't start from the end, could he?

The next morning, out in the sun, he handed Galatea the scarf she had dyed t'cheleth.

"Madame," he began, "Kabbalah is not a method to enhance one's voice; it is an enormously complex system of thought. The secrets of the maskil, or pronouncer of God's Names, are a discipline one can only learn after experiencing many other insights. Clearly, you're a spiritually gifted lady, and since you are also instinctively certain of the divine nature of *this* color, I will begin with a short lesson on this blue."

Galatea, enthralled, sat cross-legged on the ground before him, and he joined her.

"Just as a kabbalist recognizes the influence in this world of the Sephirot, God's ten emanations, so does he—or she, from today— recognize the symbols through which God's presence and plans are manifested. Saphir, the root of Sephirot, is a major symbol, it is the color of the divine, of the crystal the sages saw on Mount Sinai under God's Throne, of the Heavens and the world above—and, as t'cheleth, of the cord in the tzitzith, which allows us a glimpse of Him."

Yehezkel paused. "Now the opposite symbol to blue is *red,* or crimson, the color of blood." He hesitated. "Be indulgent with me, madame, for I'm about to make another unflattering comparison between our faiths, but what I mean to show you is the ubiquity of symbols, how the apparently haphazard way in which they litter our world is actually perfectly coherent. Just as blue is the color of Judaism—and I can guarantee you that when our exile ends, and there is once again a Jewish kingdom, its standards will be blue—in the same way, red is the color of pagans earlier . . . and Christians later."

Galatea started to protest but then decided to hear him out.

"The heart of your faith is that you were saved by Christ's *blood.* We remove the blood from all meat before we eat it. Blood is powerful indeed; it is *life,* it was sprinkled on the altar by the high priest, yet for Judaism its color symbolizes the earthly, sensual, pagan side of man. Isaiah says 'your sins are as scarlet.'"

The abbess silently considered these words.

Yehezkel went on. "So it was only *apparently* of their own free will that the Roman emperors chose crimson and purple-red as the color of power, still so dear to cardinals that you speak of *adorare purpuram.** *Edom* is Hebrew for red and is also the nickname of Jacob's twin brother Esau, who was ginger. Because it was used for Jacob/Israel's opponent, it became the Talmud's term for Rome, Israel's eternal enemy. I could use *your* Scriptures, too. Saint John, in the Apocalypse, writes 'meretrix circumdata purpura et coccinum.'"†

He concluded, "In a nutshell, madame, a kabbalist sees the battle between the angels above in hundreds of symbols; one of them is the struggle between blue and crimson. Kabbalah is a way of seeing things, and I felt happier for you to enter it through an odd awareness like this one, rather than theological talk."

Blue and crimson had played powerful roles in her visions since childhood, but that was not all. She believed that Jesus died for her sins, and that his suffering on the Cross was salvific, but in her heart of hearts, the power of the blood into which the Eucharist wine turned to save souls always had, for her, something unsettling about it. Since they were alone, she said, "I think I know what you mean by 'a way of seeing things,' Rabbi. As I told you, this blue represents God's presence for me as much as it does for you, so I'll just treasure the lesson on recognizing symbols, without dwelling too much on Christianity's choice of crimson."

✡ ✠ ✡ ✠

HERAKLION, 31ST MAY 1219

The second time they entered Heraklion was on Friday morning, after a ride that had been kinder on their haunches. The peasants who had commented on the sight of a nun riding with a Jew two weeks earlier saw her go by again, this time with *two* Jews. There was dismay among

---

*Worshiping crimson, a medieval metaphor for veneration of the pope
†"The whore arrayed in purple and scarlet"

some onlookers, the scariest thing being that all three riders, as in a satanic Sabbath, never stopped laughing.

Heraklion's Jewish quarter huddled around its synagogue by the port. Asking passersby, they soon found the home of Tofefloià Ha-Cohen, rabbi, merchant, and diplomat. They knocked on the small door and were let in. It was the typical abode of a wealthy Jewish trader, humble and somber from the outside, but rich and sophisticated inside. Galatea admired the Armenian carpets and silk cushions on the divan in the big salon. Persian and Syrian silver vases sat on low ebony tables. One wall was decorated with a fresco of David felling Goliath, which made both Jewish guests wrinkle their noses. A moment later the merchant walked in and, noticing the nun, greeted them in perfect Latin.

"Peace be with you all! Welcome to my humble dwelling. I hope the two foreign rabbis will do me the honor of accepting my hospitality over Shabbat."

Yehezkel bowed deeply. "May your light shine for many years, distinguished Rav Tofefloià! I am your humble servant Yehezkel ben Yoseph, of Fustat and Lunel. This is Rav Shlomo del Medigo of Toledo and last, though she precedes us both in grace and virtue, Countess Galatea degli Ardengheschi, abbess of the convent of San Maffìo, in Torcello."

"Torcello? Are you a Venetian noblewoman?" asked Tofefloià, immediately attentive.

"No, sir, the lands of Ardenga are in Tuscia. But the flock of nuns the Lord entrusted to my care is in the lagoon." To herself, she thought, "*Had* entrusted, is what I should start saying."

Tofefloià Ha-Cohen was the obligatory ingredient in Cretan politics. Most recently, his name was mentioned in the doge's palace for the nonchalance with which he put an end to the commercial war between Venetians and the Angeloi family that had raged since Venice's takeover of the island. He loved to quote the Book of Proverbs on the fact that "a gentle tongue can break a bone."

He was as tall as Yehezkel and dressed in the style of Jews in Islamic lands: a robe of deep purple, its neck richly embroidered, and a low yellow silk turban. A black beard rested on his chest in orderly curls. Large, dark eyes and heavy, half-closed lids gave him a languid look, belied by a penetrating gaze. "I suppose you're on your way to Jerusalem, signora. . . . Unusual as it is to see an abbess accompanied by two rabbis," he said with a smile, "I must confess the sight fills me with joy. You know, I am the strongest supporter on this island of dialogue between the three faiths. I'm convinced that when Christians mention Christ, their inner thoughts actually go to the one Creator of Heaven and earth!"

After comparing his Judaism with the sophisticated thought of the Greeks and the civilized traditions of Mohammedans, Tofefloià embraced the erudite, tolerant theological indifference that Don Sancio practiced. But for Yehezkel, if truth be told, what was admirable open-mindedness in a Christian, was unforgivable compromise in a Jew. The kabbalist kept his silence but found it outrageous that a rabbi should even speak like that. Rav Tofefloià persevered. "I am very friendly with the Latin bishop of Candia, who recently said to me—and in public, on Easter Sunday!—that he considers Jews the 'elder brothers' of Christians and dreams of the day when he will be allowed to enter our main synagogue wearing his cross!"

Unable to hold back any longer, Yehezkel blurted out, "Ha-Shem Yishmor!"* in a tone that made the meaning obvious even to the abbess. Tofefloià looked at him disdainfully, his arched nose and fat lower lip making the expression look natural.

"Aah, I see you are of the intransigent school. Are you perhaps one of those . . . kabbalists?"

Yehezkel said timidly, "With all due respect, Rav Tofefloià, one should not weigh the fundamentals of religion on the balance of reason and politics."

Tofefloià was a man of the world and had met kabbalists like this one, who wandered all over claiming to seek the road to the presence of the Lord but were in truth incapable of building a family and putting

---

*May God protect us!

down roots in one place, at least until the goyim drove them out again. He smiled and clapped his hands, anticipating the debate, especially in the presence of a beautiful nun. In an instant a servant appeared. Tofefloià instructed him in Greek and then turned to his guests.

"In Candia they make some of the best sweet wines, but none is better than the one prepared by my Jewish winemakers! Sit down; later you will tell me what brought you to my house, but now I want you to enjoy my hospitality and give me fresh news from the West."

Galatea sat on the divan, sipping malvasia and occasionally tasting a candied fruit or a pistachio nut as she listened to Rav Tofefloià treat them—in a polished but accented Latin—to his disenchanted version of events on the island since the Polis fell to the Venetians, fifteen years earlier.

"On taking Constantinople, Venice considered colonization would be too expensive and decided to impose commercial serfdom on little independent island dukedoms, granted or sold to adventurers and nobles, all distant relatives of the Venetian families at the top. I've heard it called the 'Italian solution.'"

Tofefloià took a sip of wine, a look of fondness in his eyes as he thought back to the coarseness of the Venetians. "These became, in effect, small tyrants surrounded by the sea."

"And the Greeks don't rebel?" asked Galatea, surprised. "Didn't they even defend their islands when the Venetians disembarked?"

"Oh, oh!" chuckled Rav Tofefloià at the memory. "Was it funny to see those young scions of Venetian merchant families playing Vikings in the sunny Aegean! A nephew of Doge Dandolo assembled a fleet of galleys and took *seventeen* islands from the Angelois officials, without the Greeks raising a finger!"

Galatea found the figs macerated in honey one of the most delicious things she'd ever tasted. She also found it delightful to hear the tales of military feats that in Venice made even galley prisoners proud—told by the victims of the bullying Venetian nobles. In short, the abbess was having a wonderful time.

"One of them declared himself Duke of Naxos, with celebrations worthy of the pagans of a thousand years ago. From that moment on, the Venetian families who weren't already present in Outremer lunged on the booty. Santorini went to a Barozzi, Anaphe to a Foscolo, Khitera to a Venier. And the ravenous Ghisi grabbed Tenos, Mykonos, Skyatos, *and* Skopelos!"

"And then what happened, Rav Tofel . . . ehm, Rav Tofef. . . . Oh, forgive me, this wine is so strong! I'm not used to it," stammered Galatea. Her host waved a hand to say it was nothing.

"The ferment in the streets of Candia was so intense that three years ago the local Venetian despot, another Dandolo, had to flee the island in woman's clothing to save his hide! Ah, how low the Greeks' empire has fallen! But oh, how we laughed that summer!"

Despite his wit, his guests perceived the sadness of the Cretan rabbi, a witness bitterly aware of the deathly blow that Venice dealt the Eastern Empire, now decayed to the point of being at the mercy even of nouveau riche Venetians.

The servant filled their cups. Galatea declined gently but firmly. After a few more of Tofefloià's anecdotes, Yehezkel managed to tell him of the beaching, the ransoming of the Spanish rabbi, and of his humble request: a wage for Rav Shlomo, homeless and close to hunger.

"You should have come to me right away. A leaf doesn't fall in Candia without my knowing it. I heard of the Templar cog that escaped the storm last month, but I had no idea there was a Jew on it!" Tofefloià paced the room, caressing his beard, and then said, "Rav Shlomo, you're a lucky Jew. Our melamed died last week, so if you can survive on a school teacher's wage, you can start Sunday!"

A curtain was moved aside and a slim woman of about Galatea's age stepped into the room, gently pushing the shoulders of a five-year-old child. Her simple silk dress was in the style of the damsels in the Polis. Behind her came a servant bearing a tray with a thin cake, like a wide, low biscuit. The woman's eyes questioned Tofefloià. He gestured to come in, smiling proudly, and introduced her.

"My wife, Miriam. The little one is Amos, my one-before-last. Today he turns five and starts to learn the aleph-bet. Come closer, countess, I want you to see how Jews instill the love of words in our children!"

"In the spirit of the Bible's words 'and may the words of the Torah always be sweet on your lips,'" Rav Tofefloià dipped a finger in honey and wrote a phrase on the biscuit that contained all twenty-two letters of the aleph-bet. The child could lick the letters once he had correctly pronounced each one and did so as his mother looked on with tears in her eyes. Galatea, too, found the whole ceremony touchingly sweet.

As they walked down to the harbor, Galatea and Rav Shlomo were in high spirits, possibly those of the malvasia. Yehezkel was silent; his friends guessed something vexed the Egyptian rabbi.

"What's eating you, Master Ezekiel? Don't try to deny . . ."

"The bishop called him *elder brother* of the Christians . . . Puah!!"

It was like the opening of a cataract on the Nile.

"Do you know what Tofefloià means? It means 'God plays the tambourine for him!' I wanted to shout in his face, 'Tofefloià, you're an *ignoramus*! Don't you know that all through the Bible God *always* chooses the younger brother? Have you never read of Cain and Abel, Ishmael and Isaac, Esau and Jacob, Aaron and Moses, Adonia and Solomon? Go on, Tofefloià, find me *one* firstborn who was God's chosen! The bishop wasn't complimenting Jews, he was proving that God chose the 'younger brother,' Christians! And while he was at it, he also showed everyone your ignorance of your own Scriptures!"

Galatea and Rav Shlomo laughed, amused by the outburst and impressed by Yehezkel's exposure of the bishop's devious false compliment.

Yehezkel recognized in Tofefloià one of those Jews who say "never attract the goyim's attention." After fifteen years in the West, he concluded there had always been two schools among Jews—in Babylon, under Rome or now—on the chosen people's mission. One was the school of compromise, Jews who stop telling pagans that they are pagans because it unnecessarily infuriates them. These Jews, in every epoch, soon assimilate and vanish. The other school, to which kabbalists belonged, was for denying respect to those who claim that the earth is flat and that "the Son of God came back from the dead."

The compromisers said, "Yes, we see that Christians have a theological limp, but we don't think it's nice to shout out to a lame person, 'Hey, you! Don't you see you're limping?'"

"But such an argument," retorted the kabbalists, "would apply to people incurably lame from birth, while Christians would walk perfectly well had they not been taught to limp as children by their priests."

He tried to explain to the abbess. "Madame, this man is a 'rabbi'— may he choke on his beard!—who should lead his brothers along the ways of the Torah and instead betrays the spirit of the Holy Book!"

Galatea reflected, eyeing the usual crowd forming to watch the nun and the two Jews, and then said, "I could tell you I understand your outrage, and it would be true, but don't you see by yourself that you're speaking in the exact tones of our clerics who burn Cathars, and who would gladly convert Jews at the tip of a sword?"

Yehezkel was struck dumb.

Rav Shlomo laughed. "Mother Galatea just gave you shakhmat,* Yehezkel."

Then the three parted ways. Rav Shlomo poured out his gratitude for everything they had done for him; then the rabbis accompanied the abbess to the hospital of the nuns of Saint Sergius, where she had stayed the previous time, and went back to Rav Tofefloià's.

✧ ✠ ✧ ✠

The rendezvous with Spiridione was at sixth hour on Sunday, in the dockers' tavern at the foot of the quay in Heraklion's harbor. This was the sort of place the abbess of a convent would normally never set foot in. The cries of dockworkers, the smell of rotting fish, and the

---

*Checkmate

prostitutes, already leaning over tables at third hour, should have kept Galatea a safe distance from the inn, but after the last month of adventures, she wouldn't have missed the visit to the tavern for all the world and a peacock, as they said in Tuscia.

At sixth hour on a Sunday, the place was close to what she'd always imagined a demonic Sabbath must look like. A sailor came toward them, protecting himself from the wine that literally splashed out of clients' tankards. He led the odd couple to a room in the back where some of the most unanimously condemned business in Christendom was conducted each day.

Spiridione Masarakis waited for them, sitting at a table crisscrossed with dagger marks, holding court with a smile that exposed the desolation of his surviving teeth. He was a solar Mediterranean male to whom weeping came as easily as rage. As lovable a scoundrel as only the men around that sea can be, in his life he'd been a pirate, a slave merchant, and a mercenary while seeding offspring from Gibraltar to Alexandretta. He was more or less excommunicated—not formally—but would never dare show his face in a church, at least not in the Aegean.

He greeted everyone who went by the table, gloating over the fact that he knew more than anyone in the inn about the strange couple that had twice appeared in the city. The resinous wine of the island made him overconfident, and when he saw Galatea again, he sprung to his feet. "My lady, we're made for each other! I'm ready to die for you!"

"There is no need, *sir*," answered the abbess icily. "Jesus Christ already did."

Seeing the way he looked at Galatea, Yehezkel asked him brusquely, "Well, have you found a vessel that will take us eastward?"

"Yes, my own *tareta*.* I'll take you to Cyprus myself! No, don't thank me, I have to go there anyway."

Yehezkel turned his eyes skyward, calling himself a fool for not thinking that the rubies would be too strong a temptation for such a low-

---

Taretas, Greek lanteen-rigged horse transport vessels also used for freight, replaced *dromons* in the early thirteenth century.

life. "Mmh . . . if he threatened me," he thought, "I could always tell him I hid them on his tareta where he will never find them, so he would have to protect me. But what if he threatened to torture Aillil . . . or the nun?"

"So it will only cost you ten gold bezants . . ." concluded Spiridione.

"But that's daylight robbery!" cried the rabbi.

Spiridione retorted, offended, "It is *not* robbery, but the right price to take six people to Limassol!" He glared at the rabbi, a menacing glint in his eye. "And watch your tongue, Jew! You're *in* here now, and Spiro will decide if you go out on your own two feet."

Yehezkel had an idea. "Meet me half way, as civilized businessmen do. You want ten gold bezants? Then you'll have to take on *eight* passengers, and all the way to Acre."

The abbess didn't look at the rabbi, pretending to know about the two extra passengers. Spiridione grabbed a wine jug and filled his mug, ignoring everyone else's. "Who are the other two?" he asked after swallowing a long gulp.

"A Frankish knight and his squire," answered Yehezkel evasively.

"Ha! Your champion, is he? All right, then! Eight passengers, but only as far as Limassol, take it or leave it! Five bezants on sailing and five on landfall. I'll provide sweet water and ship's biscuits; if you want other provisions, it's your problem. We sail next week, at dawn on Sunday!"

"No," said Yehezkel quietly, "in ten days. We need more time; one of the pilgrims isn't coming back."

"Oh, see the Jewish knight looking after his pilgrims like a hen after her chicks! If *you'd* accompanied those infants in the summer of 1212, they might have reached the Holy Land!" Spiridione laughed so hard he turned crimson. "He, he! But if you ask me, we would have sold them anyway. Ha, ha!"

"What infants are you referring to?" asked Galatea, horrified, speaking for the first time since sitting down. "Not the innocents who took the cross?"

Seven years earlier, Spiridione took part in the tragic ending of what was already being called a massacre of the innocents. Some incensed boys convinced a few thousand naive Frank and German children between seven and thirteen that only Christian children, innocent of the Kingdom of Jerusalem's corruption and debauchery, could free the Holy Sepulchre. The infants, fed by charitable people on the way, walked for months until they reached Marseille.

They expected the sea to open up for them as it had for Moses and the Israelites, but alas, the Lord had other plans. Most turned around and went home, but hundreds believed unscrupulous adventurers and boarded cogs to Syria, only to be cynically sold into slavery to the Saracens. Those rogues, of whom Spiridione was an example, thanked God for the children's credulity just as fishermen thank Him for a generous passage of tuna and built themselves new cogs with the profits.

Spiridione related, chuckling, of the day they sold the children. The Frank and German children, convinced they'd just arrived in the Holy Land, stared in horror at the irons that were their prize. Galatea's eyes filled with tears, and her resolve not to sail on the ruffian's boat became ironclad.

Meanwhile, the room had slowly filled up with the curious. Sailors pretended to drink as they watched the scandalous couple spewed by the sea west of Kaliviani. The pilgrims on the *Falcus* only muttered about the nun's unfortunate choice of traveling companion, but the Greeks in the inn quickly produced a more dramatic scenario. The nun defied public shame because she was already a slave to the Jew's animal sensuality—capable, as everyone knew, of awakening the moral turpitude of Eve even in a nun.

The whispered certainty had become that the poor nun, clearly under a spell cast by the Jewish wizard, was unaware of her fate: the Jew was selling her to Spiro, who would deliver her to his Saracen clients. Outrage grew among the sailors—not directed at Spiro, of course, who after all was just earning a living, but at the perfidious Jew who conceived the whole scheme.

"They should hang every Jew on the island!" cried a docker from a corner of the room.

"If we don't stop them now, they'll decide everything about our lives," said another voice.

Two of them drew closer to the table. Spiro smiled, looking forward to the moment when, defending his clients and threatening the more aggressive thugs, he would reaffirm authority over both. He was startled when the nun suddenly rose from her stool—she was taller than half the men in the room—and turned toward the crowd. In Latin, and in the tone nobles have always used with plebs, she said, "Get back to your pastimes! I am Galatea, countess of the Ardengheschis of Monte Alcino, and this is Master Ezekiel of Lunel, my personal physician. I am on a pilgrimage to Jerusalem and, for an unusually high consideration"—here her voice nearly cracked—"Master Masarakis will provide his services to us."

The mariners dispersed, but far from expressing relief for the danger the nun had escaped, their faces were those of children forbidden from playing a favorite game because adults find it too noisy or muddy or smelly. Yehezkel and Spiro stared at Galatea's smoldering eyes, still as dangerous as live embers, both clearly impressed by that lioness disguised as a nun.

She warned Yehezkel right from the alley that climbed up from the port, "You'll sail with that Greek barbarian by yourself, Rabbi! Gudrun, the armigers, and I will look for a ship owner who can be called a Christian, in the sense *I* attribute to the word!" Yehezkel had not yet seen her face quite so flushed.

"And if you'll consent to it, we'll take Aillil with us, too!"

He muttered under his breath, made a joke about Spiro, and generally avoided answering.

"And anyway, who is this Frank with a squire, uh?" she asked, still fuming, just outside the city walls.

"André de Rosson," answered Yehezkel with a straight face.

Yehezkel had bumped into the young Templar on Shabbat. The knight was left in Candia with the garrison but would have given anything to be with his brothers at Damietta. Thinking of the company's security, the rabbi had asked Rav Tofefloià to speak to the island's Templar commander, and to only do so *after* giving him don Sancio's last letter.

Galatea imagined Spiro's face when he saw the white mantle. The girlish—nay, impish—smile that spread on her face slowly turned into a full-throated laugh.

✧ ✠ ✧ ✠

Galatea never told anyone why she'd taken her vows at age fifteen. Her marriage to old Fulk, who left her a widow at fourteen, was, as Qoheleth said, "far off and exceeding deep," practically unreachable. Then hearing the rabbi's voice pronounce words in Hebrew started giving her a fleeting languor, a kind of light-headedness. Her body's reaction to his proximity became a source of fear. As she moved around the house dreamily, his voice would cause the hairs on the back of her neck to stand in terror, as if she were being charged by a bear. Buried memories, as of someone else's life, floated up like bubbles in a still pond, and Lupo's voice echoed in fiery Cretan dreams.

She'd guessed that something in her soul was about to either heal or snap. One night, after breathing in the way Master Ezekiel was teaching her to do, she made silence in her thoughts and set out to end seventeen years of disorderly flight. She would face the dark pool inside her, her very own visio secunda. Moaning out loud from the pain, she searched for the details of that day. All that was left in her guarded waking memory was the silence of Castel Romitorio in the summer afternoon, the dust suspended in shafts of sunlight filtering between the curtains.

Lupo's raspy voice called her from the floor above. She followed that memory step by step as the young girl climbed the stairs. Her stepfather had taken her roughly, snorting like an animal. She had fallen pregnant and lost the baby. Right away she had known, both in her heart and from the midwives, that she could not risk another pregnancy. A year later, she took her vows.

Albacara reminded her of Bonarina, her nanny, the only person, including her mother Blanche, who had known her terrible secret. Since the first night in her house, Galatea had been moved by the widow's quiet desperation. Albacara learned to live on the memories of Vidal, and the abbess was filled with admiration for the silent, tenacious way she got on with life, without complaining.

The day after digging her fingers in the wound in her soul that started bleeding again, Galatea was walking with the widow along the cliff's edge, when she suddenly felt the need to throw that weight off. Sitting on the grass before the waves that crashed viciously on the rocks below them, she told Albacara the little that sufficed for the other woman to understand.

"The horror, the pain," she sighed, "were no less than what one must feel being born . . . or dying!"

Galatea raised her eyes, and for a moment the sea itself seemed to draw back, appalled.

The widow was too discreet to speak of what Galatea confided, yet in the following days, having been chosen as a kind of confessor by the abbess gave her an air of self-importance that soon got on Gudrun's nerves. After all, Albacara had only just joined the company. Her demands on the mother's attentions were, literally, out of order.

Finally, the Monday of departure arrived. It was the 10th of June, and the little caravan of seven pilgrims and a trunk rode between lines of chagrined villagers. Every urchin in Kaliviani knew the rabbi's name by now, though not a living creature there could have pronounced it. The widow, still troubled by superstitious fear of the Jew, hid amulets and magical roots in every corner of her scant baggage. But even so, who was to say the infidels didn't possess more powerful charms than hers?

At dawn four days later, on the 14th, the company stood on the quay in front of Spiro's tareta. Behind them, on the rocks above the port, Spiridione stood searching the sea's face, trying to decide if the accord between wind and waves was favorable for their intended course.

For over five weeks of forced stopover in Candia, Galatea kept her distance from any kind of floating timber. She even wondered if her new fear of seasickness and storms would turn her into a recluse once back in the lagoon. Then she'd laid eyes on the tareta. At first sight, there could not have been a more neglected, derelict vessel in the quarter-and-a-half of the sea dominated by Venice.

Less than a third the size of the *Falcus* and much more slender, it could carry ten horses in its hold and had a single mast, three oars on each side, and two small castles fore and aft for defense against pirates. Yehezkel's expert eye noticed that under the chaos and dirt, standing and running rigging looked well maintained, and the hull seemed sturdy and well caulked. The air of abandon, thought the sailor rabbi, was probably intended to make the tareta look less appetizing to pirates.

"To *other* pirates," he corrected himself.

It took all the rabbi's loquaciousness, as well as the trust the abbess by now accorded him, to convince Galatea that a few days' sailing on that boat involved no danger and could even be quite pleasant.

At last came the sight the abbess had been waiting to see since the day in the tavern. André de Rosson and his squire walked up and calmly stepped onto the tareta without asking her master's permission and bringing two horses with them. Spiridione tried to look nonplussed, but the sight of the big red cross shook him more than he let on.

The company took their modest baggage on board—modest, that is, except for the chest. Stepping on deck from the gangplank, Galatea handed Spiro the widow's bundle, as if he were a servant. He turned it in his hands and then asked with a smile and a wink:

"A present for me?" She didn't answer.

Galatea's last memories of Crete were two gaunt profiles: that of the island receding in the misty dawn and that of the widow, white cap tied under her chin, face resolutely turned into the wind.

CHAPTER 12

Asher Saro Vo

Whose seed (after its kind) is inside it

ABBEY OF SANT'ANTIMO, FIFTEEN YEARS EARLIER, 26TH APRIL 1204

Despite being on her knees, Galatea teetered and felt she was going to faint. Then she thought that were she to fall senseless before the altar, the people of Monte Alcino would conclude she was being sent to a convent for unspeakable reasons, and the house of Ardenga would be dragged through the mud. Pride had the better over the young girl's senses, and with a deep breath, she regained control.

After being widowed at fourteen, the daughter of Orlando d'Ardenga, who died a glorious death at the siege of Acre thirteen years earlier, was about to become a nun at the age of fifteen.

Abbot Rainerio was celebrating the Eucharist. Galatea lowered her head, tightened her jaw, and bit her lip, contracting her thighs as if that could stop the sticky liquid shamelessly dripping down their insides. Rainerio held up the chalice in his spindly arms as the wine miraculously turned into the blood of Christ. She held back tears of rage as the abbot chanted, "Hic est enim calyx sanguinis mei novi et aeterni testamenti . . ."

Was it as red, she thought, as that on her legs? Was it sacrilege for the fullness of her month to start in church? The novice felt like a bound sacrifice. The outrageous rivulet reached her knee and she wondered if the black wool socks would absorb it. What if it flowed all the way to the floor, marking her steps with scarlet drops when she stood up?

Beads of cold sweat formed on her upper lip. Her head throbbed, and a piercing pain spread from her abdomen. It came from the center of her body, and all other sensations spun around it, giving her a kind of vertigo. The pangs bit on both right and left, as if a two-headed snake had penetrated deep into her vagina.

Her eyes darted around like an animal chased by the hunt. She looked to Bonarina for some comfort. Her nanny was in the third row, praying, head low wrapped in the yellow shawl of holy days. Galatea sighed and thought, "Jesus probably chose his apostles only among men because of this, because the weakness of a woman's body is always ready to betray her."

She went over the vows she and the other novices would soon pronounce.

"My Lord," she prayed, "please give me the strength to serve you . . . as if I were a man!"

The abbey of Sant'Antimo is, for many, the most beautiful church on the Via Francigena,* the sunlight at times giving the brown and gold veins in her travertine stone transparencies as soft as a caress.

It sits, hidden from view like a family heirloom, on the comfortable floor of the tiny valley of a brook called Starcia, a few leagues south of Monte Alcino on the road that, leaving Mount Amiata on the left, descends to the river Orcia, and beyond that to the Tyrrhenian Sea.

Inside the church, one could still smell the vinegar used to wash the floor paved with marble slabs the color of a winter dawn. The congregation

---

*Ancient pilgrimage route between Canterbury and Rome passing through England, France, Switzerland, and Italy

rumbled, worn out by an hour of fiery homily by the abbot, condemning Cathars, Beguines, Waldenses, Poor Lombards, and other heretical fraternities. Every time he paused to take in air for the next onslaught, the birds outside could be heard celebrating the arrival of the new day.

Don Rainerio, abbot of Sant'Antimo for twenty-five years, cut a fine figure aflame on a pulpit: big, spirited eyes set in cranium bones that competed to jut out the farthest, his thin body hidden by a frock that fell as straight as if empty, and a silver cross on his chest, one could have been forgiven for mistaking him for one of the heretical preachers he felt he must consign to the purifying fire while he still had time.

In the front row sat Count Lupo degli Ardengheschi, lord of Civitella, Montagutolo, Pari, and Fornoli. Fiftyish, handsome, and cynical with eyes fierce enough to intimidate a cardinal. Baldness left just a band of gray hair round his skull, a similarity to a monk's tonsure that infuriated him. Every item he wore spoke of high rank, from the colors of his mantle to the seal on his ring. Even the pouch hanging at his side bore the coat of arms of Badia Ardenga.

Next to him sat his wife, Blanche, a noblewoman from Champagne and the widow of Lupo's brother, Orlando, the *real* count of Ardenga—who for sure, had he been present at his daughter's ordination as a Cistercian nun, would not have felt the need to flaunt all those historied accessories.

Lulled by Rainerio's voice, Galatea slipped into a reverie of incense and cramps. The air in the church seemed to become denser, like transparent syrup. She recognized the familiar signs of a vision taking over: the tingling, the hairs on the back of her neck standing. She turned around again. Everyone was stoically waiting for the sermon to end. Her body quieted down some.

"Maybe I'm finally going crazy," thought the bloodied, fifteen-year-old widow.

The commotion around the abbot as he descended from the altar brought her to. The General of the Cistercian Order took his place, pronounced the ritual formula and accepted the vows of the six novices.

Before dawn that morning, with two candles lighting the empty church, the girls had approached the oak booth one at a time to confess for the last time as lay faithful. The abbot's voice softened on recognizing her, and Galatea had summoned all her courage, whispering in the semidarkness, "Father, I must confess a dream . . ."

"A dream? Again?"

"Yes, Father, another one, three nights ago . . . it was horrible. If you won't absolve me, I fear God will not accept my vows," she'd said, frightened.

"Ahh . . . I see . . ." the abbot had sighed. "So tell me, young countess, what did you dream this time?"

"Blood. The walls of a huge city, full of churches, with the blood of thousands of innocents, men, women, children, sweating from its walls. Oh Father, you should have heard the moans, the screams of pain! Tell me, why does God try me in this way? Why?"

Behind the wooden grill, the abbot was silent.

"What say you, Father? What is the meaning of such a terrifying dream?" Galatea had insisted.

"Enough, Galatea degli Ardengheschi! I've heard enough of your dreams!" blurted Rainerio, and the girl imagined the throbbing vein in his forehead. "Why do you allow yourself to be carried away by visions and dreams that can only be from the devil?" He sighed. "You're still young, my dear; you don't understand the risks you run. Don't tell anyone else, not now and not ever! *Forget* this dream . . ."

Adolescent outrage gripped the girl, who interrupted him, contravening years of rigorous education. "But Father, how can you speak like this? You *know* the things I dreamed have always come true! Twice I related events to you *before* they happened! And if, as you say, my soul is in danger, how can you ask me to just *forget*?"

Galatea struggled to keep her voice down and turned to see if any of the novices had heard.

After a moment's silence, the abbot answered. "You are right, my poor dear. There seems to be no love of truth in my advice to you, but believe me, behind it there is love for you and your family, and you'll simply have to trust me. If you were to marry again, I could assure you that these trials, as you rightly call them, would soon be a memory. But you're about to become a bride of the Lord, and you'll need all your strength in the difficult times ahead . . . yet I know you *have* that strength, Sister Galatea, so trust your spiritual director. And this time it's not advice I'm giving you, it's an order: forget! I have already forgotten. One day you will thank me."

Rainerio rattled off a list of penances and gave her a hasty absolution. Then the little window in the booth slammed shut. Galatea remained on her knees outside it, gripping a curl of carved oak until her knuckles were white. Then she stood up and went back to her place.

Mass drew to a close. It was all very moving. Six novices knelt before the altar while three boys who would be knighted at the Ardengheschis' fortress that afternoon held their swords, which had been blessed during the service, high over the abbot to represent their vow to protect the church. The choir thundered, pleaded, and wailed as Rainerio rose over the sinners and pronounced the words of absolution. A hundred eyes watched his bony hands transmitting God's forgiveness to them.

At last Galatea got up, a bloodstained bride of God, and Don Rainerio kissed her sweaty brow. She exchanged kisses on the cheek with the other novices and then with the women of her retinue and finally with her little sister Allegra. Then she kissed the hem of the abbot's habit and left the church.

✿   ✠   ✿   ✠

CASTEL ROMITORIO, LATER THAT DAY

Around sixth hour, the vast courtyard of Castel Romitorio and the meadows outside its walls were far more crowded than the abbey had been in the morning. This was because all around Monte Alcino the Christians attracted by a roast pheasant in blackberry sauce were far

more numerous than those attracted by a sermon—especially one delivered by Abbot Rainerio.

The austere fortress was on a rounded hill, separated from the town
of Monte Alcino by a deep ravine that guests had been climbing since
early morning, some on foot, some astride mules, the wealthy ones in
carts hauled by oxen with huge wheels of solid wood. Trees on the way—
holm oaks, cypresses, lime trees—were hung with flower garlands, and
the fortress was a veritable triumph of flowers, with petals strewn on the
grass, garlands on tables and windowsills, and even crowns of flowers on
the heads of the pages bearing food and drink, chased by the screams of
the women of the castle.

The occasion for the banquet was not the girls' vows, of course, but
the boys' knightings. One of them was Galgano, Lupo's son from his
previous wife and Galatea's stepbrother. He was a year older, and in him
the noble blood of Ardenga seemed to have been diluted to invisibility.
Despite being the son of counts, Galgano was so ignorant he believed
there were people old enough to have known the Virgin and the apostles,
and that God had been put to death by the Saracens. Of Jesus he knew
three things: he was born from a virgin, was crucified, and came back
from the dead. The affection he felt for God was the tenacious, canine
one of a vassal for his lord, to die for whom is a joy and an honor.

Scarcely sixteen, Galgano was feared in the county for the bullying
typical of the son of a lord. His true love was reserved for the noble lady
of his heart, who changed with the seasons, but he was explicit with peasant girls, and wordlessly forced every female shepherd he came across. His
mother died birthing him, and he was a surly boy who used dogs as targets to improve his dagger throwing. Everyone trembled at the thought of
the day when he would administer justice in the lands of Ardenga.

Before the trials of the three boys began, Galatea arrived with
the other novices, pale and aching all over. She climbed out of the
palanquin—she hadn't dared ride home from the abbey as she usually
did—and excused herself with her mother, saying she was going to lie
down because the pains of her cycle had just begun. Blanche, taken up

by her hundred guests, took one look at her and immediately agreed.

The countess nonchalantly passed her thirtieth birthday, albeit with the help of many creams and ointments for her skin. She thinned her eyebrows and washed her blonde hair in chamomile water, carefully tearing it out to widen her forehead, leaving a heart-shaped hairline, as was the fashion in Provence. That day she was wearing a dress of saffron-yellow satin, a wide belt on her waist embroidered with red hearts.

Her hat was topped by two horns, over which fluttered a vaporous veil of red silk, fixed by a silver buckle with a big ruby. A discreet choice, if compared with some of the ridiculously tall veiled cones that surmounted female heads at the banquet. Had someone watched the ladies from atop the tower, their hats bobbing up and down would have resembled birds on a beach, poking their long beaks in the sand.

Galatea lay on a big bed. After closing the heavy curtains on the noisy yard she'd tried to sleep, but the headache gave no respite, and she lay there in the dark, musing on the future. The abbot was right; she faced daunting hardships. God, she would miss Allegra, Sister Marianna, her mother, Bonarina . . . and what of riding alone on the Tuscan hills? Could she just abandon it all, forget people, landscapes, smells? Would they become distant memories? A wave of sadness, as when one thinks of the dead, swept over her. No more presences, nothing *alive* of the people in her life, just occasional news of dated, fading events. Nothing. She would be alone, alone, alone.

"Yes, but I'll be far from his eyes!"

Bonarina glanced into the room, not wanting to wake up the young countess, but Galatea saw her and called her in. She stood at the foot of the bed, head cocked as if asking for an explanation.

"Bonarina . . . I bled like a wounded animal for the whole ceremony, and I am very unhappy."

Her nanny said softly, "Come, little countess, I'll rub your back, as usual, and you'll be just fine."

Galatea slowly sat on the edge of her bed. "No, Bonarina, I'm not your young countess any more. Now I am Sister Galatea." She dragged herself to her feet and faced Bonarina. Suddenly they both realized that the girl was, for the first time, taller than her nanny. After a moment's silence, they embraced, weeping.

"If you were *my* daughter, I'd tie you to a big table and there would be no talk of going to a convent!" blurted out Bonarina, covering her mouth at once as if she'd blasphemed, but relaxing at Galatea's laugh. She undressed Galatea and laid her on her belly, fetched some chamomile ointment and, completely dressed including the white kerchief tied under her chin, climbed on top, knees astride her charge's thighs, and began to vigorously massage Galatea's loins.

Just then, Sister Marianna stepped in. Galatea jumped up, naked, and ran to embrace her. Marianna was a short, cheerful Benedictine nun, famous in all southern Tuscia for her near-miraculous skills as a healer—which she exercised in the abbey of the Santissimo Salvatore, on the other side of Mount Amiata—and was Galatea's favorite person in the world after her sister Allegra.

Various tutors had taught Galatea to read and write Italian and Latin, some music, and even a little astronomy, but none had ever made a breach in their ward's guarded heart except Sister Marianna, whose smile could melt something in the girl that everyone had always found strangely inflexible, ever since she'd refused to play with dolls.

Sister Marianna took Galatea's face, a full head above her own, in her hands. "Galatea, my dove, Sister Cristofora is going back to her convent and hasn't seen you yet, so I came up to ask you to come and say goodbye to your tutor and receive her blessing."

Galatea didn't like Cristofora's undisguised admiration for Lupo. She looked at both women, nose turned up like a child before a hated food, and then, imitating her mother's quirks to perfection, tweeted, "But of course, dear sister! I would gladly come down even if I have yet to recover from my cramps!"

Galatea was fifteen, Marianna thirty-two, and Bonarina fifty-one, but to see them laugh one would have thought they'd grown up together. When the girl was dressed, they went down to the kitchens. Standing by the cavernous fireplace, surrounded by a chaos—pots, ladles, rags, jugs, cats, children—that resembled the end of a battle, two nuns were deep in conversation. Sister Cristofora saw Galatea and came toward her, beaming with pride in the novice she'd nursed. Cristofora was so wizened yet energetic that everyone agreed she seemed the female version of Abbot Rainerio.

"My dears, this is Sister Riccarda von Stade, a Benedictine on a pilgrimage to Rome!" she boomed. "Sister Riccarda, this is the young countess of the Ardengheschi, who today became Sister Galatea and will soon depart for a Cistercian monastery in the Venetian lagoon. Oh, and this is Sister Marianna of Saragiolo, who spreads cures and comfort in all directions from the top of Mount Amiata!"

Marianna blushed, rejecting praise directed to her instead of the Lord. Bonarina slipped off to her chores, leaving the nuns to discuss spiritual matters beyond her station. Galatea asked the German nun what made her come to Castel Romitorio. Sister Cristofora didn't give the guest time to attempt an answer.

"Yesterday a knight from Champagne, headed to Syria with his squires, spent the night in town. When your mother heard of it, she sent a servant to invite him to the knightings, hoping to hear some news from your grandparents' county. As we speak, he is answering questions from the count, the cardinal, and the abbot on the kingdom of Jerusalem, where it seems he spent some years fighting infidels."

Galatea thought bitterly, "Until yesterday, I could have gone out and spoken with this worldly, exotic Frenchman myself . . . but not any longer. Nuns don't chat with knights and that's that!"

Cristofora went on, "So three German nuns, traveling under the knight's protection, found themselves diverted to your stepfather's castle! Sister Riccarda was telling us of her journey from the Rhine to here. Heretics and wandering preachers are everywhere. Lumbardy, they say, is allied with Provence against the Lord, and good Christians tremble in fear, for the Day of Judgment appears very close."

At the mention of Judgment Day, Sister Riccarda came alive. The largest of the nuns, she had big, watery blue eyes and huge hands—Galatea thought her fingers looked like sausages, which she kept crossed on her belly in a seraphic pose. She interrupted Sister Cristofora with some urgency. "Hear me out, sisters, for few women could tell a tale like mine! I was fortunate enough, as a young nun, to spend ten years in a convent at Eibingen and meet its abbess, Hildegard of Bingen, who passed away twenty-five years ago. She was without doubt the holiest woman of her generation!"

"You *knew* the Sybil of the Rhine?" asked Marianna, excited as a child.

"I didn't know the fame of my teacher had spread this far. . . ."

"Her *Liber Divinorum Operum* taught me how humours operate, and how to recognize temperaments," said Sister Marianna.

"The good Lord brought us together, sister! What a joy to discover that the book I helped copy more than thirty years ago is shining its light so far from Disinbodemberg!"

"Tell me a little about Hildegard, I beg you!" asked Marianna, visibly moved.

Sister Riccarda stared into the fireplace with the dreamy look of people to whom the world of their youths seems infinitely better than the one they live in. "Life there was more stimulating and desirable for a woman than in *any* other place. Hildegard excelled at everything, and she never did less than two things at once. She wrote heavenly music, tractates on herbs, poems; she preached sermons, but above all she prophesied, and no one *dared* doubt her visions. She described them in a book that Pope Eugene declared inspired by the Holy Spirit."

Riccarda was heating up. "Hildegard was a woman, but her actions—believe me—were those of a man! I heard her dictate a letter to Emperor Barbarossa calling him godless and evil. I saw many men tremble before her . . . and I have a warm, comforting memory of the sight!"

Galatea fantasized about the day when the famous Saint Galatea of Monte Alcino would, for the greater glory of God and through the power of her visions alone, cause Lupo and Galgano of Ardenga to tremble before her like two little birds on a windowsill, in winter.

"She . . . preached sermons, you say?" asked Sister Cristofora, suspiciously.

"Only to other nuns. Preaching to lay people is forbidden to women, as you know. But her visions gave her doubts on that prohibition. Once she said to me that she had great trust in the souls of women . . . that's how she put it: 'trust in the souls of women'!"

Marianna nodded, smiling. Cristofora clouded over like a stormy sky and was looking at Riccarda as if she'd suddenly found the source of a smell that had been offending her nostrils.

"'The nature of women, alas, is such that even if they try to do good, they can't help but sin, despite their good intentions.' That's Saint Jerome. As for women preaching, Saint John Chrysostom said, 'Woman only preached once, in the garden of Eden, and compromised everything.'" Sister Cristofora smiled the smug smile that Galatea hated. "Come, Sister Riccarda, were there any women among the apostles? If your Hildegard had doubts on that prohibition, it probably means the pope's blessing of her visions made her commit a sin of pride."

Sister Riccarda crossed her fingers over her waist, sizing up the old championess of dogma. "I've read the fathers, too, Sister Cristofora. But what I witnessed with my own eyes in my travels in the lands of the Cathars would surprise you. Among those heretics, women preach."

Cristofora scoffed, "Nothing that takes place under the skies of heresy could surprise me!"

"Even if it was men put on trial for violating servant girls? Even if it was rich women making their will out to whomever they wish? Believe me, I condemn heresy with your same disgust, but the life of women in Cathar communities is proof that Jesus took on himself not just the sin of Adam, but that of Eve, too!"

Sister Marianna's eyes widened in surprise, the smile never leaving her face. Sister Cristofora by now was outraged. "Ha! If this isn't sympathy for heretics. . . Wake up, Sister Riccarda, wake up before it's too late for you, too!" Her eyes darted bolts of righteousness like Abbot Rainerio's.

Sister Riccarda smiled amiably. "But if Hildegard was right and the souls of women are *not* from the Devil, then the heretics have unwittingly discovered God's *true* plan! Oh, Cristofora, if only you had heard their troubadours sing rhymes to the lady of their devotion! If every man loved God as they love their lady, wouldn't his Kingdom be here already?"

This time Cristofora lost her patience. "Troubadours? They're nothing but diabolical exalters of lust! I've heard the verses of those fornicators, and I've nothing in common with anyone who finds them inspiring!"

Galatea only vaguely perceived the exasperated tone of Riccarda's retort. A girlish daydream, in which she preached the word of God to adoring crowds, distanced her from the conversation. On the third tug, the faithful trying to touch her habit turned into little Allegra, who noticed her sister's distraction and was desperate for attention.

If somewhere in Galatea's features was the noble falcon that prowled Orlando's face, Allegra instead inherited Blanche's pure smile and northern softness. She was six, with curly red hair and freckles, was friends with everyone from birds and horses to squires and abbots, and loved to laugh, as if wanting to deserve her name. Allegra was the real princess of the Ardengheschis' manors, for *nobody* could resist her coquetry, and the constant exercise of such absolute power convinced her that her beloved sister would not be sent away, if only she forbade it with sufficient severity.

Right now Galatea wanted to remember a carefree Allegra, and she accepted the illusion that nothing was about to change. She curtsied to the nuns, who hardly noticed, took her sister's hand and ran out into the meadows behind the fortress, where their laughter frightened chickens and guinea fowls, while the geese, much touchier birds, chased them for a distance, angrily flapping their wings.

✡ ✠ ✡ ✠

CASTEL ROMITORIO, IN THE AFTERNOON

After handing over Allegra to a tutor, Galatea went back to the kitchens, but the nuns were gone. She thought back to the confrontation she'd witnessed between Sister Cristofora and the German nun and regretted not seeing who won the last word.

"Fornicators." Sister Cristofora had never pronounced the word before. Galatea spoke good French, and even knew a few Provençal chansons de geste, but she had never read the passionate poems troubadours wrote for their ladies. She thought bitterly that traveling with her mother between Tuscan residences, she would soon have satisfied her curiosities, but now she would seldom exit the walls of her convent, where verses written by fornicators would be found, as Don Rainerio said, when pigs would fly.

"But if the Sybil of the Rhine learned from her visions that women have the same dignity as men, well, I'll find *all* her books!" thought the novice. "In fact, I'll make Hildegard a model for my life! And one day, the visions the abbot told me to forget will be recognized by everyone as divinely inspired, and justice will be done!"

The thought of justice brought back Riccarda's words, "Men put on trial for violating servant girls." Her breath shortened. Were heretics then, the supposed emissaries of the Devil, the only ones to practice *real* justice? Had she, for her whole, brief life, been told nothing but lies?

Her head swam, and again she felt close to passing out. The bubble of excitement over the imminent journey burst after the ceremony, and melancholy set in. She squared her shoulders, drew a deep breath, and looked around. She'd wandered into the main hall, whose tall, paneless windows looked out on the court where the banquet was in progress. The tables had been dragged outside, and the empty room looked enormous. Voices and clinking glasses and knives wafted in with the afternoon heat from behind heavy curtains. Family shields, swords, and standards filled the walls of the silent hall. She looked around to impress them into memory.

She raised the hem of the white habit that now replaced her whole wardrobe, glanced around like a little bird, and pulled up her woolen socks. She was curious about the French guest but was reluctant to go into the frolicking crowd and profane her vows on the day she'd taken them. Besides, the thought of Lupo and Galgano at the table, inciting each other to mock everything and everyone, as if conversations were nothing but hunts with words instead of arrows, repelled her like a bad smell.

She moved aside the first curtain a hand's width and saw that the raised platform on which the long table of the notables was placed made her gaze level with their buttocks, not their heads. She smiled. All those important people were unknowingly in her power. She would hear every word they said, even when they leaned toward their neighbors not to be heard by the others. None of them would know that poor, indisposed Sister Galatea was eavesdropping on their malicious gossip, like an angel ready to fly to the Most High and reveal all their secrets. The childish thrill of the new game made her temporarily forget the pain in her belly.

Through the window in the corner, the closest to the staircase, she recognized the voices of Father Rainerio, Griffo de' Berardenghi, and Don Siricio, the abbey's prior. She ran to check the last window and concluded, as she'd expected, that the count, her mother, and the town's pride, Cardinal Uffredo de' Pepi—a Monte Alcino boy who'd made good—must be behind the central curtain.

After a while she'd recognized everyone at the table apart from the strangers, whom she hadn't even glimpsed yet. She thought that in Torcello she would recognize nobody. She whispered to herself, "Stop being afraid! Stop thinking like a child; think like an adult.

After a while, you'll know everyone there, too. You are the daughter of Orlando d'Ardenga, and you're afraid of *nothing*!"

Eventually she discovered that the French knight and his squires, all the chairs behind the table being taken, had brought up chairs in front of the count and the cardinal. This meant that the only position from which she might see him was a mere foot behind her stepfather. As if that weren't enough, the raised platform made it so that she could only see someone on the other side of the table if he stood up.

Summoning all her courage, she moved the curtain aside.

Lupo was the center of attention of the long table and butted into all conversations, raising his voice to partake in the more distant ones. His smile was both winning and vaguely unsettling, for he could never hide all traces of his contempt for others. The lord of Ardenga was an ambitious wolf, whose enemies went as far as to suggest he'd sent assassins to Syria to get rid of his brother and grab title, lands, and wife. In Monte Alcino people said that if Lupo were to—by some mistake—end up in paradise, he was sure to try to lie down in the Almighty's bed.

The count assaulted roast herons, hares, and baby boars indifferently, pontificating as he tore meat off the game with his teeth. Only occasionally, an imploring look from Blanche convinced him to cut the meat with his dagger and dip it in the sauces, which Lupo preferred to do with his hands.

Galatea moved her head up and down, looking for a position that would allow her to glimpse the French knight, without succeeding. But she heard him talking with Abbot Rainerio in a warm and musical voice. He was defending the honor of the Order of the Temple.

"With all due respect, revered abbot, how can you speak of him like that? He and his men were flayed on the spot for refusing to abjure their faith! And it's a *good* death one meets in the Holy Land!"

Abbot Rainerio glowered at the knight. "The pusillanimous traitors handed the city to Saladin without a fight! The seneschal of the temple had more than enough gold to ransom every Christian in Jerusalem—you can believe me, I heard it from the pope himself—but everyone knows the Templars felt less pity for those unfortunate souls than did Saladin himself!" Rainerio seemed to have a score to settle with the order.

"Templars. Bah! They're all the same; they love money more than Jews do! I heard that Philippe de Plessis, the new master, chops the hands and tongues of prisoners . . ."

"What's strange about that, revered abbot? Saracens chop the head off every Templar they capture." Rainerio was starting to find the knight rather flippant.

"Exactly! It's like a private war of theirs or something! To hear Templars talk, God created Heaven and Earth for the exclusive benefit of their order!"

Lupo didn't like the old vulture heaping insults on defeated soldiers. Besides, he could control the abbot, while the stranger was an unknown, so he arbitrarily entered the exchange on the side of the knight. "They were Christian armed monks, Don Rainerio! I won't let you besmirch their memory!" Then, to the Frenchman, "The time to take the cross is over, *mon brave seigneur*! But if you're looking for the purity and loyalty of knighthood, you're right to go back to Syria! By my beard, it's nearly twenty years since the sepulchre fell to the infidel, and no Christian is man enough to take it back! Instead, we philosophize, sing romances, and praise reason, which is in God's image . . . Puah!"

The Frenchman, grateful to the count for rescuing him from Father Rainerio's claws, applauded his sarcasm as he slapped the backs of his young squires.

"I wouldn't be surprised, *mon cher ami*," went on Lupo, "if we lived to see the Saracens watering their horses at the Lateran, with the approval of the Vicar of Peter! And maybe—judging by how Christians and Mohammedans have changed their faith at the end of battles—maybe Innocent, young and ambitious as he is, instead of martyrdom . . . he, he . . . will choose to live as a mamluk slave."

Lupo got up and mimed Innocent III waving a fan behind the

sultan amid laughter. The cardinal, as cynical a Tuscan as the count, had to blush at this insolence; his crimson cloak demanded it. "Please moderate your jibes at the Holy Father, Lupo; enough heretics indulge them these days."

Count and knight were laughing openly, and the table felt entitled to share in the joke as the clerics swallowed their bile. Finally Lupo, wiping a tear with his sleeve, regained control. "You must admit, Uffredo, it's not easy to feel respect for popes who have to wander for years from Pisa to Lucca, to Ferrara, to Verona because Roman citizens won't grant them access to the Eternal City, he, he . . . or to have respect for poor Gregory VIII, a pope so beloved to the Lord that he spent fifty-three days on the throne . . . and they were enough for him to lose Jerusalem! He, he, he . . ."

The Frenchman got up and leaned across the table to whisper something to Lupo he didn't think others should hear. That was when he saw the perfect visage of a girl in the lower corner of the window behind the count. At first she looked terrified, and then she put a slender finger to her lips, unbelievable violet eyes begging him not to betray her.

Galatea burned with shame. Orlando's daughter—worse, a nun who had just renounced this world!—caught eavesdropping on the lords like the lowliest of servants! She remained lucid enough to realize that if she just pulled the curtain shut, the knight would conclude that she *was* a servant and might alert Lupo. So she tried to make an accomplice of him and, already aware of the effect her eyes had on men, signaled to him to keep his silence.

The knight, when the count wasn't looking, winked at the beautiful wench in a nun's habit, sure that her quick reaction was a sign of noble lineage. Then, with an eloquence Galatea couldn't help but admire, he steered the conversation to how badly the faithful viewed secluded monks, saying they should go out into the world to do God's work, rather than hide behind the windows of their monasteries.

Galatea clapped her hands, won over by the charm and irony of the knight, and headed out to the court, relieved at not being caught. She climbed on the platform and curtsied to everyone and then brought up a stool across from her mother.

The knight introduced himself. "I am Arnaud de Cérisiére, sister, and Girard and Joceran de Vignory are my trusty squires. I had the fortune to visit your family's manor on my way to Acre, to do my part in the retaking of the Holy City."

Galatea had dreamed of Jerusalem for years and asked him, sincerely curious of his answer, "Tell me, Monsieur Arnaud, did you ever see any nuns on a pilgrimage to the Holy Sepulchre?"

Before the knight could answer, Galgano lashed out acidly from the far end of the table.

"Ha! *You*, of all people! Poor thing, don't you know you'll never cross the walls of your convent?"

Arnaud was about to rebuke the irreverent new knight, but the Italian-style squabble was too fast for him. Galatea immediately shot back at her stepbrother, "Your uncouth opinions no longer concern me, enemy of God! If an angel appeared to take you to Heaven, you would plunge a dagger in his gut, because it's the only thing you know how to do!"

Everyone laughed at the young novice's retort, except Lupo. Today Galgano was a knight and Galatea had left the secular world, so they could abandon all caution with words and sling them like rocks.

A heavy smell of sweat and ill-digested wine filled the air. The wine raised everyone's voice, and soon Joceran and Galgano found a way to slight each other. Lupo and Arnaud intervened before the youngsters could draw swords. Galatea heard Arnaud shout to his squire, "You never back down because you have the brains of a boar!"

Lupo slapped his newly knighted son across the face. Galatea thought they all looked like a pack of wolves, barely controlled by the oldest male. Cramps and headache had started plaguing her again. She brusquely took her leave and walked round the fortress to the small chapel behind it.

She crossed herself at the baptismal font, hurried to the altar, and recited her prayers distractedly, still prey to the day's emotions. After a life in Lupo's shadow, the peace of the cloister would be like entering paradise. "My destiny is in my visions, I *know* that! The first step is to get away from this place!"

She stood up, somewhat calmer, and crossed herself again in the falling darkness, murmuring, "In Nomine Patris, et Filii, et Spiritus Sancti . . ."

Then, walking backward, she left the chapel.

✧   ✠   ✧   ✠

As Galatea crossed herself, on the outskirts of Jerusalem a man walked briskly, despite a limp, along whitewashed walls pierced by rare, small windows.

By a fountain in an opening where three alleys met, two veiled women, wrists heavy with bracelets, carried jugs on their heads. An old man, legs naked, pulled on the reins of an unmovable donkey as an Armenian deacon in a long black habit walked past.

Passing under a low arch, the man entered a rectangular courtyard, in the center of which were a round fountain and a eucalyptus tree. Five people, two Jews and three Mohammedans, sat under the tree chatting and sipping wine in the warm light of torches stuck in iron rings hanging from the walls.

After some greetings, the man was taken to the *takhtabush,* a room open to the courtyard with a central column supporting the floor of the harem above it and two or three ample cushions on a wooden platform on one side. The man waiting on the cushions was Shimon called the Pious, head of the Jerusalem Karaites,* who had recently settled at the foot of the Mount of Olives.

The visitor made a half bow and pushed back his hood. It was a Frank, as old as Methuselah.

---

*Jewish heretical movement, started in Babylon in the eighth century, that rejected Oral Law and Talmud

"Well?" he asked hoarsely in Greek, "Did you discover anything?"

"Yes. The Hebrew parchments you're looking for were found four hundred years ago, near Jericho. The one with the circles became a relic almost right away, so the *vizir* called on the Jews to explain it. The rabbis imposed silence—on pain of death—on what the parchment said, but years later the Karaites made a Greek copy and gifted it to the Johannites. Then, eighty-five years ago, the knights from Champagne must have found the original, for they suddenly started digging in Solomon's stables."

"I knew it, I knew it!" croaked the old man. "And you don't know the half of it, Shimon! The entire enterprise to reconquer Christ's sepulchre was born of the necessity to dig under the Temple Mount to look for a parchment that would put the church in the hands of those who found it!" A sudden fit of coughing shook him.

"You shouldn't get so excited, or your strength won't suffice for what you plan to do," said Shimon.

"Oh, you needn't worry about my health, my friend," laughed the old man. "I died last year!"

CHAPTER 13

VAYEHI EREV
And There Was Evening

THE SAME 26TH APRIL 1204, IN FUSTAT, NEAR AL-KAHIRA

"We discussed *'In the beginning God created the heavens and the earth'* last Shabbat, Hezki, so stop insisting, or I won't live long enough to finish the first chapter of Bereshit with you! Then again, your grandfather was a far better man than you, and he could never repress his curiosity for secret meanings."

Moshe ben Maimon, the man who had whispered those words, was known to all Jews as Light of the East and West, Sole Teacher, and Wonder of the Generation. Maimonides, as the Latins called him, had been personal medicus to Salah ad-Din and now looked after his brother, Sultan al-'Adil. Ishmaelites, who knew him as Musa ibn Maimun, were proud of his presence on the Nile.

Sitting on silk cushions in a beautiful high-backed chair, he pronounced the phrase "a far better man than you" in elegant, punctilious Arabic, an ironic critique of his pupil's use of the Cairene Jewish dialect, an amalgam of Arabic, Hebrew, and Spanish spoken by families who came to Egypt from Spain. Yehezkel was used to his mentor's good-natured barbs and gave as good as he got, as disciples have done since time immemorial.

"As you wish, Rabbi," said Yehezkel respectfully. "Let today's lesson be on the second verse."

They were on the upper floor of a modest house by the Nile, a big room divided by a curtain, on one side a bed and on the other the study where Maimonides received patients, and where he'd written books that made his name synonymous with erudition. Rav Moshe shifted in his chair and began the lesson. "I don't intend to bore you, Hezki, with the *literal* meaning of the second verse. I would like instead to establish a connection between the primordial abyss—and through *it,* the seas—and the presence of evil in the world, as symbolized by darkness."

The words were enough for Yehezkel to forget his surroundings, knit his brows, and lower himself mind and soul into Torah study. Maimonides saw this reaction and went on, satisfied. "I want you to consider that although the first two verses are, essentially, a preamble to God's first 'creating' pronouncement—Let there be light—the sequence in the first three verses implies that darkness existed *before* light was created . . . and, by analogy, that Evil was created before Good!"

By now Yehezkel was far from the room and from Egypt, immersed in the creation. He struggled to gather his thoughts, scattered by his teacher's suggestion, and put them into words. "Yes, Rav Moshe, some sages deduced that if Good and Evil were twins, then Evil was the firstborn. But how do you plan to tie the qualities of darkness to those of the primordial waters, which, after all, were also the origin of the heavens, and of all the angelic creatures that inhabit them?"

"Ahh, well said, Hezki!" smiled Maimonides, starting to enjoy himself. "But aren't you forgetting that the heavens were created from the waters above, *after* their separation from the waters below? Supposing the qualities of darkness were present in the primordial, as yet undivided waters of the second verse, where did they end up after the firmament separated waters above from waters below? I suggest that, precisely so that the waters above should be free of those qualities, the Creator assigned them to the waters below, which, as you know, when 'gathered together' in the ninth verse, became the seas!"

The old man's visage was carved by illness, his beard, once a source of pride, skimpy and gray as if the disease had thinned his features hadn't wanted to neglect facial hair. But his eyes, black as night and always on the point of smiling, belied the air of consumption.

It being Shabbat, he was wearing his most expensive caftan, woven from the lightest camel wool, dyed a deep cobalt blue, and decorated round the neck and wide sleeves with gold thread arabesques so intricate they used to mesmerize Yehezkel as a child like flames. On his head sat a light blue turban wrapped around a central, white protuberance—a flat-topped, fez-like affair poking out from azure silk spires.

"*You* think abyss and waters are synonyms!" Maimonides accused his pupil. "Well, I intend to show that *tehom,* the abyss, is nothing if not a symbol of the future waters below, while *mayim,* the waters, are a symbol of the future waters above. That is why the Torah says that over the former was darkness, while over the latter God's Spirit already hovered. *Think,* Yehezkel, if light had not yet been created, how could darkness be over one thing and not over the other?"

The old man's eyes, while shining with the thrill of catching out the Almighty on a point of logic, were damp with the emotion that the infinite wisdom of the divine text always sparked in him. He concluded, "What the Torah is saying is that in the undivided, primordial waters both 'ideas,' as Plato would call them, were already there. Tehom prefigured the seas, and over it was the darkness that *is* the sea, while mayim prefigured the heavens and God's Spirit already hovered over them like an eagle over its brood."

Yehezkel was used to the formal elegance of his teacher's arguments and the detached way in which he presented them, so he was surprised by Rav Moshe's excited tones that Shabbat, as if the interpretation of the primordial waters somehow concerned him personally, and convincing his pupil of the association between tehom and the sea were of the utmost importance.

He nodded for his teacher to go on, but there was a knock on the door. The tingling that Yehezkel always felt in the back of his neck when studying Torah instantly vanished, as if a spell had been broken.

It was Rivkah, the youngest daughter of Joseph ibn Sham'un, Rav Moshe's prize student, who lived in Aleppo but was in Fustat that April, a welcome Pesach guest. She carried a tray with a big pot and two tall glasses. The finely engraved copper of both tray and pot shone like things a woman polishes every day. The pot had an elaborate spout and was full of a spiced apple drink, brewed before the Shabbat and kept hot on the abundant embers prepared for the holy day.

Joseph's girl was nine. She walked to the low table on one side of the study, keeping her eyes on the floor as she'd been taught. But at the last moment, as if playing a secret game, she raised her eyes and smiled at the two men. It was as if someone shifted one of the heavy curtains and let in the April sun, so strong was the contrast between the atmosphere that the mystery of creation had evoked in the room and Rivkah's mischievous grin. Maimonides shot her a mock-severe glance. She pretended to be frightened and ran from the room, a hand over her mouth hiding a giggle.

The rabbis, half a century separating their ages, poured themselves some hot cider. After a noisy sip, Yehezkel began pacing the narrow carpet between two rows of open crates brimming with neatly stacked, rolled-up parchments, tall ones in the back and short ones in the front.

Yehezkel admired Rav Moshe's disdain for luxury, evident in these unadorned quarters. Old carpets, a low table, a raised cot for medical examinations, one prized high-backed chair, a few plain ones, and a writing desk. All other available space—and much that wasn't *really* available—was given over to manuscripts. Books and parchments were everywhere, all in such order that Rav Moshe could have found any detail in seconds—in the rare case, that is, that he couldn't find it in the gigantic archive in his head.

The pause in the lesson over, Maimonides started reciting scriptural proof.

"Genesis Rabba says that God unleashed the Flood on the world by releasing tehom, for its waters push against the firmament; they keep pushing since that second day, striving to cover the whole creation again with a single, gigantic wave—something only God's love for his creatures prevents them from doing! And what of the splendid brevity of the eighty-ninth Psalm: 'You dominate the pride of the sea!'"

Scratching his chin through his beard, Yehezkel thought that Rav Moshe sounded like he was trying to prove the sea's guilt before some exegetical court. His teacher continued, a little less incensed, "But let us speak as philosophers now, as two Jews studying the mystery of the Children of Israel's exile. What does this 'curse' on the sea suggest to you?"

Yehezkel, uncharacteristically at a loss for words, looked at his teacher, bewildered.

"Let's start from the beginning," said Rav Moshe. "After its creation and nefarious return in the guise of universal flood, you practically won't find another mention of the sea in the whole Torah. In fact, the only time the Children of Israel faced it, at the Red Sea, the Lord of the Universe had to intervene himself to solve the problem. And Jonah? What do we learn from the sea's role in the story of Jonah?"

By now Maimonides was sweating and dabbing at his face with a kerchief sprinkled with an essence whose fragrance reached his pupil's nostrils. Even from a distance, as he paced the carpet back and forth, hands clasped behind his back, Yehezkel could feel Rav Moshe's agitation.

Maimonides, head resting on his chest after the outburst, was looking from below bushy eyebrows, breath raspy. In the silence that followed, both men felt the heat seeping in from every slit in the house. The old man was the first to recover.

"Trust me, Hezki, it is no coincidence that Ishmaelites, who recognize the Oneness of God, are as diffident toward the sea as Jews are, while Greeks and Romans founded their empires on control of the seas. The conqueror of Egypt wrote to the second caliph: 'The sea is a boundless expanse, on which great ships look like tiny specks; nought but heavens above and water beneath. Trust it little, fear it much. Man at sea is but a worm on a bit of wood—*dud 'ala 'ud,* he wrote—now engulfed, now scared to death!'"

Yehezkel couldn't fathom the intensity of Rav Moshe's animosity. But Maimonides wasn't through yet. "Today, too, if one reads the signs, the violent nature of Franks and Venetians is clearly one with their seagoing traditions! Every seafaring people abandoned the ways of the Lord! Aren't the brutal giants who inhabit the far north considered the best *sailors* in the world?"

Maimonides almost spat out the word "sailors," his face congested as he inspired noisily after each heave of invective. "The life the Lord of the Universe wants us to live is founded on the cycles of the *Earth*! Divine Revelations happen on the tops of *mountains*! Jerusalem, His City, is *not on the sea*! Tell me, Yehezkel, can all these be just *coincidences*?"

Yehezkel finally stopped in front of the old man, arms across his chest, looking sternly at his teacher from the heady height of twenty-one years. He was ready to begin his paean to the sea, but Maimonides raised his right hand to stop him. The rising arm trembled; Yehezkel realized his teacher had overdone it and was paying the price of his loss of composure. The old man made to get up from his chair, and Yehezkel rushed to take his arm and accompany him to his bed. Maimonides whispered, "I apologize, Hezki. I'm afraid I won't be able to hear your defense of the sea today. I don't feel well, and if I don't rest awhile I won't have the strength to visit an important patient when Shabbat is out."

As he spoke, Maimonides untied his caftan, removed the turban and stood there, unsteady, in a sleeveless tunic of white linen, over which hung his tzitzith, and a black silk skullcap.

With no warning, as his teacher slowly stretched out on the bed, Yehezkel had a sudden vision of him as a cadaver: the thinness and ashen color of his body, the skull bones visible through transparent skin. A shiver went down his pupil's back, as if that were his teacher's ghost, come back to see him from the next world of the just. He silently fetched a glass of water from downstairs, put it on Rav Moshe's night table, and left quietly, still shaken, walking backward to the foot of the bamboo ladder in a corner of the room, behind one of the many curtains that led to the roof of his teacher's house.

✡ ✠ ✡ ✠

The moment he shifted the two planks that covered the opening, the Egyptian sun engulfed him in a purifying flame. He jumped out and closed the trapdoor, fleeing the thoughts brought on by the sight of his teacher so close to the revelation of all mysteries. In truth, he was grateful for the chance to spend some time alone on that roof, not three hundred feet from the Nile and the highest in a radius of half a parasang, which, for him, was a hoard of childhood memories. Its three terraces, a few steps leading from one to the other, had been a place of childhood games, and then a refuge from enraged adults, and finally the venue of the astronomy lessons Rav Moshe gave as a still vigorous sixty-year-old.

He was already sweating. He opened his caftan and reached for his turban but, noticing how the bright white plaster covering the roof narrowed his eyes to slits, decided to wait for a drop of sweat first. The sun was still high in the west, and he'd learned to stare at its bright reflection in the river and wait for a drop of sweat to crawl from under his turban and run down his forehead and into his eye. In the exact instant the salty drop fell through his lid and burst in front of his eye, he was treated to a manifestation of the Almighty, a spinning ball of white fire that he called a corner of the Merkavah; that is, a fraction of the chariot the prophet Ezekiel described in the first chapter of his book, though he had never shared the presumptious definition with anyone.

The afternoon grew drowsy. Behind, in the distance, he heard dogs bark and children scream. His mind, lulled by soft sounds and fleeting memories, was prey to a sweet enchantment—like a daydream, but more aware. The calm euphoria that accompanied the apparent somnolence was sought by Sufis as the path to *fanaa*, the "annulment" of the world's natural forms.

He peeked at the corner of the chariot again before removing his turban, the experience leaving him languorous and grateful to God for small perfections in creation. He walked to the low wall on the side of the roof looking out on the river. Suddenly, he understood that seeing his teacher as a corpse had been an involuntary diagnosis of the incurable nature of Rav Moshe's illness. He had *seen* his teacher's imminent death, as it were, in a brief burst of prophecy. He swallowed, but the lump in his throat wouldn't melt.

In the year since Naomi took her own life he'd only been on the roof once, when Rav Moshe nodded off during a lesson. Soon he would sail to Provence. He wondered if God would allow him to ever see his Fustat again. He raised his gaze.

Five parasangs to the southwest, across the Nile, the pyramids rose higher than anything else in Egypt. He'd heard Christian merchants, in their abysmal ignorance, call the tombs "Joseph's granaries," for in their fantasies they were where Jacob's son advised Pharaoh to store grain for the coming seven lean years. Maybe his friends who held that going to study in Christian lands was folly were right after all. Shmuel, the baker's son, told him there were no hammams in Christian cities. Yehezkel retorted they must all be fabulously wealthy to have hammams in their homes. Shmuel laughed and explained that there were no hammams because Christians . . . he could hardly bring himself to say it . . . because Christians *never washed*!

He suddenly remembered the contempt with which his teacher spat the word *sailor,* and frowned. "But I never told Rav Moshe that I go sailing on the river," he mumbled.

He admitted to himself he'd been ill at ease all through Rav Moshe's harangue against the sea. Sailing had become the secret, precious love of his life. He thought grimly that he'd been wise to tell no one of this infatuation for the sea, for if every one of his teacher's opinions sooner or later became a rabbinical dictate, sailing would likely be declared a pagan practice, and forbidden to all Jews!

That night, God willing, he would go to al-Kahira for another lesson with Rav Pinhas, his new Kabbalah teacher. Rav Moshe found the discipline preposterous, based on legends and superstitions, yet despite his teacher's scepticism, Rav Pinhas ben Meshullam charmed Yehezkel. The tall French Jew with a long, narrow black beard was at once a mystic and an eccentric. Though his movements were unruffled, his eyes burned with a kind of repressed frenzy. He had taught in many lands, on a self-assigned mission to spread the vision of a circle of rabbis in the towns of Provence, Languedoc, and Cataluña who, in recent decades, had revived esoteric traditions with Babylonian roots. They had a predilection—"a morbid attention," Rav Moshe called it—for two Bible passages: the creation and the vision of Yehezkel's delirious namesake, the prophet Ezekiel.

Yehezkel thought of the day he'd studied the first chapter of Genesis with Rav Pinhas. The Lunel rabbi liked to say, "The Torah is a living creature, its life pulsating under the surface of its literal meaning." His attitude toward the twenty-two letters of the Hebrew alphabet was little short of worship, a cult of letters that Yehezkel had never encountered before and that attracted him with the same force of the patterns stars made in the night sky. He thought back to the lesson.

"I realize they are the creation of the universe and the beginning of the Torah, Rav Pinhas, but why are these thirty-one verses considered by kabbalists to be the most important in all of Scripture?"

"Ah. Now listen carefully, Yehezkel," his charismatic new teacher said. "The path to arrive in the presence of the Creator is the reverse—the reflection—of the one along which we emanated from Him. To know the stages of creation is therefore to know, in reverse, the way one must follow to return to the root of all existence." His voice, never loud in the first pace, became even softer. "This is why the secret meanings hidden in the words—in their values, their roots, their grammar—are more important in the first chapter of Genesis, and even more so in the first verse, than in the rest of the Torah. My teacher, Rav Yitzhak the Blind—may his light shine for years to come—says the deepest secrets are already present in the first word, Bereshit."

That was why an hour earlier Yehezkel, enthralled by the idea of hidden wisdom, asked Rav Moshe to linger on the first verse, which they'd already covered the previous Shabbat. But the great philosopher, knowing of his pupil's infatuation with that nonsense, impatiently denied him.

Turning to the east, his gaze fell on the three cemeteries—Mohammedan, Jewish, and Coptic—which stretched for thousands of shimmering graves between Fustat and the desert. His thoughts again turned to the imminent loss of his teacher. Yehezkel's grandfather had been the same age as Rav Moshe and his best friend. Their families fled Cordoba together when the Almohad Caliph ordered Jews to embrace Islam, and arrived in Egypt together after some years in Fez and in Eretz Israel.

"Rav Moshe was about thirty when he arrived in Fustat," he mumbled to himself, "and was known, but not famous. He began writing his Mishneh Torah while living on his brother David's trade of precious stones with the East . . ."

The moment David ben Maimon's name left his lips he fell silent, and then slapped his thigh really hard. "But of course! David drowned in a storm on his way to India, thirteen years before I was born! How could I be so *stupid* . . . Rav Moshe was bedridden for a year; the pain of losing his brother almost killed him! And I didn't understand he was condemning the sea to cope with that pain! Yehezkel, you're a simpleton . . . and an insensitive one, to boot!"

He thought back to his teacher's evident distress as he spoke of the sea's subsersive role. "Lord of the Universe! I saw his arm tremble as it rose, as if *he* were drowning, and did nothing to help him! My teacher would suffer less if David was killed by the sinister 'waters below,' symbol of evil in the world? Then I should have screamed my hatred for the sea like people on the edge of a battle! And what did I do instead? I blithely prepared to explain to him that God loves the sea as much as the mountains. And *I* am supposed to become a famous rabbi? I'm just a verbose, arrogant *nobody,* whose name shouldn't be mentioned on the same day as that of the great Rav Moshe the Egyptian!"

Later in the study, Yehezkel heard the account of the sack of the Polis, two weeks earlier, by Franks and Venetians led by blind Doge Dandolo. Rav Moshe heard it from a Yemenite trader, Sheik Yoseph ibn Abulman, who had witnessed and, God being merciful, survived, the massacre that followed.

Yoseph had the dark complexion of Jews who'd lived in the Queen of Sheba's land since before the destruction of the Temple, but not the dry physique and sharp features, vaguely reminiscent of birds of prey, of Yemenis. His role of middleman between India and Europe enriched him, and with wealth his contours had softened and rounded, until he resembled a florid Mediterranean trader. Maimonides asked him about the Sultan's reaction to his tale that morning. Yoseph, a little jaded by everything he'd seen, answered, "Rabbi, what al-'Adil most cares about are the Franks' intentions now they've taken the Polis. Will they move on Egypt, as was their original plan, or will they be content to devour a Christian ally and, like wild beasts of the desert, fall asleep until the next meal? I heard they're so busy tearing their victim's flesh from each other, fighting over who will be emperor, that no one was even speaking of sailing on eastward!"

Maimonides made a face. "Puah! I never doubted the Latins would stop in the Polis, but then I know things that not many are aware of; things the Almighty advises the Sultan to reveal to me, for the good of our people. God forbid I should boast of it, but ever since their galleys arrived in the Golden Horn a year ago, I knew the Venetians, in exchange for trading rights in Alexandria, Damietta, and Fustat, promised al-'Adil not to assist *any* expedition against Egypt."

The old man grinned as he watched the look of surprise on the merchant's rotund face. "But those rabid dogs, those of the city *inside the sea,*" he went on with a sideways glance at Yehezkel, "omitted to tell al-'Adil that they had just contracted to ship *thirty-five thousand* cross-wearing knights . . . to Egypt! Still, since their fleet departed, the sultan assured me more than once that the Venetians, crafty and deceitful as they are, would find a way to honor *both* commitments!"

"That they did," whispered Yoseph, disgusted but impressed despite himself, "that they surely did. So the attempt to invade Egypt, thank God, is still in the future, and we should all pray to see them at each other's throats for many years to come." The merchant smiled wistfully. "But I shall also pray to be spared the spectacle from as close as I saw it this time. Now forgive me, Rabbi, but there's a relative of my wife's in Fustat I absolutely *must* visit, on pain of a bout of sulking by my sweet Judith!"

Maimonides got up to accompany his guest to the door, but Yoseph stepped in front of him and grabbed his bony hand in both his chubby ones. "Bless me, Rav Moshe, I beg you! Ask the Lord to let me find peace at home! Only you saved Yemen's Jews from forced conversion by Salah ad-Din's crazy brother; whom shall we turn to when you . . ." He nearly burst into sobs, so obvious was the gravity of Rav Moshe's illness. The rabbi took his reddish cheeks in his hands, leaned forward, and whispered some Hebrew words. Then the merchant thanked Maimonides for his hospitality, wished both men a good week, and left the study.

Returning to the Shabbat routine and seeing Rav Moshe back in control did wonders for Yehezkel's mood. His teacher refreshed himself behind a curtain as the noise from the hall below grew. Yehezkel started downstairs when he felt himself grabbed by the arm.

"Where are you running, young mystic?" asked his teacher with a smile that threatened verbal sparring. "I'd like another word with you before we go down for prayers. Have you nothing to say on the news

Yoseph brought? Doesn't the behavior of those savage Venetian 'sailors' confirm my opinion of seafaring civilizations? Or are you so naive that a beautiful sunset at sea is enough to make you defend those barbarians and their connection to the waters below? Because if you'd like to do that, I'm prepared to let my honorable guests wait a little so I can hear your refutation."

The suggestion that he was too naive to appreciate the true role of the sea scalded Yehezkel's pride. In a fit of calm rage, he took the old man's arm, accompanied the teacher back to his chair, as if ready to finish the debate, and then said nonchalantly, as if expressing an afterthought, "I recognize the superiority of your approach, Rabbi, which is to subject all interpretations to the test of reason, though you allow yourself quite some leeway when you attribute an evil nature to the sea based, at the end of the day, on your rancor for the loss of your brother David."

Rav Moshe suddenly looked like a puppet whose strings had been cut. He fell back into the chair and seemed on the point of tears.

Yehezkel, as with every time he lost control of his words, was bitten by remorse as sudden and sharp as the anger of a minute before. He fell on his knees before Rav Moshe. "Forgive me, Rabbi!" he sobbed. "I was more than disrespectful; I made light of your pain! I beg you, give me the punishment I so richly deserve!"

But Rav Moshe had already recovered and, like a cat that momentarily lost its balance, pretended that nothing much had happened. "No, Hezki, you deserve no punishment. You only used your brain to refute my interpretation, as our game requires. But you went beyond anything I expected."

He caressed Yehezkel's head, which now rested on his thighs. "You know, Hezki, the way you remind me of your grandfather at your age warms this old man's weary heart. Your mind leaps like a fish, and you have the same impetuosity and love of truth at any cost that Yehezkel had."

He lowered his voice, "When your grandfather and I studied

together in Fez, we used to indulge in calculations of the date of the Messiah's arrival. I have since forbidden such calculations in my writings, so that weaker souls won't lose their faith by placing their hopes in arbitrary guesses."

Yehezkel stood up, already excited. Rav Moshe looked into his eyes for a long moment and then said, "I want to tell you of a tradition that has been in our family for twenty generations, Hezki. An ancestor of mine once affirmed, in a state of grace, that the event the Almighty decreed should be at the center of all history, from creation to the coming of his Prince, was not the freeing of the Children of Israel from slavery in Egypt, in the year 2444, it was instead the death of Moses, in 2486! No calculation could be simpler, really. At the end of another 2486 years from his death, that is, in 4972, the Messiah of David will manifest himself!"

Yehezkel, grandson of Yehezkel, stared at his teacher, mouth agape.

"Yes, young man, eight years from now. I know *I* won't be there to see it, despite your grandfather on his deathbed wishing me just such a fate. What isn't clear to me is whether the Almighty is punishing me for something, like another Egyptian Moshe—if small things can be compared to great ones," he smiled, "or whether, in his boundless mercy, he is sparing me a burning disappointment."

Maimonides knew he didn't have much time to live and concluded in a whisper, "On one hand, Hezki, I urge you not to take this prophecy too seriously, but on the other I envy you the opportunity to be in Jerusalem in eight years' time, when the Holy City will be in the grip of spiritual spasms, waiting for its Messiah!"

The buzz from below had grown louder, and Rav Moshe stood up, leaning on Yehezkel, putting an arm around his pupil's shoulder, a foot higher than his own, and they walked to the door together.

"Victory in our debate on the second verse is yours, Hezki. You saw through to the deep, irrational motivations of my interpretation. I was not aware of them myself, but when you said it, I *knew* it was true."

Maimonides stopped at the door, turned to face Yehezkel and put his hands on his shoulders. "Since I know how much it means to you, you should know that your studies in Provence will receive my blessing." He paused and gave him a long look, his eyes not smiling as they usually did. "But know also that your life will *always* be in danger among Christians," he said at last.

Then the two men went below to see out the Shabbat.

✡ ✠ ✡ ✠

Yehezkel left his teacher's house in the warm evening, astride an old donkey. The pungent smell of cloves and other spices used in the ceremony that ushers out Shabbat lingered in his nostrils, clashing now with the reek of manure that hung over the road between Fustat and al-Kahira. That pong competed in turn with the perfume of freshly harvested dates hanging from heaped branches at the foot of palm trees. A third, delicious layer crowding Yehezkel's nose was the fragrance of honey-filled pancakes some women were cooking on iron plates laid on embers and selling to passersby.

An hour later, the young rabbi was in front of Bab-ez-Zuweyla, the gate in al-Kahira's southern wall, usually swarming with humanity more than any place in the capital but now pleasantly quiet. As his donkey drank at the fountain, Yehezkel recognized the poignant nostalgia he'd felt at every stage of the ride. It was the state of mind, so often described by his teacher, of the Jew with one foot already in the next land where he will wait for his Messiah, but the other one still firmly planted in the land he is about to leave—usually against his will. Being uprooted, said Rav Moshe, produces a dizziness of the soul, caused by the absence of roots deeply planted in one place. But a Jew's roots are sunk so deep in the Torah that nothing could ever pull them out, so he is mostly immune to this vertigo.

Surely influenced by his age, Yehezkel thought that in his case that malaise wasn't even strong enough to blunt the exhilarating mood that precedes a departure. "But then, you're not leaving against your will, like Rav Moshe left Cordoba, are you?" he chided himself with a smile.

Two hours after sunset, Yehezkel reached the house of Halfon ben Yitzhak, the merchant hosting Rav Pinhas. He anticipated the secrets the French kabbalist would soon be revealing. They would switch letters and add up the values of dozens of Torah words deep into the night, and he would only go home in the morning, after grabbing a few hours' sleep on the cushions in the takhtabush.

Calculating the numerical value of words, their gematria, proved a natural talent of Yehezkel's. It soon became a compulsive habit, almost a private ritual. He instinctively added up the value of almost every Hebrew word he came across, be it in a prayer book or in a page of Talmud.

The doorman let him into the house, one of the richest in the *haret*.* Eight or nine people, Ishmaelites and Jews, sat around a eucalyptus tree in the middle of the courtyard, laughing and drinking. Seeing Yehezkel, Pinhas ben Meshullam took his leave from the merry group to sit in the takhtabush with his disciple.

After some harmless gossip, legs crossed in front of each other, Yehezkel told him of Maimonides's virulent rhetorical attack on the waters below in his lesson of that afternoon—not mentioning his untalmudic refutation—and asked Rav Pinhas for his thoughts on Rav Moshe's exegesis.

The kabbalist stroked his beard, so black it glinted with purple, smiling as if he and Maimonides shared an amusing secret about the primordial waters. Then, in precise Hebrew without gutturals, he said, "Do you remember when I told you that to know the sequence culminating in the creation of Adam is to know the path men must follow, in reverse, to arrive in the presence of the Creator?"

"Yes, Rabbi, I remember it well," said Yehezkel, already feeling the tingling in the back of his neck.

---

*Harets were cul-de-sacs starting from a street, with more cul-de-sacs branching off from the main one. They could thus be closed at night with one big wooden door, and it was the custom for them to be inhabited by members of a group, whether a community of foreign merchants, a tolerated sect, or just a rich extended family.

"Well, there's a passage in tractate Hagiga I'm surprised your teacher didn't mention in speaking of the waters. It is about a journey that four sages took into the Pardes, the garden of revelations, the orchard of secrets. A dangerous visit, which ended in tragedy for most of them . . ." Rav Pinhas paused. Yehezkel knew the passage and was already searching his memory, eyes closed, for the link with the waters. He found it and nodded, smiling, as his new teacher looked on, pleased.

"Excellent, you remembered that Akiva warned the others not to call what they would see flowing down the columns in the Sixth Palace 'water,' since on the first day—with chaos and darkness over the abyss—the undivided waters were the *only* thing already in existence. Rabbi Akiva is saying that the Torah uses words men can grasp, but here it is speaking of the formless matter *before* Creation. It is not the water *we* know, it is not the water in the seas, that Bereshit is speaking of. . . ."

Yehezkel opened his eyes wide, overwhelmed by the beauty of the gloss. He was as surprised as the kabbalist that Rav Moshe would leave that Talmud passage out of his exposition. Oh, how he would love to be able to make such an erudite objection to Rav Moshe's exegesis! Excited, he said, "I think I understand. If in the Sixth Heaven God creates light, to accede to the Seventh one must cross the darkness and chaos that preceded everything."

"Exactly!" exclaimed Rav Yitzhak. "My teacher, may his candle burn for many years, proposed that the Ruah Elohim over the waters in the second verse—since *ruah,* as you know, means both spirit and wind—was a breeze that ruffled the surface of the water, rendering it opaque. Only *after* blowing on the water did God create light, for what could be seen when the water was smooth was no longer visible!"

The kabbalist lowered his voice. "Conversely, on reaching the Sixth Heaven, one has to stop the Divine Breath, because only when the waters are smooth again one will, as only happens when water is still and transparent, see the bottom. *That* is when one will be in His presence." Rav Pinhas murmured, "I'm sure you understand that 'stopping the Divine Breath' is a concept not everyone may frequent."

Yehezkel's head was spinning as it would after two glasses of wine.

"Akiva was right to warn them," concluded the rabbi. "Climbing back up the slope of creation is, in a sense, *undoing* the creation, and the slightest mistake can be fatal, as his three companions discovered."

A gurgle of laughter came from the courtyard thirty paces from them, but to Yehezkel it sounded like the breaking of a primordial wave. He sat in front of his teacher, breathing slowly, eyes closed, mind lost in the birth pangs of the universe. In total darkness, the gale, meeting no obstacles, howled its infinite power while the waters curled in furious breakers with no coast on which to crash them.

He dragged himself back to the takhtabush and said euphorically, "Rabbi, I have exceptional news! Rav Moshe will bless my journey to Provence! With his blessing and your letter, who will stop me quenching my thirst at the holy founts in Lunel and Pokiére?"

"Posquière, Yehezkel, Posquière. Don't be rash, young man; many things could still come between you and the Merkavah. You must pray God to grant you the wisdom you're seeking."

Yehezkel lowered his head humbly and then remembered the other thing he meant to ask Rav Pinhas. "Rabbi, what do you know of a calculation that puts the arrival of the Messiah eight years from now?"

A knowing, wistful smile spread on the French rabbi's face; "2486 plus 2486?"

"They know of the prophecy in Provence, too?" cried Yehezkel, grabbing the kabbalist's arm excitedly as if that would confirm that redemption really *was* imminent.

"Calm down. I could show you a dozen such calculations, and half of them would concern dates that sadly passed with no sign of the Messiah. But there is a verse in the ninetieth Psalm, *In your eyes, a thousand years are but as yesterday when it is passed.* The only calculation Rav Yitzhak the Blind—may God watch over him—finds reliable is this: a world cycle is six thousand years, and it is again as the six days of creation, the Seventh Millennium being the Cosmic Shabbat, the Reign of the Messiah!"

The kabbalist's eyes shone with the beauty and simplicity of his teacher's calculation. "Do you see, Yehezkel? We were freed from slavery at dawn on Tuesday and are now close to the end of Thursday. The Cosmic Friday begins on Thursday's twelfth hour, the year 5000. Rav Yitzhak says God will not bring us back at the last minute, but in time to prepare for the Millennial Shabbat. He will gather us in Eretz Israel on Friday morning, seven hours before Shabbat. Can you work out the year?"

Yehezkel's expression betrayed his preference for an end to the exile eight years away—since by the Lord's counting he simply couldn't wait around all day—but he quickly did the arithmetic. If a thousand years is twenty-four hours, then one hour is forty-one years and eight months. Midday on Friday would be the year 5750, so an hour before midday would be the spring of 5708. He announced the result.

"You really have a head for numbers, Yehezkel, God bless you. Alas, yes, the Children of Israel will only return to Eretz Israel in the spring of the year Christians will call 1948 and finally start preparing for Shabbat!"

The night was nearly finished, and the cool air entering the takhtabush sharpened the feverish minds of the two rabbis. Outside, only two Ishmaelites still argued, deeply at loggerheads over something.

Rav Pinhas said, "Ezekiel's book was nearly hidden because some sages found his description of the chariot dangerously explicit. I love him exactly *because* of his candor." He smiled complicitly at Yehezkel. "You bear the name of the flamboyant prophet who saw the Merkavah— and names, as you know, are not given lightly. I imagine you know the gematria of your name?"

"Of course," answered his pupil. "Ten, eight, seven, a hundred, one, and thirty. It makes 156. What can I infer from that?"

Rav Pinhas still wore a sly smile. "What other words do you know with that *gematria*?"

Yehezkel hesitated, finding it immodest to associate himself with the other names worth 156 that he knew. Then, a little embarrassed, he said, "Yoseph and Zion, Rabbi."

"Interesting. Dreams and visions were prominent in the lives of both Yoseph and Ezekiel. I dare say they will be in yours, too."

"And what of Zion?" asked Yehezkel, hoping to find a journey to Jerusalem ensconced in his name. Rav Pinhas was silent for a while, eyes closed. Then he said, "It may be coincidence, but both Yoseph and Ezekiel traveled to Zion transcendentally: Yoseph after his death—his body brought from Egypt, as he'd asked—and Ezekiel from Babylon in a vision, carried there by an angel of the Lord. After all, Yehezkel, in gematria your name might as well be Zion ben Zion!"

Rav Pinhas fell silent again. Yehezkel felt that his next words would, at least for him, have the force of prophecy, since he also considered Rav Pinhas an angel of the Lord sent to show him his way.

"You will indeed go to Jerusalem, Yehezkel, and your journey there will be associated with dreams and visions. In fact, I believe, may God protect us, my boy! I believe your journey, like that of the prophet, will take you all the way into the Temple's courtyards!"

Part Three

Fourth
and Fifth Day

CHAPTER 14

VEHAYU LE'OTOT
And They Will Be Signs

OFF THE WESTERN TIP OF RHODES, 17TH JUNE 1219

Spiridione's tareta sailed lazily for three days, carried by a light northwesterly breeze that bore the perfume of the citrus fruit of the Dodecanese, an archipelago that reached down to those waters, but most of whose islands lay some hundred leagues north of them.

In theory, one could sail east from Candia to Cyprus in five days at most, but in recent decades those four hundred leagues had become the Mediterranean's most pirate-ridden tract, and no vessel dared to be caught far from a shore toward which to flee on sighting a black pennant. This meant coasting Crete and then hopping northeast from island to island all the way to Rhodes. After sailing along Rhodes it was a twenty-league hop to the Anatolian coast, which one followed east until it was time to head south to Cyprus, this last twelve-hour stretch of open sea being the most dangerous one.

The gentle mistral was weaker than Spiro wished for in his hurry to get to Cyprus, but the absence of fresher breezes and bigger seas favored serenity behind the prow, where the company sheltered, and the mood was that of a pleasure trip on a Holy Day. The tall, upright timber stood out against the sky as if to provide protection for the seven pilgrims, who, after surviving the beaching of the *Falcus,* considered themselves, rightly or wrongly, seafaring folk.

Among the effects of the fair weather was that after three days at sea the abbess wasn't in the least indisposed. Her mood was so cheerful she didn't even mind the howls of young Zaharias, a Cretan sailor and nephew of Spiridione, who constantly sang in a high-pitched voice Byzantine hymns the abbess called monstrous. The others tried to silence him, at times threatening to throw him overboard, but Zaharias feared nothing, and he raised his strident voice to heaven from dawn to sunset.

Spiridione's advances to Galatea in the first two days had been embarrassing even for the crew. Yehezkel feared he would have to ask young de Rosson to defend the honor of the abbess from the Greek's vulgar innuendos. At one point, Spiridione manifested the desire to "serve her in the way she would prefer." Galatea replied that she would appreciate it if his crew would refrain from blaspheming the name of God, of our Mother Mary, and of a host of other saints.

Spiro smiled the condescending smile of someone who spent his life mocking clerics of all faiths. "Please judge people by their actions, milady, not by their words! Would you condemn someone who threatens in the heat of a dispute as you would he who actually commits murder? I threaten my wife with violent death at least once a week because she cooks the worst roast fish in all Crete. Would you see me hanged for it? No? Then let my men blaspheme in peace. It's *their* way of speaking with God!"

Spiridione laughed till it seemed he would burst a blood vessel, but before the abbess could answer—and despite regretting not hearing the whiplash that would have struck him—Yehezkel interrupted to point out a shift in the wind's direction. The breeze was still light but now blew from the southwest. If it wanted to keep making headway in an easterly direction, the tareta would have to jibe its mainsail.

Yehezkel figured with this breeze Rhodes was only a league down-wind, and the best thing to do to keep away from it, as there were practically no waves, would be to drop the sail and row east, away from the island, to avoid drifting too close.

Spiridione climbed on the quarterdeck and after a minute, as Yehezkel expected, shouted to bring the tareta into the wind and lower the mainsail. The men took up their positions, one at the foot of the mast to lower the halyard and three along the sail's base to gather it in and receive the yard. But after two minutes, the rabbi realized something wasn't right. The sail wasn't coming down, and the four men were swearing as only sailors and dockers know how. Soon Spiro joined the chorus, screaming to hurry up with that mainsail if they didn't want to taste his whip. But the halyard had obviously tangled at the top of the mast, and the big, patched-up sail stayed aloft, its yard bouncing off the mast in frustration with every pitching motion of the tareta.

Then the southerly breeze freshened, pushing them toward the shore. Ten minutes later, a mere contretemps suddenly turned, as so often happens at sea, into a budding emergency. The tareta, bow to the wind, drifted quite fast, heeling over to starboard with its main-sail full of wind squashed against the mast, the rocky shore of Rhodes less than a league away. The danger was real, but the sea was still calm, which conferred a strangely ridiculous air to the scene.

"It's like being on a ship of comedians!" murmured Yehezkel.

Spiridione ordered the crew to man the six oars, a decision that confirmed his sound seamanship to Yehezkel, and then walked to the foot of the mast to see what was going on. Within minutes, Spiridione and Yehezkel realized that if the breeze freshened any more, the main-sail would catch enough wind to prevent the rowers from making any headway. Soon they would only have two options to stop drift-ing toward the rocks: send someone to the top of the mast to cut the tangled halyard, or take a knife to the mainsail to let the wind blow through it. The first solution, much preferable to ruining an expensive sail, unfortunately meant risking someone's life swinging thirty feet above deck in the bosun's chair with the boat's motions amplified by the closeness of the steep shore as the waves bouncing off it crossed the oncoming ones.

The bosun heading the crew was a stocky man with no trace of humanity in his eyes, a second cousin of Spiridione's incongruously named Theophilos. He reached the same conclusions and turned to his cousin with a pompous little speech, his broken Greek reeking of resinous wine, in which he offered to be hoisted in the bosun's chair in exchange for half the value of the salvaged sail.

As he listened to the proposition, Spiro swelled like a huge toad, his face as congested by rage as it was by laughter. Spitting copiously he screamed:

"You son of a lame and scabby dog! If your grandmother and my grandmother hadn't been sisters, I swear on every oracle in the islands I would send you to the top of the mast right now, but you'd be in no danger of falling, because I would hoist you by your neck!"

The whole eight-man crew, except Zaharias, gathered around the two, now facing each other, fists clenched, at the foot of the mast. Fear of the coming brawl froze the pilgrims in the shadow of the prow. André made a move to intervene, but Yehezkel grabbed his arm and whispered in his ear, and the Templar sat down again. All the while, the falsetto of Zaharias's voice singing hymns through the drama continued to lend the whole affair the air of a farce. The cliff was now frighteningly close. Yehezkel thought:

"If every time the nun and I leave the safety of land for the high seas we end up, within days, staring at an oncoming wall of rock, a kabbalist should draw at least two conclusions: *in primis* that our mission is strongly contrasted by certain powers in heaven, and *in secundis* that maybe we should stop provoking those powers, get off the damned tareta in Anatolia, and make our way to Syria overland!"

He started breathing the folded breath as he surveyed the situation once more. A thought floated up from the past, the voice of his teacher in Fustat arguing that going to sea was not Jewish. In what he would later recognize as a moment of superstitious fear, he asked himself, "Is being at sea so often disrespectful of Rav Moshe's memory? But Rav Eleazar sent me to Eretz Israel, how am I supposed to get there if not by sea? In any case, I can no longer just look on."

He started to untie the chest and said to the company, "*Just in case* these Greeks are crazy enough to not save their boat, we should all wait until we are no more than a hundred feet from shore before jumping in the water!"

Gudrun moaned loudly, and Garietto, ignoring the abbess, gripped her hand.

Yehezkel had a feeling that the foul-mouthed dispute was nothing more than a negotiation in the style of the Greeks, and that the two men would never let the tareta go aground in such an inane manner.

Meanwhile Spiridione found his breath again. "*You*, of all people, Theophilos, dare to blackmail me?" A shiver of pure rage shook him from head to toe, and he drew a big knife from his belt. The crew took a step back.

"I'll slit my only mainsail myself, just so I can watch you live out your days as the penniless deckhand you are and *must* remain! As for you, Zaharias, shut your mouth *now*, or I'll cut your tongue out!"

There was silence on deck.

Theophilos lowered his demand to a third of the sail's value. Spiridione agreed. "Done. Why are you standing here, get a move on, by the blood of Christ! Can't you see the rocks?"

Yehezkel leaned toward Galatea and quoted the Book of Proverbs, smiling, "People's own folly leads to their ruin, yet their heart rages against the Lord."

In a few frantic moments the bosun's chair was tied to the second halyard and Theophilos, standing on a plank, began to rise as two crewmates hoisted him up.

Without telling Spiro, whose nose was in the air like everyone else's, Yehezkel ran to the tareta's single, central tiller, to minimize her movements while a man was aloft.

Under the admiring eyes of the helmsman he replaced, the rabbi contrasted the tareta's swings with sudden sharp but small tugs on the tiller, administered when the hull was on the crest of a wave. The tareta became so steady that Spiridione instinctively turned around to see what stopped the rolling. When he saw the tiller in the hands of the Jew, he laughed out loud, "Your blasted breed never stops amazing me, Jew!"

Ten minutes later the mainsail lay on deck, rolled up around its yard, and the tareta was distancing itself from the island with regular, if impatient, oar strokes.

✡ ✠ ✡ ✠

The day of the mainsail incident ended with a sunset like a hymn to the Lord executed with colors instead of voices. The company was gathered under the prow, wedged amid coiled mooring lines and freshwater jugs. It was only a week before the shortest night of the year, and even the chilly dampness and the indefinable anxiety that accompany the approach of darkness at sea could not be felt. The tareta's prow cleaved the tranquil waters before the coast of Lycia with a soft and reassuring swoosh.

A school of dolphins gathered in front of the bow to observe the last light with them. Galatea, who had never seen dolphins before, was touched by their joyful, childlike nature. At one point the abbess even tried to feed the seagulls, but Yehezkel, like all sailors, was shocked. "Please don't do that, madame. They're ill-mannered birds, with drunkards' eyes. Don't encourage their strident attentions."

When the last sliver of sun vanished in the sea, the pilgrims, as they had done in Kaliviani, declared the world an excellent place. Aillil asked to go amidships to speak with André. Yehezkel and Galatea both gave consent, each one convinced of being the tutor the boy addressed. The misunderstanding made them smile. Yehezkel asked, "Have you noticed how our traveling together is giving less and less scandal as we move east?"

Galatea looked at him obliquely. "And you can't wait to be among Saracens, I bet, where you'll be able to pass me off as your infidel slave. Isn't that so, Master Ezekiel?"

The abbess was jesting, but Gudrun was startled. By now the young nun was truly scandalized by her abbess's intimacy with the Jew but refrained from mentioning it because of her own weakness for Garietto. Since they'd left Candia, noticing Galatea's reddened cheeks and undivided attention as the rabbi related dangers he'd survived, Gudrun started praying assiduously for Mother Galatea's soul.

The silence was peaceful and penetrating, so vast it reached to the stars sparkling in a deep blue but still luminous sky. Galatea had slept *à la belle étoile* countless times in Tuscia but now realized the night was different here. The stars were more vivid, both in color and brightness, their light spreading into the black velvet in such a way that the eye could almost make out the space around them. The abbess and the rabbi were like two children, aghast at the beauty of the starry sky at sea. Yehezkel murmured, "People who never spent a clear night at sea may know their names and positions, but they cannot claim to *know* the stars. They are ignorant of the ecstasy they inspire in the human soul."

They stared up in wonder for a while longer, and then Yehezkel whispered, "In my mind, madame, infinite stars are a reminder of creation, and creation is a reminder of the Hebrew alphabet . . ."

"Oh yes, Rabbi, this is a propitious time to learn some more aleph-bet!"

"All right, then. Do you still remember the letter *lamed* and its numerical value?"

"Of course I do. *Lamed* is the twelfth letter, and its value is thirty," Galatea answered promptly.

"And *zadik,* my favorite pupil?"

"*Zadik* is the eighteenth letter, and its value is ninety," answered Galatea with a smile, "but if there are no other pupils, Master Ezekiel, how can I be your favorite?" Yehezkel sighed. "I never taught a woman before, and alas, it's a novelty I'm discovering I favor." He lifted his eyes. "May the Lord take pity on my body, which is weak, and on my soul, which is his anyway. *Amen*!"

Galatea's laughter echoed on the water. She felt perfectly at ease and plunged right back into the game. "In Kaliviani you told me of precious jewels enclosed in Scripture as in a casket and said the aleph-bet is the key to open it and bask in their light." She smoothed her habit in the semidarkness. "Now don't tell me to be patient again, Rabbi, for if I don't see at least *one* jewel before we reach the Holy Land, I will have to think those were promises made by a duplicitous Jew to take advantage of a naive nun."

Both the German nun and the widow were doing their best to listen without drawing attention, but at this they couldn't help laughing, a little scream from Gudrun and a muffled snort from Albacara.

Yehezkel knew that "duplicitous Jew" was said in jest, but in fact the nun was right. He'd found himself hesitating every time his lessons were on the point of leaving the safe shore of philosophy and the aleph-bet to venture into the high seas of Kabbalah, and Galatea noticed.

"You're right, madame," he said, avoiding her eyes. "I don't consider you a 'duplicitous Christian,' but it is true that Jewish law forbids teaching gentiles the secrets of the Torah, nor, God forbid, its mysteries."

"I hate to confess my ignorance, Master Ezekiel, but I could not explain the difference between a secret and a mystery if my life depended on it."

Right away Yehezkel cast off on one of his monologues. "A secret is just something a certain number of people agree not to divulge. A mystery, be it hidden in the letters of a verse, in the rules of reincarnation, or in the true meaning of the resurrection of the dead, is a revelation inaccessible to uninitiated minds. Only strong, independent, and curious minds can attain the revelation of a mystery."

Galatea had waited years for someone to give an intelligible form to the hidden content of sacraments. Not even Hildegard succeeded in showing her the road she'd followed to arrive at the comprehension of mysteries. She listened to the rabbi in perfect silence, almost without breathing.

"A mystery, protected by its secrets, defines a particular mystical school. That mystery then becomes the heart of all contemplations and initiation rites of that school."

"Please, Rabbi, be kind enough to give me an example of each," asked Galatea.

Yehezkel went to the chest and fetched a candle and a small knife. He lit the candle and stood it up and then took the knife and etched a Hebrew letter into the deck. Galatea immediately recognized a *shin*, the last but one of the twenty-two letters. Yehezkel crossed his legs and started the lesson. "Very well, here is an example. Kabbalah is based on the mysteries of the hidden contents of Scripture. Gematria, or the technique of adding up the numerical values of the letters in a word, is a secret shared only by kabbalists." Then, with a smile, "At least it was until tonight . . . oh, well. Through the use of gematria, kabbalists see that when the Torah, in the second verse, says 'and God's spirit hovered over the waters,' the words 'God's spirit'—Ruach Elohim—have a total value of 300."

"Just like the letter *shin*!" exclaimed Galatea.

"Exactly," smiled Yehezkel. "Now write the number of Divine Unity before the *shin,* Madame."

Galatea took the little knife from his hand and carved out an *aleph*—the first letter, whose value is 1—before the *shin*. Yehezkel looked on, satisfied. "What you've written reads *esh,* madame, and it means *fire*!"

The instant he pronounced the word *fire,* a shooting star slowly crossed the sky above them, burning for an unusually long time. The abbess felt a shiver down her spine but clapped her hands, not in the least afraid. The rabbi wasn't to know, she thought, that for Christians fire was a symbol of the Holy Spirit.

"The Acts of the Apostles," she told him excitedly, "relate that on the Pentecost, fifty days after the Resurrection, 'the Holy Spirit descended on them like tongues of fire, accompanied by a roar like wind.'"

As she pronounced the word *wind*, Rustico farted loudly in his sleep, and both held back laughter.

Yehezkel continued the lesson. "As I remember, you liked the way the chorus of virgins in your dream sang the word *shamayim*."

Galatea softly hummed Hildegard's music for the word as the rabbi scratched out the *aleph* and added, slightly after the *shin*, the three letters that turn it into shamayim: a *mem*, a *yod*, and another *mem*.

"How would you read *this* word, madame?"

"Sha . . . mayim, of course!" guessed his pupil.

"So the three letters after the *shin* read . . ."

"M . . . ayim?"

"Yes. And do you know what mayim means? It means water!" smiled Yehezkel.

Galatea, caught in a whirl of letters and meanings, looked at him, waiting for an explanation.

Yehezkel looked as if he thought the rest explained itself. "Don't you see, madame? The second verse speaks of God's Spirit hovering *over the waters,* and here is a *shin,* worth 300 like God's Spirit, hovering above the word *mayim,* the waters!"

Yehezkel gloated like a boy showing his friend the cave he discovered in the forest. "So to those who possess the secret of gematria, the Torah reveals, through the word *shamayim,* that the sky's origin is the union of fire and water! And that revelation," he concluded smugly, "is a mystery!"

Galatea was silent for a moment and then said, "Thank you, Rabbi. You've shown me one of the jewels, and it truly shines like a *flame.* Would you show me another? Please?"

The first nightwatch was drawing to a close, and the pilgrims were asleep, but the nun and the kabbalist weren't tired. Now and then a member of the company heard them giggling. Someone snored loudly at the foot of the mast. Galatea whispered that only Zaharias could make that much noise even while asleep.

"Write, *s'il vous plait,* the letters I am going to dictate to you," said Yehezkel with a smile that his poor Naomi had been the last to see. "*Yod, yod, nun.* And then *samech, vav, daled.*"

Galatea correctly wrote both words. Then she guessed, with no help from her teacher, that they were pronounced *yayin* and *sod.* Yehezkel glowed with pride. She asked what the words meant, but he took her down the path of gematria first. "Add up their value first, madame, if you please . . ."

"10, 10, and 50 makes 70 . . . while here 60, 6, and 4 makes . . . seventy again; what a coincidence! I didn't doubt it, Master Ezekiel, but without knowing their meaning . . ."

"All right. *Yayn* is wine and *sod* is secret. The Talmud says that those who can hold their drink have the wisdom of seventy sages, for if seventy goes in, seventy comes out."

She smiled. "We say *in vino veritas.*" She made a face. "But enough of these conversations made of 'we' and 'you!' After all, what makes *me* a Christian to you is what makes *you* a Jew to me. . . Oh, I can't put it in words, Rabbi, but I'm sure you know what I mean!"

"I do, madame, I do . . ." murmured the rabbi.

They said nothing for a while, drinking in the stars and the song of the prow through the water.

Since Don Sancio's death, Galatea often brought up the document the scribe considered proof that there had been no Resurrection. One way or another, Yehezkel always managed not to give his opinion, saying they didn't know enough about the claim to comment, but the thought had not left her mind since Don Sancio put it in words.

"Rabbi, I know you don't like to talk of what is at the end of our quest, I mean *beyond* the Parchment of Circles. But the confession has given me no rest since poor Don Sancio mentioned it, and by now I have no doubt that *this* is what the hermit, ten years ago, called the enigma in Jerusalem."

She paused, not knowing how to continue or what she really wanted to ask. "You see, it's a verse in Saint Paul that makes Don Sancio's words truly frightening. It's in his letter to the Corinthians, I looked it up in the hostel in Heraklion. *And if Christ has not been raised, our preaching is useless and so is your faith.* Rabbi . . . I'm afraid . . . of what we may find. What would you do in my place?"

Yehezkel reflected and then said, "Suppose I was told a witness account exists, which claims that Moses *never* climbed Mount Sinai, *never* spoke with God, and *never* received the Ten Commandments on two stone tablets. Would I stop being a Jew? Would those commandments suddenly become childish, short-sighted advice? No, madame. Well, it's the same for the teachings of Jesus. If he was *not* resurrected, the sermon he pronounced on the Mount would still be a light to people everywhere, would it not?"

His effort to reassure her touched Galatea. She had feared that his reluctance to discuss it came from a Jewish obligation to deny the Truth of Christianity, as Jews had done since Christ's days. "All he will say," she thought, "will be, 'He wasn't resurrected because he was not the Son of God!'" Yet here he was, telling her that her faith should stay strong.

But the abbess had been taught enough theology to know that Saint Paul was right. If Jesus was not resurrected on Easter Sunday, if the tomb was only empty because some lowly Judean thieves were paid to steal the body, then Christianity really *was* just a popular, appealing superstition. She wrenched her mind from the devastating thought and went back to Master Ezekiel's Kabbalah lesson.

"Surely, Rabbi, secrets coming out when wine goes in could not be the jewel you meant to show me."

"You're right, of course. The jewel here is the number seventy, which, being the fusion of seven and ten, two numbers of great perfection, represents wisdom and authority."

"It is no coincidence, then," she interrupted him, "that the Greek translation of the Torah"—it was the first time she'd used the Hebrew word for the Old Testament—"is called the Septuaginta and overflows with wisdom and authority!"

"Ehm . . . on the Septuaginta's authority I'll tell you more," he paused, "at a more advanced stage of your studies. But your mention of translation is inspired, for the number seventy is linked to *language*. After the Deluge, men built the Tower of Babel, and the Torah says that God, to punish their arrogance, dispersed them through the world and made of their single tongue seventy different languages."

"I've often dreamed of speaking all tongues," mused Galatea, "but then in dreams dogs speak Latin and rivers flow upstream."

"Mmh . . . one can hear you're a reader of psalms, madame," said Yehezkel, smiling.

Strangely, Galatea's thirst for forbidden Jewish knowledge caused her no embarrassment. On the contrary, she felt like the Holy Spirit was descending on her as on the apostles on the first Pentecost.

"If seventy is the number of languages, then the Pentecost is even more relevant! The Acts say that 'they were filled with the Holy Spirit and began to speak in other tongues.' And that's not all, even wine comes into it! Saint Peter had to deny they were drunk and explained that Joel's prophecy on the last days was being fulfilled, when the Lord would pour out his Spirit on everyone, including babes."

Yehezkel's gut suddenly told him the conversation just took a direction that came from above. "Joel's prophecy about babes, madame," he murmured, "was exactly the one I thought of when you pronounced the first word of the Torah in the middle of the square in Torcello."

Galatea smiled. "I can see how, in your eyes, this nun might be included when Scripture says the Lord 'hid these things from the wise and learned, and revealed them to little children.'"

Yehezkel's tingling became more intense. "What Scripture are you speaking of, madame? I know the Talmud says, 'Since the Temple was destroyed, prophecy was denied to prophets and given to the crazy and the little children.' But you cannot possibly know that passage, and there's nothing else like it in the Torah."

"That's because I wasn't quoting *your* Scriptures, Rabbi. I was quoting Saint Matthew's Gospel!"

Yehezkel glimpsed the message from the world above. Teaching Kabbalah to this nun was not against God's will. If she was drawn to the word *shamayim,* he would follow her lead. He smiled and said, "Please calculate the value of shamayim, madame."

"300, plus 40, plus 10 and then another 40 . . . that's 390!"

"Good; 390 is also the value of Zachar u-Neqevah, male and female, words the Torah uses in the first chapter when it says they were *both* created in God's image. Thus gematria confirms that when husband and wife join their bodies they go to heaven, as the phrase 'becoming one flesh' also implies," he said.

The abbess felt she had to point out the different teaching of the church. "Saint Paul and Saint Augustine both think that not marrying would be better than marrying . . ."

"Ha! Augustine . . . a dangerous teacher if ever I read one! Your 'doctor' interprets the Tree of Good and Evil in a way that damns females forever, while for Judaism the Shekhinà, the Holy Spirit itself, is female!"

Suddenly, in the near darkness beside the tareta, Yehezkel noticed that a part of the line dividing the sea from the sky was curved and . . . *and it was moving*! He jumped to his feet and grabbed Galatea's hand, his other hand pointing to the horizon, "Look! Over there . . . it's a whale! Now it will shoot its spray."

Some three hundred feet from the tareta, the squirt climbed vertically into the air. They heard the whoosh, but the noise didn't wake anyone up. Galatea froze, peering into the dark, trying to make out the huge back of the monster, terrified by the thought that it might come closer.

"Oh please, God . . . we were already shipwrecked *once*," she said in a tiny voice that touched him.

"Have no fear, madame. They are not afraid of ships and don't normally attack them. I've come to think they have the same joyous character of dolphins."

Instead, the monster came closer before their very eyes, until the panicked voice of the sailor on watch shouted the alarm and frenzied maneuvers were undertaken to sail away from the leviathan.

Yehezkel knew that on summer nights, when the sea is warm, things moving through the water leave a sparkling, silvery-green trail behind them. He'd noticed it with oars, or when fish jumped out of the water, and even when urinating in the sea. But nothing had ever prepared him for the majestic splendor of the whale's dive a mere hundred feet from the tareta.

Amid the women's screams and the sailors' curses, the monster swung its tail and smashed it into the sea, raising masses of water to the height of a cathedral, and then dove into the depths. Suddenly, the surface turned into a vision as bright as the crystal under God's feet. The water literally boiled, filled with strange blue, green, and gold lights. From the center of the turbulence, long trails of luminous bubbles shot out in all directions. Other big bubbles exploded on coming to the surface. The light was pure magic, as there was neither sun nor moon for it to be coming from. The rabbi and the abbess, when the sea had slowly calmed and darkened, started breathing again in unison, taking in great gulps of air.

"Madre mia," Galatea managed to whisper after a few moments.

"I never saw anything like that in my life," murmured Yehezkel. "We're privileged to have witnessed the glory of God manifesting itself in his gigantic creature. I saw whales before, but never from this close!"

A few moments later the whale resurfaced, now some distance from the tareta, and expelled a last, leave-taking puff of water from its back.

Galatea was thoroughly enjoying herself and expected gematria to yield more miraculous revelations. The last watch of the night, the one that would greet the dawn, had already begun, but she begged him to show one last jewel.

"So be it then; hear this. *Rehem* is the root of every word that has to do with mercy. In Hebrew, mercy is *rahamim,* a word so holy to Mohammedans that in the Qu'ran the adjective *rah'man,* merciful, is used to describe Allah more than any other word."

"Is rehem written with a *caf* or with a *chet*?" she asked, already calculating the value of the word.

"With a *chet,*" he answered, impressed.

Galatea added up the letters in an instant. "It is worth 248!"

"Correct. So it won't surprise you that 248 is also the gematria of Abraham, our forefather, for no man was more merciful. But what is missing is, of course, the meaning of rehem. What word do you imagine could be the root of mercy in the Holy Tongue?"

"I don't know . . . the Latin *misericordia* comes from the Greek *kardia,* which is heart, but perhaps . . ."

Yehezkel interrupted, "No, in Hebrew mercy doesn't come from the heart. Rehem, madame, means womb."

There was a long silence. Galatea's eyes were closed as the tareta glided under the stars. "*The root of mercy is womb*!" she kept repeating to herself. The words of the hermit came back to her, 'The woman *is* the Jew, and the Jew *is* the woman.' The life of all the women she'd met in her life went by before her: the nuns, the slaves, the violated, the prostitutes, the twelve-year-old mothers, the widows. She thought of her own sterility. Fat tears started rolling from under her closed eyelids.

Yehezkel said, "No, little sister, shed no tears. You know, with the same three letters and the same gematria one writes *mahar,* which means tomorrow!"

The thought that the fate of women would change one day but she would not live to see it filled her with blind fury. She grabbed the knife they'd been writing with and stabbed the deck with all the force she possessed. The dagger oscillated, stuck in the wood.

Yehezkel jumped back in shock. She raised her eyes, sniffling apologetically, and he looked at her with melancholy tenderness. "When one wants to scream and doesn't, that's when one *really* screams."

Galatea's mood improved again as the night wore on. He showed her other jewels, and a little before dawn her muffled laugh delighted him again. After another serene silence, she smiled in the dark and said, "Rabbi, I want you to know that after fifteen years in a convent, conversing with you gives me the sensation that a little bird must feel when someone opens its cage."

Yehezkel laughed. "I'm flattered to be granted such a poetic role. I would gladly go around all day opening cages for little birds to fly out!"

For some reason, little birds and poetry reminded Galatea of troubadors. Here, finally, was a trustworthy teacher who could solve the quandary she was in about the minstrels and their songs. "Tell me, Rabbi, did you ever meet any troubadors in Provence?" she asked gingerly.

"Many. Not long after I arrived from Egypt, at the court of the counts of Foix, I was lucky enough to witness song and rhyme contests between troubadors. Those were memorable nights!"

"And tell me, do you think the rhymes about their 'ladies,' their . . . 'love' is pure or lascivious?"

"Mmhh . . . you raise an old problem, madame. Starting with the Song of Songs, that decision has been difficult to make. The Sufis, Mohammedan mystics, openly declare they are God's lovers. In my opinion—but mind you, this not Kabbalah, it is just my opinion—*all* love and *all* poetry come from God."

"I couldn't agree more! Some of the verses I read as a girl rent my heart to shreds!"

The sky was just starting to whiten in the east when Yehezkel, in a husky but melodious voice, sang a song to her that he'd learned from the troubadour Raimbaut de Vacqueyras. He sang it in the Langue d'Oc, but Galatea understood every word.

> *Keep yourself, dear keeper of the tower,*
> *Against the jealous one, your lord, wretched,*
> *More bothersome than the dawn,*
> *Since down here we discourse of love.*
> *But we are afraid*
> *Of the dawn,*
> *The dawn, alas, the dawn!*

CHAPTER 15

LE-HA'IR AL HA-ARETZ
To Give Light upon the Earth

BETWEEN ANTALYA AND CYPRUS, 19TH JUNE 1219

The reassuring sight of Antalya's lighthouse had disappeared behind them three hours earlier; the tareta was sailing southeast toward Cyprus. The atmosphere on board was quiet but tense, as these were the waters where a pirate attack was most likely.

Spiro sat on a bench on the aft castle, scratching his belly and surveying crew and passengers glumly, thinking of the Jew's rubies. Yehezkel knew that André's presence would provide the company with much needed security against Spiridione's schemes, but he couldn't have imagined how much the sight of a red cross would unsettle the old bandit. For the last four days, his mind had throbbed with memories of glory days and humiliations on Cyprus thirty years earlier. Spiro had been a rising star among the officers of the unforgettable Margaritone of Brindisi, and the cursed Templars put an end to it all.

For ten of those thirty years, Spiridione saw enough Latin brutality to put him off the pursuit of power, and the worst of it came from crazed Frankish youths, their eyes devoid of any grip on reality, draped in the white cloak with the red cross—looking, in fact, exactly like André de Rosson.

Spiro was still lost in thought when he heard the Jew's voice call out from the deck. Visibly proud of his sharp eyesight, Yehezkel pointed out a minute black sail on the southern horizon.

They had finally found their Saracen pirates.

For someone who'd spent so much time talking to sailors, Yehezkel knew surprisingly little of pirates. He knew of their predilection for capturing Jews, and since they'd discovered that rabbis were worth more silver than ordinary Jews, he knew that his black sarbel would signal the presence on the tareta of juicy prey. From Rav Shlomo and other ransomed prisoners he'd met, he heard that not a few pirates were Christians. There were Normans and galley convicts for whom joining the pirates was a lucky escape from their previous fate. Some were merchants ruined by a storm taking revenge on other peoples' goods. Then there were the renegades, Christians who "raised their finger," the Mohammedan gesture proclaiming God's Unity having become synonymous with embracing Islam.

To the kabbalist, the sighting was confirmation that his mission was closely followed by the powers above. He was not surprised at what would otherwise have seemed an extraordinary run of bad luck; he considered that at stake was the possible proof, as the nun put it, that "Christian faith was useless."

Spiridione climbed on the aft castle and came down again several times and then gave the orders Yehezkel would have given. He chose to keep sailing as close to the wind as the tareta could manage, while manning all six oars in the hope of fleeing east faster than the pirates' dhow.* Yehezkel ran below deck and grabbed an oar with more enthusiasm than the Greeks themselves.

---

*Traditional Arab boat with one or two masts and lateen sails, used in the Mediterranean and Indian Ocean

For a while it wasn't clear whether the black sail was closing in on them, and a tense silence descended on the tareta. Galatea watched the dot in the distance, struck by how tenaciously fate seemed to pick on their journey. For the first time since leaving the lagoon she wished she were in the little room of her own at San Maffìo, where her biggest source of anguish had been Sister Erminia's meanness.

"After all," she told herself, "what is a Cistercian abbess doing on a Greek adventurer's ship? Anyway, is it not a mortal sin of pride to have decided that *we* are the chosen ones who will find the hiding place of the Holy Grail in Jerusalem?"

But Spiridione was only pretending to flee the dhow. In his mind he had decided all the way back in Heraklion, that if—or rather, *when*—pirates attacked, he would keep the nun for himself and give the Jew and pilgrims to the Saracens in exchange for his freedom and that of his crew—as well as their tareta. And all that *after* grabbing the rest of the rubies, of course.

By badly trimming his mainsail—something Yehezkel couldn't notice as he pulled on an oar below—and giving secret signals to his crew not to pull *too* much on their oars, Spiridione ensured that the tareta lost speed, until it became clear that the dhow would catch them. André de Rosson excitedly watched the black sail grow bigger It would be his first combat at sea, and every infidel he would get close to was a dead man. As for himself, he didn't care if he survived or won martyrdom.

The tareta made little headway; Yehezkel hadn't caught on to Spiro's tricks and resigned himself to using the precious gift from Rav Isaiah of Trani.

When Rav Eleazar had announced that Yehezkel would sail to Eretz Israel, the little rabbi from Apulia, a land with centuries of Greek traditions plagued by pirate raids for half of every year, took him aside and gave him three projectiles of the famous "Greek fire," carefully instructing him on their use.

The secret of the Byzantines' fearsome weapon—a sticky black goo that, once set alight, didn't go out even if thrown in the sea—had been lost to the West for over forty years. Since then, the formula of the mixture—naphtha and a dozen other ingredients—had become a prize sought by adventurers from all kingdoms. The fact that Saracens were throwing Greek fire at that very moment on the Christian knights besieging Damietta was one of the reasons the armies of the cross were losing heart. In Acre or in the camp outside Damietta, one could hear people say, "Only fools insist on fighting the infidels, since clearly Jesus Christ is not opposed to them. The proof is that they took Jerusalem, and have Greek fire, and keep on winning."

The three greasy balls of incendiary destruction survived the beaching hidden in Galatea's chest. The rabbi came on deck. The dhow was twice as big on the horizon as when he'd gone below. Immediately, he made for the trunk and discreetly extracted a linen wrapping from a sealed bottom drawer.

Rav Isaiah was adamant that he must distance himself from all goyim before using the substance. Yehezkel thought the chubby Italian rabbi was being naively superstitious, but the habit of respecting one's teachers was ingrained in him, so he set out to obey Rav Isaiah's injunction. "Everyone move to the stern! I am about to fight these pirates with an ancient Jewish magic spell, and the proximity of Christians could render it ineffective!"

Now in those years, Greeks and Saracens knew Jews much better than Latin Christians did and were far less in awe of their wizardly powers. Spiridione challenged him, a sneer on his lips, "And what kind of enchantment do you intend to use against them, Jew?"

"If they're Christian, their dhow will catch fire," said Yehezkel. "If they are Mohammedans, though, I'm not sure, because they also believe in the one and only God, so the spell may not work on them."

For Spiridione's sons, cousins, and nephews the explanation was good enough, but Spiridione, a man of the world, guessed that the rabbi was somehow making fools of them all. "You have a nerve, Jew, amusing yourself with magic when your . . . I mean *our* life, is in danger!"

That was when Yehezkel twigged. "I'm the naive one, not Rav Isaiah!" he said to himself. "I thought he was being superstitious, when in fact everyone must be kept at a distance to prevent them interfering with the throwing of the projectiles . . . *in case they are in cahoots with the pirates*!"

The abbess was staring at him, violet eyes wide, incredulous and concerned. Was her teacher really about to use Kabbalah against the pirates? Would he summon spirits, like a necromancer? Would she hear his voice turn into that unearthly roar again?

Yehezkel saw Aillil get up to go aft with Galatea, grabbed his collar, and told him to stay. He told Spiro that when they were close enough, he would signal to him to drop the mainsail and turn the tareta around so that the prow, with the conjuring rabbi on it, would face the oncoming dhow. Turning his back to the Christians in the stern, he opened the linen wrapping and told Aillil to pull out his sling, which was always in the boy's trousers.

Yehezkel knew from Torcello at which range the boy's slinging was most precise, and when the war cries of the savage marauders already filled the air, he judged the moment right and signaled to Spiridione, who gave the order to stop the tareta and turn it around to welcome the dhow. It was what Spiridione was going to do in any case, as a way of signaling to the pirates that he wanted to negotiate, not escape. He was laughing out loud as he called for the mainsail to come down. It was too late now for the Jew to save the day, whatever Hebrew curses he came up with!

When the mugs of the raiders leaning from the bow of the dhow could be made out—by now Gudrun's sharp shrieks were louder than anything the pirates could muster to scare their prey—Yehezkel rubbed his flint on its iron ore mate and directed the sparks toward the projectile in Aillil's sling until it caught fire. Then he winked at the boy, nodding toward the pirate boat, some three hundred paces away. "This should be easier than hitting ducks over the willows in the lagoon!" he laughed.

Suddenly, all eyes on both vessels were following the trajectory of the burning glob of Greek fire Aillil lobbed through the air. It didn't just hit the dhow; it landed at the foot of the single structure on the boat's deck, splintering into a hundred inextinguishable flamelets.

Spiro was jumping up and down, excited as he hadn't been since Isaac Doukas called Margaritone to rescue Cyprus for him, which was the last time he'd seen Greek fire.

The first projectile failed to set the dhow alight. The pirates knew Greek fire and knew that seawater would not put it out. Christians and Jew on the tareta watched them as they flung themselves on every flame with rags and clothes, choking them before they could spread. Yehezkel saw some of them piss on the flames, one of the few things that was said to put out fires started by the diabolical substance.

The second glob Aillil threw struck the center of the dhow's lateen sail.

In seconds, sail and mast were in flames. The dhow was a hundred paces from the tareta when its mast crashed on deck, setting everything alight from bow to stern. It happened so quickly that the onlookers were as astonished as the sailors on the burning boat. The whole thing, amidst the panicked screams of the pirates, was over in the time it takes to say three paternosters.

Then the screaming stopped, and an unnatural silence fell in which the only sounds were the crackling of the flames engulfing the burning wreck and the splash of pirates jumping overboard.

Yehezkel turned aft with a triumphant smile. Pilgrims and sailors were crossing themselves repeatedly, speechless. They had been certain of death or slavery, and some even started cheering the Jew. Spiridione smiled an obscene smile.

As often happened in such cases, the survivors from the sinking ship cried out Muhammad's name and spat in the water, swore in Greek that they would accept baptism, and implored with guttural shrieks not to let them drown. Spiro—not vengefully, but knowing they couldn't be trusted—hoisted his mainsail and left without turning around. The dhow's long bowsprit vanished into a stretch of water strewn with burning wreckage and oily patches of what looked like flaming sea.

The company was shaken but understood the need for such harshness. The women would remember the desperate screams chasing the tareta as she resumed her course to Cyprus for the rest of their lives. Spiridione walked to the bow to congratulate the Jew, still irrepressibly excited to have seen Greek fire again. Erratic movements of his eyebrows and moustache made his smile at once comical and sinister. "Your excellency, my honored guest, light of Eastern and Western knowledge! Come, Master Ezekiel, at least tell me if you received the fire ready to be used, or if you know its secret formula! Please?"

Yehezkel ignored him, not without a smug grin. The Greek, eyes sparkling, wouldn't give up. "Because you see, my friend among friends, if you possess that formula, I can make you the richest Jew in Christendom in a few months!"

✡ ✠ ✡ ✙

IN SIGHT OF CYPRUS, 20TH JUNE 1219

At dawn the next day, the sixth of the passage, Yehezkel stood behind the prow, an arm around the forestay, peering at the profile of the Troodos range, some fifteen leagues to the southeast, trying to determine the right course to leave the island on port and sail around to its southern coast. In front of the tareta, he noticed the morning mist starting to thicken into the first strands of a summer fog .

"I've seen June fogs like this before," he thought. "Soon even the tops of the mountains will vanish. I'd better take a bearing of them while I still can."

He fetched the clay bowl from the chest and, checking that Spiridione wasn't keeping an eye on him, pulled out his loadstone and floated it. Once he knew where north was, he guessed the bearing of the peak and the course they should follow to clear Cape Amautis, the westernmost point of the island.

It was still early, and Galatea watched the rabbi fidget for a while before getting up and stretching by the gunwale. She noticed the thickening fog between them and the island and suddenly felt a pang of fear in her gut. Feeling them move in the breeze, she realized the hairs on her neck were upright.

"Rabbi," she whispered weakly, tugging at the sleeve of his sarbel and pointing at the whitish haze.

"It's a perfectly normal summer fog, madame," he reassured her, compensating the movements of the bowl to check the island's bearing again before the spires of fog swirling in the breeze hid it altogether. "Swirling spires?" he caught himself. "I never saw fog and breeze in the same stretch of sea before."

Later, Yehezkel would reflect that all his Kabbalah hadn't helped him to recognize that this was no "perfectly normal summer fog," as the Christian prophetess recognized at once.

While he'd been playing with his loadstone, terror descended on everyone except him. Nightmares are personal things in which events of people's waking lives entwine with the deepest contents of their souls. The fear that gripped them was not the same for everyone, rather whatever had most frightened each person in their lives approached them again. André and young Zaharias, for instance, were seeing different things, but the effect was the same: both fell to their knees, hands over faces, whimpering. Thick spires of fog swirled around the tareta as everyone fell victim to their own, private horror.

"There, look! Over there! There's a face laughing in the fog!" cried a sailor.

When he saw Aillil push his head into Galatea's lap, moaning as the nun shook like a leaf, Yehezkel understood there were evil spirits in that fog. He thought of the angels facing off in the world above and shuddered. All thoughts of the course they should set vanished, and the rabbi began to pray. He started breathing the folded breath and gestured to Galatea to do the same by placing a hand on his plexus.

He looked aft. The men were having visions, some screaming,

others curled up on the deck, their faces twisted by terror. André de Rosson wept shamelessly as before the Cretan rocks. Spiridione stood rigid at the helm, laughing and crying at once as the spirits of his victims danced around him in the swirling fog. The wind now raged through the shrouds like a sudden storm. Looking around the tareta, the rabbi came to the inevitable conclusion: only the Birchat Cohanim* could dispel such darkness. He must get them under his tallit and recite Aharon's blessing.

Nobody on board was compos mentis except Yehezkel and, to a lesser extent, the abbess. He grabbed her wrists, noticing despite the circumstances, that they felt even thinner than they looked. "We must confront a *very* powerful spirit, madame!" Yehezkel realized his voice was trembling. "This angel fell from *very* high, and probably commands more demons than a maskil could summon in a lifetime! In fact . . . this could be Sama'el himself. . . . We must gather the company under the prow, now!"

A few moments later, as he watched Galatea pulling at Garietto, who clung desperately to the mast, a strand of fog fell from above, hiding her for a moment. Yehezkel froze in a sudden, horrible premonition, sure that after the wisps of vapor dissolved, the nun would no longer be there.

He charged toward the mast, screaming "Galatea!" He'd never called her by name before. Her head snapped up, she looked at him, afraid. Arriving at the foot of the mast, he almost knocked her over. "Thank you, Lord of the Universe!" he mumbled into his beard.

When all seven pilgrims were standing under the prow, the rabbi asked himself, "But who will give the ritual answers? There is no Jewish soul to say Ken Yehi Ratzon after each verse!"

Fog shrouded the boat from bow to stern; her deck was strewn with people writhing in terror, disappearing, and reappearing with the gusts. Yehezkel thought, "Mmh . . . how many times must I be shown that Divine Providence trusts this nun more than I do?"

---

*Priestly Blessing

He explained to Galatea what he needed her to do, but she hesitated at the idea of praying to another God and not to Christ.

"It is *not* another God we are praying to!" he shouted. "It is *God the Father* of your *Holy Trinity!*" He whispered in her ear the words she would have to pronounce. The abbess haltingly repeated them.

In her heart, as she mouthed the Hebrew words for "May It Be Your Will," Galatea appealed to the Virgin, looking straight into the rabbi's eyes, which she had never seen so unashamedly frightened.

Suddenly the wind fell. The tareta, becalmed, swung gently, still wrapped by vapors. In the stern, the crew yelped like a pack of dogs under the whip, while in the bow, a forlorn group of Christian souls, led by a Jew, attempted to pit their forces against the Angel of Death.

Yehezkel's arms tried to cover the company with his black and white shawl, three males on one side and three females on the other, like Moses had done. They looked like the miniature of a biblical miracle in a triptych on the altar of a church. He told them not to look outside the shawl and stretched his arms in front of him, the fingers of both hands split in pairs in the ritual position. Then, in the voice that Galatea had been praying to hear again, he began the exorcism.

> *Creatures of the Heavens, pay attention! Hear, creatures of the earth!*
> *I, the maskil, proclaim His Glory to dispel all spirits of the angels of*
> *destruction: all the male spirits of Sama'el and all the female spirits of*
> *Lilith, howling spirits and the spirits of bastards. . . . May they all be*
> *dispelled before the blessing of Aharon the high priest!*

There was a brief silence, Aillil's sniffling the only sound from under the shawl.

"Yevaréchecha Adonai, Ve-Yishmerécha!"

(May the Lord bless you and safeguard you!)

Out of either habit or inspiration, Galatea, instead of Ken Yehi Ratzon, instinctively pronounced, "Kyrie Eleison!"

Yehezkel hesitated, startled, and then went on, "Ya'er Adonai Panav Elecha, Ve-Yichunéka!"

(May the Lord Shine His Countenance on You, and Grant You His Grace!)

"Kyrie Eleeison!" Galatea's voice rose for the second time, more assured and with a mild attempt at song. The sailors' moans still reached to the prow, but the fog started to thin out into long strands.

"Yisah Adonai Panav Elecha, Ve-Yasem Lechà Shalòm!"

(May the Lord Turn His Countenance Toward You, and Establish Peace for You!)

"Kyriee Eleeeeisoon!" This time Galatea sang the two words with passion, her voice pure crystal.

Within seconds, the sun was shining brightly, and Cyprus took up half the southern horizon, its green hills sparkling against a perfect sapphire sky. For the third time, Yehezkel thought, "If I don't stop underestimating this woman, I'll get into *real* trouble yet."

✡ ✠ ✡ ✠

Limassol harbor was full of short, fat cogs, looking for all the world like giant walnut half shells. Launches of all sizes went back and forth between the ships at anchor and the quay so heavily loaded with bags, crates, and horses that the gunwales risked being submerged. The wind carried all the way to the quay the 'Diavolo!'s and 'Porco Giuda!'s of the mostly Venetian and Genoese sailors.

By the time it disembarked, the company was well acquainted with creaking timbers, salty breezes, and merciless sun. In Venice their skins, except Yehezkel's, were white, but after two months at sea and on Crete, their wizened, reddish faces were so sunbaked they almost resembled infidels. Only Aillil was still pale, but his freckles were darker.

In the harbor the company—a first time for all except the Egyptian rabbi—set eyes on some camels. Gudrun burst out laughing at the sight of the animals. They delighted Galatea, too. Taller than a man and longer than a horse, they had huge, droopy lips and expressions that were at times monstrous, at times endearingly serene. Their fleshy lips, long eyelashes, and swinging gait gave them a lascivious air, like . . . like desert trollops! thought Galatea. She bit her lip and smiled. "In Torcello, I would have run into church to light a candle after such a thought."

A priest of Limassol's Latin diocese stood behind the official in the room where Spiridione reported the arrival of his tareta and gave an account of its passengers and crew. The cleric noticed the eccentric small group waiting outside: six Christians, two of them nuns, in the company of a Jew. "Nay, of a rabbi," he said to himself, noticing Yehezkel's black sarbel. Exiting the room where Spridione haughtily answered the official's questions, the cleric gestured to Galatea and took her to one side to discover the reason for, to use the words of Innocent's bull of four years earlier, *tam damnata commixtione.**

Yehezkel feigned indifference but then walked around the small building and, standing behind a corner not three paces from the two, caught a few words of Galatea's answer.

"It's the truth, Father. He swore to me that in Jerusalem he will embrace the True Faith! Do you think I would have abandoned the flock of nuns entrusted to my care if God had not presented me with the opportunity to convert a *rabbi* of the Jews?"

Yehezkel walked off, at first wallowing in indignation. But then a grin of pride for her sangfroid and imagination spread on his face. When the priest walked away—not before wishing the abbess success in her holy enterprise—he approached, pretending resentment. "Considering *I'm* the one teaching you the mysteries of Kabbalah, not you teaching me those of the Trinity, I find the story of my imminent conversion nothing less than a calumny!"

Galatea saw the rabbi couldn't quite keep a smirk off his face and laughed heartily. "Don't be cross with me! I had to tell that priest what he wanted to hear because his mind isn't strong or curious enough to accept the truth of things as they really are."

---

*"such an accursed mingling"

Yehezkel nodded. "You're too right, madame; the excessive zeal of certain clerics, of all faiths, can become wearisome at times, despite their good intentions." He hesitated. "This thought I can only confess to you, my friend, but sometimes I think that the Children of Israel's angry reactions to the self-righteous insistence of our prophets is not all that hard to understand."

Galatea laughed and then excused herself and walked toward Gudrun, secretly glad for that "my friend."

As they disembarked, the High Court of the Kingdom of Cyprus was in assembly in Limassol Castle, presided by the regent, Philip of Ibelin. Under innumerable arches, the walls of the huge hall were black with soot and covered with shields. The Cypriot lion above Philip's throne was a scrawny, dragon-like beast, clearly a closer relation of the English lion than of the pompous, portly Venetian one.

The regent, who ruled in place of the two-year-old king, was an aging man, overweight and bothered. More precious stones studded his robe than were in the treasury of many counts in the empire, and his expression was that of a man suffering from aggressive gout who would gladly exchange the power for which he had fought all his life for a hot footbath. In that last week of June he had a serious problem, which, if mishandled, could easily cause trouble with the papacy. For the last twenty-five years, Latin bishops sent to the island to try to convert the Greeks to the Roman creed had achieved pathetic results, and now this inopportune incident. The Cypriot nobles were anxious to settle differences without wronging anyone. But first the friar had to come to. . . .

A famous Italian friar, already spoken of as a saint, collapsed while preaching at the end of his tether in the market square. "Preaching" was too flattering a word for prancing about and pulling faces like a jester. Were it not for his reputation as a "Savior of the Church," he would have been given a dose of lashes his emaciated body wouldn't have survived. Now he lay senseless in the chamberlain's apartment.

Philip was listening intently to news of the recent arrival in Limassol of a famous medicus, astronomer, and wizard of the Jews—a disciple, it was being said, of the great Moses of Egypt.

"Well, bring him here at once!" roared the regent. "That's what Jews are for: to solve what all others have declared insoluble! And if *he* can't make the friar come to, it will mean that our island was meant to host his remains forever!"

Since Coeur de Lion conquered it thirty years earlier, Cyprus had ceased to be a schismatic island and had been faithful not to the patriarch in the Polis but to the pope. After the bloody Templar interlude, it became a kingdom ruled by the Lusignan family, loyal subjects of Emperor Frederick II.

Cypriots, like all other islanders, were a proud people who spat on invaders—Saracens, Greeks, Coeur de Lion, Templars, all of them. When, in the first decade after the fall of Jerusalem, the nobles chased from Syria by Salah ad-Din arrived, they'd been treated like all the others. The islanders' luck started when Constantinople fell to Dandolo's Venetians. Most nobles and knights ran off there, in the hope of securing more than a Cypriot village and a vineyard, and due to the disorderly nature of the lives of knights, none of them had ever been back. For the first time, the island's wealth ceased to be transferred to Damascus or Constantinople and instead remained in Cyprus. In fifteen years, trade made it so rich that Latin nobles stopping in the island gawked at the big hunts on the mountains—with hawks, leopards, and hundreds of men.

It must be said that Christian enthusiasm for reconquering the sepulchre was a shadow of the fervor of a hundred years earlier. No one seemed interested in taking the cross any more—unless, of course, it was for private gain. But 666 years had passed since the birth of Muhammad—which, being the number of the Beast, were the years he'd been allotted—and a rumor spread that a last heave would push the infidels back into the sterile deserts from where they'd emerged, screaming, on their camels.

For a year now, Cyprus had been a stage for ships and knights headed to and from the fifth campaign against the infidel. In January the previous year, when the armies had not yet attacked Egypt, Hugh I of Cyprus and his wife, Alice, left for Tripoli to attend the wedding of Bohemond IV with the beautiful Melisende. In a tragic twist like those that often plague royalty, young Hugh ruined everyone's fun by dying at the celebrations, struck down by a fever at the age of twenty-three.

As a regent to govern the unruly island, his young widow Alice—little Henry I being just eight months old—had chosen her uncle, Philip of Ibelin, by all accounts more of a notary than a monarch. When Christian forces, a year earlier, finally became large enough to attack Egypt, the papal legate, Cardinal Pelagius Galvani, stopped on his way to Damietta in August. A few days after he arrived, news came that the tower in the Nile, which kept the Christians from reaching the city's walls, had fallen. Fearing other military successes in his absence, Pelagius left forthwith.

Galatea underwent a subtle change in the week since arriving in Cyprus. Since the night Master Ezekiel fished her out of the lagoon, confirmations of the power of her visions abounded. After all, had she not found a beach for the *Falcus* to plow? Had she not, a week ago, helped the rabbi exorcise a malignant fog off the island, despite chanting *different* words from the ones he'd asked her to pronounce? The abbess started to wonder if the spiritual gifts of men had not been overestimated from way back when Christ chose only men as his apostles. Her "trust in women's soul" turned into a determination to affirm what seemed right to her *despite* men's opinions.

To Gudrun and Albacara, the behavior engendered by these thoughts seemed a lapse into the sin of pride, so common in those of noble birth. Since seeing the wealth on the island, for example, Galatea no longer wore a nun's habit, not even the white one with blue borders, but only clothes fit for a countess of Tuscia, of which half her chest—Gudrun now saw why—was filled. The women also weren't staying in a convent or in a hostel but in the villa of a French cousin of Galatea's mother. But what most bothered the women, although in Cyprus it didn't cause the scandal it had in the West, was that Galatea spent most of her time with the Jew.

The day of the High Court assembly was also market day in Limassol. The little fishermen's town had become so rich that its alleys were too narrow and its market square too small. Men and beasts shoved each other in the little available space, and brawls broke out every few minutes. The market was stranger and more wonderful than any other Galatea had ever seen. Food and slaves were sold side by side. She saw Persian carpets, stained glass from Damascus, pelts from Rus, porcelain from Cathay, painted marble vases from Arabia, pearls from the Gulf, ivory from India and Kush. There were glassblowers, fortune-tellers, fire-eaters, snake charmers. She tasted a strange, delicious fruit shaped like a quarter moon, which showed a cross when cut, called *banana*. She saw bears, panthers, ostriches, and untold things so amazing her eyes burned from looking at them. Master Ezekiel said the smell was as nice as near Christmas in Montpellier, when the spice merchants ground their wares.

The abbess was surprised to discover how much she enjoyed spending time in places where she didn't know a single soul. It was as if the spectacle of other people's lives—full and engaging to *them,* but without any role for her—had the effect of satisfying her every desire.

"Surely this is a pleasure denied to my teacher," she thought with a smile, "for there is no place in the world where Master Ezekiel wouldn't meet someone he knows. . . ."

The guards approached them respectfully. The rabbi must follow them to the regent's castle at once, and the Countess of Ardengheschi could come with them, if she so wished.

Half an hour later, the strange couple stood before the whole High Court of the kingdom of Cyprus.

Philip greeted them courteously and explained the situation. "He's a well-known Italian friar, you see, and he fainted while preaching in the square. I am told his sermons look like a tumbler's shows, but he wins over many hearts. Just before passing out again, he told my chamberlain that after living in sin with Lady Poverty for ten years, he decided to marry her, so he can no longer accept gifts, because it would be adultery!"

"Ha, ha!" laughed Yehezkel. "I am a medicus, so I would try to revive him anyway, Your Excellency. This sounds like a friar I wouldn't mind chatting with."

"You will have at your disposal any herb or essence you may need, Master Ezekiel, but you must, you absolutely *must* revive that friar! The reputation of the kingdom is at stake!"

"And may I know the name of the poor preacher whose fate is so dear to you?"

"His name is Francesco. Francesco of Assisi," said the regent.

✡ ✠ ✡ ✠

OUTSIDE THE CHRISTIAN CAMP AT DAMIETTA, THE SAME 27TH JUNE 1219

As Yehezkel made his way to the chamberlain's apartment in Limassol Castle, two of the most powerful men at the siege of Damietta walked alone outside the camp after telling their guards to wait for them but without losing sight of them.

The two were the masters of the Templar and the Teutonic orders, Pedro de Montaigu and Hermann von Salza. Their paths crossed in the camp every day, but they wished to discuss this delicate matter out of earshot.

"So what did your man tell you of my English knight, Hermann?" asked Pedro urgently. "Anything on what I need to know?"

Von Salza, as well as being a warrior monk, was an intellectual, a diplomat, and a friend of young Emperor Frederick II, a notorious atheist. He was cool to popes and to heretic hunters like Domingo of Guzman.

When Pedro de Montaigue began to suspect that one of his knights had been recruited as a spy by the Spanish monk and decided that having Bois-Guilbert watched by another Templar would be too risky, he had turned to the German. Hermann agreed to assign one of his knights to accompany the suspect and report on his activities.

"Mmhh . . . indeed," replied Hermann grimly. "You were right about the man. Near Carcassonne, at the end of April, your 'brother' Bois-Guilbert met with Domingo of Guzman."

"That does it!" cried Pedro. "I'll have him put in irons in the morning! The rest of what I want to know will come from his own lips, I assure you!"

From afar, the guards saw the black-crossed mantle hanging still while the red-crossed one danced in rage around Pedro's shoulders.

"No, Pedro, that would be a mistake," said Hermann quietly. "We can use him to find out who Domingo's man in Acre is."

"Praise be to the Baptist who sent you to help me in this race with that white-cloaked Spanish devil!" exclaimed Pedro. "How should we go about what you just suggested?"

"Simple," said Hermann. "I'll tell Brother Frutolf to stay with your knight, and you tell Brother Bois-Guilbert to go to Cyprus and Acre to recruit all the men he can find for the siege. Pelagius wants it done anyway. Just as he told me of the meeting with Domingo, Frutolf will tell me who Bois-Guilbert meets with in Acre." Hermann smiled. "Do you know, my man is so dim he still hasn't realized he is surveilling your knight, not assisting him!"

Pedro laughed. Then the two men gripped each other's forearm and walked back to their escorts.

CHAPTER 16

HA-ME'OR HA-GADOL

The Bigger Light

LIMASSOL, 27TH JUNE 1219

Yehezkel caressed and squeezed his beard—first with one hand, then with the other—as he walked back and forth across the big room, the usual Talmudic debate going on in his head.

"There are, after all, only four possible outcomes: if I cure him and he dies anyway, the goyim will say I failed their trust, if not worse. If I cure him and he recovers, they will say his sanctity was stronger than the Jew's perfidy. If I don't cure him and he dies, they will probably accuse me of poisoning him, and if I don't cure him and he gets better anyway . . ." He stopped in his tracks.

"'Don't cure him?' What am I saying? He is a sick man, and I am a medicus. I have no choice!"

Disfigured by the illness, Francesco raved softly, shivering with a fever that his brothers said rose in the afternoon and raged after sunset, often shaking him until he passed out. The rabbi observed. He was small, bone thin, and covered in ulcers. His breath was labored, and the sweat-soaked features were not handsome. Under a small tonsure, nose,

285

cheekbones, and ears all jutted out provocatively, and his curly beard was short and full of holes.

Yehezkel resumed marching. "On the other hand, he is one of the zealot friars, like Domingo, who think that burning the Talmud is God's work. If I put him back on his feet, I'll be his accomplice."

He reached the wall and turned around. "Then again, if I don't cure him I'm an accomplice in his death, and not even saving the Talmud justifies contributing to someone's death."

The minute he'd entered the room, Yehezkel had called for a basin of boiled water and administered the vapors of an infusion that would have revived people with one foot in the grave, but to no effect. After feeling his pulse in both wrists at once, he'd concluded that the man's life was in the hands of God.

Not knowing what else to try, he'd done the obvious thing. Guessing that if he came to, the friar would not allow it, he'd untied the knot in the rope around his waist and stripped him naked to wash him from head to toe. The edge of the gray-brown tunic was so encrusted with mud that at the rabbi's touch it didn't tear, it broke. He didn't like Christians who afflicted their bodies to elevate their spirits, but when he saw Francesco's poor naked body, his heart ached as it would before the embarrassed smile of a hungry child.

The water in the basin was still hot. The rabbi crumbled some herbs in it and began to rub Francesco's body with a sponge. He cleaned the ulcers, taking particular care with the red swellings around the eyes, and then applied an ointment made by mixing the herbs fished out from the basin with an Egyptian balsam whose formula was known in the West to a privileged few.

As he gingerly lifted thin shoulders to slip the tunic back on, Francesco opened his eyes.

Yehezkel recognized him immediately. In those feverish, reddened eyes he saw the languor of the lover for his beloved and understood that Francesco was a zaddik, one of the thirty-six righteous men of his generation. Three months earlier in Torcello, Rav Eleazar had smiled at him once with that look, but it had been after a whole day of fasting and meditation, whereas this little monk *just came to from a raging fever,* and already he felt that kind of aching tenderness for the whole universe!

Yehezkel bent one knee without thinking and then slowly bent the other one, too. He lowered his head, took his patient's hand in his, and placed his lips on the knuckles. Francesco raised his head and looked at his naked, clean, and medicated body.

"I . . . I don't know who you are, *messere,* but Divine Providence sent you to put me back on the road. God bless you," he murmured.

Despite his talent for languages, Yehezkel had trouble understanding the Umbrian dialect Francesco slipped into when excited or under duress.

"Sshhh . . ." whispered the rabbi, thanking God for his infinite mercy.

With a look that brooked no objections, he forced Francesco to drink a few sips of a concoction from a vial he kept in his medicus satchel. It was the middle of the night. Yehezkel thought that if the friar had broken his fever, he would survive. Then he remembered that he had yet to pray Ma'ariv.

In the corridors of the regent's palace, Yehezkel heard people speak of Francesco of Assisi as the prophet announced by Gioacchino. The thirty-seven-year-old little Italian had performed miracles in many places. Ten years earlier, Innocent III had approved a rough rule for his mendicant order, a simple text obsessed with poverty as the one and only supreme proof of apostolic spirit.

At first the pope, repelled by the very appearance of the mystical youth, chased Francesco out of the Lateran, but then, that night, he'd dreamed that the same ragged tramp was holding up the entire crumbling structure of the church. He called him back, assigning him and his brothers the mission of contrasting with their sermons those of heretical preachers. In other words, in the same summer of 1209 in which the army of Christ massacred thousands of Cathars, Innocent asked Francesco to witness to the world that the church didn't, in fact, have *anything* against love and charity.

Ten years had passed since those meetings, and Innocent had been dead for the last three. Francesco's friars in the hundreds were spreading through the empire like Domingo's. That year, the Holy Spirit instilled in Francesco the desire to pray at the Holy Sepulchre, and less than a month earlier he'd boarded a cog in Ancona with two brothers, Pietro Cattaneo and Illuminato of Rieti. In Limassol, they'd been joined by Friar Elia of Assisi, one of Francesco's first disciples, who had been in Acre for two years.

The three friars were outside the door now, kneeling in prayer on the stones of the corridor. Emerging from the room, Yehezkel reassured them on their founder's condition. All three drew back, frightened by the bearded Jewish wizard.

Francesco recovered so quickly that the next morning it proved impossible to keep him in the palace, whose luxury was to him what contact with a snake was to people who didn't share his bizarre love of *all* animals. Soon he was back in the square where the fever had interrupted his sermon.

The company was standing in the crowd that gathered almost immediately. Galatea had not been with Yehezkel the previous evening and so had not yet seen the friar. The abbess stood behind Aillil, hands on his shoulders, with Gudrun and the widow on either side and the armigers behind them. She stared at Francesco, captivated. The brownish tunic on his emaciated body was that of a monk, but the coarsely stitched patches and bare feet made him look more like one of the mystics who wandered through fairs and sanctuaries, elevating the crowds with sermons or entertaining them with songs.

Francesco was miming the adventures of Galahad. Galatea was bewitched by the range of expressions on his lean face, from the knight's outrage over injustice to the tears at the memory of a heroic death, from the exaltation of battle to the anguish of sincere repentance. And all the while, the expressions on the faces of his audience followed his own as if they all felt the same emotions.

Yehezkel suddenly appeared beside her. She shushed him before he could say a word, for Francesco started speaking of the Holy Grail, and she didn't want to miss a word. The rabbi, watching the performance from another point, asked himself if the man in whose eyes he had seen God's Spirit the night before could be the same one pulling faces—at some points dancing—in a square. Rav Moshe's words on Ezekiel echoed in his mind. "God forbid that his prophets be the object of ridicule and mockery by the ignorant, or engage in foolishness."

The very moment the thought entered his head, Francesco turned toward him and, without interrupting his recital for an instant, looked at him with the same languor as the night before. A shiver ran down Yehezkel's back.

When the crowd of Cypriots pleading for blessings and healings from Francesco, barely held back by his brothers, finally dispersed, Yehezkel introduced Galatea.

"Galatea degli Ardengheschi is a noblewoman from Tuscia, Brother Francesco, and also the abbess of a Cistercian convent in Torcello. But above all, she is a prophetess!" Then, as an afterthought, he murmured, "But were she married, she would be what we Jews call an *eshet chail,* a valorous wife."

Francesco's smile made Yehezkel blush, but the Egyptian rabbi was olive skinned, and no one noticed.

Only fifty leagues as the crow flies separate Assisi from Montalcino, and Francesco, who'd often heard of the counts of Ardenga, guessed that this must be Orlando's daughter. Then his eyes crossed Galatea's, nearly a foot above his face.

Francesco's soul was still devastated by the test the Lord put him through by sending him Chiara di Favarone. He had always taught his brothers to beware the sweet poison of women's company, but since deciding not to visit Chiara in San Damiano, he suffered the purest pains of courtly love.

He hesitated for an instant and then lowered his eyes to the ground and never—except once, nine months later—fixed them on Galatea's again. She noticed this reaction and, not for the first time in her life, wished she were not beautiful.

"Brother Francesco, your sermon was the most full of the Holy Spirit that I ever listened to!" she said.

"They're simple people, Madonna," said Francesco, his eyes on the red velvet belt around her waist. "You have to be *doing* something all the time, to keep their attention."

Galatea told herself that from the next day she would wear her Cistercian habit again.

Francesco turned to Yehezkel with an almost naughty smile. "So you think my sermons lack dignity, do you, Master Ezekiel? Let me tell you a little story. One day a man was playing a flute so sweetly that everyone who heard started to dance. Anyone who came close enough to hear his flute started dancing. Then a deaf man came along, who didn't even know what music was, and what he saw seemed to him in very bad taste, the senseless behavior of a deranged crowd."

Yehezkel was silent and then mumbled, "Yes, Master Francesco, I understand . . ."

"No, no, don't you 'Master Francesco' me. Call me 'Brother Francesco piccolo,' like my friars do."

"As you wish. What brings you to Outremer, Brother Francesco piccolo? Are you perchance a pilgrim to Jerusalem, like we are?"

Francesco started to answer, but his gaze fell on Aillil, wrenching him from the conversation. He mumbled something about angels freely roaming the earth, put an arm around the boy's shoulder, and walked off across the square under the smiling eyes of the women. Yehezkel stood there, hands on his hips as if waiting for an answer to his question.

Meanwhile, Francesco showed Aillil the feint in which the sword rises as if for a blow from above but instead is driven forward to plunge in the opponent's gut from below. The friars were speechless at the sight of their scrawny founder standing in the middle of the square, feet wide apart in a warrior's pose. Francesco urged Aillil to try the move and then, in a sudden change of heart, threw aside the branch he'd used for a sword, ruffled the boy's hair, and walked him back to where the others stood chatting.

The rabbi, noticing that the friar already understood every word Aillil grunted, felt a small pang of jealousy. Not finding the courage to address the Jew, Friar Illuminato—a quiet, introvert blond as lymphatic as Aillil—turned to Galatea. "He already learned the boy's 'song.' You know, Madonna, when we lived in the Porziuncola, before coming to Matins, he would go down to the pond. One day I asked him why, and he said he was learning the song with which frogs praise the Lord. It takes awhile to learn it, he said, but in the end he did."

Galatea nodded, eyes closed, silently thanking Divine Providence for placing her on Francesco's path. Just one more thing that would never have happened had she stayed in the lagoon.

When they rejoined the group, Francesco turned to Yehezkel as if the rabbi had just asked his question. "No, we're not pilgrims to the Holy Sepulchre. We are headed to the Christian camp at Damietta."

The company was taken aback. A preacher was going to join an army inflicting death and destruction? But before anyone could ask about it, Friar Pietro drew Francesco aside and whispered in his ear. The founder's features were suddenly transfigured with anger. He rushed over to Friar Elia and shouted at him. "Let your tongue, which spat the venom of slander on your brother, chew on excrement! Go on, Elia, pick up some shit from the ground, put it in your mouth and chew on it!"

Friar Elia's head dropped to his chest. An embarrassed silence fell on both companies. Galatea sensed an old conflict between Francesco and his earliest companion and started talking to Gudrun to downplay the outburst of monkish rigor. Friar Elia found some donkey stool nearby and bent to pick some up.

"No, Elia, not those!" Francesco's normally serene features seemed literally warped. "Those are old and dry. That's like eating earth; there are those who would do it from hunger. No, I want you to find a donkey, walk behind it until it shits and put the fresh stuff in your mouth, with all its fragrance."

Yehezkel was intrigued by this fury. Francesco's red and swollen eyes followed Elia setting off on his penance, flames of pure outrage burning in them.

A few minutes later, with Francesco already engaged in what seemed like brooding self-reflection, the two companies parted ways. Yehezkel gingerly probed Galatea on the friar's spat with Brother Elia. "You know, madame, both when he mimed kings before the crowd and just now when he raged at Friar Elia, Francesco looked like a totally different man from the one I revived yesterday. Just . . . someone else. There is something here I cannot figure out."

"Francesco is very likely a saint, Master Ezekiel, and we're privileged to have met him. I'm aching to know why on earth he wants to join the Christian armies in Egypt."

"That one puzzles me, too," smiled Yehezkel. "His own brothers didn't look all that enthusiastic when he said it, even though I'm sure they already knew of his plan."

"He is neither a jester nor the despot he looked like just now, so rest assured, Rabbi: his reason for going to Damietta is a divinely inspired one."

Galatea's tone was that of a last word, and Yehezkel took it as such.

✡ ✠ ✡ ✠

LIMASSOL, 29TH JUNE 1219

It was some days before they saw the friars again. Yehezkel was spoiling to talk to the Coptic monk Rav Shlomo had once met in Famagusta, and the next day—they had been in Cyprus for just over a week—he asked Galatea to inquire with Limassol's Latin nuns on the whereabouts of a Father Makarios. Despite Makarios being the most common name on the island, the nuns knew at once whom she meant.

The saintly Copt, sick of religious abuse from the Latin clergy, had retired to meditate in the Orthodox monastery of Kykkos, near the highest peak on the island, unimaginatively named Mount Olympus. As luck would have it, this was in the Troodos mountain range, only thirty leagues northwest of Limassol.

In accordance with her new style, Galatea took the reins of the expedition. Ignoring the loud protests, and Aillil's were very loud, the abbess decided that only she and Master Ezekiel—escorted by Rustico and Garietto—would climb to Kykkos. But this time, as Yehezkel expected, the wealth on the island made her rule out donkeys, and she asked him to find some horses.

"There are Jews in Limassol, quite a few I'd say, so how do you expect me to believe you can't procure four horses for just three days?" she told a surly rabbi.

On July 2, five days after Yehezkel revived Francesco in the regent's palace, the strange couple and the armigers mounted four Arab steeds and set out for Mount Olympus, not without jesting that visiting a seat of pagan gods before going to Jerusalem was, in a way, paying homage to the history of revelation. On reaching the monastery, they discovered that Makarios had finally renounced the world altogether and, like the hermit saints of Anatolia, left the monastery and climbed to a chapel consecrated by Saint Paul himself, in the middle of whose ruins he now sat and meditated.

They rode farther up the mountain. When they sighted the ruins, they left Rustico and Garietto to keep guard against wild beasts—so abundant in the Troodos range that locals considered it a miracle Makarios had not yet been eaten alive—and made their way among the bushes that grew undisturbed in the ruins.

Father Makarios was *very* old. A long white moustache fell down the sides of his beard, itself a dirty white. When they got close enough for the smell to reach them, it became clear the Copt hadn't washed in years, if ever. Crusts of accumulated grime covered his neck, ears, and nails, and his hair, thought Galatea, looked like the nest of a medium-size lagoon bird.

"Most Reverend Father," she addressed him, "can you help us solve the enigma in Jerusalem?"

"Aah, it's you . . ." mumbled Makarios.

"Were you expecting us, Father?" she asked hesitantly.

"You're the woman and the Jew of Gioacchino's prophecy, aren't you?" He coughed.

"Then you must also know what we're looking for," said Yehezkel with a smile.

"Ha! You're still much too cocky, Rabbi! If you don't learn some humility, you'll never find what you're looking for, whatever it may be!" said the hermit drily.

Galatea struggled to wipe a smile from her lips. Yehezkel, piqued, didn't say a word.

"Of course I know what you're looking for: the Parchment of Circles!" wheezed Makarios. "I don't know where it is. I heard even the one they call the Old Man hasn't been able to find it. If Sophia never turned her countenance toward him, it means he must be another Christian who hates women after all."

Galatea knelt down next to Makarios, a sudden urgency in her voice. "So it's true that only a woman can solve the enigma?"

"A woman *and* a Jew. That is what was written, isn't it? After all, even Christ only revealed his secret teachings to the Magdalene, the woman he took for his wife . . ."

Galatea was startled and then remembered that the hermit said the same thing. Yehezkel knew that Cathar perfecti were adamant the Magdalene had been the wife of Jesus but was mildly surprised to hear the same claim from an Egyptian Copt. Galatea pressed the hermit.

"So Christ trusted the soul of women, just as Hildegard said?"

"The soul of women. . . ." The monk raised his head. His eyes crossed Galatea's and suddenly came alive.

"Sophia is feminine, and Spiritus is masculine. That's *all* of theology right there! You Latins don't know all the Gospels. The Christians of Egypt, Syria, Babylonia, whom you call heretics, *they* are the real Church of God! They know the teachings of Miriam of Magdala, of Martha, of Salomé . . ."

Galatea thought, "First I learned that to say mercy, Jews say womb. Now I hear that Christians in the East never forgot the women around Jesus or his respect for them. Oh, Mother Elisabetta, help me ask the right questions!" The abbess was already on her knees but bent down until her lips brushed the hermit's encrusted feet. Yehezkel recoiled in disgust.

"Please, Father, let me hear one of the teachings those holy women received from Jesus's mouth."

Makarios was quiet and then recited, "'Then Salomé asked Jesus, 'When will your kingdom come?' And the Lord answered, 'When two will become one, and the masculine will become feminine!'"

Galatea was struck dumb. Yehezkel immediately took advantage of it. "For Jews, Sophia is *chochmà,* which is feminine, and the Latins' Spiritus is Shekhinà, also a female!"

Makarios was starting to enjoy himself. "Priscilla, prophetess of the Montanists, starts her book with 'Christ came to me in female form, wearing a shining robe, and filled me with her wisdom . . .'"

Galatea was in seventh heaven. If only Mother Elisabetta could have heard this holy man speak! The idea that the Magdalene had been Jesus's wife filled her with particular wonder. "But Father, why do the Gospels we Latins read never mention Jesus marrying Miriam of Magdala?"

"Don't they? Who do you think got married at Cana? Tell me, would the Lord's mother worry about the wine for the guests running out if she was not the groom's mother? John even writes, "His mother said to the servants, 'Do whatever he tells you.' Would she say that if she was just a guest?"

The old man started coughing. Galatea looked around for some water, but he gestured not to worry. "The truth is the apostles were blinded by jealousy for the anointing in Bethany, for it had been done by 'that woman,' so the Evangelists twisted it into a prostitute's gesture of tenderness for her redeemer, when in fact it was the most solemn ritual of the Jewish people: *the election of the King of Israel*!"

Makarios propped himself as if to get up, and Yehezkel rushed to his side. When the monk got to his feet, Galatea was still kneeling. He placed a hand on her head and spoke softly, his tone worried. "You must go to Egypt, my dear, to find a letter written by the rabbis who saw the Parchment in Jerusalem four hundred years ago. I was told it is kept in a synagogue in Fustat, near al-Kahira."

"But that's where I was born!" cried out Yehezkel.

Makarios eyed him as one does a noisy child. "You surprise me, Rabbi. Did you really think that God lets people be born where they will?"

This time Yehezkel decided he would not, under any circumstances, open his mouth again.

Makarios leaned on his arm. "You see, the Parchment of Circles was found with many others in a cave near Jericho. Scores of sealed jars full of manuscripts in Hebrew and Greek. In Caliph al-Ma'mun's time, the rabbis in Jerusalem examined them all, and the letter speaks specifically of the Parchment of Circles. It is in the Ben Ezra synagogue."

"Lord of the Universe! That's where I prayed as child!" mumbled Yehezkel under his breath.

The old man pointed to some bushes fifty steps away. "Help me to walk over there, Rabbi, I must relieve this mortal body one more time."

As he hobbled along leaning on Yehezkel's arm, the rabbi contravened his one-minute-old resolution. "Father, the Latins are waging war in Egypt right now, and going to Fustat would be complicated, to say the least. Would it not be more useful if we went directly to Acre and looked for this Old Man?"

"Even if he'd found the parchment, which I doubt, he wouldn't show it to you," said Makarios. "But if you told him you had the letter from Fustat, he would have to let you into his quest, wouldn't he?"

"Mmh . . . it looks like you really want to help us, Father," said Yehezkel.

"Don't be so diffident, Rabbi. Prophecies come true, but only when men realize they have to *help* them come true."

"Yes . . . maybe you're right," mumbled Yehezkel. Makarios stumbled behind a bush, and Yehezkel waited for him, reflecting, as he had done a thousand times, on the true nature of prophecy.

When they came back, Galatea was still in prayer. In a gesture typical of traveling Mohammedans and Jews, Yehezkel raised a hand to protect his eyes as he glimpsed the sun to decide if it was low enough to pray Minchà. Soon, the three clerics stood or kneeled among the ruins, the cries of swallows affectionately mocking them as they spoke with their God—that is, each one with his or her God.

✡ ✠ ✡ ✠

LIMASSOL, 6TH JULY 1219

On a fiercely hot day, three days after Makarios blessed them with moving but strange words about Mary and Jesus, but also Isis and Horus, the company met the friars again in Limassol harbor.

Once again, while his brothers were only too happy to converse with the charming abbess, Francesco, to her chagrin, was reluctant to stand too close to Galatea or to any woman in the company. This resulted in Francesco and Yehezkel's walking off to talk Scriptures while the rest of the company listened to the friars' tales of the last few days' preaching in Limassol.

"Someone gave him a copper coin yesterday," said Pietro, "and he immediately gave it to an aggressive beggar who was pestering him. I complained that widows and orphans were far more deserving of charity than that wretch, and you know what he said? 'Should I be choosier than God, who gifted it to *me*?'"

Brother Illuminato contributed his quote: "And what of the answer he gave to the merchant who asked him why he should give him a coin?"

"What did he tell him?" asked Galatea, already smiling.

"Because charity cures heartaches," said the lanky youth.

Meanwhile, Francesco and Yehezkel were walking along the pier talking ethics. Soon they came to the difference between Rabbi Jesus's "Do unto others as you would have them do unto you" and Rabbi Hillel's* *"Don't* do unto others what you would not like done to you."

Francesco argued, "Surely a positive exhortation is morally superior to a prohibition! Just think, Master Ezekiel, of a community where everyone *initiates* actions that benefit others!" said the friar with conviction.

Yehezkel smiled, "But don't you see, Brother Francesco piccolo, it would also encourage people to do what they *think* benefits others?" He stopped, grabbed Francesco's shoulders, and fixed him in his reddened eyes. "Close your eyes and imagine you're in a world ruled by your 'Do unto others.' Are you there? Now imagine that one day you walk into a village inhabited exclusively by sodomites."

Francesco made a face and then burst out laughing. "An elegant theological argument if ever I heard one! Point taken, Master Ezekiel, point taken. Tell me, did Jesus Christ and your Rabbi Hillel ever meet?"

"No, he died just before Jesus was born. But Rabbi Akiva, who taught a hundred years after Hillel, was in perfect accord with Rabbi Jesus on the choice of the most important verse in the Bible. I believe they both chose 'You shall love your neighbor as you love yourself.'"

A sunbeam shone down and lit Francesco's gaunt face. "And how do *you* understand that precept, Master Ezekiel?"

"A drunk peasant in Provence once asked me, 'Do you love me?' I said, 'Of course I love you,' but he whined, 'You say you love me, but you don't know what I need. If you *really* loved me, you would

---

*Famous first-century BC sage whose school usually issued more lenient rulings than that of his rival, Shammai

know.' I had no response. I think that only if you share your neighbor's *sadness,* do you love him like yourself. How do *you* understand the verse, Brother Francesco piccolo?"

"We all bear the same divine spark within us," began Francesco, "almost as if we were all one body. Sometimes, the hand with the hammer will miss a blow and hurt the other hand. Would you hit it with the stricken hand, to punish it? You would only feel more pain."

Francesco had mimed each word: the missed blow, the hurt hand striking the guilty one, the look of pain heaped on pain. Now, his face straight again, he concluded, "The same goes for your neighbor. If he does you wrong, he is still a part of you. If you punish him, you'll only suffer more."

Yehezkel was silent, his soul on fire, then he murmured, "Thank you, Brother Francesco piccolo. Thank you."

As the two men—a comic pair from a distance at almost seven feet and just over five—reached the end of the breakwater and turned around to walk back, a cry went up from the lighthouse.

"Templar galleys on the horizon! The Templars are attacking the island!"

Any Cypriot over thirty had memories of Templar abuse, usually memories running with blood. Both company and friars, like most people in the harbor, ran up to the ramparts on the city's walls to see for themselves if Cyprus was being invaded again.

Everyone peered at the galleys emerging from the mist on the southern horizon. Their short masts, all flying the white, red-crossed pennant, oscillated with every thrust of the oars. Soon they could make out that the galleys had no shields along their gunwales. Experienced observers decreed they weren't rigged for war and must be an embassy connected with the siege. A consensus developed that Pelagius sent Templars to squeeze more gold bezants out of Cyprus, the island being very rich and war very, very expensive.

A little later, a dozen knights of all four orders, but mostly

Templars, disembarked from the galleys, led by none other than Robert of Bois-Guilbert. They made their way to the market square, where the English knight, clearly heading the expedition, loudly announced, "Cardinal Pelagius has dispatched me to Cyprus and Acre to recruit nobles, knights, archers, surgeons, blacksmiths, and anyone else who will be useful in the coming final assault on Damietta! You know who you are; you have two weeks to get ready for war!"

The Templar surveyed the onlookers, open contempt in his eyes as he removed his leather cap, exposing a bald head. "The cardinal told me, 'Accept no excuses from pusillanimous Christians who decline to take the cross while living the good life just two days' sailing from the war! My papal mandate will see to it that their appeals will be rejected!'"

Then the knights made their way to the regent's palace. Bois-Guilbert, relishing this role, spoke down to the man on Cyprus's throne as to a trusted vassal. "Tomorrow morning, my dear Philip, in this splendid hall, I wish to see *all* the island's nobles whom you don't hold *absolutely* necessary to the defense of the island. I expect you, in accordance with the wishes of the papal legate, to deny any appeal that the men I round up may make to continue sustaining their families. There is a war, and Cyprus, as you know, has made more money from it than it has contributed."

Philip was outraged by the Templar's gall but kept silent. An excommunication from Pelagius was all he needed right now. There would be no escaping this "contribution" to the campaign in Egypt. He comforted himself with the thought that if the Latins took al-Kahira, the commercial consequences would turn Cyprus into the new Polis.

It didn't take long for Bois-Guilbert's minions to hear of the presence of a famous Jewish medicus. Robert only thought it was a good catch, but when he heard Yehezkel's name his heart skipped a beat. Domingo told him about this Jew, Arifat's friend, and warned him twice, 'If you meet him, don't underestimate him!'

Yehezkel's first thought was to ask Limassol's Jews to hide him. Then he understood that being drafted into the forces fighting the Sultan was Divine Providence providing a way to reach Fustat and find the letter. Only then did he realize what caused the impulse to hide: going to Fustat meant separation from the nun. He scolded himself, but his heart wasn't in it.

Galatea turned up after he'd decided to let himself be recruited by the Templar. She heard him out and then, for the first time since Father Makarios mentioned the missive, asked him, "Have you figured out how you'll cross the lines of this war to look for the letter that speaks of the Parchment?"

"How *I* will cross the lines? You mean you are about to abandon, to quote your words in the swamp in Torcello, 'a destiny that should have been *ours*?'"

She smiled, flattered that he should remember her exact words. "Come now, Rabbi, you didn't really expect me to accompany you in Saracen lands, did you? I'm a nun; it would be like asking for martyrdom! This is a mission for a resourceful man on his own, visiting what is, after all, his birthplace. The rest of us would travel on to Jerusalem, and when you had the letter, we would meet up again in the Holy City. At least, that's what I thought."

She didn't ask whether the rabbi meant to take the boy with him to a war or allow him to sail to Acre with the women. Before they could discuss it, a page appeared and summoned Yehezkel to the palace. Galatea went along, and soon they were standing before the knights from Damietta.

Bois-Guilbert smiled knowingly at the strange couple. He couldn't hide a smirk of delight at the sight of the beautiful nun in the company of a dangerous enemy. It was the kind of challenge he adored. "Then the noble English knight rescued the pretty Italian nun from the wiles of the Jewish wizard." His father's heart, charmed by a Jewish witch, burst in his chest. What revenge for that humiliation could possibly be sweeter than wrenching this beauty *from a Jew*?

In Bois-Guilbert's eyes, Yehezkel saw only the usual Templars arrogance, but Galatea felt the English knight's lust wash over her and gathered her wits to defend herself. Sitting not far, Frutolf was also struck by the abbess, but in a way that shared nothing with Robert's designs to repay destiny in kind. Instead, the sight of a long curl of Galatea's hair escaping the shawl over her head transfixed the German knight with the power of a mystical vision.

Frutolf of Steinfeld, like most Saxons, was brought up to believe that no sin was worse than lust, and that only life as a warrior could save a man from the wiles of women. Father Eberwin explained that *all* evil, suffering, and impurity in the world originates with woman. "I should know, I heard enough confessions. There's nothing in their heads but sin and filth. Many pass for honest and God-fearing, but every one of them, believe me, is a drooling bitch!"

Later, attending tournaments as a squire aspiring to knighthood, he met German troubadours, called minnesingers. From them, he learned the language of courtly love. "Honored, sweet sister, in me it's not the flesh that desires, but the spirit that yearns," and so on—a bizarre sentimental education whose result was, at least in matters of the heart, an overfed adolescent unmoored from reality who talked to himself in the courtly code while actually ignoring his own true feelings about most people. Despite seeing his own actions as chivalrous, Frutolf had in fact behaved brutally to every woman he ever met, except his mother.

Now, setting eyes on Galatea, he saw for the first time the purity of the lover as he'd always dreamed of her. No doubt, were she to know him, the nun would feel for him the same childlike tenderness, so different from the harshness of the whores he had grown used to frequenting. He shot a glance at Bois-Guilbert, his hatred for the English knight never more intense.

Bois-Guilbert addressed Yehezkel first, anticipating Domingo's pleasure at hearing of how he'd neutralized the crafty rabbi by sending Yehezkel off to a siege in the middle of the Egyptian desert, unable to either look for the Parchment of Circles or interfere with his own search for it.

"Aren't we lucky to have stumbled onto such a noted medicus!" he began. "You'll become even more famous if you save the lives of the kings and cardinals in the camp," he began, as if to convince Yehezkel that by dispatching him to a battlefield he was doing him a favor. "Oh, and make sure you procure all the herbs and ointments you'll need *here,* because they'll be hard to find over there. You'll be glad to hear you have two weeks, not because your services wouldn't be needed right away, but because no ships sail to Damietta before then." He turned to Galatea with an unctuous smile.

"As for you, dear countess," he said suavely, "if, as Saint Aldhelm wrote, nuns are bees who turn the pollen from the flowers of wisdom into honey for the soul, then you, noble Mother, are a queen bee!"

Galatea found his flattery smooth and hollow but smiled as if impressed by his eloquence.

Robert went on, "I've decided not to draft your two armigers, madam, so that you may safely complete your pilgrimage to Jerusalem." Galatea nodded in thanks. "But I must warn you," he continued. "They won't be allowed to carry weapons into the Holy City. In Jerusalem they will be unarmed pilgrims, like all Christians there since the infidels retook the city."

Over the next few days, Galatea struggled to find a role for Francesco of Assisi in the blue tapestry that fate was weaving. Makarios knew of Gioacchino's prophecy about the woman and the Jew, but why no mention of an itinerant saint? Everything would be simpler if Francesco were headed to Jerusalem. He might keep her at a distance, but she could still see him pray at the Holy Sepulchre. But the friar wanted to join the Christian armies in Damietta! She *had* to find out why.

Sobered by Francesco's contempt for luxury, Galatea looked more like an abbess than a countess again. A week went by before they crossed paths again, and his condition worried her. "Brother Francesco piccolo," she said, "you *must* take more care of yourself! I know you'd never let a nun look after you, but at least spare your body a little of the punishment you're unjustly meting out to it. By the way, do you really plan to travel to Damietta, as you said last time we saw you?"

"Yes, Madonna," answered Francesco, looking at the ground. "I heard that one of the Templar galleys that came from there is sailing back soon, so I plan to ask for passage for my brothers and myself."

"Forgive my brashness, Brother Francesco piccolo, but what will you *do* there, preach to Christian knights whose lives are already forfeit for the sake of Jesus Christ?"

Francesco smiled his impish smile. "No, Madonna, we're headed *through* the Christian camp and the front lines, to convert the sultan!"

Galatea's hands shot to her mouth as the company, including Yehezkel, gasped in shock. Francesco's friars, at the mention of their imminent martyrdom, suddenly stood a little straighter in their pitiful frocks. Yehezkel started explaining that crossing the lines of that bloody war was no simple matter, and that with no guarantee of reaching the tent of al-Malik al-Kamil, the attempt was little more than a complicated suicide.

But Francesco smiled as if he'd already talked it all out with the good Lord. "I know what war looks like, Master Ezekiel. My preoccupation is not how to reach the sultan's tent unharmed, but how to find someone to translate my Latin so my words may reach his heart!"

The strange couple's first thought was the same, though it took different forms in their minds.

"No one in *all* Egypt could do that better than I!" thought Yehezkel, "and if that weren't enough, I *need* to find a way through those lines to get to Fustat. My, my . . . as Rav Eleazar would say, look how hard those angels are working, up there. . . ."

"That settles it!" she thought instead. "Francesco of Assisi is going to convert the Saracen sultan, and Master Ezekiel will be his interpreter— and *I* should sail to Acre *with the women*? And miss the chance to be in frescoes and paintings of that scene in every church in Christendom? Sorry, Gioacchino: no pilgrimage, no Jerusalem enigma can stop me. I'm sailing to Egypt!"

CHAPTER 17

VaYiten Otam

And He Positioned Them

LIMASSOL, 13TH JULY 1219

One day, as Yehezkel approached the inn where they usually met to eat in the morning, he saw Galatea running toward him, holding up the hem of her white habit.

"Rabbi, Rabbi, I had a spectacular . . . no, a *celestial* dream! I must tell you about it before it fades!"

Coming from that nun, Yehezkel took the news quite seriously. "Good morning, madame. Let's go into the inn and fetch wax and stylus so I can put down what you still remember. Why did you not take notes as soon as you woke up?" he scolded.

"Oh, don't worry, Rabbi, I thought of nothing else since opening my eyes. I went through every detail of the dream a hundred times since dawn. I remember it as if I were there *now*!"

"Excellent!" said the kabbalist, adding with a smile, "It's always more rewarding to work with mystics who've learned to . . . 'handle' their visions."

"Well, this time I wonder how *you* will handle my vision. I was a bird flying over *Jerusalem*!"

Yehezkel's eyes opened wide at the mention of the city that was his numerological namesake. "How did you know it was the Holy City you were flying over?" he asked as they entered the inn.

"Oh, I just knew it. But even if I hadn't, I would have guessed it, what with desert hills all around, the Temple with the viaduct and the ceremony taking place . . ."

"Lord of the Universe, you dreamed *the Temple*! You mean it wasn't . . . it wasn't Jerusalem *today* you were flying over, it was Jerusalem when the Temple still stood on the Mount?"

"Yes, Rabbi," said Galatea, taking her usual seat on the divan in a corner of the room. "Not that I could tell you what was going on, or *when* it was all happening, but maybe *you* will understand that."

"I hope so!" said Yehezkel, starting to pace back and forth in front of the divan. "Let's proceed in an orderly fashion. We'll come to the Temple in a moment; first let's try to determine the epoch. Tell me, how big a city was there around the Temple esplanade, madame? And what was the biggest construction, besides the Temple?"

"Mmh, let me see . . . the city was quite large, but only *behind* the Temple. In front of it was a deep gulley and beyond that a hill, which I presume must have been the Mount of Olives." She clapped her hands and brought them to her lips. "Madre Santissima! I was flying over the Mount of Olives, do you realize? The largest building? Mmh . . . it was a rectangular fortress by the edge of the Temple esplanade, with crenellated walls and square towers on its corners."

"Fortress Antonia!" cried Yehezkel. "Madame, you saw Jerusalem under Roman occupation!"

"That means at the time of Jesus, doesn't it?"

"Yes! The Temple you saw was Herod's, not Solomon's." He stroked his beard.

"The Talmud devotes many pages to Herod's Temple; our sages were concerned that when the third one is built, nothing will be missing or forgotten."

"Before the ceremony," said Galatea, "the Temple courtyards were very crowded. Hundreds of people came and went, dressed in ancient-looking garb of a style I'd never seen before, even on statues. Priests in white robes were busy around an altar in front of the Temple's entrance, and the smoke from it went up in a straight, thin column. The facade of the Temple was covered in gold, so bright I couldn't look at it."

"So you were a bird, but not an eagle," murmured Yehezkel, smiling.

Galatea giggled. "Don't make fun of this dream, Rabbi; there was something truly solemn about it."

"What happened when the ceremony took place?"

"It was later. As I glided over the Mount, a figure clad in white and gold walked along the viaduct to the Temple, bearing a gold tray heaped with what looked like ash. Behind him, at the starting point of the viaduct, was a massive altar. The crowds left the courts and stood on the esplanade, lining his path. I had a strong feeling of the importance for the world of what I was witnessing . . . "

"The red heifer," whispered Yehezkel reverently. "What you saw was the high priest carrying out one of the most mysterious and crucial tenets of Judaism. A ritual to purify the whole world, exactly as you say." Yehezkel looked awestruck and not a little tense.

"But what is this red heifer? What *was* the ritual?"

"It is a mystery related to the sin of the Israelites who made the golden calf in the desert. Basically, the ashes of a flawless red heifer have the power to remove all impurity, even from contact with the dead."

Galatea looked puzzled. "But in Crete you told me Judaism is *blue,* so why is the cow whose ashes vanquish the impurity of death *red,* the color of paganism?"

Yehezkel was impressed. "It would take too long to explain, madame, but again, it has to do with the golden calf. The copper the Israelites used to harden the gold gave the calf a reddish hue, and after Moses broke the first tablets, the Torah says he 'took the calf which they had made, burnt it in the fire, ground it to powder, strewed it upon the water, and made the children of Israel drink of it.' As I said, it is a mystery."

Galatea nodded slowly and went on describing the majestic scene she'd witnessed. "The gates in front of the advancing high priest were perfectly aligned and *all* wide open, from the double gate on the edge of the esplanade to the gates between the courtyards, all the way to the entrance to the Temple itself."

Yehezkel said, "And though you couldn't see it, inside the Temple the curtain at the entrance to the Holy of Holies was drawn, too. Something that didn't happen often."

"Yes, indeed, it felt like a rare, special occasion. When the high priest stepped onto the esplanade flutes, trumpets, tambourines, lyres, and harps started playing, and a male choir, standing on a semicircular stairway leading from one courtyard to another, began to sing the first verse of Genesis to Hildegard's music, just like in my dream!" She smiled, embarrassed. "Well, Rabbi, you know how dreams are . . ."

"Those were Levites," he said. "And they did, indeed, sing the creation verses at certain ceremonies. *And* a semicircular staircase climbed from the Court of Women to the Court of Israel. The music may not have been Hildegard's, madame, but aside from that your dream is *strikingly* accurate."

"Don't mistake this for pride, Rabbi, but I'm used to that. Tell me, the double gate is on the eastern side, isn't it?" she asked. "It's the gate Jesus came in from, riding on an ass."

"Yes, at the time it was called the Gate of Mercy and was in fact *two* gates, as you saw," said the rabbi. "Now it is called the Golden Gate." Yehezkel paused, caressing his beard, and then said, "As for the deeper meaning of the dream, the red heifer ritual, in my opinion, is not the point. The Temple and the viaduct are the point. You see, your dream is connected to the Parchment, of that I have no doubt. Don Sancio said it was a map, remember? Think of the clues placed on our path so far: first the hermit's prophecy about an enigma, and then your dream of Bereshit, and then the page of Ezekiel that Hanina hid in Jerusalem, and now this dream, showing you where things were or weren't on the Mount. Do you see? When we find the map, it will all suddenly make sense!"

"I do see . . . but you just put your finger on something that is start-ing to trouble me."

The abbess looked around the inn and lowered her voice, "In Torcello I dreamed the first verse of the Bible *in Hebrew;* now I dream the Jewish Temple in the time of Christ. All right, the prophecy speaks of a woman and a Jew, but why are the shreds of revelation the woman glimpses so strictly *Jewish*? Why don't *you* ever dream a choir singing the first verse of a Gospel, or have a vision of Jesus Christ establishing the Eucharist? Something here is uncomfortably one-sided. . . ."

Yehezkel had concluded that, his own prophetic talents being sadly inadequate, Divine Providence placed a prophetess beside him as a con-duit for the heavenly forces supporting his mission. But by now he knew how the proud nun would react to that explanation of the Jewish con-tents of her visions, so he said, "The only answer I have is what Rav Shlomo said in Crete: mysteries are only accessed through the sacred language of Scripture. If your part in the quest is rife with Jewish words and symbols, it must be because the Parchment of Circles is itself in Hebrew, and if you're destined to solve its mystery, you must first—how can I put it—*adapt* your gift to that language."

Galatea was silent for a while and then said, "I'd still like to hear what Brother Francesco piccolo thinks of my dream; his interpretation would comfort my Christian heart . . . Brother Francesco may not be as learned as you, but by your own admission, he's so full of the Holy Spirit it overflows on those around him."

"I agree, madame. There's a side to him I can't fathom, but the Lord's hand is firmly on his head!"

Galatea smiled. Then, making to get up from the divan, exclaimed, "Come, let's go out and look for him! I dread what he'll think of a nun who dreams of animal sacrifices in the Jewish Temple, but I still can't wait to hear what he'll say!"

"Just a minute!" Yehezkel held her back. "Sit down, madame, you only just started telling me what you saw. *Every* detail of your dream could be the difference between finding and not finding the confession!"

Her voice was suddenly cooler. "Ah, so you think the confession *does* exist, after all . . . but then, didn't Jews deny the Resurrection from the first day? So why did I expect . . ."

"No, madame! Don't put words in my mouth. We've spoken of it before and decided we will only know if the fabled confession exists *if* and *when* we find what the map leads to. I said confession, but I might as well have called it the Holy Grail!"

The air crackled between them. Galatea grunted an acceptance of his explanation and tried to think of more details of the dream. Then, suddenly, she went back to the topic of their most recent spat. "Have you given any more thought to the question of Aillil?" she asked out of the blue.

Bois-Guilbert was sailing to Acre, so Yehezkel had suggested they ask for a passage for the women and the armigers. Galatea disliked the idea from the first moment, but the real issue of contention was Aillil. When he'd told her the boy would be coming to Egypt with them, she had been outraged. "*I* decided to sail to Damietta with you and Brother Francesco, but I am an adult! To take a thirteen-year-old to a battlefield is simply *irresponsible*!" she exclaimed.

Now Yehezkel sat silently in the semidarkness of the inn and then answered gloomily, "Yes, I thought about it, and I still think sending him to Acre with the women would put him in greater danger. You can't imagine the dreadful tales I heard of life in Acre since Jerusalem fell. What happened to those children who took the cross seven years ago is happening every day in that city."

"The Templar and his Teutonic toady don't inspire any confidence," she conceded. "Anyway, I suppose after Brother Francesco preaches to the Sultan . . . well, either the heathen king accepts the Light of Christ, or we all win martyrdom, and Aillil becomes an infidel's pretty blond toy. Isn't *that* what awaits us?"

"No, madame," laughed Yehezkel. "You heard tales full of prejudice and hatred. In fact I heard the new sultan, al-Malik al-Kamil, is an open-minded Mohammedan, a lover of philosophy who admires Averroes, as poor Don Sancio did and as I do . . . to a point. I rather think he'll recognize a fool of God in Francesco and do him no harm, even if he should not accept the Light of Christ."

Galatea was relieved. Resigned to thwarting her wishes, Yehezkel said, "I told you, madame, the reason Aillil is coming with us is that I'm responsible for my friend's only son and will not let him out of my sight. Besides, Arnald is probably outside Damietta, with almost every other knight in Outremer, so as soon as I arrive I will likely return the boy to his father and be discharged of my obligation, free to go and look for the letter in Fustat. That is, of course, after Brother Francesco's mission in the sultan's tent goes whichever way God plans for it to go."

He resumed pacing. The abbess smiled, somewhat mollified. "I'm learning to appreciate the elegance of the Averroist position, Rabbi, which I understand as trusting that things will follow God's plan, but without needing to claim advance knowledge of that plan."

Yehezkel stopped in midstride and bowed in an elaborate Saracen curtsy, his right hand opening out toward her after touching his heart, lips, and forehead. "Madame, no philosopher I know of could have expressed the attitude more simply than you just did!"

She blushed and was about to say something modest when the rest of the company joined them at the table. Once *again,* Gudrun found her abbess alone with the Jew and glared disapproval. Galatea, excited about the dream, barely gave them time to dunk bread in cups of watered wine before dragging them out in the street, already crowded and hot at third hour. Assigning an armiger to each woman, she dispatched the two pairs to look for the friars, setting off in another direction to do the same with the rabbi and Aillil.

An hour later, the abbess stood before the friars under a big lime tree on the edge of town, relating the dream to Francesco. The little friar was enthralled, but his brothers listened with growing diffidence to her awed description of the Temple whose destruction Jesus had prophesied.

"I don't know the Hebrew Bible as well as Master Ezekiel," started Francesco, "but . . ."

Yehezkel butted in, "There's another dream in the Bible connected to the Temple, Brother Francesco piccolo, but to the *first* Temple, for the dreamer was none other than King Solomon. In that dream, God granted him a 'wise and discerning heart.'"

On an impulse, Galatea asked, "Does the Bible say what King Solomon *did* when he woke up from that dream?"

"Strange you should ask," answered Yehezkel. "I remember the verse, because it makes the king look like any one of us. It says, 'Then Solomon awoke and realized it had been a dream.' If I remember right, he offered up some sacrifices and then gave a feast for all his court."

"That's it!" she exclaimed. "That's how I feel about *this* dream: everyone should celebrate with me! I'll give a feast like King Solomon, but instead of inviting 'my court,' I'll invite every poor person in Limassol!"

Francesco almost looked at her and started clapping from joy. "Mother Galatea, if giving a banquet for the poor is what this dream inspires you to do, then I have *no doubt* it came from God!"

Yehezkel smiled at the thought of Francesco attending a banquet, but the prospect of music, dancing, and poems appealed to him. It would be like the old days in Languedoc! "Don't forget, madame, that the galley taking us to Damietta sails in just over a week," he said.

"You're right, of course. I'll have to find a place for the feast and the people who will arrange it all . . . Brother Francesco piccolo, can I count on you and your brothers to spread the word, as Saint Luke says, 'in the streets and alleys of this town, and bring in the poor, the crippled, the blind, and the lame?'"

"We'll be delighted!" said Francesco. "We're here to spread the Gospel, which is the Good News, and what could be better news to the poor than a feast where they can eat their fill?"

As Yehezkel expected, Galatea's hardest task was convincing Francesco and his brothers to join the revelers at a banquet. She pointed out that it was a feast for the poor, so how could Lady Poverty's own husband fail to attend?

At first Francesco seemed immovable, but then Brother Illuminato said in a timid, high-pitched voice, "But Father, the rule you wrote for us says we should never be choosy about food, but obey the Lord's words in Luke, 'When you enter a town and are welcomed, eat what is offered to you.'"

Francesco looked strangely vulnerable for a moment and then smiled. "You're right, Illuminato. If I see myself not as a guest, but as a mendicant friar in front of whom some food has been placed, I shall run no risk of falling into the sins I committed in the banquets of my youth."

Yehezkel made a face and said, "Brother Francesco piccolo, I've heard you call your body 'flesh that will soon die and is hostile to the soul.' Well, let me tell you that body and soul were created by the same God, and to believe that one is hostile to the other is a grave theological error. Christian hermits who mortify their flesh too severely destroy what was created in God's image."

Francesco looked up at the rabbi and said, seriously, "My brothers and I are no hermits, Master Ezekiel. We walk the world to win souls to the Lord and help the poor in any way we can. As for my body . . . you're right there, it may look like I don't show it the compassion I feel for all creatures, but that is because of a deliberate choice I made to imitate the suffering of our Lord Jesus Christ."

Friars and abbess nodded approval of the perfectly evangelical retort. Yehezkel lowered his head and said, a little condescendingly, "Still, the way you treat your body is disrespectful to God's creation."

After a silence, Francesco said, "No, Rabbi. My suffering is my own choice—indeed, it is my salvation. My desire to imitate Christ may cause pain to my body, but I suffer *pleasantly*. I know it sounds crazy, but there's so much joy in the pain I feel that I delight in my sickness!"

Yehezkel relented, smiling. "You sound like a lover speaking of his sleepless nights. The Sufis claim that love of God should be as sweet and painful as the longing for one's lover. Tell me, did you ever meet any Sufis?"

Francesco glanced at his brothers. "Actually, yes. Five years ago, on a pilgrimage to Santiago de Compostela, I met a Mohammedan, as raggedly dressed as I was, who said he was a disciple of one ibn 'Arabi. He was an infidel, but he said 'Love is my religion and my faith'—Christian words if ever I heard any! God forgive me for praising a heretic, but I learned more about faith from him in the two nights we spoke than in the thirty years I'd lived until then."

Yehezkel said, "Ibn 'Arabi . . . 'the greatest sheik'—I heard he teaches his doctrine in Damascus now."

Francesco said, "I know that some among the infidel understand that God and Love are the same thing, but until it is shown to them that the God of Love sent his only Son to be the sacrifice to end all sacrifices, they will continue in their blindness . . . as will you, Master Ezekiel."

Yehezkel shuffled his feet and said nothing. He'd been on the point of suggesting himself as the interpreter chosen by Divine Providence for Francesco's sermon to the sultan but decided there would be better moments for it, perhaps during the passage to Damietta.

✡ ✾ ✾ ♛

LIMASSOL, 22ND JULY 1219

Bertrand of Bar-sur-Aube—Blanche's cousin, whose villa the abbess and the women left for a local convent after meeting Francesco—offered his property and its servants for her improvised imitation of King Solomon. He only asked that the knights from the Templar galleys be invited too, in case the town's poor, after quaffing enough Cypriot wine, should become ungovernable.

The abbess supervised the preparations with Cistercian rigor. In the largest hall, low tables for three hundred destitute guests were laid under the arches. A long raised table at which nobles, knights, and clerics would sit was covered with a red cloth rampantly embroidered in white; the wall above it hung with shields, spears, and the skins of wild beasts.

When Galatea was satisfied that everything was ready for the next day, Yehezkel took the company to Limassol's Jewish quarter—close to the port, as in every city around the Mediterranean—to introduce to them Yehudah al-Harizi, a Spanish poet and sometime diplomat he recently met there.

Al-Harizi was an erudite Jew in his fifties, one of the polyglot—penniless, perennial pilgrims roaming the Levant—whose culture and sensibilities nearly always exceeded those of their hosts. His satirical works were known in Spain, but he had to work as a schoolteacher to survive. When he saw Galatea, al-Harizi bowed deeply in the same heart-lips-forehead homage Yehezkel had paid her earlier.

"Sincerely *enchanté,* madame. Rav Yehezkel was not exaggerating..." Galatea blushed. "My name is Yehudah al-Harizi, and I am, for lack of a subtler expression, a Jewish troubadour."

"How exciting!" said Galatea. "I hope tomorrow night we will hear you sing some of your verses."

"I'm afraid my verses are in Hebrew or Arabic, madame—but for you, I'll happily sing someone else's."

Soon Yehezkel was deep in conversation with al-Harizi in a boisterous mix of Hebrew, Arabic, and Spanish. Now and then the two men burst out in howls of laughter, slapping their leg or each other's shoulder. The abbess admitted to herself that she envied Jews their complicity, which made strangers living thousands of leagues from each other instantly behave like old friends, if not family. When she stood next to Yehezkel again, Galatea whispered, "If we ended up in hell, Rabbi, you'd know someone there, too."

"Maybe," laughed Yehezkel, "but for sure I wouldn't speak his language!"

As fate would have it, the banquet took place on Saint Magdalene's day, tenth anniversary of the massacre at Béziers. The first ones to arrive, late in the afternoon, were the knights of the orders and their sergeants. When they become acquainted—Frutolf shaking like a teenager on being introduced to Galatea—and the countess had been toasted for her inspired idea of holding a feast for the poor, the gates were opened for the crowd outside, and enough people came in to fill the tables.

Ragged men and women of all races sat on the floor, many with the kind of rapacious features that so often go with harsh lives that some wonder if one of the two—but which?—brings on the other. When they were seated, servants began bringing dozens of platters bearing roast boars, kids, herons, hares—each one swimming in a different, but always fiery, sauce—and everyone began noisily gorging themselves.

An hour into the feast, the friars walked in and sat among the beggars. Francesco kept his promise not to stay away, but the wealthy surroundings made him uncomfortable. He looked happy to see the town's dispossessed having a good time, but his plate was empty and he barely sipped at his wine.

Yehezkel and al-Harizi heard their fill of the complacent chatter on the top table, so excused themselves and went to crouch on the floor next to the Italians. Yehezkel told Francesco that some of that roast meat would do his poor body nothing but good. "I thought Brother Illuminato had convinced you to eat what was put in front of you."

"True, Master Ezekiel," said Francesco, "but *your* plate is empty, too. Why is that?"

"Neither of us can eat what was not selected, butchered, and cooked according to the Law."

"Mmh . . ." Francesco hesitated but couldn't resist. "Did you never hear Christ's words: 'What goes *into* someone's mouth does not defile them; what comes *out* of their mouth, that is what defiles them?'"

Yehezkel didn't respond to the good-natured taunt. Since deciding that the spirited friar *had* to accept him as his interpreter, he had started to slip away from theological confrontations.

Suddenly, al-Harizi made a joke about Pope Honorius's ripe age, something to do with incontinence, and the mostly Greek crowd roared with laughter, as Francesco covered his ears in mock scandal. Yehezkel decided it was time to approach the knights about a passage to Acre for women and armigers. He stood up, gestured to al-Harizi to follow him, and made for the top table. Meanwhile, Bois-Guilbert took advantage of the Jews' absence to sit next to Galatea.

"I know an inn in Acre, countess," he said with a complicit smile, "where a Tuscan cook makes the sort of bean soups you were brought up on!"

"Sorry to disappoint you, Brother Bois-Guilbert," she said, "but I won't be sailing to Acre with you."

"You won't?" asked the Templar, startled.

"I have decided to follow Brother Francesco piccolo in his mission to the king of the infidels."

Robert thought, "God's teeth! I send the Jew to Damietta, so she finds an excuse to go with him! His spell on this nun is as powerful as the one that bitch, Rebecca, cast on my father!"

Out loud, he sneered, "Soon there will be more clerics than knights at that siege! That the mother of a Cistercian house should go on a pilgrimage to Jerusalem I find laudable, Madonna, but following a crazy preacher in search of martyrdom into a war? That's nothing short of insane!"

"Had I been an abbot, instead of an abbess," snapped Galatea, "you would have found my choice to follow my preacher on a holy expedition no less commendable than a pilgrimage! Is that not so?"

The Templar smiled. "Women wish they were men, and you make no secret of it! But no man, I'm sure you'll concede, would ever wish he was a woman."

She glared at him, "Pah! You might as well have said no man would ever wish he was a slave!"

Al-Harizi, standing behind them, intervened on her behalf. "Don't you know, my good knight, that troubadours pine incessantly over their inability to attain the moral purity of women?"

Robert turned. "Women are only moral by coercion, señor. If the daughters of the empire's nobility could marry the men they fancied, we would all be governed by languid minstrels and dark-eyed outlaws! As for troubadors, I find their laments nauseating. They all sing like their teeth ache!"

By now Frutolf had swallowed more insults from the Templar than rain down from a besieged town, but his master assigned him to do his bidding, so he'd never reacted to such arrogance as it would have deserved. Chagrined to hear that the lady of his thoughts would sail to Egypt, he'd relished Bois-Guilbert's disappointment at her escaping his clutches. But by insulting her, the bastard went too far. "Brother Robert, apologize to the abbess for calling her insane, or I shall be bound by my knightly vows to defend her honor," he growled. Frutolf's lower lip protruded on one side as if he'd had a pebble in the corner of his mouth for a long time. The heavy German accent of his Latin and his dramatic tone made Bois-Guilbert burst out in a condescending laugh.

"Ha, ha, ha! Sheathe your blade, chivalrous knight, I was only jesting! The lady herself will tell you so."

Galatea nodded in Frutolf's direction, more in thanks for his readiness to be her champion than to confirm Bois-Guilbert's claim to have meant no offense. She knew he had. The moment passed, but Frutolf's impulse convinced Yehezkel that the German was the answer to the nun's mistrust of the Templar. In the humblest tone he could muster, he turned to Frutolf and said, "Honorable knight, I seek your protection for two women headed to Jerusalem. If you will see to it that they reach Acre safely and find a caravan to the Holy City, God will surely reward you for it!"

Frutolf readily accepted to look after the women, to Bois-Guilbert's immediate scorn. "I'll vouch for the pilgrims *myself*, Master Ezekiel! Mother Galatea needn't worry her pretty head about them. Instead, she should worry that her *own* head remains attached to her neck in the infidel's camp!"

Frutolf was doing what he did best, feeling sorry for himself. "I'm committed to looking after two pilgrims while the Jew sails to Egypt with the lady of my thoughts! Perhaps one day I'll slit open the belly of this verbose Jew for the liberties he takes with the queen of my soul. Surely killing a Jew is no more a sin than killing a Mohammedan: they're both infidels!"

The German's spark of knightly honor mitigated Galatea's misgivings at the thought of Gudrun and Albacara at the mercy of those ghouls. In any case, leaving the women in Cyprus, albeit with Rustico and Garietto, was worse than entrusting them to the knights. After all, these two had crosses on their mantles!

When food—after a final, glorious blancmange—stopped coming, musicians started to play. Wine flowed freely, and the dancing was wild. It was a hot night, and girls fanned themselves, opening the necks of their blouses and holding cool metal dishes to their cheeks. Galatea went out for some air. Light from inside poured all the way to the lane. Big earthenware oil lamps sat among the columns, and shadows danced on the walls. The yard smelled of meat, mingled with the fragrance of mint, cinnamon, and hot wine spices. People came and went, and she heard muffled laughter, music, and occasional imprecations.

"Ezekiel is simply too big," she thought suddenly, a bit tipsy. "He takes up so much space when he moves. He's like an untamed falcon that cannot open its wings in a room without knocking over a chair or a jug."

Finally, on the 30th of July, the galley heading for war embarked both its conscripted passengers and the few eccentrics who needed no coercion to join the armies—that is, the friars and Galatea.

For two weeks, Gudrun and Albacara were torn between relief at not joining the abbess on a journey to possible martyrdom and sheer terror at the thought of completing their pilgrimage without her. Not to mention the abbess asked them to find storage for her trunk in Acre.

The adieus on the quay were heartbreaking. At the last moment, faced with Gudrun's desperation, Galatea was on the point of changing her mind and sailing to Acre, but in the end she reminded Gudrun of her vow of obedience, and that she was her Mother Superior, even in Cyprus.

Aillil was beside himself with joy for three reasons: first, his father might be outside Damietta and his dream of a lifetime about to come true. Second, they were joining an army besieging an infidel city—with war engines and real kings! Third, and possibly most exciting, they were about to board a galley, the kind of ship he always dreamed of sailing in.

Six months earlier, when he'd left Montréal, he'd been truly tired of being too young for everything and wondered when he would acquire the confidence that adults showed when faced with threatening developments. Now, he was probably the only thirteen-year-old in Christendom to have single-handedly sunk a pirate ship, and the thought of his father teaching him to look after himself on a battlefield filled him with elation. Back in Montréal, he would have his own tales to tell in front of the fire.

The last to show up were the Italian friars. When everyone was on board, Yehezkel watched the galley's Genoese crew prepare to cast off. He heard Francesco's voice soar as he and a knight from Provence sang a French ballad. The friar couldn't resist taking a few dance steps across the deck as a few knights clapped their hands. They looked like anything but a galley sailing to war.

They cast off and slowly rowed out of the harbor. Then the rhythm of drums and oars picked up; the galley surged forward. Even Galatea, by now undaunted by waves and slippery decks, was thrilled by the speed of the slender ship whose prow threw spray all the way to the quarterdeck. With Cyprus shrinking on the northern horizon, she asked Yehezkel, "This is a roundabout route to Jerusalem, isn't it? How long will it be before we set course for the Holy City again?"

"Actually, I did some calculating last night, madame. It so happens that we spent precisely forty days on Crete *and* precisely forty days on Cyprus. I don't look forward to them, but I fear it will be forty days again before we leave Damietta. You know how much they like that number, up there . . ."

✡ ✠ ✡ ✠

THE SAME DAY, IN JERUSALEM

Just as the Templar galley exited Limassol harbor, in Jerusalem a young Bedouin sheikh of the tribe of Saud advanced on his knees along an endless carpet leading to the slipper he would have to kiss.

The slipper was that of Haj Abû Haydjâ' al-Hadhbânî's, a Kurd who was Jerusalem's vizier by appointment of al-Mu'azzam 'Isa, caliph of Damascus and brother of the Sultan. Five months earlier, when al-Mu'azzam ordered the demolition of Jerusalem's walls—in case the city was ceded to the Franks to get them to leave Egypt—the vizier's residence moved from the patriarch's palace. The carpet was now in the fortress of King David, next to the main gate in what was left of the city's western wall. Al-Hadhbânî sat on a raised platform on cushions covered in Damascene silk. On his head was the white turban that is the privilege of those who have been on the Haj. The Saudi sheikh he summoned was the director of the restoration work ordered by al-Mu'azzam 'Isa on the Esplanade where the al-Aqsa Mosque and the Dome of the Rock rose. In the last week or two strange events had been frightening the workers there.

"What's happening on the Haram al-Sharif?"* barked the vizier.

The foreman was already on his knees but now bent down until his forehead touched the carpet. "Peace be with you, Your Excellency. May God grant you a life as long as time itself!"

The vizier gestured impatiently for him to answer the question. The sheikh went on, "Your humble servant sent stone masons twice to fix a section of the paving about three hundred steps north of the dome. Both times, the workers fell sick the day after they began work in that spot."

---

*Arab name for the Temple esplanade, literally: the Holy Precinct

"From what did they suffer?" asked al-Hadhbânî.

"Fever, vomit, vertigo, nightmares . . . and visions. One of them is dead, and another two are moribund. The city is murmuring, Your Excellency. They say Allah doesn't want that spot touched."

"And since when is Allah's will determined by people in the souk's alleys?" snapped the vizier. He stood up, irritated. "Call my ulema!"* he shouted to the guards around the platform.

Three bearded old men wearing white turbans walked in and listened to the foreman carefully, asked many questions, and then stepped aside to whisper among themselves. Finally, the eldest one stepped forward. "Your Excellency, the Qu'ran says that Shaytān† hides even under one's nails . . ."

Al-Hadhbânî stopped him right away. "I've no time for qu'ranic derivations! Are there *ruah'in*‡ on the esplanade or aren't there?"

"There are, Your Excellency," answered the alim. "A small dome will have to be erected there in honor of the Prophet, who must have chased away a ruah in that spot. The workers will have to be changed every day, and when the work is done, it will be best to just stay away from there!"

---

*Alim (plural: ulema), Arabic for scholar; came to denote arbiters of sharia law, well versed in *fiqh* (jurisprudence)
†Arabic for Satan
‡Ruah (plural: ruah'in) is Arabic for a spirit in the sense of invisible entity, as in "evil spirit" or "spirit of the dead"

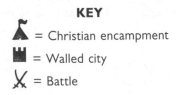

Damietta

al-Adiliyah

Färiskür

Lake

Manzalah

NILE

DELTA

Sharamsah

Baramun

Mansurah

Fifth Crusade, 1217–1221

KEY

▲ = Christian encampment

▥ = Walled city

✗ = Battle

CHAPTER 18

HA-HOSHECH

The Darkness

OUTSIDE DAMIETTA, IN THE EASTERN NILE DELTA, 2ND AUGUST 1219

The man was on his knees on the riverbank, hands tied behind his back. He shouted a war cry again.

"Allah-Huu . . ."

Before he could say Akbar, a knight standing behind him kicked him between the shoulder blades with an iron-clad foot so violently his neck snapped. The man fell forward, lifeless.

Galatea gasped in shock. It wasn't the first death she had witnessed, and the man had been an infidel, but the casual brutality took her breath away. On that bank of nothing but sand and reeds, the scene had the frozen starkness of one of her visions. All she could think was, "Thank God Gudrun isn't here."

Yehezkel, standing beside her, remembered the premonition he'd had outside Carcassonne ten years earlier, that other wars were in store for him. "And that God would see me through them alive," he murmured to himself.

Francesco, who had seen battle in Italy, recognized the look of pained surprise on a man struck by a deadly blow, and felt pity for the Saracen. He heard his brothers mumble a prayer for the man's soul and wondered briefly if Jews and Mohammedans also prayed for the souls of infidels, as he had taught his friars to do. He would have to ask Master Ezekiel.

Aillil held his breath in fear and excitement, happy to feel Galatea's hands on his shoulders.

They had made landfall at dawn in al-Jiza, a small fishermen's village on the coast. The Christians were digging a canal from the shore to the Nile to bring vessels closer to the camp, but it wasn't completed yet, and the village had no harbor, so the galley dropped anchor half a league offshore, and overloaded rowboats crawled to and fro from first light, carrying men and provisions. Serfs hurried to load timber for war machines, iron for new blades, sacks of grain, and quarters of salted meat on carts so they could reach the camp before the sun rose much higher.

Saracen children tugged at the knights' clothes, avoiding Christians from the camp, by now inured to their pitiful near nakedness, concentrating instead on the newcomers, more likely to be moved to pity. Young girls offered their bodies with smiles frozen by embarrassment, only to be chased away by shrieking Italian and Frankish whores, who had set up shop in the camp over a year before.

The new arrivals marched in the sand with their carts for over an hour when suddenly, after climbing the back of a high dune, the entire fresco of the fifth holy war for Jerusalem was unveiled before their eyes.

The Nile's eastern branch filled the horizon under a giant half sun the color of egg yolk. On an island in the river near the closer bank stood the tower whose capture had cost hundreds of Christian lives a year earlier. Beyond the river, a league from where they stood, a narrow strip of land separated the Nile from the huge Menzaleh lake beyond. In the middle of the strip rose the city of Damietta, smaller than they imagined it, but with fabulously high, impregnable walls.

They rested briefly on the dune's crest as a sergeant described Christ's Army, laid out south of the city across the strip between river and lake. The tents stretched without end, beyond anything any of them had ever seen. From west to east, the sergeant pointed out the standards of John of Brienne, the king of Jerusalem, followed by those of Frankish and Pisan counts. Then came the encampments of Templars and Hospitaliers, and further still Spaniards and Provencals. Finally, at the eastern edge of that sea of tents, nearly on the shores of the lake, was Pelagius with the Romans and the Genoese.

Sliding down the steep side of the dune, they made their way toward a bridge of planks laid over flat boats that crossed the Nile upstream of the city. After crossing it, the column finally entered the camp, already crawling with activity. They stumbled as if lost, mouths agape in wonder at unknown coats of arms and weapons they'd never seen in their countries. The heat was fast becoming unbearable, the trunks made heavier by the burning sand in which their feet sunk at every step.

They were walking past a smith's tent, the hammers already singing on the blades, when they heard shouts from the river. Knights and sergeants emerged from tents and ran toward the source of the noise. The group joined them and a few moments later stood in a rapidly growing crowd along a stretch of riverbank where eight Saracen spies had been caught in the nets an hour earlier as they tried to bring Greek fire and bread to their besieged brethren by swimming underwater.

Galatea knew war would not be pretty but had not been able to watch the spies being tortured, as everyone around her seemed happy to do. Two of them were flayed alive, right there on the sand. She asked Yehezkel, voice shaking, why they didn't just kill them. The spies, he conveyed grimly, may have possessed information on the true situation inside the city, obtained through pigeons, but it was more likely that what they were witnessing was pure revenge, the anger of the besiegers taken out on some brave but unfortunate men.

Then the last of them was forced to his knees, tried to shout defiance toward the *kuffar,** and earned his martyrdom.

✠ ✠ ✠ ✠

The crowd dispersed slowly.

By now the newcomers heard of the disastrous toll, especially on the Templars, of the mamluk attack two days before, on the 31st of July. Yehezkel heard loud moans emerge from some tents, and as they entered the Templar section, he realized the wounded must be so many he would be lucky to secure a refuge for the night before he was compelled to start performing duties as a medicus.

Galatea asked about nuns in the camp and was advised to seek out the bishop of Acre, Jacques de Vitry, who supervised the activities of clerics with the campaign. As luck would have it, Francesco of Assisi and Jacques de Vitry had met five years earlier in Provence, when the latter was not yet a bishop. The Frenchman was preaching against the Cathars, while the Italian was on the pilgrimage to Spain on which he'd met a disciple of al 'Arabi. Each was taken with the quality of the other's faith, and Francesco had been happy to hear of Jacques's rapid rise to bishop of Acre, as well as principal preacher of the first real effort in thirty years to retake Jerusalem from the infidel.

The moment he heard Jacques was in the camp, Francesco asked where his tent was and set off to greet his friend, dragging everyone along. The tent was not far from Cardinal Pelagius's, which meant they had to trudge to the eastern edge of the camp. As they passed Frankish, Italian, and Spanish tents, a vague anxiety crept over the strange couple, as if coming to Egypt instead of going on to Jerusalem was a mistake, and the spectacle they had just witnessed an omen of things to come.

They crossed the city in the sand for an hour. By the time they glimpsed the pennant on the cardinal's tent, knights, squires, and artisans from the ship had dispersed to quarters where their mother

---

*Arabic for infidel, unbeliever

tongues filled the air. Catching their breath, a new, different company of seven—now comprising Yehezkel, Galatea, Aillil, Francesco, and his three friars—approached the bishop's tent.

Jacques de Vitry, despite not having returned to Europe since his arrival in Acre three years earlier, had heard of the near miraculous success of Francesco's mendicant order. When a page announced the Italian friar was asking to see him, he jumped up joyfully from the letter he was writing. "Francesco of Assisi is outside my tent? Bring him in immediately! And whoever is with him, too!"

Jacques and Francesco embraced like old friends. Then the bishop, who was nearly sixty, held the little friar's face in his hands, more like a father than a friend, and said, his voice cracking with emotion, "Francino, didn't I tell you that your friars would fill the earth like the stars fill the heavens? Didn't I? How many friars have you got today?"

Francesco blushed but didn't answer. A moment later Brother Elia, unable to contain his pride, blurted out, "Almost five thousand, Your Excellency!"

Francesco's next words surprised everyone, as his words often did. "You know, Jacques, a little after we met, the way people chose to follow my example, the fact that so many wanted to join me . . . it made me afraid the devil might have a hand in it. I asked myself, 'Has Satan sent these multitudes to distract me from the love of Christ?'"

The bishop laughed. Francesco introduced the new company to him. The bishop had a short, white beard and kind, intelligent eyes. Yehezkel noticed his welcome, warm even to the Jew among his guests. As he'd expected, his medical skills were foremost in Jacques's thoughts.

"Master Ezekiel, it must be God's work that you arrived *today*! Surely you heard of the way Pedro of Montaigue saved the day on Wednesday?"

"We heard that the sultan's mamluks entered the Templar section of the camp, Your Excellency, but that's all we know," said Yehezkel.

"I'll tell you everything. But first *you*, Francino, must tell me what you're doing here!"

"I came here to stop this carnage," asnwered Francesco, quietly.

Jacques stared, incredulous. "How do you propose to do *that*?"

"Once I've preached to the sultan and he has seen the light of Christ, there will be no need for war."

For a few moments, the bishop was speechless. Then he gathered his wits and said, "God can do anything he pleases, Francino. At the end of days, He will convert Satan himself. But we both know how unlikely it is that al-Kamil will accept baptism, which makes your enterprise sound more like a quest for martyrdom than an inspired mission." Jacques paused and then cleared his throat. "We'll speak of it later, my friend, when we're alone. Now to the grim situation in this cursed desert. What do you know of recent events?" he asked his guests, gesturing for a page to bring refreshments.

"In February the Franks . . . I mean the Christians," stumbled Yehezkel, "took the sultan's camp at al-Adiliyah, where we are now, when he rushed to al-Kahira to deal with a treasonous sheikh, and his new camp is at Färiskür, four leagues upstream from here. After that, I heard no more for months because we were mostly at sea or stranded on Crete."

Galatea rolled her eyes. Jacques sat down on the stool behind his scriptorium and invited them to do the same wherever they could, in the relatively spartan tent.

Yehezkel went on. "Then, in Limassol, which is where we met Brother Francesco piccolo, I was forcibly recruited, along with a hundred others, by a Templar knight."

"Well," began Jacques, "I shan't bore you with skirmishes and defections in May and June. Leopold of Austria sailed home, and many nobles were tempted to do the same. To make them stay, Pelagius extended the indulgences granted to those who take up the cross to cover parents, siblings, wives, and children."

A twitch of the nose betrayed the bishop's disapproval, but Jacques knew better than to criticize the papal legate in front of strangers. He waited as his guests gratefully drank some water and then continued,

"A month ago, some Coptic monks came to the camp bearing a Saracen book of prophecies. Pelagius had it translated and announced that it prophesied Damietta's fall to the Christians, as well as events that had already taken place, like the capture of the tower in the Nile. Since then, he has relentlessly assaulted the city, with no results and grave losses."

It was becoming obvious that, had he been alone with Francesco, the bishop would have aired his real opinion of the legate. Francesco thought it would do him good to vent his frustration. "Don't hold anything back, Jacques," he said. "Mother Galatea and Master Ezekiel deserve your trust as much as I do."

Obviously relieved, Jacques continued his tale in a different tone. "Some details convinced Pelagius the book was divinely inspired—maybe it said a Spaniard would lead Christians to victory—so he began to trust its prophecies more than the advice of the king of Jerusalem and the masters of the orders." Here the bishop shared a wry smile. "To be blunt, I think it's the Italians he listens to and then dresses up their advice as prophecy."

The heat in the tent was becoming fierce. Jacques stood up to remove his mantle and then went on. "So he began his senseless attacks. First, Pisans and Venetians assailed the walls from their galleys, banners flying, trumpets blasting, and reed pipes playing. It was quite a spectacle, but the infidels rained down Greek fire on the ladders and forced them to withdraw. Also the sultan, at a signal from the garrison, moved downriver from Färiskür to harass our camp so we wouldn't be able to assist the Italians."

A page stepped in and announced that the bishop of Paris, Pierre de la Chapelle, was asking to see Jacques de Vitry. Galatea reflected that the stifling view of the lagoon from her little window in San Maffio was replaced by the toing and froing of the most important men in Christendom.

"I'm busy with guests now. Ask him to come back in an hour," said the bishop. Francesco started to object, but Jacques, knowing he would, shooed off the page before the friar could open his mouth.

"I have reasons to keep the bishop of Paris waiting, Francesco. Where was I? Oh yes, Pelagius attacked twice more in July, this time from the camp. Encouraged by intelligence of dire conditions in the city, he dragged petraries and ladders near the walls. But before dawn, while the Italian guards were sleeping, eight Saracens sortied and burned the machine nearest the wall, slaying seven of its defenders."

Jacques sipped some water and then winced as his tale came to recent events. "Two days ago, the pompous ass ordered another attack. This time, mamluks forced our knights back and rode in among the Templar tents. Mercifully, Pedro of Montaigue, their new master, and Hermann of Salza, the master of the Teutons, are skilled leaders. They managed to regroup their troops, and in the end, despite heavy losses, the enemy was pushed out of the camp. I believe we lost between a hundred and a hundred and twenty valorous knights. An enormous price to pay for an action that brought us *nothing*."

"Just who *is* this cardinal?" asked Yehezkel, knowing the bishop wouldn't mind his irreverence.

Jacques sighed. "When Innocent made him bishop of Albano, he called him a 'prudent and honorable man.' I was told that a few years ago after Dandolo sacked the Polis, he strutted around there arrogantly, closing churches and jailing Greek monks." The bishop looked forlorn.

After a brief silence, Galatea changed the subject. "Forgive my lowly concerns, Your Excellency, but do you know where in the camp a Cistercian abbess on a roundabout pilgrimage to Jerusalem might find a tent with other sisters?"

"You're the one who must forgive me, Mother Galatea!" said the bishop. "I should have thought that you just stepped off a galley and have more immediate needs than hearing bitter accounts of war."

Galatea realized she sounded frivolous and material, like all women. "Oh no, Your Excellency!" she cried. "On the contrary, the progress of the siege affects the prospects of Brother Francesco's mission, which is the reason I came. I'd much rather be apprised of developments than rush to take some sand out of my shoes!"

Jacques gave her a "so you're not just fetching" look and said, "Mmh . . . the prospects of Brother Francesco's mission . . . I'm reluctant to predict what Pelagius will make of *that*, Mother, but it's safe to assume he won't allow a *woman* to join such an expedition."

Galatea lowered her head in apparent resignation. Yehezkel knew better.

Jacques suddenly looked weary, older than his years. "This is a war, Mother, and there are some forty thousand men in this camp. I'm sure you're not naive, but you must know that though there are nuns here— my page will lead you to their tent shortly—there are at least a hundred prostitutes for every nun, so you can imagine the attitude of these men, especially the . . . lower types, to any woman they come across. *Bref,* Mother Galatea, it would be better if you didn't move around the camp alone."

To be sure, armies and whores have gone together since ancient times, but for some reason *this* siege, perhaps because it was always clear it would be a long one, attracted more harlots than had ever been seen together in a place where the main business was killing. In the large, gray brothel tents as well as in the brocaded ones of the nobles, hundreds of women plied their trade. Shiploads of them came from the beginning of the war: smiling, elegant Latin whores from Venice and France; sensual, avid Greek whores from Cyprus and the Polis; fiery-eyed Armenian whores; veiled and bejeweled Persian whores with their own slaves.

Then there were the madwomen, visionaries at times seized by convulsions, some of them possessed to lie with any man, even if they had no money to pay. One was heard to say she'd done it with Saint George himself. Finally, there were the women from Acre and the crumbling kingdom of Jerusalem. These were widows who had lost everything and came in the hope of finding a protector among the thousands of Christians encamped in the Delta. Yet even the older, more withered ones found dozens of lovers, because nobody thinks of beauty when death is strolling around, and no one wants to wait. Even so, there weren't enough for such an army, and they often had to appeal to the king's guards to escape the soldiers' thuggish ardor and grab a few hours' rest. With time, Galatea felt pity and understanding for each and every one of them, perhaps more than Francesco could.

Of course, also common in the Christian camp was that *other* plague of soldiering life, which found its victims among pages and young squires, even in the tents of nobles. Aillil was unfortunate in this respect, since his blond hair and fair complexion—which still refused to darken after four months of travels—would almost daily make him the object of stupefying propositions to which he would respond with spitting and insults, not because he found them revolting, but because the idea of being taken for a girl infuriated him. But it was at Damietta that the boy, with a Venetian friend, would also lose his virginity in the tent of a Circassian whore.

On leaving the bishop's tent, they found a small crowd gathered outside, patiently waiting for the famous miracle-working friar to emerge. Most were Italians who had heard much about Francesco in their country and were eager to hear him preach, or at least receive his blessing.

Jacques's page was ready to escort Galatea to the tent where a dozen nuns were lodged, while Yehezkel heard of a Jewish merchant somewhere in the camp and intended to look for him, but when they saw a crowd waiting to hear Francesco, force of Cypriot habit and sheer curiosity for what he would say to the soldiers made them both linger.

"There's no point pushing to get closer," Francesco's voice rang out in the space before Jacques's tent. "Those destined to hear my words will hear them even from the back, and those whose fate is not to be touched today won't hear them even if they are a palm from my face."

Since the time of his conversion, Francesco's disposition was against war, even Saint Augustine's "just war" and most of all, with repugnance, against "holy war." Yet he also vowed obedience to the church, which emphatically supported holy war against the infidels. So Francesco steered clear of the subject as much as he could. In Christian lands that wasn't difficult—and even then, Provence was an open sore—but being opposed to war while surrounded by forty thousand men incensed with hatred of all infidels was a different matter.

Even worse, Francesco knew of Jacques's impassioned support for the struggle to regain Jerusalem, so when he saw him emerge from the tent and stand next to the abbess and the rabbi, he knew that anything said against the war would be construed as undermining troop morale and embarrass the bishop. He foresaw such a situation and resolved to avoid preaching to Christian soldiers on his way to the sultan's camp but at the same time trusted the Holy Spirit, as he always did, to guide his tongue if he did speak to cross wearers.

"My brothers," he began, unusually subdued, "fifteen years ago, before my conversion, I was a knight in Assisi and worshipped at the altar of chivalrous virtue, just like you. Then God spoke to me in dreams and visions, and though at first I misheard his message, in the end I understood that he wanted me to follow Christ's instructions to his apostles."

A naughty smile broke through Francesco's meek demeanor. "So now I bring *everyone* the Good News, and if the cardinal will allow me to cross the line between the camps, I intend to bring Christ's Truth to the sultan of the Saracens himself!"

The small crowd was struck dumb, as stupefied as everyone Francesco shared his plan with. As Jacques predicted, the only direct knowledge those soldiers had of Saracens convinced them that if the little friar entered their camp, he would either be killed or enslaved. A bemused buzz rose from the thirty or so cross wearers listening.

Francesco went on. "I'm not a priest, so I'm not allowed to comment Scripture for you, only to preach for the conversion of your hearts, and to do that to Christians ready to die for Christ would not only be superfluous, it would be offensive! So while my brothers and I are among you, we'll engage in our fraternity's other task, which is curing the wounded and comforting the sick." He slipped the hood off his head. "Any one of you can of course assign to us the most menial of tasks, since we are friars minor and submitted to *everyone,* but I beg you not to impose military chores on us, like working on war machines and the like. And above all, I ask you to pray for us, that we may succeed in our mission to open the sultan's eyes to Christ's Holy Light!"

Yehezkel saw the bishop of Acre shake his head, but with a smile.

A cynical warrior, probably a mercenary, provoked Francesco loudly. "Hey, holy man! I'll give you a golden bezant if you can tell me exactly where I can find God!"

Francesco, as usual, needed no time to think of a retort. "And I'll give you *two,* if you can tell me where it would be *impossible* to find Him!"

The crowd laughed heartily, starting to warm to the plucky little friar and his deranged project. Yehezkel turned to Galatea to solicit her thoughts on Francesco's noncommittal little speech, when he saw a crimson-clad figure approaching between the tents, a small retinue behind it. He knew at once it was the cardinal. He touched the bishop's shoulder and pointed to the little procession. Jacques turned at once to welcome the most powerful man in the Christian camp, second in authority only to Honorius III.

Pelagius Galvani wore all his insignia, the edges of his crimson robe embroidered in gold. Having chosen to serve God rather than have to serve men, he was now papal legate a latere, meaning he'd literally emerged from the pope's side, and since at the Lateran Council, four years earlier, Innocent declared that popes were no longer vicars of Peter, but of Christ himself, this entitled Pelagius to behave as if he had emerged from the flank of our Lord.

Walking stiffly next to him was a taller cleric with the typical constipated expression of "right hand of power" figures. The company would later discover he was the cardinal's secretary, Oliver of Cologne, a German preacher whose engineering skills had been crucial in the capture of the tower in the river.

Jacques greeted Pelagius and introduced the new company, heaping praise on the Italian friars. As he told the cardinal everyone's name, impressing Yehezkel with his memory, Pelagius turned his nose up at the friars' mud-encrusted habits, dispensed his only welcoming smile to the Tuscan countess, and reserved his most disapproving stare for the Jew. Turning to Francesco, he said, "Yes, Brother Francesco, I heard of the Rule that Innocent granted you, and of the success your order has met with since. Well, if your famous love of poverty inspired you to come, you'll find yourself at home here, as we're short of *everything*, and you're most welcome to share our wants. But if you came to preach love of martyrdom and fierceness in combating the infidel, then I shall authorize your sermons *myself*!"

Francesco lowered his head, but not his standards. "My mission is to preach the Gospel, your Eminence, not war," he said in a small voice.

The cardinal's lips narrowed to a line drawn by contempt itself. "And you think these cross wearers need *your* words to get closer to Christ?"

"No, your Eminence, but Sultan al-Kamil does. It is to *him*, if you will allow me to reach his camp, that I intend to preach Christ's Gospel."

The cardinal burst out laughing, boisterously imitated by Oliver but somewhat more hesitantly by the other attendants. The crowd, in contrast, was silent.

"NO, Brother Francesco! I will *not* grant you martyrdom, nor will I let such a famous friar become a joke by handing himself over to the enemies of Christ! You and your brothers can stay if you wish, but the only way you'll meet Saracens will be if you borrow the armor of a wounded knight and join a group of warriors in our next engagement. *That* will convince everyone that you love Christ more than *any* sermon!"

Pelagius turned to the bishop of Acre, his expression making it clear that the friar was dismissed. "Jacques, I came to discuss what we learned from the spies we captured this morning. Perhaps we could go into your tent for a moment."

"Of course, your Eminence. And by the way, don't give Francesco's plans too much importance. His enthusiasm is as pure as rain, and it falls where it will . . ."

By now it was early afternoon on the 2nd of August in the Nile delta, and for most Westerners the heat was hard to comprehend. As Pelagius and Oliver entered the bishop's tent, Galatea tried to comfort Francesco, telling him he should have expected the cardinal to oppose his plan. After all, they'd heard enough about him from the bishop. "The simple fact," she concluded, "is that all men would be tyrants if they could!"

Francesco was again tempted to look her in the eyes. His gaze rose to her neck before he stopped.

Soon they all parted ways and went to look for a tent in which to set down their things and refresh themselves, knowing it would be some time, if at all, before Francesco won his way with Pelagius.

✡ ✠ ✡ ✠

Like many new arrivals, the young squire ignored the warnings about the sun and sweated all day, dragging crates and pitching tents. At Vespers, he leaned against a cart and asked for water. His comrade answered, "When I have a moment to spare, I'll bring you some." An hour later, the youngster was still sitting there and when someone took his hand, it was as cold as steel.

Evening fell with the usual, unsettling abruptness. The faint light of torches spread hesitantly through the stifling humidity in the camp, which smelled of smoke and roasting meat. Here and there in the sea of silent gray tents, a small band of knights and footmen sat around a fire in the twilight. Before them a jester juggled wooden balls or told obscene jokes amid muted, guttural laughs.

Then night fell. From a few tents the sound of soldiers singing, vielles playing, and whores laughing could be heard, softened by the fog. Homesickness inspired the singing, and choirs of popular songs—here Flemish, there Italian—rose from the camp, at times so vibrant they caused alarm among the sentinels on the besieged city's walls.

The newcomers noticed the smell as darkness fell. It didn't come from the latrines, nor from the river. Heavy, sweet, sickening; it was everywhere in the camp and made some retch. Soon they understood that the breeze, which had been blowing the smell of the decaying corpses in the besieged city out to sea, dropped with the sunset, and the smell of death would be with them until dawn.

They were so exhausted they felt sure that despite the countless novelties, the famous men they had encountered and the general war fever, they would fall asleep the moment they laid their heads down. But what heat, smell, and flies couldn't accomplish, the memory of the tortured spies did for each of them. They lay awake in the night, the clinking of cups and blaring of songs mingling with the screams of the Saracens etched in their minds.

The camp that night was immersed in a thick, humid mist. The sentinels on Damietta's ramparts kept watch, but all they could see was a vast, whitish fogbank from which only the tips of the tallest tents poked out, their pennants sagging like so many wilted flowers.

CHAPTER 19

YOM REVI'I

The Fourth Day

OUTSIDE DAMIETTA, 10TH AUGUST 1219

The new company had been in the camp for a week. Yehezkel and Aillil slept in the Templar section and Galatea in the tent called the nunnery, while the friars, having refused the bishop's offer of a plain, gray mendicants tent, slept in the open or where someone offered them a corner of his quarters.

The Cypriot and Frankish knights discovered how hard it is to pitch a tent in sand, got used to the stench from the latrines, and learned to save water and shelter from the sun, at all times. Like everyone else, they already hated the indifferent Egyptian sun that seemed to rise mercilessly behind the same dune each morning, bringing nothing but more deaths. Even the more sensitive souls grew used to the funerals that added new crosses to the camp cemetery every dawn. Yes, they knew that the soul of a man who took the cross was saved even if he died of the fever, but they all thought that dying while attacking the sultan's camp would surely profit the cause of the Lord much more than dying among spittle and boils.

From the day after their arrival, Aillil started asking everyone if they had seen or heard of Arnald Arifat of Montréal. Being in the Templar section of the camp, he soon found a knight who knew his father had entered the order four months earlier, in Provence, and was attached to one of the platoons patrolling pilgrim routes in Syria. Aillil was disappointed, but soon the excitement of life in the camp, and the knowledge that Rav Yehezkel was headed to Jerusalem anyway, made him temporarily forget the reason he embarked for Outremer.

That dawn, the horses in the nearby stable tent woke Aillil before first light. He heard distant sounds of trumpets and sentinels calling out to each other as the camp slowly came alive. He jumped up from his pallet, shot a glance at a still snoring Rav Yehezkel, and ran out, without even washing his face, to meet the other boys at the usual place on the western edge of the camp.

He'd fallen in with Marco, a Venetian boy, and two other teenagers in the camp with the ease typical of their age. For the boys, war in the desert was a huge, fantastic game—while adults, despite endless oaths and songs in the weeks before landfall, soon lost their enthusiasm and became glum.

A different handful of boys—some squiring their fathers, most of them the sons of prostitutes—ran to the sea each dawn to bring back news of ship sightings. If the masts flew crosses, it meant reinforcements; if they flew Italian ensigns, it meant victuals—so the boys who'd learned to recognize pennants relished being the first to bring the good news to camp. Besides, splashing around in the warm Mediterranean was so irresistible that when their turn came, they didn't walk the three leagues to the sea, they ran.

"I am lucky to find kids here," thought Aillil as he ran. "Adults at war don't look at me."

They'd been running for half an hour, the heat still bearable as a delightful breeze blew through their shirts, when the sea appeared behind the crest of a dune. The sun was still low behind them, and the water wasn't yet the sparkling, brilliant blue that Aillil loved, but it was

smooth and transparent as glass, and the four boys ran into it, screaming in pure joy.

Around them, the day's activities stirred. Since the Christian armies
had arrived, palm trees had disappeared, both on the seashore and along
the Nile near Damietta, to replace the siege engines destroyed by Greek
fire from the city's ramparts. This was why the riverbank seemed so
bare to the newcomers who had witnessed the capture of the spies.
Along that stretch of the Nile's eastern branch, only papyrus reeds were
left, just as sprawling bushes of prickly pear cactus were the only things
growing on the shore where the boys were swimming.

When the boys tired of water games and had their fill of ripe prickly
pears—in August they were the color of local sunsets and sweeter than
honey—they gathered news of the morning's arrivals, donned the cloth
caps they'd brought against the sun, and ambled back to camp, the heat
already too intense to even think of running.

When he wasn't playing with new friends—which meant "borrowing"
real weapons to stage mock tournaments—or speaking with soldiers
willing to make an effort to understand him, Aillil divided his time
between his mentors. The first, of course, was Rav Yehezkel, who spent
the days in the tents of his patients, dividing his time, ointments, and
herbs between nobles, knights, and squires, strictly in that order.

Most patients bore siege wounds—embedded arrowheads and Greek
fire burns—but others suffered from desert fever, a wartime plague that
caused red spots, bloody noses, diarrhea, and delirium, usually killing
its victims in a couple of weeks. Yehezkel had a measure of success with
this fever, bringing some knights back from the final stage by forcing
them to constantly swallow big ladles of water.

Aillil's second mentor—his preferred choice—was Galatea. He
would wait for her to emerge from the "nunnery" and accompany
her on rounds of the camp, the only escort she would accept to show
compliance with the bishop's advice. The abbess did, mostly, keep her
distance from the soldiery, more from fear of their conversation than

of lecherous attentions, and usually either followed Francesco and the friars or spent her time with the camp prostitutes, in the tent where they slept or took respite from their ordeals. There, too, Aillil would sit at her side, straining to hear what the prostitutes were confiding to her.

By this time, Aillil had visited his musk-scented Circassian whore twice, the first time with Marco, the second by himself. The second time, she'd refused his coins with a smile that made him giddy. He was nearly fourteen and grew up listening to troubadours sing about the true love of their lives, but only after encountering the mystery of a woman's body did he understand all the talk of love he'd heard most of his life. That morning, a Venetian woman about the same age as the abbess was saying to her, "I survive on next to nothing, Mother, just so I can say 'no' to the men who don't stir something in my chest. You're a nun, so you probably don't know what I speak of . . ."

"On the contrary," said Galatea with a smile. "I'm a nun, but not an oblate. I was a widow when I took my vows, and I know *exactly* what you mean. Men may all have been created in God's image, but there's no denying that some of them, well . . . came out better!"

The prostitute made a face. "*All* men created in God's image? Don't make me laugh, Mother! There are men here who can't get it up if they don't smell fear, and it must be *real* fear, not faked! Are *those* in God's image, too?"

Galatea thought of Lupo and said nothing. Aillil looked puzzled. Later, he would think that the words of that prostitute explained why women everywhere were so often violated, but when he heard them in that tent, they made no sense to him.

On arriving in the Templar camp, Aillil had the pleasant surprise of finding Iñigo Sanchez and André de Rosson among the knights at the siege. After hearing how they'd survived the mamluk raid of the last day in July, the boy finally found, in the subject of women, something to talk about with the Spanish knight besides arms and blood. The next time they met, he asked, his delivery even more halting than usual,

"What . . . what is the difference between doing it with a prostitute and doing it with one's true love?"

Iñigo laughed. "I always knew you were a smart one, Aillil! This business of women is strange indeed. Even if you've had hundreds, one comes along, gets into your gut, and there's no way to get her out!"

Aillil looked a little worried at the prospect. "So . . . so what can one do?"

"Mmhh . . ." Iñigo pretended to mull it over. "Die, I think. Yes, that's it. I'm pretty sure that if you die, your love pains just go away!" he guffawed.

Aillil looked at his friend and somehow knew that, though said in jest, the answer was the truth. "Do you have a woman at home?"

"*One*? I'm chased by a pack of bitches the moment I set foot in Castille, my boy!"

"What about André?" asked Aillil. "Is he married?"

"Who, *Brother* André? The man couldn't fornicate if you locked him up in a barrel with three sluts! Sometimes I wonder if he is . . . you know, of the *other* kind! But you won't repeat that, will you, boy?"

Aillil's third and most recent mentor was Francesco of Assisi. The little friar kept his promise not to preach to the soldiers. Instead, the friars made themselves useful tending the wounded. His quirky, polyglot way of raising a footman's morale soon endeared him to the whole camp. The friars, whose shabby tunics and talk of love reminded Aillil of every Cathar perfectus he met as a child, moved around the camp looking for the losers, those who for one reason or another had fallen through the web of wartime solidarity that, coupled with discipline, holds an army together.

One day, Aillil saw Francesco patiently listen to the story of an Italian squire who had lost everything. Like many, he'd gone through the money from home in a few weeks and slowly abandoned all scruples to survive. He borrowed money he couldn't return and moved to another section of the camp; he even sold sick horses meant for butchering as healthy mounts.

Francesco sensed that the young man was no thief and tried to correct his downward spiral. "You must seek service with a knight who will pay for your keep," he said. "But the important thing, Jacopo, is to turn your heart around and stop ruining your good name. Do your *utmost* to repay those you swindled. Once you have sincerely repented, the Almighty will help you."

"But what will I do until the Almighty decides to help me?" whined Jacopo.

Francesco smiled. "He will also help you to wait until He helps you."

Desperate as he was, Jacopo couldn't help laughing.

✡ ✠ ✡ ✠

OUTSIDE DAMIFTTA, 20TH OF AUGUST

Occasionally, in that scorching August in the delta, Aillil's three mentors would spend time together. One day they were all standing on a rickety pier jutting out over the Nile when Francesco asked Yehezkel to teach him the blessing Mother Galatea told him about, the one with which he'd chased away the demons on the tareta taking them to Cyprus.

"I'll gladly teach you the verses, Brother Francesco," said Yehezkel. "They come from what you call the Book of Numbers and were the words with which Aaron the high priest blessed the Israelites in the Sinai desert. Not that far from here, come to think of it." Francesco laughed.

Galatea thought, "If Brother Francesco pronounced that blessing, it would probably bring peace to the *entire* world!"

Yehezkel smiled. "Jewish Law actually prohibits you—and even me—from pronouncing this blessing, for we are not Cohanim, priests, but so be it. First, you'll have to learn the proper position to assume."

Francesco suddenly looked serious. "Position?"

"Your head should be covered by a prayer shawl, but the point is that none should look at your hands while you are pronouncing the blessing, so any cloth will do just fine."

In one of his prankish impulses, Francesco wrenched the blue shawl from Yehezkel's shoulders and covered his head and arms with it, but not his hands. Yehezkel smiled and continued, "Now raise both arms and keep them stretched out before you, covered by the shawl. Split the fingers of both hands in the middle, so there is a V separating two pairs of fingers." He helped him assume the pose. Arms raised, the shawl over them, Francesco stumbled to his right and faced Galatea.

All of a sudden, she realized she was looking at her vision in Torcello, before the hermit's prophecy, and everything fell into place. She had glimpsed Brother Francesco reciting the Priestly Blessing on the Nile bank, but the blue had been that of Christ's mantle. Francesco was the returning Christ! Her hand flew to her mouth, overwhelmed by the revelation, but Yehezkel was already going on.

"Now repeat after me. I'll say the Latin meaning, too, but you just try to pronounce the Hebrew. Yevaréchecha Ha-Shem Ve-Yishmerécha, which means May the Lord bless you and safeguard you."

The ease with which Francesco pronounced the Hebrew words surprised everyone.

"Ya'er Ha-Shem Panav Elecha, Ve-Yichunéka," continued Yehezkel, "which means May the Lord shine his countenance on you and be gracious to you."

Francesco's emotion grew as he repeated the Hebrew phrase.

"Yisah Ha-Shem Panav Elecha, Ve-Yasem Lechà Shalòm—May the Lord turn his countenance toward you and give you peace!" concluded Yehezkel.

Francesco pronounced the end of the blessing and then took off the shawl and repeated the last three words in a tone of shock and awe. "Ve-Yasem Lechà Shalòm means 'and give you peace'? I can't believe it! God once whispered those very words in my head and told me they were to be our future greeting, and now I find they're a blessing in the Old

Testament! I love my ignorance dearly, Master Ezekiel, but sometimes I can imagine what a sublime pleasure it must be to truly understand the role of *words* in God's plan."

Galatea blurted out, "Oh, Brother Francesco, if only you knew! Master Ezekiel has been teaching me a little Kabbalah . . . the light that shines from the twenty-two Hebrew letters is . . . it's the light of my visions!"

At once, she realized she'd spoken like a hapless victim of the Jew's assaults on her faith. Francesco smiled and said, never looking her in the eyes, "Don't worry, Mother Galatea. I don't know what Kabbalah is, but if it is akin to what Sufis practice, I'm all for learning from heretics and infidels. *D'ailleurs,* I had my own Sufi teacher, as I told you."

Galatea was first relieved and then emboldened. She turned to Yehezkel. "Master Ezekiel, won't you show Brother Francesco piccolo two Hebrew words with truths in them, like the ones you showed me on the tareta? And please, choose two jewels that I have yet to see."

Yehezkel lowered his head and caressed his beard for a while as he thought of the right examples. "You should know, Brother Francesco," he finally began, "that all Hebrew words are built from a root of three consonants. I won't go into details—Mother Galatea already understands some of the principles—but here is an example that I trust will convince you that Hebrew is not like any other language: the word for charity is tzedakah, and its three-letter root is tzedek, which means . . . justice!"

Francesco looked up at the rabbi with childish glee, a smile spreading on his weathered face.

Yehezkel said, "If the root of charity is justice, the Holy Tongue is saying that when we give to the poor, we are in fact redressing an injustice. The very *word* tells us that the money isn't really our own."

"A tongue that teaches ethics . . . that's nothing less than a miracle!" mumbled Francesco. "I beg you, Master Ezekiel, show me the second jewel."

Yehezkel glowed with pride as he sought out the best word for his other jewel and then said, "Latin expresses the concept of responsibility by fusing the words 'response' and 'ability.' Clearly, for the fathers of the Latin tongue, responsibility is the capacity to answer for what we say or do. Fair enough, but in Hebrew, responsibilty is *achraiyut,* whose three-letter root is *acher,* which means 'other.' So for the Father of the Hebrew tongue, the Creator of Heaven and Earth, responsibilty is in effect 'other-ability,' the capacity to stand in the other person's shoes."

Francesco breathed deeply, eyes closed, and said, "Master Ezekiel, your knowledge of letters, words, and tongues is . . . let me ask you a brash question: if God overcomes the cardinal's hostility to my mission, would you agree to accompany me to the sultan's tent and translate my words?"

Galatea sucked in a breath. Yehezkel silently thanked the powers above and said, "I'd be honored, Brother Francesco piccolo. Simply honored. As for the cardinal's hostility, I've given it some thought, and I may have come up with a way to . . . help God overcome it."

"Oh, please share your thoughts," said Francesco eagerly.

"Well, as your interpreter, I would get to speak to Saracen officials in the sultan's camp. I could find out things that Pelagius is dying to know, like what reinforcements the sultan can count on, and *when.*"

Francesco's hands shot out as if to reject what he was hearing. Then, incredulous, he whispered, "You, a Jew, would *spy* on the Saracens and report back to a Christian *cardinal*?"

"No, no, Brother Francesco piccolo!" laughed Yehezkel. "That's just what I would say to Pelagius to convince him to let us go! And so he won't react like you just did, I'll ask, in exchange, for an honorable discharge from my duties here." He paused. "But I wouldn't be coming back. I was thinking that if you do . . . return, you could tell Pelagius I was held back by the sultan. After all, the Saracens need physicians as much as the Christians do, and being born in Egypt makes me his subject."

"Brilliant, simply brilliant!" exclaimed Francesco. "I knew that if you'd 'given it some thought,' Master Ezekiel, a solution could not be far."

"Maybe," smiled Yehezkel, "but don't underestimate the cardinal's, ehm . . . *disesteem* for both of us."

Later that day, the new company waited outside the cardinal's tent as Yehezkel's pessimism was confirmed, and he failed to obtain a mandate to spy on the sultan.

Six months earlier, after losing his first encampment, al-Kamil offered to return Jerusalem and the coastal strip to the Christians if they removed their infidel presence from Egypt, but Pelagius refused.

True, the sultan had razed Jerusalem's walls before making the offer, yet many in the Christian camp—the king of Jerusalem, understandably, more than others—seethed over the cardinal's rejection of what was, after all, the campaign's main objective.

All this made the information Yehezkel was offering to procure even more important to the Christian leader, but Pelagius was sure Damietta was on the point of falling—which was why he was reluctant to attack the sultan's camp—just as he was sure that what Francesco of Assisi really sought was martyrdom. So he heard out the rabbi, said he would think about it, and dismissed him. When Yehezkel emerged from the tent, the company immediately knew from his expression that Pelagius hadn't budged.

In the following days, Francesco became wrapped in gloom. Pietro told Galatea in worried tones that he talked of leaving the camp at night, alone, and walking south until Saracen sentinels apprehended him. To the rabbi, Francesco said the only thing he could do was fast and entreat God to let some light into the cardinal's heart.

✡ ✠ ✡ ✠

OUTSIDE DAMIETTA, 28TH OF AUGUST

It was noon, and Francesco had been weeping for a day, a night, and half a day.

Tears silently flooded his face as he sat on the hard-packed sand in a corner of Jacques de Vitry's tent. His brothers had seen him like this before and knew that only prayer could give him the strength to repel the demons darkening his mind. He hadn't eaten or drunk in two days and ignored all attempts by friars and bishop to grab a corner of his soul and heave him out of this melancholia.

That afternoon, Brother Illuminato found Master Ezekiel and reported on the father's condition. The rabbi rushed over to the bishop's tent. He went in, greeted Jacques, and knelt beside Francesco.

"What's come over you, Brother Francesco? You know how much God loves *joy* better than anyone I've met! What shook your confidence in his Good News, my brother?"

On hearing the rabbi's voice, Francesco raised his head. "Oh, Master Ezekiel!" he sobbed. "Good News? I only see bad news everywhere. For whom did God create his blessed Eternity? Who will adore him when the earth is empty of souls and hell brims with the damned? Can you tell me that?"

"What chased every shred of hope from your heart?"

"I had a . . . a vision, Master Ezekiel," stammered Francesco. "The worst in my life. You know Pelagius is going to attack the sultan tomorrow . . . well, two days ago I saw the outcome. They *must not* fight tomorrow! It was terrible . . . there were bloated bodies everywhere." He burst out in tears again.

Since refusing Yehezkel's suggestion a week earlier, Pelagius had yielded to an ill-advised plan to attack the sultan. Realizing that the growing complaints could turn into open rebellion, he'd given in to Frankish and German nobles, defying the Italians, and divided the army into three units: one to guard the camp, one to man the ships, and a third, the largest, to march on al-Kamil's camp at Färiskür.

Yehezkel stepped aside with Brother Illuminato and whispered to him, "If he tells the leaders of his premonition, they'll lock him up to protect the morale of the troops. If he *really* wants to save knights and soldiers from the death he has seen, he'll have to warn them himself!"

Brother Illuminato reflected and then knelt beside Francesco and said, "Father, don't give too much importance to the judgment of men. It wouldn't be the first time they call you crazy, would it? Do what your conscience tells you, and fear God, rather than men!"

Francesco gazed at his unassuming young brother, and in an instant, before their eyes, horror before a prophetic vision turned into something between missionary zeal and the rush for water when a house is on fire. Francesco jumped up, wiped the tears off with his sleeve, and planted a kiss on Brother Illuminato's tonsure. Then he bowed his head to Yehezkel and the bishop and rushed out of the tent.

Running alone through the camp, he found an open space amid the chaotic preparations for the next day's battle and called out for the men to stop and listen. Maybe it was the work he'd done in the month he'd been there, or maybe it was the need for saintly words before facing death, but many stopped, and more ran over from other quarters, shouting, "Francesco! It's Francesco!"

When the rest of the company caught up with him, Francesco was declaring feverishly, "*Don't* fight tomorrow! There are auspicious days and inauspicious days! You *cannot* oppose God's will! Obstinacy brings disaster! By counting only on your own forces, you forfeit heavenly help! If you seek victory, you must only do battle when the attack is divinely ordained!"

The mostly Italian soldiers started to heap scorn on the jinxing friar. They knew that marching orders had already been given—so most of them, as kindly as they could, urged him to shut up.

Francesco knew a knight's faith, knew they were gifting their lives to their Supreme Lord, and became desperate. If he couldn't convince them, he must try to frighten them. "Listen, brothers! I had a revelation of the defeat that awaits our forces if we fight tomorrow! This will cost the lives of thousands! I beg you, speak to your leaders, ask them to delay the attack, if only by a day!"

Overwhelmed by his vision of death, Francesco began weeping again. The soldiers, torn between pity and embarrassment, walked away. Undeterred, the friar ran to another point in the camp, an increasingly worried company on his heels, and began to shout his warning again.

Before long Yehezkel and Galatea concluded that if they didn't get Jacques to stop him, soon the cardinal would. At dusk, the bishop's personal guard gently but firmly accompanied Francesco to Jacques's tent. The bishop begged him to stay in his tent for the night. Francesco reluctantly obeyed. The company sat on the ground around him in a corner of the tent, hoping to distract him from despair.

News of what Francesco was preaching on the eve of a battle reached Pelagius, and an hour later Oliver of Cologne was asking to speak with Jacques. Oliver was a lanky fifty-year-old cleric, only slightly less opinionated than his master. He asked to speak with the Italian friar, more out of curiosity at the words of ill omen than anything else, but when he saw the Jew and the abbess sitting among the friars, he became cagey. "I hear you object to the day our cardinal has chosen for the attack," he said to Francesco, "but not, surely, to the fact that the Army of Christ is going into battle against the infidels!"

"As I already told the cardinal, Master Oliver, I believe in preaching to the infidels, rather than killing them," said Francesco in a quiet voice.

"I believe in that, too, Francino," said Jacques, "I tried to preach to some in Acre. The problem is that Mohammedans' faith is so *fierce* that preaching Christ to them is an infallible way to win martyrdom. It has become like those Roman aqueducts that suicides seek out to jump from."

Oliver bluntly pursued the friar. "Cardinal Pelagius believes you're such a case, Brother Francesco. Tell me, what did the soldiers say when you told them not to fight tomorrow, eh?"

Francesco answered, "A famous Roman, I forget which one, once said, 'Dulce bellum inexpertis.'"*

"Wrong again, friar! War is to men what motherhood is to women!"

---

*"War is delightful to those who have no experience of it."

Galatea spoke for the first time, something the German preacher hadn't expected. "Oh no, Master Oliver, men love war because it allows them to look serious," she said drily. "They love it because it's the *one* thing that stops women laughing at them."

Francesco chuckled openly. Oliver looked startled to see Yehezkel and Jacques joining in.

The bishop turned to Yehezkel. "Rabbi, you can speak freely in this tent. Please tell us what Jewish wisdom teaches on the question of martyrdom—or, as I believe you call it, Sanctifying the Name."

"I'm not sure the answer will be to your liking, Your Excellency . . ."

"Give it to us anyway, *mon brave Rabbin,* and leave it to us to decide," said the bishop sternly.

"Well, when an Almohadi tyrant was forcing Jews in Fez to accept Islam some fifty years ago, Moshe ben Maimon the Egyptian, light of Judaism and my first teacher, may his memory be a blessing, ruled that Mohammedans are 'believers in the one and only God, who accept many precepts of the Torah and recoil from worshipping images. A Jew should not give up his life so as not to accept Mohammed. He should instead keep the Torah in secret.'"

Oliver said coldly, "I admire your tact in choosing the example, Master Ezekiel, but your teacher's words imply that if the alternative were Christian baptism, then a Jew should hurry out of this vale of tears and collect his reward for his fidelity to Yhavhè. Is that not so?"

Yehezkel lowered his head. Francesco, Jacques, and Galatea were listening intently. "In effect, too many things in the Christian faith coincide with what we call 'idolatry,' sir. If, in order to stay alive, a Jew must bow before images of men and women, drink blood and affirm the existence of a Triple Divinity, it would be better for him to proclaim the Sanctity of God's Name."

His voice was trembling, but he had not raised it. He continued before the speechless Christians. "But I'm a medicus who believes in a merciful God, one who *never* demands of humans to sacrifice their lives. Never, for any reason. Our Father Abraham taught us that. Therefore I don't condemn those who are converted by force, only those who freely abjure their faith."

A silence followed these blasphemous words. Galatea thought he may have called *her* a pagan, but at least he had the guts to do the same to three famous and powerful Christians.

"Are we going to listen to this obstinate Jew deny and insult revealed Truth?" hissed Oliver.

Francesco found a dig at the German's pompous indignation too hard to resist. "My brothers," he said, "have you noticed how martyrs, for *us,* are those who go out to convert the heathen, while *he* speaks of the martyrdom of the converted?"

"That is the natural order of things, my good friar," said Oliver.

"No, Oliver," said Jacques. "Francesco, in his 'divine folly,' put his finger on something that betrays the decay in our faith. It's been almost a thousand years since Christians were martyred *not* while preaching their faith to others, but for refusing to *abandon theirs.*"

"A thousand years," said Oliver, "which proved Christ is the *only* Truth, Jacques, so how could anyone be forced to abjure him? Surely you don't think this a mere battle between men, with no role for God?" He turned to Yehezkel with a haughty smile. "On one hand I pity your blindness, my poor rabbi." The smile veered to a sneer. "On the other, I resent the impunity an eternal curse bestows on your stiff-necked race. If a Christian pronounced words less offensive than yours, we'd send him to Europe on the spot, into the arms of Brother Domingo, to be tried for blasphemy, heresy, and I know not what else. Wouldn't we, my good bishop?" His Teutonic laugh echoed through the tent.

"I met your Domingo once," said Yehezkel matter-of-factly. "Almost exactly ten years ago, when he wasn't yet the pope's favorite monk."

Mocking Domingo in such company was a boyish mistake. Luckily, Jacques noted how generous the rabbi was with his opinions and swiftly changed the subject, before a good medicus would be lost to the cause for slandering Domingo of Guzman. "I presume, Master Ezekiel, that the Jews in Fez wanted to know if they should follow the example of their brethren along the Rhine, seventy-five years earlier, many of whom took their own lives not to be baptized by the mobs headed to Jerusalem. Is that not so, Rabbi?"

With about the same restraint of a moth diving into a torch, Yehezkel answered, "Yes, Your Excellency, and wasn't it that Sanctification of the Name by hundreds of Jews that sparked Christian jealousy and provoked the recent thirst for martyrdom among you?"

Another silence followed. Again Francesco broke it, but this time his tone was tinged with outrage at the rabbi's provocation. "Do you really think Christianity lacks martyrs to prove the purity of its faith, Master Ezekiel? Are you implying that anyone in this tent would hesitate to give his life in testimony of Jesus Christ?"

"No, Brother Francesco, I know your faith is as strong as ours. What I meant was that what befell the Jews of Germany a century ago was like a taunt, like daring Christians to show the same steadfastness."

Francesco's outrage turned to puzzled curiosity, but Oliver's grew to red heat.

"Tell me something, Rabbi," Oliver hissed, "and this is pure reason now, which I'm told Jews love. Before the evidence of Christianity's success, before the powerless wandering of the Jews in these ten centuries, shouldn't you be asking yourselves some questions? Saint Augustine said that your curse will last until the return of your Victim. So tell me, how do *you* explain having become like Cain?"

Yehezkel found the comparison deeply offensive, which was the German's intent. "We *know* the meaning of our exile, Master Oliver," he said, "and faithfully wait for the Messiah to deliver us from it. We pray for a more concrete redemption than anything Jesus ever offered. Christianity never taught anything but resignation. It is a religion of night, and death, a moon shining on the tombs of the ancient peoples that Rome destroyed. Its mission is a kind of Judaism for pagans and will finish on the day Israel, the Sun, wakes up to new life . . ." Yehezkel was panting. His whole life since leaving Egypt was in his next reckless words. He had no choice but to finish what he'd begun.

"You torture us, you burn us alive, and then run into your churches to be moved to tears singing the psalms you stole from us! How could the usurper of a revelation not yearn for the death of its legitimate owners? Were it not for the promise the God of Israel made to us, you would have slain every one of us long ago. I'll tell you what, *Master* Oliver: you go your idolatrous way and we'll go our way, and when Judgment Day comes, which we both believe in, God will be obliged, by his own promise, to reveal which one of us was right!"

Oliver's face was flushed, and if he'd had a weapon, he would have drawn it. "Watch your tongue, Jew, or we'll make do with less famous physicians!" Then he repressed his anger and laughed. "Ha! To me, it rather looks like you're the one, not Brother Francesco, seeking martyrdom in Damietta, so you can enter Jewish legends as Rabbi Ezekiel the Egyptian, the only Jew to forfeit his life while saving those of wounded Milites Christi! Ha, ha!"

Yehezkel stood straighter, as if ready to forfeit his life for the God of Israel there and then. Jacques wondered why this wise and well-read Jew was so intent on provoking the German cleric. He decided the night before a battle was no time for such confrontations. His bishopry in Acre taught him to mediate, when necessary, between the faiths.

"Oliver, I beg you, don't let the quarrel escalate," he said, "for the sake of the quiet contemplation that should precede a battle on behalf of the Lord. Master Ezekiel's claim that we 'stole' King David's psalms from the Jews pains me, so in all humility, I suggest we all sing the verse about the 'tents of the righteous' before we part, Jew and Christians together, in a gesture of reconciliation."

"On one condition!" spat Oliver. "That the Jew sing the psalm in *Latin,* like we will. The *new* owners of those songs, the Verus Israel, now sing them in Latin—and so will the rabbi!"

Yehezkel examined the challenge from a halachic point of view. "First," he thought, "my faith is not in danger. Second, the psalm in Latin is a meaningless tongue twister. And third, if I refuse to sing it in Latin, the goy will put me in irons and send me to Italy."

He nodded to Jacques, without looking at the German. At a signal from the bishop, everyone in the tent, except Aillil, intoned the fifteenth verse of Psalm 118:

"Vox iubilationis et salutis in tabernaculis iustorum."*

Francesco wept openly as he sang of the joy in the tent. His brothers, who knew how unfailing his premonitions were, had to make an effort not to weep with him over the coming defeat.

The auspicious singing done, Oliver took his leave with a foolishly premature statement, "Why is this the tent of the righteous? Because there can be no doubt that God is on our side!"

Jacques smiled. "Most important is not that God be on our side, Oliver, but that we make sure to be on His . . ."

Yehezkel decided to stay after Oliver left the tent, so he could thank the bishop. "I'm grateful for your indulgence, Your Excellency. I don't know what came over me. I dare not think what my words would have caused, had Oliver's master been present."

Jacques laughed. "Yes, that would have been worth watching! Still, I think Pelagius would have been less angry with a Jew calling him a pagan than with a Christian preacher predicting defeat in his personal war against the sultan!" he said, darting a glance at Francesco.

Then Galatea kissed his ring, Yehezkel and Aillil bowed their heads, and the three left the tent.

✡ ⸮ ✡ ⸮

Later that night, King John of Jerusalem toured the camp, as was the custom on the eve of battle.

Every tent had a bivouac burning before it, and the sudden flicker of flames revealed faces straining to see the king: wizened old veterans, bearded knights, pimply adolescents—all shining with the joy of a long-awaited feast. His guard sounded their trumpets when he

---

*Shouts of joy and salvation resound in the tents of the righteous.

entered a section of the camp, and soldiers came running to hear and see the only king to have so far graced that war with his presence.

John of Brienne, a brave and generous king, was sixty-four that summer, his long white beard like that of a saintly hermit. He seemed to be everywhere that night and spoke with everyone who addressed him, in the accessible tones of one of their comrades. Everywhere he went he repeated his plea that every cross wearer do his duty in the morning, not for the love of their king, but for the love of God.

The soldiers didn't know it, but King John was ill. The cause of his sickness wasn't known, but on the 31st of July he'd been under the walls and been hit by Greek fire. His guard put the flames out right away, but a combination of age and the effects of the burns weakened the old warrior. Pages ran into his tent all day bringing hot stones, hot wine, bits of wood to clean his teeth. He kept his strength by drinking the blood of birds, he only accepted the blood of hawks and buzzards, so the birds had to be brought from Acre and their throats slit in the camp.

In those days, the king was the one force capable of uniting riotous barons and being a model for his people. He was the only one who would never lie to them, the only one they could always trust. If a king betrayed his soldiers, as Philip of France had done by leaving Acre before Coeur de Lion, the sky was sure to fall on their heads. English knights had mercilessly mocked the Franks: "Where is your King, then?"

Outside Damietta, John was admired for his courage, while absent kings were slandered, whether for departing early, like Andrew II of Hungary, or for not showing up at all, like young Henry III of England or Emperor Frederick II. King John spoke with feeling. "*Now* is the time to prove that Christ is the True God and Mahomet a piece of rotting straw! Through your efforts, Jerusalem shall be retaken and the infidels chased from the Holy Land once and for all! And what of your comrades, your friends who died in this year-long siege? Must not their blood be avenged? Let no one in the future dare suggest that we didn't repay that debt of honor! For every Christian who died in this cursed, soggy land, we shall send tens—nay, *hundreds* of infidels to hell!"

After the king left, two inebriated footmen talked by the fire.

"What did you *say*? One-eyed Bohemond of Antioch, now he's married to a Lusignan, could attack the king's forces in Acre while he's here? Pfff, the very idea of Bohemond attacking the king! A rabbit might as well attack a bear!"

"Still, the king is old," slurred the other. "What if he dies tomorrow? I've never lived through a king's death, but everyone knows it can bring trouble, sometimes even war . . ."

"Bring war? This is *already* a war, you dunce!" snapped the first footman.

CHAPTER 20

VE-OF YEOFEF

And Let Birds Fly

FIVE LEAGUES SOUTHWEST OF DAMIETTA, 29TH AUGUST 1219

All eyes were fixed on the helms and brightly colored shields shining in the sun. High-pitched cries rose everywhere as thousands of fists shook threats at the infidels. It was the glorious, once-in-a-lifetime spectacle of the advancing Army of Christ.

Above the troops, flying standards heralded nobility on the march, some banners so heavy that special, gigantic workhorses were brought to bear them—England's leopards, France's fleurs-de-lis, the Holy Roman Empire's two-headed eagle, and behind them the coats of arms of all the great European houses, dozens of flags with vertical, horizontal, and oblique bands of all colors. At the head of the army, the count of Jaffa, the baron of Hebron, and the prince of Galilee flanked King John of Brienne. Over their heads, above all other banners, flew Jerusalem's powerful five silver crosses—also the emblem of the Lusignans which would have accompanied the King of Cyprus had he not been but an infant.

The king's white Arab steed, walked by his squire, sniffed the air nervously, exchanging whinnies with a cadet's horse. It trotted in full battle armor, heavy engraved iron plates covering its flanks and a strapped-down iron mask over its head. The king wore a hauberk of the finest chain mail, which reached below his knees but was split up to his waist, both in front and behind, to ease riding. His helm was not a vain, royal iron cylinder, just a simple pointed cap, but so shiny one couldn't look straight at it.

After reaching its lowest point a week earlier, the Nile had begun the buildup to September's floods, overflowing its banks for the first time the day before. Twenty-thousand men marched in waterlogged sand under their lords' colors. Horses slipped in the sludge, their hooves sinking in mud to the fetlocks, spraying armors and shields. The heat was unbearable, the sun beating on helms and hauberks.

Their shirts and bodies soaked in sweat, skin one big blister, blood pulsing in their ears, the men shouted their war cry—"Hyerusalem et Sancta Crux!"—at the top of their voices, but it could hardly be heard over the clinking of armor and weapons, the shouts of squires, and the sucking of hooves pulled from the mud. The din was such that had God thundered, no one would have heard Him.

In al-Kamil's army they faced a formidable enemy. Salah ad-Din, conqueror of Jerusalem, founder of the Ayyubid Dynasty and uncle of the present sultan, formed and trained his army in Egypt back when he thought that to unify Egypt and Syria he'd have to fight Nur ad-Din, the last Zengid sultan. But his lord died, and within ten years Damascus was his.

The core of Salah ad-Din's force was the Turkish and Kurdish cavalries—the Arab regiments, mostly Bedouin, having auxiliary roles. Many warriors were not vassals of their emir—a kind of Saracen general—but proud independents, deployed in the middle of the battle formation. Behind them came the emirs with their mamluks, the sultan's mamluks being only the third layer.

After seeing the incensed, frequently reckless behavior of Christian regiments, the sultan's emirs devised a classic ruse to be used if the infidels attacked the camp. When the Franks charged, the center of the Saracen front hastily retreated. Most Christians paused, unsure what to do, but a hundred Cypriots in the middle of the lineup, recently arrived and hungry for glory, were sucked in by the enemy's false retreat. In an instant, the mamluks surrounded them and began slaughtering them.

In a stroke of incredibly bad luck—or, as the Saracens would have said, by the will of Allah—just as the knights closest to the Cypriots tried, unsuccessfully, to come to their aid, King John was seen turning with his men and galloping off toward Damietta. What happened was that he'd received a report that a band of Bedouin were attacking the Christian women bringing water from the river to the edge of the battlefield. Such cowardly, barbaric behavior infuriated the old king, who'd rushed to the riverbank in rage. But when the Roman contingent, already in shock from being next to the space where the Cypriots had been, saw the king in apparent full flight, they remembered Brother Francesco's words and turned their backs on the enemy. Despite Pelagius and Jacques screaming their lungs out to stop the feckless Italians, panic soon spread among the crosses. That was when al-Kamil gave the order to attack.

At most battles, spectators—sometimes dozens, other times thousands—stand at what they consider a safe distance from the fighting. During attempts to take a town, they cheer from high buildings with the enthusiasm of people whose lives literally depend on the outcome. In larger clashes, they often seek out nearby hills from which the movements of troops can be discerned. But however hard they try, they never grasp who is winning and who is losing. Worse, in the open, the high spot they chose may suddenly acquire tactical importance, and not a few spectators are known to have paid for their curiosity with their lives.

On the left bank of the Nile, opposite the village of al-Huran, was just such an elevated place. The absence of bridges for several leagues made the spot enviably safe, as the armies would do battle on the other side of the river. The company, with nearly a hundred curious clerics and women, reached the rise before the clash between the armies began and watched the disastrous developments.

"And now? What's happening now?"

Francesco's eyes were too sick for him to make anything out from that distance, so he kept asking his brothers to tell him what was happening.

"The Cypriots are lost, Father," said Pietro. "And now the Romans . . . what are they *doing*? God have mercy on us all, they're turning their backs on the mamluks!"

When the shameful rout became clear, his brothers fell silent and Francesco began to weep, his example soon followed by nearly everyone on the sandy knoll.

When they judged the tragic outcome of the attack on Färiskür to be irreversible, the onlookers made their way back to camp to look after the wounded—not as fast as the fleeing footmen on the other side of the river, but fast enough to watch the Saracen onslaughts being contained by the military orders, aided by many French and English knights, who took turns in a desperate rear guard action.

The Templars assembled in platoons of ten or twelve and charged the oncoming mamluks, crying, "Non nobis, Domine, non nobis, sed tuo nomini da gloriam!"*

While they fought to the death, taking dozens of mamluks with them, the next platoon, this one of Teutonic knights, would gather for their charge. The operation to give cover to the retreating army was organized by King John, and it was only thanks to his efforts, though at the cost of dozens of knights, that the whole Latin campaign didn't end in disaster on that 29th of August.

Hundreds of footmen, especially among the newcomers, drank

---

*"Not to us, Lord, not to us, but to your Name give glory!" from Psalm 115

their whole ration of wine in one swig in the morning, to brace themselves before death. Many of them, in the chaotic rout, died from the force of the sun, baked drunk in their armor, without having delivered a single blow.

More than three thousand footmen fell on that day, as did two hundred knights of the orders, plus a hundred other knights from various lands. Al-Kamil also took many important prisoners, among them the counts of Beauvais and Epoisse and Gautier de Némours, grand chamberlain of France. Later, it would be written that the best men of that generation met their death at the battle that Brother Francesco implored them not to fight.

✡ ✠ ✡ ✠

The bodies stretched endlessly in every direction. From afar, it looked like a swarm of giant locusts had settled on the dunes east of the Nile. The stretch of desert was an immense open grave, the thousands of decaying corpses nothing if not a biblical vision of divine retribution.

Aillil and the stretcher bearers followed Yehezkel as he stepped through the battlefield, looking for signs of life among the dead. Here and there, they thought they saw a leg or an arm move suddenly. The stench made the air unbreathable despite the cloth masks Yehezkel made for them. With each step, Aillil distracted hundreds of big flies from their gruesome banquets, his eyes following the emerald-green cloud as they took flight.

Crows and jackals moved among the bodies as huge birds circled above the desolation, diving into the melee of scavengers, not caring if their claws dug into carcasses or live creatures. Huge black crows Aillil knew, but the other, horrid birds were like nothing else he'd ever seen. Enormous wings and long, fleshy necks with no feathers on them except for a collar round the base, and deadly looking hooked beaks. Monsters that should have been carved in stone looking down from the sides of cathedrals, not flapping their black wings before his eyes while tearing flesh from human corpses in that hellish landscape.

Their discordant, raucous cries covered every other sound on the plain by the river.

"But why does God *do* such things?" asked Aillil in a small voice.

"If you start asking that sort of question," answered Yehezkel, "you can end up in the most frustrating confusion, Aillil. Still, I'm glad you asked it . . ."

Hours later, the little group turned to accompany the last stretcher, bearing the fifth wounded knight Yehezkel decided might survive, back to camp. The worst of the wounded were taken to the tent where his friend Ugo had set a priority among the stricken warriors, so that urgent care would go to those who had, by his discernment, the highest likelihood of surviving their wounds.

Ugo de' Borgognoni was a medicus from Lucca of about Yehezkel's age. The son of nobles, he taught surgery at the university in Bologna and decided that a war would be a good place to widen direct experience of wounds. Ugo and Yehezkel argued endlessly all through August over the best approach to embedded arrowheads, and a jovial camaraderie— fed by the dark humor that physicians at war often use to cope with their grim surroundings—grew between them.

Yehezkel had learned his medicine in Fustat from Moshe ben Maimon, who was a follower of what physicians would later call the *dry* method of treating wounds, which consisted of washing them in boiled water and the strongest available liquor, stitching them up immediately, and wrapping them in clean dry linens. The results this method achieved in the days after the battle converted Ugo de' Borgognoni to Saracen medicine once and for all.

Most wounded were entrusted to the care of monks and nuns, and the only moments of relief the Italian medicus enjoyed in those exhausting first days of September were the exhilarating flare-ups between Master Ezekiel and the monks over most of the patients in the big tent. One morning, in the presence of Ugo and Mother Galatea, a

Benedictine monk called Brother Gerard was attempting to draw blood from a wounded English knight. Yehezkel wouldn't hear of it.

"I tell you I *know* what this man needs: a good bleeding!" cried Gerard. "Can't you see how flushed his face is? Experience has taught me that when all else fails, a purifying draining of blood, and then another one, and one more, is what brings healing to the body!"

Yehezkel's smile told Ugo that the thunderstorm he'd been looking forward to was about to break. "Believe me, my good monk," began the rabbi sweetly, "this man needs all the blood the Saracens were good enough to leave *inside* his body. I've nothing against drawing blood from a congested patient, but the color you see in his face is only due to the heat in this tent. This knight will have much greater problems recovering, if you leech him now."

Brother Gerard, hands on his hips and the truth necessarily, since he was arguing with a Jew, on his side, defended the tradition the Salerno school transmitted to him. "I'm no village priest, sir! I am aware that there are circumstances when drawing blood is discouraged. But both moon and tides have been growing for three days, and bleeding a patient is only normal . . . whatever they may think of it in the synagogue!"

Yehezkel's nostrils widened imperceptibly to all—except for Galatea. "Since I've lived in Christian lands, Brother Gerard," he said, voice nearly making the tent cooler, "I've seen unspeakable horrors passed off as 'medicine.' I witnessed limbs hacked off with axes to cure ulcers that would have healed with a simple poultice! I saw a woman's head cracked open and her brains spilled because they said she was possessed by a demon, when the poor wretch was only suffering from nightmares and should have changed her diet." Yehezkel caught himself and exhaled to calm down.

"I could go on, Brother, but there isn't any point. I can't stop you bleeding this poor man, but perhaps Master Ugo will, as he is in charge in this tent." Yehezkel turned and marched off, fuming.

One of the wounded Templar knights who spent some days in the tent was Iñigo Sanchez. From him, when he'd recovered enough to speak, Aillil discovered that André de Rosson was dead, struck by an arrow during a rear guard charge.

"I'll miss him," wheezed Iñigo as Aillil bent over him, "but at least he'd already achieved his greatest ambition . . . to be called a brave man by established brave men."

He coughed up a little blood. "I shouldn't complain . . . he earned his martyrdom, saved his soul. If I think of the eternal flames he's been spared, I couldn't ask more for him . . . but what can I do? The flesh is weak, and I had grown fond of the young fool!"

Aillil didn't feel the aching void he'd felt when Don Sancio died, but later he remembered André's outrage for small injustices and once more agreed with the perfecti in Montréal: when it comes to the young, death always picks those who least deserve to die.

The day after the disaster, as physicians and scavengers roamed the battlefield, Pelagius seethed with rage at the Italian friar whose doom-saying caused the Roman contingent's dishonorable conduct. In truth, the cardinal was secretly pleased by the outcome of the battle: now the nobles would quit harassing him and press on with the siege, as he wanted, and as the Mohammedan book of prophecies indicated was the only way to victory.

But the friar's defeatist words had to be punished. Pelagius hadn't wanted a famous holy man to suffer martyrdom under his watch, but now he had a vision of his journey back to Italy. The papal legate's ship, destined for legend, the precious casket with the body of the soon-to-be-sainted martyr on her deck. This led his mind to the problem of how to secure the body from the Saracens after they were done burning, or beheading, or dismembering, or hanging poor Brother Francesco.

The cardinal thought of the fame the Italian's Imitatio Christi—after all, his most ardent wish—would procure for Pelagius Galvani. He smiled. Not to speak of the information the Jew promised to deliver in exchange for an honorable discharge. If al-Kamil was really weak, as soon as Damietta fell he would march on al-Kahira. There would be no limit to what the church could demand from Venice and Genoa for such a prize! He had to seem distraught by the disaster, but not everything was as bad as it looked.

Pelagius summoned Yehezkel and Francesco, and soon the tall Jew and short friar stood before him. "I wrongly interpreted the prophecies in the Arabic translation," he said. "In hindsight, as is often the case with prophecy, I understand that both Francesco's mission to the sultan and the rumors of an army massacring the Saracens in the east are events described in the book. I just hadn't recognized them!"

Yehezkel's heart missed a beat. His curiosity made him speak out of place. "I've not come across this rumor, Your Eminence. Can you tell us more?"

Pelagius would normally have scorned the brazen request, but the Jew was now in his employ. "Hordes of savages on small horses attacked the Khwarezmian Empire from the east," he said with ill-disguised delight. "They kill everyone, including women and children, in every city they take. A letter I just received says Samarkand has fallen, and the sultan fears they'll ride on Baghdad next."

The cardinal beamed at the vision of the enemies of the Cross defeated in every corner of the world. "The letter from Rome says these must be the armies of Prester John, the powerful eastern king who became Christian and wrote a letter to the emperor in the Polis fifty years ago . . . well, maybe it's his son. Anyway, now I see that this menace in the east is also foretold in the book."

Yehezkel had heard of the famous Prester John in Montpellier, but having spoken with enough Jewish merchants back in Egypt who traveled to the farthest eastern lands, he knew that no such king ever existed, and the only Christians that far east were a few scattered followers of the heretic Nestorius. He thought of the recent fever among Jews over the imminent arrival of the Messiah of David and couldn't help wondering if the warriors laying waste to Mohammedan lands in the east might be the ten lost tribes of Israel coming home as the prophecies said they would in the last days.

Pelagius interrupted his messianic musings. "Anyway, that is not why I called you two. I've decided to allow you to cross the lines to Färiskür."

Before he could say another word, Francesco was on his knees, kissing the hem of his crimson robe. "God bless you, good Father, for being humble enough to open your eyes to His plan!"

Pelagius stepped back from the ragged heap of cloth. "So far, your visions have proved their power as a curse, Brother Francesco!" he sneered. "Now we'll see if they can shine as a blessing. If the sultan accepts Christ, I swear I'll give up my cardinalate and become a penitent friar of your order!" His laugh was harsh. Then he turned to Yehezkel.

"As for you . . . I don't trust you, Rabbi, but you live in Provence, so remember: if you don't bring back the goods you promised, you'll be hunted down as a deserter. Unless, that is, you decide to stay in Egypt. But even then, watch your step, *Master* Ezekiel. I could come after you in al-Kahira, you never know . . ."

Yehezkel thought Pelagius displayed the spite of men who never grew to be as tall as their childhood friends.

The cardinal wasn't finished with him. "Oh, and one more thing: the fact that you're to be Brother Francesco's interpreter doesn't relieve you of your duties to the wounded. You will both leave only when every one of them has been tended to. You, Francesco, will take just *one* of your friars, and you, Master Ezekiel, your page."

He dismissed them, face suddenly sad. "You may go now; I have a hundred funerals to officiate."

A few days later, al-Kamil, thinking the Christians' losses would make them see reason, and keener than ever to rid Egypt of the Frankish invaders, sent messengers renewing his offer of March, sweetening the deal by offering to return the prisoners he'd just captured. Again, King John and the orders—except the Temple—urged Pelagius to accept, and again the cardinal refused.

Francesco had to choose which of his brothers would accompany him to face likely martyrdom, but his problem paled in comparison to Yehezkel who had to deal with Mother Galatea's obstinacy in the face of hard realities. The abbess immediately started looking for a way to circumvent the cardinal's limit on the size of the mission. Pelagius would never allow the abbess of a convent, especially a noblewoman, to join the suicidal enterprise. There was nothing for it; she would have to go in disguise.

Huddling with Dorina, a muscular Venetian whore who'd become her closest confidante in the camp, she came up with a credible plan. Yehezkel would ask the cardinal to allow a fifth man to join the expedition, an armed squire to defend them from stray Bedouin who might attack on their way to the Saracen camp—and that squire would be Galatea, dressed as a man.

Yehezkel considered the risks involved, secretly proud of her initiative and courage. When he smiled an agreement, Galatea marched off to the brothel tent to ask Dorina to cut her hair and hide her breasts under tightly wrapped linens. Noticing his admiring smile, she jested, "It's easier to leave than to be left behind, Rabbi."

✡   ✠   ✡   ✠

A week passed between the day Pelagius summoned them and their departure from camp.

Near the end of their time in Damietta, when all that could be done for the wounded had been attempted, a young Templar squire approached Yehezkel and told him that Pedro de Montaigue, master of the Order of the Temple, wished to speak with him.

Yehezkel had completely forgotten about Don Sancio's letter to the new master. On arriving, he'd thought he would ask for an audience to deliver it, but then a thousand things pushed it out of his mind. He followed the squire to the Templar encampment. The master's tent was large but spartan.

Pedro de Montaigue was a Spaniard, as big as Yehezkel, who also wore a black beard, but his head was shaved, like the more rigorous

Templars. He'd been elected master exactly a year before, on the death of his friend Guillaume de Chartres, but had been in Provence at the time and only joined the siege in January, leading—and surviving—all the Templars' engagements since.

But this time the order's losses had been dramatic. Not since the siege of Acre had so many Templars fallen in one battle. The weight of the blow on Pedro's morale was evident on his face. He told the page to leave and once they were alone directed Yehezkel to a low divan in a corner of the tent.

"We both have little time to waste, Master Ezekiel, so I'll come straight to the point. I was fortunate enough to learn from the cardinal of his deal with you, and that you claim to have credible sources in the sultan's camp. Well, you see, I have such a source, too, so I thought the two of us should speak, to avoid damaging each other's . . . operation."

Yehezkel was taken aback by Pedro's outspokenness, especially as he had also decided to play all his cards at this meeting. He wouldn't get another chance to speak with the person most likely to know the identity of the Old Man, so on the way there he'd decided to mention the Parchment of Circles and watch Pedro's reaction. Now the master, by asking for the name of his contact in al-Kamil's court, was turning the tables. Yehezkel thought furiously and then said, feigning confidence, "I'll tell you the name of my old friend who is close to the sultan, but only *after* you tell me what the Parchment of Circles leads to, and if the Old Man has found it."

Pedro stared, and then his big shoulders dropped and he looked as if he'd just conceded a joust. "Guillaume knew about theology, heresies, secrets," he mumbled. "I was always just a fighting man. I'm going to trust you for two reasons: first, I know you're a friend of Arnald Arifat, who brought the Parchment to Syria ten years ago."

Pedro sighed deeply and then stood up and started pacing in front of the rabbi. "And second . . . I can no longer bear the pressure from Domingo of Guzman to hand over the Old Man and whatever he found! You know of the parchment, and there's no way *you* could be

Domingo's man, so I think I'll benefit from your advice on this whole mess, because what to do with the Old Man and his search has become a curse for me!"

Yehezkel thought, "If the Templars have really been blackmailing the popes for almost a century, then the current master is nothing if not a master of dissimulation!"

He caressed his beard, considering how to react to Pedro's apparent frankness, and then said, "I agree that in Domingo we have a common enemy, Master Pedro. I'll be as open with you on what we know of the parchment, *and* as discreet with everyone else, as you will be with me." After a pause, he added, "But first, please, tell me what you know of the mysterious Old Man."

Pedro sat down again, relieved by his newfound alliance with a clearly informed Jewish player. "Even *I* don't know who he was before faking his death and moving to Jerusalem. Guillaume and I were friends from the old days, before going to Acre, but I was never as interested in mystics and heretics as he was. Anyway, Guillaume met the Old Man some twelve years ago when he'd just arrived and was moving around Jerusalem, asking everyone about maps of the Holy City. He had officially been dead for two years, and his greatest fear was bumping into someone who knew him."

Pedro paused. "I think Guillaume knew who the Old Man is . . . but he never told me."

A knight poked his head into the tent and asked the master if he was ready for the funeral. Pedro looked down and told the page to say he was unwell and would join them later. He resumed his tale. "When we entered the order, Guillaume was already a disciple of the Old Man's personal heresy and helped him become a chaplain, first in isolated outposts and then in central positions. Ten years ago, the Old Man became powerful enough to arrange Guillaume's election as the next master."

Pedro hesitated, careful not to reveal any secrets of the order to the rabbi, but then went on. "As you already seem to know, the Parchment of Circles is in fact a map. Arnald brought it to the Old Man during Innocent's war on the Cathars, but the Old Man says the relic is not the real thing. I cannot tell you what the real map leads to, but it is something . . . of great importance to our order. Unfortunately, the pope ordered Domingo to find the map before we do. I recently learned that 'God's Dog' even had the gall to infiltrate one of his men in *my* order!"

Everything the master said tallied perfectly with what they'd learned from Sancio. Yehezkel wanted to somehow reward Pedro for his forthrightness. "Some rabbis in France and Portugal heard of a secret cabal inside the order of the Temple, a group . . . opposed to Christianity," he murmured.

"That was *him* again!" cried Pedro. "Once Guillaume was master, he gathered a dozen brothers with Manichean leanings—you know, the sort who go to Jerusalem dressed as pilgrims to meet with heretics and plan a theological orgy of all religions! *That* was when Domingo was unleashed on us and sent monks to find out who Guillaume was meeting with in Acre. Oh, but I put an end to that! First thing I did on becoming master was to disband his Baphomet rubbish and expel all the knights involved!"

Pedro was quiet for a moment, clearly fearing he'd said too much.

"I will try to meet him," said Yehezkel. "Don Sancio said he's the chaplain of Château Pèlerin now. But tell me," asked Yehezkel on a whim, "how old do you think the Old Man actually *is*?"

"Oh, he looks a hundred and twenty, but I believe he 'died' at around eighty and must be ninety-four or ninety-five."

"I presume you know why the Old Man says the Cathar Parchment is not the real thing."

"Because it is in Greek. He says the real thing is in Hebrew."

"I *must* meet the Old Man," whispered Yehezkel intently. "And in any case, whatever it is they're both after, I hope he finds it before Domingo!"

"Is your advice to keep protecting him from the pope himself?"

Many have said that the three most powerful men in Christendom in those days were the emperor, the pope, and the master of the Temple. Yehezkel savored his momentary influence over one of them. "Master, you said that what the map leads to is 'of great importance to the order.' Well, if the map is in Hebrew, something tells me that were I to join the Old Man's quest things could start to move. I'm sure you would only have to hold off Honorius for a few months."

Pedro winked. "Now you can tell me, Rabbi. Who is your old friend in al-Kamil's court?"

"Fakhr ad-Din al Fârisî," said Yehezkel, naming the sultan's personal adviser and spiritual guide.

Pedro whistled softly. "Your source is more highly placed than mine," he said, and stood up. "I am pleased with our conversation, and will follow your advice concerning the Old Man."

Pedro offered Yehezkel his wrist. "Brother Rupert here will give you a laissez-passer with my seal on it. It could come in useful when you're in Syria."

Yehezkel bowed deeply to the bearded man with the big red cross on his chest and left the tent.

The next day Yehezkel related to Galatea what Pedro had revealed about the Old Man. She was as surprised as he'd been that the master should refer to what the map led to as 'something of great importance to our order.' After all, if the confession existed, it would lay waste to Christianity.

"The focus of my prayers and meditations has been Brother Francesco piccolo's mission, Rabbi," she said, "but what you tell me reminds me that we're here because of the enigma in Jerusalem, much as I find it hard to believe that the holy friar has no role in that quest."

"If he comes back alive from his mission," said Yehezkel, "he may decide to complete his pilgrimage. Then we might meet him again, perhaps in Jerusalem. So there may yet be a role for him."

"Tell me, after we find the letter in Fustat, how do you plan to go to Jerusalem?"

"The simplest way is to join a Bedouin caravan. They take money from passengers, just like ships."

"So they should. After all, camels are known as ships of the desert, are they not?" she quipped.

Yehezkel laughed. "Remember Spiro? Well, the Talmud says 'All camel drivers are wicked, all sailors are righteous,' so we can expect the Bedouin to make Spiridione look like a God-fearing man!" They shared the fearless laugh of people who feel the touch of the Lord's hand on their heads.

Galatea, in artful disguise, was a credible squire. Her shoulders were wide for a woman, and her chest nowhere near as buxom as Gudrun's. The problem, of course, was her eyes. Anyone seeing them, a Christian in one camp or a Saracen in the other, would instantly know that squire was a woman. So she practiced being a melancholy squire, head low and eyes on the ground, to the great amusement of Yehezkel and Aillil, who knew how much this nun was used to holding her head high. Yehezkel told Aillil he must treat her as a man of his own, lowly rank at all times, but Aillil found that hard to do.

One day, as she tested her disguise by doing squirish things around camp, Yehezkel, looking from a distance, caught himself wondering what his life would have been like if instead of sweet, silent Naomi, he'd married a woman as unpredictable, rebellious, and proud as this nun.

Francesco, to no one's surprise, chose Brother Illuminato to sustain him in the sultan's tent. In his month at camp, the friar had won some souls to his mendicant order. As was often the case in Italy, they were well-off, educated men—in fact, two of them were young clerics in the bishop of Acre's retinue. Jacques didn't like it one bit. When taking his leave from Francesco in his tent, he blessed him, embraced him, and kissed him but then said, with unexpected harshness, "Francino, are you at all aware of the unhappiness you bring to the families from which you wrench your followers, who so often abandon parents, wives, and children to marry Lady Poverty like you?

And do me a favor, don't bring out the 'This is my family' Gospel."

Francesco looked pained, but his answer was ready, "When I was in my father's house in Assisi, there was a medicus who cured everyone for love of God, without asking any money. What I saw was that people trusted and respected him *less* than the ones who leeched them of both blood *and* money. The unhappiness they cause to fathers and wives is the price these sick souls pay when they come after me to be healed. And they heal, Jacques, because they believe in the most expensive medicus they found."

Rattled as he was by the loss of two of his brightest students, Jacques couldn't help smiling.

The departure was postponed by a day because of Ugo's sudden plea to Yehezkel to help extract two arrowheads from the shoulders of an Italian knight, a nobleman from Lucca close to his family. This gave Aillil time to say goodbye to Iñigo.

The Spanish knight was recovering fast and grabbed the boy by the shoulders. "Good luck, Aillil! When you become a knight, as I've no doubt you will one day, just remember this: the difficult thing is not to kill a mamluk, it's to convince him that he's dead!"

They both laughed hard, like the old friends they had become.

At dawn the next day, the 12th of September, the small band set out, accompanied for a few hundred yards by a crowd of well-wishers. They all knew of Francesco's plan and were divided in their opinion of how it would play out. Some were sure that with God on his side the friar would prove to the sultan that only Christ could save his soul. Others, though aware of being men of little faith, thought instead that they would never again see any of the five men leaving the camp.

The squire who was supposed to protect friars, rabbi, and page should anything happen in those five leagues walked a few steps in front of them, eyes on the ground, dressed in light chain mail, an expensive sword hanging at his side. Yehezkel quickened his pace, flanked him, and whispered, "Madame, your demeanor is so manly that if I were a

Bedu scouring these dunes, I would probably leave this little group well alone."

Galatea smiled. "Rabbi, do you know why Ugo de' Borgognoni asked for your assistance yesterday?"

Yehezkel looked at her, puzzled. "No, why?"

"Well, last time," she said, "on the galley sailing from Limassol, you told me you'd added up the days we had stayed on the two islands. Well, this time *I* did the arithmetics and guess what? We spent forty days outside Damietta, but only because we left today. Yesterday it would have been thirty-nine days!"

Yehezkel whistled his surprise and admiration. "My student makes me really proud, madame!"

For just one moment, the squire stopped looking at the ground, and his dangerous, forbidden eyes swept the delta of the Nile as if he owned it.

✡   ✠   ✡   ✠

BOLOGNA, 12TH SEPTEMBER 1219

As the five figures left camp walking south, a monk with an exaggeratedly wide tonsure sat at his scriptorium in the preachers' house in Bologna, poring over a parchment. With Domingo was Reginald of Orléans, his most trusted brother and the only one who knew of the Parchment of Circles.

"Here it is, Reginald, listen!" said the Spanish monk as he started reading from the most ancient one of the dozen parchments on his desk. "In the year 809 from the Incarnation of our Savior, I, Timothy, Metropolitan Bishop of Seleucia, came to know from the Jews of Jerusalem that ten years ago, in a cave near Jericho, a collection of jars was discovered containing hundreds of Hebrew parchments bearing Old Testament and other sacred writings, including two hundred *unknown* psalms by King David and *two apocryphal Gospels.*' Gospels *in Hebrew*! Do you grasp the import of this, Reginald?"

He was corroded by illness, but his indomitable spirit egged him on, and the search for the map gave him the strength to ignore fever attacks.

"Timothy says the Parchment of Circles was among those found in Jericho. He says it mentions 'the Heart of the Messiah' *in Hebrew,* specifying *where it is buried*!"

He put down the folio and frantically searched for the other one to show his partner the connection he'd made. He rummaged for a while, sweat dripping from his forehead. "By the Holy Womb of the Virgin, here it is! This is a letter on the Bogomil heretics that a Greek monk called Euthymius Zigabenus wrote to Pope Paschal more than a hundred years ago."

Reginald couldn't help thinking that there was no longer a single document in the whole papal archive that Domingo couldn't lay his hands on, if he so wished.

"Come and read this. Euthymius says that the Bogomils received the Parchment of Circles, which is now in Cathar hands, from the Paulicians—and that *it is in Greek*!"

Domingo raised his hand to underline what emerged from collating the two documents. Reginald saw his arm tremble as it went up and rushed to his side, but the founder waved him away.

"Do you *understand,* Reginald? The parchment I chased for ten years is in Greek; therefore, *it is not the original*! Someone in Jerusalem, four hundred years ago, made a Greek copy of it!" With age, the blue of Domingo's eyes had, if anything, become deeper, and now they were glowing.

Just then, a novice knocked and introduced an emissary from Pope Honorius. A Cistercian monk walked in, greeted the founder, and blurted out, "The Holy Father just had to move to Viterbo with the whole court, *again*! Rome is once more in the hands of the friends of the Antichrist, Emperor Frederick!!"

CHAPTER 21

HA-TENINIM HA-G'DOLIM

The Great Sea Monsters

BETWEEN AL-ADILIYAH AND FÄRISKÜR,
12TH SEPTEMBER 1219

A league into the crossing from safety to danger, the new company of five walked in a different formation from when they'd left camp. Francesco was now flanked by Yehezkel on one side and the squire with the downcast gaze on the other, while Brother Illuminato and Aillil chatted a few steps behind the trio.

The way from Damietta to Sharamsah was usually an ample, well-trodden path among irrigated fields, but in September—God being merciful—all branches of the delta burst their banks. The resulting swamp was life giving to the crops but made traveling on foot a slow, messy affair. Twenty-foot puddles dotted the muddy trail, which, a little farther on, disappeared altogether.

Yet the delta in that season was also a spectacle from some far-away magical land, for the Nile was covered in bright vermillion lotus flowers rising from big, round leaves floating on the water. As well as covering the river, colonies of the scarlet jewels were scattered over puddles and fields like spots of blood. As he looked at the big flocks of birds arriving in Egypt for the winter, Yehezkel mused that to *them,* the flowers must look as if the whole delta had developed a sudden rash.

Yehezkel was saying, "So I hope your friars aren't destined to hunt heretics like Domingo's preachers are doing. In a disputatio in Provence ten years ago, he swore to me that he would build an order of learned, polyglot monks, who would refute and convert not just Cathar heretics, but Jews and Mohammedans, too! I hope your friars never collaborate with his, Brother Francesco piccolo."

"Domingo and I?" Francesco laughed. "No, Rabbi, that would be like crossing eagles with chickens! I'm wary of books, unlike him, and don't enjoy debating God's attributes. For me, everything there is to learn"—he waved his arm in a sweep that embraced the delta—"is written right here; no need to know how to read to understand it. Who needs tractates and summae? Life has few certainties: the sun that warms you, the rain that wets you, the wild fruit you pick. The rest is chatter, vanity . . . nothing!"

Yehezkel made a face. "No, my brother. This is like your disregard for your body. Worse, for study is more than a need of the mind. You're wrong to see only vanity in it. Ignorance is dangerous. It favors man's evil inclination, while rational thought is the divine attribute that separates man from animals."

Francesco had encountered objections to his love of ignorance before but had never lost confidence. "You're right, but when what you call 'rational thought' is applied to Scripture by theologians, it ends up *choking* faith! The prophets say that truth will be hidden from the wise and learned and revealed to little children. Why? To confound the vanity of scribes and philosophers! There is something pure and upright in man's heart, Rabbi, which deserves more trust than any syllogism."

"Oh, Brother Francesco piccolo," interjected the abbess in chain mail, "you just said something I have known since my heartless tutor taught me what a syllogism is!"

"Don't think I don't know what you are talking about," said Yehezkel, "or I wouldn't have undertaken the path of Kabbalah, instead of following the precepts of the Law without asking questions on their purpose. But let me get back to Domingo for a moment. Did you ever meet him?"

"Once, at the council in Rome four years ago, and believe me, it would be hard to find two Christians with more different views on preaching the Gospel than Domingo and I."

"That much I've seen for myself, Brother Francesco, but you say you're sworn to obey the church in every way, which means that popes could use your friars in any way they see fit. Fighting heresy, for example, as they're already doing with Domingo's."

After a moment, Francesco said, "That *is* one of my fears, Rabbi. But our communities, if *I* write their Rule, won't lend themselves to 'theological service.' Domingo's will be convents of academic excellence where wily teachers are trained. Not so *our* convents, where my friars will grow up in the modesty of a peasant family, deriving peaceful hearts and good cheer from that frugality and becoming living examples of Christian love, more convincing than the most sublime sermon!" He smiled. "Domingo's friars won't be able to live in similar poverty. Books are expensive. He calls his a 'mendicant' order, but his friars will never know a precarious tomorrow, or insufficient food, or threadbare habits. More, I foresee times when a proud display of *learning* will be the ruin of the church."

Yehezkel mumbled, "Only fools despise wisdom and instruction, says the Book of Proverbs."

"In this respect you're like Christian theologians, Rabbi. You cite Scripture all day, only instead of the Gospels, you quote the prophets. If I'd put myself to it, I could probably have learned enough Bible to do the same. Instead, if I could, I would hide all commentaries to Scripture, because I find that when a man knows too many things, his wisdom is always greater than his compassion. And you know what? Studying the revealed Truth is a virtuous thing, but sometimes it is also a means to subjugate those who haven't studied and don't know the *words* to ask for justice."

"Mmph . . . we'll have to agree to disagree on this one, Brother Francesco. There's no such thing as a Jew who can't read or write, so you see how vast is the chasm between our visions."

Francesco said, "Perhaps Mother Church needs both learned monks like Domingo," and with a quirky smile, "and crazy fools like me!" He seemed lost in thought for a minute and then said, "But will agreeing to disagree suffice to compel you, Rabbi, to translate faithfully what I say to the sultan . . . even if you should disagree with it? Will you swear to do that?"

"I'm not allowed to swear, Brother Francesco, but I can assure you, and let the abbess be my witness, that lies and dissimulation are alien to my . . . conduct."

"I've no need for Mother Galatea's testimony, much as I trust her judgment. Your pledge to truthfully convey the words of my sermon is more than enough for me," said Francesco.

Brother Illuminato suddenly caught up with them, grabbed Francesco's arm, and ran ahead with him in a kind of inspired frenzy.

An hour later, halfway between the camps, the friars still walked two hundred feet before the others when the monster emerged from the river, straightened the stubby paws that supported its scaly trunk and almost comically ran into the center of the path not a hundred feet in front of them.

Nile crocodiles are the biggest and most dangerous lizards in creation. The one that faced the friars that day, thought Yehezkel later, must have weighed over a ton and been more than twenty feet long—of which at least the front five were jaws. It squatted in the middle of the trail, waiting for its prey to make a move.

Everyone froze on the spot. Yehezkel, who'd grown up on the Nile and seen such beasts before, was the first to recover his wits and immediately began breathing the folded breath. He remembered fishermen catching crocodiles by putting chunks of meat on metal hooks and tying the beast's jaws shut as soon as it fell for the bait. He shouted to the friars not to move a muscle and frantically looked around for something, anything, to act as a hook and a bait.

Galatea was transfixed by the monster. Even from that distance, the size of its teeth was terrifying. The scales covering its body were like black tiles, ending in a crested tail at least as long as she was tall. She thought the dip halfway along the profile of its jaw made it look like it was grinning, which added to the overall impression of a lizard from hell. Aillil said to himself that if Egypt was a land of monsters like the birds on the battlefield and this wingless dragon, then Rav Yehezkel could not leave for Jerusalem one minute too soon. Galatea also mused, absurdly, that if Brother Francesco was going to be martyred not at the hands of infidels but by the jaws of a wild beast, like the first Christian martyrs in the Circus Maximus, this had to have some deep, important meaning.

Then, under everyone's incredulous gaze, Francesco walked toward the crocodile, talking to it in his Umbrian dialect. The beast didn't move but opened its jaws wide and made a strange gurgling sound, as if to warn the holy man of his impending, gory dismemberment.

Yehezkel caught up with Illuminato and heard Francesco say to Fratel Crocodillo that it should let them through, because the sultan was waiting to receive the Light of Christ. The monster thrashed its huge tail twice, ludicrously evoking the image of a playful puppy. Then, with Francesco less than ten feet from it and everyone ready, breaths held, for the coming horror, it blinked both green eyes, turned its snout away from the friar, and slowly trotted back toward the Nile.

Francesco turned to his audience, an ecstatic smile on his face. "Brother Crocodile didn't really mean to hinder our progress. He just came out to say hello!"

Brother Illuminato had just witnessed his founder perform yet another miracle. He fell on his knees and praised the Lord. The squire, little taken as she was with genuflection, did the same.

Yehezkel was as relieved and grateful to the Almighty as the others yet found the time to reflect on how the words of his biblical namesake were constantly relevant in that journey, whether at the climax of a storm at sea or facing an Egyptian crocodile. He recited the verses under his breath, "Human one, sing a lament for Pharaoh, king of Egypt. Say to him: You consider yourself a young lion among nations, but you're like the sea monster! You thrash about in your rivers, roil the waters with your feet, muddy your rivers. But I will put hooks in your jaws!"

"The little Italian monk," said Yehezkel to himself, "didn't even need hooks."

Once they thanked the Lord for his mercy, Yehezkel quoted the prophet to them. Brother Illuminato immediately said that al-Malik al-Kamil was clearly the Pharaoh, king of Egypt, of Scripture, and the miraculous taming of the monster a "figure" of the sultan's imminent conversion. Galatea, struck by the allegory, prayed for the young friar to be right.

✡ ✠ ✡ ✠

IN SIGHT OF THE SULTAN'S CAMP AT FÄRISKÜR, 12TH SEPTEMBER 1219

A rumor in the Christian camp claimed that the sultan promised a gold bezant to anyone who brought him the head of an infidel. The edict, if true, would have made it hard for Francesco to survive his first encounter with the Saracens, but when he'd heard of it he confidently quoted a psalm, "Though I walk through the valley of the shadow of death, I will fear no evil, for Thou art with me."

Now, as he walked ahead with Brother Illuminato, the sultan's camp less than a league away, he tried to prepare his partner for the possibility that the encounter with Brother Crocodile had *not* been a symbol of how their mission would end.

"If we win martyrdom for witnessing Christ, Illuminato, you

must not be afraid of dying. Dying is just being born again. Your mother's womb prepared you for life, and your life prepared you for death. You'll find yourself on the other side, *tout simplement,* like you found yourself in this world the day you were born. Drop worldly weights, my brother. The lighter your soul, the higher you'll rise in His presence."

Perhaps through the sentinels' overconfidence two weeks after a victory, they weren't challenged by anyone until, as they crested a rise in the trail, they sighted the Saracen encampment in the distance. Their first reaction was to duck behind a dune and cautiously poke their heads out. The camp was smaller than the Christian one, but white cylindrical tents were arrayed as far as the eye could see. The first thing they noticed were the birds circling an area between them and the camp, occasionally diving down to feed on the corpses of mamluks evidently not important enough for anyone, even long after the battle, to have removed from where they'd fallen.

Then they saw them. Inside a whitish halo of dust lit by the sun's glare, the swords and shields of a group of guards glinted menacingly. Again, Yehezkel began to breathe in long, draining exhalations.

Suddenly, in the still air of the September morning, Francesco jumped up from behind the dune and ran toward the guards, immediately followed by Brother Illuminato, who only paused for the time it took him to cross himself. Yehezkel sort of expected Francesco to do something like that. He raised his sarbel with a disgusted grunt and gave chase, closely followed by Aillil and Galatea.

By the time the two ragged Italians came close, the mamluks had already realized they presented no threat. Two infidel monks, by the look of them—unarmed and clearly crazed by the sun. But wait, more infidels were running behind them, and one of them had a sword! The guards thought, gleefully, that even scouring the edges of the infidel camp, they would never find an easier reward.

Francesco threw himself at the feet of the first mamluk, raising a cloud of dust. The guard smiled down at him. He wore a sleeveless, green padded overcoat with a dagger in his waist and carried a lance and a round shield that shone like silver. Francesco shouted, "Soldan! Soldan! Take me to your soldan!"

The mamluk kicked him in the shoulder, both for the pleasure of humiliating a kafir, and in case he might be faking submission and hiding a weapon. Francesco fell on his back in the sand, still screaming "Soldan! Soldan!" A hundred feet away, Yehezkel saw Francesco on the ground and went into action.

"Take your hands off the *rahib*!* He is an emissary to the sultan from the Frankish kings!"

Yehezkel shouted the words in court Arabic, the language in which mamluks serving the Ayubbid sultan were given their orders. As well as using the power of the maskil to throw his voice at them, he'd imbued it with an arrogance that identified him as a member of that court.

The first mamluk was so worried about who the onrushing Jew might be that he leaned down to help Francesco get up. Yehezkel's intervention made it obvious that Francesco's theatrical surrender as a way of reaching al-Kamil's tent had been unnecessary—little more, in fact, than a search for humiliation by the mamluks. The friar looked embarrassed.

One of the guards saw Galatea's eyes and gasped but still demanded that she hand over her sword. Then they discussed among themselves whether to tie the prisoners' hands, decided not to, and marched them toward the tents.

They walked for another hour, first through unimpressive defense positions, then amid hundreds of white, round tents with vertical sides and conical roofs. At last, they came to a vast clearing at the center of the camp, where the sultan's tent was pitched. This was an oversized Bedouin tent, a hundred feet across, made of wide, colorful bands of fabric stitched side by side. Six mamluks of the sultan's personal guard

---

*Arabic for "monk"

stood outside wearing pointed helmets with a band of animal fur at their base and bearing ceremonial axes with elongated double points, the blades decorated with religious etchings.

The traffic of emirs and notables constantly arriving to see al-Kamil made the cardinal's tent look like the headquarters of a provincial war, but Pelagius after all, thought the rabbi, was only running a military campaign, while al-Kamil had to keep administering an empire that stretched to Yemen in the south, to Mount Ararat in the north, and to the African coast in front of Sicily in the west.

They waited to be summoned and then entered escorted by the mamluks. A wide entrance with raised flaps led into a main hall and several trapeze-shaped spaces under the same roof. Al-Kamil's throne was in the middle of the tent, and the guards forced them to their knees as soon as they were before it. The three-step platform was simple, but the cedar chair on it was a wonder to behold. Its tall back was pierced with elaborate open-work carvings, and its armrests were roaring lions. Above it was a silk baldachin, red folds falling on all sides. More guards, as heavily armed as the ones outside, stood on either side of the platform.

Al-Kamil—his full name, al-Malik al-Kamil Naser al-Din Abu al-Ma'ali Muhammed—was a portly man of about Yehezkel's age, with a black beard and dark and kindly but penetrating eyes. His flowing red and green robes were of rich fabrics and fashion, but quite somber.

He was still intrigued by the friars, when Yehezkel spoke in Arabic without having been addressed. "*Salaam Aleikum,* most honored king, Prince of All Believers and Cornerstone of Islam!" Then he pronounced the traditional Jewish blessing upon seeing a monarch. "Blessed be the Lord, who imparted from His wisdom and from His honor to a mortal!"

Al-Kamil peered at him and said, "I recognize you! You're the childhood friend of Fakhr's son, Ahmad, the pupil of Musa ibn Maimun, my uncle's and my father's *tabib.** What was your name

---

*Arabic for doctor

again? And anyway, what on earth are you doing in the company of these *rahibeen*?"

"My name is Yehezkel ben Yoseph, Commander of the Faithful, and I'm honored that you remember my face. I was born in Fustat and am your faithful subject, but I was forcefully conscripted by the Franks while practicing medicine in Cyprus. I offered my services as an interpreter to the smaller one of these monks, who came here to speak with you, and whose name is Francesco of Assisi."

Francesco heard Yehezkel's name and then his own and understood that Master Ezekiel had made the necessary introductions. Not knowing how the rabbi described the purpose of his visit, he was silent, waiting for the sultan to speak. Al-Kamil gestured for all of them to stand up.

"So pray tell, Messer Francesco," he began, flaunting one of a few Italian words he learned from Venetian merchants in al-Kahira, "are you a messenger from the Frankish nobles who have invaded my kingdom, or have you instead come—as many others before you—to accept Islam and swear allegiance to Allah and his Prophet Muhammad?"

Yehezkel immediately translated the sultan's words into Latin. The friar—whose face had already lit up in a smile on hearing 'Messer Francesco' in Italian—answered confidently, "Yes, we are messengers indeed, sire, but not from Frankish nobles, from God!"

Again Yehezkel translated, and al-Kamil leaned back in his chair, hiding disappointment behind a smile. He had hoped that this might be an eccentric embassy from the enemy, maybe even a low-profile acceptance of his latest offer. He turned to Yehezkel, "If they come from God, why did you tell the guards they were coming from the Frankish kings?"

Yehezkel held the sultan's gaze. "Because if I hadn't, Commander of the Faithful, the mamluks would have killed them." Al-Kamil looked startled but then smiled. "Well, yes . . . now that you mention it, they probably would have."

Francesco hadn't understandood a word of the exchange, but something told him that Master Ezekiel and the sultan knew each other, and he realized that the Jew's role would be more influential than he expected. He closed his eyes and entreated the Holy Spirit to turn his words into flames that would keep burning from one tongue to the other.

"Sire," he began when the exchange between the two had petered out, "if you will listen to our words, you will be enlightened, but if you will *believe* our words, then we will consign your soul to God. Because I tell you, in truth: if you die professing the law you follow now, God will *never* receive your soul! For the law of your Mahomet, a perfidious deceiver, is worth nothing!"

Brother Illuminato and Galatea gasped, the mystery of Francesco's true intent finally solved, but al-Kamil, thankfully, didn't notice them. Yehezkel set to work at once to save the friar's life.

He had told Francesco that unless he was seeking martyrdom, insulting Muhammad was the *one* thing he must not do. Now, as he translated the part on consigning al-Kamil's soul to God, he feverishly sought a phrase to replace the insults to the Prophet, whose name the Sultan had recognized. "For the Law of your Mahomet is useless, so vague that men have twisted all justice out of it!" he finally said, cursing himself for replacing Francesco's Latin words with twice as many Arabic ones.

Francesco knew what he had said and expected the sultan to react with outrage, if not fury. Instead, al-Kamil looked bemused, and for a moment the friar asked himself if the Jew had betrayed him but then pushed the thought from his mind. Meanwhile, al-Kamil was finding himself strangely charmed by the idea of a conversation with those Christian Sufis.

"What you say about the prophet's Law is interesting . . . and provoking," he said severely. "I see you dress like Sufis do, so I expect the sermon with which you intend to save my soul will be full of Love and annulling oneself for the sake of others."

Yehezkel translated the first words dishonestly, warning the friar to watch his tongue as if reacting to the insults. As he'd hoped, Francesco was struck by the sultan's mild-mannered tolerance and seemed inclined to abandon his original intent to provoke him.

Then al-Kamil's irony on Sufis made the monk smile and convinced him to debate the infidel king instead. "Call your wisest theologians, sire," he began, "and I will prove to them, with solid arguments, that Mahomet's Law cannot save your soul!"

Al-Kamil smiled condescendingly. "It would take more than solid arguments to shake my faith in Allah, Messer Francesco, but I believe in preaching Islam to the infidel. The Holy Qu'ran tells us to say to the people of Scripture, 'We believe in what was revealed to us *and* in what was revealed to you, and our God and your God are one and the same—to Him we are both submitters!'"

Al-Kamil looked straight at Francesco as he waited for the interpreter to catch up, and smiled when he saw the friar relishing the qu'ranic verse on their gods being the same. Then he stood up, arranged his robe, and summoned his four principal ulema to the tent. The Christian Sufi may not have been sent as a channel for negotiations, he thought, but that didn't mean he couldn't *become* one, if handled properly.

As they waited for the greatest authorities in the Ayubbid empire on Qu'ran and sharia,* al-Kamil seemed to notice for the first time the tall squire with his eyes on the ground.

"Why does your squire look so dejected, Tabib? Is it because we took his sword away?" he jested.

Yehezkel knew that once in al-Kamil's tent, hiding Galatea's sex would be impossible and decided to confess the little trick they'd played on Pelagius before the sultan found out for himself. "Commander of the Faithful, the cardinal heading the infidels—may his name be rubbed out of all books—would never allow this Italian noblewoman to accompany the monks on such an expedition, so I . . . I convinced her to dress up as my squire!" he lied, hiding behind the Arabic to shamelessly appropriate Galatea's idea as his own.

---

*The moral code and religious law of Islam.

Al-Kamil was amused and called out to the squire. Galatea looked up, and right away the sultan gestured for her to come closer. Yehezkel chose not to tell al-Kamil that the noble lady was also the abbess of a religious house, but now, seeing the look in his eyes, he called himself an idiot. If she was just a Christian noblewoman, she was legal war booty! With one word, if he so wished, the sultan could put her in his harem! How *could* he have been such a fool?

Four rigid figures in long black robes walked in and bowed to the sultan, their beards and turbans vast white expanses between which the small, dark stains of their faces looked almost lost. The oldest one, unsteady on his feet, was Fakhr ad-Din al-Fârisî, who recognized Yehezkel but only acknowledged him by a lowering of the eyelids. Al-Kamil welcomed them into the tent.

"Honorable friends, these two infidel monks had the temerity to come here to preach their religion to me. I want you to help me show them the light of the Holy Qu'ran."

The four scholars bowed again, and the first one to speak—the youngest, thought Yehezkel—at once declined to assist al-Malik in his intent. "My lord and king, not only does sharia forbid listening to the preaching of kuffar beliefs, it decrees death for the kaffir who dares preach to believers!"

The second one chimed in, "If you want to be called Defender of All Believers, you must have these two *worms* beheaded without further discussions!"

Yehezkel translated both comments in Francesco's ear. When the friar heard he'd been called a worm, he blurted out joyfully, "Thank you, thank you, Your Excellency! I don't see how I could become a better creature than a worm! Just look at it: it accomplishes its Creator's will without ever destroying anything!"

Yehezkel pronounced Francesco's retort in Arabic, with a straight face. Al-Kamil laughed.

The third alim gave the Sultan's request a little more thought, and said, "I will give the kuffar a brief introduction to the revelation of our

Prophet—peace be upon Him—as you ask, but debating with them the merits of our religions, which is what I suspect you would like to see us do, well, that does indeed go against half a dozen injunctions in the Holy Qu'ran."

The last one to speak was Fakhr. He sounded very tired. "Naser, I'm too old for the words of a Christian monk, however courageous, to endanger my faith. Let my colleagues run away and protect themselves as the law prescribes, I'll stay and listen to him with you." The old alim paused and smiled. "And help you confound him, if you should lack for words."

"Let it be as you say!" grunted al-Kamil, disappointed at the lost opportunity for another disputatio like the one he'd presided over with Coptic monks in al-Kahira.

The three ulema fled the tent. Francesco knowingly watched the old Saracen clerics deliver their harsh judgments to their king, all the while praying for the Holy Spirit to inspire him. Then, when only Fakhr remained, he said almost slyly, clearly working up to some *coup-de-scéne,* "Actually, I'm glad there will be no disputatio with your sages, sire. You said solid arguments wouldn't convince you that only Christ can save your soul . . . well, for me, too, faith is above and beyond reason."

He stopped to allow Yehezkel to translate and then went on in the ringing, prophetic voice that always startled everyone coming from such a small man, "To replace your sages, sire, have some brushwood brought in and have them light it—this tent is big enough for a small fire. Then we will let God be the judge of our religions, and I shall prove Christ to you by walking into the fire when it roars, protected by nothing but my faith!"

At first, when Yehezkel told him what Francesco came up with, Al-Kamil was speechless. Then he exchanged whispers with Fakhr on the platform. A giggle escaped him as he turned to the friar. "No, Messer Francesco, I will *not* allow you to walk into a fire in my tent. First, because I would prefer to debate the foundations of our religions, as I've done with other Christian clerics, than watch you play with fire.

Second, because if fire didn't burn you, word would get out and some of my troops may want to embrace your religion. Unfortunately, sharia commands the execution of anyone who abjures Islam."

As he translated, Yehezkel recognized Fakhr's elegant irony in pointing out to the monk that if he gained any converts, this would instantly make martyrs of them. But the sultan hadn't finished. "I have to go now, Messer Francesco, but I would enjoy speaking with you some more tomorrow, with the help of the tabib here." He gestured to Yehezkel to translate and turned to the old man.

"Fakhr, how do I stop your colleagues branding me an apostate for talking with a Christian monk? In fact, won't they assail me like wasps just for not putting both of them to death?"

Fakhr smiled. "Easy, Nasser. Declare him a Majnun.* The Sunna holds that by taking away his mental sanity and responsibility, Allah conferred the greatest of all graces on the Majnun, the inability to sin. If you have sympathy for the monk and you find that he speaks nonsense and says everything just to mock this world, you can declare him a fool of God and let him live."

Al-Kamil smiled, relieved. "You're priceless, Fakhr. I don't know what I'll do without you when . . ."

"Oh, you'll manage, Naser. I've no doubt."

Al-Kamil took his leave of the monks. "You'll be assigned a tent, and no one will touch a hair of your beards." The word reminded him of the beardless squire, and he turned to her. "You will be lodged with other women in the camp, my lady, but before I leave, may I ask whom I have the honor and pleasure of hosting in my makeshift encampment?"

Yehezkel translated. Galatea curtsied to the sultan and introduced herself. "I am Countess Galatea degli Ardengheschi, abbess of the convent of San Maffio in Venice, sire."

When Yehezkel translated, al-Kamil's displeasure was evident. "Convent? You are a member of a religious order?" He glared at Yehezkel.

---

*Crazed, possessed

"Why didn't you tell me, Tabib? Why did you only say 'Italian noble-woman'? Surely you're not thinking of . . . selling her?"

Yehezkel wished the ground would open up and swallow him, like the Israelites who rebelled against Moses. "Forgive your clumsy servant, Commander of the Faithful. What I thought was tactful turned out to be tactless."

Al-Kamil ignored him and turned back to the squire, whose mix of chain mail and violet eyes he found far more beguiling than the monk's puerile attempts to consign his tent to the flames of hell. "And why would a noblewoman," he asked her, "who is also the head of a women's religious house, take up arms to protect extravagant monks?"

Galatea smiled. "We Christians have a long tradition of women caring for wandering holy men, sire. Jesus was but the first of them. Before I met Brother Francesco, I was on a pilgrimage to Jerusalem."

"Ahh, Jerusalem!" said al-Kamil dreamily. "I first saw the Holy City when I was seven, and my uncle Salah ad-Din took her back. Ninety years earlier the infidels inflicted a massacre on the city, but when we rode in, my uncle spared everyone, to show the world who is more civilized."

As Yehezkel translated, the sultan watched the infidel thorough-bred's glowering eyes. He turned to Yehezkel with a bitter smile. "Your oversight nearly changed her life, Tabib. She's a female priest, so I can't touch her, but had she just been a follower of the Majnun monk, she would have become by far the most beautiful of my wives."

Yehezkel thanked the Almighty from the bottom of his by now besotted heart.

Twice the next day and once more on the third, Francesco spent time with the sultan and explained to him the scandal of Christianity, the victory over death of a man who was also God's only Son. He told of how accepting that His death had been the ultimate sacrifice that absolved men of their sins would instantly save his soul and allow it to enter God's Kingdom.

Although he'd heard Christians espouse their creed before, al-Kamil listened graciously. The very idea of God having a son made his blood curdle, and he was amused to see the Jew straining, as he translated, to disguise his own distaste for the monk's beliefs. But Francesco's inspired sincerity and flowery tongue touched him, and twice he was moved to remind him that Jesus and his mother Mary were deeply revered by the only true religion—that is, by Islam.

On the second day, al-Kamil gently pushed the friar to talk of the war. He was pleasantly surprised to discover that Francesco was opposed to it and believed that Christians and Saracens should live side by side, free to mingle and preach their religion to each other, if they so wished. This, al-Kamil told him, was also the opinion of Sufis, of whom he was not as critical as his ulema.

"Will you bear an embassy to your cardinal," said the sultan, "to help bring an end to this war?"

"Cardinal Pelagius is not impressed with my mission . . . or my style of preaching, sire. But I'll gladly convey your embassy to the bishop of Acre, who is influential and a good friend."

Yehezkel couldn't resist the opportunity to air his own plan to save Damietta. "I hope the Commander of the Faithful will forgive my insolence if I express an uncalled-for opinion, but I had many conversations with the nobles I was curing in the infidel camp, and I was hoping for a chance to tell you my impression of the situation there . . . politically."

The sultan was immediately attentive. "Go ahead, Yehezkel ibn Yusuf. I'm listening."

"The cardinal is certain that Damietta is close to falling. That's why he refused all the offers you made to give them Jerusalem if they leave Egypt. But many important people there don't share his certainty and want to go home. Especially after the disaster of two weeks ago." Yehezkel hadn't yet said anything al-Kamil didn't already know. Then he unveiled his idea. "My lord, Christians are so superstitious they're more like pagans than believers! Add to your offer that you'll return the wood captured by your uncle at Hattin, which they call the True Cross and hold as the Relic of Relics. Offer a thirty-day truce to consider the offer. They'll accept the truce, but the offer will split their camp right down the middle! It wouldn't surprise me if fights broke out between factions!"

"It's a good idea, Tabib. Fakhr thought of something similar . . . but there's a problem. My brother and I know our father received the wood from his brother, who took it from the infidels, but when I asked al-Muazzam to send it, he came back saying they couldn't find it! The confounded officials chose a hiding place for it, and no one alive remembers where the place was! Can you believe it, Tabib?"

Yehezkel was silent, squeezing his beard as he considered the quandary. "Tell me, Commander of the Faithful, what would be the difference between confessing *now* to the Franks that the True Cross has been lost and confessing it *after* they leave Egypt?"

Al-Kamil smiled knowingly. "Only the fact that if I offer the wood now I would be lying, because I already know I don't have it."

"Exactly. But suppose you had not yet asked your brother to look for it, then your offer would be made in good faith, for you would still think you had it *somewhere . . .*"

The sultan smiled admiringly. "My father used to say that your teacher, Musa ibn Maimun, was the smartest man in the world. A little of that may have rubbed off on you, Tabib."

Yehezkel looked so pleased with the compliment that Francesco and Galatea regretted not having followed the exchange.

The sultan went on. "I shall follow your advice. You'll remain in camp until the infidels react to the offer, and if they behave as you predicted, you'll be rewarded. Is there anything in particular your heart desires?" He grinned in complicity and, had Yehezkel not been a Jew, would have winked. "After all, Tabib, renouncing my wartime claims on your Italian countess is reward enough, is it not?"

Yehezkel blushed under his beard, pretending not to grasp the insinuation, and then took his chance. "Actually, my lord, there *is* something I would appreciate. A letter with your seal on it, giving me permission to carry out searches on the Haram al-Sharif, both above and below ground."

"Mmhh . . . and what exactly would your *searches* in that holy place aim to find?"

"All I know, my lord—and even that only from rumors and speculation—is that whatever it is, it would be the undoing of Christianity."

The sultan's dark eyes searched his face. "Something tells me you're not exaggerating, Tabib. All right, if the cardinal accepts the truce but not the offer, you'll have your letter with my seal."

On the third day, the sultan told Francesco his new offer, asking him to convey it to Jacques de Vitry. At the mention of the True Cross, the friar's face lit up like a small sun, confirming to al-Kamil the relic's power over Christian hearts. Then, to express his esteem of the Christian Sufi, he offered him various gifts, but Francesco predictably refused everything.

The one thing Francesco and Illuminato accepted during their three days in al-Kamil's camp were the delicious meals cooked for the guests and brought to their tent. During one meal, Francesco told Yehezkel how taken he was with the camp's muezzins.

"The calls to prayer that spread among the tents here five times a day are sudden, piercing reminders of God even in the middle of war," he said, "so much more direct and *personal* than church bells!"

On the 15th, the time came for separation. The two friars and the escort the sultan insisted on were headed back to the Christian camp, while Yehezkel, Galatea, and Aillil would remain in Färiskür.

Galatea asked Francesco for his blessing.

The little monk hesitated, as if uncertain that blessing her without looking her in the eyes was possible, and then asked all three of them to kneel down, put his hands on Galatea's and Aillil's heads, with Yehezkel in the middle, and pronounced, "Ego vos benedico, in nomine Patris, et Filii, et Spiritus Sancti!"

As they got to their feet, Francesco unexpectedly fell on his knees before Yehezkel, saying, "I want your blessing, too, Master Ezekiel! Please don't refuse me!"

Yehezkel looked embarrassed. No one had ever asked him for his blessing before. He was about to say something self-denigrating, but Francesco grabbed his right hand in both of his and pressed it on his head. Unable to decline, Yehezkel pronounced the Priestly Blessing.

The friars walked out of the camp, surrounded by the mamluk escort. Yehezkel and Galatea watched Francesco's tiny, frail figure, his back a bit rounded, one shoulder slightly higher than the other, sudden shivers of fever shaking him as if he were ruffled by an invisible hand.

CHAPTER 22

PRU U'REVU

Be Fruitful and Multiply

ACRE, 15TH AUGUST 1219

"Frutolf, these women are your wards," said Bois-Guilbert as soon as the passengers disembarked on the quay in Acre. "I advise you to accompany them to the Benedictine convent of Saint Anne's." Then he turned to Rustico and Garietto. "As for you two, find yourselves a hostel for pilgrims, they're everywhere!"

The Templar galleys left Limassol a week after the one headed back to Damietta. Flying on the water at eight knots, they made the passage to Acre in just twenty hours and after passing under the Tower of Flies on the end of the breakwater waited for the massive chain between outer and inner harbors to be lowered and then entered the port of what had become the new capital of the Latin Kingdom of Jerusalem—at least until a Hero of the Cross reconquered the Holy City.

Bois-Guilbert convened the knights of the other orders to a rendezvous the next day and marched off with the Templars, their sergeants, and squires into the passage leading to the order's castle. The tunnel was a new addition to Templar possessions in the city. Four hundred yards long, domed and heavily guarded, it passed under the Pisan quarter and connected the port with their castle in the southwestern corner of the city. The Templars would have loved their own harbor in Acre, but steep castle walls rising from the sea confer a strong military advantage, and one just doesn't build landing quays at their feet.

St. John d'Acre—or Acre, as everyone called it—capitulated to Salah ad-Din without a fight after the sultan's victory at Hattin and his capture of Jerusalem. But it had only been in Saracen hands for two years when King Guy of Lusignan besieged it, first with the help of the Italians and later the kings of France and England.

The siege of Acre was unique, with Saracen troops besieging the Frankish besiegers. One year after the kings retook Acre, every institution in Jerusalem, from the royal palace to the headquarters of the military orders to churches and monasteries, relocated there, bringing the city's population from twenty thousand souls to nearly fifty thousand almost overnight.

Luckily for the Latins, trade in merchandise from the silk road continued to fill Acre's coffers and enabled the construction of sorely needed new buildings. Venetians, Genoese, and Pisans had their own quarters in the city, each with a marketplace, warehouses, baths, a bakery, shops, and dwellings. Acre became intolerably crowded, and tensions between the Italian communities grew. Everyone knew that at any moment the frequent brawls could turn into urban warfare.

But chaotic and violent as it was, life in Acre, amid the pageants of marriages and coronations of Latin nobility, had gone on unperturbed until two years earlier, when, for the first time in thirty years, Christian kings started arriving to retake Jerusalem. A year earlier, the Frisian and Burgundian fleets had arrived with their thousands, and mayhem and confusion in Acre was complete.

Adding to the dangers was a gruesome recurring event, almost peculiar to Acre: assassinations by the Hashashin. These were a heretical offshoot of a Shiite sect, the Ismailis, devoted to their sheikh to the point of instant, unprepared martyrdom. Their name was said to derive from the hashish they ate before going on a mission. The sheikh of fifty years earlier, Rashid ad-Din Sinan, became famous as the Old Man of the Mountain by giving unpredictable orders from his fortress in Syria, which resulted in the death of many important players in Outremer, both Christian and Saracen.

Rumors were rife in Acre that the masters of the Temple secretly met the sheikhs of the Hashashin to determine which leaders had to be eliminated, and these were often Saracens, since in Outremer it was not uncommon for warriors to dispatch their brothers in Islam, too, if their understanding of the prophet's plan differed from their own and, above all, if the price was right.

Gudrun and Albacara were warmly welcomed at Saint Anne's. Unarmed pilgrims could still travel to Jerusalem, and the convent had become an important way station for the women among them. Their first concern was to entrust the big trunk with the Ardenga blazon, with Rustico and Garietto's help, to a warehouse in the Pisan quarter. After a week without her, both women had nearly overcome their physical need for Galatea's presence, which had different roots, but resulted for both in the same paralyzing fear of every horse, knight, or sword—not to speak of the occasional Saracen—they crossed in Acre's alleys.

On the Day of the Virgin's Assumption, choirs blaring from dozens of churches, the women emerged from hearing Mass in Saint Peter's, the main church in the Pisan commune, and were making their way back to Saint Anne's. Despite its being the middle of the day on a crowded street, two Hashashin waited for them in a doorway and when they walked past pulled them inside and gagged them before anyone in the street noticed they were no longer walking along.

The women at once feared for their lives. They were so shocked they needed no subduing and were pushed, gags in their mouths and wrists held roughly behind their backs, down a dark corridor. A glimpse of the Saracen features of their captors confirmed that their time had come to give up their souls. Shaking with panicked sobs, they reached a dingy room where they were thrown on a bundle of hay in a corner and locked up with no explanations.

✡ ✠ ✡ ✠

ACRE, 22ND AUGUST 1219

Bois-Guilbert didn't believe for a moment that the Jew couldn't have used his connections in Cyprus to avoid being drafted, or that the crazy friar was the real reason the abbess chose to go to Damietta. They had *wanted* to go to Egypt! Domingo warned him about that Jew, and he was ready to burn in hell if those two weren't after the parchment!

After mastering his jealousy and crippling desire for revenge on the Jew, he'd reasoned more coldly, and it came to him. The two women would tell him why the perverts went to Egypt!

"The Hashashin kidnapping a German nun and a Venetian widow in the streets of Acre will go almost unnoticed," he'd thought. "Sure, the oaf Frutolf will raise hell, having sworn to protect them, but once I have the information I want, I'll free them myself! He, he! Brilliant!"

He found himself, as always, diabolically clever. He'd meant for the women to stew in their terror for a few days but hadn't counted on Garietto being in love. Albacara and Rustico agreed in Limassol to provide a cover for the two youngsters, who could not be seen alone. That day Garietto arranged for all four to meet at ninth hour near the building site by the seawall where Saint Andrew's, which would be the biggest church in Acre, was being raised.

After waiting an hour, Garietto and Rustico, their scant weapons as visible as they could make them, walked to Saint Anne's to inquire after the women. They were told the two had not returned from Mass and after a frantic exchange in their lagoon dialect decided to look for the Teutonic knight who gave his word to Master Ezekiel that he would protect the women.

On hearing of the disappearance of his wards, Frutolf made his way to the Templar keep to speak with Bois-Guilbert. His master told him not to answer his brothers' questions on his assignment with the Templar, which made him feel important at the time, but now he had to speak with Bois-Guilbert, and the fact that he couldn't enter the Templar castle was one more instance of the humiliations he had not foreseen when he'd obediently accepted the mission. When Bois-Guilbert finally came out to see him, Frutolf told him with a certain urgency in his voice that the women had disappeared.

"The Venetian armigers of the countess are questioning everyone who was at the Mass in Saint Peter's. Soon they will go to the Venetian authorities and report them missing . . . or worse."

"Pipe down, Frutolf," said the Englishman condescendingly. "I had the Hashashin kidnap the women because I need to find out what the Jew and the abbess spoke about."

Frutolf was aghast. "You knew they were *my* wards and had them kidnapped?"

"You're an ingrate, Frutolf!" shouted Bois-Guilbert, turning the tables on the German. "I could have tortured them myself! If I had the Hashashin use their potions on them instead, it was so that *you* wouldn't break your pledge to the Jew . . . as if one had to keep promises made to servants of Satan!" He spat on the ground, looking even more outraged than Frutolf was.

"Now they'll tell her my protection was worth nothing . . ." mumbled the German, distraught.

"Aha! So *she's* the one that worries you, my poor besotted knight! Well, I can't blame you; the damsel is worthy of sleepless nights. But let me tell you, Frutolf: if I were to put a girl in your bed tonight—tall, shapely, and with long black hair—and tell you it was the Tuscan countess of your dreams, you wouldn't know the difference."

Frutolf was silent and then whispered, "Get what you want out of them, and then *let them go.* Understood?"

Bois-Guilbert smiled, thinking he would have to ask Master Pedro for a different partner.

The first day they'd been given nothing but bread and water, but their hands had not been tied, so as soon as they'd been thrown into the makeshift prison, they'd removed the gags from their mouths and started moaning in high-pitched, broken voices.

"Why not kill us outright?" sobbed Albacara. "They did so to enough Christians on Candia!"

"They must want something from us," Gudrun said, unusually lucid. "Remember the 'parchment' Mother Galatea and the Jew kept speaking of? That's probably what they're after."

"By the Holy Blood of the Virgin!" the widow cried. "Do you think they'll torture us?"

"I don't know. But when the mother told me we were going to Jerusalem, she said martyrdom at the hands of infidels could not be ruled out." They embraced each other, weeping in the darkness.

The next day, a bowl of meat with a thick sauce made them hope that someone was concerned about their well-being. They could never have imagined that the reason for the lamb stew was that the resin, which the Hashashin obtained by pressing the pollen of hemp flowers, was harder to hide inside bread.

The effects of the hashish on them were like an evil spell. At first, their heads swam, and they tripped when trying to stand up. Then their captors' laughter echoing behind the door sunk them into terror-filled fantasies in which defilement preceded death. At one point, Gudrun worked her lips, straining to form a word, but ended up blowing uselessly in Albacara's face. She started crying silently.

Still later, a little less anxious, Gudrun slid into more agreeable fantasies: Garietto freed them, sword in hand, and they accomplished their pilgrimage in Jerusalem. Even before being fed the resin, Gudrun possessed enough imagination for three young nuns, so in her incredibly vivid vision, back in Venice, their pilgrimage was followed by annulment of her vows, marriage, and a flock of blond children.

Just then, they heard the lock slide, and in the dim light from the doorway they made out Brother Bois-Guilbert entering the cell. Behind him was Frutolf, who insisted on being present when the women regained their freedom. Despite slurred speech, Albacara exclaimed, "Praise be to the Virgin! I knew the Mother of God would not abandon us. Thank you, Sweet Mary!" Gudrun was crossing herself over and over.

"You're lucky I have friends in the Saracen order that kidnapped you, my ladies!" began Bois-Guilbert, setting his trap.

"Why on earth would they kidnap *us*?" asked Gudrun, already standing up and straightening her habit, certain that the knights would now lead them out.

"Ehm . . . I'm afraid I've not yet obtained your release, Sister," said Bois-Guilbert. "The Hashashin want information about the Jew who charmed your abbess into submitting to his plan, and they won't let you go until you give it to them."

"I knew it!" cried the widow. "I always knew Mother Galatea was too trusting of that Christ killer!"

It was how Bois-Guilbert had hoped they would react. He saw Gudrun hesitate, uncertain whether to believe his words, but before the girl could say anything to the older woman, Albacara gushed, "You were right, Gudrun, it's the parchment they talked about with Don Sancio!"

"Who is this Don Sancio?" asked Bois-Guilbert immediately.

"Don Sancio de la Palmela," said Gudrun.

"They met the old master's secretary?" asked the Templar, incredulous. "Where? When?"

"He died in my house," said Albacara. "A week after the beaching of the cog."

"God knows what *he* told them," mumbled Bois-Guilbert. "Father Domingo must hear of this."

Gudrun heard the name but said nothing, increasingly sure that the Templar was not to be trusted.

"They want to know why the Jewish wizard and his captive abbess went to Egypt," said Bois-Guilbert with a new urgency. "Just tell them that, and we're all out of here!"

Gudrun wondered, "And who told these Saracens that Mother Galatea and the Jew went to Egypt?"

Albacara was quick to take the bait. "It's a letter! A monk in Cyprus told them there was a letter in a synagogue in Fustat. They wanted to see it badly; that's why they joined the friar."

Bois-Guilbert was exultant but tried not to show it. He'd been right, as usual! He'd found a lead that would make Father Domingo jump for joy; he just had to find a trusted messenger to deliver the news.

"Did they say anything about the letter? Who wrote it, or to whom?" he pressed the widow.

"Those are *his* questions, not the kidnappers'!" thought Gudrun. "No," she interjected, deciding to stop Albacara from spilling any more beans. "I heard them speak of the letter, but they never said who wrote it."

"But the letter was about the parchment they were looking for, was it not?" said Bois-Guilbert.

"Yes, yes," said the widow. "They said they would take it to Jerusalem and show it to the Old Man."

Bois-Guilbert blanched. "Almighty God, the Jew knows of the Old Man!" he thought, horrified. "Now we really *are* behind in this race!" His head spun with the implications of the Jew's reaching Syria and meeting with Domingo's archenemy, the chaplain of Château Pèlerin.

In any case, he'd found out enough. He'd meant to release the women after questioning them, in case the German lost control altogether. Despite the success of his scheme, he decided to punish Garietto for interfering by reporting the women's disappearance to Frutolf. The next day he summoned both armigers and gave them summary notice that they were on the list of people being recruited from Acre for the final assault on Damietta.

Garietto and Gudrun were devastated by the news. Bois-Guilbert had promised Galatea he wouldn't draft the women's escort, but the man clearly had no honor, and Gudrun prevailed on the widow to seek refuge in the Venetian commune and sever all contacts with the knight.

Early in September—too late, God being merciful, to take part in the disastrous attack on the sultan's camp—Garietto and Rustico embarked for the war. Gudrun and Garietto said their adieus on the quay. She took out a small silk bag that had lain hidden in Galatea's trunk and closed his hand around it.

"Take this, Garietto. It's a *real* relic my grandfather brought from Jerusalem. Woven into the bag is a thread from the Virgin's tunic! Wear it close to your heart; it will protect you from every blow in battle."

The big blonde started to weep. "I'll take the bag, my beloved," murmured Garietto. "But most of all, I'll take these tears with me . . ."

✡ ✠ ✡ ✠

CHÂTEAU PÉLERIN, ATHLIT, 12TH SEPTEMBER 1219

On a spur of rock jutting into the sea, separated from the shore by a wide moat, Château Pélerin was the strongest fortress the Temple had ever possessed in Outremer. Fifteen leagues southwest of Acre, it was completed just one year earlier, and many halls inside its walls were still unfinished.

A ditch, eighty feet wide and twenty feet deep, was dug across the base of the promontory in such a way that the sea could be made to flood it from either end. Behind the moat, the castle was defended by a wall with three-hundred-foot square towers, one in the middle and one at each end. But its real strength lay in its own small port, which enabled it to receive supplies under siege.

On that September day, Arnald Arifat approached the fortress from the south. Despite the master of Provence effortlessly exposing him as an agent of the Cathar church, he'd decided to contact the Old Man anyway. After the treaty between Salah ad-Din and Coeur de Lion, the coastal strip from Ascalon to Tyre was all that was left of the Latin Kingdom, but it had still been a risk for him to leave his squire in Ascalon and ride sixty leagues northward alone. He'd waited a long time for that meeting and didn't want anyone to know he would see the Old Man—nor, God forbid, ask questions about it.

Slowing his mount, he rose in the stirrups and gazed at the waves crashing on the breakwater that sheltered the little harbor. A beauséant* flapping in the wind above the near tower reminded him that he'd been wearing a Templar cross for four months. "I don't regret that decision," he thought with a smile. "Mostly because I wasn't subjected to the stricture of monkish life I feared most: abstinence!"

The two knights guarding the descent into the dry moat greeted him as he rode past, and soon he was entering the gate at the foot of the southern tower. He took his horse to the stables and then went to look for the Commander of the House to inquire about the chaplain's whereabouts.

He was told the Old Man was supervising the laying of foundations of the small round chapel that would soon go up in the keep. Arnald found him in a shed next to the hole over a hundred feet across that five workers were digging on the southern edge of the vast courtyard. Arnald peered at the figure in the semidarkness. He recognized the cleric to whom he'd given the Parchment of Circles ten years earlier, but only just. The Old Man now looked like life had been breathed into his corpse just before it could begin to seriously rot. Folds of ashen, shriveled skin hung from his skull, but the look of mild amusement in his eyes made him unmistakably the same man. Then the cadaver spoke.

"Ah, look who's here, Arnald Arifat, the blond troubadour who fights Rome with Father Boson. What a pleasant surprise . . . and wearing a red cross! Tell me, how is the old sage in Narbonne?"

"I don't know, Father; he was well enough when I last saw him, five months ago. By the way, what *is* your name, Father? Or should I call you Old Man, like everyone seems to do?"

"He, he . . . nice try, Arnald, but I'm not yet ready to reveal who I am—or rather, who I *was*. When I find the parchment, then I might be tempted to let my real name bask in some of that glory."

---

*The Templar standard, in battle or on keeps, was a vertical rectangle, the lower half white, the upper one black.

Arnald remembered the master of Provence calling the Old Man "a crafty bastard."

"What do you mean, when you *find* it? I brought you the Parchment ten years ago!" he blurted out.

"Ahh, you're right, of course, and I still have it," wheezed the Old Man. "But unfortunately, the parchment you brought me, the one your Cathar bishops received from the Bogomils, is a Greek copy of the original!"

"But it was drawn in Greek by Saint John himself!" exclaimed Arnald, trying to keep his voice down but visibly shaken by the demotion to "a copy" of a relic he considered holier than the True Cross.

The Old Man leaned forward, smiling kindly. Arnald thought of smiling skulls in Sicilian crypts. "I'm sorry, Arnald," he said. "I know how *crucial* those two circles are to your church's view of history. But I've spent *fifteen* years chasing that map—I mean that parchment. I discovered the original was found near Jericho four hundred years ago. It was identical, but *in Hebrew*. You see, the original is a *map,* but once the words on it are translated into Greek . . . they no longer lead to anything!"

Arnald took a step back and scratched his beard. "If the real Parchment is a map, what does it lead to? Why does everyone want it so badly?"

The Old Man burned with the desire to unburden decades of secrets, but if the Cathar in front of him was certainly an enemy of Rome, he was now also a knight of the Temple. Pedro de Montaigue could make him repeat every word he was told.

"And Pedro is *not* Guillaume," the Old Man reminded himself. "But Pedro already knows what the map leads to. I must simply avoid telling Arnald anything I haven't told the new master," he thought.

"All right, Arnald," he said out loud, grinning in anticipation. "The Cathars' version of the Parchment may not work as a map, but you and Boson trusted me enough to let me keep it for you, and it was helpful in my unfinished search for the original . . . so if you'll follow me to my scriptorium, I'll repay my debt to the Cathar church by telling you the story of the Parchment of Circles—and I mean the *real* story!"

The two men crossed the courtyard, the Old Man taking short, determined little steps, to a long building on its western side that looked out on the sea. The scriptorium was on its first floor and was so full of books and parchments that Arnald thought it looked out of place in those bare military quarters.

The chaplain sat him down by a window and went to fetch a Bible. "You're a Cathar," he began almost gleefully, "so you've always known that Jesus wasn't the Son of God, but a man like you and me. A prophet, to be sure, as the Saracens also admit, but a man. And like all men, he did *not* come back from the dead!" He put down the Bible and whispered in the knight's ear: "*That* is what everyone is after, Arnald: the written proof that there was *no* Resurrection!"

Pleased with the knight's wide open eyes, the Old Man turned to a worn page of the codex. "Did you ever read these verses?" He recited a passage from Matthew. "Some of the guards went into the city and reported to the chief priests everything that had happened. When the chief priests met with the elders and devised a plan, they gave the soldiers a large sum of money, telling them, "You are to say: '*His disciples came during the night and stole him away while we were asleep.*' If this report gets to the governor, we will satisfy him and keep you out of trouble." So the soldiers took the money and did as they were instructed. And this story has been widely circulated among Jews to this very day."

The Old Man paused for effect. "The Parchment of Circles leads to the confession by the thieves who stole the body. Its discovery would make the very foundations of Roman Christianity crumble to dust!"

Something twigged in Arnald's memory, but he couldn't put a finger on it and didn't want to lose a word of the Old Man's account, so he said nothing. The chaplain went on.

"I spoke with every sect that was in Jerusalem when the Jericho trove came to light. I even spoke with the keeper of Saracen records. I discovered that the rabbis prohibited Jews from revealing the true nature of the Parchment but that the Karaites, some years later, gifted a Greek translation of it to the Johannites, who were convinced it was the work of Saint John himself. That copy made its way to Thrace and ended up in the hands of Bogomil—who was, as you surely know—the Bulgarian founder of your religion."

Arnald nodded silently and then said, "But how can you be sure it was a translation, Father? Couldn't the Jericho trove also have included a parchment drawn by Saint John *in Greek*?"

"Mmh . . . the question of whether Saint John wrote in Hebrew or Greek is a fascinating one, Arnald, but the fact remains that the Parchment was drawn as a *map,* not written as a prophecy."

"Who says so?" By now Arnald was almost pleading. "If you haven't found the Hebrew original, how do you *know* it is a map? Or that a Hebrew original even *exists*?"

"That's not a bad question," said the Old Man, standing up slowly to put away the Bible. "Well, for a start, several people *independently* told me of a letter, written by the rabbis in Jerusalem who saw the Parchment at the time it was found. Apparently they wrote it was a map, which led to a document that would put an end to Christianity and that the Messiah would make use of it on his arrival. It seems that letter is somewhere in Egypt."

At the words "put an end to Christianity," Arnald again felt the twinge of a distant memory. He made an effort to remember where he'd heard the phrase, but every Cathar perfectus he'd ever met believed Rome was Babylon and was always predicting the end of Christianity, so he soon gave up.

The Old Man went on. "As for how I *know* that an original exists, I entered the Temple as a Cistercian chaplain in Montpellier thirty years ago, knowing nothing of any parchment, simply driven by a scholar's desire, nurtured for years, to find the *first* circular map of Jerusalem, the one that must have given rise to the dozens I'd seen in Europe since my childhood in . . . never mind, where I was a child is not important."

He grinned and sat back down on the stool in front of Arnald.

"What matters is what I discovered in Montpellier. A hundred years ago, when the Order of the Temple was founded, rumors were already rife that the real Parchment was somewhere in Jerusalem. The first nine knights, with the pretext of building their stables, spent eight years digging under the esplanade looking for it but found nothing."

The chaplain looked around as if to make sure no one could hear and whispered,

"Then, in 1127, at the Council of Troyes, Saint Bernard convinced Honorius II that the order had found the Parchment and, through it, the confession. The concessions the Temple has extorted from popes ever since have been exorbitant. And you wonder *why* everyone wants that parchment so badly?"

"Saint Bernard of Cîteaux *lied* to the pope?" asked Arnald, incredulous.

"Listen, I met Bernard; in fact he was my first teacher, eighty years ago," said the Old Man. "To save his Cistercian houses he would have sacrificed Rome, not just a pope—but Jerusalem, *never*! He wanted his Templars to hold it forever, or at least until Christ returns. He was lucky to die thirty years before Salah ad-Din took it from him."

"There's just one thing I don't understand, Father," said Arnald. "You and I have our reasons to hate Rome; we know why *Roma* is the reverse of *Amor*. But the Temple is Saint Bernard's and the pope's creature . . . why on earth would *they* ever threaten the very survival of Christianity?"

"Another far from stupid question. You see, after Godefroy took Jerusalem, Christian knights spent thirty years speaking with all kinds of heretics: Syriac monks, Jewish-Christian sects, Sufi brotherhoods, Manicheans of all sorts. Some of them began to contemplate a kind of synthesis of the three faiths, which would put an end to all wars, and soon found that if such a new religion could be spawned, the demotion of 'Christ the Son of God' to plain 'Jesus the prophet' was an obligatory step in constructing it."

Arnald smiled, thinking back to conversations with Yehezkel on whether such a truly ecumenical faith would ultimately be practicable. He suddenly wished his kabbalist friend could speak with the Old Man while the cleric was still alive. "I have a good Jewish friend in Languedoc," he said, as though this had something to do with new religions, "a rabbi, medicus, and kabbalist. I wish he were here to help you in your quest. He's supposed to be somewhere in Syria with my thirteen-year-old only son. I don't know if he'd help you *find* the Parchment, but if you already had it, for sure he would be the man to understand what those Jerusalem rabbis understood four hundred years ago!"

The Old Man looked seriously interested. "A kabbalist? Yes, I heard of those 'Jewish Sufis' before, in Montpellier, but I confess I don't know much about them. They pronounce names of God, don't they? What is this rabbi's name, anyway?"

"Yehezkel ben Yoseph, Father, but back in Provence everyone calls him Master Ezekiel."

"And why did my speaking of knights who wish to inspire a new religion that will truly bring peace remind you of your Jewish friend?"

"Because he sometimes claims to be an Averroist—you know, a follower of the Saracen philosopher who holds that no religion possesses the whole truth. But do I detect a trace of sympathy in your words for the plans of those enlightened knights, Father?"

The chaplain grinned. "You do indeed, Arnald. I've promoted them for decades and made enemies in the process, both here and in Rome." His collapsed features twisted in disgust. "Rome gives off a truly bad smell, Arnald," he said bitterly. "Greed, arrogance, simony, and sodomy reign there, but what do its popes worry about? Heretics! Domingo and his friars wrap the hands of heretics around hot coals, tear out their nails and beards to convince them that the way they think about God is mistaken. It's all so . . . stupid!"

Arnald let him vent a little and then turned back to the Parchment. "Do you think the original never left Jerusalem?"

"I don't just think so, I'm sure of it. A hundred years ago, circular maps of Jerusalem began to be seen in Europe. North and south were often differently placed, but they all bore the same mistakes with respect to the real city, so they obviously shared the same original. And at the time, your Greek version had been far from here for centuries. Clearly, a copy of the Hebrew original was made."

"Have you found no indication of where in the city the original might be?" asked Arnald.

"I've been concentrating on the records from the days of the first king, Baldwin I, but . . . "

The name Baldwin finally shifted something in Arnald's memory and he let out a short cry. "HA! I have it. It was Robert de Bassonville!"

"Uh? What *are* you talking about?" said the chaplain.

"I just remembered who used the phrase 'put an end to Christianity!' Abbot Boson once told me the story of a convert, a Frankish noble from Dieppe, Robert de Bassonville, who became a Cathar believer in his old age, thirty or forty years ago. He married Adelisa, an illegitimate daughter of Roger II of Sicily, but one the king loved so much it seemed he'd told her a secret, which Adelisa revealed to her husband, and he later confided to Abbot Boson."

The Old Man had never heard of any of them—except Roger of Sicily, of course—but listened intently all the same, hoping for a clue, any clue, to the whereabouts of the Parchment.

"Well, what Roger told his daughter," Arnald went on, "concerned his own mother, Adelaide of Vasto, the woman Baldwin I took for his wife in a second marriage."

The chaplain let out a short gasp. "Uh, I know all about *that* story! Arnulf, the Patriarch of Jerusalem, was deposed because he officiated that wedding despite knowing that Baldwin was *bigamous,* because Arda of Armenia, his first wife, was still alive! When the king fell ill, he got so scared that he had the marriage annulled and Adelaide sent back to Sicily!"

"Exactly! Her son Roger never forgave the kingdom for the slight! Thirty years later, he refused to join half the kings of Europe in the second campaign against the Saracens."

The Old Man urged him on: "So what was the secret Roger learned from his mother?"

"She'd read Baldwin's private diary and told her son the king found a document that, in his own words, 'would put an end to Christianity!' Roger told Adelisa of the diary to perpetuate the knowledge of its existence, since finding that document was his only hope of avenging his mother's humiliation."

The Old Man was euphoric. He got up and started pacing the room, short steps and hunched back making him look like a piece on a chessboard. A hooded bishop, thought Arnald.

"King Baldwin chose to hide it! I should have guessed," the chaplain was murmuring. "This time I have it! Just when I thought I wouldn't live long enough to set eyes on it . . . "

"I admit it sounds like Baldwin was talking of the confession," said Arnald, "but Roger said nothing to his daughter of where it might be."

"Aah, but the king almost certainly wrote that in his diary!" cried the chaplain.

"And where do you plan to look for King Baldwin's hundred-year-old private diary?" asked Arnald.

"But in the Royal Treasure, of course," said the Old Man. "Where else?"

CHAPTER 23

VAYEHI EREV

And There Was Evening

THE SULTAN'S CAMP AT FÄRISKÜR,
16TH SEPTEMBER 1219

Galatea bent down to straighten her *sirwâl*.* A mamluk caught a
glimpse of a slim ankle and thought, "See how Allah is merciful, even
to depraved sinners like me!"

On her first night in the camp, al-Kamil ordered that she be taken
not to the prostitutes' tents, but to the one housing the wives of several emirs. The women there, quickly taken with her noble demeanor,
crowded around and lent her clothes, which quite became her, despite
being a little short, since the tallest of the Turkish and Kurdish ladies
there barely came up to her chin.

A loose, long-sleeved dress with a short slit in the front and an
ornate belt fell just below her knees. Colored bands of Arabic inscription adorned its arms and the hem of the skirt. Under it, she wore a
white ankle-length sirwâl, lined in red, and low black slippers. Finally,

---

*Loose drawers similar to pajama bottoms, reaching to the ankle and held up by a draw-
string called a tikka.

a veil went over her head and round her neck. Seeing her walk around the camp dressed as an Egyptian woman—not so differently, that is, from the way his Naomi used to dress—Yehezkel found Galatea more feminine than when she'd worn a nun's habit or the extravagant dresses of a Tuscan countess. Glimpsing the contours of her body now sparked the same stirring in his loins that he'd felt while holding her senseless in his arms in Torcello and on the *Falcus*.

Communication with the women being limited to a few courteous hand gestures, Galatea's days in the camp were a time of isolation and silent contemplation, both second nature to a Cistercian nun, but to which she had devoted precious little time during the heady events of the last six months. In the light of the little Kabbalah she learned, she reflected on Brother Francesco turning out to be the man in her vision. It occurred to her that this was the perfect occasion to question Aillil, who visited the ladies' tent every day, about the true beliefs of Cathars.

She did, and the doctrines Aillil learned from perfecti as a child soon made her understand why the heresy won so many Christian hearts. After all, neither Christians nor Jews, as far as she knew, had a really satisfying explanation for human evil. Neither were prepared to admit that Satan was the equal of God, both insisting instead that he, too, was a fallen angel. How much easier and free of contradictions it must be to consider God wholly good, but faced with a wholly evil *uncreated* adversary, a Satan so powerful it was actually *he* who created the whole bloodied, unjust universe around us, in which all are, in effect, prisoners!

After witnessing al-Kamil's placid response to Brother Francesco's missionary fervor, Galatea became enough of an Averroist herself to refrain from trying to correct Aillil's Cathar view of the world. Let him believe what he'd been taught, even if it was that there isn't one God, but *two*! That it would make any difference to the fate of his soul was something—may God forgive her!—she no longer felt sure of.

By now it was clear, she thought. They all preached the same thing: Gioacchino, Francesco, Sufis, and Cathars all preached a coming era of love! In those lonely days she became intimately convinced, with the wordless certainty of dreams, that in Francesco what was taking place was not simply an Imitatio Christi, but the Second Advent itself!

Then she suddenly thought, "But if Jesus Christ has returned like he promised, and fifteen years ago I was solemnly declared a Bride of Christ, then . . . then Francesco is my husband!"

She gasped. "Now how did *that* thought enter my head? Are priests, and not Hildegard, right about women after all? Oh, Mother of God, stop me thinking, for I am made of flesh and cannot help sinning!"

Six days after Francesco returned to the Christian camp, Yehezkel was summoned to the sultan's tent.

"Get up off your knees, Tabib," said al-Malik with a wide grin. "The Franks, like you predicted, have accepted the truce and asked for more time to consider the new offer. But tell me, what will happen to you *now* if you set foot in a kingdom where the long arm of that 'cardinal' can reach you?"

Yehezkel smiled. "I took the liberty of asking the rahib to tell the Franks that you detained me, my lord, because I am your subject by birth, and you needed more physicians for your wounded."

"Ha, ha! You're giving me ideas, Tabib . . . but no, I don't want to interfere with your search in al-Kuds. How do you plan on reaching the Holy City from here?"

"No, Commander of the Faithful, not from here. First I have to find a document in a synagogue in Fustat, so I thought we would sail up the river."

Al-Kamil laughed. "I like your style, Tabib! If those bloody Franks—may Allah curse them to oblivion!—didn't feel they had the right to impose their trading privileges on the rest of the world, I'd probably be taking a cruise on the Great Mother Nile myself . . . though no one in my harem is a match for your stunning Christian lady!" He laughed again.

"I love the Great Mother Nile," said Yehezkel, "more than any other waters I've sailed in, and that includes most of the Mediterranean."

"A sailing Jew!" laughed the Sultan. "I don't believe the *ummah* has known many of those!"

"You're right, my lord. My teacher, Musa ibn Maimun—may his memory be a blessing—always opposed my love for the sea. He said God lives on mountains."

"He was a wise man," said al-Kamil. "Here, this is your authorization to search the Haram al-Sharif. I hope your erratic behavior won't make me regret signing it."

"May Allah keep you alive as long as time exists!" said Yehezkel, bowing deeply. He took the rolled-up letter, thanked God in his heart for how things had gone in the Egyptian camp, and left the tent.

Yehezkel told Galatea the good news, asked her to get ready to sail in the morning, and then found Aillil and walked to the riverbank village of Färiskür with him to look for a jalabah. As happens to villages close to besieged cities, in the six months since the sultan's camp had moved there from al-Adiliyah the daily passage of men, arms, and victuals coming down the Nile from al-Kahira had turned Färiskür into a bustling little town.

He was looking for a decked boat so that Galatea could sleep below while he, Aillil, and the jalabah's owner slept on deck. He knew that September breezes would blow from the north, pushing them south to al-Kahira, and would have preferred a jalabah with two sails that opened out like a butterfly's wings. That would have guaranteed them enough speed to overcome the current even when the breeze behind was light, thus avoiding having to zigzag their way up the river with constant stern tacks, jibing the sail every time they approached a bank.

It didn't take him long, on the crowded riverbank quays, to find Ahmed ibn Suleiman, a cheerful man with a droopy moustache and spindly legs poking out of Yemeni-style trousers. Ahmed owned a decked jalabah and, for a fee Yehezkel found reasonable, would take the rabbi and his companions to Fustat. Yehezkel examined the boat, and the two men agreed on a time of departure.

As he walked back to the camp, Yehezkel reflected that he was about to return to Fustat for the first time in fifteen years. Images of his father, Naomi, and his teacher floated up before his eyes. He sat down, overcome by nostalgia. "All the people I loved are dead," he thought. His mother had died when he was a child, and for some strange reason the memory of her funeral was sharper than that of her face.

He was startled by the sudden thought that he must not shed tears in front of the nun. Then his mind turned to the search in the *geniza** and something that emerged from the whirlwind of memories unsettled him. He'd grown up praying in the Ibn Ezra synagogue and remembered the curse that lay on anyone who dared to remove any writings from its geniza. His mind jumped on the challenge.

"The simplest way to avoid the curse is to read the letter in the geniza and leave it there," he thought but then followed that through. "But Makarios said the Old Man wouldn't collaborate unless I showed the letter from the rabbis. But surely the Templar master will *tell* him to collaborate, won't he?" The next thought made his face drop. "What if the synagogue elders forbid me to even enter the geniza to avoid a curse on their community?" He wondered if mentioning Rav Eleazar of Worms would have any effect on the rabbis of his hometown and decided it wouldn't. He went as far as considering a nighttime burglar's expedition into the synagogue. At this, his alter ego burst out, "What? And bring a flame into a room full of parchments and papyri? Have you gone *mad*?"

---

*A geniza is a storage area in a synagogue.

Finally, he decided that Divine Providence would find a way to help, stood up, and entered the camp.

✡ ✠ ✡ ✠

FÄRISKÜR, 22ND SEPTEMBER 1219

By the next morning, with everyone on board and Ahmed casting off, Yehezkel forgot both sad memories and geniza preoccupations. A breeze in his nostrils and the war in another world, he relished the four sublime colors of the Nile Valley for the first time since arriving in Egypt: the yellow desert, the green irrigated valley dotted with date palms, the purpley blue of the Nile, and the whole scene topped by the whitish sapphire of the Egyptian sky. Unable to contain himself, Yehezkel started declaiming.

"Madame, Aillil: before you is the mother of all life, the great Nile, without which Egypt would not exist!" Ahmed couldn't help laughing at the strange sound of his Latin. Galatea and Aillil were smiling.

"My teacher—may his memory shine forever—used to say that in this land, the Nile is never far from the eyes and never far from one's thoughts. But look! All around us are dozens of jalabahs like this one—to me, the river's true beauties! Their sails, full of breeze under thin, arched bamboo yards, make them look like graceful white butterflies. See, their hulls are the same size, in proportion to the sails, of a butterfly's body in proportion to its wings! They may move on the water, but from afar you can almost imagine them suddenly begin to flap their sails and take off, a cloud of white butterflies flying over the river!"

"How poetic, Rabbi!" exclaimed Galatea, touched by this dreamy vision.

For an instant, inadvertently calling him "Rabbi" despite Aillil's presence made her feel as if they were a family and there were, in effect, no strangers. She shook her head hard to dispel the notion that they could *ever* be a normal family. Sometimes there were limits even to dreams.

Yehezkel started rushing around the jalabah, tugging on sheets and halyard until he was satisfied that their single lateen sail was propelling them as fast as the breeze would allow. Ahmed nodded approvingly as he squatted by the hatch that led belowdecks, preparing some pomegranate drinks. Then the sailor rabbi sat down next to his Christian partner again and reminisced.

"These jalabahs are what made me fall in love with sailing when I was a boy." Smiling at the memory, he went on, "My heart would miss a beat when a gust of wind filled the sail, but the pull on the sail didn't yet overcome the boat's weight and the water's grip on it. Then, the next instant, the jalabah wrenched itself free of those reins and surged forward, and a scream of pure joy would erupt from my throat, to the great amusement of the sailors on board."

Galatea thought of the sudden surge of the galley leaving Limassol and knew what the boy felt.

"I took part in maneuvers on board whenever they would let me," went on Yehezkel, "and one day the owner of a jalabah told me that if I should decide not to become a rabbi, he could make a good sailor of me, and after saying it he laughed so hard he knocked one of his mates into the river!"

Galatea's laugh, as usual, crossed languages better than a sermon by Brother Francesco, and Ahmed's face, when he heard it, lit up in a nearly toothless grin. They sailed upstream until nightfall, a wonderful northeastern breeze pushing them along the bends in the river as they drank in the landscape and enjoyed the day as if they hadn't just spent a month and a half in the middle of a brutal war.

As the crow flies, al-Kahira is about a hundred leagues—parasangs, as they were known in the East—from Damietta, but along the winding bends of the Nile's eastern branch, which sometimes doubled back on itself twice in a row, a boat had to cover almost double that distance, and the jalabah's best speed meant it would be at least a week before they reached Fustat.

Farther upstream, closer to al-Kahira, the river's banks would become solid—made of earth, sand, or rock—but in the delta its edges mostly vanished into a smelly, humid, insect-ridden swamp, a place that at night seemed noisy and dangerous to Galatea, the dense bamboo and papyrus surely hiding crocodiles on the prowl. Much as she was excited by the days and moved by the sunsets, the abbess would later recall nights in the delta as among the most harrowing times of the whole pilgrimage. When, before darkness, Ahmed would steer the jalabah close to the swamp and throw its grapnel anchor overboard, Galatea would wrap herself in every stitch of fabric she owned and go into hiding below.

The jalabah's passengers were twice woken in the middle of the night by strange screeching and warbling sounds echoing out of the swamp. No one, not even Ahmed, could imagine what they might be, which contributed to Galatea's anxiety. As if all that weren't enough, experience in the Venetian lagoon had taught her that mosquito bites left swellings on her delicate skin that took days to disappear. But her mood always improved when the sun rose and the jalabah left the marshes for the middle of the river. She had sailed on a cog, a tareta, and a galley in the space of six months and moved around on Ahmed's little sailboat with a confidence that impressed the Egyptians, both Saracen and Jew.

"Actually," she said to herself after a compliment from one of them, "for a Tuscan girl who grew up riding horses, I don't make such a bad sailor after all."

One day the jalabah was sailing around a bend not far from the village of Zifta, halfway to al-Kahira, when suddenly, through some gaps in the vegetation, they glimpsed a collapsing ancient temple. Ahmed had seen it before and didn't pay it much attention, but his passengers, curious as monkeys like all kuffar, excitedly asked him to drop anchor so they could go ashore and explore the ruins.

Fear of crocodiles and snakes limited the time they spent on the muddy bank, but it was enough for them to step onto the remains of a paved plaza and walk around the half of the temple that had not fallen into the surrounding swamp. It was clearly a construction from the time of the pharaohs, the mysterious symbols of their tongue—depicting everything from eyes and hands to birds and palms—carved into many stones. They saw statues of hawks and dogs, and Yehezkel explained that the pagan ways before Islam were collectively known as *jahiliyyah,* which he translated as "the days of ignorance."

In hindsight, after living under the wing of the Angel of Death in the Christian camp, witnessing the slaughter of the 29th of August and running the risk of joining Brother Francesco's martyrdom, the lazy, peaceful days on the river were a badly needed, refreshing pause in a hectic pilgrimage.

✡ ✠ ✡ ✠

FUSTAT, 29TH SEPTEMBER 1219

On the seventh day, after sailing past the point where the Nile splits into its two branches, they sighted al-Kahira. Beyond the fertile fields on the right bank, three parasangs to the south, the vision took shape like a trembling mirage. From that distance, in the late afternoon haze and with the sun behind them, the city looked like a snowcapped mountain—an illusion, explained Yehezkel, created by the two palaces in the center of the city. Built in front of each other, they had by now four thousand rooms, haphazardly built on top of each other, and the whole structure was whitewashed every year, so that it looked like a shining white hill emerging from the mist.

It was a sight to make one's heart sing. As they sailed past it heading for Fustat, a handful of parasangs further upstream, they had to maneuver among hundreds of jalabahs and narrowly avoided more than one collision. Even as he frantically jibed the sail—untying its sheet, raising the yard until it was vertical, and then quickly passing it onto the other side of the mast—Yehezkel kept up a stream of lyrical lore about Egypt's jewel. Galatea and Aillil both rolled up their eyes mockingly.

"I never saw Damascus or Baghdad," he intoned, "but the Jewish medicus of the Hunchback's Tale, in the Thousand and One Nights, calls al-Kahira Great Mother of the World. Where will I ever find a more moving sight," he said, "unless one day the Lord, in his infinite mercy, allows me to see Jerusalem?"

In front of Fustat, the Nile is so wide it contains the whole island of er-Roda; Island of the Rich, as Egyptians call it. In effect, the richest men had marvelous palaces and gardens built there since the time of the pharaohs. Now, too, the island's mansions were no less luxurious than those of Western kings.

As Galatea watched the fabulous residences, Yehezkel told her that when the Torah says, 'And the daughter of Pharaoh came down to bathe at the river,' it is speaking of the palace on er-Roda, so it was among the reeds before them that Moses was saved from the waters.

When they finally disembarked and paid Ahmed his due, Yehezkel took them to the house of his teacher's son, Avraham ben Moshe ben Maimon, who had been appointed nagid, head of the Jewish community, on Rav Moshe's death by the previous sultan, despite being only seventeen. Avraham welcomed his old friend, gave Galatea and Aillil a guest room in his house, and then kept Yehezkel up all night with questions on the Kabbalah he learned in Provence.

Yehezkel grew up with Avraham, who was four years younger, and had watched his friend turn, perhaps as a reaction to his father's famous rationalism, into a soft-spoken mystic, influenced by Fustat's Sufi schools to the point of writing, "The mystics of Islam walk in the footsteps of the prophets of Judaism." Before leaving for Provence to avoid taking another wife after Naomi's death, Yehezkel took comfort from a rabbinical opinion in which Avraham recommended postponing marriage until spiritual perfection is achieved.

The next day, the 30th of September, was Yom Kippur, and Yehezkel spent it fasting and praying in the synagogue of his youth while Galatea and Aillil visited the Coptic church of Abu Serga, Saint Sergius and Bacchus, inside the Roman fortress of Babylonia, built on the spot where the Holy Family rested on their journey into Egypt.

Unfortunately, the Nile was high, and they could not descend into the crypt.

When Yehezkel emerged from the synagogue in the afternoon, he found Galatea waiting outside, a little worried by his haggard look, to accompany him to break his fast.

Yehezkel knew that Maimonides had died some six months after his departure for Provence, so the first thing he did on meeting Avraham was to inquire after Rav Moshe's grave. On hearing that five years earlier the body had been taken to Eretz Israel and reburied there, he rejoiced for the soul of his teacher but also regretted the lost opportunity to visit his grave.

Despite the disappointment, the next day he went to Fustat's Jewish cemetery to visit his own father's grave. He asked Galatea and Allil to wait outside the plot, and they watched from a distance as the rabbi placed some pebbles on the tombstone and recited a prayer.

As black crows squawked ceaselessly around them, Galatea caught herself thinking that the somber, low tombstones, identical except for the inscription, contrasted sharply with Christian crypts and mausoleums, which betrayed a habit of continuing to compete for prestige, even from under six feet of earth.

Another embarrassing comparison between the customs arising from their respective faiths happened when Yehezkel, a day later, entered a *beit midrash,* a Jewish house of study, to consult the Book of Kings about a detail in her Cypriot dream that baffled him. Galatea waited outside, but soon curiosity drew her to peer in through a window. Yehezkel was sitting at a table, his head in a book, when someone announced it was time for Mincha, the afternoon prayer. The Jews who'd been studying in pairs, or eating, or joking in the big, bare room full of nothing but books and parchments, suddenly stood, faced Jerusalem and started to pray. In an instant, the room turned into a synagogue. Galatea was startled.

When the rabbi emerged, she confided to him the comparison the sight had provoked. "You know, Rabbi, we Christians, in order to pray, have to first surround ourselves with altars, sacred paraments, silver utensils, and the smell of incense."

Yehezkel laughed. "As usual, madame, the sharpness of your mind shapes your natural intuition. The observation you make shows two things: first, that *real* prayer is between you and God, something you do in your soul, so you should be able to do it anywhere, even on a ship's bowsprit."

Galatea smiled at the memory of the rabbi deep in prayer, tied to the forestay of the *Falcus*.

"And second," he went on, "that turning the room you're in into a synagogue confirms the notion that God is everywhere, while the dramatic difference between churches and other places makes it easier—for simple people—to conclude that in the tavern God is absent."

Galatea thought of the Age of the Spirit that Gioacchino and Brother Francesco said was arriving and for an instant wondered if Jews weren't already living in it. Then her teacher surprised her again.

"Having said all that, when we still had *our* Temple in Jerusalem, we were also very fond of altars, sacred paraments, silver utensils, and the smell of incense. I guess the fact that we've learned to do without them is one of the lessons of exile."

They looked at each other and smiled their complicit, Averroist smile.

Jewish sacred books that are no longer usable cannot be thrown out because they contain the name of God, so they are put in a geniza, from the Hebrew meaning "to store," usually in a synagogue's attic or basement. In the year of the Lord 882, the Jews of Fustat bought and renovated the derelict Coptic Church of Saint Michael, turning it into the Ibn Ezra Synagogue, where Yehezkel had prayed as a boy. For three centuries Fustat's Jews stuffed such writings into a hole high up in the wall of the women's section, and through it into a small attic under the roof.

The way Divine Providence helped them was to ensure that

Avraham ben Moshe would be the nagid, so that if *he* decided to allow them into the geniza, no rabbi or notable in the community, curses notwithstanding, would dare to object.

The day after visiting his father's grave, Yehezkel explained to Avraham the importance of finding the letter from the Jerusalem rabbis on the Parchment of Circles, which he'd been told was in the geniza.

"You're joking, Heski!" said Avraham. "Even if you manage to enter the room with no one stabbing you, can you imagine what three hundred years of books and parchments thrown in through a hole will look like? A needle in a haystack would be easier to find than that letter!"

"I know, Avi, I know. I'll very likely spend three days in there, cover the inside of my lungs with dust, and come out empty-handed. But I trust in help from above. And you know, Kabbalah is teaching me to recognize that help."

Avraham smiled and authorized his friend to discreetly enter the geniza.

When she heard that Yehezkel would go in there but would not be allowed to remove a thing from it, Galatea demanded to go also.

"I dressed as a man to leave the Christian camp, so I can pretend to be a Jewess to see the letter!"

"And just *what* Jewess will you be, madame? How will you answer questions from other Jews in the synagogue? Your disguise wouldn't hold up for a minute," said Yehezkel, knowing he couldn't win.

Galatea pondered his objection, an embarrassed smile slowly spreading on her face.

"I'll be your new, *very* shy Italian wife," she finally said, grinning. "A wife who *never* speaks to strangers."

For a moment, Yehezkel speechlessly entertained the fantasy of her converting and really becoming his wife. Then he resigned himself to force majeure, not before thinking, "Go on, admit it, anyone else looking for a needle in a haystack would be grateful for the presence of a prophetess with the visionary powers of this nun."

"If you open your mouth in there, you will ruin what's left of my reputation as a rabbi," he said.

"Don't worry, Rabbi, in the presence of others I'll be as talkative as a tomb, but *if* we find the letter, I'll expect you to read it to me immediately, in Latin, in the geniza. A later summary will *not* do."

Yehezkel grunted agreement, thinking that, after all, Jewish prophets had all been grumpy, too.

When the day came, Yehezkel decided not to disturb the hole in the wall that tradition elected as the geniza's only access and to look instead for the door leading to the attic that must once have existed and later been walled up. He examined every mite of the wall, scratching away plaster where he thought it hid something, and eventually found it. Avraham's servant kept women out of the upper floor as Yehezkel took down a section of the wall, one brick at a time, until he could crawl up the mercifully well-preserved wooden steps behind the proper door, followed by Galatea, and at last enter the geniza.

The mountain of books crumbled slowly away from below the hole and into the center of the attic, as Avraham predicted. But on the opposite side of the room, in the dim light from the hole, Yehezkel saw some shelves up against the external wall of the synagogue, also full of books. He guessed that an attempt had been made early on to store parchments and books in an orderly way, perhaps even archive them, before the process degenerated into a lazier "throw them in the hole" practice.

He pointed at the shelves; Galatea nodded and followed him over. She lit the safest source of light they had thought to bring, a small slipper-shaped bronze oil lamp, and by its weak but steady light, Yehezkel began to look for indications of what was on the shelves. The help from above Yehezkel counted on was punctually delivered.

Sections of the shelves had labels nailed to them bearing names of cities, presumably those from which the rolled-up parchments on the shelf had come. Baghdad, Jerusalem, Tiberias, Trani, Marseille, Cordoba, Toledo, Pumpedita . . . here was a collection of four centuries of missives from rabbis in every important center of Jewish study and legislation in the world. A veritable treasure trove!

Yehezkel whispered something to Galatea, sat by the shelf marked "Jerusalem," and began to carefully unfurl the parchments on it, one by one. A few crumbled in his hands as he opened them, but most were readable. He rolled each one up again and replaced it on the shelf as soon as he understood it was not what he was looking for.

After an hour of repetitive work, Galatea had just refilled the oil lamp when Yehezkel let out a muffled cry and gestured to bring it closer. He was holding a parchment rolled up inside another one, the inner one visibly much older and frayed than the outer one. He gingerly put the older one on the shelf and started reading the newer one, the letter from the rabbis. As he read, his eyes darted to the older parchment on the shelf with what to Galatea seemed almost a look of fear. When he finished, he let out a deep sigh.

"What does it say? Come on, you promised you wouldn't make me wait!" blurted Galatea.

"Rav Nachman of Jerusalem writes that he and his companion brought with them the page from the Book of Ezekiel"—he looked at the scroll on the shelf again—"that Hanina bar Hezekiah hid in Jerusalem after removing it from the version in the collected Holy Writings."

"That's exactly what Elisha ben Abuya accused him of doing," whispered Galatea in the semidarkness.

"That's not all," said Yehezkel. "Father Makarios was right . . . Rav Nachman writes that the rabbis used the Parchment of Circles to find the page but refused to explain the map to the Abbasid governor, who confiscated it, and two of them had to escape to Tulunid Egypt."

Yehezkel peered into the letter to find the passage again. "You see, madame, he writes, 'The man who made the map was a heretic, so it was dangerous to reveal the place to the authorities, but we found it and took the page to safety from Christians. But the other two things we left in their hiding place, for when Messiah comes.'"

"'The other *two* things?'" gasped Galatea. A detail of the story that Don Sancio recited on board the *Falcus* was escaping her, and she knew it was important.

"Im ha-Shemen," said Yehezkel. "Elisha said Hanina had hidden the page *with the oil,* remember?"

"Now I do. I never asked you about it, Rabbi, but what oil was Elisha speaking of?"

"I have a hunch about that, but it would be too fearsome a thought . . ." murmured Yehezkel.

"Go on, you can say it. It's not as if I'll go and tell the rabbis here that I think you must be crazy!"

He laughed. "Well, somewhere in the Temple was the Holy Oil of Anointing, made in the desert at the time of the Exodus 'after the art of the perfumer.'" Yehezkel looked incredulous himself. "Moses anointed Aaron with it; Samuel anointed two kings with it, Saul and David. The Talmud says it was inexhaustible, that it was always the *same* oil."

"But the rabbi says 'the other *two* things.' One is the oil, and the other? It could be the confession."

Yehezkel changed the subject. "Here's another interesting passage. Listen: 'Rumors in Jerusalem say that the Parchment of Circles is a map leading to an object that belonged to Yeshu ha-Nozri.'"

"Madre Santissima!" exclaimed Galatea, barely repressing a little shriek. "The Holy Grail!"

They'd rarely mentioned it, but both knew Chrétien of Troye's chanson, and Galatea had spoken about the meaning of the tale with Brother Francesco. Her head spun. Francesco was the returning Christ, and they were going to find the hiding place in Jerusalem of the Cup of the Last Supper!

"Rabbi, is the frayed parchment you put back on the shelf the page from Ezekiel?"

Yehezkel nodded, put down the letter, and reached for the twelve-hundred-year-old rolled-up skin.

EZEKIEL CHAPTER 43

Canonical Ezekiel   Censored Ezekiel
Quotes from Ezekiel and Bible (1:1)

1 Then the man brought me to the gate facing east, 2 and I saw the glory of the God of Israel coming from the east. His voice was like the roar of rushing waters, and the land was radiant with his glory. 3 The vision I saw was like the vision I had seen when he came to destroy the city and like the visions I had seen by the Kebar River, and I fell face down. 4 The glory of the Lord entered the temple through the gate facing east.
5 And in the vision that I saw, the glory of the God of Israel (43:1) was in the Prince himself (44:3), and the Prince was a Son of man (2:1), as I am, but clothed in white linen (9:2) and with a golden sash around his chest (Ap. 1:13), and upon that man was the Spirit. 6 And the radiance around the Prince was like the appearance of a rainbow in the clouds on a rainy day, 7 such was the appearance of the likeness (1:28) of the Prince, when he entered the temple through the gate facing east. 8 And the Son of man sat down to eat bread in the presence of the Lord inside the gateway (44:3) facing east, and while he ate bread in the presence of the Lord a woman approached him. 9 And the woman spoke to him and said: "The hour has come for the Son of Man to be glorified" (John 12:23). 10 And the woman anointed his head with the sacred anointing oil, a fragrant blend, the work of a perfumer (Ex. 30:25). 11 She poured some of the same sacred anointing oil that anointed God's servant David king over Israel (2 Sam 5:3) on the Prince's head and anointed him, to consecrate him. 12 The oil flowed down to his feet, and the woman wiped it lovingly with her long hair (John 12:3). 13 The glory of the God of Israel was upon him, and he looked like glowing metal, as if full of fire (1:27), while the woman anointed him with the sacred anointing oil and wiped the flowing oil with her long hair. 14 This was the vision I saw of the Prince, the man anointed by the God of Jacob (2 Sam 23:1), sitting in the gate facing east. Then the vision I

had seen went up from me (11:24) 15 *and the Spirit lifted me up and brought me into the inner court, and the glory of the Lord filled the temple. 16 While the man was standing beside me, I heard someone speaking to me from inside the temple. 17 He said: "Son of man, this is the place of my throne and the place for the soles of my feet. This is where I will live among the Israelites forever.*

A long silence followed Yehezkel's translation of the missing page. He was a little disappointed, not having recognized what he'd just read, but Galatea's eyes were wide open in surprise and awe. "Elisha was right, Rabbi! Elisha was right. . . . This page was hidden because it speaks of Jesus Christ!"

"You mean the woman anointing the Prince?"

"Yes. The very words you just read were used by the Evangelists to describe the anointing of Christ by Mary Magdalene. 'The woman wiped it lovingly with her long hair.' God, how I know those words!"

Yehezkel looked piqued. "Don't forget, madame, that the Evangelists *knew* the Book of Ezekiel."

"But it was one of *your* sages who thought the prophecy was authentic!" retorted the abbess. "So much so that he removed the page!"

"Exactly, madame. *Because* the Evangelists knew the prophecy, they made Jesus fulfill it word for word in their tales. Hanina hid the page because it would convince thousands of desperate and gullible Jews of Ezekiel's 'endorsment' of Jesus as the 'Prince' of prophecy."

Galatea reflected for a moment and saw the point. She said, "And the use the Evangelists made of the prophecy could still be made today. Couldn't it, Rabbi?"

"That, madame, is probably why the Jerusalem rabbis came to hide the page in this geniza."

"It must also be why Elisha made the map in the first place," mused Galatea. "You told Don Sancio that Elisha abandoned Judaism, didn't you? Well, if he had become a Christian, he would want this to be found again, wouldn't he?"

"You're no longer my disciple, madame. You're working this out as fast as I am!"

Galatea blushed. "A woman and a Jew will solve the enigma in Jerusalem, said the hermit." Then, fixing her eyes on his, "Will you destroy it, Rabbi, so it can never be used to convert Jews again?"

"What? Me, destroy a page of my namesake's book? Never! Mmh . . . how much oil is left, Madame?"

"Maybe a half hour's worth."

"Excellent. I brought what I need to write. I'll copy both pages now, and then we'll be out of here."

Two days later, when the excitement of their find stopped plaguing their conversations, Yehezkel suggested that they take two donkeys—being dhimmis,* they couldn't ride horses in Ayubbid Egypt—and ride to al-Kahira. But not in the daytime—at night because he wanted them to see the mosque of Ibn-Tulun, and that was something that *had* to be seen at night.

---

*Literally "protected," the term for Jews and Christians under sharia, who cannot be converted by force but are to be exploited and humiliated

Part Four

The
Sixth Day

CHAPTER 24

NEFESH HAYA

Living Creatures

FUSTAT, 12TH OCTOBER 1219

The odd couple discussed whether, in al-Kahira, Galatea should pretend to be Yehezkel's European wife, as she'd done to enter the geniza, or reveal that she was a Christian nun. Avraham had made inquiries and been told that, despite the war in the delta, the Venetian *funduq** in the capital was not closed. The news caused Galatea to opt for traveling as her true self.

"But madame!" Yehezkel cried out. "People in Fustat have seen you dressed as my wife. If now you go out dressed as a nun, I dread to think what rumormongers will dream up to explain it!"

"Mmh . . . I was hoping I wouldn't have to bring this up, Rabbi," said Galatea coyly, "but what will you tell your Jewish hosts in al-Kahira, when they find out your 'wife' needs a room to herself?"

Yehezkel looked flustered, but only for a moment, and then smiled and said, "I'll say it's your time of the month. A Jew cannot touch his wife during those days."

---

*A foreign trading post, often occupying a whole enclosed neighborhood of a city

"Really? Not even to beat her?" jested Galatea. "And what if we stay more than a few days?"

"That shouldn't be necessary. I want you to see the Pearl of Egypt, of course, and to buy us a passage to Syria in a Bedouin caravan I'll have to find Maître Chalabi, a merchant in the souk I used to know—if he is still alive, that is. My guess is that we'll be back in Fustat in three or four days." He paused, and then added, sympathetically, "A long time, I fear, for you to refrain from opening your mouth in public, since my wife, of course, would speak Hebrew."

Galatea acknowledged the jab with a smile. She considered the problems that being a Christian in a land at war with Christians would cause and compared them to the tranquility that Avraham ben Moshe's knowledge of her identity afforded her in Fustat, and then gracefully conceded the round to her teacher.

After rising from recalcitrant donkeys in Crete to an Arab stallion in Cyprus, Galatea was demoted to riding a donkey again between Fustat and al-Kahira, and being a Venetian abbess wouldn't have made any difference, since a Christian and a Jewess are both dhimmis. But at least this time Aillil had his own donkey and didn't have to ride behind her. Egyptian donkeys turned out to be placid, almost philosophical beasts, so the countess made light of the umpteenth humiliation.

Leaving Fustat at dusk, as Yehezkel insisted on, they trotted into the sweet countryside. The huge sun was setting into fields of rice and cotton dotted with fruit trees and palms. Aillil and Galatea remarked on the wonderful mélange of fragrances that Yehezkel remembered so well from his youth.

After a while, they got to know their mounts and assumed more relaxed postures. Suddenly, in the last light, ghostly ruins rose from the vegetation. Yehezkel told them the massive stones were all that remained of el-Askar, the capital of the Abbasids of Baghdad, and of el-Qata'i, the capital of the Tulunids, who had broken free from Baghdad.

Plants swarmed over stones that had been palaces. The two adults, as darkness mercifully engulfed the ruins, mumbled the first words of Sancio's beloved Qohelet, "Vanity of vanities."

They resumed the ride in the semidarkness, and soon the magical shafts of light around the mosque of Ibn Tulun, the reason Yehezkel wanted to travel at night, came into view. The mosque built by the founder of the Tulunid dynasty had no equal in all Dar-al-Islam. Walls made of well-fired red bricks, four hundred feet long, enclosed an enormous courtyard and were pierced, every three or four feet, by small windows with pointed arches. Grates carved in stucco in decorative geometric shapes filled each window.

As the reddish light from hundreds of torches in the courtyard passed through the windows, the grates splintered it into myriad shafts that beamed out in all directions before fading into the night.

Galatea and Aillil stared for several minutes, bewitched by the beauty of the sight.

"Three hundred and sixty-five windows, and no two grates have the same design!" exclaimed Yehezkel, as proudly as if he'd designed the building himself.

"I'm grateful to you, Rabbi," said Galatea, "for not letting me ride past this wonder during the day."

From there on, the road was called Shari el-A'dham, and as it approached the southern gate of the city, the Bab-ez-Zuweyla, it gradually filled with stalls, shops, and small mosques. The sugar and spice traders along its length had given the Shari el-A'dham its new name: Sukkariah.

Bab-ez-Zuweyla, like the other gates built by the Fatimid sultans a hundred years earlier, consisted of massive, foot-thick wooden doors, flanked by two powerful square towers, closing access to an arched passage through the walls. The towers were connected by an arch above the passage, and inside were three floors of lodgings for archers, with arrow slits on each floor.

With the evening crowd strolling around, Yehezkel asked his companions to dismount and lit a torch, as prescribed by the Law to attest the honesty of his intent in entering the city.

They proceeded along an almost deserted al-Ghuriya, with the Greek haret on the right.

The mamluk guard had already closed the gate of the haret Yahud for the night, and Yehezkel had to pull out some baksheesh. It was a different man from the one who'd stood there fifteen years earlier, he thought, but uniform and haughty attitude to dhimmis were the same. The guard pocketed the money, shot a look at Galatea, and asked where they were headed. Yehezkel mentioned Nissim ben Nahray, and the mamluk pulled the gate ajar and waved them through.

Yehezkel had sent a note to Nissim from Fustat, conveying his need for a few days' hospitality in the city, telling his old friend of his marriage to a taciturn French Jewess, and adding a line to explain the presence of his Cathar friend's son. When they reached his house, Yehezkel tied the donkeys to rings in the wall in the street—knowing that no one who had any use for his right hand would dream of stealing them—and reminded himself to arrange for someone to feed them.

Nissim ben Nahray traded mostly with the Maghreb, using both caravans and ships, and his house was so large that one reached its courtyard through an arched passageway, as if entering a keep. It had two floors, the top one a big harem with its own entry up a stairway in the courtyard. They were led into a hall on the ground floor, with a small fountain in the middle of black and white marble, and a divan—a raised wooden platform covered with cushions—on one side.

After a few introductions—Galatea impressing Yehezkel with the way she pronounced "shalom aleichem," the greeting she rehearsed—a servant showed the rabbi's new wife to her room. Then Nissim, a portly man whose fashionable dress reminded Yehezkel of Tofefloià, called for wine to celebrate the unexpected return, after fifteen years, of his "personal rabbi"—and with such a stunning new wife!

•••

The next two days were Galatea's first real encounter with Islam. Yehezkel had lived the first twenty years of his life under Ayubbid rule—the first ten, in fact, under Salah ad-Din himself—and as he showed her around the city, he gave her a brief introduction to the intricacies of Qu'ran, *hadith,* and *siras.*

"You see, madame, Islam's constant, dominating thought, as its name says, is submission to Allah—or, as you call him, God the Father. *Everything,* from the rising of the sun each day to the point on a branch where a bird lands, is decided by him alone. I once read a Shiite tractate on geometry that stated that 'two parallel straight lines are two lines that meet where it pleases Allah.'"

Galatea laughed. "If they didn't want to seem disrespectful, they could have said it was Allah who decided they could never meet!"

"But that's exactly the point, madame! The very next sentence in the tractate said, 'And if somewhere, some day, two such straight lines should meet, how great is the power of Allah!'"

Galatea laughed again, but this time she said, "I think I understand!"

The souk in the Pearl of Egypt was, as she had expected, as rich as Venice's and even more Eastern than Limassol's market. Its alleys were lined with hundreds of *dekkakin,* shops that were no more than holes in a wall with mastabas in front of them, stone or brick platforms on which the shopkeeper sat on cushions, legs crossed. Without ever moving from that position, the trader hawked his goods, haggled with clients, drank cider, gossiped with passersby, and joked or quarreled with neighbors. Galatea told Yehezkel she would have been happy to watch one snappy old spice trader for a whole day.

But snake charmers and street magicians she'd seen before. What intrigued her were strange figures, between monks and beggars, wandering the souk, who put her in mind of Brother Francesco piccolo. In the middle of their foreheads was a big, dark stain, and a bowl and a sling hung from their rope belts. Despite shaven heads, they stunk like goats. She asked the rabbi who they were.

"They're called dervishes. They are the Shia equivalent of Sufis," said Yehezkel. "The bowl symbolizes the Fount of Wisdom, and the sling is for chasing away Satan. They ask for charity, foretell futures, and sell talismans and charms with holy words on them. The language, I can assure you, is the only difference between what these dervishes preach and Brother Francesco's sermons."

Galatea smiled. "What's the dark stain on their foreheads?"

"That's no stain, madame; it's a callus! It's called a *zebibah,* and it grows above the brows of those who don't just touch their foreheads to the ground when they pray, as is prescribed, but *slam* them down." He grinned. "I heard that Domingo of Guzman whips his back with bunched-up iron chains when he prays."

"*Please,* Rabbi, not the sermon on punishing one's body again," she graciously cut him off. "Rather, why don't you tell me something about Sunnis and Shias? What's the difference between them?"

Humbled by her frankness, he said, "Mmhh . . . not as easy a question as it may sound. I suppose you Christians would call it more of a *dynastic* than a theological dispute—or, better said, feud. It boils down to who should have been the Leader of the Faithful after the Prophet died. But then wars and martyrs piled up until it felt almost theological, if you see what I mean."

"Of course I do," she said wryly. "Don't forget we've had our share of schisms and antipopes. But is there really no difference in the way they tell the story of Mahomet, in how they read the Qu'ran?"

"The closest thing to a doctrinal difference you will find," said he, "is probably in their *shahadas.** The Shias, after acknowledging the oneness of God and Muhammad's prophethood, add the words, 'And Ali is the wali of God.' Ali was Muhammad's cousin and son-in-law, and wali is a guardian, a protector. Shia is actually short for Shiatu Ali, the Party of Ali. But thirty years after the Prophet's death, when he'd been the Fourth Caliph for five years, Ali was killed in the war against Yazid,

---

*Statement of Islamic creed declaring belief in the oneness of God and acceptance of Muhammad as his prophet

the Ummayad pretender. Since then, as you can imagine, Sunnis have called his followers heretics."

"I see. And what does the name Sunni come from?"

"The Sunna is . . . well, everything the Prophet said and did. So since a Muslim must base his thinking and behavior on those of the Prophet, I suppose you could translate Sunna as orthodoxy."

Galatea, seriously trying to understand the bewildering world she'd entered, clarified. "The Fatimids were Shias, and they ruled until fifty years ago, when Salah ad-Din, a Sunni Kurd, reestablished orthodoxy in Egypt?"

"As I've said before, madame," smiled Yehezkel, "it would be hard for *any* teacher to have a better pupil than you!"

✡ ✠ ✡ ✠

AL-KAHIRA, 14TH OCTOBER 1219

On the second day in al-Kahira, Yehezkel had an idea he thought would please his friends. He decided a visit to the hammam was the best way to steam both desert war and Nile swamps right out of their skins—in fact, out of their very souls!

Hammams were the thing Yehezkel missed most since moving to Provence. One of his Ishmaelite friends was the barber of a splendid Fatimid hammam. A barber shaved faces, cut hair, let blood, and headed the attendants who washed and massaged clients. He burned incense twice a day to purify the place, made sure that no lepers were allowed in and that no one ate beans or peas in the hammam, and that anyone intentionally revealing his private parts was promptly ejected. But above all, the hammam barber, being privy to the hidden talk, was the hub of a town's news and gossip.

Aillil reacted enthusiastically to the idea, but Galatea was wary, both out of a Western diffidence for excessive contact with water and because women there would likely move around naked and expect her to do the same. Eventually, Yehezkel's description of the sense of purification and cleanliness that followed a visit to the hammam convinced her to attempt the experience. She went on a day reserved for women, the rabbi accompanying her to the entrance. She was led down an arched passageway to the dressing room and from there, a towel round her chest, to the harara, the hot room where massages were administered.

This was a beautiful round hall, circled by columns and walled in colored marbles, with a few pools, stone benches, and steps everywhere. Discreet shafts of sunlight streamed in from windows in the domed roof. Amid clouds of steam, Egyptian women sat unveiled, some in light patterned robes, some naked but for a cotton cloth round their loins, all gossiping, laughing, suckling their children, or painting their faces after their ablutions. The muted echo in the harara repeated their every word thrice.

Having spent half her life in a convent, Galatea understood the appeal that the atmosphere of half-light and seclusion held for women as a quiet, temporary refuge from the world of men, but despite much smiling, her attempts to communicate failed miserably, and when she shed her towel for a massage, she became, as she'd feared, the object of the unwanted attention of every woman in the hammam.

It wasn't just her milky complexion. Egyptian women shaved their bodies from armpits to pubes every ten days or so. After much giggling and pointing to her bushy black hairs, a lady found the courage to approach her. Eventually, through gestures pointing in succession to Galatea's chest, to a silk veil on a marble bench and to the prosperous breasts of a nearby matron, the woman succeeded in explaining to the infidel wretch that her pitifully small breasts were Allah's punishment for not wearing a veil.

"That's the last straw," thought the abbess, "the one that broke the camel's back!"

She gave the bitch the smile she'd always reserved for the bishop of Torcello, turned around, picked up her towel and marched out to the dressing room.

On the third day, Yehezkel set out to find the shop where he'd last met Maître Chalabi—as the shady character insisted on being called, as if he were some kind of scholar. The rabbi walked quickly, Aillil close behind, trying to find the right alley, but Galatea was constantly distracted by sights so incredible she had to stop and verify it was not just her imagination running away with her.

At one point, she lost sight of the other two. "I'm tall, and so is he," she thought, "so surely I'll catch a glimpse of his turban in the crowd. Besides, he'll notice I'm no longer behind them . . . won't he?"

But this time she'd stopped too long, and they were nowhere to be seen. She was alone. A Christian woman alone in the capital of the Saracen empire. A shiver ran down her back. "Where will I look for him? On which desert trail, in which oriental city, on which battlefield swarming with crows and vultures?" Her breath was getting shorter, and she got a grip on herself.

"Don't panic, Galatea degli Ardengheschi!" She reflected on the options. "I can't find Nissim's house again without revealing that I don't speak a word of Hebrew and 'ruining what's left of his reputation.' But even so, I can find the Venetian funduq and somehow make my way back to Fustat. Once there, I'll ask for the home of the *rais,* and he'll be there, waiting for me." She frowned. "He won't be happy, to be sure, but I think he'll be relieved I wasn't kidnapped and sold into slavery." She smiled. "At least I hope so."

Luckily, her moment of anxiety kept her from moving from the spot where she'd stopped. As she finally turned to do so, Yehezkel was standing behind her, smiling. "It seems that Aillil knows better than you, madame, not to lose sight of the person who can lead him back out of the souk."

Later, Galatea would find her dependence on the rabbi, even in a Saracen land, excessive, but right then she was so relieved to see his burly figure that it was all she could do not to embrace him.

Yehezkel continued his search and eventually found Maître Chalabi in the same rickety wooden house where he'd conducted his business fifteen years earlier, the space doubled by the absorption of the shop next door. Chalabi, a ruddy Copt in his early fifties, was a Levantine merchant so busy making money that his pointed beard seemed like a visual invitation to his interlocutors to get to the point.

A worldly, widely traveled dealer, Chalabi spoke passable Latin and four other languages and traded in everything under the sun, sometimes for a commission, other times buying and selling the goods—be they spices, jewels, slaves, services by the underworld, or the oldest commodity in any souk: information.

As the rabbi ducked to enter his lair, Chalabi recognized him and got up to greet him. "Yehezkel ben Yoseph, what an unexpected pleasure!" he exclaimed. "How on earth did you get here from Provence despite the war, through Alexandria?"

Chalabi led his guests into a private room, where Italian merchants often clinched deals that would get them excommunicated if their pope ever got wind of them.

Yehezkel decided to reveal Galatea's true identity to Chalabi. He'd considered passing her off as his wife with the Bedus, but then thought the reaction of a desert dweller on discovering, in the middle of the Sinai, that he was harboring a Christian woman, was unpredictable, but unlikely to be cordial.

Within minutes, before Yehezkel could mention caravans to Gaza, Chalabi's attention shifted from his old Jewish acquaintance to the Italian noblewoman, whose first smile awoke his womanizing instincts in a way no female had done in years.

"I'm honored and *enchanté* that such an important Madonna is in my shop!" Galatea found his nasal singsong amusing. "A contessa, no less, and the head of a religious house. If your king of Jerusalem does not invade Egypt, I invite a *hundred* notables to a big dinner, just for the welcome you deserve!"

Chalabi wooed the abbess for ten minutes with a humorous account, in a mixture of Latin, French, and theatrics, of the shortcomings of his Cairene clients. Yehezkel fidgeted in his chair. Eventually, Chalabi's knowledge of events in the Delta gave Yehezkel a pretext to interrupt the Copt's vain monologue.

"Maître Chalabi, perhaps you could share with us the latest news from the war?" he interjected.

Chalabi turned to him with a knowing smile and answered in Latin, ever the perfect gentleman. "Sorry, Yehezkel. My first thought was to question you on why you traveled through a war to come here, but the *charme* and grace of your . . . companion lead me astray!"

Galatea blushed. Yehezkel started finding the room stuffy.

"The war goes well, I hear, but the capital slides into panic because of rumors that Damietta will fall within days. The sultan—may God grant him long life—had a marvelous idea, certainly inspired by Allah, when, four weeks ago, he offered to return their True Cross to the Franks if they leave Egypt."

Galatea, whose knowledge of Outremer had grown in leaps and bounds, noticed that Chalabi, being a Christian, said "Franks" and not "infidels." Chalabi went on. "Rumors say the offer sowed discord in the Frankish camp, and the truce the Franks accepted expires in three days' time. If they refuse the sultan's offer and Damietta falls, they're sure to march on al-Kahira." He grimaced. "Many wealthy Cairene are already packing and moving to their upriver estates."

He looked at Yehezkel. "And you must have heard of the blood-thirsty armies threatening Baghdad from the East . . . these are such end-of-the-world times I'm not at all surprised to see you here, Yehezkel!" He laughed a high-pitched, slightly frenzied wartime laugh. Yehezkel thought Chalabi must be making more money from the war than the Venetians themselves but said nothing.

He had to relieve his bladder, but Galatea laughed enough times at Chalabi's jokes that he worried about leaving her alone with him, even for a short time. He scolded himself for being jealous of a woman who not only wasn't his, but *never would be*. Sobered, he stood, asked Chalabi where he could attend to a bodily need, and left the room.

When he came back the two were laughing heartily, as he'd feared.

The youthful glint in Chalabi's eye would normally have amused him, but his outlook on life was grim. Chalabi seemed instead in an excellent mood, end of the world notwithstanding. He got up and slapped the rabbi on his ample back.

"Yehezkel, I just had the idea that solves your problem! Madonna Galatea told me you are headed to Jerusalem, and you look for a caravan to take you to Gaza."

Yehezkel shot Galatea a look of reproof, but Chalabi shushed him before he could say anything. "A Christian nun and boy in a Bedu caravan. Trust me, Yehezkel, I understand your problem, and you came to the only man who can solve it! I have just the clan for you. But I'll need time to find their sheikh and speak with him. You go back to Fustat, and come to see me in November."

"She even told him we're staying in Fustat!" he thought, outraged at her naïveté, then caught himself. "Calm down. Chalabi always knew you live in Fustat. Try to keep feelings and reason separate."

Galatea also seemed convinced they had come to the right person. Perhaps, he thought, it was because Chalabi was the first Christian— albeit a Monophysite heretic—that she'd set eyes on since Francesco left Färiskür: a whole month of Jews and Ishmaelites! But whatever it was, the abbess looked so pleased that he found himself wanting to leave the place.

He put up with the never-ending leave-taking and then herded Galatea and Aillil outside. On the way back to the haret Yahud, Galatea confessed with an embarrassed smile that she'd not been able to refuse a small *cadeau* Chalabi insisted on giving her.

Yehezkel stopped abruptly and turned to face her. "May I know what it was, madame?"

She pulled a small silk bag out of a pocket, loosened its string and poured onto the palm of her hand a single, brilliant pearl. It was perfectly round and the size of a small olive. Yehezkel was no expert on pearls, but anyone could tell the big translucent jewel was worth a fortune.

That was when he knew something had happened between them. After the times he had saved her in those six months! Something constricted his throat, as if the air had just filled with fine dust. He began to cough and the next instant, without any warning, images of Chalabi forcing himself on the nun floated up before his eyes. Had he caressed her? Had he kissed her? Or had even *more* happened in there? That pearl was a sign of gratitude for *something*!

That last thought did it. Yehezkel lost control, and his bitter anger gushed out.

When it was over, Galatea stood there, trembling. "Is that my teacher's opinion of me? Headstrong, capricious, selfish, an *ingrate*?" Each word had been a dagger in her heart. "If he really considers me such a shrew, then there's nothing for it, I've disappointed his hopes, lost his esteem. What will become of me now? Perhaps being covered in mold in my convent is what I deserve." She was silent, hands shaking, suspended between outrage for the humiliation and an overpowering desire to weep.

As she stood there, Yehezkel emerged from what felt like a possession. He realized nothing could have happened in the shop in Aillil's presence, and a moment later saw a sack of flour that had fallen off a porter's shoulder and exploded on the street stones, causing the fine cloud that had choked him. He saw what he had just done and fell on his knees before the abbess.

"I beg you, forgive me, madame!" he cried, his voice breaking, "Not one word came from my heart! It was what fury does to me when it takes over, like a demon clawing at the edges of my soul." He hesitated and then plunged on. "I can't hide it, madame, I was furiously jealous of Chalabi in there, and when I saw the pearl, I . . . " He looked at her, unable to continue.

Galatea smiled, immensely relieved by the apology, and chose not to comment on his jealousy. "Remember when Brother Francesco poured out his fury on Brother Elia?" she asked. "You said there was 'something about him you couldn't fathom.' Perhaps at times a demon claws at *his* soul, too."

She stretched out a hand to help him back to his feet, and they returned to Nissim's house.

The next day a certain coolness still hung between them. Of course, the rabbi's confession that he was jealous had not left her cold, but she willed herself not to dwell on its implications.

Yehezkel couldn't get a detail of her dream in Limassol out of his head. It was connected to the red heifer, so he decided to glance through the appropriate tractate of the Talmud in a house of study; maybe something would jolt his memory.

Cities with many wooden houses, both in Christendom and Dar al-Islam, are plagued by fires, but al-Kahira in those years was particularly known for fires breaking out somewhere every single day.

Turning a corner in the haret, the three saw a small crowd of Jews pointing and shouting outside the house of study, from whose first-floor window smoke emerged and rose to the sky. They ran toward it, and Yehezkel learned that an old rabbi was still inside and someone had just run in to rescue him. A chain of people passing buckets had already formed, and though no flames were visible from outside, the smoke pouring out of the windows was getting thicker and blacker.

Just as Yehezkel was about to rush in, a man came down the steps of the entrance carrying a minute, bearded figure in his arms. The old rabbi wore an embarrassed smile, as if surprised that his time had not, in fact, come. A shout of joy rose from the Jews in the alley, by now more than had been in the house.

It only took five minutes for the celebration over the rescue of the rabbi to turn into lamentations for the fate of the Sifrei Torah, the Torah scrolls that were in the Holy Ark in the hall.

"That was quick!" thought Yehezkel, "We Jews are such a lachrymose lot!"

He saw a single tongue of fire through an upstairs window and decided there was probably enough time to bring out at least the two or three scrolls in the ark. He turned to Galatea. "I'm going in there to rescue the scrolls. *Please,* madame, whatever happens, don't come in! You couldn't help me if you did. Keep an eye on Aillil, and I'll be back as soon as I can."

He decided his blue scarf was too narrow to wrap the scrolls in and borrowed a large, black Bedu shawl that a woman nearby was wearing. He grabbed one of the buckets of water moving from hand to hand, dunked the shawl in it, pulled it out dripping, wrapped it round his head and ran into the burning building.

Galatea had no intention of disobeying him, but the minutes went by, and the dousers' efforts seemed to have little effect. Flames could now be seen dancing in the windows. Then, to a fearful shout from the crowd, the floor of the upstairs room, which was the ceiling of the main hall, caught fire with a sudden, great roar. Smoke poured out of the entrance, and people began to shout for Yehezkel to come out.

Suddenly, Galatea recognized the signs of a vision taking over. The air became thick, sounds receded, time slowed. A hall full of smoke came into focus before her eyes, its floor covered in scattered books and chairs. The rafter that had held up the ceiling was burning in the middle of the floor, a wrought iron chandelier lying next to it. A foot of Master Ezekiel's blue scarf poked out from underneath.

For the first time in her life, driven by the urgency, she *willed* a vision away before it ran its course. The scene slowly vanished, and she saw the entrance again. The ceiling was burning fiercely now, and for a moment she thought it was like looking at hell from underneath. The more she waited, the more dangerous it would become. She lifted the hem of her habit and made to run into the house but suddenly felt someone's hand pulling her wrist to drag her away. She turned, saw no one there, and understood the vision had not finished with her.

She remembered Master Ezekiel's folded breath and started breathing it, waiting for something else to happen. When nothing did, she told Aillil not to move and rushed in. She ran down a corridor, dodging bits of burning wood that fell from the ceiling, and came to the hall of her vision not five minutes earlier. The rabbi, scarf still round his neck, stood in the middle of it, contemplating the three scrolls he'd laid in the black shawl on the table.

Galatea looked at the rafter above his head, already in flames at both ends, and shrieked,

"Yehezkel!!"

He looked up in shock. No woman had called him by name in over fifteen years. For a moment, he thought she'd ignored his instructions again, but his outburst of the previous day still weighed on his soul. He relished her slip of the tongue and thanked the danger that had caused it. "What's going on, Galatea? Why did you come in?"

He realized he had to shout to overcome the roar of the fire raging on both floors of the house.

She looked unaware of having used his name. "I just had a vision out there. The rafter above your head, the one with the chandelier, was on the floor, burning! You must come away from there *this instant*! Please, take the scrolls and leave this place, before we both burn to death!"

Yehezkel knew better than to underestimate her visions, yet for a few seconds he stood there, debating what would be worse for a holy text between the touch of gentile hands and burning to a cinder. Then he called himself an idiot and said, "We don't have much time, madame. I selected five codices, but I couldn't have carried them *and* three scrolls. Now that you're here, we can save them all!"

As they bundled books and scrolls in the shawl, Yehezkel's scarf slid off his back. When they reached the door and turned at the sound of the rafter crashing down, they saw Galatea's vision turned into reality, with the blue scarf under the beam. And just as in the vision, Galatea felt someone pull her wrist, dragging her out of there. Now she knew it was her teacher, who would be lying dead, crushed under the rafter, had it not been for his pupil's divine gift.

For a kabbalist—explained Yehezkel later that day, as they made arrangements to ride back to Fustat—her saving him from fire after he'd saved her from water symbolized the special relationship between their souls, as implied in the prophecy of the woman and the Jew. She could not but agree.

He also told her, in admiring tones, that contrary to her dreams of Bereshit or the Temple, this time she hadn't been the passive recipient of a cryptic revelation but had at once understood its import and acted to change what might have been.

"A kabbalist can only dream of achieving what you did after decades of study and practice," he said.

Those words soothed the abbess more than any Egyptian balm. The crisis of the day before wasn't forgotten but assumed the traits of the trial that precedes a breakthrough in the growth of an apprentice.

In the three weeks they spent in Fustat before returning to Maître Chalabi's shop, they felt more like a couple than ever. Criticism was open while affection was hidden, as in a true friendship.

"I don't need to sing troubadour ballads to her," he thought one day. "I may not recite teary verses, but she knows that I love her. She is neither stupid nor selfish, just . . . a little crazy, no more than is needed to make life tolerable."

For her part, Galatea used terms like "perfect confidence" and "secret understanding" to describe their relationship and often argued with herself over the role their feelings for each other had in the hermit's prophecy and in solving the enigma in Jerusalem.

"We are blind instruments of an irresistible destiny . . . No, Galatea!" said Mother Elisabetta in her head, "that is exactly how men and women attribute to fate what is in fact the fruit of their sinful passions!"

In Torcello she'd once heard of a tradition on the Apocalypse that said that the Antichrist would be born in Babylon from a nun seduced by Satan. Autumn in Fustat was as delightful as any part of their journey so far, but one day the abbess reflected on that tradition and reached a dismaying conclusion. "I'm a nun, and Yehezkel was born in Fustat, the site of a fortress the Romans called Babylonia. In the sultan's camp I understood that Francesco is my divine husband. Does it mean that if I commit adultery with a Jew, the result will be the birth of the Antichrist? Am I destined, should I surrender to temptation, to bear the son of the Devil?" She looked at the pyramids in the distance, her breath short.

"Madre Santissima!" she moaned. "Why couldn't I just stay in my convent and eat sardines in vinegar?"

CHAPTER 25

KOL REMES

And Everything That Creeps on the Ground

AL-KAHIRA, 7TH NOVEMBER 1219

The first time, Aillil only saw her eyes.

The girl was hiding behind a hanging fold in the tent of the Bedu sheikh they'd come to meet. Only her eyes showed through the gap in her niqab, but they were too far for Aillil's weak sight when he sat with Yehezkel and Galatea in the middle of the tent. But when he stood up to relieve himself outside, he walked past one of the two posts holding up the tent and saw the big brown eyes, hiding behind veil after veil, staring at him so hard that he knew at once those eyes would rule his life forever.

When he reentered the tent, the hungry brown eyes were still there. He took a step toward the girl, wanting to see her face, but Yasmine nimbly retreated into the depths of the tent. Aillil wasn't too upset. They were riding to Syria with this clan, so he knew he would see her again. He wondered how he would communicate, and his first thought was to enlist Rav Yehezkel.

"Or maybe Mother Galatea would be better," he thought. "She's a woman; she could vouch for my noble intent . . . but wait, *she* doesn't speak the girl's tongue, either! No, it has to be Rav Yehezkel."

Still shaken by the willful intensity of the girl's gaze, Aillil went back to sit by the rabbi. As Yehezkel translated niceties between sheikh Twalia and the abbess, the boy thought dreamily that he needed to see those eyes again more than he'd ever really needed anything else.

Aillil never felt strongly about any of the things his peers got excited about, not heresy or saving souls, not holy war and killing infidels, not even the knightly code of chivalry, which in the last years he pretended, even to himself, was his ideal. No, apart from finding his father, the only thing in the world he *really* wanted was to see that girl again, and to remove the veil over her face and hair!

Yasmine was the oldest daughter of Twalia ibn Salem, the sheikh of a clan of the Muzziena Bedouin tribe that Chalabi approached to take the three to Syria. The reason the Copt told Yehezkel it was the perfect clan for them had been revealed on meeting Twalia in Chalabi's shop a week earlier. After the trader's introductions, the sheikh addressed Yehezkel in pure, ancient Arabic.

"My clan is honored to have been chosen to escort to Syria a disciple and close friend of Musa ibn Maimun, may his memory live forever, after bringing the master himself to his final resting place!"

Yehezkel's jaw dropped. "You took my teacher's remains to Eretz Israel?"

Twalia ibn Salem nodded with a proud, nearly toothless smile. "Your teacher saved my father's life twice and refused to be paid. Your community knew of his wish to be buried next to his father in Tiberias, so after watching over his body for ten years, they asked our clan to bring the casket safely to the shores of the lake, to be buried where the great man wished."

Yehezkel was moved to the bottom of his soul. "May the Lord reward you and your clan for the holy duty you absolved!" he exclaimed to approving nods from Mâitre Chalabi.

As Chalabi expected, Yehezkel felt they could not be safer on a journey across Sinai than in a Muzziena caravan. Before the meeting, the rabbi warned himself to keep jealousy in check lest he harm their chances of making a deal, but on hearing what the Copt arranged he'd been so grateful that Chalabi's verbose attentions toward the abbess hadn't bothered him in the slightest.

But the cheerful atmosphere of the gathering was soured when Chalabi glumly reported the news that Damietta had fallen two days earlier. It seemed that three thousand people were found alive inside the walls that two years ago sheltered some sixty thousand Egyptians. Hunger and pestilence turned the once thriving city into an open-air cemetery.

"They say al-Kamil has written to the caliph in Baghdad that if he won't send forces to help Egypt, the whole ummah will face catastrophe," Chalabi reported. "But the caliph, as everyone knows, has other problems. Some of the savages from the East are already camping on the banks of the Tigris."

Yehezkel's first thought was that if the sultan was forced to give Jerusalem to the Christians, the only thing he could count on for any search in the Holy City would be Pedro's laissez-passer. Still, he was pleased to see Galatea not at all uplifted by news of a Christian victory—after all, *her* side in the war Brother Francesco called a "useless massacre."

"The caravan will depart in three weeks," said Twalia, noting he was still waiting for part of the goods he would transport to Syria, so they decided that the next week the passengers would visit the clan's camp to acquaint themselves with both people and camels.

A week later, they mounted their donkeys and rode to the edge of the desert, just north of al-Kahira, where the clan pitched their camp—and where Aillil saw Yasmine for the first time.

Later that day, they met Hussein the camel puller, the only member of the clan outside the sheikh's family they were introduced to.

Everything about Hussein was like a miniature: a short man with a short beard and short, muscled legs. The only large thing about him were his eyes, black and shiny like fat olives.

Galatea later discovered that Hussein tried to feel up every female he got close to, from little girls to old hags, and often carried the bruises that were the price of his reprehensible habit. Fortunately, from the day he set eyes on her, something about the abbess made him repress such beastly instincts.

The reason Hussein's habit didn't get him chased out of the clan was that good camel pullers were hard to come by. They had to be experts on camels because, as Twalia put it, "there is no good doctor for a camel when he is sick, so a camel puller must learn how to keep it well."

And Hussein loved his camels. Later that day, he introduced the three passengers to them, assigning each one to an animal, rather than the other way round. In big caravans, with several eighteen-camel files of heavily loaded beasts, passengers would alternate between riding on top of a load and walking. Luckily, Twalia's clan only possessed one file of camels, and each passenger had a nearly load-free animal to ride. Also, to Yehezkel's relief, Twalia said the caravan would cover no more than ten leagues in a day.

As she gazed at the munching female that would be her mount for a month or so, Galatea suddenly felt herself grabbed above the hips and lifted off the ground. Two iron arms were holding her in midair, proffering her like some sort of sacrifice before an altar.

"You could have warned me you were going to help me onto the saddle, Rabbi!" she exclaimed, scandalized by the affront to her dignity. Galatea had ridden horses and donkeys in her life—and now had sailor's legs, too—so the problem as the animal rose on its legs wasn't keeping her balance in the ample stool-shaped saddle; the problem was that she hadn't expected to be lifted quite so high. The moment she saw the camp from almost ten feet in the air, vertigo raised its ugly head. The abbess closed her eyes and gripped the saddle's big horn with all the strength in her body.

Hussein sensed something wasn't right and refrained from calling to the camel to start walking.

Galatea, eyes still closed but head no longer spinning, said to herself that she had no choice: she couldn't walk to Jerusalem. A moment later, she opened her eyes and said, "I'll be all right, Hussein."

Hussein walked her camel in a circle, and Galatea experienced first-hand why the beasts were called "desert ships." Hussein laughed at the awkward positions she assumed on the saddle, in much the same way Galatea might have laughed at his spelling—but for the time being, she thought, it was not her turn.

Her overfed, undisciplined camel was a real princess, curling its lips in disdain. Hussein, with Yehezkel's translation, instructed Galatea to keep talking to the animal to get it used to her voice. Then, in painstaking stages, he taught her the commands to make her camel bend its forelegs, sit down, rise again, trot, and stop. When Galatea climbed down, quite spent, Hussein whispered the last command in her ear, the one to make the camel break into a gallop. She must pray to Allah, translated Yehezkel, that she would never have to shout that last command.

With the help of Yehezkel's translation, Hussein then held a lesson on camels for Galatea and Aillil that belied his reputation as a dirty little man best forced to live with his beasts. He showed them the large leathery pads that are a camel's toes—"able to grip any surface that Allah invented"—and how it can keep sandstorms out by sealing hermetically its nostrils and double eyelashes. He explained that camels don't store water in their hump, as Westerners seem to think, but fat, and that if the hump shrinks, the camel is sick.

They were fascinated—even Yehezkel was impressed by the exposition—and Galatea was happy to regain some respect, after her initial diffidence, for an animal she'd have to get along with, like it or not. As Hussein concluded their lesson, Galatea felt someone's eyes on her back and turned to see a young Bedu in a dirty djellaba sprawled on the sand, his back leaning on the side of his seated camel. He was chewing on a long blade of grass, his lower lip sticking out, and staring at her with an air of lewd bravado. She was so amazed by the resemblance between animal and owner that she nudged Yehezkel to point it out to him. At first he didn't grasp what she meant, and then she whispered "The lips . . ." and he burst out laughing.

Aillil told his mentors of the young girl he'd seen—whose eyes he'd seen, he corrected—and how those eyes made him feel. Both of them warned him that seducing a Bedouin girl could cost him his life, but he looked at them as though they hadn't understood what he'd said. In any case, on that first day in the Muzziena camp, he did not set eyes on her again.

✡   ✠   ✡   ✠

AL-KAHIRA, 27TH NOVEMBER 1219

It was another two weeks before the caravan moved off. The passengers joined the Bedus two days before departure. The clan numbered some fifty men, women, and children, and a third of the camels' loads consisted of their tents and fodder for humans and animals.

On the trail along the eastern edge of the delta, past the city of Bilbeis, it took the caravan a week to reach the Sinai and venture into the desert. By that time, the passengers had grown used to both spending hours perched on swinging camel humps and to the routine when the sun set behind them and the clan pitched their camp—the traveling one, without the sheikh's big tent—for the night.

The landscape from up there seemed to Galatea to run past her as she sat still, but she knew from the ache in her hips that the opposite was the case. After a while she found that camel logic wasn't so different from horse logic and eventually reached a number of unspoken understandings with her mount.

But the fact that riding a camel for ten leagues every day seemed tolerable was due to the proximity of the Nile. As soon as they entered the Sinai, the daily marches trudging over wind-whipped dunes and across endless plains, where the weirdest mirages shimmered through the heat, seemed more than they could bear. The wind blew all day, carrying sand that struck their faces, every grain feeling like a hot spark from a fireplace. Soon Galatea was forced to ask one of Twalia's wives to lend her a niqab. Desert sand became the unwanted companion of every second of each day. They breathed it, swallowed it with their food, and drank it with their water, a fine layer of it floating on every liquid. Galatea even felt it between her buttocks as she walked. All the while, the heightened danger as the distance from towns and villages increased was evident throughout the clan. Fear of raiding parties kept everyone tense and alert, eyes searching the horizon even when dazed by lack of sleep. Those first few days spent on trails not far from the eastern branch of the Nile now seemed like a pleasure ride.

That week also gave Aillil a chance to meet Yasmine. When Yehezkel had first approached her, the girl shocked him by saying she knew exactly why he wanted to speak with her. She also wanted the blond boy with a mystic's gaze for herself, but her father had already promised her to a cousin, and anyway Aillil was an infidel. But driven by her own beguilement, she'd agreed to meet him, on condition that the rabbi be present and that the meeting be hidden from the clan.

It had not been easy to arrange, but in that first week the caravan often camped beside villages—both to avoid using their own water and to pray in a mosque—so one day Yehezkel told Yasmine to find a pretext to go to the well in the evening and turned up there with Aillil as if by chance. Yasmine removed her niqab and smiled a bitter-sweet smile at Aillil. The boy knew what she'd said to Yehezkel about him being an infidel, and the moment he saw her face was the first time the thought of becoming a Mohammedan entered his mind.

After that, the two youngsters secretly met behind the sleeping camel herd many nights, despite the danger they knew they were running. Soon they discovered that mutual bewitchment provides a hundred ways to overcome differences of language. Hussein taught Aillil to chew jasmine flowers before kissing her, laughing as he did so. During the day, when Aillil looked at Yasmine from afar, he understood the chansons of the troubadours who sang stories of wildly beautiful princesses. Every time she walked out of a tent, it was as if all the torches had been snuffed out.

Then one night, near the Bir el Malhi well, it happened. The teens became lovers, and though they'd not yet learned a dozen words of each other's language, the life-and-death decision to never part was as clear as in a long, poetic missive. One memory of the night that would never leave Aillil, even years later, was when, though his soul had just risen to heaven, he worried that his weight might be oppressing her and tried to roll off her sweat-covered body. At once Yasmine's legs wrapped themselves tightly around him and kept him where he was.

In the morning, on his camel, Aillil thought languidly, "So this is what love is . . . now I understand why men and women chase each other mindlessly, why husband and wife care so much for each other; now I understand *everything*!"

In the camp at Damietta he discovered what a wonderful thing a woman's body was, but doing it with Yasmine was different. This was the enchantment Iñigo spoke of, the one from which only death can free you.

Almost from the first day, Aillil was enlisted as Hussein's apprentice. For a boy who'd grown up in the green valleys at the foot of the Pyrenees, his love of the desert was as sudden and intense as his love of Yasmine. Hussein the camel puller, like Yehezkel and Don Sancio before him, found that the boy made up for the shortcomings of his senses with a kind of sixth sense, as well as with an almost uncanny ability to trust his own intuitions.

With a little help from Yehezkel, but mostly through gestures and facial expressions, Aillil acquired a world of skills from Hussein. He learned to navigate the desert the way Bedus do: by the stars, by familiar landmarks, and by stone markers left on previous treks. Little escaped

Hussein's eye in the desert. If wild animals were scant at a water hole, the water in that oasis was probably brackish or bitter, yet he always knew where good water was. Shrubs told him when it last rained, and how much. Signs left in the sand announced who had been there before them, and when, as well as their directions of arrival and departure, the size of their flock and sometimes even the ages of their camels.

The animals they saw in the wild delighted Aillil. Most beautiful were the oryxes, their long, straight horns like sharp spears God carelessly wasted on grass eaters. They saw herds of wild donkeys and wild pigs, not that different from the boars in Languedoc, but with bigger and nastier tusks. Day after day, Aillil absorbed desert lore as the sands absorbed rain, his Arabic vocabulary growing daily.

His questions to Yehezkel on Mahomet grew frequent, and he was happy to find that Mohammedans, just like Cathars, considered Jesus a prophet, but not the son of God. The rabbi didn't know that the love between the youngsters had been consummated, but Aillil's sudden curiosity for sharia made him suspect that the young man's feelings for Yasmine were more than a passing infatuation.

"In Montréal I didn't understand girls," said Aillil to Yehezkel one night. "They laughed at things my friends and I didn't think were funny. They mocked me when I hadn't provoked them. Yasmine is the first one . . . I'm not afraid of. She doesn't speak my tongue, but she *always* knows what I'm thinking."

✡ ✠ ✡ ✠

Around the middle of December, two weeks into the desert trek, they crossed a bigger caravan going west. Two of its passengers were Jews, and they spoke with Yehezkel for a while before both caravans moved on. Galatea noticed that the rabbi's face grew dark. With a reckless maneuver she would later be proud of, she brought her camel next to Yehezkel's and asked what was troubling him. Yehezkel waved her away with a smile. "It's nothing; I'll tell you tonight."

But before evening came and she could hear what caused her teacher's gloom, she went through the most frightening experience of the desert journey—except for the arrival in Gaza. As she'd suspected from the day she'd first mounted it, her camel had a crazy streak that Hussein forgot to mention. That evening, as the sun dropped behind them and Galatea relished the thought of dismounting, the beast suddenly took off at a gallop, away from caravan and trail.

The command Hussein taught her to stop the camel sounded something like "Heut!" and as she bounced on the saddle, hanging on for dear life, Galatea shouted it over and over to no avail. She heutted imperiously, she heutted mellifluously, she heutted like a lioness, but it was all useless. The beast chose martyrdom in the wilderness, and the caravan looked more distant with every second.

Her strength waning, she was already desperate enough to consider attacking the animal to force it to slow down and jumping off it, when she caught sight of another camel: Hussein nonchalantly perched on its hump, legs crossed as if sitting by the fire, galloping right behind and slowly catching up. Within minutes, Hussein had stopped the runaway, and both camels were making their way back to the caravan at a leisurely trot, Hussein wearing an only slightly embarrassed grin.

That evening, by the campfire, Yehezkel told them of the group of Latin monks who had gone by on that trail a month earlier, on their way from the Christian camp at Damietta to Jerusalem. The Jews in the other caravan spoke of their tragic end. There had been six. First they were attacked and robbed and then sodomized and beheaded. Galatea gasped and hid her face in her hands.

The news of that martyrdom finally convinced the abbess that the Last Days, as Gioacchino called them, were upon them. The thoughts that entered her head that night felt like they were not her own.

"Francesco is my rightful husband *and* the returning Christ. If my fate is to conceive the anti-Christ with a Jew born in Babylon on a desert trail far from anywhere, then tenderness toward Yehezkel, even sisterly affection, is a weakness that can make Satan's plan succeed. What

I should be doing to thwart that plan is to leave the rabbi and seek out my heavenly husband. With him, I'll be safe from the Devil's plots. But where is Francesco now? And how could I leave Yehezkel and betray our quest, after everything he's done for me? And what of the prophecy, was *that* the Devil's work, too? Oh, Mother Elisabetta, where are you?" she whimpered, alone in the maidens' tent.

Two days later, Yasmine was bitten by a scorpion while gathering shrubs not far from the camp.

Aillil's eyes always followed her as she performed chores in the camp, so when he saw her walk out into the rocky plain by herself, he at once took a roundabout route to join her. When Yasmine jumped back from a parched bush, clutching the hand stung by the scorpion, Aillil instinctively lunged and crushed the fleeing armored spider underfoot. Then, seeing her short breath and panicked expression, he ran toward the camp, shouting "Rav Yehezkel!" at the top of his voice.

The first thing Yehezkel asked was, "Did you kill it?" Aillil nodded uncomprehendingly, and the rabbi charged off in the direction the boy came from, his ward hot on his heels. In a minute they reached the spot where Yasmine lay moaning on the ground, muscles already starting to twitch.

Yehezkel had only once applied the antidote to a scorpion's sting he had learned from Rav Moshe: the juices of the scorpion itself. He smashed the big female, the color of ripe dates, between two stones and forcefully rubbed the repugnant pulp into Yasmine's slightly reddish and swollen hand. Aillil understood why the rabbi asked if he'd killed the monster and prayed to God—*any* God, he thought, and meant it— that the rabbi's repulsive cure would save his only love. He watched Rav Yehezkel sweep up the girl in his arms as if she were an empty dress and followed them back to the camp.

For the next two days, the caravan's journey brusquely interrupted, Yasmine hovered between life and death in Twalia's tent, looked after by the Jewish tabib. She was conscious, but her speech was slurred, her eyes shifted erratically, and her muscles, even those of her face, twitched uncontrollably.

Aillil pestered Yehezkel to think of a way for him to see her, but his mentor denied him lest the boy's anguish might alert the sheikh to what had been going on between his daughter and the unseemingly pale young infidel. During the first night, Aillil could take no more and asked Yehezkel, in solemn tones, to tell Twalia that if Yasmine lived and the *sheikh* allowed him to marry her, he would accept Allah and his Prophet, convert to Islam, and become a member of the clan.

To Yehezkel's great surprise, Twalia consented, either moved by Aillil's prostration or because he didn't really think his daughter would survive the poison. Aillil was allowed into Twalia's tent and never left Yasmine's side again, holding her hand despite the disapproving looks from the women.

Pain twisted her lovely features into grimaces that tore his heart to shreds. He stared at her, pushing back the tears. "Is this God's punishment for our sin? But then why her and not me? And why is it a sin to touch a woman's body? Does God send scorpions to punish those who surrender to temptation? Well, outside Damietta I saw men do it with mares, and *they* didn't die! It's just the way life is."

He dabbed at the sweat on her brow. In his mind's eye he could see every expression of that face he chose to remember: Yasmine laughing, Yasmine worried, Yasmine annoyed, Yasmine sleeping.

"If I lose her now," he thought, "I'll spend the rest of my days summoning a thousand images of her until I convince myself that she's still beside me, even if it makes everyone think I'm crazy!"

God being merciful, Yehezkel's remedy worked, and on the third day Yasmine came to and wept with joy at the news that Aillil would become her husband and stay with the clan. When Aillil told the rabbi of his vow, Yehezkel joked, "It's a good thing she lived! Now you don't have to go back to Provence and live with the ghost of a Bedouin girl!"

Twalia decided that the conversion would take place in the mosque in Arīsh, a Bedouin town on the coast, and once Aillil—who would meanwhile be given his Mohammedan name—raised his finger to proclaim the oneness of Allah, the wedding would take place forthwith. A young goat was butchered and roasted that night to celebrate Yasmine's surviving Satan's assault. Yehezkel was the hero of the evening around the fire, being compared several times to his teacher, the great Musa ibn Maimun.

Everything in Arīsh went smoothly, and when they moved on, the happiness of the fourteen-year-old newlyweds seemed to give the whole caravan a jauntier step. They were two-thirds of the way to Gaza, but several days behind schedule, what with scorpions and marriages.

One morning, counting back to their departure on the 27th of November, Galatea realized that the next day would be Christmas. Aillil's decision to become a Mohammedan had both delighted and rattled the abbess. Albacara, in Crete, feared that the Jew would drag her into his theological blindness and make her reject Christ. Now it was the young Cathar heretic, instead, who had changed his religion and become an infidel, just like the ones his own father hunted down "for Christ's sake." Sometimes God's plans, she thought, were truly obscure.

Now that Aillil was no longer a Christian—not even one caught up in a Manichean error—Galatea was the only person in the caravan who believed that this was the night the Redeemer was born.

At first, remembering Christmases in Tuscia when the voices shouting, "Peace on earth among people of good will!" had literally shaken the ground, she felt desperately alone. In that Bedu camp, nobody knew or cared it was Christmas Eve, but somehow that only made her feel *more* Christian than she'd ever felt before. For a moment, she understood the inner strength that allowed Jews to preserve their faith among gentiles, her head almost spinning with the realization. Late that night, sitting by the spluttering fire as it went out, she told Yehezkel it was Christmas Eve. He said nothing but placed his hand on hers, smiling with empathy.

She thought, "Yehezkel and I live almost like man and wife by now. Our adventures have made us drop the masks we wore when we met."

Suddenly, her eyes wide open and staring into the fire, she had a fleeting vision. Yehezkel was dressed as the sheikh of a Bedu clan, and she was his wife, wearing a niqab and dismantling a tent as the sun rose on the desert. She snapped out of it and turned to him.

"Know that I'll never be your beast of burden, Yehezkel!"

The rabbi was getting used to that woman jerking normality from under him like a carpet. "I don't know what in the world made you say that, Galatea, but I would really like for you to call me Yehezkel from now on . . . and I'll call you Galatea. I think we've *earned* that much intimacy, don't you?"

She was silent, her face lit by the waning fire, and then turned to him and nodded, smiling.

After a little while, she said, "Yehezkel, may I ask you for some . . . spiritual advice?"

Yehezkel was surprised, though not as much as he would have been six months earlier. "Of course, Galatea. I just hope your dilemma is not one that would elicit different responses from our two faiths," said the rabbi, guardedly.

"It's about Brother Francesco," she said, lowering her voice despite the wilderness around them. "And also the feverish expectation among Jews you told me about, of the imminent arrival of your Messiah."

Yehezkel knew the nun sitting next to him was a prophetess and was immediately attentive.

"Christian Scriptures reveal that in the Last Days, Christ will return," she went on. "Well, I've . . . I've had signs that Francesco of Assisi and the returning Christ of the Second Advent are *one and the same*!"

Yehezkel said, "And where, pray, does the Jews' Messiah come into this . . . vision?"

"Priests say that when Christ returns, Jews will recognize him as their Messiah and claim he is not the same Son of God they crucified the first time around. I've been wondering, Yehezkel . . . could predictions of your Messiah and of our Second Advent be referring to the same event?"

"Mmh . . . I mean no disrespect, Galatea, but if someone claims the Messiah has arrived, isn't claiming he will also, at some later stage, come again, the perfect insurance against having been wrong?"

She smiled. "I can see how your use of logic must have sent Domingo crawling up the walls!"

The distant chorus of hyenas and jackals from the darkness around camp gave her next words an apocalyptic ring. "Still, I have a strong sense that both events are very close, and the excitement among Jews seems to confirm it."

Yehezkel recalled the prophecy in Rav Moshe's family and said, "I'll tell you a cautionary tale on such predictions, be they of our Messiah or of your Second Advent. An old Jewish tradition claimed that when God freed the children of Israel from slavery in Egypt, he wanted that event to be at the center of history, from creation to the coming of the Messiah. Jews know the date of the Exodus, and doubling that date gave a year which, in your calendar, was one thousand two hundred and twelve."

"Oh, dear!" said Galatea with real sympathy. "That must have been awful for a lot of believers."

"Mmph! The fever and expectation survived nonetheless," said Yehezkel. "The frenzy was such that eight years ago, a year before the prophesied date, *three hundred* rabbis uprooted their families and schools from England and France and moved to Jerusalem! You see, for them the Latins losing the city to Salah ad-Din—who allowed thousands of Jews to live there again—was nothing if not a sign that preparations were underway for the Messiah's arrival!"

"So what did they do when . . . when nothing happened?" asked Galatea.

"Oh, most of them are still there; they simply decided that the date must have referred to the *birth* of the Messiah, not to his manifestation, so now they walk around Jerusalem, peering at the expression on the face of every seven-year-old they meet."

Galatea laughed out loud. Hussein raised his head and then let it drop again. After a while, she said, "You asked me for the secret of my good mood. Well, a big part is that I feel—thanks to the Lord, but also with your help—I feel like I am party to mysterious, epochal events that are unfolding. And you know what the strangest thing is? That I always *knew* I was destined to find myself in the middle of them. I knew it from my very first vision as a child! Oh, Yehezkel, it's all so exciting it takes my breath away . . . and you wonder why I'm in a good mood?"

✡ ✠ ✡ ✠

NEAR GAZA, 5TH JANUARY 1220

In early January of the year of our Lord 1220, the caravan was two days from Gaza and the end of its journey. Twalia decided to camp some five hundred yards from a wadi where water could be found, because the place was full of roughly dug, shallow graves that he found sinister, and for some years he'd preferred not to spend the night there. So at dawn, Yehezkel and a young Bedu took two camels and rode to the wadi to fill some goatskins with water before they moved on.

The blessing from heaven was in minute detail: the fact that the wadi was east of the camp, so that when, halfway there, Yehezkel turned around, he saw the tips of the Templars' weapons glint in the rising sun, just above the crest of the dune behind the Bedus' camp.

War made attacks on isolated Bedouin caravans by small groups of Templars and their sergeants a common occurrence. Yehezkel started breathing the folded breath, his mind racing through options. In a minute the knights would charge down the dune. There were twenty Bedus of fighting age in the camp, but even small squadrons of Templars had been known to overwhelm a hundred well-armed men.

"It will be a massacre. Perhaps they won't even spare Galatea," he thought, horrified.

Then it came to him. Arnald hadn't been at Damietta, and a knight told Aillil his father was with a platoon patrolling Syrian routes.

"God's mercy knows no limits. If someone up there really is protecting us, my friend is one of those knights!" He was just turning his camel around, when the charge began.

There was no time to ride back. In an instant, he understood what their last chance was. The distance was big but worth trying, and the windless dawn would help. He stayed on his camel to raise the source of the shout and deepened his breathing, as a fearful scene unfolded some three hundred yards from him.

Four knights and five sergeants, white mantles flying behind the former, brown ones behind the latter, charged down the dune. Yehezkel kept breathing as he watched panic spread through the clan, everyone running, some jumping on camels and galloping away. The more breaths he took, the more powerful his voice would be, so he waited for the last moment before calling out to his friend.

The first knight was a hundred feet from the nearest Bedu when the cry shattered the desert dawn. "AAARNAAAALD!!!"

The commander of the platoon *was* Arnald Arifat of Montréal. On hearing his name and recognizing Yehezkel's voice, he jerked on his reins and raised his swordless arm to stop his comrades. The animal dug its heels and a spray of sand rose over the head of the Bedu who had been about to lose it instead.

When Yehezkel returned to the camp, Aillil/Ahmed had already met his father and told him of his life-changing decision. Another Templar, with a less curious mind than his, might have wept over the loss of a son, but Arnald had last seen his boy aged three and fragile as a bird, so the mere sight of the strong, sunburned, freckled teenager filled his heart with joy. He embraced him and blessed him and his new wife. Then he thanked his Jewish friend profusely for Aillil's miraculous recovery.

"If only my poor Esmeralda could see him now! Oh, Yehezkel, how will I *ever* repay you?"

"Mmh, I may have one or two ideas on that," said the rabbi as Galatea grinned knowingly.

On being introduced to her, Arnald performed the same heart-lips-forehead homage the abbess had now received thrice, but her reaction, though struck by how handsome Aillil's father was, was muted, as she was still recovering from seeing a dozen knights charging down a desert dune directly at her, easily the most frightening sight she had ever beheld.

By now Twalia's clan were convinced that whatever blessing Allah bestowed on his teacher had been passed on to Yehezkel ibn Yusuf, who had just saved the clan single-handedly . . . and with one word!

Arnald decided to stay with the Muzziena clan, say goodbye to his son in Gaza, and escort his friends north to Château Pélerin. Had the Old Man been there around the fire that evening, he would surely have appreciated the sight of Templar knights breaking bread with a Bedu clan.

Arnald asked Yehezkel to teach him the Templar battle cry in Hebrew, since it came from a Psalm that King David had certainly not written in Latin.

"With pleasure, my friend!" said the rabbi. "Your cry is: Non nobis, Domine, non nobis, sed tuo nomini da gloriam. The Hebrew original is: Lo lanu, Adonai, lo lanu, ki le-shimcha ten kavod."

Arnald thanked him and repeated the phrase until he'd memorized it.

Considering the horrific tales she'd heard about desert dwellers in Torcello, by the end of the journey the abbess found the Muzziena an honorable people, if with a slightly aggrieved sense of what honor *is*. In any case, she felt sure that Aillil's life with them would be richer than among his Cathar peers. As she sat by the fire reflecting on this, Yehezkel tapped her shoulder.

"Here is a question to put your kabbalistic skills to the test, Galatea. We didn't stay in al-Kahira for forty days, like we did in Crete, Cyprus, and Damietta. Can you tell me why?"

"This is a tough one," said Galatea. "How many days *did* we stay in al-Kahira, then?"

"Let's see, we arrived on the 28th of September and left on the 28th of November, that makes . . . sixty days! Can you find a symbolic meaning in that?"

"Mmmh . . . no, I can't," said she. "But now tell me, instead, when the fortieth day in al-Kahira was."

"That's easy. It was . . . the 7th of November!"

She smiled and said, "That's the day Aillil first met Yasmine. It's not always about *us*, Yehezkel!"

✡ ✠ ✡ ✠

ROME, 5TH JANUARY 1220

That same night in early January, as Aillil was finally reunited with his father, Domingo of Guzman had just arrived in Rome and was lying in state in his coffin, listening to a De Profundis.

Lying in a custom-made casket when his mood was dark was a habit he'd picked up from a pious nobleman in King Alfonso's court, a certain Count of Olivarez who, since *also* being made Duke of San Lucar, was known to Spaniards as El Conde Ducque. When he wanted to remind himself of his mortality, Olivarez would summon a choir, have forty big church candles lit all around his coffin, and stretch out in it. Then he would meditate on transience while the choir sang the De Profundis.

Domingo tried it, and his Spanish soul was enraptured with the experience. On this night he felt certain he didn't have more than a year to live. Where better to reflect on the imminent revelation of all Truths, including where he'd gone wrong and sinned, than *in* his grave?

From the outside, even according to his critics, his mission was an unmitigated success. He was conferred the title of Master General of the Order of Preachers by Honorius, and as master, he had just sent letters to all convents announcing the first general chapter of the order, to be held in Bologna on the next Pentecost. True, soon he would be in the arms of his Creator, but his work was done and was, God willing, irreversible! So why was he lying in this coffin, eyes closed, and arms crossed on his chest?

"Because there is no news from Brother Roberto!"

In October he'd heard of how Master Ezekiel brilliantly escaped Cardinal Pelagius's clutches in Damietta. Then, of course, once out of reach, he'd simply stayed in the sultan's camp!

Sure, he'd be hunted down for treason and desertion in Christian lands, but the Jew knew that. What was more, as Brother Roberto conveyed to him by trusted messenger, the Jew *wanted* to go to Egypt because of a document about the Parchment that was hidden in a synagogue there!

"I'm in my coffin because that Christ killer is ahead of me and might find the confession before me. Worse, I could be dead by the time the rabbis of Europe set about using it!"

Domingo knew that the Old Man, whoever might be hiding behind the honorific, had been looking for the Parchment for years. He'd pressed Honorius to force the Templars to give up the old chaplain to his preachers, but there were limits to the pope's power over the Temple—as he knew only too well.

Cencio was in wandering exile—O tempora!—but as soon as he was back in Rome, Domingo would have to see him and find a way, with Roberto's help, to stop the Jew before he got to Jerusalem!

Unless he was already there. ¡Madre de Dios! Where *was* Brother Roberto?

CHAPTER 26

VE-YIRDU

And Let Them Have Dominion

CHÂTEAU PÉLERIN, 27TH JANUARY 1220

Near the end of January, after a week in Gaza and a leisurely ride up the coast, stopping in Askelon and Jaffa on the way, the three friends reached the fortress on the sea. The abbess—trotting between the two men, quietly happy to be on a horse again—was soon charmed by Arnald's earring, blond curls, and sunny smile. His lighthearted troubadour manner made her feel like a countess wooed by a handsome knight, rather than the visionary nun on an enchanted pilgrimage she really was.

In Gaza, Arnald took leave of his son, after promising to seek out the clan whenever he was in the Sinai. In light of the Old Man's struggle for a synthesis of the three faiths, the irony of his own son embracing Mahomet's religion had not escaped him. On the way north, he'd discussed it with rabbi and abbess and found himself in total agreement with their Averroist outlook—in fact he'd wondered aloud if it wouldn't be a good thing for *everyone,* as the Old Man claimed, if Jews and Mohammedans were proved right about the Resurrection, after all.

During the journey, Yehezkel and Arnald exchanged accounts of events in the ten years since they'd last seen each other. Galatea heard Yehezkel relate to his friend, as delicately as he could, of Esmeralda's illness and death at the siege of Carcassonne. She avidly listened to the tales of their respective adventures, all the more enjoyable for the disenchanted light the two shone on the characters they'd met.

"Oh, Yehezkel" said Arnald, "you *must* tell the Old Man of your *disputatio* with Domingo of Guzman! The Spanish monk is his sworn enemy, his nemesis, and the only thing he still fears—his words—is dying before beating him to the real Parchment."

Neither Jews nor Cathars believed that Jesus was resurrected, so Arnald didn't hesitate to tell Yehezkel what the Old Man discovered, hoping Galatea would not be too distressed to hear of the confession. The strange couple's reaction confounded him. They already *knew* what he thought was the best-kept secret in Christendom: that the Order of the Temple blackmailed the church, pretending to have found a document they did not in fact possess. To explain their knowledge, they told him of Sancio's deathbed revelations and of the letter from the Jerusalem rabbis they read in Fustat.

"Our purpose in seeking out the Old Man," said Yehezkel, "isn't just to help him find the Parchment; it is to *decipher the map and find the confession*!"

Arnald was shaken. He stammered, "I feel caught in events much bigger than my puny little life."

"Welcome to the company, Arnald!" jested Galatea. "That's how I have felt all the time since April!"

Yehezkel pressed for every last bit of information. "So you heard no more from the Old Man after he told you in September that he would look for Baldwin's diary in the Royal Treasure?"

"No, nothing. I was in Askelon all the time, and he said he couldn't trust anyone with information on the Parchment, because Domingo's men were everywhere."

"He was right about that!" said Yehezkel. "In the camp outside

Damietta, your master told me that the Spaniard has even infiltrated an agent in your order."

"Trust me, that wouldn't be hard to do, these days," said Arnald. "Did he know who the traitor is?"

"If he did, he kept it for himself," answered Yehezkel.

"You know, Pedro's relationship with the Old Man—I mean which one bows to the will of the other," said Arnald, "is what I never understood. After all, how come Pedro didn't do anything about the Old Man in the year and a half he has been master?"

"You forget that Pedro wants the Parchment, too," said Yehezkel, grinning. "He told me it leads to 'something of great importance to the order,' so since the chaplain's chances of finding it are greater than his own, Pedro probably thinks *he* is the one manipulating the Old Man."

"Mmh . . . I told you how easily the master of Provence humiliated my ambition to become a spy," said Arnald. "Sometimes my head hurts just trying to keep up with everyone's lies and plots. I'm a simple knight, Yehezkel, and the clash between the Old Man and Domingo goes right over my head."

"I know just what you mean, Arnald," smiled Galatea. "I often think Divine Providence must have slipped up when it chose *me* to solve the enigma in Jerusalem . . ."

Arnald laughed. "The Old Man says the Templars dug under the esplanade for *eight years* looking for the Parchment and found nothing." He turned to Yehezkel. "What makes you think that ghost of a man and the three of us are going to find it?"

That gave Yehezkel an idea. "Listen. Could you find out if the order has maps of the tunnels they dug a hundred years ago? That would be enormously helpful."

"I never heard talk of such maps, but then I've only been a Templar for nine months. I asked myself how to repay you for saving my son and bringing him here, my friend, and now I know: if such maps exist, rest assured that I'll find them and copy them for you!"

"If they do exist," murmured Galatea, "I bet the Old Man knows where they are."

"But of course!" said Arnald, impressed. Yehezkel grinned at the newcomer's reaction to the nun's astute conclusion.

Arnald had told them that no one deserved the epithet "Old Man" more than this chaplain, yet when they entered the scriptorium and saw him, they were amazed at his decrepitude. Yehezkel was reminded of the vision he'd had of his teacher a few months before his death.

"Oh, so this is your 'kabbalist' friend," said the Old Man, a residual trace of hope in his raspy voice. "Welcome, Master Ezekiel, welcome to my lair. Arnald says you'll be an invaluable aid to my quest. But first tell me, please, who is the fetching noblewoman with you?"

Galatea introduced herself and complimented the Old Man on the most powerful castle she'd ever set eyes on, as if the rickety old figure before her were its commander and not its chaplain.

"My friends have found the letter from the rabbis on the Parchment!" said Arnald excitedly.

"Have they really?" said the Old Man, smiling wistfully. "I do hope they can help me understand the Parchment of Circles before I leave this frustrating, overlong life."

Yehezkel couldn't believe his ears. "You *have* it?" he cried.

"Yes, I have it. It's been in my hands for a week, but its cipher escapes me . . . and sleep, now, too."

"How did you find it?" asked Arnald. "Did King Baldwin's diary lead you to it?"

"Yes, but Divine Providence had a role in how I finally laid my hands on it, after all these years. Even a man who is a heretic in the eyes of most heretics, as I am, has to admit that much."

The disappointment of finding the map but failing to decipher it soured the chaplain's expression. He sat down and explained, "When Damietta fell two months ago, the king of Jerusalem and Cardinal Pelagius quarreled over possession of the city, until two weeks ago, when John of Brienne, enraged, left for Acre with his barons and the Teutonic master."

The Old Man paused to catch his breath. Arnald thought his voice trembled in a way it hadn't done before. The chaplain knew better than anyone else that his time was up, and his bitterness showed. "The king's chancellor denied me access to the treasure, but when John arrived in Acre—despite the strain on this wreck of a body—I went to the palace and, with a scholarly pretext, obtained permission to look at Baldwin's diary. It was easier than I'd hoped. Everything was right there, black on white. Anyone could have read it in the hundred years since he died, had they only cared to do so."

The other three didn't need to ask him what the king had written; their eyes spoke for them.

"It's an incredible story," the Old Man began, "that starts in Calabria in the summer of 1070, exactly a thousand years after the destruction of your Temple, Master Ezekiel. Three rabbis from Jerusalem, during a vicious dispute with some local Benedictine monks, blurted out the secret of the confession. One of them said the body was stolen and proof would emerge when the Messiah will arrive, thanks to a map that had been drawn to find it. The monks, terrified by the threat, ran off north the next month, in search of rich nobles and clerics who could find the cursed map and destroy it before *it* destroyed Christianity!"

The silence in the scriptorium was such that had an insect flown in, all heads would have turned.

The Old Man wheezed on. "They founded an abbey at Orval, near Bouillon, which is why Godefroy was among the first nobles to be alerted to the terrible danger. It may even be that Urban II's campaign to recover the sepulchre was really motivated by the search for the map, but Baldwin's diary doesn't say. . . . Anyway, in 1110 two surviving founders of Orval, two monks who had exchanged insults with the rabbis forty years earlier, came to Jerusalem on a pilgrimage, and to check on the search. They told King Baldwin the story from the beginning—and this is where it gets unbelievable . . ."

The Old Man started coughing. Galatea rushed to his side, but he waved her away and continued. "The monks thought one rabbi had said 'αλ μα μην που το πέτρα,' or 'al ma min pou to Pétra'—more or less 'anything but Peter!' But of course, how would Calabrian Benedictines know who al-Ma'moun was? When Baldwin heard the Greek phrase, he understood at once that what the rabbi had actually said was 'Al-Ma'moun pou tou pétra;' that is, 'Al Ma'moun put it under the Rock'!"

"But of course!" cried Yehezkel. "The letter in the geniza says the Parchment was confiscated by al-Ma'moun's Abassid governor! That reckless rabbi even told the monks in Calabria where the caliph had *put* it, but they were too ignorant to understand him! Truly the ways of the Lord are mysterious. So what did King Baldwin *do* with the Parchment when he found it?" Yehezkel was an excited boy again.

"That's the ironic part," said the Old Man. "He wrote that he showed it to a few people and then put it back where he'd found it, afraid of the fate that would befall a Christian king who found the confession! Which, by the way, confirms my theory on the source of circular maps of Jerusalem. One of the people Baldwin showed it to—apart from his wife, that is," he said, glancing at Arnald, "must have made a rough copy, and the knowledge that it was a map of the Holy City did the rest."

The Old Man allowed himself a proud but brittle smile. He may not have deciphered the Parchment, but at least he'd solved the mystery of the origin of circular maps that had plagued him for half a century.

"And *you* entered Omar's Dome in Ayubbid Jerusalem and removed the Parchment from under the Rock? *By yourself*?" asked Arnald, incredulous.

"It wasn't that hard," said the Old Man. "I dressed as a Mohammedan and was even revered for the obviously long life Allah bestowed on me. The hardest thing was moving around the esplanade that the restoration works of al-Muazzam 'Isa have turned into an immense building site."

The Old Man smiled as he thought back to what had surely been his final visit to the Holy City. "I went into the dome and prayed to Allah with everyone else, as I've learned to do over the years. Then I hid in a corner and waited for nightfall. Finding the niche in the gallery around the base of the Rock was child's play. But believe me, pathetically weak as I have become, if anyone had stood between me and the Parchment in the dome that night, I would still have killed him!"

"You are a braver man than a good portion of the knights I ride with every day!" said Arnald.

The Old Man smiled. Yehezkel pulled out the copy of the rabbis' letter he had made in the geniza. "Listen, Father. Four hundred years ago, a rabbi wrote that the map was drawn by a heretic. We think it must have been Elisha ben Abuya, because of a page of the Jerusalem Talmud that we deciphered with Don Sancio on the *Falcus,* before we had to beach the cog in a cove on the western end of Crete."

"Wait, wait, Rabbi, you're losing me. First of all, where is Don Sancio de la Palmela now?"

"I'm afraid he's no longer with us, Father. He was swept onto the rocks in the cove and passed away in a Cretan village ten days after the beaching."

The Old Man sighed. "I survived another good man . . . will only the evil ones outlive me? I know that page of Talmud. So you discovered who those weird, Persian-sounding names belonged to?"

"We did. They were encoded with a cipher called ATBASH. Elisha ben Abuya was accusing Hanina bar Hezekiah of hiding a page from the Book of Ezekiel, 'together with the oil.'"

"The *oil*?" The Old Man looked up, excited. "You're on to something, Rabbi!" he exclaimed. "One of the writings on the inner circle of the map says 'the Oil!' What else makes you think Elisha drew it?"

"Well, he says that Hanina hid the page because it was a prophecy 'fulfilled in the life of Yeshu ha-Nozri.' Some sages hold that Elisha became a Christian, and Galatea here says that the page from Ezekiel does, in fact, describe Mary Magdalene anointing Jesus in Bethany, in the very words of the Gospels. So if Elisha became a Christian, he would want that prophecy to be found, wouldn't he?"

"Aahh . . . so those names were encrypted because Elisha spoke of Jesus!" said the Old Man. "But surely if he was Christian, he would *never* have drawn a map that led to the confession!"

"Yes, I thought of that," said Yehezkel, "and decided there was only one possible explanation: Elisha *didn't know* the confession was in the hiding place with the page and the oil. Let me explain: Hanina put the oil, the page, *and* the confession in the hiding place just before the revolt against Rome; that is, thirty years after the death of Jesus. But Elisha lived eighty years later, over *a hundred years* after the Crucifixion! He must have discovered the hiding place of the page and the oil—the only things he mentions—but *not* the presence with them of the confession! And in his day, under Emperor Hadrian, Jews could no longer enter Jerusalem, so he couldn't go and verify what was *in* the hiding place."

Galatea quietly fumed. "Why, in *nine* months," she thought, "he never shared the reasoning he just expounded on Elisha and the confession! 'Perfect confidence' indeed! Ooh, but he'll get what's coming to him. This time he's really *asked* for it!"

The Old Man smiled. "Seems Arnald was right that your help would be the key to this riddle."

Everyone burned. Yehezkel wanted to decipher the Parchment as badly as the other three wanted him to do so. The Old Man abruptly put an end to the discussion of who had drawn it. "Come, now," he said, standing up wearily. "Let me show you what the whole world is looking for."

A tall library covered the eastern wall of the scriptorium. The Old Man got down on his knees, removed a codex from the lowest shelf, and laid it on the floor. Then he slid his hand where the book had been and pulled a hidden lever. He stood up again and finally, with a smile to his audience, leaned on the side of the bookcase. The heavy piece of furniture slid soundlessly sideways, revealing a small door in the wall behind it. They all stared in disbelief, for they knew that on the other side of that wall was the courtyard.

The Old Man gestured for them to follow and vanished, absurdly, *into* the wall.

What the Templars had done—the Old Man himself conceiving of a whole secret *room*—was to build a straight, extremely narrow stone staircase *inside* the thirty-foot-long eastern wall. It climbed diagonally from one end of the wall to the other, giving access to a loft hidden between the ceiling of the scriptorium and the roof of the building.

The space inside the wall was so narrow one had to turn one's shoulders to avoid getting stuck while climbing. When all four had crawled into the loft—where Yehezkel and Galatea had to keep their heads down—the Old Man lit an oil lamp and raised a plank in the floor, the map's last defense. He brought the Parchment of Circles to the table in the center of the room.

Once unfurled, the Parchment was about a foot square, its edges frayed and crumbling. Illuminated by the lamp, the circles were precisely drawn and still clear, but the Hebrew writing on them—four phrases on each circle, plus one in the center—was faded and not easy to make out. Yehezkel pored over it for five minutes, which, to the others, felt like an hour. At last he straightened up and hit his head on a roof beam.

"Ugh! Yes, I can just about make out what he wrote. What we must do is copy the words exactly, but bigger, so we can see them easily as we try to solve Elisha's riddle." Then, as an afterthought, "Father, do you have an old-fashioned wax tablet somewhere, that we can erase over and over? Elisha was a kabbalist, they say, and one of the finest minds of his generation. This is not going to be easy . . ."

"Of course I have wax tablets. Arnald, be a monkish knight; go down and fetch a couple of them. In the chest by the fireplace."

מקומו
His Place

שכינתי
My Spirit

לב המשיח   נשמה   השים   השמן   קורבן הלב
Heart of the Messiah   The Soul   The Heavens   The Oil   Sacrifice of the Heart

שופט בני החשך
Judge of the Sons of Darkness

בירושלים
In Jerusalem

The Old Man turned to Arnald. "I know how your Cathar perfecti read this. They say Saint John's cycles start on the left side of each circle, going round the bottom first, and they consider the inner one the path of the single soul, while the outer one is the Fate of Humanity."

"That's right, Father. On the inner circle, a soul must be judged for the darkness it contains; only then can it be anointed with the Holy Oil and rise to join His Spirit. On the outer one, the Heart of the Messiah—not the Son of God, but the Messiah nonetheless—is sacrificed in Jerusalem and rises to His Place. And the Heavens in the center represent the eternal wellspring of both circles."

As Arnald explained Saint John's theological summation, Galatea pulled on Yehezkel's sleeve, her eyes glinting with excitement in the light from the lamp. "Yehezkel, have you added up the phrases?" she asked urgently.

"Yes, I have," answered Yehezkel with a grin. "It's the first thing I always do."

Turning to the Old Man, he jested, "Did I introduce my outstanding pupil to you, Father?"

"Gematria!" said the chaplain, lightly slapping his own cheek. "But of course! I only thought of the *meaning* of the words, not their numerical values!"

"I told you Elisha was a kabbalist," said Yehezkel. "Every single phrase on the horizontal axis of the map is worth three hundred and ninety-five. That *cannot* be a coincidence."

"Have you already added up the phrases on the vertical axis?" asked the Old Man feverishly.

"Yes, of course. Give me a tablet, and I'll show you all the values."

The chaplain stood behind Yehezkel as he wrote on the wax tablet with a small scimitar-shaped stylus. After a few moments, he sucked in his breath. "790 is twice 395!" he cried. "Any two phrases on the horizontal axis are worth the same as 'My Spirit' or the 'Judge!'"

"That's not all," said Yehezkel. "'His Place' and 'In Jerusalem' *also* add up to 790! Arnald, can you still defend the idea that this is only a prophecy and not . . . something else, too?"

Arnald smiled, the quest for the Parchment's real meaning drawing him in despite himself.

Yehezkel said, "I think the way to read the map is to follow the sums. For example, what adds up to 790 should be read together. If you do that, 'His Place In Jerusalem' is practically the Parchment's title! Also, one should read 'My Spirit Judges the Sons of Darkness,' since both are worth 790. Elisha is playing games with us here. But we have a card to play, too."

"What card is that, Rabbi?" asked the Old Man.

"We already know *where* on the map the treasure is!" smiled Yehezkel. "Elisha said that Hanina had hidden the page 'with the oil,' so he must have drawn the map to show where the oil is!"

"You mean . . . you mean each phrase on the map is a place in Jerusalem?" asked Galatea.

"Well . . . isn't that how maps work?" said Yehezkel, who was enjoying himself immensely.

"Interesting," murmured Arnald. "Could that mean that phrases with the same value . . . are places at the same distance from each other on the ground?"

"Eureka!" cried Yehezkel. "I think you have it, my friend!"

"But *where* are the places on the ground?" asked the Old Man.

"Well, the moment I saw the Parchment," said Yehezkel, "my first thought was: 'If the center of a map is the Heavens, it can only mean that's where the Kodesh Kedoshim was!'"

"The Sancta Sanctorum of the Temple?" asked the Old Man. "That would put the oil 395 . . . 'units' east of it. What units of distance would Elisha use, Rabbi?"

"Wait a minute," interrupted Arnald. "Where on the map does it say east? The oil could be north of the Heavens, for all we know . . . or south."

"You're right, Arnald," said Yehezkel, "but let's follow the Old . . . the chaplain's thought through." He turned to the Old Man. "Elisha would use cubits, I think; everything in the Talmud is measured in cubits. That's from the elbow to the tip of one's fingers—almost two feet, I'd say."

"Let's see," said the Old Man. "If the Sancta Sanctorum is the center, the oil is some eight hundred feet east of it. Assuming the Rock under which I found the Parchment is where the Sancta Sanctorum was located, as everyone always has, then what is on the esplanade eight hundred feet east of it, Rabbi? I don't remember anything in particular . . ."

Yehezkel scratched his beard. "I was never *in* Jerusalem, Father, something I hope to remedy soon, with God's help. But I *do* remember the dimensions of the Temple courtyard, and eight hundred feet is about the distance to the eastern boundary of the esplanade."

"So the oil is on the edge of the esplanade? That doesn't make sense," said the Old Man.

"It would be easy enough to verify, though," said Yehezkel. "A cubit is also the length of an average step, so one would only have to count 395 steps eastward from the Rock under the dome. But then what do you do, start digging?"

"Ha, ha!" laughed the chaplain. "Al-Mu'azzam's mamluks would whisk you off before you had even unpacked your shovel!"

Yehezkel leapt at the chance. "No, Father, that wouldn't be the problem. Don't ask me how I got it, but I have a written permission from the sultan himself to search the esplanade, even belowground. Of course, if I knew where someone had already dug tunnels . . ."

The Old Man smiled. "Oh, what luck! I *happen* to have the maps drawn by Hugh de Payens a hundred years ago! I'll be happy to let you copy the overview map that shows the access to each tunnel."

"I accept gratefully, Father, although *this*," said Yehezkel, pointing to the parchment on the table, "is what we must carry a copy of. There's an enigma in Jerusalem, as a hermit once said, and the time to solve it has finally come! Arnald, is it too much to ask you to escort us to Jerusalem?"

"Of course not, but as a Templar I won't be allowed into the city. Besides, I've been absent without leave for long enough to get in trouble as it is."

"Excellent," said the Old Man. "You'll stay tomorrow and leave the next morning. For now, I'll assign comfortable cells to you so you can clean up and rest a little. The meals in the refectory are a monk's fare, but if you come to my apartment at twelfth hour, I'll have someone prepare a proper Italian dinner for the four of us. After all, we must celebrate unlocking the secrets of the Parchment!"

✡ ✠ ✡ ✠

The siege of Damietta over, Château Pélerin's garrison reverted to its contingent of fifty knights, thirty sergeants, one hundred archers, two hundred squires, and forty Saracen slaves. Every corner of the castle throbbed with activity, from training jousts in the courtyard to residual construction works, but the Old Man seemed to live in a château of his own, somewhere in the Midi, and the sacristy in which they ate a delicious candlelit dinner that evening easily deserved the name "apartment." The chaplain's tastes and habits were not those of a monk, and Yehezkel wondered if at some point he would get a chance to ask about his real identity.

The Old Man was in an ebullient mood as he poured Cypriot wine in four silver goblets several times during the meal, never looking a day over eighty. "I feel young, I tell you! I like to think I've improved with age, like good wine. My heart is lighter and my mind clearer at ninety-five than at thirty or sixty. I emerged rejuvenated from each molt, laughed at the skin I'd shed, and moved on. Despite the wisdom of old age, I am as unpredictable as a madcap youth. That's why my moves always surprise the Spaniard!"

Galatea, already a little tipsy, said, "Arnald says that in your youth you were a pupil of Saint Bernard. So how did you come to embrace Cathar and Manichean teachings on Sophia and against Rome?"

"Arnald also says," butted in Yehezkel, "that you favor those working for a new religion that would keep our common father Abraham's lesson on justice and charity, and scrap what came after him."

"Non est peccatum nisi contra conscientiam,"* recited the Old Man softly. "That would be *my* new religion! I was too young to hear him teach in Paris, but Pierre Abelard was my ideal thinker."

"Then it figures," said Galatea, "that you became a good friend of Father Makarios."

"Oh, you met the one *I* used to call the Old Man? Is he still meditating on a Cypriot mountain?"

"He is," said Galatea. "He was the one who told us of the letter in Fustat."

"*I* told him about that," grinned the Old Man. "But to answer you on the love of Sophia, I always had nothing but contempt for Saint Augustine's disesteem of women. You know, his works were only translated into Greek a few years ago. What a good, long theological run the Greeks had without him! What a shame the cursed Venetians thought of spreading his sick ideas in the Polis!"

"But Augustine also said Jews shouldn't be killed," said Yehezkel, "since exile is their punishment for refusing to accept Jesus as the Messiah. In a sense, we Jews owe him our survival in Christian lands."

"True, but look at what Innocent is doing with his bulls on Jews now!" objected the Old Man.

Yehezkel sighed. "Our life in Christendom can only get worse, Father. Had Christians corrupted the sense of the Torah, but gone their way with *their own* holy texts, like Muhammad, their faith wouldn't be a menace to us. But Christians—confound them!—went their way with *our* holy texts! They call themselves Verus Israel, heirs to Mount Sinai,

---

*There is no sinning except against one's conscience.

when they stole those traditions from the legitimate beneficiaries of that revelation. What feeds their hatred for us is that the more learned among them *know* it."

"You're right," said the chaplain. "But they understand nothing of the power of the Holy Tongue."

"Indeed," said Yehezkel. "Now that reminds me of the strange ideas of a kabbalist in Gerona, Father."

"Do tell, Master Ezekiel," said the Old Man eagerly, mindless of the evening turning to night.

"The Talmud calls Jesus a magician," began Yehezkel, "who cured people with a power he'd acquired. A pronouncer of Names, a drawer of circles—in effect, were he to live in Provence today, a *kabbalist*! Well, a rabbi in Gerona teaches that the Incarnation and the Trinity arose from mistaken interpretations of kabbalistic concepts that were correct in themselves. In other words, Jesus wasn't a magician, but a kabbalist who took a wrong turn, a rabbi whose Kabbalah was full of errors."

"Jesus, a kabbalist . . . what a fascinating thought, Rabbi. I wonder if you might do something for me . . ."

"After showing me the Parchment of Circles, you can ask me *anything* you wish, Father!"

"Well, just as I had no rest until I discovered where circular maps of Jerusalem originated, there's a mystery concerning Jesus that has plagued me since I first read Saint John's Gospel."

His audience of a Christian, a Cathar, and a Jew leaned forward, intrigued.

"In the last chapter of his Gospel, after the Resurrection, John says that Jesus went to the shores of the lake, and with his help some disciples caught 153 fishes." He repeated, "*One hundred and fifty three fishes.* John is a dozen verses from the end of his tale, it's the last thing Jesus does in this world, so how could a detail like a precise *number* be devoid of significance? And in a Gospel as riddled with symbols as John's!"

He paused, not really daring to hope for a solution. "I've played with that number for decades, as have others before me, but this idea of Jesus as a kabbalist changes things. What if Saint John was one, too? Tell me, Rabbi, can gematria be used, how shall I put it, *backward*? Can a number lead to a particular word?"

"Mh . . . John's Gospel is in Greek," said Yehezkel. "I've heard of gematria applied to Greek, but secrets can only be apprehended through things like gematria in Hebrew, the Holy Tongue of Creation."

"But didn't Jesus speak Hebrew?" asked the Old Man, surprised. "He was a Jew, wasn't he?"

"Yes, he was," said Yehezkel, "but Jews then, outside of prayers and Torah readings, spoke Aramaic."

"Still and all, could you show me how to arrive at a word from the number 153 in *Hebrew*?"

"I can try that, but you'll have to fetch a wax tablet again," said Yehezkel.

Ten minutes later they followed his lesson as he played with letters and numbers for them. He scratched 1 5 3 on the tablet. "Since every letter in the Hebrew alphabet has a value, I could write 153 with four, five, or even ten letters, but I will do it with the smallest number, three. Not just because we all like a three-letter word, but because with three letters there will only be eighteen possible combinations, while with even just four letters, there would be . . . oh, dozens and dozens!"

The Old Man's bony hand went up immediately. "Wait, wait, Rabbi! How could there possibly be *eighteen* ways of combining just *three* letters?"

"It's because they're not always the *same three*! You see, if the total is to be 153, then one letter—the *gimel,* which is worth three—will always have to be present. But making up the remaining 150 with two letters is something I can do with *six* different letters! I can use 100+50, 90+60, and 80+70! On top of that, changing the order of the letters will result in a different word! Here, I'll show you the combinations."

He started scratching, and soon the tablet was covered with figures like a dish invaded by ants.

100+50+3	100+3+50	50+3+100	50+100+3	3+100+50	3+50+100
90+60+3	90+3+60	60+3+90	60+90+3	3+90+60	3+60+90
80+70+3	80+3+70	70+3+80	70+80+3	3+80+70	3+70+80

"As you see, Father," said Yehezkel, "there are eighteen. Now I'll substitute Hebrew letters for the numbers." He started scratching out each number and writing the equivalent letter in its place. It took him just over five minutes, and the result was a sequence of eighteen "words."

"These are not all *words*," he said and then corrected himself with a smile. "At least, not in *this* cycle of the universe. They're just *all* the combinations of three letters that add up to 153." His audience was puzzled.

"Now we have to see which ones *are* words, and for that, I'm afraid, one has to know Hebrew."

Yehezkel began scratching out the words that, in this cycle of the world, meant nothing in Hebrew. The nonwords vanished under Yehezkel's strokes. In a remote corner of their minds, the three assorted Christians wondered if they hadn't embarked on a magical, possibly dangerous Jewish ritual. The mystery of the 153 fishes permeated the silence in the apartment, the only sounds coming from the spitting candles and the little scimitar on the wax.

In the end, Yehezkel raised his head, smiling. He had rubbed out all eighteen words. "None of those words mean anything in Hebrew," he said. "But I believe *one* of them does tell us what your Evangelist meant by that number. You see, John knew that his readers, the ones who would wonder why Jesus's disciples caught *exactly* 153 fishes, knew Greek better than Hebrew."

They all stared at him like children about to receive the most extravagant gift in the world. The Old Man, who had toyed with the riddle for the best part of a century, wasn't even breathing. Yehezkel wrote a single, large, three-letter Hebrew word on the tablet and handed it to Galatea. "How would you read *this* word, the fifteenth one of the eighteen, my brilliant pupil?"

Scratched in the wax were an *ayin* (70), a *gimel* (3) and a *pey* (80).

ע ג פ

Galatea, her heart skipping a beat from surprise, whispered, "A . . . gà . . . pe!"

"Correct, my friend! It seems the message John left the followers of Jesus in the number of fishes was the same selfless love that he came into this world to teach them."

The Old Man's eyes were moist. "It is as you say, Rabbi; there can be no doubt. The proof is that in the verses that follow, Jesus asks Peter three times if he loves him—using agàpis!"

The Old Man stood up and faced his three new friends. "Now I know *this,* something no theologian knows: I can repossess my real name before I lie down and die. Now, thanks to you, I am truly Doctor Universalis! And in any case, if you two find the confession, I want my real name to be remembered as that of the man who found the map that led to its hiding place."

"Doctor Universalis," murmured Yehezkel. "Where have I heard that title before? But of course! At the University in Montpellier! You . . . you are Alain de Lille!"

"At your service, my good friends. I died in the year of our Lord 1203, in the abbey at Cîteaux, and I can testify that no man is freer than a dead one!"

Galatea's laugh restored the gathering's celebratory mood after the brief spell of Gospel Kabbalah, but Yehezkel's face darkened as memories of Alain de Lille's reputation surfaced in his mind. "But you were a well-known, respected theologian . . . who wrote things that pleased the church." He suddenly remembered one. "By my beard, if I'm not mistaken, you even wrote a Contra Judeos!"*

Alain smiled. "Bernard of Clairvaux taught me to stay in the good book of the powerful. The man was so cunning that by the time I was

---

*Against the Jews—most Catholic theologians, at some point, wrote a tractate to refute Judaism with this title

twenty he'd *made* his own pope! My orthodoxy was always a facade—behind it, my mind was as free as Abelard's! I only stopped hiding my distaste for Catholic dogma after I moved to Montpellier, where a whole different world opened up to me."

The rabbi's expression softened. "I knew that world, too, Master Alain. Curious, tolerant, sensual . . . But Simon de Montfort destroyed all that for good, ten years ago. It no longer exists."

"Master Ezekiel, don't despair," said Alain softly. "This darkness is just a pause, before the iron wheels of circumstance grip firmly once again, pulling to Jerusalem!"

"There is something, Father," said Galatea, "that Don Sancio never explained. How did the Templars get to know of the confession, and of the Parchment of Circles?"

"Bernard, or *Saint* Bernard, I should say, *loved* ancient manuscripts. He heard of the confession and tasked *his* Templars with finding it. They dug under the Mount for nine years but came up with nothing, so at the Council of Troyes, in 1127, Bernard told Honorius II that the Templars had the document, and there was nothing left for him to do but recognize the order, with the rule he'd written for it."

Yehezkel looked puzzled. "But why would an . . . upright saint like Bernard *lie* to a pope and put the church in the hands of warrior monks?" he asked.

"I'm not sure. I was told it was to do with saving the Cistercian order from financial ruin, but I rather think he wanted his monks to have a military arm to fight heretics, infidels, and antipopes. You see, when Bernard decreed who was pope and who was antipope, people in Rome just didn't listen, which enraged him. He wanted a militia because he feared what would happen when Honorius II died."

Before retiring to their cells, on an impulse from Arnald, the only knight at the little cryptological feast, they raised their goblets to the genius of Elisha ben Abuya.

✡ ✠ ✡ ✠

ACRE, 27TH JANUARY 1220

While Yehezkel was solving the mystery of the fishes, Frutolf was in his master's quarters in the Hospital of the Teutonic Order near Acre's eastern wall.

Hermann von Salza had left Damietta two weeks earlier with John of Brienne, when the legate's arrogance became too much for the king of Jerusalem to bear.

"So, Brother Frutolf, what other slights did you suffer from the English Templar?"

"The most vulgar you can imagine, Master. I gave my word to a Venetian abbess that I'd protect two women traveling with her while they were in Acre. So what does *Brother* Bois-Guilbert do? He has the women kidnapped by the Hashashin a few days after they disembark!"

"Why on earth would he do that?" asked Hermann. "Surely not so he could have his way with them?"

"No, no, he wanted information for Domingo of Guzman. The women came from the West with the abbess and a Jew. From what I garnered, Domingo and a Templar chaplain they call the Old Man are looking for a certain Parchment of Circles, and Bois-Guilbert is Domingo's arm in Outremer."

"Mmh . . . a Parchment of Circles. Pedro didn't mention it. As for this Old Man, who is *he*?"

"To hear the Englishman, he's the principal head of a heretical hydra hiding *inside* the Temple."

"Scheiße! I have enough problems with heretics in *my* order without worrying about Pedro's, too! The reason I called you, Frutolf, is that you were actually surveilling the Templar for their master, and you did an excellent job, too. Thanks to you, he now knows, as you just said, that the agent Domingo infiltrated in his order is Bois-Guilbert. Do you know who he met with in Acre?"

"The Templars wouldn't even let me into their castle here. He was busy recruiting people for the siege, but of course he stopped doing that when Damietta fell. But if he's been exposed as a spy, Master, I'll be grateful not to have to do his bidding any more."

"Not only is that the case, Frutolf, you're about to avenge every humiliation he inflicted on you. Pedro de Montaigue has asked me to have the traitor arrested and, if he resists, executed."

"Forgive my insolence, Master, but wouldn't there be consequences if a Teuton killed a Templar?"

Hermann smiled. "I always underestimated you, Brother Frutolf. Yes, there would be; that's why you're to go to Jerusalem disguised as a pilgrim and offer your services to the abbess you mentioned."

Hermann seemed unsure of his next words and then said, "You will protect them, and if Bois-Guilbert is desperate enough to follow them there out of uniform, you will eliminate him—in which case, as you see, he won't be a Templar killed by a Teuton, but a pilgrim killed by another, maybe over a woman. And don't worry; if it should come to it, I'll make sure the vizier lets you go."

Frutolf could hardly believe his good fortune. His mission, assigned to him by his master, was now to be Galatea degli Ardengheschi's champion, to protect the lady of his thoughts!

He grabbed Hermann's forearm, at the same time bowing his head, and then left the big study.

CHAPTER 27

Zahar U'Neqevah
Male and Female

ON THE CLIMB TO JERUSALEM,
30TH JANUARY 1220

A dreary chant rose from the barefoot and bareheaded pilgrims, their staffs swinging their way up the side of a hill. The three riders caught up with the column a little before Tulkarm. Two Templar knights—eccentrically faithful to the order's original, hundred-year-old mission—escorted forty or so penitent souls, two white mantles with red crosses being enough to deter raiding parties of even a dozen Bedus.

Coming up behind them, Arnald slowed down to exchange words with his brethren while Yehezkel and Galatea peered at the pilgrims. Their distant gazes bespoke the sobering sights they'd witnessed in the two thousand leagues they had walked, but their eyes also shone with the feverish expectation that from the next hilltop, they might finally glimpse Jerusalem.

As they rode on, Yehezkel said, "We'll never thank you enough for these mounts, Arnald. The pilgrims will walk for another week to reach Jerusalem while we, with God's help, will be there tomorrow."

"Le cheval, comme chacun sait, est la part la plus importante du chevalier!"* laughed Arnald.

They left Château Pélerin at dawn after spending the previous day resting and discussing with Alain—who swore them to secrecy on his identity—the precautions they should take to avoid Domingo's agent in Jerusalem, for, whoever it was, he would have to dress as a pilgrim to enter the city and would thus be harder to spot, while they would be as obvious as they'd been for their whole journey.

They arranged to communicate through a Templar in pilgrim's clothes who would loiter just north of the city, by the ruins of the church of Saint Stephen, destroyed by Salah ad-Din. Arnald bristled at the words "Templar in pilgrim's clothes," something as compatible with the Rule as murder was with the Ten Commandments, but then considered the unusual circumstances and said nothing.

Finally, and most important, they discussed with Alain what they would do with the confession, should the Lord help them find it. They eventually agreed—Galatea with some reluctance—that the Saracens were the best guardians of a relic so dangerous for the church. They would take it to Damascus.

The night before, Yehezkel copied a map that showed every tunnel the order had dug between 1119 and 1126. The Templars started digging in Solomon's Stables, in the southeastern corner of the esplanade, and reached deep into the bowels of the Mount. As Yehezkel labored by lamplight in the secret loft, they all laughed at the thought of the *real* Parchment of Circles, a hundred years earlier, safely ensconced under the Rock as knights dug tirelessly, and uselessly, twenty feet below it.

The rabbi, besotted with maps since childhood, lovingly copied the one with the points of access to the tunnels, all the while wondering if the knights named after the Temple ever found any of the Temple's treasure, which he knew had been hidden in prearranged spots under the Mount by the high priest during the siege by the Romans.

---

*"The horse, as everyone knows, is the most important part of the knight!"

✡ ✠ ✡ ✠

"So you always thought Elisha didn't *know* the confession was hidden with the oil, did you?" she began, as if expressing a mild, scholarly interest in a detail.

He felt the ice in her voice and braced for what was coming.

"Well, of course I would have told you of my . . . supposition, but really, the thought only occurred to me in the last few days, as I reflected on Elisha's accusation *only* mentioning the page from Ezekiel and the oil, but ignoring something as important as the confession."

"Uuhh! Don't lie to me, Yehezkel ben Yoseph! You 'reflected on Elisha's accusation' from the minute Don Sancio told us of the confession! Why not just admit that you don't trust this Christian nun with the knowledge that the confession *exists*?"

Yehezkel thought she looked more upset than when he'd called her a pagan.

"And this idea of handing it to the Saracens! If I were an accomplice in *that,* would I not be a renegade to my own religion?"

Yehezkel heard real anguish behind the anger. "My friend," he ventured gingerly, "if there was no Resurrection, then surely you would be a renegade to a *false* religion."

"That's it!" she thought. "He's made his move! Now he'll say, 'Become a Jewess, and marry me.'"

Yehezkel, instead, murmured, "But if accepting that truth is too hard for you, I suppose you can claim the confession is a fake document, concocted by the Jews to deny that Jesus defeated death."

Startled, she thought, "And here he is, instead, providing me with a way out of my quandary! Why do I always think this man is after my soul? Is it the bile I heard from all those priests about Jews?"

"That's what I'll do," she said. "At least until we find out if there *is* a confession. After all, if you trust *me* not to hand over the page from Ezekiel to Christian clerics to be used in converting Jews, I suppose I should accept your decision to entrust the confession to Mohammedans."

With that, she steered her horse toward Arnald's. Yehezkel smiled, relieved. Then a bizarre thought entered his mind for the first time. "The Jerusalem rabbis left the confession in its hiding place for when the Messiah would arrive . . . And now *I'm* going to find it?"

The next morning they climbed the first hill from which Jerusalem could be seen.

Arnald told them that King Baldwin, moved by the joy pilgrims felt on reaching it, renamed the village on the hill Montjoie. Jerusalem, from there, was an ivory-and-ochre stain, perched on a crest of the mountain range a handful of leagues south of them, its minarets jutting out against the ice-blue winter sky.

Galatea was moved by the sight. She was meditating on the approaching end of her pilgrimage, when suddenly she saw Yehezkel pronounce some words in Hebrew and tear the collar of his sarbel. She would later discover he'd cut the edge of the garment with a knife so it would tear easily when custom prescribed the gesture of mourning, on first catching sight of Zion bereft of Jewish sovereignty.

She asked what he'd said, and he told her he had thanked the Lord for keeping him alive until the moment he set eyes on Jerusalem and then quoted a sage of the Talmud, "Jerusalem is a desert. . . ." Even from that distance, the rubble of the city's walls, torn down by al-Mu'azzam 'Isa a year earlier, could be made out.

"Jerusalem lies open to any attacking army, a defenseless maiden on the side of a road," he said. Then he unexpectedly straightened up and started singing a joyous melody borrowed from a troubadour. "Od yishama be'arei Yehudah uvechutzot Yerushalaim, kol sasson vekol simchah, kol chatan vekol kalah!"

"What's that you're singing?"

"It's Jeremiah. 'Again shall be heard in the mountains of Judah and in Jerusalem's courtyards voices of joy and voices of gladness, the voice of a bridegroom and the voice of a bride!'" His voice broke. "I have a vision before my eyes, Galatea, like the ones you're used to having.

Thousands of young Jews are walking around the streets of Jerusalem, their heads high, and . . . and they're speaking Hebrew!"

She said sympathetically, "It's the undying hope of your people, isn't it, my friend?"

"No, Galatea. This is no mere hope. I *know* it will happen. If somewhere in the world everyone should speak the Holy Tongue as a normal, everyday language, the benefit to humanity would be immense. But if that place was *Jerusalem* . . . well, that would mean the Messiah of David was about to arrive!"

His friends smiled, their bemusement tinged with admiration for Jewish steadfastness.

"I already told you, Yehezkel," said Galatea softly. "When Jesus Christ returns triumphant, Jews will hail him as their long-awaited Messiah."

Inspired by the sight of Jerusalem, Yehezkel drew a breath and retorted, "After the centuries of hating Israel—and all those yet to come—I wonder how your theologians will react when God, one day, will gather his people in their land and protect them from their enemies with miracles, his arm stretched out as in the Exodus, to prove to Gentiles that he'd never forgotten his promise to Abraham."

Later, Yehezkel heard from the villagers that *their* name for the place was Nabi Samwil, since both Jews and Mohammedans believed the prophet Samuel to be buried under the small dome on top of the hill. Yehezkel jested with his friends that the prophet's spirit must have come over him earlier in the day.

✡ ✠ ✡ ✠

JERUSALEM, 31ST JANUARY 1220

After taking leave from Arnald by the ruins of Saint Stephen's and returning the order's horses to him, the two entered the city from the gate the Latins called Saint Stephen's and Salah ad-Din renamed Bab el-Amud* but that was starting to be called Damascus Gate. They

*Gate of the Column

approached it separately, and Yehezkel did not use the sultan's letter or draw attention to himself in any way.

In the generation since the founder of the Ayubbid dynasty took al-Quds, Saracens and Jews streamed back until her population surpassed thirty thousand souls. But when, a year before, al-Mu'azzam 'Isa razed her walls, thousands again fled the now defenseless city for Acre. Still, despite half her homes being empty, her streets and markets were still lively and crowded.

Galatea was told by some nuns she'd met on the ride from Gaza to Château Pélerin that the safest and most tranquil place for her to stay in Jerusalem was the Abbey of Our Lady of Mount Zion, just outside the southern walls. The prioress of this abbey, Marie de Saint-Clair, was happy to host mothers of religious houses on a pilgrimage to the holy places.

Yehezkel on the other hand, to find a place to stay, only had to walk into one of a dozen synagogues that had sprung up since the Christians were chased out. The three hundred rabbis who'd come from Europe nine years earlier, of course, were not among those who'd fled the city, certain as they were that the upheavals of war were nothing if not the birth pangs of redemption.

Mamluks and assorted Saracen warriors were everywhere, but this didn't prevent the strange couple, once they took up their lodgings, from getting lost in the markets and chatting with people—Galatea with Christian pilgrims, Yehezkel with almost everyone else. They avoided being seen together too often and postponed both a reconnaissance on the Haram al-Sharif and Galatea's first visit to the sepulchre until they were more familiar with the city.

They expected their every thought to be occupied with finding the places on the map, but at first their conversations were instead about Galatea's sorry, humiliating life as a Christian in Ayubbid Jerusalem. The Jews, though dhimmis, were a pillar of the city's commerce, and Yehezkel was their respected Egyptian guest, but the abbess was just one more barely tolerated Christian pilgrim, a category whose lives at that time resembled those of stowaways on ships.

Salah ad-Din ordered the big iron cross the infidels dared to install on top of the dome to be dragged around the city behind a donkey, before being melted down. Similarly, church bells—whose sound is an abomination to Saracen ears—were smashed and melted. Most churches in the city—including the biggest one, Saint Anne's—became qu'ranic schools, and in the few Christian holy places allowed to survive, the lives of Greek and Syriac monks became as bitter as unripe olives.

But pilgrims were treated worse. If they ventured outside the walls, to the Gethsemane or to Mount Zion, children pelted them with rocks from afar and spat on them from close up. Yehezkel said the Saracens were a civilized people, and Galatea complained bitterly to him of their behavior. But her anger at ignorant folk—who, she knew, were much the same everywhere—paled in comparison to her outrage at the shameless frauds perpetrated on pilgrims every day with the trade of false relics.

On first retaking Jerusalem, the Saracens hadn't allowed the rare Christian pilgrims into the sepulchre, but they soon found them well heeled and gullible, and a thriving trade of false relics grew around their holy places. Ecstatic pilgrims bought hundreds of thorns from Christ's crown, hairs of his beard, phials of the Virgin's breast milk, and countless fingers of Saint Peter. But perhaps the pièce de résistance of the Saracen imagination was Christ's foreskin, known to hapless pilgrims as the Holy Prepuce.

One day, as they discussed why pilgrims pretended to believe in the authenticity of such obviously fake relics, Yehezkel said, "A real relic, of a truly holy man, has powers. These pilgrims, I think they know the objects are fake, but they serve as mementos to remind them of their pilgrimage."

Galatea made a face. "If it makes them happy. I suppose it feeds what locals call artisans."

In Jerusalem Yehezkel frequented and studied Torah and Talmud with four rabbis who'd arrived nine years earlier from Europe: Samuel ben

Shimon; Joseph ben Baruch; his brother, Meïr; and Shimshon ben Abraham. It took a week for the four to see that Yehezkel was a kabbalist, but no charlatan, and only then did he confide their quest to them. Meïr ben Baruch was the only one sympathetic to Kabbalah, and Yehezkel discussed the clues in Elisha's map with him late into Jerusalem's cold February nights, but all four rabbis recognized at once the connection between finding the confession that would put the lie to Christianity and the imminent arrival of the Messiah of David.

The anticipation of that arrival had gripped the Jewish third of the city like a fever for a decade. When the Exodus in the Middle of History calculation joined the ranks of unfulfilled prophecies, many rabbis, as Yehezkel had predicted, coped with the chagrin by supposing that 1212 had really been the year of the Messiah's birth and began to follow Jewish children born in Jerusalem in that year from so close that their parents eventually complained to the nagid.

The rabbis took Yehezkel to pray at holy sites that Jews in exile had only heard of in doubtful tales. One such place was the synagogue known as the Cave, a hall below the Temple Mount that had been used as a synagogue for centuries under Islam. The Latins turned it into a cistern, but Salah ad-Din reopened it. Yehezkel felt the messianic thrill of praying twenty feet below the esplanade, in a spot a stone's throw from where the Ark of the Covenant once stood in the Kodesh Kedoshim.

Another thing that moved him deeply was seeing the Temple esplanade from the Mount of Olives. Praying on the flank of the hill east of the city on Shabbat had become a custom of Jerusalem Jews, both the Westerners and those, by far the majority, from Yemen, Babylonia, and the Maghreb.

This time Galatea was with him, watching the dome that replaced the Temple in her dream. Yehezkel braved the open reproach in the eyes of many Jews at the sight of a disciple of the great Moshe ben Maimon defiling the holy places with his Christian concubine.

"God punishes me twice," he thought glumly. "Once by soiling my reputation in the Holy City and a second time by denying me what they all think me guilty of. Just what did I do to deserve this?"

Meanwhile, in that first week of February, Galatea found a kindred spirit in Marie de Saint-Clair. The Frankish nun was an enthusiast of Hildegard of Bingen and expressed trust in the soul of woman more articulately than Galatea thought she could ever do, yet the abbess still decided to follow the rabbi's advice and didn't mention either parchment or confession in her conversations with the prioress.

Marie told her much about Jerusalem. She learned, for example, that the only church outside the walls still allowed to function—apart from the one next door to where they sat—was the Church of Saint Mary of Jehosaphat, in the valley of that name, a few steps from the Gethsemane, also known as Saint Mary's Tomb, since ancient Christian traditions told of Mary ascending to Heaven in body and spirit from that place three days after her death, just as her son had done.

Salah ad-Din had destroyed the upper structure and used the stones to repair the city walls, but the real church, which had always been underground, was allowed to survive—perhaps because of the Qu'ran's loving veneration of the Mother of Jesus. A small niche indicating the direction of Mecca had even been installed in the cave for Mohammedan prayers.

Marie said that local traditions spoke of catacombs even deeper than the cave where Mary's casket was worshipped, since her family's tomb had been dug at the foot of the Mount of Olives much earlier than her time. On hearing of this, Galatea exclaimed, "I always knew I had to come to Jerusalem, but until I came here, I didn't know how many things I already knew without knowing they were about *this* place."

As with the glimpse of blue shawl over Francesco's arms, she was now realizing that childhood visions she'd never understood were visions of places in Jerusalem. This was what started Galatea's slide into the dreamlike state that would culminate, that Passover night, in her Eucharistic revelation.

But something else, also little short of a miracle, happened before she solved the Jerusalem enigma. One day, in the throng on the Street of the Chain along the German hospice built by the Latins, now called Muristan, Galatea thought she glimpsed Gudrun's blonde tresses. She sprinted forward and caught up with two women as they rounded the corner into the perfume market.

"It *is* you! God be praised!" she cried.

Gudrun melted into her arms, weeping, as Albacara fell on her knees, praising the Lord.

Galatea was flushed with joy. "It's been six months, but you're *alive*! May the Virgin keep you both! *That's* why I hadn't found the courage to enter the Holy Sepulchre . . . I was waiting for *you*!"

The three kept hugging each other, crying and laughing at the same time, as women sometimes do. Gudrun had lost weight and, though still florid, was now a Nordic beauty. Albacara looked as if nine months of adventures rekindled the smouldering embers in her eyes that life in Candia covered with ash. When they'd regained their composure, the three went to the abbey on Mount Zion, and Galatea heard the story of their time in Acre, of the kidnapping by the Hashashin, and of the potion they'd been fed. Gudrun could not hold back tears as she told the mother that Bois-Guilbert had sent both armigers to Damietta, and that she would probably never see Garietto again.

But above all, Galatea heard of the two knights questioning them before freeing them. At the end of the tale, without a word, she rushed out of the abbey to look for Yehezkel, knowing she'd just discovered who Domingo's agent inside the Temple was.

"Uuhh . . . if I had that Englishman in front of me, I'd drive a stake through him like a pig!" she said, the goriness of the thought surprising her as she ran to the new Zion Gate, followed by the other two.

Yehezkel also shuddered to hear Bois-Guilbert's words, "Father Domingo must hear of this," and went straight out of the city, to the ruins of Saint Stephen, to pass the news on to Alain de Lille. They also decided to redouble their cautions, but to go up on the Mount as soon as they could.

At last the day came for the women to visit the tomb of Christ and be absolved from their vows. Yehezkel made up an important meeting to avoid having to tell Galatea that a Jew couldn't enter a church, which the Talmud considers an impure place of pagan worship. In the crowded patio before the sepulchre stallkeepers sold their blasphemous wares to pilgrims, but it was Friday, and Mohammedans streaming into the nearby mosque of Omar were far more numerous than the tremulous Christians.

Yehezkel told her of the second of the Four Rightly Guided Caliphs, Omar ibn Al-Khattāb, who conquered Jerusalem and asked to be shown the tomb of Jesus but then told his ulema he would pray outside, so that his followers wouldn't turn the sepulchre into a mosque because he'd prayed there. As he'd predicted, a mosque dedicated to him stood on the spot where he had thanked Allah, two hundred feet in front of the church.

The Latins had restored the sepulchre forty years earlier, placing its two parts under one roof. In the new choir between the Chapel of the Golgotha on the east side, and the tomb with its pierced dome on the west side, was a long marble altar. Centuries of kisses and tears had dug a depression in its center, and a small cross in a circle carved on one side marked the spot where Joseph of Arimathea and Nicodemus laid the Lord's body to wash it, after detaching it from the Cross.

Probably not by choice, for the deposition must perforce have taken place between Cross and tomb, the first thing Christians encountered on entering the last station of their pilgrimage was the spot where Christ's tortured body had been deposed, the women wailing all around. Every pilgrim, memory full of a hundred paintings of the Lamentation, cried their heart out at the thought that *this* was where it happened. Galatea, Gudrun, and Albacara were no exception.

When they were ready to leave the holy place, Gudrun had to look for the widow and eventually found her sitting on a stone bench in the patio, chatting with a Venetian pilgrim she had met inside.

✡   ✠   ✡   ✠

JERUSALEM, 27TH FEBRUARY 1220

They'd been in Jerusalem for four weeks, and her stones were beginning to speak to them.

"Jerusalem's stones are the only stones in the world that can feel pain," Yehezkel had told her.

Galatea felt as if the boundary between reality and vision in that city were blurred. It was as if a touch of madness were mixed into everything she did. She started to think that everything she saw around her was a sign somehow connected, even if not clearly, with her personal destiny. Clouds shifting shape were messages that only a stupid detail prevented her from grasping, like a name just out of memory's reach. Cobblestones, stains on walls, bird flights, even chains of camel and donkey turds started to seem vital clues about Francesco and the confession that she absolutely *had* to decipher. Every little thing contained a secret, and every secret concerned her mission in Jerusalem.

At first she tried to hide what was happening from Yehezkel. After all, he was as anxious as she was; why alarm him with her kabbalistic excesses? Then one morning she told him, almost absentmindedly, "You know, don't laugh at me, Yehezkel, but lately I've been hearing voices."

"Really?" said Yehezkel, intrigued. "Are they intelligible?"

"Well, they don't actually speak. In the middle of the night, a loud voice calls my name . . . and you know the funny thing? I *know* the voice but can't remember who it is . . . it's irritating, but it's happened so many times I've almost grown fond of the irritation." Yehezkel caressed her shoulder, laughing.

By the time they felt ready to explore the Mount, they had both—like generations of pilgrims before them, even in the time of the Temples—fallen in love with the city, her olive and orange gardens, her alleys and markets, her terraces, and most of all what the light did to her when the sun was low. Yehezkel loved her inhabitants, too—all of them a little crazy, not one of them boring.

"You see," he told her one day, "Jerusalemites—Saracens, Christians, Jews—are more often people of thought than action, because along the paths of thought, one sooner or later understands that *all* answers are in the stones of Jerusalem. And in my opinion a city where every passer-by is a philosopher, every shop owner a prophet, every inn-keeper a visionary . . . is a wonderful place!"

Jews were allowed on the Haram, unlike fifty years earlier under the Latins, when Yehezkel's teacher put his life at risk climbing there in disguise. But his Christian companion had no right to be up there, and Yehezkel thought he would have to pull out the sultan's letter at the gate on the northern side of the esplanade. But the mamluk guard stared at Galatea's eyes and waved them through.

So they went. The thousand-foot-long, trapeze-shaped plaza was swept by a chilly wind. The city was not big, and though the Haram wasn't her highest point, the Judean hills all around, their desert colors bright in the sun, drew their eyes the minute they emerged from the maze of alleys. Everywhere masons and carpenters were busy carrying out al-Mu'azzam's restoration projects, and the air was full of hammers striking, Arab workers shouting, crows squawking, and the occasional braying of a donkey.

They tried counting 395 steps eastward from the Rock under the dome, but after 300 they reached the eastern wall, beyond which was a sheer drop to the cemetery below. After that, copies of the parchment discreetly clutched in their hands, they wandered the esplanade from one end to the other, Yehezkel occasionally looking at the map, scratching his head under his turban, Galatea at his side, and raising a thumb to line up a spot on the Haram with something behind it. The two tall mystics were taking long, purposeful strides, when suddenly a voice shouted out to them in Arabic, "Don't pray! Hey, you two, you're not allowed to pray to your false gods up here!"

Three ulema, dressed in long black robes and prestigious white turbans, were running toward them, shouting. Yehezkel had expected something like this. They were from the Waqf, the religious foundation established by Salah ad-Din to govern the holy places on the Mount. Much stricter than mamluks, these clerics' understanding of the Holy Qu'ran was that making the lives of infidels miserable gives Allah more pleasure than all the charity in the world. Yehezkel faced them without a trace of apprehension. "We are *not* praying. And we have permission to be here. From Sultan al-Kamil."

"Careful, Jew. If what you say is not true, you won't leave the Haram al-Sharif alive."

Yehezkel pulled out the letter and handed it to the cleric, who examined it with growing surprise. "Now I've seen everything!" said the alim, aghast. "We fight Christian unbelievers for 120 years over these stones, and now a *Jew* is the only one with permission to search them? Puah!" He spat on the holy ground and walked off, disgusted, with his underlings in tow.

They spent another hour climbing up and down the few steps between the levels of the plaza. Then Yehezkel, passing in front of the Golden Gate, suddenly realized that the workers there were not restoring the double portal, but walling it up. He ran closer to make sure and then told Galatea he would have to ask Rav Shimshon why al-Mu'azzam gave such a peculiar order.

An hour later they reluctantly left, no closer to solving Elisha's riddle. But the spirit of the place penetrated their souls like a vapor. Babylonians, Persians, Maccabees, Romans, Greeks, Saracens—who hadn't fought over that tiny Mount? Galatea told him she could feel presences in the place, as when one smells a fragrance for an instant, and then it's gone.

Yehezkel didn't possess her gifts but knew the history of his people enough to feel overwhelmed.

✡ ✠ ✡ ✠

JERUSALEM, SUNDAY, 15TH MARCH 1220

The pilgrim Albacara met in the Holy Sepulchre was a Venetian, and he courted her for weeks.

He was a mild man named Marco, who made money, lost his wife, and decided to spend the rest of his days in Jerusalem. He and the widow were in their early fifties, and Albacara fought hard not to give in to the dangerous dream of not growing old alone. She knew she was a plain woman and refused to live through the loss of another man.

But he told her his love was real and that the light in her eyes was the same that had been in his wife's. One day, he told her his love was a locked door that kept out the passage of time, making her look to him as she looked when she was sixteen. Albacara consulted Galatea on his sincerity, spent sleepless nights, and in the end agreed to marry him. Perhaps the will to do something with what was left of her life, in case it shouldn't be that long, had something to do with it.

A clandestine Christian wedding ceremony was not easy to arrange. A monk of the Holy Sepulchre agreed to officiate, and they chose a secluded but meaningful spot by the church of Saint Anne, in the northeastern corner of the city. This was the site of the Bethesda pools, where Jesus had healed a cripple. The Greeks built an enormous basilica over the pools, supported by seven incredibly tall arches, but it had been destroyed two hundred years earlier. The Latins, finding it in ruins, built a small chapel perched on one of the arches. Salah ad-Din had contemptuously knocked down the ceiling of the chapel, but now the Ayubbid vizier pretended not to notice that Christians were again praying in the roofless structure.

On the day of the wedding, in mid-March, the sky had the color and weight of lead. A few pilgrims converged inconspicuously on the ruin-filled pools, passing by an ancient, immense laurel tree in front of Saint Anne's. During the ceremony, Galatea was so moved by the eyes of the kneeling couple, twenty years older than she was, that she stepped across the derelict chapel to hide her tears from Gudrun.

Meanwhile, Yehezkel stood outside, thinking, "She met Aillil in Torcello, and he's happily married to his Yasmine. Then she met Albacara in Crete, and she's happily marrying her Marco. I bet Gudrun ends up marrying Garietto, too, and she and I will be the only ones left to nurse our love in secret, like lepers hiding their wounds."

Halfway though the ritual, a cold rain started pouring down, as it often does in Jerusalem in March. The chapel offered little protection, and the pilgrims knew that mamluk guards would soon arrive, urchins having surely reported the unusual assembly of infidels. But the Nuptial Mass had started, and everyone, though soaked and scared, went on singing. Galatea thought the pouring rain added something sublime to the sound of the choir. Yehezkel later agreed.

At the start of the Passover month of Nissan, a rumor spread that a shofar* had been blown on the Mount of Olives. Many rabbis taught—based on a verse in Zechariah—that this was how the arrival of the Messiah would be announced. Within an hour, Jerusalem's Mohammedans, whose fear of the Day of Judgment is genuine and intense, were gripped by apocalyptic terror, while Jews were in a state of joyous frenzy, as if those were the last minutes before redemption would be upon them.

Yehezkel was studying in the house of Rav Shimshon ben Abraham, the oldest of the four rabbis he'd become friends with, when two students burst into the room, excitedly bringing the news that a shofar on Har Ha-Zeitim had just announced the arrival of the Messiah.

Rav Shimshon was seventy years old and considered a sage by all Jerusalem rabbis. He got up, went to the window, opened it wide and stood there for two minutes, looking out. Then he gave his verdict. "No, I don't see a renewal of any kind out there. Go back to your studies!"

---

*Ancient musical instrument used in Jewish religious rituals, traditionally made of a ram's horn

✡ ✠ ✡ ✠

VITERBO, 15TH MARCH 1220

On the same day in the middle of March, Domingo visited Honorius III's court in exile in Viterbo.

When Innocent died right there in Viterbo four years earlier, the conclave—which for the first time was literally locked up until it produced a new pontiff—elected Cencio Savelli, already sixty-eight at the time. Since Innocent had become pope at the unripe age of thirty-six, Romans cynically remarked on the Holy Spirit's frequent reapprais-als of what was best for the church.

Honorius would be back in the Lateran before long, having con-vinced his erstwhile pupil, Frederick II, to threaten the Romans with a military visit should they keep harassing their pope. It cost him the promise to crown Frederick emperor the following month but took much pressure off him. Things in Egypt weren't going well, and he still hadn't prevailed on his unruly protegé to do his Christian duty and go there. In short, Domingo couldn't get the pope to take the threat posed by the confession as seriously as it deserved.

Honorius was seventy-two now and a wise, saintly pope. Domingo thought that his red stole over flowing white beard and soft, white kid-skin gloves looked like blood on the snow.

"Your Holiness, Your Beatitude, Your Serenity . . ." he began, grinning.

"Oh, don't mock an old man, Domingo. I could be your father . . ."

Domingo's chiseled features became deadly serious, his blue eyes stormy. "I received more news from Brother Roberto, Holy Father. It's worse than I thought; the Jew met the Old Man at Château Pélerin at the end of January and then went to Jerusalem with the renegade abbess. I fear they may be a step from finding the confession—and we *can't* let that happen!"

The prospect seemed to worry Honorius more than usual.

"Pedro de Montaigue promised to send me the Old Man in chains. I'll have him do it at once!"

"It's too late for that, Holy Father, I fear they've already deciphered the Parchment of Circles! The Jew is going to find the confession, and we can't very well invade Jerusalem to stop him! I suppose Robert could chase him there dressed as a pilgrim, but it will take a month just to get the order to him, and by then the cursed parchment will be in their hands . . ."

Honorius looked even older than his years. "What do you think they'll do with it, Domingo?"

"Good question, Your Holiness. I've asked myself what *I* would do in the Jew's place," he smiled, "though I doubt I could ever really think as *they* do—and came to the conclusion that he'll try to take it to the sultan's brother, in Damascus."

"Then tell Brother Roberto to take a squadron of Templar knights and surreptitiously patrol the roads to Damascus! Pedro cannot deny me this emergency measure!"

"Good idea, Holy Father; I'll send a message to him immediately! I hope it reaches him in time. And what should I tell him to do if he finds them?"

"Whatever he needs to do," said the pope curtly. "That parchment must *not* see the light of day. The Templars' claim that they already found what the Jew is looking for gave me little sleep in the last four years; you know that. What do you think I should do about *them*, Domingo?"

"Ideally, Holy Father, we should just find the confession and destroy it," said the Spaniard. "But if we fail in that, the only thing for it will be to destroy the Order of the Temple . . . however long it takes."

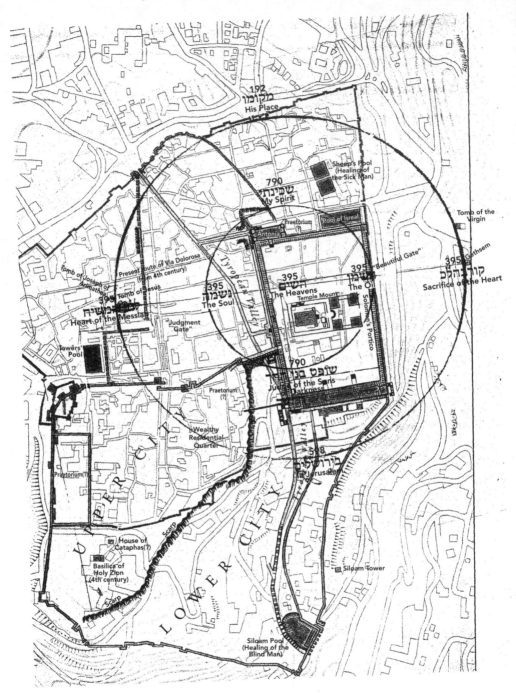

The Map
Courtesy of Carta, Jerusalem

CHAPTER 28

VAYEVARECH OTAM
And He Blessed Them

JERUSALEM, MARCH 1220

As Passover approached, Galatea gleaned clues about the map in increasingly unlikely places. Yehezkel decided it was high time he introduced the nun to the Jewish luminaries probing the map and told them of her irreplaceable role in the quest. These, after all, weren't superstitious, provincial rabbis who found frequenting Christians reprehensible. Rav Shimshon, before making aliyah,* was the head of a Jewish school in Sens and met regularly with Christian clerics in the French town.

Galatea agreed to go to Rav Shimshon's the coming Friday, despite being a little apprehensive at the thought of Jewish sages examining her spiritual credentials—including, she feared, the origin of her visions. It was her second time in a Jewish home, this time on Shabbat eve. She was touched by details that spoke of a homely, unceremonial holiness—from the prayer the rabbi's wife pronounced over the candles to the family's

---

*The immigration of Jews from the diaspora to Eretz Israel. Literally, "the act of going up" (to Jerusalem).

joyous singing before the meal. As they sat down to eat, Yehezkel told her that the blessings Rav Shimshon pronounced—first over wine and then over bread—were the Jewish root of the Eucharist, though the Apostle Paul changed their order.

Rav Shimshon spoke fluent Latin and French, and the conversation was less intimidating than Galatea had feared. At first, inevitably, it concerned the war. Damietta had been in Christian hands since November, so why didn't the Franks press their advantage? Wasn't the sultan going to give them al-Quds to stop them marching on al-Kahira? And if he'd refused to give up Jerusalem, then why *weren't* the Franks marching on al-Kahira? In Rav Shimshon's view, all this could only be explained by the imminent arrival of the Messiah. Would God's Prince show up in Jerusalem while she was in Christian hands? Unthinkable.

Jerusalemites knew more than Christians in Damietta on the nature of the threat to Baghdad from the East. Rav Shimshon said that Samarkand, on the caliphate's eastern frontier, had fallen to the Mongols.

At one point Yehezkel told Rav Shimshon of the workers he'd seen walling up the Golden Gate.

"Yes, I heard of it!" The old rabbi laughed gleefully. "There's yet more proof, if any were needed," he said. "Mohammedans know that both our Scriptures and those of the Christians say the Messiah will enter the Temple from the east, so his ulema told al-Mu'azzam to block the only opening on that side!" He laughed again. "I find their behavior at once blasphemous and pathetic!"

Yehezkel smiled, but something about the Golden Gate still bothered him. "Another thing I saw up there, Rav," he said, "was a small dome on eight slender columns, some three hundred feet north of the big one, that looked brand new. Is it part of al-Mu'azzam's restorations? And if it is, do you know why his ulema prescribed a new dome just *there*?"

"Ah, yes," said Rav Shimshon. "A peculiar story. It happened in . . . when was it? The end of July, I think." He shifted on his chair.

"The workers fixing the pavement there repeatedly fell sick; in fact, one of them died. The vizier consulted his ulema and was told to build a small dome there, because the Prophet must have chased out a ruah in that spot."

"Surely you mean a *jinn?*" asked Yehezkel.

"Qubat Ru'aheen is what they called the little dome, though I agree; it must have been a jinn."

"If it ever happened," said Yehezkel, adding, "that is, if their Prophet was ever here at all." Yehezkel chuckled, as if only now understanding Rav Shimshon's mirth on the closing of the gate.

Something that wasn't yet an idea was sneaking its way into Yehezkel's mind, and on their third visit to the esplanade, he stood under the Dome of the Spirits, turning slowly and staring into the distance, one direction at a time. For a while, Galatea listened to him mumble phrases from the map, and then she went to sit on a low wall by the wide steps leading down to the lower level just west of the small dome.

She wasn't wearing her white cap that day. The men of the Waqf, having heard of the sultan's letter, stopped following them around the plaza, so she was less discreet, but it was her constant dreamlike state that caused her to forget the cap. The north wind whipped her hair, which had grown to her shoulders again since she'd cut it to become a squire.

Yehezkel was looking at the lead tiles covering the dome, thinking how ridiculous it seemed to even *suppose* that the Holy Temples could have stood anywhere else.

"Everyone knows," he said to himself, "that Omar cleared the rubbish Christians threw on the esplanade and then went up with an erudite Jewish convert, Ka'b el-Akhbar, to determine where the Temple once stood. That was where, fifty years later, Abd el-Malik built the Qubbat al-Shakhra. Everyone has always taken for granted that the dome is where the Temple was."

He turned to the Golden Gate. The workers had walled up half the space under the arches. Soon, the olive grove in the Valley of Jehosaphat he could see through the remaining gap would vanish. And those ruins next to it. Suddenly he froze, gripped by something he'd only experienced during storms at sea. Time seemed to stop, and the contours of things were intolerably sharp. His eye discerned the details of a leaf hanging from the column in front of him as clearly and effortlessly as the towers on mountains several leagues north of Jerusalem. He rubbed his knuckles into his eyes and took a deep breath.

"What did I just say? Which word gave me that sense of touching something in the dark? I'm almost there; the mosaic's tesserae are all in front of me. Keep calm, Yehezkel, and 'think of it from tomorrow,' as Rav Moshe used to say. Your soul already grasps what your mind can't yet see."

He looked around as he sifted through his previous thoughts. Galatea sat on the wall smiling at him, her hair now tied in a tail. He turned to the Golden Gate again, the wind in his beard, and found it.

"*That* was it! I thought that in a week's time the olive grove I can still see under the gate's arches will no longer be visible. Why did that thought strike me so? What *is* that garden?"

He turned around again, a familiar tingling in his nape.

"Galatea! Galatea!" She felt the urgency and rushed to his side. "Galatea, what is that patch of olive trees I can just see through the bit of gate they haven't yet walled up? Are those the ruins of a church just beside it? Has that place meaning or holiness for Christians?"

"I should say so, Yehezkel! That's the Garden of Gethsemane, where Christ prayed the night of the Last Supper and was arrested by the guards of the Sanhedrin," she said. "I prayed there last week."

"Yes, now I remember the scene in the night, when Judas tells the guards which one is Jesus."

"Pilgrims there are moved to tears," she said gently, "but not at the thought of his arrest, rather because of his prayer to his Father while the apostles slept. It was there that he accepted his fate."

Yehezkel felt the tingling again. "Do you remember that prayer?"

"I may get a word wrong, but in Mark's Gospel, he prayed, *Abba, Father, all things are possible for You. Take this cup away from me. Nevertheless, not what I will, but what You will.*"

"I like that!" smiled Yehezkel. "His admission of weakness before God reminds me of Moses. *True* prophets are weak, like all humans." He repeated her last words, "*Not what I will, but what You will,*" and it came to him. "Wait a minute, you could call that a 'sacrifice of the heart,' couldn't you? But then, what would be on the other side?"

He turned around and looked for something as far to the west as the Gethsemane was to the east. He saw the domes of the Holy Sepulchre. His head spun back and forth twice, followed by Galatea's. There was no doubt: a straight line from the garden to the tomb went *right through* the spot where they stood.

"*Oh, my God . . .*" murmured Galatea. "If the Gethsemane is the Sacrifice of the Heart and the Holy Sepulchre is the Heart of the Messiah, then . . . then the Heavens . . . is right under our feet!"

"Trampling on the Heavens will get us into trouble yet, you'll see . . ." said Yehezkel, a wide grin spreading on his face. "Come, my friend, let's count 395 steps east from *here!*"

They did and ended up *inside* the Golden Gate. Or would have, if workers, ladders, and materials hadn't filled the space around the structure. Still, it was clear that had they taken the last twenty of the 395 steps, they would be standing under the gate's disappearing arches. Yehezkel was euphoric.

"Of course! I'm surprised Alain didn't think of it! He knows the Gospels better than I do; he should have realized that a Christian Elisha would call the Gethsemane Sacrifice of the Heart!"

They walked back to the Qubat Ru'aheen, Yehezkel debating with himself—but out loud, mindful of Galatea's temper—the implications of what Elisha was suggesting. "If the Kodesh Kedoshim was under the little dome, it could mean that Omar, despite being advised by a Jew, wrongly identified the site of the Temples. *Or* it could mean that the converted Jew remained Jewish enough to mislead his caliph on this one, so that no abominations would be built on that spot. Then again, it could mean that Omar knew where the Temples stood but decided that Muhammad flew to Heaven from *another* spot, three hundred feet south. There's no end to the possible explanations."

They stood once more under the little dome, gathering their thoughts. Galatea spoke first. "Surely, Yehezkel, if the Sancta Sanctorum was here—I'm thinking of my dream now—then the Gethsemane must also be where the Altar of the Red Heifer was."

"Of course!" said Yehezkel. "Or maybe somewhere just above the Gethsemane. And look at how Elisha relished the parallel between the ashes of the heifer overcoming the impurity of death and Jesus's sacrifice absolving humanity of its sins—overcoming the impurity of man, as it were."

"And the place where they crucified and buried him he called Heart of the Messiah," said Galatea, turning round again. Seeing the sepulchre, she added, "We counted 395 steps east, but we could never do the same walking west, Yehezkel. Within a hundred steps, we would be in the city's alleys!"

"True," said Yehezkel. "But in any case, we only counted the steps to the oil, not to Sacrifice of the Heart, so we can't yet be sure we're right. By the way, here is a greater conundrum: the oil is the hiding place, so even if we *are* right, *where* exactly in the Golden Gate do you suppose the oil is hidden?"

"Mmh . . . we need more confirmation before we tackle that one," said Galatea. "First we must find a way to verify, without actually counting the steps, that the sepulchre is as far to the west of this dome as the Gethsemane is to the east . . ."

"*Yess*! You're priceless, Galatea, simply priceless! The Holy Spirit is never far from your lips!"

She was about to ask what she'd just said that was so priceless, but Yehezkel grabbed her hand and sprinted south toward al-Aqsa. All she could do was run with him.

Her words reminded him of his astrolabium, an object so precious it was in his pouch even on the Temple Mount. He had to find a place on a line perpendicular to the Gethsemane-sepulchre horizontal axis of the map they had just identified, the farther away and the higher off the ground the better, and then hold his instrument horizontally, instead of vertically as at sea.

Using the astrolabium as a simple goniometer would allow him to measure the angles between dome and olive garden on one side and dome and sepulchre on the other. If the angles turned out the same, then so were the distances. And best of all, they would have confirmed it *without* having to count the steps, as his personal prophetess said!

Twenty years earlier, the Ayubbids had built a women's mosque west of al-Aqsa. Looking south from the Dome of the Spirits, Yehezkel's eyes fell on its minaret. They ran the length of the plaza, stopping before they reached its southwestern corner to brush up and straighten each other's clothes. He covered her hair, as he expected Waqf officials to object strenuously to the idea of two infidels climbing to the top of a minaret, even if it was just to "take a look."

He was right. The vizier had heard of the Jew with the sultan's letter and knew he couldn't win. He either disobeyed al-Kamil's orders or provoked his ulema, who argued, not unreasonably, that "freedom to explore" didn't mean "freedom to desecrate." In the end, al-Hadhbânî ordered the Waqf to arrest the Jew, but *only* if he practiced a religious ritual, or even mumbled what looked like a prayer.

Yehezkel found a compromise. The cleric at the foot of the minaret would climb to the muezzin's platform with them, to ensure that what they did up there was really geography, as they claimed, and not some Jewish celebration—or worse, propitiation. As they climbed the spiral staircase inside the tower, Yehezkel thought, "Not only are they walling up the eastern gate, they fear *anything* Jews do on the Mount!" He smiled. "Mohammedans seem to believe in the coming of our Messiah more than we do!"

The position was perfect, but measuring an angle precisely while holding an astrolabium horizontally is tricky, so he took two bits of wood he'd picked up in the plaza and arranged them on the platform's low parapet so they would hold up his instrument as he knelt behind it and sighted the map's landmarks without needing to touch it. Galatea and the cleric watched him, intrigued, as he set up his makeshift goniometer and measured the two angles.

After the second measurement, Galatea saw his face light up. *Elisha's map was deciphered!*

Back down on the esplanade they were overtaken by sheer, unhinged joy. They unabashedly took a few Provençal dance steps, holding hands high in the air and spinning round each other, as the cleric from the Waqf looked on in silent outrage. Then, feeling like kids playing the most exciting of games, they sat under a big cypress and planned their next move.

Galatea said, "You know, I can see the map now. Where we are sitting must be roughly where Elisha placed the Judge of the Sons of Darkness, whatever that meant to him."

"But it's the oil we're after, Galatea," said Yehezkel. "If my astrolabium worked from here, I think we should look for somewhere in the southeastern corner where we can use it again, to check if the Golden Gate is really halfway between the Dome of the Spirits and the Gethsemane."

"Sounds logical to me. Let's go, then!" cried Galatea, grabbing his hand and dragging him off. They ran eastward across the plaza with childish enthusiasm, looking for all the world like a pair of young lovers indecorously chasing each other in a holy place.

"Apart from the issue of respect," thought the Waqf official watching them as they passed before al-Aqsa, "they should know they no longer have the age for this sort of thing."

Soon they were standing on the ramparts in the extreme southeastern corner of the esplanade, a spot from which—Yehezkel told her—more than one priest or heretic had been thrown to his death. Leaning out, she looked at the desert descending to the Dead Sea in the distance and murmured, "The shrubs look like stubble; that's what does it. It may be holy, but the Judean desert looks like an old man's unshaven cheeks."

Yehezkel walked about a hundred feet north along the top of the eastern wall before the Dome of the Spirits reappeared from behind the Dome of the Rock, which had been hiding it. He would have liked to be higher up but set up his instrument and found the angle between the little dome on the left and the Golden Gate in front of him to be exactly equal to the angle between the gate and the olive garden on his right, at the foot of the Mount of Olives. There could no longer be any doubt: the equidistances were those Elisha had drawn on the Parchment of Circles!

They rested awhile, breaths short and heads spinning, already wondering where in the Golden Gate to look for the oil. The gate was a large structure, with walkways and chambers beside the two arches. The idea of brandishing the sultan's letter and starting to dig in the middle of a gate the authorities were busy closing seemed too much even to them.

"In my dream, the Levites began to sing as the high priest bearing the ashes crossed the threshold of the gate. It was where the viaduct from the altar ended."

"I'm on a different line of reasoning," said he. "First, we know that the rabbis who wrote the letter in the geniza found what Hanina hid. Second, when Elisha drew the map, the Romans had destroyed everything: there was no more Temple, no more viaduct, no more Altar of the Red Heifer— but above all, there was no more Gate of Mercy! How could Elisha be sure that with the map what Hanina had hidden could *still* be found?"

"Because it was underground!" she cried. "Yehezkel, you're the best! I have yet to see you let down your teacher!" Without warning, she took his face in her hands, smacked a loud kiss on his forehead like a mother with her child, and ran off toward al-Aqsa.

Yehezkel stood there, unable to breathe.

The idea of a hiding place *below* the gate suggested to them the possibility of a gallery beneath the path the high priest followed, both when

entering the Temple with the ashes of the red heifer and when exiting it
with the scapegoat to be sent into the desert on Yom Kippur.

"King Solomon dug chambers and hiding places deep inside the
Mount, so a tunnel *could* exist from the time of the first Temple," he
said. "In any case, none of the tunnels the Templars dug—according
to Alain's map—is even close to the Golden Gate. Besides, if a tunnel
exists that passes below the floor of the Valley of Jehosaphat, it must
be so deep that its entrance would have to be at the bottom of a well!"

His astrolabium didn't indicate any idea of where, on the Mount of
Olives, the Altar of the Red Heifer had been, for without a landmark to
sight, like the domes, "so many degrees east of the Golden Gate" meant
a vague patch of ground around the dozen olives next to the ruins of the
Church of Gethsemane, another Latin chapel the Ayubbids tore down.

"If a tunnel *that* deep has its access near the grove," he went on,
"we'll have to look for caves, cracks in the limestone, anything that
leads down . . . a long way down."

He peered at the Gethsemane from atop the eastern wall. "Galatea,
what's that other church I can see pilgrims going in and out of, just
across from the Gethsemane on the path that climbs the Mount?"

"I prayed there last week," said Galatea. "It is Saint Mary of
Jehosaphat, but people call it the Tomb of Mary." On pronouncing the
word tomb, she remembered the catacombs Marie had told her about.
"But of course . . .Yehezkel, we just found the way to the tunnel!"

They were too exhausted that day to descend into the Valley of
Jehosaphat, and in any case Yehezkel wanted to speak with Rav
Shimshon before they did, so they went back to their rooms, quietly
elated in the knowledge that, just like the rabbis four hundred years
earlier, they had just solved Elisha's riddle.

Rav Shimshon was excited to hear of the equidistances on the
Mount, but the idea that the Temple had not been where the Dome of
the Rock was sat uncomfortably with him.

"What you're saying is not without its logic, Yehezkel," he opined, "but I still believe Ha-Shamayim in the map is the Rock under the dome."

"It is your right, Rav Shimshon," said Yehezkel. "But tell me, in the days of the Temple the eastern gate was called Gate of Mercy, but do you know if the Talmud says anything else about it?"

"Well, now you mention it," said Rav Shimshon almost reluctantly, "it's not in the Talmud, but a bizarre, six-hundred-year-old tradition exists on the eastern gate." The old rabbi seemed to struggle with an unwelcome, obstinate fact that could no longer be denied. "In the year Christians call 614, the Persians took Jerusalem from the Greeks and carried off their holiest relic, the True Cross. Fifteen years later, Emperor Heraclius led a holy war against King Khosrow and almost took his capital. Not surprisingly, the resulting treaty stipulated the return of the True Cross. Knowing he'd bring it back to Jerusalem, Heraclius arranged extravagant celebrations for the spring of 629. He would personally carry the Cross onto the esplanade through a new double gate in the eastern wall, whose construction he ordered before leaving to sign the peace."

Galatea and Yehezkel sensed that Rav Shimshon wasn't happy to be divulging this story. Yehezkel was listening intently, his smile implying that he knew what was coming.

"Ehm . . . the tradition claims that the workers who dug the Golden Gate's foundations," concluded Rav Shimshon, "found remnants of a previous gate in the very spot Heraclius picked for the new one—the remnants, it was said at the time, of Solomon's Shushan Gate."

"I knew it!" cried Yehezkel. "Don't you see how it all fits, Rav Shimshon? Elisha's map, the Shushan Gate, the sick workers. . . . Come on, Rabbi, you know it wasn't 'spirits' that made those workers sick last summer, it was digging on the site of the Kodesh Kedoshim! The Dome of the Spirits, not the Dome of the Rock, is where the Temple was!" Then, with a grin, "And I bet they're walling up the Golden Gate because they *know it,* because it's right in front of that little dome."

"It's true," smiled Rav Shimshon, "that they began to bury their dead outside that gate when they heard that Jewish priests may not walk through a cemetery. Evidently they didn't know that the Messiah cannot be a cohen, since he must be from the tribe of Judah."

Yehezkel mused aloud, "The original Gate of Mercy was destroyed by the Romans along with the Temple. Isn't it strange that the gate Emperor Heraclius built five hundred and fifty years later was *exactly* on top of it? I wonder if he knew what he was doing."

✡ ✠ ✡ ✠

JERUSALEM, FRIDAY, 27TH MARCH 1220

It was a week before Passover, and thousands of Jews in Jerusalem were caught in a habitual spring-cleaning frenzy. The very next day they went for an underground inspection.

As they crossed the rocky, windswept Valley of Jehosaphat, Galatea said jauntily, "So this time you're going to enter a church, eh? When the three of us went to the sepulchre, you invented a meeting with important rabbis so you wouldn't have to come with us."

"But . . . but I really did see some famous rabbis that day."

"Oh come, Yehezkel! *Everyone* in Jerusalem knows Jews don't set foot in churches. Did you really think I wouldn't hear of it? Yehezkel, you still don't treat this nun as your equal!"

Yehezkel's pride almost moved his lips, but the whole previous year crushed it underfoot, and he was silent as they approached the portal of the church.

The crypt that harbored Mary's tomb, cut out of an existing cave, was entered by descending a wide, gently sloping stairway. Sunlight and the outside world receded with every step down, as a powerful smell of incense and melted wax drifted up the vaulted, candlelit slope. The chapels on both sides of the stairway were crowded with lamps and candles as only Greek chapels can be. Galatea dragged him to the chapel of Saint Joseph, Mary's husband, on one side, and then to that of Joachim and Anne, Mary's parents, on the other, which also hosted the sixty-year-old tomb of Queen Melisende of Jerusalem.

Voices singing a psalm in Greek wafted up from the crypt. By the time they reached it, it was as if the Valley of Jehosaphat—indeed, all Jerusalem—had ceased to exist. They turned the corner and saw Mary's casket. Hundreds of candles and countless lamps hung from chains in a cluttered, glittering sanctuary, as if the holy objects of an entire cathedral were squeezed into the tiny cave. Altars covered in gold and silver were everywhere: Greek, Latin, Armenian, Coptic, even a niche pointing to Mecca. Galatea felt like she was *inside* a reliquary.

Only a handful of pilgrims and the young, bearded Greek pope were there. Despite the cool March day, the deacon kept wiping sweat from his neck and forehead. As Yehezkel spoke with him, Galatea wandered around, staring at paraments that made her abbey in the lagoon look like a hermit's hut. The humidity and smell felt as stifling as in a crowd. Then Yehezkel came back, dragged her to the Armenian altar in the eastern corner and whispered, "He confirmed that when Saint Helena declared this to be the Tomb of the Virgin, it was known to have been a family tomb in Herod's time. I said we want to see the deepest part of the cave, but he waved me away. Come with me, and I'll show him the sultan's letter."

The pope was as outraged as his Saracen counterpart that a Jew should be in possession of such a document, and the two black-bearded men glared at each other for almost a full minute. Then the Greek looked at Galatea's eyes and relented. He took a key in his minuscule sacristy, in effect a niche in the rock behind a hanging curtain, and with it, he opened a low door in the northern wall they hadn't even noticed and stood next to it, waving them in.

The next thing Yehezkel heard, as he bowed to enter the chamber, was the loud slap on the pope's face. He turned round and saw her shout at the deacon, a hand still on her buttock, "You're a perfect example of the reason Jerusalem has been lost to the heathens!"

The Greek cleric, who understood her Latin perfectly, retreated to the main crypt, a plump hand over his swelling cheek.

Inside the catacomb, Yehezkel examined the floor by the torchlight, looking for ways further down. Finding none, he started removing earth with a brush from each square foot, searching for a crack. His patience was rewarded, and soon they were lifting a stone trap door. Before them was what they'd hoped to find: a spiral stone staircase, probably from the time of King Solomon, going straight down into darkness.

The excitement made them forget deacon and pilgrims. They started gingerly descending the ancient steps, Yehezkel leading the way and Galatea holding the torch, trying to shine it ahead. They knew the tunnel had to pass beneath the valley, but they were both surprised, and not a little anxious, to be going down for so long. After what seemed like ten minutes, they finally emerged in a round hall, some fifteen feet across, where men a foot shorter would have stood comfortably.

When they'd caught their breath and smiled at each other to raise their spirits, Yehezkel said, "There must be air ducts somewhere, or this torch couldn't burn down here, and we couldn't breathe. This is sophisticated work; it wouldn't surprise me if it really was King Solomon who had it dug." He looked around the chamber. "The tunnel must be behind one of these walls, the one facing west, but even if I had known where west was at the start of that stairwell, it's a mystery now."

"It's a pity your astrolabium can't help us down here, isn't it, Yehezkel?"

"You've done it again!" cried Yehezkel. "It's as if my brain needed *your* thoughts to move!" He searched his pocket and pulled out the pouch with the loadstone and its calamus. "You're right, the astrolabium can't help us, but we will still 'navigate' our way into the Temple!"

In minutes, the sailor rabbi poured some of their drinking water into a hollow in a stone, floated the calamus on it and determined where west was. The last people there had been the Jerusalem rabbis who deciphered the Parchment before them, and he felt sure they had not rebuilt the wall to perfection. Galatea watched as he used a knife to carve off a twig from their torch and lit it.

"Even a weak puff of air will move a small flame," he explained and began to run the twig along the west wall, very slowly, a finger's breadth from the stone. It wasn't long before the flame moved, and he found the crack through which a breath of air came.

For the next half hour, they worked up a sweat demolishing the small but well-packed pile of stones blocking the entry of the tunnel. At one point, she realized that one of his grunts was a suppressed laugh.

"Why do you laugh?" she asked.

"Oh, it's nothing worthwhile . . . " said he.

"Let *me* be the judge of that, Yehezkel."

"It's just that Saracen letters help me search aboveground, and Christian catacombs give me access belowground. I feel a hand over my head, if you know what I mean."

"What I *do* know is that you're starting to prophesize, too, Yehezkel, because the hand you'll feel over your head in a minute will be *mine*!"

Their laughter echoed down the black gallery that had slowly opened up before them. "Now what? Do we count 395 steps?" she asked, her breath getting shorter.

"Mmh . . . we can try that, too," said he. "But we can't be sure this precise point is the Sacrifice of the Heart. But if the tunnel follows the viaduct above, then the Golden Gate must be above its midpoint."

"True. But how do we find its midpoint?" she wondered.

"I thought we would come back here with a long . . . a *seriously* long string and unfurl it as we advance. If the tunnel, as I think, leads to a point under the Kodesh Kedoshim, I will recognize the place, and measuring half the string we unfurled would tell us where the tunnel's midpoint is."

"But Yehezkel, where will we find a piece of string a *quarter of a league* long?"

"The weavers in the market will tie thin twine together for us until the ball is big enough for the job."

"Maybe," said she. "But please, let's go back up now. I'm shattered, dirty, and starting to choke. I feel the weight of earth above my head."

"I know what you mean; it's like being halfway to Hell. This torch is nearly out anyway. Let's go!"

✡ ✠ ✡ ✠

They returned with the twine two days later and found the gallery to be wider, straighter, and better finished than they expected. The smooth rectangular stones of the walls all looked the same, so if the oil was hidden behind one of them, they would have to know precisely at which point of the tunnel it would be worth looking for the right stone to dislodge.

They counted 395 steps, all the while unfurling the twine and feeling like the ancient Greek hero hunting the Minotaur. When the count was up, they examined the stones by the light of the torch. Finding nothing, they walked on. As they did, Yehezkel turned to her and said, "Galatea, do you know what we just did? We entered the Holy Temple's courtyard through the Gate of Mercy—even if underground. And what's more, we entered it from the east, from the Mount of Olives! We just did something prophecies are full of!"

The thought had never really left his mind since first entering it during the ride to Jerusalem, but only now, as he walked down the tunnel for a second time, unfurling twine, did he consider the outrageous idea that *he,* Yehezkel ben Yoseph, might unknowingly, *unwillingly* even, be the Messiah of David.

"Rav Pinhas's words fifteen years ago were so precise; he said: 'I believe your journey, like Ezekiel's, will take you into the Temple's courtyards.' His prophecy is coming true. If I also find the confession, will that mean *I* am the one they've all been waiting for?"

Yehezkel turned and saw Galatea looking at him, no fear whatsoever in her eyes. He took her hand for a moment and then went back to unfurling the twine as they walked on. As he'd feared in his heart of hearts, when most of the twine was gone, the tunnel ended abruptly in a pile of rubble collapsed from above. They looked at each other wordlessly, bitter disappointment in their eyes.

"Perhaps when the Romans set the Temple on fire," he said at last, "the falling stones made things collapse down here, too. But if you ask me, that's not it. I'm sure the high priest ordered the destruction of the tunnels, so that the hiding places could not be reached."

Their ball of twine was useless now; they dejectedly wound it up as they retraced their steps.

To make matters worse, Yehezkel couldn't help pursuing his messianic musings. "Would a pile of rubble have blocked the *real* Messiah?"

CHAPTER 29

HINE NATATI LACHEM

Behold I Have Given You

JERUSALEM, MARCH 1220–NISSAN 4980

Galatea was cooking, alone in the big kitchen in the farmhouse in Marsiliana. They had been married for five years and had a son and a daughter. Yehezkel, for marrying a Christian, was no longer a rabbi, while Galatea, for marrying a Jew, was no longer a nun. Excommunicated by their respective communities, they lived on a hill in Maremma, a backwater in the south of Tuscia. He'd been in Outremer for six months, and she was doing her best to raise Moshe and Francesca as little Averroists.

A noise in the yard made her turn around. His big shoulders blocked the evening light in the doorway, and she ran to him. The vision dissolved. "I really must get a grip on myself," mumbled Galatea.

She was standing with Gudrun, Albacara, and Marco in the Saracen cemetery just outside the Golden Gate. Albacara's husband of a week reminded them of how the Virgin's parents, Joachim and Anne, met at that gate when she'd just found out she was pregnant. As she listened to the story, Galatea drifted into a daydream, as she so often did in those last days before Passover 4980.

Yehezkel, too, despite the upset in the tunnel, hadn't been able to dismiss the blasphemous thought that he might be the Messiah. In fact, he'd even found verses in Ezekiel predicting what the Ishmaelites were doing. *Then He brought me back to the outer gate of the sanctuary which faces toward the east, **but it was shut**. And the Lord said to me, 'This gate shall be shut; it shall not be opened, and no man shall enter by it. As for the Prince, because he is the Prince, he may sit in it to eat bread before the Lord; **he shall enter by way of the vestibule of the gateway.*** Could the little hall at the bottom of the stairwell be Ezekiel's "vestibule"?

He told no one but briefly considered bringing some bread to eat in the tunnel next time.

Rav Shimshon argued that if the tunnel no longer reached its destination under the Kodesh Kedoshim, they would have to calculate its total length from Scripture to find its midpoint. So they pored over the Book of Kings for Solomon's Temple and the Talmud tractate of Middot for Herod's.

Yehezkel drew a map of esplanade and Temple, correcting details of boundaries if they didn't agree with Galatea's dream, and marked the distances from Scripture: Court of the Women, 135 cubits; Court of the Israelites, 11 cubits; Court of the Priests, 127 cubits; Temple building, 60 cubits. Total distance from eastern to western wall of the Temple's perimeter: 333 cubits. They both liked that number.

Now came the tricky part. Yehezkel knew the dimensions of the esplanade from the Waqf, and used the geometry of a trapeze to calculate its width at the point of the Golden Gate and the Dome of the Spirits: it was 546 cubits. The difference between 333 and 546 was divided between space *in front* of the Temple compound, between the Gate of Mercy and the entrance, called Court of the Gentiles, and space *behind* the Temple, a corridor running between the rear of the building and the western edge of the esplanade.

In the end, the length of half the tunnel was determined by how that difference of 213 cubits was split between space in front and space behind the Temple, a numerical conundrum that gave them no rest in the last days before the feast. Yehezkel drew the esplanade over and over, thinking to himself that he was obeying Ezekiel to the letter. *Make known to them the design of the temple and its arrangement, its exits and its entrances . . . write it down in their sight.*

Feeling close to Elisha, they also didn't neglect the kabbalistic approach, playing with numbers and letters to see if 213 could be split in a meaningful way. In this feverish state they walked around Jerusalem, both stepping in and out of private chimeras, while the city around them prepared for her messianic—nay, apocalyptic Passover.

Despite her lack of walls, hundreds of Jews were toiling back to Jerusalem, unafraid of finding death there; in fact, content if their dust might finally mingle with the soil of their native land. Galatea was happy to find that Christian Easter, to be discreetly celebrated in the Holy Sepulchre, would fall two days after Passover, so that she could accept Rav Shimshon's invitation to attend their seder, the ritual Passover supper. Yehezkel told her of the secret seder in Torcello the night she'd fallen in the lagoon, and she found it hard to believe how much her life had changed in one year.

Easter, for Latin pilgrims, was so low key as to be clandestine. Salah ad-Din's successors treated Greek monks as more legitimate than Latins—after all, they were in the city from before the arrival of the Franks—and allowed them to run the surviving churches. The Greeks celebrated Resurrection Sunday on the same date, but their strange Holy Fire rituals made the few Latins in Jerusalem feel like they were witnessing the rites of another religion.

As for Galatea, celebrating the Resurrection while searching for the confession that denied it ever happened was no easy position to be in. Gudrun and Albacara knew that the parchment she and Yehezkel were looking for led to an object that had belonged to Jesus Christ—maybe the Holy Grail itself!—but Galatea never mentioned the confession to either woman.

One day, close to Easter, she looked at them and thought, "What if we find it? Will *that* be the gift I bring my sisters from the Holy Land? The denial of their faith? These are not the epochal events I was destined to be involved in! But no, I must keep faith. Brother Francesco will find a way to turn the denial of Christ's Resurrection into its affirmation and definitive proof!"

Her theological quandary was painfully obvious to Yehezkel, who knew it would only be resolved, one way or the other, by the use that would be made of the confession. Would the *real* Messiah take it to Damascus, as he'd agreed to do with Alain? Would he not instead bring it back to Rav Eleazar of Worms, to use as a weapon in keeping Domingo's paws off the Talmud?

Then, the day before the seder, Gudrun sighted Frutolf.

She'd gone to pray in the Holy Sepulchre by herself, every strand of blonde hair tucked away, as she'd learned to do among Saracens, when suddenly, in the small crowd that filled the church in the middle of Holy Week, she'd glimpsed his big, square head, a foot above those of other pilgrims, turning one way and the other as if looking for someone. She'd ducked out of sight, her heart nearly bursting through her ribs, and managed to leave before the Teuton, disguised as a devout German pilgrim, could see her. Or at least she hoped she had.

The news threw them into near panic. They hadn't yet found the hiding place in the tunnel, and here was Bois-Guilbert's henchman, looking for them. The Templar was Domingo's man, and it was the end of March, so the Spaniard must know that the Old Man and Yehezkel had met. There was nothing Domingo wouldn't do to stop them from finding the confession. The only logical conclusion was that the Teuton was there to eliminate them before they could reach the prize.

Yehezkel sought an escape route. He procured three donkeys, since Albacara had decided she would remain in Jerusalem with Marco. Then he asked Rav Shimshon for an exemption from the prohibition to travel during the Passover Holy Day, should they have to run for their lives. He also asked which direction it would be best to take. Rav Shimshon advised against the roads to the sea, whether to Jaffa or Acre. Better to go north to the Galilee, or south to Askelon and Gaza. The German knight, when he found out they had left, would almost certainly charge down to the coast.

Finally, the 27th of March arrived, Passover Eve. The Jerusalem rabbis, surrounded by families and devotees, would spend the whole night commemorating the Children of Israel's liberation from slavery in Egypt. Eighteen people attended the seder in Rav Shimshon's house, just as in Torcello a year earlier, and even there, on the rich table laid out before them, Yehezkel and Galatea kept a wrinkled copy of the map he'd drawn of the Temple's courtyards.

Galatea couldn't help thinking, several times during the meal, that this was the Jewish feast Jesus had been celebrating in the Last Supper. She followed the songs and prayers with as much concentration as she could muster, Yehezkel leaning over now and then to explain what Rav Shimshon was doing.

Late in the night, when they had finished eating and the last of the four ritual glasses of wine were poured, Galatea felt the habitual signs of a vision taking over. She pulled weakly at Yehezkel's sleeve, and he turned, noticing immediately that she was an even whiter shade of her usual pallor.

Rav Shimshon finished the blessing, and everyone raised the fourth cup and drank from it. Yehezkel, thinking some wine would help her overcome queasiness, urged Galatea to do the same. She did, and as the cool wine entered her mouth she felt it turn into warm, dense blood. She gagged, managed to swallow, and then slowly sank into the *visio secunda*.

Yehezkel sensed something was wrong. He and another medicus among the guests fussed over her, but though she breathed regularly and sat upright, staring ahead, Galatea was no longer with them.

✡ ✠ ✡ ✠

MOUNT OF OLIVES, MARCH A.D. 66

Some of the trials conducted by the Sanhedrin's judges shortly before the revolt against Rome concerned accusations of blasphemy and heresy. Not surprisingly, some of the alleged heretics were followers of Yeshu ha-Nozri. These fiery preachers, mostly Galileans, claimed for years after Yeshu's death that he was the real Messiah of David and had not died but was resurrected.

Many claimants to messiahood filled the streets in those times of oppression and martyrdom, and the Sanhedrin viewed them as harmless exponents of a mild heresy. But lately some of them, influenced by the converted pagan Saul of Tarsus, started preaching that Yeshu was the Son of God, and that his blood had been a salvific sacrifice. This new notion was too much for Sadducees *and* Pharisees, and the trials began.

That cool spring day, with skirmishes between those zealous for the Law and Roman troops already spreading like fire on the mountains around Jerusalem, Hanina bar Hezekiah, a senior judge and respected sage, with five of his seventy colleagues, was passing judgment on three such paganizers. For political reasons, the trial was being held in the open air, in a meadow on the Mount of Olives, instead of in the Chamber of Hewn Stones in the Temple, the Sanhedrin's courtroom.

Standing before the six judges was Shimon bar Cleophas, Yeshu's first cousin and leader of a group that had recently started calling themselves Christians. On his left stood Yohanan ben Zebadyah, known among the heretics as Yeshu's beloved disciple, while on his right was Mattityahu, an acolyte who'd only joined the group after the Romans executed Yeshu.

Unfurled on the table before Hanina was a Greek parchment, a life of Yeshu that the heretics called a Gospel, redacted by one Luke of Antioch, a pagan disciple of Saul. The parchment had been confiscated from Shimon, and Hanina read it. He immediately recognized Ezekiel's touching prophecy of the Messiah's anointing, lifted straight out of the prophet's book and, in the heretical Greek writing, fulfilled in the person of Yeshu, *their* Messiah.

In the last few months, Hanina had saved Ezekiel's book from becoming apocryphal by reconciling certain statements the wayward prophet made with the dictates of Torah. A week earlier, after reading the heretical Gospel, he and other sages felt forced to remove from the canonical version of the book the page the heretics used, lest it help them gain converts to their Greek "salvation."

But the fanatics did something else, too, something much worse than stealing a passage from a prophet, or even calling a man Son of God, something for which Hanina was about to emit, for the first time in his life, a death sentence. He stood up. "Are you really in possession of the vial of Holy Oil that was stolen from the Temple thirty years ago?" he asked Shimon. "Do you realize that in order to anoint your poor sacrificial lamb, you rendered impure the oil that is meant to anoint the true Messiah?"

Bar Cleophas looked at him with a forgiving, almost paternal smile. "Yes, we have the alabaster jar, but we did *not* steal it."

Hanina sat down heavily, his mind searching for a way to enforce the Law yet save the heretics' lives. "By anointing an ordinary Jew with *that* oil," he said at last, "you've condemned yourselves to be cut off from the Children of Israel in eternity, as it is written. But tell me, if you want your lives to be spared, do you still have the oil?"

"Rabbi, your hatred of Rome prevents you from seeing God's will. The Holy Oil has already anointed the true Messiah, and he has already come back from the dead and risen to Heaven, just like Eliyahu did."

Hanina sized him up from head to toe as if he would have to wrestle him to the ground. "Shimon bar Cleophas," he said then, at once angry and sad. "I am seventy years old, and in this short life I have already seen six of these 'saviors' come down from the Galilee. *Six,* do you hear? Each one of them lived in poverty and condemned wealth, spoke in riddles, chased away evil spirits, healed the maimed, and *loved* to argue with priests in the Temple! Guess what, Shimon: half of them met a grisly end, and the other half were never heard of again. Tell me, what was so special about this Yeshu ha-Nozri that you decided *he* was the real Messiah of David?"

Shimon was about to answer, but Yohanan, the beloved disciple, preceded him.

"Yeshu wasn't just the Messiah of David, he was God's *only Son,* and he defeated death!"

"Have you *lost your mind,* man?" shouted Hanina. "Don't you hear, in your own words, the idolatry that snaked its way into your heart? What speaks through you are those cursed Greek divinities, wrenching you from your people! And for what? So you can try to make a God out of a man who will be forgotten in two generations?"

Yohanan lifted his robe off his threadbare sandals, as if to walk away, and said, "There will not *be* two more generations, Hanina bar Hezekiah! We will return the oil, so that you and the Sanhedrin will not take our lives—but only so that we can spend them spreading the Truth, certainly not because we wouldn't be ready to sacrifice them to witness Yeshu!"

Hanina bar Hezekiah intended to hide the oil, the page from Ezekiel, and Samuel's horn in the niche he'd prepared at the midway point of the tunnel, precisely below the gate through which the Messiah will enter the Temple, so he would find them there. But after hearing the dangerous talk of the heretics, he'd decided to punish their vainglory; he went into the Sanhedrin's archive and retrieved the parchment he'd signed himself, thirty years earlier, condemning to thirty-nine lashes the thieves who confessed to removing Yeshu's body from the tomb. They clearly said that Yeshu's followers paid them so they could claim he'd been resurrected.

Hanina added a few words on the end about the same heretics stealing the Holy Oil and, that very night, went into the tunnel dug under the Valley of Jehosaphat by his father's namesake, King Hezekiah, almost eight hundred years before. Though the Messiah wouldn't need documents to show heretics their error, Hanina was contributing to the realization of God's plan, described in detail by Ezekiel: *the Messiah will come from the Mount of Olives and enter the Temple from the east, to be anointed there by the high priest or by a prophet.* As he descended the spiral stairway, Hanina thought to himself, "This is not the Temple reconsecrated by the Maccabees, rightful priests, and kings of Judah. This sanctuary was built by the same Herod who massacred the whole Hasmonean dynasty, an Idumean whom only the impure call king! But down here everything is as Hezekiah left it, down here the Messiah will find things in purity, waiting for him. Then Ezekiel's prophecy can be truly fulfilled!"

He reached the midway point of the tunnel, removed a smooth triangular stone in the left wall—all other stones in the tunnel were rectangular—and placed the two parchments, the oil, and Samuel's ivory horn inside the niche. Then he carefully replaced the stone and climbed back up to face the inevitable war.

✡ ✠ ✡ ✠

When she came to five minutes later, Galatea smiled weakly and apologized for having worried them.

Then, secretly proud of the kabbalistic feat in front of her teacher, she grabbed the stylus and drew a צ—*tzadiq*, the eighteenth letter, which is worth 90 and means "just"—on the corridor behind the Temple.

It took Yehezkel a second. If there were 90 cubits behind the Temple, then there were 123 in front of it, and 333 plus 123 makes 456, the number of steps they would have to count to reach the hiding place.

Galatea leaned back in her chair, exhausted, and whispered, "The real radius of the map is Bereshit."

The gematria of Bereshit, they both knew, is 913, and twice 456 is 912. In other words, Elisha was saying that the tunnel is "Bereshit" long, and between its two halves of 456 cubits is a central cubit housing the hiding place.

"HA!" cried Yehezkel. "Of course, Bereshit! That's what you dreamed in Torcello!"

They were both too excited to spend the rest of the night at the seder table. Besides, if they found the confession, leaving Jerusalem at night would give them an advantage over the German knight that they sorely needed. All this went through their minds without their needing to exchange a word.

They stood up. "I'll get the donkeys, you get Gudrun," said Yehezkel, smiling at the involuntary jest.

He was so busy considering possible scenarios—including the need for some silver dinars to bribe the mamluk guarding the church against parament thieves—that it didn't occur to him they were going to the Gethsemane in the middle of the night after eating their Passover meal; in other words, doing exactly what Jesus did on the night he was arrested.

Galatea, instead, remembered the phrase in Mark, *And when they had sung a hymn, they went out to the Mount of Olives,* and once again felt she was involved, with Yehezkel and Francesco, in Christ's Second Advent, to which this reenactment of the Gospels was a prelude.

The Passover moon was as full as it had been in Torcello, its light bathing the deserted valley as the three led their donkeys across it. Everything went smoothly, and after the mamluk took a generous baksheesh to turn his back, they descended the stairway to the little hall. Gudrun suffered noisily from the weight of earth above her, but once they started counting steps down the tunnel, its walls flat and regular, Galatea told her to think they were in the corridor of a castle, and the girl calmed down a little.

As they counted the 456th step, Galatea gave out a little cry. "Look! There, on the left, one of the stones is a triangle!"

In a minute, Yehezkel had pried out the triangular stone using the chisel he'd brought. They stepped back from the putrid, twelve-hundred-year-old puff of air that emerged from the niche, and Yehezkel carefully took out a parchment, an alabaster jar, and an ivory horn. While he read the parchment, Galatea turned the two objects in her hand by the light of the torch, still unsure of what she was holding.

From the moment she'd solved the enigma, Yehezkel considered the possibility of denying that the confession was the confession. Now, as he read Hanina's letter, he saw the stroke of luck that would allow him to do so. What he held wasn't the thieves' confession, but the record of the sentence meted out to them, though it did say that the thieves confessed. The stroke of luck was that the judge who signed it was Hanina bar Hezekiah! It would never occur to Galatea that the man who hid the oil and the judge who condemned the thieves were the same man!

"As I suspected all along," he said, trying to inject disappointment in his voice, "there has never *been* a confession. This parchment, written by Hanina, only describes what he was hiding here and why."

"Mmh . . . I was afraid it would come to this," said Galatea. "I simply have to take your word for it that this parchment is not the confession."

"No, no, look! You know enough Hebrew by now to recognize Hanina's name! Look at the signature at the bottom of this letter!" he said, handing her the parchment.

Galatea examined it and, in effect, recognized without much difficulty the name of the sage whom Elisha accused of hiding the page from Ezekiel—which, of course, was no longer there, having been taken to Egypt. She thought of the rabbis' words in the letter in the geniza: they'd left "the other two things" for when the Messiah would come, so those must be the two objects she was holding.

"Why did Hanina hide the oil?" she asked, apparently mollified, in reality breathtakingly relieved. "Does he say anything about that? And what is this horn?"

Yehezkel had discussed at length with Rav Shimshon the probable nature of the oil and decided to be sincere about what Hanina wrote. "That is the Holy Oil of anointment," he said, "compounded by Moses according to the art of the perfumer. It anointed every king of Judah and Israel. And this," he took the horn from her hand, "is the horn of the prophet Samuel, of which it is written, *Then Samuel took **the horn of oil** and anointed him in the midst of his brothers; and the Spirit of the Lord came upon David from that day forward.*"

Galatea and Gudrun, certain that something hidden all the way down there could not be a fake relic, were struck dumb. The oil that anointed King David! The horn of a biblical prophet!

Yehezkel hadn't finished his little show. "But that's not all. Hanina writes that the Holy Oil ended up in the hands of Yeshu's followers, who used it to anoint him as their Messiah—which is both why he decided to hide it and, between you and me, why a Christian Elisha later drew a map to find it again."

Only then did Galatea realize that the vial she was holding was an *alabaster jar*! The thought that *this* was the oil used by Mary Magdalene in Bethany took a moment to sink into the minds of the two nuns. Galatea was the first one to give out a gasp and fall to her knees. "*Hallelujah*!" she cried. "I've lived to hold the oil that Mary Magdalene poured on Christ's head!"

Seeking a gesture of worship greater than anything she'd done before, Galatea placed the jar on the ground in front of her and, like she'd seen Mohammedans do, stretched out full length before it on the floor of the tunnel, her face touching the ground. As she stood up again, she said, "I can die happy now; I've been absolved of *all* my sins!"

"I would rather you didn't, my friend, so let's put all three things in the pouch and get out of here!"

They did as he suggested and rushed out of the tunnel.

They rode north along the Kidron Valley under the full moon, and Jerusalem was soon behind them as they headed across Samaria to the

Galilee, by way of Nablus. Yehezkel had told Rav Shimshon glumly that even if their destination confounded the German, a man and two women crossing the mountains with no escort were asking for trouble. In a sense, he thought, it was almost safer for them to be traveling at night.

"Don't look so worried, Yehezkel," she called out to him from her donkey. "The dangers are there, I know, but we carry two relics that would be enough to protect us from Salah ad-Din himself!"

"If only it were true . . ." thought Yehezkel. "Actually the third relic, the one I've lied to you about, which can vanquish Christianity, makes us the most sought-after little caravan in all of Outremer!"

CHAPTER 30

VAYEHI CHEN
And It Was So

NAZARETH, 2ND APRIL 1220 19TH NISSAN 4980

The power of the relics must have been great, for they were not attacked in the four days it took them to cross Samaria. They decided to pass through Nazareth, not because they knew where they were headed, but because the nuns' yearnings were those of all Christian pilgrims. On Wednesday, they sighted the town, nestled at the foot of its green hill.

Yehezkel argued that even in the absence of the confession, they should take the oil, the horn, and the copy he'd made of Ezekiel's prophecy to Damascus anyway, for if Domingo ever got his hands on them, he would use them in massive campaigns to convert Jews. Galatea agreed but suggested they stop in Nazareth first, since it was on their way, and Christ spent his childhood there.

Yehezkel was strangely quiet for most of the journey. As they approached the town, he said, "I was supposed to find proof of the Talmud's antiquity, and what did I find instead? A page from a prophet plundered by the Evangelists." He smiled wistfully. "Fine example of a Jewish hero, aren't I?"

She was silent and then said softly, out of Gudrun's earshot, "You're the bravest man that ever lived."

He drove his donkey next to hers and took her hand but said nothing.

After taking Jerusalem, the Saracens drove Christians out of towns in what had been the Latin Kingdom, including Nazareth, but in the three decades since, a few had returned. Also many Jews arrived after the Latins left, so that the town's population was now as mixed as Jerusalem's, but Greek and Syriac Christians there weren't treated nearly as harshly as in the Holy City.

They rode into the market square. A big terebinth tree stood in its center, its branches forming a roof, ten feet off the ground, wide enough for twenty people to shelter from the sun. Twice that many were gathered around a figure. They hopped off their mounts and went closer. All three were surprised to see Brother Francesco preaching to the crowd as Illuminato kneeled by the tree roots, praying, but in Galatea's case it was more than mere surprise. Here was the returning Messiah . . . and the Holy Oil of anointment was in the pouch hanging at her side!

When he saw them approach, Francesco gestured to his audience to bear with him a moment and ran to greet them. He embraced the rabbi and bowed to the nuns, without looking into Galatea's eyes.

The crowd listening to him was a fresco depicting Ayubbid Outremer. Closest to the tree—because they understood Latin and many knew of the holy man from Assisi—were Latin Christians who had returned to Nazareth. In the next layer were a dozen Jews who had fled Jerusalem a year earlier, who also understood him and sensed the Christian preacher's thirst for martyrdom. Milling outside the two groups was a crowd of Saracens, who understood not a word of the friar's sermon but knew from experience that this was another infidel mystic trying to convert them to his faith. Most of them hoped it would end badly, preferably with some kafir blood being shed.

"My cherished friends! What a perfect delight it is to see you again!" beamed Francesco.

Now they were closer, they could see the toll his ailments had taken in the six months since Färiskür. His eyes and smile were still arresting, but every inch of his body exuded weariness.

Sitting under the terebinth, he told them of his pilgrimage. "I fled Damietta in November. Seeing what the two-year siege did to the city was painful, but even worse, Rabbi, was watching the Army of the Cross once they were done plundering. The greed and cruelty of supposed 'brothers in Christ' was too much, so we went to Acre." The friar laughed, his way of saying that Acre hadn't been much better.

"In the end, I chose to obey the pope and not go up to Jerusalem in time of war."

"*That's* why we didn't see you," said Galatea. "We spent two months in the Holy City." She paused. "I'm . . . sincerely sorry you could not complete your pilgrimage."

"On the contrary, Mother, I *am* about to complete my earthly pilgrimage!" said the little friar. "A week ago, in Acre, I received news that in the faraway lands of the Maghreb, five mendicants of our order won the palm of martyrdom. Now I can claim with certainty that we have at least five *true* friars minor!"

Yehezkel and Galatea didn't like what those words implied. Yehezkel thought, "If he insults the Prophet again to 'win the palm of martyrdom,' I won't be able to pull off the trick in the sultan's tent with this crowd!"

Galatea said, "I hope I've misunderstood the intent behind your words, Brother Francesco piccolo. In any case, you and Brother Illuminato look like you haven't eaten in days, so if you'll excuse us, Gudrun and I will just go over to those stalls and buy some bread."

Yehezkel caught her eye and discreetly pointed to the pouch. She smiled reassuringly, stood up, took Gudrun's hand and walked off.

When they were gone, Francesco said to Yehezkel, a new hint of desperation in his voice, "There was also a letter from Chiara waiting in

Acre, Yehezkel. Apart from the turmoil letters from that saintly woman always cause in my soul, she writes of worrying developments in the order. Satan has sneaked his way in there, Rabbi, and I'm too weak to face him down. It will be a greater help to them if I offer up my life for Christ here, trying to convert the Saracens."

Yehezkel considered his friend's position from as many angles as he could and then said, "No, Francesco. I can feel how tired you are, but martyrdom, how can I put it . . . is also a 'saintly' way of quitting! If you *really* want to imitate Christ"—it was the first time Yehezkel had ever used the word—"well, in my opinion, what *he* would do is bow his head in humble submission, go home, and save the order."

Francesco looked at him like the spiritual teacher he'd always had to do without. "And when they force me to 'correct brothers who err,' like the ones who want to stay married to Lady Poverty, what will I do then?"

"Ah, Domingo tried that one on me! He used Ezekiel's verse on the wicked man's blood being on my hands if I don't correct his ways. Not that he was looking for Cathars to burn—not that night, anyway—but he would have liked a rabbi's endorsement of *his* interpretation of the prophet."

"I'm sure he didn't get it," smiled Francesco. "How did you pull Ezekiel to your side . . . Ezekiel?"

"Simply by reciting the next verse to him. *But if you do warn the wicked person to turn from his ways and he does not do so, he will die for his sin, but you will be saved.* The prophet makes it clear that a good example is sufficient to absolve one from responsibility in the wicked man's conduct."

"An inspired exegesis, my brother. But I already know they'll find a way to blame me. All they do is keep asking me for a Rule the pope will approve. A Rule, a Rule . . . " The shabby little monk threw his arms in the air, discouraged. "As if the light my friars must spread in this world could be spelled out in the third subsection of the second paragraph of *a Rule.*"

As the two mystics under the tree discussed Francesco's quandary, the third one, with her younger sister, had already bought a large pita, still warm and fragrant. But before going back, Galatea wandered in the square for a while, reflecting on the *real* reason she decided to buy this bread. It was because the Gospels said that when Mary poured the oil over him, Jesus was eating in a Pharisee's house in Bethany, while Ezekiel's hidden page specified, *And the Son of man sat down to eat bread.*

In those twelve months—unbeknownst to her—Yehezkel's Talmudic debating style had rubbed off on the abbess, and she started arguing for and against the crazy idea that had entered her head the minute she'd seen Francesco under the tree: to anoint the New Christ with the same Holy Oil that once anointed Jesus!

"No one deserves to be anointed with *this* oil more than he does!" she thought. "Besides, it may be the opportunity Divine Providence is giving me to use it. And what of the choir-like repetition of Gospel circumstances? I ran out from my Passover meal in the night, and to the Gethsemane! Jesus was anointed before entering Jerusalem to seek the palm of martyrdom, which Francesco so clearly yearns for."

The thought of reenacting the Gospels made her consider her own role.

"On the other hand, why was *I* chosen to anoint the new Messiah? The Magdalene was a prostitute . . . Do my feelings for Yehezkel make me the new Magdalene? Oh, my God . . . the Magdalene wiped his feet with her hair, and mine barely reaches my shoulders! Imagine the crowd's laughter should I try to do that to him! Besides, what would Yehezkel think of my using the oil in that way, and without even consulting him. I've let Hildegard's visions get the better of me; I'd better put the whole idea out of my mind."

But the thought of Hildegard had already swung the jury in her head the other way. "Wait a minute. Did you learn nothing from Hildegard, from Gioacchino, from Father Makarios, from solving the enigma?" She stopped in her tracks, a hand over her mouth.

"Mary Magdalene was a prostitute, and I was violated by my step-father! *Those* humiliations entitle us to be the prophetess who anoints the Messiah! Yehezkel said Cathars believe the Magdalene was Jesus's wife—the hermit and Makarios said so, too. Well, I already knew that Francesco is my heavenly husband. As for the problem of my hair, in one Gospel she wipes his feet, but in the other two she pours the oil over his head. Yehezkel said all the kings of Israel were anointed on their heads . . . Yes, that's what I'll do!"

She recoiled from glorifying her role, but the fulfillment of her own destiny was clear to see. "Ezekiel's prophecy of the anointing is found after a thousand years—and I'm there! The oil that anointed Christ is found again—and I'm there! Now Christ himself returns to Nazareth . . . and here I am! Who could ask for more evidence?"

Suddenly, she could feel heat emanating from the pouch against her hip. It was time.

She took the pita to Francesco and asked him to recite a blessing over it before she gave some to the Christians in the square. He mumbled some words over the bread, and she asked him to eat some himself. He hesitated and then put a piece in his mouth. That was when she uncorked the alabaster jar and poured all its contents into Samuel's horn and from there over Francesco's tonsure.

The thick ointment ran into the dirty curls around the bare top of his skull, as the air filled with the resurrected fragrance of twelve-hundred-year-old spikenard. Francesco slowly tilted up his head and, for the first time since meeting her in Limassol, looked straight into Galatea's eyes for a long moment. She knew that was the look Jesus had given the Magdalene.

Some oil dripped on Francesco's foot. Galatea changed her plan and freed her hair, which was in fact long enough to wipe it as the Magdalene had done. Francesco understood her intent and tried to stop her, but when his hand touched her hair to move it away, the memory of Chiara's hair in his hand when he'd cut it, in San Damiano, swept over him—and he froze.

The people closest to the tree, who'd seen Galatea's gestures, froze on the spot, whatever their faith. Anointing someone's head with oil is a potent symbol in the tradition of all three faiths, and a puzzled but outraged buzz rose from onlookers. They had mixed feelings. On one hand, bestowing such an honor on a sleazy infidel preacher sparked uncomprehending hostility; on the other, there was instinctive reverence for a scene that felt important, at once mystical and historic. It felt . . . biblical.

But soon more intransigent Mohammedans were calling on their neighbors to punish the arrogance of the infidels, anointing each other before everyone, shamelessly proclaiming themselves what they were *not*. The crowd's rumble grew unfriendly. Yehezkel and Galatea started breathing the folded breath.

Then, head still dripping oil, Francesco stood up and stepped toward the crowd.

He raised his arms, fingers splayed in the Priestly Blessing position, and slowly, in a voice that reached to the stalls, blessed the crowd in Hebrew, to Galatea's Kyrie Eleison and Yehezkel's Ken Yehi Ratzon.

The animosity dispersed like smoke in the breeze, and after a moment, so did the bewildered crowd. Friars, nuns, and Jew sat down, a little shaken.

They all knew that Francesco forfeited the chance to complete his Sequela Christi only because the mob wouldn't have lynched just him and Illuminato, but no one said anything. Yehezkel tried to push Francesco's heart further from martyrdom.

"I reflected on your problem, Francesco. The answer may lie in your leadership of the order. If you go back—but *abandon* that leadership— and continue your personal mission, leaving decisions on the future of your friars to those you deem worthy, then you're doing what Ezekiel said, leading by example *only* without correcting anyone. In other words, my friend, solve the problem by continuing to be yourself!"

Francesco reflected, swollen eyes closed, for what seemed like a long while. When he opened them, they interrogated Illuminato. The young friar smiled, clearly grateful to the Jew for his suggestion. Francesco stood up and embraced Yehezkel, his head ending up on the rabbi's wide chest. "You're right, Yehezkel. Something bothered me anyway about taking the place of Providence and deciding by myself when to leave this vale of tears."

The grateful smile Galatea gave Yehezkel was enough for him to subsist on for the rest of his days.

Francesco stepped back and looked at the rabbi. "Before we part, there's one question I *must* ask you. But I want the truth, Yehezkel. Did you betray my words to save my life, in front of the sultan?"

"Yes," said Yehezkel immediately. "Just as you would have done to save mine in front of Domingo."

Francesco laughed. The two grabbed each other's forearm like knights and were standing like that when they heard Galatea's shriek.

She'd gone to pick up the alabaster jar she emptied into the horn and found it full again. She held it up for them to see. Francesco was the first to fall on his knees. Galatea wept openly; Gudrun laughed, Francesco and Illuminato thanked Christ over and over as Yehezkel mumbled kabbalistic blessings.

It took them ten minutes to acknowledge the world around them again. By then, Galatea had taken another unilateral decision. She went up to Francesco, proferring the prophet Samuel's ivory horn. "I want you to take this, Brother Francesco. Pilgrims buy all kinds of fake relics in Jerusalem, but *this* horn was used by the prophet Samuel to anoint King David! Don't ask me how I know; suffice it to say that we found it hidden in a tunnel fifty feet below the Dome of the Rock! Please take it."

Yehezkel was startled at the thought of Samuel's horn going to Italy but said nothing.

Francesco looked in her eyes and decided to visit Chiara the moment he was back in Assisi. "I'll take it, Mother Galatea, though I'll *never* need a reminder of the miracle I witnessed here today."

"One more thing, Brother Francesco," she said. "If you should sail to Venice, ask after a place called Island of the Two Vines, near Saint Erasmus. Ten years ago, I met one of Gioacchino's monks there, and he predicted what happened in Jerusalem. It is the holiest place in the lagoon."

"I'll pray there, rest assured," replied Francesco, already looking stronger than he had an hour earlier.

Then they blessed each other and parted ways, the two friars heading back to Acre and Italy, the other three riding east, toward the Sea of Galilee, which the Gospels also call Lake of Gennesaret.

✠   ✡   ✠   ✡

SEA OF GALILEE, 5TH APRIL 1220

Three days later, at the end of an afternoon of spring squalls and sudden outbreaks of blue sky, they sighted a round little guard tower, perched on a spur of rock jutting over the eastern waters of the lake.

Yehezkel wanted to visit Rav Moshe's grave in Tiberias, but it would have meant renting a boat afterward to cross the lake, which would have left too easy a trail to follow. So they had ridden their donkeys around the south side of the lake and up its eastern shore.

No horses were tied outside the tower, so they decided to rest a while inside it, where they would be less visible. Leaving the donkeys below, they climbed the stairway to the terrace. Dusk approached as they gazed at the lake below and the mountains of the Lebanon to the north, their peach color blazing against the darkening blue, as bright as if a fire were burning inside the peach. They reminded Galatea of the Alps lit by the last sun in September, a sight she'd grown to love in Torcello—and there weren't many.

As they sat there, Yehezkel quietly clung to his messianic speculations. "I found the confession, it's here with me, shortly to be in safe hands, so who can say I won't be the one to show the world the error of Christianity?" The thought gave him pause. "And how does that error make Galatea any less a 'valorous woman' than she is?"

The sound of a galloping horse broke the silence. They jumped up and looked out from the ramparts. A Templar knight was riding toward the tower as fast as he could, his white mantle flying behind him. Yehezkel's first thought was for the laissez-passer in his pouch, signed by Pedro of Montaigue in Damietta.

"This shouldn't be a problem," he said to the two women.

Bois-Guilbert was waiting for his platoon to return from patrolling the northern shore and saw them approach from the terrace. There was no doubt, it could only be them. He'd laughed, gloating over the unsought-for advantage of being on God's side, and immediately left the tower in the hope that seeing it empty, they would shelter inside it. The prey, of course, fell into the trap.

They expected a Templar to address three pilgrims decorously, especially when they recognized him, but Bois-Guilbert jumped onto the terrace, sized up the opposition, and grabbed Gudrun. He pulled her to his chest, put a dagger to her throat, and then snarled at the other two, "I bet you thought you'd made it! Now you'll hand over to me what you found in Jerusalem, or the blood of this innocent nun will be on your heads!"

Galatea didn't hesitate. She slipped the pouch from round her neck and gave it to the knight.

Bois-Guilbert took it with one hand, keeping the dagger at Gudrun's throat with the other. "I want to know *exactly* what is inside it. It is my condition for letting you live. All three of you."

There was a silence. Then Galatea, unable to bear the terror in Gudrun's eyes, blurted out, "The Holy Oil with which Mary Magdalene anointed Christ in Bethany and a missing page from the prophet Ezekiel, predicting that anointment."

The Templar's victorious cackle rung out in the fading light. He threw Gudrun back toward them and the two nuns embraced, weeping.

"I don't know if that's what the Parchment of Circles led to, but Father Domingo will know what to do with these things. A page of a

Jewish prophet that speaks of Jesus Christ! I can just see him converting *masses* of Jews with it! As for the oil, I guess it will anoint popes from now until the end of time!"

Bois-Guilbert had been keeping his eyes on the big Jew, and Galatea caught him totally by surprise when she lunged at him and in one, smooth sweep wrenched the pouch from his hand and flung it over the ramparts into the lake below.

There was nothing they could do, but still they all watched it arch into the air, as if to memorize the point in which it splashed into the waters of the lake.

The Templar's voice was full of cold, self-righteous anger. He looked skyward. "Oh Father, I couldn't find a Jewish harlot, so I found a Jew *and* a harlot, instead. Now I'll kill them both, and you'll finally be avenged!" He turned to Galatea.

"I was going to kill you anyway, renegade bitch, but now I think I'll have some fun with you first!"

He drew an incredibly long sword and placed its tip under Yehezkel's chin. "I wanted you to watch me force her, Jew, but you're too unpredictable, so I'll have to kill you first."

Yehezkel stepped back to distance the blade from his neck, but he was at the edge of the terrace. He thought, "Well, if I'm the Messiah, it seems I am of the Christian kind, who only come to be killed."

Suddenly, he heard something at the foot of the tower. He shouted the first thing that came into his mind, loud and slow, to cover the noise from the stairs, in case it was a Saracen who could help them. "Non nobis, Domine, non nobis, sed tuo nomini da gloriam!"

"What the fuck are you shouting, Jew? You're about to die, so say *your* prayers, not ours!"

Yehezkel saw Frutolf's big head rise above the last step, his eyes aflame like a German Saint Michael.

"Maybe you can kill *me* and get away with it," he said with unnatural calm, "but the man behind you is a *real* knight, and he won't take it kindly if you lay a finger on the nuns."

"Ha, ha! How typical of a Jew to try deceit until the last second of his life! But it won't help you this time, Jew. I'm *not* about to turn around!"

Something deep in his Teutonic soul had prevented Frutolf from abandoning his mission, and he'd traced their every move to that tower. He stepped onto the terrace and said, without raising his voice, "If there is a master of deceit here, it is you, Bois-Guilbert, not the Jew."

The Templar spun around, unsure if words could save the situation at this point.

"Frutolf, if you won't let me kill these heretics, at least help me tie them up and take them to Acre!"

Frutolf drew his sword, which looked even longer than Bois-Guilbert's.

"I'm through listening to your lies, Englishman. My master says you're a spy for Domingo of Guzman and a traitor to your order. Your time is up, Bois-Guilbert."

"That's true, but you're too blind to see what it means! Yes, I work for Domingo, and no man alive is closer to the pope than he is! If you want to become someone, Frutolf, you had better join me!"

"But you swore an *oath*!" said the Teuton, his anger rising.

"No oath is valid when sworn to enemies of the faith! The Temple has become a snake in the bosom of the church. Help me tear out the rot and purify once more the Body of Christ!"

"Enough! You've trampled over everything a knight should honor and defend! I'm going to kill you not for lying to me for months, not for threatening the lady of my thoughts, but because it is *intolerable* that a knight should betray his order! Defend yourself, Robert de Bois-Guilbert!"

The bout began in the bright moonlight, the onlookers shouting support for their champion. The duel on the minute terrace didn't last long, for Frutolf was a foot taller and fifteen years younger than Bois-Guilbert and was fighting for chivalry itself. After a few parries, the Teuton disarmed the Templar in a clash of blades so loud it seemed to echo off the hills around them. Then, with a scream of pure rage, he sunk his sword through the chain mail on Bois-Guilbert's chest.

Instead of the look of surprise that Yehezkel had seen on men who realized they were dead, Bois-Guilbert, arrogant to the last, clutched the point of the sword with both hands with animal desperation, trying to deny it entry into his body, and the blade, as Frutolf pushed it in with both hands, cut off most of his fingers. Then he lay against the parapet, mouth spurting blood and fingers bunched in his lap.

A minute later Frutolf was on his knees before the abbess—apparently asking for absolution for the killing she'd just witnessed; in reality wordlessly dedicating to her his revenge over Bois-Guilbert.

Suddenly, he heard the sound of the Templar platoon returning from its round and thought, "What my Master tried to avoid, a Teuton murdering a Templar, is what I ended up doing. Now these knights will arrest me and take me to their castle. Maybe *this* is what I had to do to get in there."

Galatea spoke before he even thought of asking her to justify his actions before the Templars. "What you just did was a noble deed, Frutolf of Steinfeld, and I shall bear witness to that before the knights who will be here shortly. I am an abbess and a countess, so if I tell them that I *know* Bois-Guilbert was betraying their order, they will do nothing to you—at least not until they find out if I speak the truth."

Frutolf was as euphoric as if he'd just single-handedly freed Jerusalem.

"Madonna, you can't imagine . . ."

"I shan't be doing this for a sense of justice alone, Frutolf," she interrupted him before he could gush any courtly love words. "The three of us need an escort to reach Acre in safety. Are we agreed?"

"Of course, my lady. It goes without saying, my fairest, noblest muse!"

With a mischievous smile, Galatea placed a kiss on his vast forehead. The German closed his eyes, overwhelmed; Gudrun frowned, and

Yehezkel found that, for the first time in a year, he wasn't jealous.

He pulled her to one side. "Have no regrets over the pouch, Galatea," he said. "It's all part of the plan of the God of Israel . . . who—it has been granted me to understand—is also the God of Christians."

The presence of Bois-Guilbert's slumped body and the clinking sounds of the knights dismounting at the foot of the tower gave his next words a strange, somber weight. "When you threw the pouch into the sky, my friend, as if you wanted to return it to the Heavens that gave it to us, my eyes followed its arch and I had a numerical vision: Rav Yitzhak the Blind's calculation is the right one. In the fullness of time, when the arch is complete, the pouch will be found and the Holy Oil will anoint the true Messiah!"

"When the arch is complete," she repeated. "I'm afraid I don't understand, Yehezkel."

"Arch in Hebrew is keshet: *kof, shin, tav.* Do you understand now?"

"Yes," said she. "A hundred, plus three hundred, plus four hundred. You're saying that in eight hundred years, in 2020, the oil will anoint the true Messiah." She took his arm gently.

"You know, speaking of the true Messiah . . . I thought Francesco was the returning Christ, and that the oil had done its work, but I was wrong. Now I understand what Gioacchino meant when he said that the Jew and the woman will be redeemed together in the Last Days. What he was saying was that the true Messiah . . . *will be a woman*!"

Yehezkel smiled, finally tamed, and kissed her lightly on each eye.

Then they went down to speak to the Templars.

The Holy Grail was lost, but in Acre Gudrun was reunited with Garietto and the abbess with her trunk.

CHAPTER 31

וירא אלהים את-כל-אשר
עשה והינה טוב מאד
ויהי ערב-ויהי בקר יום הששי

And God saw everything He had made,
and behold, it was very good.
And the evening and the morning
were the sixth day.

✡   ✠   ✡   ✠

Ἔστιν δὲ καὶ ἄλλα πολλὰ ἃ ἐποίησεν ὁ Ἰησοῦς,
ἅτινα ἐὰν γράφηται καθ᾽ ἕν, οὐδ᾽ αὐτὸν οἶμαι τὸν
κόσμον χωρῆσαι τὰ γραφόμενα βιβλία
ἀμὴν

And there are also many other things that Jesus did
that, if every one should be written, I suppose that
the world itself could not contain the books that
should be written. Amen.

ACKNOWLEDGMENTS

I had two objectives in researching and revealing these true events of eight centuries ago: the first was to follow in my father's footsteps. He was a *talmid chacham,* that is a learned scholar of Torah and Talmud, who left us exactly thirty years ago. A few held him for a somewhat heretical kabbalist, while others diagnosed him as a manic depressive with messianic delusions. The second objective was to make my mother proud. She is a ninety-five-year-old Auschwitz survivor who is fortunately still alive and probably the only person happier than I am to see this novel finally come off the press.

Apart from my parents, I would like to express my gratitude to the several people, in no particular order, who most contributed to that happening. Rav Moshe Lazar, who instilled a love for Jewish Scriptures in me that keeps me studying them to this day; Elisabetta Dami, whose words nearly twenty-five years ago—"I think you and I must have met in the Middle Ages. You were a rabbi and I was a nun"—gave birth to the idea of the novel; Professor Asher Kaufmann, whose hypothesis that the Temples were 300 feet *north* of the Dome was the basis for the map hidden in the Parchment of Circles; my sister Chaja, a strong reader who made useful suggestions on the first draft of each chapter; Stefano Magagnoli, the first editor to believe in the story and the one who gave me the best advice, though it took me two years to put it in practice (beginner's ego, I guess); I'm grateful to the whole team at Inner Traditions, who did a superlative job, with special thanks to Jon Graham for deciding that this novel would not be out of place in his publisher's catalogue; heartfelt thanks to Peter Hubscher, who fell in love with my strange couple and did an amazing amount of work to promote the book; and finally my agent, former business associate and best friend Marinella Magrì, last but far from least on this list, for without her this book, like much else, would still be in a drawer.